EXILED
BY
IRON

ALSO BY EHIGBOR OKOSUN
Forged by Blood

EXILED BY IRON

EHIGBOR OKOSUN

HARPER
Voyager

Harper*Voyager*
An imprint of
HarperCollins*Publishers* Ltd
1 London Bridge Street
London SE1 9GF

www.harpercollins.co.uk

HarperCollins*Publishers*
Macken House
39/40 Mayor Street Upper
Dublin 1
DO1 C9W8
Ireland

First published by HarperCollins*Publishers* Ltd 2024
1

A catalogue record for this book is available from the British Library.

ISBN: 978-0-00-861594-9 (HB)
ISBN: 978-0-00-861595-6 (TPB)

Printed and bound in the UK using
100% renewable electricity by CPI Group (UK) Ltd

For you who gifted me a voice,
and you who protected it,
and you who helped me find the shape of it,
and again, you, who taught me to hone it.
May this voice move mountains,
And reach across seas,
To you in search of your own.

———

CONTENTS

YUSA

LLEYRIA

AENYLSED CAVE

MATTIASJORD

STUGAART

NORDGREN

BENIN SEA

BENIN

PORTO PISCHU

WYLDEWOOD

YOMO
BUNDÉ

GINAÉ

LOKOJA

ABIYE

BENIN FOREST

OYO

OLD MAIDUGURI

SAKU

ZAIN-RIVERS

NNOZINI

MANAPANÉ

OSHOMALU

IKOLÉ

BIA-HYANG

BIKU

ASHÉ SEA

SAYAJI-ISLAND

REY'HATI

EL'TERNÉ

MYARRIS

UL'TARRA

THE KINGDOM OF IFÉ

UMU-A'TEA SEA

ASHKENAYA

A REMINDER OF THE EVENTS IN
FORGED BY BLOOD

ABIDÈMI ADENEKAN AND HER PEOPLE, THE OLUSO, ARE HUMANS WITH blood magic that manifests in many forms, from manipulation of ice and water to teleportation to visions and prophecies. Dèmi and her mother, Yetundé, are Ariabhe Oluso who possess wind and healing magic and live out a meager life as the town's healers in the small village of Ikolé in Oyo, a central region in the Kingdom of Ifé.

TWENTY YEARS PRIOR, the Eingardian Empire, another region populated by nonmagical Ajes, subjugated Oyo in a bloody war that resulted in the murder and enslavement of countless Oluso. Though their magic is powerful, Oluso cannot murder another human for any reason, or else the spirits through whom Oluso draw their power will sever their spirit bonds, causing the killer to lose both their magic and their sanity, while their descendants are born as Aje from that moment forth. Despite the Oluso incapacity for bloodshed, the Eingardians fear the Oluso and believe they are dangerous and barbaric, dehumanizing them, enslaving them, and pushing them to the margins of society.

ONE DAY, AN Eingardian woman brings a sick Aje boy to nine-year-old Dèmi's hut pleading for their help to heal him. Yetundé warily agrees, and after the healing ritual is completed, she leaves the boy in their hut as he recovers, with Dèmi to watch over him. Dèmi feels a strange connection to the boy, Jonas, and befriends him. Then, Eingardian soldiers attack, attempting to capture Dèmi and her mother for their unlawful use of blood magic. Dèmi witnesses the captain of the guard, Mari, revealed to have past history with her mother, murder her mother in cold blood.

Feeling betrayed by Jonas, who is now exposed as an Eingardian noble of note, she leaves her home and childhood behind, running for her life. As she escapes, however, she is mortally wounded, and in desperation asks the Aziza, the spirits of the forest, to save her, knowing that they will exact a price from her one day.

NINE YEARS LATER, Dèmi has found a new surrogate family of fellow Oluso in the city of Benin: Oluso guardians, Will and Nana, and their newborn daughter, Haru. Dèmi and her best friend, Colin, a mysterious and charismatic Oluso with strong yet unstable magic, receive training and tutelage from the elderly Baba Sylvanus and spend their days getting into trouble while attempting to protect their fellow Oluso. On a routine trip to the Benin marketplace, Dèmi encounters a slaver selling two young Oluso children. Unable to stand idly by while seeing her people treated like livestock, she helps the children escape. The jailbreak seemingly draws the attention of Lord Tobias Ekwensi, an Oluso who works as an onyoshi—a broken Oluso who has traded his services tracking his fellow Oluso in exchange for comforts the Eingardian Army provides. He confronts Dèmi in her home and offers her a proposition: kidnap the Eingardian prince and use him as a bargaining chip for the freedom of the Oluso . . . or she, along with the other Oluso in the house, will be arrested if she refuses. Dèmi accepts, and with the help of Colin's teleportation magic, infiltrates Benin Castle, where the prince is known to be visiting.

WHILE COLIN RUNS interference, Dèmi breaks into the prince's quarters, intending to knock him unconscious, but she comes face-to-face with the boy from the day her mother was murdered: Jonas. Jonas, now a man, is dissatisfied with the way his uncle, Alistair Sorenson, rules the kingdom, and fears his uncle's plans for the Oluso. He agrees to go with Colin and Dèmi willingly, hoping the action will serve as recompense for Dèmi, who is still angry his presence drew the guards to her village and inadvertently caused her mother's death. Colin hurriedly teleports them to safety but is unable to get them to their destination, forcing them to journey on foot.

STILL RAW FROM the betrayal a decade ago, Dèmi distrusts Jonas's motivations and binds him with her magic as they work to evade patrols searching for the kidnapped prince. Desperate to avoid capture as they travel toward their goal of a rendezvous with Lord Ekwensi in the northern Oyo city of Old Maiduguri, the trio run into a forest rumored to be a passage to the Spirit Realm. They find themselves sucked into this realm, where they encounter magical beings such as tree spirits, powerful water-spirit humanoids called the omioja, and the Aziza. After Dèmi risks her life, and Jonas aids her in saving a young omioja from a vengeful and deadly water spirit known as a mami wata, the Aziza queen, Ayaba, invites the trio to stay. Colin is discomfited by his sense that Jonas desires Dèmi, as he, too, wants her heart.

MEANWHILE, DÈMI BRACES for death, believing that Ayaba will make good on the life-debt promise that Dèmi made as a child, but instead the queen asks for Dèmi's help to save the Aziza and the other spirits. Ayaba reveals that because the Spirit Realm exists in parallel with the Physical Realm, their homes are being destroyed by Eingardian consumption of and disrespect toward the lands they inhabit. Dèmi promises to help the spirits, and in return, the Aziza assist the trio in getting to their destination by supplying them with gwylfins—large, sentient dragon-like beasts that fly them to the next city on their path: Lokoja. Before they leave, Ayaba pulls Dèmi aside and cautions her against becoming too involved with Jonas or Colin, telling her of a prophecy she has received that one man would bring her death and the other would bring her despair.

THEY LAND IN Lokoja and meet with an informant of Ekwensi's, Etera, an Aje executioner tasked with killing his fiancée, an Oluso named Sanaa. Upon meeting Etera, Dèmi is unsettled to find herself speaking directly to Ekwensi through his use of skin walking—a taboo magic that allows him to inhabit another's body at will. Dèmi is further discomfited by the fact that Ekwensi is able to wield magic despite having previously broken his spirit bonds when he killed soldiers while defending his village from the Eingardian invasion twenty years before. She has little time to ponder her concerns, however, as Ekwensi charges them with saving Sanaa, who is set to be executed later that day.

Dèmi leaves Jonas and Colin to secure the escape route as she descends into the dungeon where Sanaa is being held along with other Oluso who are waiting to be sold into sexual slavery. Despite Ekwensi's protests, Dèmi refuses to stand by and let her fellow Oluso die or be enslaved, but in her attempt to rescue all of them, they are captured by Mari.

DÈMI IS CHAINED with iron, a metal known to seal Oluso powers and cause them pain akin to torture. She and the other Oluso from the dungeon are led to a square on the outskirts of the city for immediate execution. She watches helplessly as Elu, an Angma Oluso who chooses to keep her explosive magic inside to protect her fellow Oluso, is ultimately burned to death with molten iron. Too late, Dèmi remembers a bead that Will gave her before she left Benin, which—when broken—would summon him to Dèmi in case of emergency. She breaks the bead, but nothing happens, so she prays to Olorun to save them, at which point Colin materializes holding a knife to Jonas's throat. Colin uses his hostage to negotiate the Oluso out of their chains, but a battle breaks out and they must devise another means of escape. Will and Nana finally arrive and Dèmi insists on evacuating all nineteen Oluso prisoners before they themselves escape, so they stall for time as Colin and Will teleport out groups of Oluso. Exhausted from all the magic they've expended, they are defenseless as Will prepares to transport the last of prisoners out of the square. The soldiers launch a volley of arrows at them, but they are halted in midair by Jonas's hidden iron-blood magic. This revelation, coupled with the self-sacrifice of Elu's sister, Cree, who uses her light magic to first blind the soldiers and then detonate herself, lets them narrowly escape.

WHILE WILL AND Nana attend to the freed Oluso, Dèmi, Colin, and Jonas make the rest of the journey to Old Maiduguri. Jonas confesses his heart to Dèmi, apologizes for her mother's death, and for keeping his secret identity and magic hidden. Colin questions Jonas's commitment to the

Oluso cause for freedom, given his proximity to the colonial forces that underpin the kingdom.

FINALLY, THEY MEET up with Ekwensi and turn Jonas over into his custody. As part of their payment for helping Ekwensi, the lord tells Dèmi about her father, who was known as Iron Blood Osèzèlé and hated by his fellow Oluso, including Dèmi. Osèzèlé was the last remaining iron-blood Oluso, suspected of betraying his brethren and single-handedly winning the war for the Eingardians by using his magic to sacrifice 50,000 Oluso at once in Benin, the capital city of Oyo. Ekwensi admits that this story is incomplete, and that the truth is Oyo was already losing the war, so Osèzèlé sacrificed 50,000 *willing* Oluso to turn the other 400,000 in Benin into Ajes, thus sparing them from murder or enslavement by the encroaching Eingardian Army.

WITH THEIR PART of Ekwensi's plan complete, Colin and Dèmi make to depart, though Dèmi has grown closer to Jonas over the course of their journey and is conflicted as they part ways. Before they can take their leave, they are met by the king of Eingard himself, Alistair Sorenson. Colin moves to teleport himself and Dèmi away, but before he can, the king recognizes Colin as the son of Royal Council member Lord Kairen. Fearing what would happen to Colin's father if it was known his son was Oluso, and under threat from the king, Colin and Dèmi accompany Jonas and Alistair to the Eingardian capital of Nordgren.

IN THE CASTLE at Nordgren, Dèmi, Colin, and Jonas share a tense meal with the king, where he reveals that he recognizes Dèmi for who she really is—the daughter of his first love, the former Princess Yetundé of Oyo. To Dèmi's further dismay and confusion, Mari enters, having survived the explosion in Lokoja, and declares that Dèmi should belong to her since she also once shared love with Yetundé. Jonas attempts to intervene on Dèmi's behalf, but Alistair tells Jonas that Iron Blood Osèzèlé was the man who is responsible for putting Jonas's mother in a coma for the past eighteen years. Dèmi is pushed to the brink as the king also admits to killing Osèzèlé, and she attacks Alistair, thinking to garner the freedom for the Oluso by killing him. She is quickly subdued, shackled with iron, and thrown into the dungeon.

IN THE DUNGEON, Dèmi meets pregnant Oluso women who are being forcibly bred to see if their children can be made into iron-bloods by being born and surviving life in an iron cage. In nearly two decades of experimenting, only one child has lived past infancy, a girl named Malala. Ekwensi arrives soon after, revealing that Malala is his child, and the source of the magic he's been using to thwart Alistair's machinations though the magic comes at the cost of Malala's lifespan. When Dèmi confronts him over the use of his daughter's magic, he questions her commitment to garnering the Oluso freedom at all costs, insisting that she has to be willing to sacrifice anything for true freedom. He then releases Dèmi from her shackles and Jonas's nursemaid, his now-undercover ally, takes her place in the dungeon as a decoy. Dèmi escapes the dungeon by means of a secret passage and the help of Jonas, who is set to be officially named the heir to the kingdom at a gala that evening.

JONAS PLANS TO use the succession gala as a means to smuggle Dèmi out of the castle. She accompanies Jonas as his personal guest at a masquerade, where she meets Jonas's fiancée, Elodie, and reunites with Colin. Knowing she feels betrayed by his secret regarding his parentage, Colin tells Dèmi about his mother, Eyani Al'hia who ruled Berréa, the region to the south of Oyo as the Scourge of T'Lapis. His father, Lord Kairen, once Eyani's concubine, slowly murdered all of Eyani's court and tricked a young Colin into poisoning his own mother over several years under the guise of offering her a sleep aid. Soon after, Colin's magic manifested and his father tried to assassinate him as well, but he thwarted his father using the battle techniques his mother taught him. Ever since, Lord Kairen begrudgingly decided to accept Colin's existence.

JONAS TAKES DÈMI away from Colin and Elodie for a dance, during which they kiss and Dèmi comes to the realization that the strange attraction she's been experiencing toward Jonas since the moment they met is because they are destined Oluso mates. Jonas has known ever since that first meeting in her hut.

THEIR DISCUSSION IS cut short by King Alistair Sorenson's announcement of Lord Ekwensi's promotion to Regional Lord of the Oyo region and Jonas's official appointment as heir to the throne of Eingard. The partygoers are then shepherded out of the ballroom into an arena for "entertainment." There, the king gives a speech that stokes the crowd's fear and hatred of the Oluso as three hundred shackled Oluso are brought out onto the arena floor. The king announces that the Oluso will be unshackled and tasked with killing one another in a battle royale until there are just a few survivors, and those few will be rewarded for their great deeds in service to the kingdom.

LORD EKWENSI OBJECTS to the wanton killing, so the king strips him of his titles and land and prepares to execute him, but Jonas uses his magic to disarm both the king and Mari. The king orders the Oluso in the arena killed, but Jonas undoes their shackles and Ekwensi springs into action. He calls down lightning from the sky to strike the stadium, sending the audience scrambling in fear. Ekwensi calls for the Oluso to take back their freedom by force, but Dèmi stops them before things go too far and challenges Alistair Sorenson to a trial by combat for the kingdom's crown. Full of hubris and seeking to restore his subjects' confidence, he accepts with one condition: Dèmi must wear iron to seal her magic. They begin to fight, and Dèmi is quickly overmatched. Colin and Jonas attempt to interfere and save her, but Ekwensi stops them. Moments from death, Osèzèlé appears to Dèmi in a vision and unlocks the iron magic within her. She impales the king with a number of iron spikes and subdues him but refuses to deal the deathblow in honor of her spirit bonds and her mother's vow to pursue true justice. Ekwensi steps in and calls lightning down to smite the king, reducing him to a blackened lump. He incites the Oluso to war, promising them a new way to kill without losing their spirit bonds and magic. He gives them a choice— side with Dèmi, who refused to kill the king who oppressed them, or join Ekwensi and take back their humanity by force. The vast majority of the arena Oluso follow Ekwensi as they set out to build their army, and Dèmi faints.

WAKING AFTER TEN days of unconsciousness, Dèmi is eager to begin her rightful reign as queen and set about the work of rebuilding the kingdom and freeing the Oluso. She quickly discovers that the powerful Royal Council is no less distrustful of her, and many outright challenge the legitimacy of her rule. Jonas thinks to force the Council to accept Dèmi's legitimacy by dissolving his engagement to Elodie and pledging to marry Dèmi instead. Frustrated, Dèmi leaves the Council chamber with Jonas and runs into Colin, who is clearly envious of Jonas's status as Dèmi's mate. After a heated argument, Colin confesses his love to Dèmi and disappears to join the ranks of Ekwensi's army.

ASSURED OF THEIR goals but entirely unsure of how to achieve them, Demi is nonetheless determined to forge ahead toward a brighter future with Jonas beside her.

PROLOGUE

BEFORE

THIRD YEAR OF THE GREAT WAR, THIRTY-THREE YEARS
BEFORE ALISTAIR'S BETRAYAL

THE CREATURE OPENED ITS MOUTH AND CRIED LIKE A NEWBORN BABY.

Afèni paused momentarily as the sound echoed through her ears. It all felt so real, the sniffling cries that spoke of hunger and longing, the curling pitch that invited the hearer to extend their arms out for an infant who needed warmth and love. She could see her youngest, Lola, with puffed cheeks like ripe kola nuts reaching for her, nestling into her lap as though she were a happy child of a year. But the glittering eyes staring out of the razor-sharp skull in front of her were frostier than an Eingardian winter, nothing like Lola's wide, brown ones that drank in the world. So she drew her blade, put away the specter of her lost child, and advanced again. It was time to end this.

But as she took a step forward, the creature drew back, flapping its bony wings as though it could ward her off with the gale they generated. She touched a finger to the Oluso mark on her neck—a red flower nestled in the eaves of a crescent moon—and the wind spirits gathered around her like stars overtaking the night sky. She clenched her fist and the wind spirits surged forward like arrows, sending out tiny bursts of concentrated air that exploded near the creature's body, knocking it from side to side until it crashed against the copse of fallen trees on the hill behind.

The creature screeched, revealing rows upon rows of deadly sickle-like teeth studding its generous jaw like diamonds glittering in cave walls.

Afèni tightened her grip on the hilt of her blade and lowered herself into a near crouch. One of those teeth had been enough to cut through an entire battalion of her soldiers, the best of the Oyo Royal Army. Three had destroyed half her Council, five Oluso closer to her than a ragtag group of politicians from disparate regions throughout the entire Kingdom of Ifé should be. She had mourned them all—golden-haired Brigitte, who laughed harder than anyone else and fought just as bravely, whether in the battlefield with her ax or in the courts against her fellow Eingardians who resented the growing prosperity of the other regions. Green-eyed Ts'alisi, whose songs about her desert home in Ismar'yana were enough to draw even the most taciturn of listeners into a smile. Cheeky Jae Hyuk, who told as many jokes as he invented new ways to wield his shadow magic. Brooding Unagbona, who had as many anxieties as visions of the future. Calm and collected Maluly, who favored her native Berréan rapiers and could kill with so many different kinds of weapons but preferred to cook for people, enemies and lovers alike.

"Run, Ola rè!" Brigitte had screamed as one of the creature's teeth drove into her back. As Afèni's vanguard, she was tasked with protecting her queen. But Afèni had not been prepared for the way her friend's gray eyes shifted into fathomless pools of ash, the smile plastered on her ruddy face reduced to a flat, unmoving line. She had known even before her friend's body drove at her with her beloved ax that Brigitte herself was long gone. The creature had taken her mind, and with it everything she once was.

The creature in front of her now slunk back even farther, the rattle of its bones drawing her out of her reverie. Her own bones ached as though in echo, warning her that exhaustion loomed. Most of those who had seen sixty name days were safe at home in their beds or surrounded by a wealth of children and grandchildren, gathered like precious pearls beading a crown. Some had fallen prey to the ripples of the Great War that tore through the kingdom, yes, but there were many still who had yet to suffer a drop of blood. She'd made certain of that. Yet here she was, tangling with ghosts, spending down what was left of her life thread in battle.

She took another step forward, careful to keep her gaze pinned to the creature. It slipped through the copse of trees, its whiplike tail scraping the ground in steady bursts like the nose of a hound in search of something. Afèni knew better than to trust its retreat, but she couldn't help but wonder why the creature hadn't sent its fearsome teeth after her. Finally, the creature's tail slapped against the bark of a tree stump in the clearing, the remains of a once-proud iroko tree, and stopped, drawing its head back on its long, snakelike neck.

It was now or never.

Afèni stabbed her fingers to her neck, imagining a fire that would burn even brighter than Ts'alisi did when she died buying Afèni time to escape. This creature was nothing like the ones that had attacked Benin Palace—it was bigger, more fearsome and intelligent—and so she imagined a flame that would burn as badly as the lava in Mount Y'cayonogo.

Flames gathered on her skin, gold-red illuminating the rich earthen shade, a fire ready to consume everything that gathered in its path. It surprised her, even now, how easy it was to summon Shango's gift, how simple it felt to wield an ancestral spirit's magic as though it were a mere trifle. This magic alone had cost the lives of most of her children, but it sang so easily at her fingertips, as though it were good for nothing other than to light celebration candles.

If this works, we will have something to celebrate, she thought.

Stepping back on one foot, she swung her hand like the arm of a catapult, flinging a ball of pure heat at the creature. The creature flapped its bony wings closed, crouching over the tree stump. The flame connected with the edge of one wing, and the creature lifted its head, crying out in what sounded eerily like a human scream. A woman's.

Afèni burst forward then, screaming as she charged the creature with her blade. Her heart pounded in her ears, the rush of power swirling in her veins, making her feel as though she could strike the earth itself and split it forever. She leapt at the creature, ignoring the ache in her body, the voice in her head warning her to stay careful. The time for caution was long past. Her blade met the creature's tail in a shower of sparks, and she leaned in, coating the body of the blade with some of Shango's fire. The creature held fast, screaming even louder as the flames jumped from the blade onto its skeletal rib cage. Then Afèni felt something slithering, knife-hot against her spine, bone scraping against skin. Suddenly, she was flying through the air, speeding toward the body of an ashen birch.

She slammed into the tree with a thud, blinking against the pain that burst against her skull like an ax demanding its due. Her bones sagged as though at peace, happy for the chance to rest, but her body sang its pain, blood pooling at the back of her head. She had no time for this. Afèni rolled upright, sucking in deep breaths, wincing against the stab of pain that pierced her chest. Another broken rib. Temi would be disappointed.

How many times must I beg you to be careful, Mother?

She could almost hear her eldest daughter's stern voice, feel her warm, steady hands. But as her vision cleared, she saw that there was no healing magic bathing her skin. Temi was as dead as Lola.

Afèni was alone.

She took a step forward, gritting her teeth as fresh pain engulfed her. She had promised the ancestral spirits she would find a way to subdue rather than harm this creature. She'd lied. It was perched in a high tree now, studying her as though it could read her thoughts. She could imagine what Damini would say.

Ogbon ju agbara lo, Mama. *Wisdom is greater than strength.*

Her third youngest had been wiser than many of her generals, but it was still his mother's cunning that robbed him of what should have been a long life.

She put her blade back in its sheath and made to go. Perhaps she had erred, tracking the creature all the way here, clearly disturbing its territory. Maybe it was time for her to let it all go. Most of the creatures were dead now, vanquished by Shango's flame. This was the last as far as she knew.

The creature cocked its head, the action so like her dead son's that she nearly stopped. But she kept on, putting one foot in front of the other. It flew to another branch, watching her leave.

Now.

She whipped around, running full speed at the tree stump the creature had abandoned. The creature screeched, a thunderous cry that shook the ground. But she was already drawing both hands away from her neck, pulling a fiery notched bow into existence. The arrow lying against the string of flame would cause nothing short of an explosion.

The creature leapt off the tree.

She aimed at the stump.

The creature swooped down.

She loosed the arrow.

Then, just as the creature's talons grazed the air above her head, she bent away, rolling onto the ground. But it was for naught. The creature disintegrated in a burst of violet flame and reappeared as the arrow approached the stump, driving its body at the arrow.

The creature went up in a blaze, bone charring in an instant. It flapped its wings, rising like a bird of legend into the sky, then it plummeted to the earth, crashing into a heap.

Afèni sucked in another lungful of air, breathing past the haze of smoke and heat that gathered around her face. Finally, it was over. Three long years in bitter war finished.

The fire raged, but it did not spread onto the nearby grasses, keeping the creature as its pyre. The creature's eyes hollowed into empty sockets, and only then did Afèni skirt around its body to get to the tree stump it had perched on.

The stump it had so clearly been guarding.

Afèni peered into the hull of the stump and gasped. There, lying in the swell of dark wood, was a sleeping baby. Silver-white hair fell gently over golden cheeks the color of ground cassava. Tiny hands wriggled against a round face as the child stirred from its sleep. She reached out a finger to touch it, her heart racing faster than the flames devouring the creature. The baby opened honey-brown eyes and looked back at her. She staggered, nearly falling to her knees. The child gurgled as though she had done something funny and waved his little hands in the air.

Tears pricked Afèni's eyes as she reached for him, drawing him to her. He nuzzled against the hard copper of her breastplate, batting shell-like hands against her breast. He rounded his mouth, sucking in air and she realized then that he was hungry.

"I can't feed you, little one," she whispered. She had fed all her children at the breast from the time they were born. She'd been head-strong, even wrapping Lola to her chest as she charged into battle the first time the creatures attacked, even though her royal mother had disdained the practice.

Sacrifices must be made for greatness. That is the code we live by.

She wondered now if her long-dead mother, Empress Yomi, would be proud to know that her daughter had sacrificed all but one of her children for power. Sacrificed her own heart for that of their people.

The baby sucked the air again, making a noise halfway between a gurgle and a wail, and Afèni clicked her teeth at him.

"Pèlè, pèlè. I'll get you food."

Placing the child back in the stump, she took out the bowl in the pack strapped to her back, dumped all the water from her skein into it, and waited.

Two faces appeared on the surface of the liquid, swirling like shadows covering the face of the deep. A young man with a hardened body that denied his role as a scholar stood next to a willowy woman with pale skin and long dark hair.

"Ola rè, you're bleeding!" the man exclaimed.

"I'm all right, Sylvanus," Afèni answered, brushing her fingers against the wound still oozing in her scalp. "The creature is dead."

"With hope, this will keep the Ajes from rebellion," the woman said. "They are flooding the streets as we speak, clamoring for a sacrifice."

Afèni wanted to laugh. It was comical, really, how history seemed like a snake engulfing its own tail. Her mother had turned a blind eye as the other Oluso slaughtered the Fèni-Ogun, risking their spirit bonds out of fear of iron-blood magic. Now, the Ajes, humans born of broken spirit bonds, were fast outnumbering the Oluso, demanding that they sacrifice themselves to give the Ajes a firmer sense of safety.

The child roared into a full-blown wail and Afèni gathered him up again, pushing away her thoughts.

"I thought you just finished a fight," Sylvanus asked.

"I need help," she answered. "Tell Markos to send you to Sayaji Island, the northernmost strip. Bring Edwina with you, Folaké has decided to wean Yetundé."

The woman frowns, the slits in her neck flapping with the motion. "Human children can be weaned after a few months?"

Afèni shook her head. "No. My daughter just resembles my mother. She thinks it will make the child weak. Be grateful, Xiaoqing, that our lot is not yours."

Xiaoqing opened her mouth to ask something else, but just then the child wailed again and Afèni sat back against the stump, soothing him.

He looked to be about the same age as her granddaughter, Yetundé, a bright little star she had gotten to hold only once. It was understandable that Folaké could not forgive her. She had, after all, traded the lives of all of Folaké's siblings, eight out of her nine children, for the ancestral power needed to defeat these creatures. Even Lola, the child of her later years, and the apple of her eye, was not spared. The spirits had demanded and received their due.

Folaké would understand in time. Or she wouldn't, and the kingdom would suffer.

She stroked the little boy's face and he latched onto her finger, trying to bring it to his rooting mouth. She smiled at him, pressing a kiss to his forehead. But as she did, the magic in her blood leapt to the surface of her skin, buzzing like a horde of worker bees tasked with protecting their queen.

She pulled away immediately, nearly flinging the child back into the stump. Then, taking a deep breath, she placed him in her lap and peeled back the wrapper bundling him. There, on his chest, was a flower in the eaves of a crescent moon. She gasped. The boy was not just Oluso but Fèni-Ogun. The way his magic had pulled hers out of her confirmed that.

She laid the boy on the ground and got to her feet. The water in the bowl rippled and Xiaoqing looked up at her.

"Ola rè," she said. "Sylvanus will be there soon. They just left." Then, seeing the pinched look Afèni wore, she asked, "What's wrong?"

"Xiaoqing, do you remember the bodies that started washing up on your shores years ago? Oluso who all died in a similar fashion?"

Xiaoqing nodded. "I know of the acts those few cowardly Oluso committed. The Fèni-Ogun are Olorun's children too. We omioja are tasked with aiding all of you."

"I found one."

"What?"

"This child is Fèni-Ogun."

The omioja woman blinked up at her. "That is good news, yes?"

"No. People have reason to fear the iron-bloods. Not all of them are innocent. Some were kind and wonderful, yes. But others—they were close to wreaking destruction on our world."

Xiaoqing narrowed her eyes. "Many of you are not innocent, and still, we help you. Listen to yourself. You found a baby. What harm could it cause?"

Afèni dragged her hand through her curls, her mind racing with thoughts that peppered her like stones. The creature had protected this baby—the same creature that had laid waste to their kingdom for the last three years.

"You're right," she told Xiaoqing. "He is harmless. I need to pick him up."

She knocked over the bowl of water with her foot and the image of Xiaoqing disappeared. She didn't want to be tempted to change her mind.

Drawing her blade from its sheath, she walked over to the baby. He blinked at her, reaching out both hands, and she positioned the blade over his chest. Her heart ached. Her fingers shook with the knowledge of what she was about to do.

But what choice did she have? Her daughter, Folaké, would come to power soon. She would not be able to handle the storm that would ensue if people found out there was an iron-blood still living.

The Fèni-Ogun had been the brightest of all Oluso, children of Olorun who could shape the very earth with their will and sometimes control the magic of other Oluso. Many iron-bloods had been unjustly—at least some would claim that; Afèni didn't have the luxury of living in such a naïve world—killed in the last five years. This boy was likely the last. But for all her disagreements with her mother's callousness concerning the

Fèni-Ogun massacre, Afèni understood that iron-bloods could not be allowed to run around unchecked.

Sacrifices must be made for greatness. That is the code we live by.

She shuddered. Then she lifted her blade, her heart drumming with fear that gathered in her like a hurricane, drowning out everything else.

"Please," a woman's voice said, cutting through the noise in her mind. "Please, save him. Save my baby."

She looked up. There was no one around her, save the still-burning corpse of the creature. She saw now that the creature had moved the remnants of its head. It now faced her, eyeless holes burning into her skin, hotter than any ancestral flame. As she watched, it opened its mouth again and the voice crept out.

"Please. Save my child. Help my Osèzèlé . . ."

Afèni flung aside her blade, putting her hands on her head. Suddenly she could feel the creature's presence in her mind like a grasping hand trying to ensnare her will. It drew memories out of her: Lola's wrinkled face as a baby freshly born; her children gathered around her, kissing her cheeks and hands to mark her sixty-fifth name day, not knowing those hands would soon be stained with their blood.

Afèni's throat tightened. She wanted to weep; she still had not done so. She wasn't sure she could. There was no time to mourn in war, only to maim, kill, destroy—survive.

She let out a small chuckle. "All right, you win," she barked at the dying creature. She relaxed, letting her shoulders drop, and the creature's presence in her mind receded. It already knew what she couldn't admit until this moment: she could not do this evil, not for anything in the world. It was ironic that she had made such a bargain with the spirits, promised them the lives of her children so she could save countless others. But she could not kill this child.

Almost in answer, the creature's head crumbled into a pile of dust, its remains fluttering on the wind.

The baby wailed, loud and clear now, and Afèni snatched him to her breast, holding him close.

"I'm sorry," she whispered over and over. "I'm sorry."

And she was. Somewhere along the way she had begun to believe what her mother said—that power to destroy your enemies was the only thing that would chase away your fears. Her mother feared iron-bloods like Croiden Aurelius Schulson, who could bury a village with a wave of his hand, so she'd turned her back on the suffering Fèni-Ogun. Afèni, too, had cheated the spirits and harmed the creature instead of quelling its anger as the spirits asked. She was no better than her mother.

She got to her feet, pressing another kiss to the child's forehead. There was still time. She would send the child away with Sylvanus and Edwina. At the very least he would have people to care for him and hide his origins. When he came of age, he could train with Sylvanus, hear the story of what happened to his people. She would right this wrong.

Starting now, she promised herself, she would learn the hardest lesson of all—hope.

PART I

ÌYÁ-ILÉ

TORN

There's nothing out there. Will sent us on a fool's errand—

"Shh!" I clap a hand to Jonas's mouth although the words had actually passed between us without a sound, blossoming in my mind like fireflies winking into a darkened night. It's been a year. One year of knowing Jonas as my mate, of wondering every time my heart thuds against my chest whether the feeling is mine or his as well. One year of waking tangled up with each other, unsure of where I begin and he ends. One year since he's been able to slip into my mind like a dagger caressing its sheath.

"Sorry," he whispers, his breath tickling my fingers. "Talking seemed more conspicuous—"

I shake my head in a quick motion and he falls silent. Moving slowly, I inch closer to the agbayun bush we've been hiding behind since the sun's rays first beckoned at Rabbit Hour. The moon is shining now, her silver light barely visible through the veil of clouds smothering her like a shroud. Wolf Hour is fast approaching, but save for the eerie violet flames burning through the trees in the clearing, nothing has changed. Until now.

Straining against the bush, I still, not daring to breathe. Then it comes, a crackling rattle, like kokulu when they turn their heads all the way around, jewel-blue eyes chattering with excitement as they scent their prey. I crawl into a crouch, the honeyed smell of agbayun berries curling against my nostrils. In the haze of the flames, the fruit glow red against milky-white flowers, like blood dripping through pierced skin.

"What is it?" Jonas asks.

I glare at him this time. What does he not understand about being quiet? The sound comes again, faster and louder, rhythmic rattles that echo through the burning leaves. The flames grow brighter, but the branches and leaves remain unconsumed. Then, at the edge of the clearing, something flits by. I clutch the bracelet on my arm and imagine a dart, sleek and long, with a curved, sharp edge like an arrow. The bracelet blazes golden, peeling itself from my skin, twisting and curling until it resembles the dart in my mind. I scan the clearing for jewel-bright eyes, a slim, bony frame, and a ridged, whiplike tail, knowing the only chance we'll have to survive a kokulu is to strike first.

The bush to our left rustles. Rolling to my feet, I whip out a hand to pull Jonas up, but he is already standing, one hand on the sword hanging from his back, tensing forward in a mirrored pose. The leaves give way, and a flash of white springs across my vision. Flicking my wrist, I shoot the dart forward, hoping to hit the hollowed part of the kokulu's skull, the soft ridge in the bone right between its jeweled eyes. A small face topped with silver-brown hair pops up instead, and a child spills out through the bush. Jerking abruptly, I fling the dart just wide enough that it flies right by his cheek, burying itself in the tree a few paces behind.

The child screams, then catches himself, slamming his head into the dirt in a frightened bow. "My apologies, My L-liege," he stammers. "I was s-s-sent with a mes-s-s-age."

I step back, breathing hard. The rattling is gone.

"I'm sorry," I gasp in answer. "I didn't know you were there. I didn't mean—"

The boy begins to pray. "Ah Raah Dhathi," he cries, calling for Olorun, Father of Spirits and Skies. His words arrive in near song and inhaled trills—it's T'chera, a language spoken only in the ridged valley where Oyo and Berréa meet. "*Save me from the many deaths that hide at this woman's hands,*" he pleads.

I flinch. I'm used to Ajes being afraid of Oluso like me, treating those born with blood magic as beasts and monsters to be exploited and slaughtered. Despite spending all my life at the mercy of those Ajes, I have never felt like the monster they imagine. To this boy, though, I am no doubt a walking nightmare.

I open my mouth to tell him I'm harmless, then snap it shut. That's not entirely true, and even though I mean him no harm, though I've tried my hardest not to harm *anyone*, a handful of assassination attempts in the past few months have taken the matter out of my hands. It's laughable. People make us into monsters, and we become more monstrous when we fight back. There's no way to win.

Jonas recovers first. "Raise your head," he says softly. "We won't harm you. I promise."

The boy does not move.

"Raise your head," Jonas repeats, this time with the command of a man born to be king.

The boy obeys, trembling all the while. He shies away from Jonas's offered hand, unfurling with the bush at his back. He's lanky but wears his height like an oversized coat, hunching as though he can fold himself in half. His pale skin isn't strange here in Lleyria, half a day's ride north from the Eingardian capital of Nordgren, but his coiled silver hair and gray-green eyes mark him as double-caste, with more than one mixed bloodline. No doubt he's one of the many refugees fleeing toward the capital in hopes of avoiding the drums of impending war.

"Who are you?" I ask, palms up in an attempt to soothe. I can barely hear my own words over the thundering of my heart, but I try to slow them down, fill them with soft apology. "Who sent you here?"

And why were they foolish enough to do so when they suspect this forest is filled with ancient beasts?

I swallow that last part though. No doubt the town's elders failed to share that with the boy, same as they did with us until a series of unexplained deaths forced them to ask for aid. They probably thought a refugee's child expendable.

The boy shifts toward Jonas as though he can shield him from my gaze. "I am a humble messenger, my liege," he says, words tumbling out in a quick rush. He breaks into another bow. "My name is not worthy of your notice."

"You're from Manapané?" I ask, keeping the gentle hum in my voice.

The boy looks up at this. "How—"

"I have a friend from there—Amara. When she speaks, it almost sounds like she's singing. I've always envied that."

The boy cocks his head, considering. I offer a brief smile—my palms still up in a gesture of peace—and speak one of the few phrases I know in T'chera: "Ngisi kaya omi erinbi gaja."

The boy bursts into a strangled half laugh before slapping a hand to his mouth. Jonas lifts an eyebrow.

"I charge like a buffalo, but love like an elephant," I say, grinning. "I frightened Amara when we first met."

Jonas smiles. "What was so scary about you?"

"I wasn't exactly merciful to the woman selling her on the market." I flash another smile, but the memory of Amara stuffed into an iron cage designed to burn her every time she transformed at her owner's request vanquishes the lightness of the moment before.

Pushing past the ugly memory, I turn to the boy. "You've a message for us?"

Jonas slips his hand in mine, giving a gentle squeeze. I squeeze back.

The boy touches his ear, then the bottom of his chin before holding his palm up, saluting us the way T'cherians greet respected elders. "The tall woman—the captain of the guard sent me. The search is done. They asked you to come down for a report."

"Is that all?"

He nods. Jonas and I share a look. We knew, when the Eingardian Royal Council approved our joining this excursion, that the situation must be dire. So we did things our own way, interviewing the townspeople, trudging uphill to investigate these flames that appeared with the wave of death that has swept Lleyria. So far, though, we've seen nothing. But to hear that the guard has found something not even a day since we've been here, after months of nothing to report—something is off.

Jonas shrugs. "Maybe we brought better luck."

"Let's hope so." I nod at the boy. "Thank you. Go back safely."

"Namiz'en. I am Namiz'en, Your Holiness," he chirps, then he stops, frowning. "I mean, Your Grace. No—my lady?" His voice is husky but high, still brimming with the energy of boyhood. He can't have had more than thirteen name days.

Jonas chuckles, his throaty laugh cutting the tension in the air. "It's okay," he says. "I don't know what to call her either. I call her 'my queen,' but she gets annoyed with me."

I roll my eyes at this, but my lips are already curving into a smile. "We're not married yet. Or so your Council likes to remind me."

He snorts. "An error we will soon remedy."

I laugh and turn to Namiz'en. "Call me Dèmi." I tap the corner of my mouth then point to my heart, offering the T'cherian sign of heartfelt thanks. "Ah Raah Dhathi keep you on your return." Then I lower my voice, weaving steel into it. "Go. Don't stop for anything. Run until you get down there."

Namiz'en dips his head in a parting bow and scurries away, cutting through the bush as though we are the rumored beasts lurking in Lleyria Forest.

"All that work to put him at ease, and you go and scare him again," Jonas tuts.

I say nothing, watching as Namiz'en's silver hair is swallowed up by the dark that rings the clearing. If the townspeople are right and the kokulu—a beast that once hunted even the most powerful Oluso for sport—is in this forest, fear is an appropriate gift. O dara lati beru ati ki o wa laayé ju iku lo ni iku alaibowo, iku alaanu.

Better to fear and live than die an irreverent, merciless death.

"What now?"

"We go," I say. The forest is silent, except for the flames roaring on, mocking us. "Who knows what they found?"

"Or who."

I look up at this. "You think it's Ekwensi? Or—"

I stop, the memory of the last time I saw Colin coming alive in my mind. His mischievous hazel eyes glittering with hurt and hope. His warmth as he held me before dissolving into the stifling castle air. I swallow, throat suddenly tight. It can't be him. Colin grew up with an Oluso mother, with the ancestral knowledge of the Great Spirits. He wouldn't unleash a kokulu on a town. At least, not knowingly.

But it's also been a year. One year since Lord Ekwensi killed Alistair Sorenson and ended his despotic rule. One year since many Oluso, dreaming of a world where they no longer had to be hunted, joined hands with Ekwensi to start a revolution. One year since Colin left me behind to join him.

Jonas squeezes my shoulder and I sigh, brushing away the memory of Colin's bitter smile. "It could be Mari," he says. "She has family in these parts. You never know."

I flick a finger and my iron dart rips out of the tree bark, shooting back toward my heart. As it arrives, I throw my arm up and it transforms once more, morphing into the ringed, snakelike bracelet Nana gifted me as a betrothal present. Mari disappeared after that disastrous day when I took on Alistair Sorenson and won, escaping with no concern for her fallen lover or the many lives she'd manipulated and destroyed. It *could* be her—this felt like her style.

"We should go," I snarl, snatching my ogbene from the ground. If I meet Mari Strumblud again, she will beg for the mercy of a quick death. I might even show her the same courtesy she showed my mother and kill her in front of her loved ones.

Jonas takes one of my hands, stopping me as I struggle to tie the woven cloth bag to my waist.

"We need to hear their report before the Council gets to it," I argue.

"And we will," he says, tipping my chin up. "But we can't go down there like this."

"Like what?"

"Oko mi, you've been like this all day."

I snort, annoyed, but my cheeks heat all the same at him calling me "my darling," and in Yoruba at that. Jonas never stopped with his Yoruba lessons, even after becoming king-elect. Often, when we're alone, he'll speak it to me and, just for a moment, I'll imagine I am home in Oyo again, watching children dance as Mummy sings during the Winter Festival. But it's summer now, and these days I struggle to remember the twinkle in her voice, the way she would light up as she wove tales for me, whole tapestries of our history and ancestors' memories. I have spent so many months in Eingard, wishing for the blistering kiss of an Oyo sun, anything to fill the bone-deep ache for home that grows with each passing day.

I meet Jonas's piercing dawn-blue eyes, scowling. "I've been *what?*"

"Nervous, jumpy, worried—other adjectives."

I rock back on my heels, pulling away. "That's not fair. You know why—"

"I know that we planned to come here, to figure out if the Council was hiding anything, together. I know that what the townspeople told us, and the timing of the kokulu coming back, is eating at you."

He snakes an arm around my waist and draws me in, brushing my cheek with his free hand. "I also know that we have to trust each other to get anywhere, and that we haven't been alone—without an attendant, guard, retainer, what-have-you—in months."

I swallow, heat spreading from my face down to my breasts and lower belly. "We have been alone," I protest weakly. "Just not as long as we would like."

"Hmm," he murmurs, kissing my forehead.

"You have to admit—the timing *is* suspect."

"I admit that." He kisses my neck.

I try not to squirm, the brush of his lips sending warm tingles down my arms. "And we're still in the dark about so much."

He cocks a head toward the crackling flames. "Strictly speaking, that's not exactly true." He nuzzles his nose against mine, his ash-blond hair tickling my cheeks.

"Then what is?" I whisper, daring him.

"This."

He slips a hand into the waterfall of braids cascading down my back and cradles my head. His lips crash into mine, soft yet demanding, unspooling my focus. My skin burns everywhere his fingers touch. I throw my hands behind his neck and drag him down, filled with a need to have his skin on mine. He bows over me, bearing down like the bower of a tree over a sapling, the heft of his body bending my frame, molding me into something pliant and supple. Each kiss is a sunburst, drawing me out of shadow, insisting I be seen, felt, and touched. The air is hot despite the sticky, wet night, and we gasp for breath as we meld with each other, aching. The Oluso mark on my wrist sparks, the magic in my blood thrumming to a rhythm matched by his.

The rattle starts again, so close my ears ring with the sound. I stop nibbling on Jonas's bottom lip and freeze. This time though, the sound does not stop, growing in intensity, crashing through the clearing like a wave. I lower into a crouch.

"What's wrong?" Jonas's gaze is fixed on me, alert. Gone is the heavy-lidded desire that made his eyelids flutter a moment ago.

"Don't you hear it?"

"Hear what?"

I stiffen. "You can't hear it? Even if you look into my mind?"

He shakes his head, and now he spins, searching the clearing. "I feel your fear. Nothing more."

The rattling stops, but now there is a shriek, a spout of braying laughter. Jonas edges closer to me. "I heard *that*."

The flames flare, and suddenly the twisted yew trees burning within them resemble a mass of wizened faces fused together, mouths open in silent horror. The branches shake like grasping hands reaching beyond, begging to be set free. The laughter twists into cackles and hisses. Jonas and I stand side by side, weapons at the ready.

I remember now the tale the okosun sang the year I came into my magic; of Queen Afèni forging an immortal flame from the fury of the Spirits and using it to destroy the kokulu. I shook with excitement as I recounted the tale for Mummy later, bursting with pride that my great-grandmother had been a fearless warrior, hoping I would become the same.

"Dèmi, that tale is tragedy," Mummy whispered then, gathering me into her lap. "The kokulu are not mere monsters to be vanquished."

"Then what are they?" I say, steeling my jaw in defiance.

"A vengeance. One that Afèni paid handsomely to defeat. The Spirits do not give without exacting a price."

She pauses as though she wants to say more, but when she tries to speak another shriek pierces the air, and the memory dissipates. I grasp at it, trying to remember her face, her voice—more. It's been so hard to do that lately. But the memory is gone.

The shrieks grow, rippling into a storm.

Jonas touches a finger to the mark glowing faintly through his light-colored shirt—a flower resting in the eaves of a crescent moon, the sign of an Oluso. The iron short sword at his belt obeys, whipping itself out, poised like a scorpion readying to sting.

Then silence. The flames die out in one fell swoop, the night engulfing us. Twisting my palm, I call the wind spirits and within a moment they are there, hovering above, glittering stars in the devouring night. The wind howls as something slices past the trees. We barely have time to pivot when balls of violet flame explode out of darkness into the sky west of us.

"The town!" Jonas shouts, but I am already running, calling on the threads of my magic, feeling its ferocious warmth burn through me until my skin blazes with green fire and our legs are wrapped in wind. Anything to get us there fast.

We tumble down the hill bracketing the bush, not stopping even as brambles catch at our skin and tug at our hair. We land on the trail winding through the larger mountain face and leap onto the rocky ledge that overlooks Lleyria. The town is spread in parallel and intersecting lines, its order belied by white limestone roofs lashed to timber houses, beset on many sides by sloping stone buildings. Cobblestones end abruptly in muddy streets, and the spiked logs that serve as the city walls are patched with beaten sheets of metal.

Beyond the winking golden specks of lanterns in the town streets, those violet apparitions swarm like bees converging on a honeyed hive. Winged shadows glide and swoop between, dragging massive tails that chatter and click like cowrie shells. The townspeople, wispy dolls from this distance, twist their gazes up, some lifting their hands as though in supplication.

Stretching my magic, I forge a vine that lashes Jonas's wrist to mine. We scramble a few paces back and sprint full-speed at the ledge. As we catapult off, the wind spirits gather around, flinging us forward like arrows speeding off a bow. Before we drop to the gilded city gates, the first flame falls, and the shining eyes of a kokulu sparkle as it jets past, maw spilling teeth that streak toward the people below, driving into their bodies with deadly precision.

We land on the city walls as people start to run, screaming as they flood through narrow streets. A man dives into the safety of his home, a kokulu tooth protruding from his back, but within moments the stone walls are ablaze with violet flame, roaring like an inconsolable child.

As the flames fall and the kokulu descend into the streets, screaming their fury and delight, the last of Mummy's words from that fateful night spark in my ears.

Never forget—the kokulu are messengers, a sign of what's to come. When the Spirits grow restless and evil rules the land, they rise to bring a message of death. If you ever meet one, Dèmi, your wisdom is in your survival.

Run.

BREAK

THE SKY IS FALLING, BALLS OF VIOLET FLAME SPARKING AS THEY SLAM into the ground, setting off an inferno that licks through the city streets. The townspeople scatter as the earth cracks and splits, falling away from their feet. The flames bathing the ground spit dark clouds that writhe into a shadowy veil, devouring the breezy night air.

In front of me, a woman stands transfixed, a young child in her arms, watching the chaos with a rueful, dreamy smile.

"Move!" I scream, leaping off the city wall. I knock her to the ground just as another kokulu dives, claws snatching at the place where she'd stood a moment ago. The little girl in her arms is wailing, but the woman's gaze is blank, brown eyes fixed on the darkening sky. Now I see the glowing tooth embedded at the base of her throat, sparkling like an amethyst on a wealthy woman's neck. I wrestle the girl away, jumping back as the woman goes up in a blaze.

A shriek erupts behind me and I whirl, but Jonas is there, sword clashing with the elongated jaw of a kokulu. It jerks back, tail whipping at us, but there's a flash of cerulean and Jonas's short sword darts up, parrying the tail. The girl's terrified cries grow louder, her pale face turning red with the effort. The kokulu rears its tail again, then as Jonas's blade flies to meet it, it pirouettes, twisting around and stretching its cavernous mouth. As the blade meets bone, shooting off white sparks, the kokulu unhinges its jaw and spits hundreds of daggerlike teeth.

"Dèmi!" Jonas shouts, but once more I'm ahead of him, already clutching the iron ring hanging from my neck, calling on the spirits.

The wind spirits converge, knitting into a wall that gathers around us. The kokulu's teeth ricochet off the wind wall, slamming into the stone outposts near the gate, kicking up a storm of dirt and rubble. A few slip through cracks, driving at us. The girl burrows against my chest, screaming. Rolling to my feet, I clutch her to my waist and yank my father's ring off its chain. The ring radiates golden flame, twin to the fire now racing up my arm. As the teeth dart near, the ring transforms, stretching until it resembles a spear with a jagged edge on one side, as though it's been split into two. I lash out with the spear in a wide arc, turning on my left heel, striking down the teeth coming my way. The iron screeches as it clashes with bone, but the teeth fly into the dirt, erupting into smaller orbs of violet flame.

"You didn't mention demon teeth when you signed us up for this," Jonas huffs as he cuts down the few spinning around him.

I swipe at the sweat dripping down my face. "Thought it'd be better to see them yourself."

"I didn't think you'd be lying. The town elders are fools."

"For what?" I turn, slapping away an errant tooth. "Struggling to believe the kokulu existed at all? Or using it as an excuse to revive Oluso raids?"

He stabs the tooth with his short sword and it wriggles, dancing like a live thing. "It won't work. The laws have changed, the raids won't be coming back. Not if I have anything to say about it."

I clench my jaw, thinking of the hatred in the town elders' eyes this morning, the way they talked to the walls—Olorun's blood—even the dog that wandered into the chief's rooms—anything to avoid acknowledging me even as they begged for aid. Oluso may not have been found in Lleyria for more than a century, but the fear is alive and well. It's only worse now that Ekwensi has shown that Oluso can kill without losing our magic and sanity. It doesn't matter how many times I argue that he might be a special case—an aberration that defies the original spirit bond to which Olorun bound all Oluso to. It sounds like excuses even to my ears. No doubt the Council is hoping I will die here. I smirk.

Good thing Will warned us in advance.

Jonas slips his sword back into the scabbard hanging from his back.

"The Council won't get away with this. Not this time." He smiles grimly, his eyes creased with worry.

I turn my back to him, scanning for the kokulu that attacked us. Nothing. The teeth scattered around us lie dormant, the flames consuming them as bright as festival lights, mocking us with their jovial hue. Save for the woman's still-burning body a few feet away, no one is in sight. Beyond us the city is ablaze, violet twisting with stone and timber like ivy growing over a wall. Screams echo from the distance, warring with deafening rumbles broken only by thunderous claps. But the street is quiet.

Too quiet.

The girl begins to sob again, her small hands clutching at my neck. She's frail but with a dimpled face that still boasts baby fat—seven name days at most. I abandon my spear and it hovers, radiating golden light that cuts through the darkness. I stroke the girl's dark hair, murmuring reassurances. She wails even harder, mumbling words that are hard to understand.

"What is she saying?" I ask. We need to move, meet up with the guards that were supposed to be protecting this city. But we can't leave this child, not with her guardian dead.

The girl blubbers, spilling a chorus of words, but I shake my head. I'm a fast learner, but a year in Eingard has not been enough to pick up all the local dialects. At first it was a shock to realize that, although the Royal Council under Alistair Sorenson's rule mandated everyone speak the standard dialect of Ceorn, Eingardians outside the capital had their own variations on the language. Then again, all that mattered to Jonas's uncle was Eingardian blood. Destroying the languages of the rest of the Kingdom of Ifé was more important than ensuring everyone in his region spoke the right dialect of the "proper" tongue.

"It's all right. We won't hurt you," Jonas says, taking the girl from me. He rubs her back, whispering softly. "What hurts, little one?"

The girl answers and he listens, the skin between his brows pulling tighter as she speaks. Then she scratches at the ill-fitting trousers covering her legs and he beckons me over.

"Something bit her. When she and her cousin were running away."

I swallow and move closer, waving a hand slowly before pointing to the girl's trousers. She flinches and clutches at Jonas, whispering in his ear. He places a hand on her shoulder and gives a small squeeze.

"I'm a healer. I won't hurt you," I say.

Another tremor ripples through the buildings. The timber backing lashed to the city gates creaks in protest. The girl collapses. There's a gash on her knee, creased, mottled, and bumpier than a cut should be, oozing dark liquid. I peer closer, and right then, the bump moves, making a squelching noise that sends a shudder down my spine. I call up my magic, green fire swirling at my fingertips. I need to examine the girl closer, confirm I'm not imagining things.

"Wound's infected," I say.

The tremors shift into a rhythm, the beat of a thousand footsteps marching in tandem. I scarcely have time to extinguish the flame in my hand when guards sporting iron breastplates and purple-and-yellow cloaks erupt from the mist, arrows nocked.

A man's voice rings out. "In the name of the king, I order you, identify yourselves!"

"I *am* the king," Jonas announces, stepping forward just as a guard spits, "Meascans. They're behind this."

The guard swerves, training his arrow at my throat. "Hands where I can see them."

I stiffen at the insult, that familiar coil of rage spreading through my tightening muscles. This guard chose the wrong day.

He steps closer, barking, "Hands where I can see—"

Another voice drowns his. "Put that bow down. Now."

The guard snorts, but others move to obey, lowering their weapons, shuffling to the sides of the wide street like grass parting against an onslaught of wind. A woman stands in the center, a head taller than the rest, iron spikes threaded through the thick braid running down her scalp. The secondary braids on the side of her head are plaited into half suns, the beads hanging from them threading back to the middle braid to form rays. Her pauldrons are lion faces, mouths carved into a vicious snarl. The sun symbol on her breastplate announces her as Mina, the former leader of the capital wing of the Eingardian Army, and Jonas's new head general. The three jagged streaks under her left eye, stark white against the richness of her brown skin, mark her as Oyo-born, from the northeast Lani tribe of warriors.

"I won't repeat myself," she says, yanking out the nzappa strapped to her belt. She tosses the curved ax from palm to palm and it gleams, catching the light coming off my spear. "What's it to be? Your pride or your life?"

Next to me, the little girl whimpers, folding as though she can make herself disappear.

The guard eyes us. "You're making a mistake, Captain," he scoffs, barely sparing Mina a glance, let alone a respectful salute. "*It* may look like one of your people, but meascans are not known for showing mercy. Look what it did to the child."

I bristle and my spear responds, flying straight to me. Everything happens all at once. The guard releases his arrow, but the arrow halts midair, a thread of cerulean twining around it. Mina hurls her nzappa and it catches the guard's bow, cleaving it in half. It spins back into her hand, but not before the smaller curved blade on the back licks his hand, leaving an angry gash. He drops with a howl. A few other guards cursing my dirty-blooded magic move to try their luck when Jonas steps in front of me, brandishing the insignia that's been tucked under his collar. At the sight of the sun insignia, the guards fall to their knees crying, "My liege."

My spear pulses in my hands, straining against my fingers, begging to be unleashed. The iron magic in my blood sings with rage, building a fire in my chest. I try to beat it down, hold myself together.

"Dèmi?"

I meet Jonas's concerned gaze, hear the question he wants to ask without him saying a word, *Can you hold it?*

No remonstrances, no accusations of my failure to contain a power I didn't even know I had a year ago.

Closing my eyes, I inhale, imagine myself in the Spirit Realm the way Baba Sylvanus taught me. Seven breaths and the fury drains from me like water seeping into the earth. I slam the end of my spear into the ground and it collapses into a ring again, searing itself to the chain around my neck. I'm in control—for now.

"Forgive us, my liege," General Mina starts. "We merged with the local Lleyrian guard. They don't yet know your face." She clears her throat, then adds, "Or my lady's."

"They don't even know the difference between a captain and a general," I mutter, glaring at the bleeding guard. The others have the good sense to avoid my gaze. I don't want to frighten anyone, or prove these Ajes right, make them believe the Oluso are monstrous after all. But sometimes I'm too worn out to care. Sometimes their fear is better than any begrudging respect I might win from them someday. Their fear keeps them out of my way, and keeps us both alive.

"Rise, Mina," Jonas commands. She obeys, tucking her nzappa away. "The city?" he asks.

"Five beasts sighted. Vanished now. Arrows didn't work. They weren't interested in us."

"The people?"

"Fifty-eight dead, thirteen of ours. Followed your orders—evacuated most this morning. Dead are stragglers, naysayers who refused to go. Bodies burning or disappeared."

"Fifty-nine," Jonas corrects, nodding at the charred smudge spread across the cobblestones. The woman's body is gone, consumed as though it never were. Only the little girl at my feet, rocking with her hands over her ears, left as remembrance.

"Children? We found this one," Jonas says, scooping the girl into his arms. She hangs limp like a newborn kitten, eyes closed. I still need to heal her.

"There were a group of refugee children. Late evacuations. The beasts went straight for them. We lost ten men defending."

"But you sent one to us," I snap, anger burning through every word. "A boy from Manapané."

Mina frowns. "We did not. At least—I did not."

Jonas and I share a look. Mina was the only person who knew we were in the forest today. We led everyone else to believe we were returning to the capital. If she did not speak to anyone—

The ground shakes, knocking us all off balance. Jonas drops to one knee, nearly dropping the girl. The kokulu teeth lying on the ground rise, twirling in place before gathering to each other, birthing a larger flame as they clash and meld.

"Protect Their Royal Highnesses!" Mina shouts, but the guards rush forward, creating a chasm of bodies between Jonas and me. One even brandishes her sword as though to ward me off.

"It's the meascan," someone whispers, loud enough for me to hear. "You saw what she did with the arrow."

I jump to my feet before one of them can take a swing at me. I have never hated the Council's decision to continue hiding Jonas' status as an Oluso—and the fact that he went along with it—more than I do right now.

"Mina," I warn. If she doesn't convince these guards we're on the same side, and soon, I am going to have to defend myself and they will not like what I might do . . .

But she's already shoving a few of the guards out of the way. "You fools! Protect both His and *Her* Royal—"

A thundering crack swallows what's left of her words. A kokulu's face emerges from the gathering mass, a deep-set skull with a spiked crest protruding from the top of its head, its elongated jaw adorned once again with those deadly teeth. Before I can even blink, the face lances through the guards separating Jonas and me, setting fire to those too slow to jump out of its way. The smell of burning flesh and rot chokes the air.

Rearing back, I forge my spear again, throwing it as the kokulu arrives at Jonas, weaving around him like a masquerade dancer. The spear slams into the side of the kokulu, splitting its jaw, but the monster merely spins, streaking toward Jonas after turning in a wide arc. Jonas tosses the girl to a nearby guard and meets the kokulu straight on, slashing at its nose. But the creature passes through, detaching its jaw fully and sweeping past. Too late I see the luminescent mark on the girl's knee, the mottled violet matching the flames still emanating from the kokulu's skull—the injury I hadn't yet had a chance to deal with because of these annoying guards.

I skid into Jonas. He yanks me away from the scattered mess of teeth that fall in my wake. The guard carrying the girl drops her unceremoniously to the ground, scrambling from the now-stilled kokulu face floating a mere breath away. Mina lunges forward, swinging her nzappa at the creature, but the girl jerks her head toward her and Mina freezes, suspended in midair, the fierce look in her eyes swiftly morphing into terror. The guards behind her follow suit, bodies stitched in place, marionettes dangling from an invisible string.

"Well done, my child," the girl says. Gone is the twinkling, breathy voice that spilled out in bursts of a Ceornian dialect. Her voice is sharp, scarcely above a whisper, yet it carries a weight that echoes through our bodies. She rises to her feet, cracking her limbs into odd angles, a snake shedding old skin. She twists her head until her eyes fix on me, her pupils now a fathomless white. When she smiles, pale pink lips stretch into a too-wide grin. My skin prickles, and I fold my trembling fingers into fists. Jonas places a hand on my arm as though to shield me, but I feel the quiver on his skin too.

"You are Osèzèlé's, are you not?" the girl continues.

"What if I am?" I answer, forcing my voice to remain even. The mention of my father's name is enough to make the ribbon of fear in my belly unspool into horror. My spear, still buried in the kokulu's discarded jaw, rattles.

"Who are you?" Jonas shouts.

The girl tilts her nose up, sniffing like a dog. "Ah, Afèni's too." She tuts. "We should have checked, slaughtered *all* her children."

"Who are you?" Jonas asks again, this time through clenched teeth.

The girl ignores him, muttering to herself, ". . . the second child, was it not? The lame-legged one . . . she looked at us with such contempt . . ."

He tugs at the short sword at his waist and I feel his voice in my mind like a soft, reassuring caress. *Can we take it down without harming the girl?"*

She's dead, I volley back, willing away the dread creeping up my throat.

You can't know that. What if we strike the kokulu—get it away from her?

I swallow hard. Whatever is controlling the girl knows who I am. And all I hear are echoes of my dead mother's warnings like a ritualistic chant, *Run, run, run!*

Jonas's fingers tighten on my arm. "Dèmi? We have to try."

I shake my head, mind racing. "The wound on her leg—there's a kokulu tooth in there. If we cut it out, we might save her."

The girl cocks her head, peering at Jonas. "You stink of Osèzèlé's magic too." She licks her lips. "Let's have a taste." She beckons, and he's dragged into the air, speeding towards her. Shit.

Calling on the wind spirits, I fling a focused gust at her. She flips backwards, drifting upright, and Jonas falls, dropping to his feet. When she turns to face us, she is no longer smiling. She waves a hand and a few teeth rise from the pile, boring into the surrounding soldiers' necks. They straighten, but now their faces are slack, pupils wild and frenzied. They stagger toward us, closing in with raised swords.

Diving for my spear, I drag it up in time to meet the first soldier's blow. Jonas parries another and knocks a third to the ground with a sweeping kick. The female guard from earlier lashes out, catching me in the side, and I scream, bringing her and a few others to their knees, blood dripping from their ears. I sneer, satisfied. The Lleyrian guards didn't even know to avoid an Oluso's magical scream, and yet they thought to challenge me.

Jonas cracks his head against another soldier's. His assailant falls, and another takes their place, jumping onto his back and stabbing his upper shoulder. He buckles, gasping against the pain, and I'm there, slamming the blunt end of my spear into the soldier's back and knocking him out.

"I'm starting to think we should kill them," Jonas growls, gripping his bloodied shoulder.

I grin. "Changed your mind about everyone being worth saving?"

He grunts as I yank the dagger from his shoulder. I splay my fingers over the bleeding wound. "Hush, this is going to hurt."

Pulling at the threads of my magic, I coat his wound in a steady stream of white flame, careful to feed in only a little bit at a time. Iron-bloods draw the magic out of others, and my mate is no exception. Losing too much magic here might mean we end up dead, but I can't fight this battle half-worried that he might die. He clenches his teeth against the pain, wincing as the muscles fuse back together.

General Mina's howl breaks my concentration. She crashes onto her feet, a glowing kokulu tooth studding her brow like a decorative ring, her possessed gaze trained on us.

"Middle of the skull, between the eyes!" I yell, shoving Jonas forward. "Go."

He springs for the kokulu head, and I crouch, sinking my fingers against the cracked cobblestone. General Mina advances toward me. My heart thunders wildly, exhaustion pulling me into its depths. I've used so much magic. I have to end this—now.

Taking a deep breath, I reach for my iron magic, pushing everything I have left into this. If Jonas doesn't strike down that head, it won't matter whether I'm in control or not.

A familiar rush of warmth floods me as my power grows, filling me with the urge to command the earth itself, carve it up and shape it and everything around me to my will. I try to rein it in, chanting the words Baba Sylvanus taught me, words my father apparently spoke every time he struggled to control his iron magic.

Emi li omi li apa odò. Emi ni ina gbà eeru. Mo wa jinna fidimule. Mo se apéré irin bi ò sè nsè mi.

I am water in the arms of a stream. I am fire embracing ash. I am deeply rooted. I shape iron as it molds me.

Mina hurls her nzappa at Jonas. Golden fire races down my arm and a tremor ripples through the stones under my fingers, pieces of flinty iron rising from them. The iron particles close around Mina's nzappa, peeling it apart as though it is little more than wrinkled paper.

Jonas darts through an opening between two soldiers, racing for the head. A figure emerges from the corner of my eye. I whirl, deadly magic at my fingertips, and stagger back as I lock eyes with the man across from me.

Colin stands at the edge of the street, cloaked in smoke and shadow, his face golden in the light of the burning flames.

I step forward, stricken.

"Dèmi!"

Jonas's shout roars like an alarm bell. I spin around as the girl waves a hand and a possessed soldier rushes him, sword aimed at this heart. Striking my fist against the dirt, I draw more iron and shoot it forward. It warps into a shield, blocking the blow. Jonas drives his sword through the center of the kokulu's skull, impaling it between the eyes. The girl screams as the skull shatters, and the sound resonates, bursting glass in nearby windows. The moving soldiers and Mina drop to the ground. The girl closes her eyes, her body bent in half like a broken doll.

I leap back, avoiding a collision with a falling soldier. Then I sweep my gaze around, searching. There is nothing at the edge of the street save rubble and the acrid, nauseating stench of burning flesh. Colin—if he was ever there—is gone.

The girl drops from the sky, eyes rolling back into her head. Jonas dives to catch her.

But as she nears his arms, she seizes, body hovering in midair. Violet flame sparks on her skin and her hair rises in wild tendrils, fluttering about her face. Now I see the glint in her eyes, the piercing look that speaks of an ancient spirit, ageless and malevolent.

"Consider this parting a gift. We'll meet again," she says, curling her mouth into a ferocious smile. "Rivers of blood await you, sleeping moon."

She disappears, winking out of existence like a smothered candle. The pyres surrounding us cease, and we plunge into darkness.

ENTREATIES

"You refuse to reverse the law? Bring back the raids? After what you saw in Lleyria?"

Lady Ayn leans out of her chair, spittle flying as she shouts. Her usually stiff face is flushed, the red darkening the wrinkles in her pale skin.

"We don't know if the events in Lleyria had anything to do with the Oluso," Jonas responds in as even a tone as he can muster.

"As far as you know."

"As far as you know too," Jonas counters.

"I know that your weapons won't work on the kokulu," I add. "Magic is our best bet."

"You would say that, wouldn't you, meascan?" she snarls.

"Lady Ayn," Jonas snaps.

I take a breath, steady myself, although all I want to do is call the wind, knock that vicious smile off her face. It's one thing for isolated village guards to use that word. But for a member of the Council? Yet one year has not softened Lady Ayn's tongue, and there are eleven other sets of eyes watching me, weighing whether I'm worth the risk after all. A young Oluso queen was gamble enough. But one they cannot mold— or cudgel with iron at the very least—is a dangerous existence, worse even, than Ejo-Maré, the mountain spirit suspected of luring townsfolk to certain death by appearing as the person they desire most. The Council may be skeptical about the work of spirits, but perceived disrespect is a worse, unpardonable insult.

Except when that disrespect is aimed at me.

But I can't give them reason to doubt me further. So, I fold my voice until it comes off as measured, confident. I play the game. "The kokulu are ancient. Queen Afèni united the regions of Ifé with the common goal of defeating them. Believe it or not, Oluso and Aje once fought together against them. I dare say the Oluso protected the Aje from the brunt of that war."

Lady Ayn rolls her eyes. I tamp down the urge to morph the ornate iron choker she's wearing into flesh-rending spikes.

"The kokulu we encountered last night did something I've never heard of," I continue, turning away from her. "It possessed a child."

The man settled on the throne in the center of the room finally stirs, giving me a sharp look. "What do you suggest?"

"We send a message to Oluso elders. Gather information. There's so much we're still missing from Afèni's time. Especially since—" I lick my lips, searching for a way to mention how Alistair Sorenson, the brother of the man now enthroned, set fire to four hundred years of historical records and hung the royal okosuns by their tongues in his bid to conquer Oyo. It doesn't suit me, all this dancing around the truth, but I promised Jonas I'd try things his way.

"Since we've mismatched records," Jonas finishes smoothly. "Grandfather ordered the court scribes to focus only on Eingard's history during his time. We don't have any useful information in our archives."

Right. Those archives are filled with military propaganda praising the might of Eingard, treatises on why Oluso are little more than magic-wielding beasts that need to be put down, and several entries from Jonas's grandfather detailing his quest to find a cream that would restore his waning sexual prowess.

Jonas flicks a look at me at that last thought and I shrug, sending him a mental reprimand.

If you really want me to maintain my composure, stop reading my mind. I'm allowed to think what I want about that bastard—these ones too.

His reply accompanies a low chuckle. *Fair enough.*

Markham rises from the throne, crossing to the lower end of the dais. "Then who would you consult? Who are these . . . elders?"

I straighten, assuming the poise of the politician again. "Baba Sylvanus—he helped raise me. General Tenjun. He is well respected for the peace treaty that ended the border wars between Goma and Eingard—"

"The treaty that kept us from receiving the fertile lands we'd won in skirmish," Lady Ayn interjects.

I tense. Of course Ayn sees the former king's attempted conquest of the Gomae region as a mere skirmish. After Eingard conquered Oyo, Goma and Berréa, the eastern and southern regions of Ifé, surrendered, fearing an invasion. Alistair Sorenson, the former king, marched on Goma anyway, leaving bodies and chaos in his wake.

"Mother, Uncle Alistair's forces got whipped and you know it," Elodie proclaims with a bemused smile. "They routed our forces without killing a single soldier. Impressive, if you ask me."

Ayn turns her frosty glare on her daughter, and for once, I'm grateful for Elodie's presence in this room.

"You would do well to remember only to speak in turn," Lady Ayn chides, rubbing a bejeweled finger against the neck of the songbird sitting on her shoulder.

"Words spoken out of turn make for poor song and bad omens," Elodie parrots dutifully.

But Jonas has had enough. "You should take your own advice," he declares. "Dèmi was still speaking." He nods at me. "Who else beyond Sylvanus and Tenjun do we consider?"

I pause for a breath, knowing they'll see this as a trap waiting to spring. "Ekwensi."

They all erupt at once, voices clamoring for supremacy.

"—I knew you were in league with—"

"You can't be serious—"

"—trust the man who turned our kingdom into—"

I raise my voice. "I'm not saying we should trust him, but we can offer a truce. If the kokulu come back in full force, we will *all* suffer devastating losses. The kokulu don't care for politics. *They* don't bother negotiating the murder they commit."

Lady Ayn throws her fan to the floor, and the bird on her shoulder twitters in alarm, hopping off to perch on the edge of her seat. "You think us foolish? You think we don't know what you're doing? Filling the capital with your people—"

"*My* people," Jonas interrupts, eyes flashing a warning. "The Oluso are my people too. And Dèmi will soon be your queen. It would behoove you to remember that."

"I remember that you broke your betrothal to *my* daughter for a woman whose meascan family nearly ruined this kingdom."

I grit my teeth, trying to remind myself that she's not worth it. Retaliation is not worth it over a mere insult. Not after what I've suffered all year.

"Lady Ayn!" Jonas shouts. "I will not warn you again. Do not insult my mate or her family."

Elodie sighs. "Mother, Auri and I agreed to set our betrothal aside. He loves Dèmi, anyone can see that." Her gaze falls onto us, and for a moment her blue eyes spark with emotion as she adds, "He pledged himself to her so quickly, when he couldn't be bothered to grant me a commitment ceremony."

Jonas has the audacity to flush, ears turning bright pink. "Elodie," he says, tone softening a little.

She shrugs. "It's all in the past, Auri. The royal coffers aren't enough to keep me in style anyway." She laughs, a tinkling sound that sets my teeth on edge. The other Council members share looks before following suit, some of the tension easing from their shoulders. Elodie catches me staring and winks.

I turn away. It's times like these, when I look at her slim, pale face, the braided golden hair that adorns her like a crown, when I see how easily she handles the Council despite only joining officially half a year ago, that I feel most ashamed and out of place. I remember, that despite how kind she is to me in public, how much she chases after me to offer advice, Elodie is not my friend. She is "Queen of the Court"— a nickname the Council would still like to fashion into prophecy. She is a reminder I do not belong here. That, after all, is why her mother invited her in.

"You may forgive, my dear," Lady Ayn sniffs, "but it should infuriate you that this whelp took your place. Her bitch mother ran off after being impregnated by that murderous, dirt-blooded savage—"

My power surges as my last shred of self-control rips like a hut mangled by a wind storm. The rings on her fingers heat, iron scorching her papery skin.

She howls. Elodie snatches her wine goblet off the side stool between their seats and dumps the rich liquid on her mother's hand. Lady Ayn exhales as a hiss of steam rises from her burned fingers. The guards posted at the perimeter of the room swarm me, weapons drawn.

"Stand down," Jonas commands them, wresting me to him. "Everything is under control. Back away."

"Insult my mother one more time," I cry from behind Jonas's shoulder. "You'll understand the meaning of ruin then."

It's the first time outside of a fight that I've used my magic to hurt someone. But what is more frightening is the swelling excitement in my chest, the knowledge that I enjoyed it. For once, I'm glad the Council has always ignored my pleas. No Oluso can kill without suffering loss of their spirit bonds and condemning themselves to a creeping madness and slow yet painful death, but in this moment, Lady Ayn is afraid I might risk it.

"Oko mi, look at me," Jonas mutters, framing my face with his hands. His voice fills my mind, drowning out my rage. *Please, please, just wait a moment. This is what she wants, to see you lose control. Just wait and trust me, please.*

I stare back, defiant. *What should I wait for? For more of her insults? For the rest of this farce to play out?*

This isn't you, he volleys back. *Remember our goal. We—you are the voice of the Oluso. Every time you lose control here . . .*

He trails off, but I don't need to hear anything more. He's right. Like it or not, I am the representative of the Oluso, the mirror meant to reflect the actions of all my people. If I fall here, we fail. If we fail, I condemn them. Shoving down the magic welling up in me, I exhale. I am in control once more.

Lady Ayn sneers at Jonas. "You pledged to make this kingdom safe— instead you bow to these meascans. People will die because of your foolishness."

"Yet it was *yours* that nearly got my son killed," Markham roars from the throne, his voice a clap of thunder. Everyone falls silent, not daring to breathe. He rounds on her, the fires from the kudu horn hanging on the ceiling casting him in bronze. "You have yet to explain yourself, Camilla."

Lady Ayn opens her mouth, then registering the telltale tic in Markham's jaw, the way his mouth is drawn tight, she lowers her head. "Forgive me, my liege. The situation in Lleyria was pressing. We could not wait for your return."

"You risked the heir out of mere impatience? What would you have done if things went wrong?"

She says nothing. Another Council member coughs. The answer is in front of us, plain for all to see. Markham sits on the throne ruling as regent while Jonas and I stand in the midst of the council circle like petulant children awaiting a scold. Jonas may be heir, king in name, but at the end of the day, the Council's votes and that gnarled circle of gold passing through Markham's wispy blond hair dictates who has the power in the room.

"Answer me, any of you," Markham demands. "What were you thinking?"

Ayn lays a hand over her burned fingers, the mask of composure now in place. "Lleyria is a key, strategic city. We could not afford to lose it."

"You can't afford to lose its mines," I seethe. "Iron and precious jewels are the Ayn family trade."

She narrows her eyes. "I didn't know my family was of such interest to you. Looks like we've uncovered another motive for magical beasts appearing in one of our best areas—sabotage."

"Enough," Jonas commands. "We stay on topic. We can't accuse the Oluso of this. Or we risk starting a war. We need their help. Do you all agree?"

Silence.

He turns to Markham. "Father, *you* must at least see the wisdom in my words."

Markham does not respond. I know him well enough by now to know that his silence is consideration. The slight furrow in his brow tells me that he is parsing our words, imagining all that comes with our recommendation. But then he takes his place on the throne, folds his hands under his chin, and it's clear we have lost.

"For now, we wait and watch the situation," he announces finally. "Keep all information about these creatures to this room only. We do not alert Ekwensi, nor do we alarm the local people." Lady Ayn settles back in her high chair, victorious. "We must not antagonize the Oluso." Her smile slips into a scowl.

"For now," he repeats, the words echoing through the room.

I want to scream at this cowardice. Instead I curl my fingers into fists and let my nails bite half-moons into my palms. I'm the fool for expecting anything to change. What good was risking my life to depose Sorenson, winning the right to rule, when all it meant was catering to another Aje, tying myself to a council that still believes it gets to decide our freedom?

"So, we are in agreement then," Jonas declares. "The Oluso raids remain illegal. And we consult the Oluso elders on the kokulu issue."

Again, Markham does not answer.

Sometimes the laws Jonas and I fought for seem little more than paper idols peeling off the side of thatched houses, symbols meant to ward off evil. They're meant to grant the Oluso freedom from persecution, but every patrol day we uncover something new—an Oluso forced to work in iron mines, a child rumored to cry precious pearls smuggled into a noble house. It wasn't enough for the Council to plead for concessions; begging for enslaved Oluso to continue working as paid servants; arguing that Oluso asewós in pleasure houses could not be liberated without causing riots. The very idea that Oluso might be free, that the Aje world might change, is unbearable. Why grant the Oluso freedom when they can continue profiting off our bodies and minds? And so they haunt us like anjonú, ghouls born from the souls of unvenerated ancestors, feasting on our patience and goodwill, promising us a taste of paradise. And I'm not sure how much more I can take.

Jonas brushes his palm against my wrist, but I don't look up. He was the one who asked me to trust him. He needs to find us a way out of this mess. The kokulu won't care that Ajes now rule Ifé. They will kill until they've satisfied themselves. I shudder, remembering the possessed girl's smile before she disappeared. At the very least, I need to see Baba Sylvanus, get a better understanding of what is happening.

"Perhaps we're discussing this from a limited perspective," Lord Kairen mutters, speaking up for the first time all morning. He strokes the earring decorating his ear, the action so like Colin's that I swallow, pushing back the ache gnawing in my chest.

I searched the streets of Lleyria, looking for any signs my friend had been there after all. Nothing.

"Maybe war is what we need," Kairen adds, his expression brightening as though he's just solved a riddle.

"A war between whom, exactly?" I ask, not bothering to mask the hostility in my voice.

He chirps on like an excited child who has discovered a secreted sweet. "If these creatures wreak more havoc, Ekwensi may reconsider, join forces with us. War makes for interesting bedfellows."

"Certainly," Elodie quips. "I hear your son is in league with him."

Kairen purses his lips before answering stiffly, "I have one son, my heir, Matéo, who waits in T'Lapis. Nicolás was excised from our ancestral line the day he took up arms in rebellion."

I scoff. Even now this bastard denies Colin. I feel ashamed for thinking them similar for a moment.

Jonas speaks, cutting his eyes at me before I release the scathing remark burning on my tongue. "Ekwensi has no reason to help us. Oluso have a better chance of surviving kokulu."

"More reason to suspect your kind," Lady Ayn mutters.

I ignore her, taking Jonas's hand instead. "What if we reveal you're Oluso?"

I wait, heart in my throat. If everyone knew Jonas was Oluso, things would change. The Ajes would think twice about disobeying the new laws. The Oluso would be more likely to report violations. At the very least it would present a different option than joining Ekwensi. Perhaps with this, too, Ekwensi could see a path forward and fight with us to eradicate the kokulu.

"You see it now?" Ayn barks gleefully. "She wants to tear our kingdom down. She always has."

Jonas ignores the shrill voice and strokes the back of my hand. "I don't think that will work. Not now."

"Why not?"

"We still need public support. We're passing laws, having a betrothal—I just need more time to make sure it all goes well."

And you think this is going well?

I hold his gaze, catch the lurking anxiety hiding behind the confident façade he wears. I do understand. Most of Eingard has been raised to hate Oluso without question. Even if they could accept their king as one, there have been many changes in their lives of late. Alistair Sorenson is dead, and there are daily reports of Ekwensi's army growing. The new laws protecting Oluso have been in place for a little less than a year. Yet the presence of a few Oluso—delegations from the other regions led by Nana, who arrived last week for our betrothal—caused a stir.

But I am also tired of understanding, of hiding behind pretty words and political dances, fickle promises and fanciful treaties. I am tired of suppressing my desires.

I want Jonas to tear off that mask, ascend that dais with me, and reveal himself as my Oluso mate. I want him to forget the nobles and courtiers and everyone who must be considered for political reasons and think for a moment about us alone. I want him to hold my hand and show the world the glory of our magic swirling, melding together to birth a glorious flame.

Then, I'd believe we stand a chance to lead both Oluso and Aje—that we have the power to change the world.

He presses his forehead to mine, forgetting for a moment where we are. "We will have that and more." He places a kiss on my hand, a plea. "Soon."

I nod. It's not enough. But it has to be. For now.

Markham glowers at us. "If you're quite finished, we have other matters to discuss?" He waves and the guards step back, sliding into their places against the Council room walls like decorative ornaments festooning a cake.

The message is clear—the issue is dismissed. We have no power here, not enough to command the guards, or push on the issue of the kokulu. Markham has moved on, and so has the Council.

I grit my teeth, wishing for a moment, that one of those creatures would suddenly appear, spark into life like cinders, and unfurl a blaze of terror in their hearts.

"Yes, there is trouble with one of the central cities, Gaeyak-Orin," Lord Islington begins. "The waters are failing to produce fish—"

"These are Inner Council matters," Markham interrupts, arching an eyebrow at me.

Jonas moves to protest, but I place a hand on his arm. Offering the Council members a perfunctory bow, I leave the room. I need to leave this place before I end up becoming the monster they suspect me to be.

I'm not even three steps into the outer corridor when Elodie calls after me.

"You're in a hurry," she says, amused blue eyes scouring my face. The guards shadowing her hover closer as she leans in, touching my shoulder with a gloved hand. "And you seem exhausted too. I told you not to get too close to Lord Ottamen. His breath would rot corpses."

I pull back, crossing my arms. "What do you want?"

The smile on her face recedes into a controlled, courtly mask, and shame stirs in my heart like sparks spewing from flames.

In the past year, Elodie has been nothing but polite, seeking me out at Council dinners and court parties, inviting me on several occasions to spend time with her. But there is something about the way she watches me, eyes following my every breath and movement, like a merchant poring over a prized jewel, aware of every crack and imperfection. Sometimes our eyes will meet and she'll stare, face twisted in an expression so stark my heart seizes in fear. When I blink and search her face again, her usual smile is there, plastered on like a practiced illusion, but I know what I saw.

"You are tired," she says, dropping her lingering hand. "Perhaps you would like a rest? I had hoped to chat today, but I shouldn't keep you. The ceremony is so soon."

"It is." I flick my eyes at a passing attendant carrying a tray laden with silks. "The head maid asked me to return to my rooms early. Good-bye, Lady Elodie."

Her mouth quirks into a half smile. "You're not even curious about what I have to say?"

"And what is that?" I ask, keeping my voice as airy as I can manage. Her guards are still eyeing me with unabashed distrust.

"I hear Oyo-born people care about fortunes, so I just wanted to wish you good fortune."

That's it?

I nod my thanks, offering her another bow before hurrying to the corridor. I feel her eyes on me with every step, clinging like leeches to my skin. As I slip out of sight, though, I'm reminded of Oya, the premier wind spirit who harnesses the gales, and the carved wooden statuettes sold in Benin markets that showcase her beauty and radiance. Oya's eyes are always closed, twin orbs in a serene face. Her arms dance out and back in welcome, her indigo-dyed skirts billowing in an imaginary wind. But when you turn those statues over, Oya's eyes open, her welcoming arms now jubilant talons that hang over the souls of the dead like a cage, her skirts the web that drowns them, pulling them into a world where light is a forgotten dream. And the look on her face?—pure hunger, greed that promises you she will leave nothing behind if your soul ever becomes hers, a look not unlike Elodie's.

I shudder and walk faster.

INTRIGUE

I RACE THROUGH THE CORRIDORS OF CHÂTEAU NORDGREN, COGNIZANT OF the two shadows stalking me, moving with such speed that their iron breastplates whistle against the breeze.

The corridor splits ahead. I swerve left instead of following the path to the solar Jonas and I share. The guards following pick up speed, breaths hitching like dogs on the hunt, moments from sinking their teeth into their prey.

Up ahead, more shadows await; broad, misshapen lumps hidden under a shroud of damask cloth. A marbled hand gripping a dagger, a remnant of the Sorenson statue that once presided over this corridor, peeks out from underneath the cloth.

Speeding into a sprint, I snag the dagger with one hand and shove it back, flinging myself into the recess that opens as the stones shift between the covered statues. I slip into the secret alcove, crouching low as the guards chasing me thunder past. I remain there for a few breaths, heart beating so fast the stone underneath my fingers seems to throb as well. Then, before they think to double back, I drag myself out of the thick curtain of cloth and run in the direction of our solar. The royal guard can be persistent when they want to be, and being found means losing the only quiet I'll have before the betrothal.

When I finally glimpse the swell of oak peeking out of the sea of gray stone walls, I dive for the door's handle, clinging to it as if it's a lucky piece of driftwood rescuing me from ceaseless waves. Since the day Ekwensi murdered Alistair Sorenson, the doors on the castle floors housing nobility are fashioned from iron masked with bronze paint designed to convince the viewer the entryway is nothing but wood. Any Oluso who harbors dreams of joining the royal retinue or infiltrating these walls is in for a painful, vomit-inducing awakening, courtesy of the Council. Jonas and I alone are able to walk in this castle without pain, spared by our status as iron-bloods. Still, Jonas insisted on crafting our bedroom door from my favorite kind of timber produced in Benin, so I could remember the scents of home.

The room is empty, the fire in the hearth long snuffed out. The pewter dishes are still covered in ash, stacked at the hearth where I left them two days ago. The hairs on my arm rise. Where are the attendants?

Something shifts in the corner of my eye, a shadow lurching. I spring forward, leaping out of the way as an ax whips by my head and embeds itself in the door. The wood splinters, pieces of the òwón landing in my hair and on my nose. But I don't have a moment to breathe in the tangy, honeyed scent of my favorite wood because my assailant dives at me, slashing at my waist with a double-edged dagger.

I jump back but the blade rips through my top. A rectangle of cotton flutters to the ground exposing my navel to the piercing chill. The assassin comes at me again, spinning into a high kick that I block with crossed arms, pushing them off balance. They stumble for a moment then pivot, circling me. I mirror their movements, waiting for an opening. This is the seventh assassination attempt in the last six months alone. If there's anything I've learned, it's that magic is wasted until I understand who and how many people I'm fighting. Losing stamina when fighting off one killer is bad; getting magic drawn out of me when there are many lying in wait, eager to finish the job, is dire stupidity.

The figure across from me is clad in a white, close-fitted suit capped with a common mask they sell at Eingardian markets—an ashen face with scarred cheeks, a toothy, grinning mouth, and antlers sprouting from its helm—the bridal mask. Through the generous eye slits, I glimpse a flash of seawater green.

"Olorun's blood," I curse. My assassins have hailed from all around the kingdom. Eye color alone is not enough information.

"They told me you were a blasphemer," the assassin taunts. Her voice is gravelly, like cave waters that burble deep in the mountains. Her Ceorn is well pronounced, but with an edge, a lilt that tells me she once spoke another tongue before succumbing to Eingard's.

I narrow my eyes. The fact that she recognizes Olorun, the Father of Spirits and Skies, can only mean one thing.

"Olorun forgives his children who curse. He has no room for those who kill their brethren," I blurt, pulling my staff from the air.

I launch at her, swinging my staff in a wide arc. She dodges, somersaulting onto our dining table. I sweep the end of my staff at her legs, but she is faster, leaping overhead. As she crosses above me, I spy the Oluso mark at the hollow on the back of her neck, its flower a faded, wispy red. She darts for the door, pulling her ax from it. I thought I had purged the castle of onyoshi, the broken Oluso who served as Alistair Sorenson's hunting dogs, sussing out their fellow Oluso on raids, but clearly I missed this one.

"I freed the onyoshi from a lifetime of bondage," I cry. "Why would you come after me, sister?"

She flings her ax in answer. I throw up an arm, and the wind lashes around it, creating a barrier of white flame. The ax bounces off, clattering to the ground. But as I drop my arm, she's there, dagger slashing at me. I stumble back to avoid it, careening into a chair.

"One man's bondage is another's freedom," she says, kicking at me. "That was the first lesson they taught me." Her foot catches me in the ribs, the blow unleashing a burst of pain that stabs through my chest. I grunt and roll upright, edging away.

She charges me again. My heart is pounding in my ears, my iron magic pulsing, begging to be freed, but I wait, let her feint forward with her dagger, then I dodge, stepping into her, latching onto her shoulder and elbow. Driving my foot into her instep, I pin her in place and thrust her arm back, past her ear. She howls as the bones snap, cracking as they break.

But it is not enough. She slams her forehead into mine. I fall backward, crashing against the table. Pain splits my skull like a hammer and I blink rapidly, trying to clear my blurring vision.

"Weak," she jeers, mocking me. "Sorenson broke us more than that. We had to learn to fight in chains."

The black spots in my vision gather to form another shadow, one slipping out from behind a curtain, closing in on us.

Shaking my head, I try to right myself, but my assailant drives her foot into my chest, knocking me to the ground. "I fought for what I had here. I didn't need your *liberation*."

Her mask is shattered, clay shards peeling off like pieces of eggshell as she speaks. "You never thought that maybe we were happy? Living out our madness in comfort?" Another kick. Now I glimpse a wide forehead, snatches of honeyed skin. "It was far better than the painful life most Oluso are destined for."

The second shadow creeps closer, and I catch a glint of burnished copper gleaming in the fading afternoon light.

The assassin looms over me, none the wiser. I gasp as she digs the iron soles of her boot into my ribs, crushing the air out of me. "They said you'd be tough to put down. Said you were full of surprises."

"Surprise," calls the man behind her.

She turns as he brings the copper vase he carries down, striking her over the head. She sags to her knees and slumps to the ground, blood dripping from her dark, matted nest of hair.

"You're late," the man says, reaching out a hand to help me up.

"Is that why you didn't help sooner?" I growl.

Mikhail shakes his head matter-of-factly. "Ekwensi trained me himself. I know not to get involved in magical fights. Not until I'm sure I can win, anyway." He arches his back, stretching his wide shoulders. "Besides, I was waiting for you first. This one slipped in after me. I've been here since Gull Hour."

Jonas and I were just entering the Council chambers when the castle bells rung five times, so Mikhail has been here a while.

He crouches, placing a finger on the neck of my fallen assailant. "Dead. What do you want done?"

"You killed her?" I cry.

He rolls her over, draws back one of her swollen eyelids. The whites of her eyes are laced with red veins. Poison.

I swallow. "She was onyoshi," I admit, settling into the chair nearest to me. The thought of another Oluso, broken or not, hating me enough to risk death to murder me, is new and disconcerting. "Her magic threads were very faded," I continue. "But that's why the Council sent her, isn't it? They'll mark her down as Oluso all the same if I bring attention to this— use it as ammunition to argue we're all unstable." I pound my fist against the table and leap to my feet. "We need to get her out of here. Bury her somewhere. We don't even know her name."

"Dara," Mikhail supplies. He pulls the sheet off the bed in the center of the room and drapes it carefully over the dead woman. "She was one of Sorenson's favorites. She and Ekwensi never saw eye to eye. Always competing for the former king's favor."

I nod, unsure of what to say. It's the first time I've been able to put a name to one in a line of many faces that have attempted to murder me.

Mikhail shuffles me to the hearth, drawing me away from the body. Clearing the ash-laden bowls to the side, he strikes at a piece of flint with his short sword. When it sparks, he dumps the cinders onto the pile of kindling and short sticks in the hearth, then he scoots closer, coaxing up a whisper of a flame.

"You might need more close-combat training," he teases, gray eyes twinkling as he regards me now. "Seemed like you were about to lose that fight."

I scoff. "Try escaping the royal guard, or fighting a deadly assassin after living off that rubbish excuse for porridge you Eingardians use to starve your brides. Then we'll talk."

Mikhail chuckles, broad shoulders shaking so hard, the mace strapped to his back creaks with the motion. "I happen to like griej. It's great in winter."

I plop down across from the soldier turned Guard commander. "You eat it then. I'm sure Lady Ayn would be pleased if you thinned out a bit. She could even find a traditional dress for you to wear so you can perform the betrothal in my stead."

Mikhail has the audacity to grin even wider. "Don't tempt me. I might wear it just to see her face." He fluffs his wavy chestnut hair, framing the long tresses hanging down his face in imitation.

I let out a chuckle of my own, shoulders slumping as my muscles relax. Then I remember the dead woman lying only a few feet away from me, and my body feels tight once more. "What do you have for me? Did you ever locate the boy?"

We had checked through the refugee children we rescued in Lleyria, but Namiz'en was nowhere to be found. None of the children remembered a boy from Manapané either. Another ghost.

He straightens, eyes hardening to flint as he gives his report. "Warlord Uzai reported providing safe passage for two thousand refugees. Mostly Aje, and a handful of Oluso from Biku, Bia-Hyang, Manapané, and Rey-Hati."

I nod. "Ekwensi attacked all the Eingardian strongholds in those cities, freed the Oluso there."

"The cities have also suffered increasing Harmattan storms in the months since," he adds. "No one is certain why. The Cloren Oluso were able to warn the people before the sands took hold."

I frown. Harmattan season is half a year past. There is no reason the swelling dust storms should be viable now, especially not for the coastal cities of Lower Oyo and West Berréa. I should send a message to Ayaba, the Aziza queen who watches over human life and seasons. If anyone would know about this, it's her.

"There's more," Mikhail announces. "A tenth of the refugees Uzai helped boarded a junket in Saku and sailed for Wyldewood. The vessel was rerouted to Mattiasjord midjourney. The children you found in Lleyria are the remnant of that group."

My frown deepens. "How did they end up several miles north in another city? All the adults just disappeared into thin air?"

"I spoke with a contact in Mattiasjord, the new vice chancellor," he starts.

I raise an eyebrow, but he is already waving me off. "We slept in the same cot at the orphanage. Cadena would die before giving me up."

I nod, but it's hard to reel in the unease that settles in my gut like a well-fed cat. Mikhail is one of the only Ajes I trust, but that trust was earned. "Anything worthwhile?" I ask.

"The elders in Mattiasjord received a secret missive with the Council's seal. They conducted a meeting with the Lleyrian elders the day the ship arrived. Cadena wasn't allowed in. The refugees disappeared after that."

"So, it's all connected," I mutter. "The Lleyrian elders behaving strangely, the disappearance of the refugees. Something drew the kokulu to that place."

"The what?"

I shake my head. "Something I hope you'll never have to fight. Worse than fighting ten Oluso at once."

He lifts both eyebrows. "It must be gruesome if even you are afraid."

I ignore his implication, instead asking the question that's been lurking in the back of my throat, waiting for its moment to be freed. "Was he there?"

I know it pains him, the thought that the man he owes everything to might be out somewhere killing his fellow Ajes, but I need to know.

Mikhail sighs, pinching the skin between his eyes. "Lord Ekwensi wasn't sighted. He's rumored to be in Gaeyak-Orin actually."

"What of any others? Known associates?" I ask, voice dipping low.

He pins me with a sharp look before responding, "No sign of Colin either. Nothing since the attack on Porto Pischu."

Just last month, we received reports of merchants attempting to sell orphaned Oluso children in the northwestern city, a day's ride from Nordgren. When we arrived, there were no okri to be rescued. Instead, what awaited us was a garden of statues—frostbitten husks that had once been slavers, their terrified expressions and attempts to escape immortalized in unforgiving ice. A surviving food merchant described a heavily tattooed young man with a single, winged ear cuff and a grim aura who led the attack—Colin.

I lick my lips. I know Mikhail wants an explanation, but I'm not ready to give one. Not yet. "You're certain?"

"Absolutely."

I hesitate, then lower my voice into a hushed whisper, "Did Ekwensi leave any message for you when he left? Perhaps how to get in contact with him or . . ."

Mikhail answers abruptly, "No. And even if he did, I wouldn't—"

Footsteps ring out then, loud thuds that slap against the stone like warning bells. Voices follow, royal guards shouting orders. We're out of time.

TRUCE

THE DOOR SCRAPES BACK, SMASHING INTO THE WALL. I SPRING TO MY
feet, one hand on the bone blade tucked into my belt while Mikhail
straightens to attention, all traces of camaraderie between us gone. As
far as the Council is concerned, he is merely executing their orders to
keep a close watch on me, nothing more.

A flushed Jonas stands in the doorway, breathing as though he's
been running for days. He rushes over, hands fluttering over my head,
waist, back. "I sensed you were in danger. What happened?"

A guard saunters into view behind him, standing on the threshold.
I snap my fingers and the wind shoves the door back, slamming it shut.
I exhale then, allowing my rigid muscles to slacken. "I'm all right. Just a
bump on the head."

He touches my cheek, brow furrowing as he peers into my mind.
"Someone on the Council must have kept track of a few onyoshi. I'll talk
with Lord Islington, see what we can find out without getting caught."

I squirm away. It's still a shock every time, knowing someone else
can delve inside me, pull out my darkest secrets.

Sensing my discomfort, Jonas drops his hand. "Mikhail, can you
handle the disposal without being seen?" He nods toward the sheet
covering Dara's corpse.

Mikhail looks from me to Jonas before responding, "Yes, my liege."
He is undoubtedly confused, especially since the mental bond between
me and Jonas is a closely held secret, but he recovers quickly, plucking
a tin whistle from the inner pocket of his leather vest, a gift from my

guardian Will. "I'll send for Mina. We'll take the body to the hills on the outskirts, give Dara a proper burial. It's Harvest Festival, no one will look too closely at guards transporting extra sacks of grain."

Jonas nods his approval. The two clasp hands, gripping each other's thumbs. "Thank you, my friend."

Putting the whistle to his lips, Mikhail blows out a few notes. No sound arises, yet the whistle takes on a faint glow. He replaces it in his vest, then stoops, wrapping Dara's body carefully in the sheet. Her face, unencumbered by the mask, is deeply lined, her honeyed skin pock-marked with age spots.

"She celebrated twenty-three name days last year," Mikhail says, as if he, too, can hear what I'm thinking. "She aged faster because of the torture. They all did."

Hefting Dara's body on one shoulder, he moves to the swath of wall left of the hearth.

"Mikhail," I call out to him as he tugs on the bottom arm on the sconce sprouting from the wall. "Do you have *nothing else* to share with me?"

Mikhail pauses before answering. "Ah—yes. There was another report. A larger group of refugees headed to Wellstown. I already sent riders out. We should know more soon."

Behind me, Jonas tenses, fists clenching, lips pursed. Every movement of his body is etched in my mind, as familiar to me as my own. I know he's already discovered what I really want to say, so I ignore him, and ask again, bolder this time. "Ekwensi left you nothing?"

Mikhail shakes his head. "Nothing." The wall gives way, receding into a secret passage, and the stench of rot and damp permeates the room, spoiling the air. General Mina rises out of that shadowed abyss, still dressed in her battle-worn armor. A light akin to the glowing aura of Mikhail's whistle emanates from the ear clip lashed to her left ear.

"My liege, my lady," she salutes. She takes one glance at us, notes the way Jonas is boring holes in my back while I face forward, arms crossed, and she hastens to the mouth of the passage, taking one end of Dara's tightly wrapped corpse without another word.

Mikhail cannot hide his amusement. "One more thing!" he exclaims as Mina tugs him into the waiting darkness. "Add a draught of goat's milk and a slice of butter next time. The griej will sing right down."

The wall groans closed behind them, but not before I break into a smile.

Jonas leans down, threading his arms around my waist. "I'm sorry, oko mi."

"What are you sorry for?" I bluster, levity warping into annoyance. "Sorry that the Council was going to have me murdered . . ."

"I didn't know," he interrupts. "If I had, I would've—"

"Or that the Council opposes us on every single little thing," I continue, cutting him off, "and yet we court their approval!"

I never got that time to myself after all, time to let the energy in my body melt away until I could think. Yet another thing this place has robbed from me.

I raise my voice, anger lacing every word. "We can't keep going like this, Jonas. The Oluso can't afford for us to play politics. You asked me to trust you. I did. But look where we are. The Council has all the power, we have—"

"Allies," he declares. "We have allies." He spins me around, framing my shoulders with his hands. His eyes are shining, gold flecks threaded through the blue glimmering like sunlight cutting through the dark of the ocean. "It may look like we're losing, but I promise you, we're not. We've already swayed a few Council members."

"Two," I counter.

He beams. "Three, from my uncle's court. Remember how impossible that felt a year ago?" He stalks over to a wooden chest on the nearby table and flings it open. The crystals inside are dark, their gleaming surfaces drawing in the light. He tosses me a toothy fragment and I catch the obsidian with one hand.

"Theru Al'Jai sent that over. Best volcanic glass straight from the mouth of Mount Y'cayonogo."

I whistle appreciatively, anger temporarily forgotten. "We can sell these to the merchants, make enough money to resettle all the freed Oluso in Nordgren."

He nods. "This is just the start. There are lower nobles in Eingardian cities joining our cause. Generals, warlords, people from all over Ifé—Oluso and Aje—are coming to us little by little. In time, we'll be able to eliminate the worst parts of the Council, make sure we're not reliant on them for resources. We are building a movement, a revolution that will last."

I turn over the raw crystal, marveling at the way it catches the light. It feels so sturdy in my hands, solid. But I'm tempted to open my hand and let it fall, watch whether it will shatter or survive. In this way too, I wonder if our plans are little more than this—untested and hopeful, standing just at the edge of daring. Has our revolution truly even begun?

Jonas tugs me over to the balcony. "Tell me what you see."

"I'm not in the mood for games," I retort.

"Go on," he urges. "I promise this has a point."

The capital city of Nordgren stretches before me like an Eingardian wedding dress; ornate iron wrought bridges dangling like jeweled ornaments over the stream winding around the castle like silvered thread; stone buildings, each as intricately patterned as buttons, lacing over polished cobblestone streets; peat and wood cottages clustered on rolling hills spreading wide from the center of the city in a full skirt; looming mountains that hang over like a veil, changing color with every whim of the shifting sky.

This city is breathtaking every time I look at it, a masterpiece I'm sure I could spend a lifetime studying. Then my eyes drift to the white stones gathered in a heap like an altar, the ruins of the arena where Alistair Sorenson nearly murdered three hundred captured Oluso.

I press my fingers tight against the railing, grateful for the frosty wind that nips at my nose and cheeks, bringing me to my senses. It's so easy to forget, to look at this beautifully embroidered city and lose track of the seams, the invisible threads that pulled all this together. Oluso bodies were the scaffold this city was built on, our blood the dye that colors it.

"What do you see?" Jonas asks again.

"Beauty," I answer. "Life. And all the pain, injustice, and sacrifice it took to achieve it."

"Then you've already won," he declares. "You know that there are things worth fighting for, people worth protecting, whether they love us or not. You know evil hides, arrays itself in finery and pretty words. You'll never fall for the things a seasoned Councilperson would, focusing only on what benefits them. You'll always ask if a gift for you means someone else's loss. That is what makes you who you are. That is why you will be a great ruler."

"A great ruler would be willing do whatever it takes for her people."

"You are more than willing, always." He draws me closer, shielding me from the wind. "This is why I fell in love with you."

I stiffen. It's precisely this that makes me wonder whether we're on the right path after all, whether my reason is clouded by my emotion, whether the situation we're in is as dire for Jonas as it is for me.

He places my hand against his heart. "Trust me, oko mi. I won't let you down."

His presence unfurls in my mind then, like a flower bud opening into bloom, inviting me to look. His thoughts and emotions unspool in a steady stream as I venture in. Fear: a growing urgency, the worry that all we're doing is not enough, that someone might betray us at any time. Anger: a memory of an Oluso child we buried a few weeks before. Frustration: that his father still sits as regent. Rage: that the Council dared attempt to kill me. Grief: for his mother, who lies in a frozen state just a few rooms away, for the harshness of the world we live in.

And then—

I hitch a breath as another emotion roars into my mind—a certainty, a song, a claiming—Desire, as fiery and consuming as an inferno.

He runs a finger along my collarbone. Heat stirs in my lower belly. I shift my hips toward his. He yanks me up, depositing me on the small end table we sometimes use for meals. I hook my legs around his waist as his lips burn onto mine.

We kiss, tongues lashing, breathing in hot, harried gasps. He slips a hand under my blouse and cups my breast. I bite back a moan and grind my hips against the bulge of his arousal.

"Olorun's blood," he curses. I freeze for a brief moment, the specter of Dara's face bubbling to the surface of my mind. Then Jonas shoves his free hand into my trousers, and rubs two fingers against the silken fabric of my ibante, stroking the nub at the apex of my lower lips. The assassin's face drifts away like a rank perfume. I lift my hips higher, glorying in the joy of being alive. I won't let the Council take this from me too.

I moan aloud as he works his fingers faster, thrusting them against the fabric. He strokes my puckered nipple at the same time, and I buck, crying out—

"This is what you've been doing while I've been waiting to dress you?"

Nana stands in the doorway, fingers tapping against the frame. Jonas and I jerk apart instantly.

"If you had completed our ceremonial rites, I would approve." my guardian declares. "But since his people require things done their way, I'll give you three seconds to get inside."

"We were just—" Jonas blusters.

"One . . ." Nana counts.

Leaping off the table, I obey. As I pass into the room, the heat filling my skin dissipates against the piercing chill, the sensation of his body on mine a forgotten dream. Now, without desire to distract me, all I am left with is the storm of doubt brewing in my heart.

Trust. I turn the word over and over in my mind like a gambler's coin and hope I made the right bet.

TROTH

"Are you trying to drown me?" I gasp, spitting out another mouthful as Nana pours another jug's worth of water over my head. "I've passed nineteen name days now, I'm more than old enough to share a bed."

She slaps my fingers with the bijwi and I hiss, shoving my fingers into the cool of the bathwater.

"Hold still," she chides, dragging the stone comb through my unbraided locks. "I should've beaten you at least, if I knew going to Lleyria meant you'd neglect your hair."

I giggle, sinking against the walls of the wooden tub. "Don't let Ayn hear you. She'd offer money to watch."

"Dèmi, I'm serious."

"So am I. Did Baba send anything back?"

She lowers her voice, although the attendants have still not returned, a mere half bell before the betrothal. No doubt they're keeping away, fearing my unclean magic would taint their very souls. Perhaps they're still hoping to discover my corpse.

"He's on his way. He's decided to attend the ceremony in light of your news."

"This must be serious if it got Baba to change his mind." Baba is one of many who cautioned me when I agreed to Jonas's proposal. "Is possession a new kind of kokulu power?"

She combs through a particular knot and I tense. When she speaks again her voice is a taut string. "K'inu. The correct term is K'inu—a devouring spirit. The kokulu are vessels. The K'inu control them."

"Why haven't I heard of this?" My mother, who raised me to know our ancestry, taught me everything she believed a young Oluso should know. It's not likely that she would have left something out, no matter how frightening it was.

"Our elders feared what would happen if we spoke of them. The K'inu are descended from the Spirit Realm. They interact with our spirit bonds in a way that is more . . . elemental. Mentioning their names is enough to attract their attention."

"So what do we do?"

"We wait for Baba."

She works rose oil into my hair, smoothing the ends, pulling now-detangled locks into a polished braid that runs around my head like a crown. She, in turn, is already resplendent, black hair braided in a similar style, jewels glistening from between the plaits. Her angu lies flat against her chest, the square jacket collar embroidered with blossoming violets, the bird pattern on her rolled-up sleeves seemingly in flight, whipping up and down as she works. Her outer skirts billow as she begins working on the other side of my scalp. But her majestic appearance doesn't hide anything. Not from me.

Her eyes are ringed with shadow, her golden cheeks sunken. In the week since she arrived, she has never slept a peaceful night in this castle, fearing instead that the Eingardians will wake one day and decide to finish us off. I can't bring myself to tell her of the attempts in the last few months alone—the poisonings, accidents, and wild coincidences—and the scene tonight. If she'd been here, she would have beaten Dara handily. Nana becomes even more frightening when people go after her family.

I sigh. She is already sacrificing so much, leaving Haru with Will to be here with me. And I know all this talk of the K'inu is only adding to her worry.

"Can you tell me about you and Will?" I ask shyly. "Before you were betrothed? What was it like?"

Maybe this distraction will be enough to soothe our tumultuous minds.

She cracks a grin, the dimples around her eyes meeting in a kiss. "You mean before we married? Will skipped the whole betrothal process altogether. We married within a week of meeting."

"A week? You eloped?"

I try to picture calm, proper Nana—the Nana who dutifully writes letters to her parents every month detailing Haru's progress—stealing out of her family home to marry a wandering craftsman she met just the week before. Will only settled in Benin after they met. These days, he holds Nana, covering her like a winter coat every market day when her letters are sent back unread, still sealed in the wax coating she worked so hard to create.

"'Elope' is not the word. Will came by when I was buying silks for my mother. He spoke to me in that gruff voice of his. That was all it took."

I run my hand over my neck, suddenly aware of its nakedness. "Was it the bond? The magic?" I run my teeth over my lip. "Or did you know—"

"Is that what you fear? That you don't love him? That the magic is all there is?" She searches my face, brown eyes full of warmth and worry.

I don't have to ask which "him" she means.

"I love him," I say quickly. "I do love Jonas. I'm just not sure about any of the rest of it."

She picks up an inyun from the stool next to the tub. The pin is slender, a butterfly carving erupting from the end of the silver body. There are three more pins next to this one, all from varying materials—gold, bronze, white jade.

"Nana. Those are your mother's," I protest.

Nana ignores my protests and pushes the first pin through the braided puff at the front of my head in answer. "What do you fear?"

"She gave those to you for your wedding present," I try again.

Nana selects the bronze pin next, this one bearing the head of a tiger. "Is your fear greater than your will? Does it rule you?"

I flare at this. "Nothing rules me. I'm just tired of the Council's games. Our wedding was to take place today and now it's at winter's end. We're to go through the betrothal because it's proper."

Nana's lips draw tight and I know she's arrived at the same conclusion I did long ago—the Council wants more time and chances to eliminate me.

"The Council is irrelevant," she insists, threading the gold pin through. Its deer head shimmers in the dim torchlight. "Once you both pledge the sacred words and share a bed, it is finished. You are bonded. Oluso have never needed petty ceremonies."

She winks mischievously. "Perhaps I shouldn't have stopped you earlier."

I groan, lacing water-wrinkled fingers over my heated face. "Take that back, please, I don't want to discuss this with you."

She giggles unabashedly. "I did worry you wouldn't know what to do, but my worries were misplaced. No need for the talk on intimacy then."

Jonas and I have contented ourselves with breathless kisses often leading to explorations—quick forays where we writhe, hands and tongues running over skin and under clothes. Today was one of the few times we've gotten closer, drunk on the scent of one another, standing on the precipice of more. One shred of cloth, one quick motion, and we would be joined, woven together in a way that would be difficult to untangle. Then there's also Jonas's steady presence, the way he slips past the curtains of my mind and pulls me into his, pushing me into a level of intimacy I didn't know was possible . . .

All this talk is reminding me how much I want this all and him so badly. But I fear I'm living in a dream that will soon crumble, that my world is nothing but a bubble floating on a gracious wind, desperate to live its brief yet tenuous life before exploding.

I cradle my knees to my chest. It's all so much.

"What happens after all this?" I mutter. "We bond together. We rule the kingdom. Then what?"

Nana takes my face in her hands. "My dear, no one can know the future."

"You're a Cloren."

She lifts a corner of her mouth in a half smile. "Even Clorens run into our visions blind. We never know when the future might change. We can only promise that the sun will rise, but even then we can't be sure of when." She pauses, her eyes stilling into dark pools, reflecting the barest flicker of light from the lantern. "My sister was a Cloren, the strongest of our line, and she still died. No one foresaw that."

Nana's sister died the week before she met Will, a drowning death off one of their father's fishing boats. I wonder now if that is part of why she recognized Will as her mate so quickly, if grief became a sieve that stripped away the noise of the world, left her with nothing but a deafening hunger for the person who would bring warmth into her frozen heart. I wonder, too, if that is why, beyond the discrimination against half-caste children, her parents refuse to see Haru. Perhaps they fear glimpsing the daughter they lost in the granddaughter they never wanted to have.

I touch Nana's hand softly, hoping I can draw her away from the remembrances keeping her tethered to the world beyond. It takes her a moment to look at me, really see me, but I am rewarded with a soft smile that brings a dusky bloom of color into her cheeks.

I hesitate before asking, "Did you see anything about today . . . about me?"

"Nothing yet."

She offers the final pin without another word and I straighten. At the head of this pin is a white jade elephant, tusks gleaming, its deep-set eyes knowing. In Goma, white jade is the most precious stone, used only in marriage and memorial ceremonies between families. Gomae Oluso pass down pieces of themselves to their children by storing a portion of their souls in white jade. This pin is Nana's gift to me, a reminder that we'll always be family, but also a challenge.

"You don't have to go out there today. If you tell me you want to leave, I'll call Will and we can disappear immediately."

"But Jonas—"

"The bond is unfinished. Jonas could track your sign, but it would take time to find you. We can go on the run, leave all this behind. It's up to you."

I meet the bright sparkle of her gaze, knowing she means every word, that she loves me no matter what I decide. If I am unsure, if I am tired and want to put this burden down, she won't blame me.

"What of the Oluso? All the people who will suffer if I break my word now?" I ask in a near whisper.

"There are no simple answers, my dear. Marrying Jonas isn't the only path to our freedom. But if you trust Jonas enough to be engaged to him, trust that he'll keep fighting for us. *You* don't have to be involved."

I mull her words, consider the things I'm most afraid of. I shudder, remembering the young girl's face, the emptiness in her eyes as she—no, the K'inu—spoke through her. I think of what it's been like walking through the castle with strangers' eyes chasing me, every look a mirror of the next, fear and distrust carving faces into masks of hate. Then I think of Jonas, of the way his shoulders draw in when he is worried, the way his mouth winds tight and dawn eyes turn to darkened skies when he is hurt. Once he realizes I am no longer here waiting, that he'll be in this fight alone, what look will he wear?

I take the pin.

Nana produces a jar of white clay from the folds of her angu. When she places the jar on the stool, I catch a glimpse of the knives secreted in the inner sleeve of her puffy, long-sleeved top.

As I thread the pin through the crowning bun in the middle of my head, she traces the clay over my face and neck, whispering ancestral knowledge into my skin; three dots on my brow for wisdom to know what life to lead; two stripes running down from my right eye and ending in a sharp curve on my cheek to warn those who would harm me of the strength of my spirit; a lattice of swirls that cover my neck like lace—to snatch joy from life's unpredictable depths.

I step out of the bath and into the ibante she holds. While she wraps the thick undercloth under my arms and festoons it at my waist, I take a brief glance at the mirror in the corner of the room. The clay stands out against my brown skin, turning my face into a fierce mask.

"My mother couldn't give me her approval when I left to marry Will, but she gave me her love," Nana says, placing her hands on my shoulders. The shelled ornaments dangling from the animal heads at the end of the inyun click together as I lean against her, tinkling like bells.

"Today, I give you your mother's love and mine."

She lifts an aso okè, golden lilies sprouting from the soft, sky-blue lace drawing the light. The dress is long with a scooped neck that leaves room for my markings to be seen. The top flares out to the sides, drawn up by golden ribbons that run back into a larger bow at the open back. The bottom is a puffed, full skirt with a lace train that ripples as it moves. I still, tears stinging my eyes. All I see are Mummy's fingers, her laughter as she stitched the cloth together, her assured smile when she promised that, one day, she would make me something of my own to wear, something I could dance and glory in.

"Yetundé left this with Baba just in case."

I swallow, unable to speak. Mummy was always planning, thinking ten steps ahead. The fact that she left this for Baba all but confirms what I have battled to accept over the last year: Mummy knew she would die, and she wanted to prepare me for it. I wonder what she would think now that I can no longer remember her face.

Nana grips my chin, draws my gaze to hers. "She is watching. Today, when you walk out there, *if* you walk out there, she will be with you. As will I."

I dab at my tears, careful not to smudge the clay. "I'm ready. The Council won't win."

She lowers her head in a slight bow. "Then it is my honor, as your guardian, to dress you."

I laugh this time, gratitude and joy swelling in my chest. Gomae mothers dress their daughters before sending them off during wedding ceremonies. It is a way to signal to the ancestors that their child is beginning a long journey, and to ask for their protection.

Nana helps me into the dress, pulling the golden straps over my shoulders and tying them neatly in a bow at my lower back. She clasps the ringed bracelet on my wrist and slips the bone blade Ayaba gave me into the hidden side pocket stitched into the end of the skirt.

A knock comes at the door. "My lady," an attendant calls, "the time for the ceremony is here. Could you let us in to dress you?"

Nana smirks. "What petty tricks. Do they leave preparations so late for Eingardian brides?"

She places my father's ring on my neck as the door opens and eight different attendants, all in variations of the same starched blouse and long skirt, come in. The leader, Cariadhe, flushes at the sight of me.

"Apologies, My Lady. We did not mean to come so late as to have you dress yourself. Did you need anything?"

Taking Nana's hand in mine, I lift my chin and smile. "Not to worry. I have everything I need."

BONDS

WE SWEEP DOWN THE CORRIDOR, ATTENDANTS AND GUARDS FLANKING US like soldiers in a battalion. When we reach the large room in the west corner of Château Nordgren, I take a breath before walking through the forbidding iron doors that Nana holds open with a piece of protective cloth. She grimaces at the indignity but says nothing as we pass into the waiting Great Hall. I pause on the landing, taking in everything. The room is packed, a myriad of faces—earthy, ruddy, rusty, golden, and pale—pooled into uneven, swelling compartments. The Eingardians, arrayed in midnight colors, huddle like crows near the raised stage in the center of the room. A few break tradition with jewel-tone dresses and vests, rebels who offer me nods of approval or even smiles. But the rest remain uneasy, the tension radiating from them like an angered boar rearing to charge the wanderer in its territory.

I descend the spiral staircase leading onto the main floor, grateful for the kiss of cool marble on the banister—another gift from Jonas, who insisted on changing the room to make it more hospitable for attending Oluso. I may be Fèni-Ogun, and now, with my iron magic awakened, I am somewhat comfortable with the metal that once ringed every arbor in this room, but the metal remains a threat to the Oluso, leeching life and inflicting wounds with only a simple touch. Just one of many things that still needs to change—one of many things Jonas and I will change.

As we reach the center aisle, the few Oyo-born in the room crowd in to get a look. They are a whirlwind of color, swanning about in highly stylized aso èbi. The women nod as I pass, their blue and green gèlès waving like flowers dancing on the wind. The men tip their jaunty filas or pull off crimson okpu abus that bob as they wave to me. The Gomae attendees offer bows, uniform black hats with flared plaits swinging next to braided heads adorned with twinkling ornaments. Their rich, silken clothing stands out against the gray stone walls, and I linger a moment to admire their white inner shirts subsumed by rich blue over-gowns secured with slim black belts, or like Nana, billowing blush-pink skirts that scream for attention. The Berréan delegation win the day with light-colored gauzy fabrics that drape over shoulders and jewels that drip from ears and decorate fingers and toes.

As we glide toward the dais, I catch different looks from hopeful to joyous, frightened to disdainful, all on a multitude of faces varying in region and color. But I see, too, a few glowing marks, blazing flowers set in crescent moons winking from exposed necks, arms, legs—the Oluso are here and they stand with me.

Taking Nana's offered hand, I step onto the dais, turning to survey the gathered people. I twist my mouth into what I hope is a smile and try to ignore the sweat dusting my fingers, the prickling on my arms. Fear gathers in my belly, clawing at my insides, but I take focused breaths and work to quiet the thundering in my heart.

The doors to the right of the main hall open. Jonas saunters in, a score of guards following behind him. He is triumphant, a golden crown hemming his flowing blond hair, a silken mantle emblazoned with the royal insignia streaming behind him and kissing the ground as he walks. He sports a white tunic capped with golden epaulets, a woven thread of gold-and-blue rope running from his tucked collar into his front pocket. His trousers are fitted, hugging his powerful, muscled legs, and his leather boots shine as he steps toward me. When our eyes meet, the fear in my belly melts into quiet relief, and I reach out a hand.

He is across the room in a few quick strides, placing a kiss on my fingers before twining his with mine. As I stare into the eyes of my mate, I make a vow then and there to hold on to the joy of this moment, to find hope despite the exhausting trials of the past year.

Oko mi, you look . . .

Exhausted? Tired? I offer.

Radiant. Captivating . . . He licks his lips. *Delicious.*

Heat flushes up my cheeks and neck. It's times like this that I am grateful for the mental bond. I don't know what I would do if anyone heard him say these things out loud.

Nana coughs as though she heard him, and we look up to find all eyes trained on us. The lower door opens underneath the staircase and an elderly man with earthen skin and a white peppered beard slinks into the room—Baba. He scans the room, his wooden staff turning with him. His eyes are reptilian slits, no doubt from a transformation that ended moments before he walked in. When he catches sight of me, he nods his acknowledgment, but he looks up, searching the upper balconies before sliding into one of the back rows.

Before I can investigate further, an attendant blows a trumpet and the now seated guests rise for the Council members filing in. Many are dressed in the same dull colors as their counterparts, but a few—Lord Kairen, Markham, another Council member from a smaller township—are bedecked in full celebratory dress. Lady Ayn is the most surprising, in a crimson gown that sets off her auburn hair. Behind them, twin Eingardian priestesses follow along, their long, flowing robes weighed down with necklaces made of bones twisted with rocks and tree branches. And then there's Elodie, golden hair neatly gathered into a high chignon, wearing a frosted white gown similar to the traditional Eingardian wedding dress. She waves at me, grinning all the while. I falter before giving an answering nod, shaking off the unease that curls around my heart like a fist. It doesn't matter what the Council or *she* wants—Jonas chose me.

Markham takes his place on the throne at the end of the dais while the Council members settle into seats hemmed in by a low partition. One priestess takes her place before us, waving an iron baton with feathers lashed to the end. I step back instinctively, curling into a battle stance, but Jonas takes my elbow, whispering, "Urgun dhu. Old Eingardian custom for blessings. She will brush our faces with the feathers, nothing else."

"Do you do this for all your betrothals? What happens when the iron touches the wrong person?"

A single tap of this ceremonial stick is enough to coax an Oluso into a scream. No doubt the Eingardians worked these into their ceremonies with the intent of flushing out hidden Oluso.

"We use these for high ceremonies between noble families," Jonas admits, rubbing his neck sheepishly. "I never asked why. I thought it was a holdover from worshipping the gods."

"Lucky you, being iron-blooded, then," I mutter. "They would have caught you long ago if not for that."

He stiffens, and I regret those hasty words instantly. I squeeze his hand. "I'm sorry. Just nervous. You didn't deserve that."

"I absolutely did," he says, giving my hand a reassuring squeeze. "It's strange, remembering that iron, the iron that always brought me comfort, is poison to our kind." He flicks me a bright smile. "Good thing you're here now. We can be different together."

The priestess standing on the upper level of the dais begins to speak, and I lose my chance to answer.

"Midé's Day shine upon you, brethren."

"May your day be filled with hope," comes the customary reply.

"We gather for the joining of the two before us, to ask the spirits to unite two souls opposed in nature . . ."

The baton-wielding priestess waves her baton over her head, jabbing it into the air as she moves into a dance. The flowers and thorns encircling her flaxen hair bob as she weaves around us, cutting invisible enemies with her short staff. She grunts as she dances, humming in a shrill tone.

The other priestess moves forward, carrying a bronze bowl in one hand and a red ribbon in the other. As she approaches, swerving neatly past her twin, her stern voice rises, clashing with the high tones of her sister's. ". . . May the spirits grant remedy and make you balms for the other's sorrow, shelter for the world's troubles . . ."

Now her twin begins to sing, careening in High Ceorn, and though I received a year of instruction in it at the mandated school in Ikolé, I can only understand a few words.

". . . ward . . . joining . . . spirits . . ."

The first priestess dips her hand in the bronze bowl and sprinkles a clear liquid over Jonas. The scent of honey and roses tickles my nose, but there is something sharp and cloying underneath. She turns to do the same to me, gray eyes studying me, but I struggle to focus, overwhelmed with the cacophony of stones clashing with wood and bone, and the words spilling out of her sister's mouth.

"... protect ... burden ... awake ..."

The priestess seizes my hands, binding my right palm with the ribbon until the skin between my little finger and thumb is covered. "Be steadfast, be faithful. To him you are bound, as a circle meets no end, so you shall sustain."

Jonas responds with the partner vow, pledging his loyalty and declaring his commitment to marry me. "I will run at every beckon; I will heed every word. I am one in this circle; I choose this winding road. My spirit shall not waver, in this life or the next."

She loops the end of the ribbon through his left palm, repeating the first verse. "Be steadfast, be faithful. To her you are bound ..."

Her sister whirls closer, pale-blue robes brushing my side. She swings the baton and I jerk forward, the skin on the back of my neck prickling. Jonas grips my shoulder in support. "You all right?"

"Yes, I—"

"The vow," the priestess insists.

"Yes." I run my teeth over my lip, trying to pull the words out. "I will run at every beckon; I will heed every word ..."

I catch a flash of red as Lady Ayn sits forward, her fan working furiously, though the air in the room is decidedly cool.

"... I am one in this circle; I choose this winding road ..."

The singing priestess twirls, her shrill voice dying to low embers. As she spins, the iron catches the dying light streaming from the arched windows behind the dais. Beyond her, the Council members hover with stony faces, perched like vultures before a slaughter. My tongue is suddenly heavy, my chest devoid of air. Once I say these words, Jonas and I are on the path to fully becoming mates. His people, his customs, will all become mine, whether I like it or not.

The ghost of Colin's voice caresses my ears: *Will it be enough, Dèmi, to live with him? Love is one thing, but can he give you a home?*

Nana steps onto the dais, tapping her forehead with two fingers. Her message is simple—to remember I have a choice.

"Dèmi?"

I look up at the man standing before me, his shining eyes belying the tremble in his voice as he spoke my name. He waits, smile still firmly in place, but I see the slight pinch in his forehead, the way the free fingers on his right hand are clenched. I know, without peeking into his mind, that he is terrified, afraid of what I'll do next. So I reach for the feeling, that song that murmurs in my heart, thrumming with joy and hope.

I raise my voice, push until it echoes through the room. "My spirit shall not waver . . ."

The singing priestess jumps, robes curling like thorny vines. She darts at me, baton raised, but Nana is faster, throwing a hidden dagger. The woman collapses, blood spilling from the wound in her back. Her sister steps back, flinging the ceremonial bowl at Jonas's head. As he catches it, she rushes in, long needles flashing between her fingers. I drop, pulling Jonas with me as I sweep her feet out from under her. She falls, then rolls herself up and she's ready again, circling us.

Markham leaps to his feet, but the guards close around him, obscuring him from view. Shadows drop from the balconies, dark blurs cutting across the ceiling. I whip in time to see Baba slam his staff into someone running up the main aisle. The crowd erupts into screams as the assassins land, striking at those in their way. Jonas throws a hand up, silver-blue flames engulfing the curved swords in the assassins' hands. Iron screams as the swords bend, wrapping themselves around their masters' arms. The guards rushing to Jonas's side stop, shock evident on their faces.

"The Council's not going to be happy!" I yell.

He grins. "I'm tired of putting their happiness first."

The priestess flings her darts, and I pull my staff from the air, striking at them with my free hand. She unsheathes a poniard from a strap on her thigh and rushes us. Nana dives for her, parrying her blade with another dagger. Nana shoves her back with the force of her blow, and I jab the priestess in the thigh. She pitches forward into a roll, but Nana is there, pouncing with another attack.

"Don't tell me this is another Eingardian tradition," she grits out.

A roar tears through the hall as an onyx-skinned lion shifts into existence, its knowing brown eyes the only sign that marks it as Baba.

Jonas tuts, "Pissing off lethal Oluso? Let's hope not."

People swarm the doors, rushing to get out, but a few Oluso hang back, meeting the assassins blow for blow. A Gomae Oluso grips the wooden benches surrounding him and they transform into full trees, vines and branches reaching out to ensnare everything in their path. Many Council members abandon their seats, scurrying through the side door, but a handful stay seated, watching as though they've ordered entertainment.

"Protect the people," Jonas commands. The guards skitter into action, shock forgotten. But as they rush into the fray, they clash with both assassins and Oluso.

"No! Just the intruders!" Jonas screams, but his voice is lost in the din.

We leap from the dais, rushing into the main aisle, when hooded figures sporting beaded bracelets—one wooden, one silver—catapult over, flinging more of those long needles at us.

When I block with a gust of wind, Silver twists in, punching Jonas's shoulder. I tug him back with the ribbon still linking our hands, then slam my staff down on the second assassin. He takes the blow with crossed fists, the carved fox faces on his wooden beads spinning. Then he charges, swiping at me with those needled fists. Jonas yanks me away, but the sudden motion pulls us off balance and we knock into each other, our tangled limbs further trapped in the ribbon binding our wrists.

Silver advances, but Nana springs over, twin daggers slashing at him. He sidesteps away and edges back. I wriggle my bone blade free from the pocket in my skirts, dragging it up and slicing the ribbons that bind Jonas and me just as the abandoned priestess yanks the dagger from her sister's back. The fallen woman groans, but the priestess steps over her, gaze trained on us.

I scramble to my feet as both assassins surge toward Nana, needles pinched between their knuckles like talons. The priestess springs forward at the same time, boxing us in, but Jonas clenches his fist and the blade sprouts a silver-blue flame before darting from her hand into mine. I round on the men, and Fox Bead rears to a stop as Silver vaults in. Nana hurls her dagger, pinning him in the upper arm. He cries out but the sound is strange, a gurgle where another might have screamed. The priestess scrambles off the dais and into the crowd.

"Jonas!" I toss him my staff.

"Already there," he says, catching it and launching after her.

Fox Bead pulls the dagger from his comrade's arm just in time to deflect Nana's flying blade. He dances in, throwing quick punches that she blocks with her elbow and forearm. I dart forward, and he weaves back, abandoning the close fight.

He and Silver draw wooden batons from holsters at their backs, gripping them by their fist-length handles. When they shift into a stance, hinging back on one foot while rearing forward with the other, Nana gasps. The terror in her voice is enough to root me in place.

"What?"

"We need to stop them from moving." She rips the necklace from her throat and smashes the icy bead hanging from it. A blue wisp curls from the shards like smoke, a portion of her mate, Will's soul, and she inhales, drawing it into her mouth. Then she peels off her oboi, wrapping the thick belt between her fists. "Now. Build me a shield."

I'm burning with curiosity, but I don't question it, slamming my hand against the marble floor as the men leap for us. The wind spirits respond, gathering to us like fireflies on a summer night. Pivoting on his heel, Fox Bead clicks a lever on his holster. A spear explodes from it, sailing through the wind still gathering, and lodges into the stone wall behind us. The assassins grip the thick rope attached, hanging on as the wind swells into a gale.

"That enough?" I ask, but Nana closes her eyes. The Oluso mark on her forehead glows, the amber flower rippling into an ice blue reminiscent of Will's magic.

The air takes on a new chill, frost unfurling over the windows until the reddening sun is a glimmering blur. Ice spreads from Nana's feet, racing along the floor, and I trip before wobbling back into position. In that moment, the wind dies out and the assassins crash. Ice creeps over their arms and legs and I watch with amusement as Silver struggles to free his hand from the floor. Everywhere, people slip and slide, trying to catch hold of a bench or wall that might anchor them. Jonas escapes it all, standing on a bench, the staff in his hands separating a guard from a young Oluso.

Then an assassin stabs an Oluso with one of the needles. The fire in the old woman's hands dries into ash, and she crumples instantly. The assassin pivots, leaping from bench to bench, headed toward Jonas.

Yanking my ring from my neck, I wrap it in wind and blast it forward as Jonas looks up. As the assassin dives in, my ring expands, ripping the iron from the side benches and doors until it's a sizeable shield. The needle ricochets off the shield, but I close my hand into a fist, and the shield transforms into a cage that swallows the assassin.

Then, a silvered blur flashes past. I turn. Nana stands, eyes open, pupils swallowing the whites of her eyes. She opens her mouth, but no sound comes out. Sticking out of her shoulder and the base of her throat are several slim needles. The Oluso mark on her forehead pales to a dull, sickly yellow, and then she's falling, crashing onto her knees, the ice at her feet melting into a puddle.

"No!" I dash to her as a needle flies by my nose.

Fox Bead presses his baton to his lips, the hole on the other end of it spitting another needle. I roll into a crouch, reaching for the threads of my magic. Golden fire sparks at my fingertips as I stretch a hand toward the Council box. The iron rips away with a screech, transforming into a spear that rams into the assassin's chest, breaking him out of the half slab of ice encasing his legs and pinning him to the pillar behind us. He screams, the cry echoing through the room. The few assassins still standing grind to a halt. The guards pounce on them immediately, forcing them to the ground.

I dash to Nana's side, stepping over Silver who quivers on the floor, body still trapped in ice. She breathes in short, gasping wheezes, and I wrap an arm around her shoulder, pulling her tight against me.

"Breathe, Nana, hold on. I have you," I plead, reaching for the needles.

She pushes feebly against my hand. "Don't touch," she croaks. "Poison."

"I know." Placing my hand on her forehead, I call for the ancestors, reaching into that deep well that brims with my healing magic. Nothing happens.

"No, no, no." I try again, and though green fire races up my arm, bathing Nana in its light, my magic pools at my fingertips and palm, clawing against my skin.

"Baba!" I scream. A hawk swoops down. Wings recede into long arms, and curved beak and sharp eyes shift into the wizened face of Baba Sylvanus. He completes his transformation as his feet grace the ground.

"She won't heal. No matter what I try—"

"Stop, Dèmi." He shoves me away, gathering Nana into his arms.

"What's wrong with her?" Jonas asks, sliding to a stop near the dais.

Baba puts two fingers to Nana's throat, then he pulls back her sleeve. Black lines cover her arms like a tattoo, splintering and cracking into a veinlike pattern. He whistles between his teeth and I swallow, trying to hold back the tears blurring my vision.

"Baba," I whisper, imploring.

He shakes his head. "Bitna. Venom I haven't seen since Afèni's time. It spreads through the blood, blocks spirit channels. She won't be able to use magic, and neither will Willard. As she sickens, so will he."

"Why can't I heal her?"

"I don't know. Perhaps"—he stops, face scrunched tight—"perhaps it's because you need them both—Willard and Nana. They're mates. If you were fully bonded, too, maybe . . ." He trails off, stricken.

"We can complete the ceremony now," Jonas says, "if that's all it takes—"

"It's not. Bitna comes from the Spirit Realm. It's a death curse designed to take a life. To remove it, you need a talisman soaked with the blood of the one who cast it. Or you need to offer the caster's life as sacrifice."

I spring to my feet, stalking over to Fox Bead. His blood runs in a steady stream down the pillar, curling over the decorative indents like vines choking a wall.

"Give me the talisman and I'll let you live," I snap.

He blinks at me, then shuts his eyes, body slumping to one side. I fly at him, wind swirling around my arms and legs, and rip his hood from his face. He startles and I jerk back instinctively. His eyes are sunken, his cheekbones jutting against his sun-beaten skin. His mouth is cracked, graying against an overly red tongue. The smell of koko chokes the air between us.

It takes all I have not to slam my fist into his face. "The talisman. Give it to me."

"I don't have it," he rasps.

I curl a finger and the betrothal bracelet Nana gave me separates into five spikes. "Try that again."

He leans his head back against the pillar. "Do what you please."

"Dèmi, don't—" Jonas starts, but I rear back, gathering the wind to me. The benches quiver as the wind grasps at them. I don't waste my breath on a chant this time. My iron magic flares, singing as it consumes me, setting me ablaze. Iron peels away from windows and doors and swims into the storm.

"Give me the talisman." My voice is a roar now, my skin prickling with heat. My heart beats wildly as power and rage flood through me, licking through my senses.

Fox Bead manages a half smile. I drive a dart into his shoulder. His scream tangles with the whirring in my ears, and blood spurts from his mouth, but all I can think of is Nana lying like a broken doll on the ground below.

"The talisman."

"Dèmi!"

I drift closer, hovering a dart above Fox Bead's heart. "The talisman, or your life. Which will it be?"

His bloodshot eyes spark in challenge. "Kill me," he spits. "Take my life and reap your reward, *meascan*."

I don't ask again. I punch the air and the dart lurches forward, piercing his chest. Then, just as the blade breaks skin, the dart takes on a silvered aura and freezes in place.

Jonas seizes me by the wrist, his touch like ice on my burning skin. "Let him go," he commands. "You are not a murderer."

"You let go," I growl, shoving at him with my free hand. "He's killing Nana."

He wobbles, unused to channeling my wind magic, and I use the opportunity to pour out more magic, willing the dart to dig into Fox Bead's body, gnaw at his flesh until there's nothing left. The dart inches forward and Fox Bead's scream is now a wail of pure anguish. Then Jonas pushes into my mind again, and the dart unhooks itself, drawing out of the assassin's body.

My iron magic flares, desperate to take control, but Jonas's presence is like a rope ensnaring me, dragging me away from my prey.

"This isn't you," he insists, pulling me to him. "Remember the Oluso bonds."

I struggle against him, filled with a need to consume, to rage until there's nothing left. "Let me go."

"Dèmi, look." He spins me, and I catch sight of the scene below. The benches are in tatters, smashed against the wall. Ribbons and cloth hang from odd angles, shredded and torn. Water sloshes with dark red, the river of blood pooling at the broken doors. A few people are huddled against the walls, taking cover, but the rest stand in the corridor at the back, watching me with horror.

I fall, the flames on my skin winking out all at once, crashing until Jonas sends a burst of air that ferries me safely down. Baba still cradles Nana, keeping a hand on her pulse.

"She's still breathing. We have time. A few days, perhaps a week," he says, as though he heard the questions tumbling through my mind.

I nod, but as I step toward them, Silver peeks out from behind a cracked bench, baton at his lips. He puffs his cheeks, but I swerve, hurling a spike at him. It impales his throat with a sickening thud, and he crumples, slamming into the floor. Blood pools around his head, and right then pain lances through my chest, a cold knife flaying me open.

I sputter, choking on air. Jonas races to my side as pain spreads over my back, tattooing itself on my skin.

"Breathe, oko mi, breathe," Jonas begs. His hands are warm against my icy skin. "What's happening to her?"

Baba taps Silver lightly with his staff, but the assassin does not move. Bending, he peels his cloth mask off. Silver's face is similar to Fox Bead's, the lack of wrinkles by his eyes deeming him the younger man.

Fox Bead mutters something, and I make out some clipped, jumbled sounds. Baba leans closer, listening.

"You killed his brother," he translates.

Just then the ground underneath me rumbles, tremors shaking my entire being. A voice pierces my ears, thunderous and bombastic as a thousand gangan drums announcing the start of war.

To the winds, my child, you will go. Your bonds are now broken, so you have chosen, an exile without an end.

I scream.

As the voice dissipates, the pain devouring me intensifies until I can no longer tell where I end and where it begins. Then, suddenly, blessedly, it stops, melting away like mist.

The knowledge of what I've done takes hold. Silver is dead at my hands. I am a murderer. My spirit bonds are sundered—broken.

"I'm sorry," I whisper. "I'm sorry."

I crawl to Nana, who lies perfectly still, her golden skin decidedly pale, the slow rise and fall of her chest the only sign of life. Gathering her to me, I stroke her raven hair. Jonas wraps his arms around us, and I let the tears I've been holding fall. I cry, wailing as though no one is watching, letting the sobs wrack my body. Jonas murmurs into my hair, looking as though he wants to take it all back, undo the horrors of this evening. But I can't negate the thoughts that ring in my head like an insistent bell: Nana is dying, and—now that I've broken the sacred bond of the Oluso—so am I.

I close my eyes, then jerk them open again as another realization brings me to a seizing halt—we never finished the binding ceremony.

TREMORS

I STAND AT A CROSSROADS MARKED ONLY BY THE SLIM IROKO TREE AT MY side. To the left is darkness, a fog that tickles my back, beckoning me into its grasping fingers. To my right is a glade reminiscent of Benin Forest. Water spirits skim the surface of the river cutting through the glade, the sounds of their laughter high and robust. But when I take a step in that direction, they stop in place, stitched into the night like carvings etched in wood. Tinkling laughter curls into stilted cries that echo. I try to move back, but my body will not obey. An omioja at the edge of the glade turns slowly, sea orb eyes glowing as they latch onto me. She takes a step toward me, the shells in her coral pink tresses shaking as her feet slap the ground.

"Come closer, little one," she whispers. Gone are highly defined cheeks, the sweet curve of a mouth that graces omioja faces. Her mouth is an open, greedy thing, cracking her face in half.

I whirl and dive into the fog as her laughter chases me. A hand closes on my arm and I startle, falling out of the Spirit Realm.

"What did you find?" Baba asks.

"I was lost." I breathe hard, sucking in air like I've run for hours. "In Benin Forest this time. But everything was wrong."

Baba listens to my tale of the omioja who came after me, gnawing thoughtfully on a chewing stick. "You're untethered," he answers when I finish. "We need to try something else."

He returns to the stone mortar in the corner of the room, and I settle by Nana's cot, dismissed. I know Baba is only trying to help, but the dry way he says things, as though I don't already know that my trouble accessing the Spirit Realm is all of my own making, stings. Then I turn my attention on Nana, and hurt melts into guilt.

I sponge Nana's face, careful as I run the cloth over the lines spreading across her skin. Her head lolls as I lift her chin and clean under her ears. The lantern at her bedside announces the arrival of a spiral trailing her navel, and I watch as the tattoo grows, slithering toward her hip.

Baba bangs the pestle against the mortar, sending kanuwort mixed with palm and cedar oil flying onto the stone walls. He scoops a handful into a bowl, stirring in small strips of biwa to sweeten the taste, then he hobbles to the cot, tapping me with his cane.

"Her face will vanish from all your staring."

I rise but hover at the foot of the cot, watching as he picks Nana's head up and dips a finger's worth of tincture onto her tongue.

"How long?"

"A week if Olorun shows mercy. At the rate this is spreading, maybe three days."

I rock back on my heels trying not to let those words drive me into the pit of despair. Nana is dying, and it's my fault. My back is on fire, the pain that began in the Great Hall growing with every passing breath, but I can't give up now, not when every moment I waste is one that Nana— the only other mother I've ever known—might not have.

"Jonas and I will finish the bonding tonight," I declare. "I'll try healing her again."

Baba cocks his head, the feather in his beard waving as he faces me. "You will not. Do not trifle with the Spirits Dèmi."

"They don't ask when they trifle with us."

The pain in my back intensifies as though in warning, and it takes all I have not to hiss. Baba puts the tincture down, rounding on me.

"Let me see."

"It's nothing, Baba."

"Abidèmi."

His voice is quiet yet insistent, a sheath hiding a well-honed blade. I know too well that I am letting fear rule me, as though denying the pain I'm in can erase what I did in the Great Hall. But I still see the rush of blood, the way Silver's body collapsed into a heap.

"Atanakpà nogbè élamhè ole mu ékuolè khuòn uwah. What do I always say?"

A tiger that hunts must carry the carcass home in its mouth.

I lift my head, meeting Baba's steady gaze. His placid expression is the same as when we met, when he threw me, a girl of only ten name days, a staff before striking at me with his own, forcing me to defend myself. Baba has never shied from life's hardships, always pushing me and Colin to do the same. Even now, with all I've done and Nana as she is, he goes about what needs to *be* done rather than consider what *has* happened, burying the worries that plague his heart.

"I'm ready," I sigh.

He squeezes my shoulder before fetching the second lantern from the table by the screen. I hold my breath as he examines my back, each light touch enough to make me wince. He presses down a ridged knot that's sprouted in the middle and I convulse, falling to my knees as pain washes over me. I inhale, snatching at lungfuls of air, but the air itself claws at my nostrils and throat, fighting to leave my body. My vision goes blurry and the dark creeps in, swallowing me up. Then the wooden door creaks against its rusty hinges and someone wraps their arms around me, pulling me into the light.

I shudder as the darkness clears, blinking up at a concerned Jonas. His touch is an icy balm quieting the fire still raging in my chest. I bury my nose against his neck.

"Dèmi, what did you do?" Baba asks. His mask of calm is gone, his eyes wide with terror.

"I don't know. I couldn't stop myself in the Great Hall, just like Lleyria."

He bursts into motion, dragging over the mirror tucked neatly behind the screen. He thrusts the lantern closer as I squint, adjusting to the sudden light clouding my eyes. Jonas releases me, and I sit at the base of the mirror, turning my head as far as I can. There in the shimmering glass trapping bits of moonlight and shadow in its depths is my back—brown like kola nuts, but with raised, glistening silver skin lacing into the pattern of a tree. The roots dance up from my lower back and the trunk reaches high, grasping at the nape of my neck. Branches splinter from the trunk onto the greater expanse of my back, the smallest ones curling into my sides. And there, at the spot Baba touched, dangling from a lower branch, is a welt lashed out in the shape of a leaf.

Jonas whistles through his teeth. "I take it you've never seen this before."

"I'm from Afèni's time. I've seen many an Oluso after their spirit bonds shattered. But this?" Baba shakes his head gravely.

I dart away from the mirror and Jonas throws his overcoat over me, insulating me from the chill now tickling my skin.

"We must seek Ìyá-Ilé's help."

"Oh, just go to Ìyá-Ilé? How are we to find her?" I cry bitterly.

When the first Oluso came into the physical realm, the spirits granted them Ìyá-Ilé, the Mother Tree, as a guide. For a time, Ìyá-Ilé moved with them as they spread across the world, blessing the ground they walked upon with flowers and trees, weaving spaces for her children to thrive. But though the Aziza and tree spirits still litter the forests, Ìyá-Ilé disappeared after that fateful battle when Afèni banished the kokulu.

"Ask for guidance in the Spirit Realm. Pray Olorun favors you."

"I just tried that! The spirits do not welcome me. You saw for yourself I was lost—" I start.

"And you will make it right," Baba declares. "I did not raise you to be a coward. We need the guidance of the spirits to defeat the K'inu. At the very least, Ìyá-Ilé may be the key to saving Nana. My brews can only delay the poison's spread."

A knock comes at the door. "My liege, a message from His Highness. Your presence and the Lady's is requested in the Lower Halls."

I get to my feet. Markham may have renamed the east dungeon as the Lower Halls, but I still have memories of being trapped down there, waiting with pregnant Oluso who spent their days wondering if they or their babies would survive.

Baba's voice drops to a whisper. "Hide the marking on your back. Don't go anywhere alone. You're vulnerable with broken spirit bonds."

"I won't leave her alone," Jonas answers, gathering me to him.

The attendant pounds on the door again. "My liege, if you'll excuse me—"

"Wait just a moment!" Jonas shouts.

"Stay with him," Baba says, nodding at Jonas. "He is the key to returning to the Spirit Realm. If your magic falters, your bond with him will help pull you through. Strengthen that, and you'll have everything you need."

"Strengthen our bond?" I ask. Baba throws me another wry look. I swallow, cheeks burning. Jonas's ears turn red as he considers Baba's meaning.

Baba reaches into the collar of his agbada, plucking out three streaked brown feathers, molten gold fumes rising from them like vapor. He folds one into Nana's hand, then hands one to me. The last he throws at the threshold of the door, and it stitches itself to the frame.

"I can't trust that they'll leave me be once you pass through those doors. Send for an attendant, someone you trust."

Panic sets my heart racing. "Where are you going?"

He pulls me into a brief hug. "To marshal our forces. The K'inu have returned. The Oluso must gather if we are to survive this trial."

"And Nana?"

"Once you settle things here, I'll bring Will to you. Olorun willing, all will be well."

"My liege—"

Jonas yanks open the door and the harried attendant stumbles in. He recovers himself, mopping at the sweat pooling on his brow.

"Call Edwina," Jonas commands. "Tell her to bring strong cloth and herbs. When she returns with you, we will heed my father's summons."

The attendant scrunches his forehead, worry sending fresh color into his youthful face. "My liege, I cannot return empty-handed—"

"I would hurry if I were you, then. My father does not like to be kept waiting."

The attendant manages a bow before streaking out of the room like a bird escaping a fox, the ruffled fabric at his throat jumping as he scuttles past the waiting guards.

"Edwina?" Baba asks.

"She was Mummy's nursemaid."

His eyes cloud for a brief moment, then he breaks into a smile. "Ah."

Edwina slips in, carrying a basin full of strips of cloth. As she passes through the frame, the feather embedded in it flashes a rich ochre, then the light winks out. The protection spell is firmly in place.

As she catches sight of me, Edwina drops the basin, grabbing my shoulders. Her slim, brown face is etched with worry, her words spilling out in a flood. "My lady, I never meant to leave you. They told me the Council was taking charge of your preparations. This old woman would be no use."

The attendant hovers on the threshold. "My liege—"

Baba's feather takes on a deadly crimson.

"Enough." Jonas moves to the door. "You've done your work admirably. Now, give us a moment." The young man backs away as the feather fades to white, unaware of how close he came to injury.

I pat Edwina's hands. "I'm all right. But I need you to help Nana. Don't let anyone else into this room. Can you do that for me?"

She turns her attention to the cot, the ridge between her brows deepening into a chasm. "Yes. Anything else?"

Baba brandishes the tincture as though he's presenting flowers to his lover. "If she wakes, feed her this. She may try to spit it out, but give her every last bit."

Edwina's worried expression melts into a smile. "Still making nasty brews, Vanus?"

"Always," Baba says with a wry smile.

I quirk an eyebrow at Baba, but he ignores me, pushing me to the door. New footfalls echo down the corridor, swimming toward us. There's no more time to waste.

Sparing a brief glance at Nana, I hand Edwina the lantern and follow Jonas out. We walk quickly through the narrow corridor, following the attendant, who darts down passageways and into rooms like a fleeing rabbit. The guards hem us in, the extra ones who came in search of us taking the lead when we reach the tower at one end. We press on down a winding staircase, skimming our fingers along the decaying, crumbling walls, a string of lanterns cutting into swaths of shadow shifting on stone. Then we come to an abrupt stop at a small door at the base, filing through it one by one.

The smell of iron and rot permeates the east dungeon. Wrinkling my nose, I hurry past the cells strewn with rat feces and broken metal cuffs. It's been several months since I've been down here, but time has not been enough to erase the horror of this place in my mind. Markham waits at the central command room, a map rolled out on the table before him, bookshelves on either side of him boasting well-kept tomes, names carved into leather backs in elegant Ceornian script. On the floor next to the table, Fox Bead lies lashed to an iron pole, blood pooling underneath him. His eyes are closed, his chest barely moving.

Markham's armor creaks as he whirls to face us. "Took long enough."

Jonas bows. "We had to appoint a caretaker." At his father's perplexed frown, he adds, "For the woman."

Markham relaxes slightly, but the way he studies us, as though we are loyal hunting dogs that have bitten their master, reeks of doubt, or worse—betrayal. He narrows in on me.

"I need information. Can you heal this one?" he asks, scuffing his boot in Fox Bead's direction.

I look to Jonas. Markham has never shown any interest in magic, preferring to keep me at arm's length. I don't blame him, knowing that every time he glimpses magic, he undoubtedly thinks of the wife who lies two floors above, trapped in a dreamless sleep. He knows now that his brother rather than my father is to blame for what happened to Jonas's mother. But he is wary of magic nonetheless.

"The others proved useless. They had no tongues."

"Had?"

Markham's mouth settles in a grim line. "Poison."

"Bitna does not work on Ajes," I counter.

Something akin to guilt flickers in Markham's eyes, then just as quickly, it's gone. "Shodsgrass," he supplies. "In the water skeins strapped to their backs. No odor, no taste."

Jonas frowns. "Shodsgrass? From Ellaria?"

Now the pieces fall into place. I think of Lady Ayn's gleeful smile, the way she sashayed from the wreckage of the Great Hall, a peacock displaying for all to see.

"They had Council help," I declare. "Lady Ayn has cousins in Ellaria—"

"Many Council members have ties to Ellaria," Markham interjects.

"But *here*, in Eingard, we don't throw gauntlets without cause. We operate with evidence, witnesses."

I draw my lips into a mirthless smile. "I'll give you one then." Skirting round the table, I kneel by Fox Bead, splaying my fingers over his oozing wound.

"Dèmi—" Jonas warns.

But it's too late. I pull at the threads of my magic, pushing the fire gathering at my fingertips into the assassin's chest. The fire roars, leaping from my fingers onto the man's tawny skin, but even after skin and sinew knit together, my magic does not fold quietly into the well of my spirit. It charges through, gushing out of me, warmth twisting into a drowning frost, numbing my fingers and skin. I try to pull away, but my muscles are rigid, near paralyzed.

Jonas yanks me back. "I don't think Father meant you should heal every scar he has," he says, summoning a levity into his words I know he doesn't feel. "Just make sure he's well enough to talk." He throws an arm around my shoulder, obscuring my trembling, and I sink against him, grateful.

Markham doesn't spare us a glance, though, his attention riveted on Fox Bead who is easing up, straining against the pole lashed to his spine. The guards do not move from their positions, none of them the wiser. But I know that this is yet another gift, a direct consequence of killing Silver. My magic is out of control, and things will only get worse.

Markham raises a hand and two guards deposit Fox Bead into the waiting chair, positioning the pole beyond the chair's wooden back so Fox Bead grunts in pain as his arms twist behind him. I wince, remembering Elu, the Angma Oluso the Eingardian Army tortured, dangling on a platform in Lokoja. But Elu had done nothing but try to save lives— Aje and Oluso alike. This man nearly killed Nana. I steel my jaw and look on.

"I am Markham of Eingard. But I'm sure you already know that. You came into my hall tonight and attempted to murder my son. Why?"

Fox Bead raises his chin, peering out from a curtain of wavy brown hair. His face is covered in stubble, but the scarred cross marks at the corners of his mouth still stand out, mottled pinkish flesh stitching a warning against his weathered skin. The amber flecks in his brown eyes mark him clearly as Ashkenayi. He turns his head, gaze roaming until it lands on me. When he speaks, white dots flash on his reddened tongue, a clear sign of koko withdrawal.

"Blessed are the children of the Many-Faced One. He who reaches into darkness, She who gathers up the lost, They that bathe the world in bounty."

Markham scowls. "What is this?"

"The Ashkenayi call Olorun the 'Many-Faced One,'" Jonas answers.

"Meaning?"

"It's a litany. He's thanking Dèmi for healing him." I shoot him a wondrous look and he shrugs. "I pay attention in our lessons."

I have spent the better part of a year recounting our histories, the stories I've gathered from Mummy, Baba, and the okosuns I've met, for Jonas. So often those history lessons devolve into furtive romps in our private solar or stolen kisses in the corridors. It's funny to discover that he's been listening after all.

"Who are you?"

I snap my attention back to Fox Bead. When he doesn't answer Markham's question, the guards shove his head farther down. His arms strain against the pole, his shoulders erupt, bone jutting out from skin like rocks breaking through dirt.

"It doesn't matter if you kill me," he croaks. "My brother has returned to the Many-Faced One. Nothing else can harm me."

Markham leans closer, hovering inches from Fox Bead's face. "I've fought Ashkenayi like you before, and you see, I learned something interesting." He raises a hand and a guard rushes over with a pouch. Another two drag over a pail sealed with an iron lid. Markham reaches into the pouch and pulls out the silver beads, and now I spot the wolf's head engraved on one of them.

Fox Bead lunges. There's a crackling, a decisive snap as he strains for those beads, arms bending at unnatural angles. Markham steps away and a guard slams the flat of her blade against Fox Bead's knees, knocking him down. He howls, arms dangling uselessly behind him, and I dig my fingernails into my palms to keep from reeling.

Markham runs a finger over the wolf's head. "I've heard these are a kind of family tribute. But too many of you turn into berserkers over these cheap trinkets. You do something to these beads, don't you? Today I'll find out what."

Now I remember a tale Colin shared after a short jaunt in Ashkenaya. He'd raved about a kind of magic a few Ashkenayi possessed, the power to put their essence and memories into beads, much like Oluso stored portions of their souls away. Which means . . .

Markham is toying with Silver's heart.

"Give it back," Fox Bead rasps.

"Are you ready to talk, then? Let's try again, shall we? Who are you? Why did you come here?"

Fox Bead squirms, but he answers in a rush of words. "I am Maranya. From the House of Sand. My brethren and I"—he pauses to wet his cracked lips—"were given an opportunity to earn our freedom. If we managed to kill the girl and your son."

I straighten at this. The House of Sand is famous for covert assassinations, so deadly that the legends of their exploits traveled to Oyo even across the Ashé Sea. This explains Nana's fright. Perhaps if I hadn't spiraled out of control, we might not have survived intact.

Except I didn't, did I? I think, the pain in my back answer enough.

"Who sent you?" Jonas blurts the question, but his face is already hardening, the arm I'm clutching taut with attention. There are few people influential enough to summon a rival nation's assassination squad to an Eingardian betrothal. If nothing else, Maranya's silence, the way he hangs his head as though he's waiting to die, is confirmation enough. The Council is involved.

Markham removes the pail lid, revealing a sunset of bubbling liquid threatening to spurt out of its container. He dangles the silver beads over the molten iron.

"Who sent you after my son?"

Maranya's voice cracks as he begs. "I don't know their names, just their faces. So much was given us by letters. My brother maimed and his tongue stripped. We were not to return empty-handed."

The beads drop closer to the molten iron. The iron sparks as it jumps, licking upward and landing on the side of Markham's breastplate. The metal gives way, burning a small hole.

"Father," Jonas cautions, but Markham ignores him. "Describe them," he urges the assassin. "Those who sent you."

"A woman. Very tall—"

"Was she wearing fine clothes? What color was her hair?" The questions spill from my lips before I can rein them in. If there's even a small chance I can use this to catch Lady Ayn out, I can get an antidote and save Nana.

"Hair like yours. Skin like the desert sands. Dressed in leathers and fur. She wore a gold medallion."

My stomach sinks, hope snuffed in an instant. I know no one by that description.

"And the poison? Did she say anything about that?"

He considers briefly then shakes his head. I rock back on my heels, mind whirring. If there is no talisman, I need to visit the Spirit Realm and find Ìyá-Ilé as soon as possible. Only the Mother Tree can save Nana and Will now, and every moment I spend here instead of searching for Ìyá-Ilé pushes them closer to death.

"There was another, but I saw her only once," Maranya adds. "Ghost-like, dark hair, crooked nose. She had a scar across her face."

That describes someone I know perfectly.

Mari.

Despair gives way to hope and I can't control the smile that blossoms on my face. Markham falters, dropping the beads, but I wave a hand and the iron pail tips over, spilling onto the floor. Almost immediately, my back is on fire and I tighten my grip on Jonas's arm as tremors ripple through me. The silver bead skims the surface of the pail, bouncing safely near me.

Maranya draws his feet in, grunting as he works to keep the iron from touching his skin. "I have answered everything you ask."

"This second woman, did she know anything about the poison?" I ask, drawing in a sharp breath. The pain recedes, fading like smoke wisping over a fire.

"She laced our weapons with her own blood."

I frown. There's still a missing piece to all of this if Mari of all people could get her hands on an Oluso extinguishing poison. This makes one thing clear though—she is the curse caster. The person I need to kill is her.

"If you saw a portrait of this person, could you identify them?" Jonas asks.

"I will never forget." He lifts his chin, rage contorting his features. "She cut my brother's tongue out herself."

Markham stands unmoving, mouth held in a grim line. The facts are clear; somehow Mari sent multiple assassins to a betrothal ceremony organized by the Council and protected by several layers of Council-appointed guards. Either Mari's assassins have infiltrated the ranks of the Royal Guard, or someone on the Council has betrayed us. And since the Royal Guard are hand-selected by Council members, it's likely the latter.

But I say nothing, let Markham consider things in silence. In the last year, he's transformed from general to politician, working frantically to grasp the fragile threads of power cast adrift from his brother's passing. To his credit, he's always listened to what Jonas and I have to say regardless of whether he agrees.

A flourish sounds. The guards part as Mina stumbles in, Lady Ayn bobbing in her wake. I snatch up the beads, slipping them into my skirt pocket as Markham turns his attention to the newcomers. Maranya's lips curl in a grateful, pain-soaked smile.

The bandages wrapping General Mina's left knee—a souvenir from Lleyria—shift as she kneels, presenting a roll of paper. "Urgent message from Nyzchow, Your Highness."

Lady Ayn rips it from her hands, thrusting it at Markham.

"Ekwensi razed Wellstown. The city is no more."

EXPOSED

THE PROCLAMATION HANGS IN THE AIR. THE GUARDS COME ALIVE, BUZZING like hornets whose nest has been disturbed. Before now, Ekwensi has been sighted all over Eingard, liberating imprisoned Oluso from keeps throughout the region, but he's never harmed a city.

Markham unfolds the paper, face darkening as he reads. "Thousands dead. An attack at Pig Hour—"

"During the betrothal," Ayn finishes.

I let the words wash over me, fear stirring my heart as I realize what this means. Jonas takes my hand, but I can feel the sweat on his palm, the way he shifts as though he's preparing to fight.

The ten metal balls at the base of the agoo itanji rattle as Markham leans against the table. The eleventh ball, halfway through the spiral maze that makes up most of the contraption's body, clinks against the canal walls, inching toward the waiting bowl, where its descent will mark the start of Snake Hour. Only five of those balls littered the metal base when I left my rooms with Nana, brimming with trepidation and hope. The world has changed in so little time.

"It's as they intended. Occupy our forces, then strike." There is excitement in Lady Ayn's voice, a relish that sets the hairs on my arms tingling. "Those flying things were spotted as well."

"If the kokulu are involved, we can't lay this solely at Ekwensi's door," Jonas chimes in. "They left Lleyria in shambles after mere moments. Send scouts to Wellstown. We need more information."

I recall Mikhail's report now. There were refugees en route to Wellstown. If they reached Wellstown safely, it would mean the kokulu attacked yet another Eingardian city housing refugees. Something is amiss. Somehow, the Council has brought about this ruin.

"Ekwensi is in league with those creatures. As he is with the assassins," Lady Ayn insists. Her gaze flickers briefly to Maranya, whose eyes are now closed, head sunken against his chest.

"You're lying," I snarl through clenched teeth. "I saw you during the betrothal. You didn't move from your seat when the attack started."

"I was afraid for my life."

"Or you knew they wouldn't harm you," Jonas remarks, fixing Ayn with a pointed look. "This man confessed to working with Mari. You were closest to her."

She laughs, but the sound is hollow, forced. "Tell me, dear *prince*, what would it serve to throw my lot in with assassins? If you or Markham are harmed, I lose everything."

I close in on her, letting malice drip into my words. "Tell me where Mari is. Give me that and I won't hold you responsible for the attack today."

"I will not have my loyalty questioned," she sneers, eying me disdainfully. "Your kind just destroyed one of our major cities. The guards protecting the perimeters of this one hail from my lands."

"Enough."

Markham's voice is quiet, but there's enough weight to give us all pause.

"Father," Jonas says softly, "Ashkenayi warriors can't be bought by just anyone. Our neighbors would like nothing more than chaos to destroy Ifé. At the very least—"

"I am your king," Markham thunders. "One who has tolerated much. From *all* of you." He sweeps us with an imperious look. "I took this mantle to succeed where Alistair failed. I resolved to listen to you all, but I implore you—don't take my regard for granted."

He tosses Mina the seal ring on his middle finger. "Lock the capital down. No one is to enter or leave. All are under suspicion."

"Nana is dying!" I cry. "I need to get her help. If you'll let us through—"

"Send forces to Nyzchow," he continues, drowning me out. "I want a headcount of every refugee approaching the city." He hesitates a moment, then plows on, voice filled with certainty, "Give the order—round up every Oluso in Nordgren. Send them to Branach Keep."

The bravado I felt moments ago dissipates, dread ensnaring me in its place. I've given up so much, spent months in this miserable place, all for a peace that has shattered over the course of one night.

Mina stands frozen, looking from Markham to Jonas.

"Your Highness," Jonas pleads, "this is too hasty. The Oluso fought with us in the Great Hall. Send scouts to Wellstown, confirm the reports first."

Ayn dips into a curtsy, her face aglow with triumph. "The nobles have gathered seeking answers, Your Majesty. They fear the enemy is in our midst."

Markham slams his fist into the table, and the ink bottle jumps. Blue liquid spills through the fresh crack splintering the oak, but most of it swims over the map, blotting out half of Nordgren in one fell swoop. He erupts in a string of curses.

I speak, putting away the fear that is curling in my belly, screaming that it's too late. "We Oluso did nothing to deserve this. If Ekwensi destroyed Wellstown, he did so of his own volition. Calling for us to be imprisoned will make people believe Ekwensi was right."

"Dèmi is correct." Jonas puts his hands out as though he can hold his father back. "If we do this, we lose the Oluso's trust—everything we've worked for in the last year."

"Everything *you've* worked for," Markham accuses, stabbing an accusing finger at Jonas. "You. You promised me they were harmless. Thousands are dead."

"More will die from this decision. The Oluso won't be willingly imprisoned. We'll lose soldiers and people trying to enforce this order." Jonas swallows, then adds, "You would need to imprison me too."

"What would you have me do?" Markham shouts. "The Oluso are safer imprisoned. If I do nothing, do you think the nobles will wait? They will hunt the Oluso themselves. They saw you in the Great Hall. They'll come for you too!"

"So be it."

They stand close, breathing hard, faces mirroring masks of anger tied down by fraying strings of self-control.

Ayn slaps her fan closed with a resounding click. "I'll not wait and allow my own to be brutally slaughtered. When Alistair died, Markham, I placed my trust with you. I convinced wary Council members that you were best for regent. A third of the soldiers protecting these walls"—she spreads her arms wide—"all hail from the Ayn family keep."

"What do you want from me, Camilla?" Markham asks. His face is gaunt, the lines stretching around his temples and mouth multiplied since Lady Ayn arrived.

"Loyalty."

"Loyalty." He repeats the word, lets it fill the air. Then he whips out his sword, crossing the room in two strides, headed for Maranya.

"No!"

I rush forward, but the guards move in, blocking my way. Markham stabs at Maranya's chest, but Jonas is there, parrying his father's blade with his, sparks shooting off as Markham's blade is repelled. Maranya's eyes jolt open and he digs his feet into the ground, trying to shove himself away.

"You would oppose me? For someone who tried to murder you?" Markham cries.

"We would oppose you because we need him alive. He holds key information. We need him to save Nana's life."

Shifting his weight to his back foot, Markham springs forward, bringing his sword down, this time on Jonas's waiting blade.

"When you are king, you'll understand that one life is a small price to pay for thousands."

Jonas absorbs the force of the blow, then redirects the energy, shoving Markham back. "Never a wrong time to impart wisdom, is it, Father?" Jonas quips, mocking.

The guards spread out, making space for the fight, but the ones around me keep their focus on me, blades hemming me in. I spread my feet wide, attempting to call magic to my fingertips, but a fresh wave of pain envelops me, stopping me in my tracks.

"What happens when the price demanded is ten? Ten thousand?"

Jonas spits. "There will always be more lives in need of saving and lives we sacrifice in exchange."

"Naïve boy." Markham dashes in, turning at the last moment and using the flat of his blade to slam Jonas's back. Jonas stumbles, then catches himself in time to fend off another barrage. Markham speaks, each stream of words punctuated by a flash of his sword.

"Disloyalty destroys an army. A soldier who distrusts his battalion dies. A battalion that maligns their general perishes. Wars are lost—"

He knocks Jonas's sword out of his hands, then kicks his son in the chest. "By generals who believe themselves wiser than their rulers."

Turning on his heel, he plunges his sword at Maranya's chest, but there's a flash of cerulean flame and the sword shivers in midair, pausing before it can hit its target.

"I won't let you do this," Jonas gasps, one hand outstretched. "Or imprison the Oluso."

Markham sighs and lets go. His sword remains firmly in place. "Then you must compromise," he says finally. "I won't take back my order. Doing so is telling every Eingardian that I place the needs of others over theirs."

"We have done nothing. You can tell them that!" I scream. "We nearly died this evening."

In the glow of the torches, Markham's face is golden, resolute. His sandy hair takes on a red hue, much like his brother's. But the most frightening thing is how sharp his eyes are, the gray in them brackish pools intent on devouring everything in sight.

Sugbon lakooko eso, o ni lati te orun re ba ki irugbin re le wa laaye. A proud iroko tree during fruiting season still bows its neck for its seed to survive.

If Baba were in this room, looking at Markham, that is what he would say. Gone is the sympathetic general weighing his options. In his place is a consummate politician who will do what it takes to hold on to power.

Markham's next words fall like a blade: "In times of crisis, we unite against a common enemy. That is how we win. Not with faulty claims made against people who have proven themselves loyal."

Common enemy?

I want to laugh, but the sound is strangled in my throat. For months I've folded myself into neat compartments like the beaten flour cakes Eingardians love, diminished myself to an airy lightness for Ajes to consume without fear, all in hopes that one day they would see my humanity. That perhaps the Oluso might be more than monsters in their imaginations.

Ayn swans over to me. "Ferdinand's son was spotted with Ekwensi in Wellstown." She cocks her head, tapping her fan against her chin. "What was the boy's name? You two were once involved, no?"

"Colin," Jonas supplies, brow creasing into a frown.

"And what will the nobles say when they hear of our would-be queen's association with him? Would they believe her innocence then?" She stabs the fan in my direction. "She couldn't even finish her vows."

"That's not true!" I protest, but the words ring hollow even in my ears. I hesitated, stood with Jonas at my side and wondered if our bond would be enough. I am paying for it now.

Jonas's gaze settles onto me. For a moment, we stare at each other, grasping as we have so often for the comfort of our bond, taking refuge from the waves of hostility around us. I ease the walls of my mind, let him feel the desperation clawing at me. From him I sense a raging storm of worry tangled with fear—for me, for Nana, for everyone outside these walls unaware of all that is to change. But I find a seed of something too, an errant thought that slips into my mind like a star racing across the sky—an image of me hand in hand with Colin, overlooking the ruins of an Eingardian city.

"You believe them, don't you?" I choke, my voice struggling out against the knot in my throat. "After everything? That I would betray you."

"I don't. I know you." His face twists in anguish. "But they don't. They'll believe anything their fear dictates. Oko mi, please—"

"Don't call me that."

I close my eyes, shutting him out of my mind.

There is a howling in my ears, a grief for the dream I nursed for the past year. Every day since Alistair Sorenson died, I've woken up with a childish hope, held it closer to my breast as I've languished in this place, spun it lullabies and ditties while dancing past assassination attempts and slights, clutched it tight during lonely nights when Jonas is called to Council duties and I sit under the moon, trying to remember the taste of home. But the peace I've been fighting to birth is dead, and in its place is a whispering voice, begging me to unleash the fire burning inside until this room is blood and ash.

But I push that voice away, hanging on to the dying embers of that hope. "Get me a talisman and I'll do whatever you want. I'll kill Ekwensi or die trying. Just leave the Oluso alone."

Now that I've broken my spirit bonds, there's no telling what will happen next. It might take me years to die, madness slowly consuming me, or months. But I can't let Nana, Will, and all the other Oluso suffer for my choices.

Yet Jonas overrules me. "Send the Oluso into exile. Past the city gates."

"You can't—" I object, but he continues.

"I'll take a battalion along, escort them safely through. They know who I am now, so they'll have an easier time trusting me. While I'm gone, you can fortify our defenses, reassure the nobles. Dèmi will stay here. No one is to harm her. That is my compromise."

Markham nods his assent. "Agreed."

Jonas drops his hands, clenching them at his sides as Markham catches his unfrozen blade and rams it into Maranya's chest. The assassin sputters, taking labored breaths. Lady Ayn beams her approval.

"Stop it!" I scream, fury singing through my every pore. I surge forward, skirting under the crown of swords hemming me in, each step like shards of glass biting into my skin. Then I stumble against the iron pail and go down hard, fresh pain lancing through my joints like daylight piercing the dark of a cave. Jonas springs toward me, but the guards press in, a halo of weapons trained on my back.

Markham pulls his sword free and Maranya gasps as the chair tips over, iron pole screeching as it hits the floor. He slumps, blood gushing from the gaping wound in his chest, body curling in. For a brief moment, his eyes meet mine.

"Set us free," he wheezes.

Then his eyes roll back into his head and his jerking legs slow to a stop. He stills, blood trickling through the slits in the stone, and with it, my hopes of finding Mari.

I bite the inside of my cheek to keep the tears stinging my eyes from falling. I will not give them my tears. I will not let them see how much they've taken from me tonight.

Mina bows as Markham repeats Jonas's order, shooting me a sympathetic look before leaving the room. Lady Ayn sweeps out, guards trailing after her like ducklings.

Markham places a hand on Jonas's arm. "Today you've shown you have what it takes to rule. The Council won't forget this. Come up and address them. We'll wait for you."

Then he leaves, taking the rest of the guards with him.

Jonas snatches me up, engulfing me in his arms and I slump against his chest. Even though I have the steady song of his heart under my fingers, his warmth soothing the pain wracking my body, I keep the door to my mind closed, leaving him on the periphery aching for the comfort of our bond.

"Oko mi?" he whispers, tipping my chin up. "Say something."

"They'll try to find a way around you," I answer. "I wish—" I pause, trying to force down the lump in my throat. "I wish you wouldn't trust them."

"I have to trust some of them at least. Or none of this would be worth it." He presses his forehead to mine, rubbing my arms. "I'll get the Oluso to safety. It's a day's ride to Yusa. I'll put them on a ship bound for Oyo. Make sure the Council can't hurt them."

"And Nana?"

"Let's journey to the Spirit Realm tonight. Find out what we can. Once I'm back from Yusa, I can convince Father to let us go, at least to heal her. We'll make it."

I nod. Everything tonight has confirmed what Ekwensi told me—the Eingardians would never choose peace, not when they could have power. Jonas may want to support me, to fight for a future together, but in this thorny forest masquerading as a home, there will always be pits—fertile ground for doubt to grow and spread its rot to everything around us.

But I put on a smile and let Jonas wipe away the tears staining my cheeks. When he leans in to kiss me, I hold on tight, savoring the feeling of his lips on mine. This will be the last time I let him see me like this, the last time I give in to my wanton desires. I can't trust him—not while he still believes in process and compromise. The laws will always shift to suit those in power. Compromises are little more than delays, creeping blights that take more and more until the inevitable arrives. The Oluso can only be freed if we take our freedom by force. I see that now.

The eleventh silver ball lands in the base of the agoo itanji with a rattle. The bells of Château Nordgren come alive, ringing through the courtyard with such fervor that I shake.

"I'll be back," he murmurs softly against my lips. As he rises to his feet, he adds, "I'm sorry."

"I am too."

He walks to the door, stopping in the frame to steal a glance at me, then he passes through and I am alone, Maranya lying a few feet away from me.

Pulling my bone blade from my skirts, I squat and use it to peel the wooden beads adorning his broken wrist out from under the iron pole.

Set us free.

"I will," I whisper to the empty room. I owe Maranya that much after taking his brother's life. Tucking their two bracelets together, I leave the room, heading into the abandoned corridor. I am certain now, promises be damned—the moment Jonas leaves for Yusa, I will escape this castle, and I'm taking Nana with me. I'm going to find Ekwensi.

BEHEST

THE MOMENT JONAS WALKS INTO OUR PRIVATE SOLAR AN HOUR LATER, I pounce. He barely has time to register the sheer aso owosun hugging my breasts and hips when I grab his collar and yank his head down to mine. He mumbles against my lips as though he has something to say, but once I sweep my tongue into his mouth, he relents, leaning into my embrace. I may not be able to trust him, but I still need him to access the Spirit Realm, find out how to keep my body from falling apart so I can make it to Ekwensi intact.

I stroke a hand against his neck, trailing my fingers down until I meet the silk fabric of his shirt. Then I pull back, giving him a full view of the pearl-white buttons beading the ikomu that cups my breasts.

He swallows, taking in the way the fabric splays open just under my ikomu, revealing my navel and the sliver of cloth wrapped about my hips and butt.

"The Oluso are safe," he breathes. "We won't leave until the morning."

"I heard from Mikhail." I don't add that I deceived the Royal Guard commander into aiding my escape, telling him I needed to send Nana away in secret.

"We ride at Crow Hour."

I skim my fingers along the high waist of Jonas's trousers. "You have a lot of time then."

"We'll talk about the meeting later?"

Dropping his hand, I stride to the waiting bed in the middle of the room in answer. The satchel I tucked away just moments before I heard him unlocking the door is almost completely out of view, but the edge of my bone blade peeks out at the top, the gleaming white shining in the light of the hearth across.

I whirl at the edge of the bed, blocking my satchel from sight, and shrug the owosun from my shoulders. He watches me, dazed, but when I tuck my bottom lip between my teeth and offer the string holding my ikomu together, he throws off the scabbard hanging from his back and reaches the bed in three sharp strides.

He slips a hand behind my head, but before he can kiss me, I place a finger on his lips.

"Spirit Realm first; we can enjoy ourselves after."

He rubs a hand against his reddened cheeks. "Of course." But he sits back on his knees, moving his hand to my shoulder. "Are you all right? With everything that happened down there—"

"I'm fine," I snap.

He flinches, then quirks his mouth into a half smile. "It would make sense that you're not. If Maranya lived, we could have gotten more information on Mari."

"Or threatened Ayn," I add. "Used that to get the talisman."

Now that Maranya is dead, the only path left to helping Nana and Will is through the Spirit Realm. And though I've sat on this bed for some time willing myself into its swelling embrace, all I find is fog and shadows, mocking laughter chasing me as I stumble in the dark.

"It was a gamble," Jonas explains, rubbing small circles over the surface of my palm. "One I wasn't comfortable taking with you."

I close my eyes, try to tamp down the fury burning its way up my throat. But he keeps going.

"Dèmi, I know that choice wasn't mine alone to make—"

"Then why did you make it? Why did you trust your father?" I cry.

"I had to keep them from overwhelming us," Jonas answers.

It is the softness of his voice, the evenness of it, that sparks my ire more than anything. "The Council was involved in Lleyria," I charge. "They clearly did something to bring the kokulu to Wellstown. Can't you see this is all one big trap?"

Jonas sighs, running a hand over his stubbled cheeks. "The Oluso were in immediate danger. I was focused on that. Besides, we didn't have the evidence to accuse them. Mikhail's riders haven't returned."

The hair on my arms prickles, and the warmth in my belly gives way to stifling anger. "Evidence? You want to play games with evidence now? Evidence that the Council can just claim is false?"

"We needed time!" he yells.

I rear back in surprise. He flushes, clearly embarrassed. He's never raised his voice to me before. It seems we're both discovering new things about ourselves.

"We needed time," he says again, whisper-soft now. "Time to regroup, figure out what to do. That's all."

But I refuse to back down. "Time is the one thing we don't have. Can't you see? How much longer until the Council decides the Oluso need to be conquered once and for all? You gave away Nana's best chance."

I take a breath, swallowing against the knot in my throat. Jonas is stricken, his face pale and eyes sparking with grief. When he speaks again, his voice cracks, as though he's swallowed several blades.

"I'm sorry. I couldn't throw my father's opinions away. I did the best I could with what I did. I'm sorry it makes life harder." He takes my hands, folds them to his chest. "But we'll find help for Nana and a solution for the Oluso together. So, tell me, please, oko mi, how can I make this right?"

I settle back, suddenly ashamed. I can feel his presence waiting at the threshold of my mind, skimming against my consciousness. All he wants to do is connect, to help carry the burdens that have weighed me down my whole life, but I can't trust that he can. He still believes Oluso freedom can be won with laws and treaties, but I know iron swords that speak their will onto Oluso flesh only understand the language of power. And right now, I need more. I need an army that will fight at my back to overthrow the Council and stop them from using the kokulu. I need resources to hunt down Mari. I need Ekwensi.

So I pull Jonas's hand to my breast and say, "Strengthen our bond. Get me to the Spirit Realm. Everything else we'll discuss later."

He hesitates a moment, then dives at me as though desperate to erase the ugliness of the moment before. As our lips collide and his fingers tear at the thin layers that form my ikomu, I hear a single thought ring through my mind like a bell.

Whatever you want, oko mi, I'll do it. I would pull this city apart, brick by brick to protect you. Believe me.

I rip his shirt open, scratching him in my haste to peel it off his shoulders. He palms my bottom, jerking me onto his waiting lap, and I lean into him, rocking my hips against his. He groans, then sucks my bottom lip between his teeth.

The threads of magic stir beneath my skin, drawing up with every brush of his fingers. He pulls back the curtain of my braids and lets his gaze roam over my bare breasts.

My heart swells as he looks up at me and murmurs, "You're so beautiful. O ma rewa o. What did I do to deserve you?"

He cups my right breast, stroking it softly. My nipple strains against his fingers, begging for attention. He glances at me again, dawn eyes bright with desire, and I pull his head closer, inhaling as he darts his tongue over the waiting nub.

My magic leaps at his touch, warmth spreading over my skin, and I can see the path to the Spirit Realm now, the glimmer at the edge of my vision.

He closes his mouth over my breast and sucks hard, tonguing the very tip at the same time. I throw my head back, bracing my hands on his shoulders. For a moment, I forget my ulterior motives, lost in the throes of bliss and arousal. I want—need more—now.

I claw at his trousers and he rises on his knees, yanking them down. His cock springs free, and I shove him back, pinning him to the bed with a hand. Lacing my legs around his hips, I grind hard against his cock. He draws back with a curse, but I am on fire, magic rising up in me like a wave, enveloping me altogether.

"Dèmi." Jonas whispers my name. I meet his eyes for a bare moment before I find myself in the dark of the Spirit Realm, standing by the iroko tree again.

This time, however, Ayaba awaits me.

As the Aziza queen rises from the arbor embedded in the hull of the tree, her wings unfurl, shedding light into the dark fog. Her white-gold eyes burn into mine, and she wrinkles her nose. "I see you are ill prepared."

I look down to find I am still naked, a purpling bruise puckering my right breast where Jonas nipped me.

She tosses me a piece of cloth. The gossamer robe drips from my fingers, the cracked brown-and-moss-green pattern resembling the skin of the iroko tree. I pull it on hurriedly as Ayaba paces, her halter necklace of cowrie shells and animal bones rattling.

"Come," she commands when I finish. She glides away, braided silver hair spilling out of her kofia as she goes.

I race after her, dodging various vines and branches that appear as we delve deeper into the Spirit Realm. The ground is uneven, strewn with pebbles and jagged rocks that bite my feet as I go, but I dare not stop. Apart from the light falling from Ayaba's wings, everything is mired in fog, darkness pressing in on either side of us, lying in wait. Once or twice a creature darts across my path, but I only catch a glimpse of long, spiny ears and an equally barbed tail before it's gone. Then we reach the mouth of a cave with luminescent blue orbs littering the ceiling, and I stop in awe, taking in the sight.

"Time unspools herself in haste, so listen carefully," Ayaba says, turning to face me. Her amber skin, smooth and dewy as a flower petal only a year before, is creased. Her full lips cut a fine line. Though hundreds of years old, she still retains the appearance of a young woman, but it's clear that something has happened in the time we've been apart.

She stretches out her hands, and light streams forth, twisting into myriad shapes; a ghostly forest that burns without ceasing; a city swallowed by encroaching sands; restless sea waves that batter junkets racing toward land, tossing them to and fro.

"The evil that plagues your realm has visited mine as well. Our forest homes are burning, our sands shifting. The seas cry out for help."

"The K'inu can enter the forest realms?" I ask, eyes widening in surprise. This explains Mikhail's observation about the increasing number of Harmattan storms.

She sighs. "Their very presence disturbs the balance of our realms; physical, spiritual, and in-between. The time I warned you of has come.

We need your help, as a child of the Aziza, to vanquish this evil and set things to rights."

I curtsy, placing one fist over my heart. "Your enemy is mine, Olá re." The Aziza saved my life when I was a child of nine and have helped me through more difficult situations. I owe them more than I can repay. If the K'inu are affecting the Aziza and smothering the land itself, it is all the more reason why I must join hands with Ekwensi and stop the Council in their tracks.

She touches my shoulder lightly. "But that is not the only reason why I brought you here. Your ancestors lament your unravelling bonds. Many would not answer when you called."

I nod, not trusting myself to speak. I knew killing would untangle my Oluso bonds, but it stings to hear my own ancestors want nothing to do with me, each word from Ayaba like stakes driving into my heart. I want to ask about Mummy, but I am suddenly afraid, wondering if she, too, is ashamed of me.

Ayaba's fingers tighten on my shoulder. "I have watched you all your life, omoyé. I understand the choice you made today."

I soften, letting out the breath damming my lungs when she calls me her child. At least Ayaba hasn't abandoned me.

"The best I can give you is a hiding place, no more." She points to the heart of the cave. "But hear this, omoyé: whoever you see in there, do not touch them."

"Who is inside?"

"Even I don't know."

I swallow, then ask, "Can you show me the way to Ìyá-Ilé? I need her help. My loved ones are dying."

She sweeps back, burnished-gold gown waving as she steps aside. "My mother will call you in her own time. For now, she asks that you walk this path. When the time comes, you will need the blade and mask I once gifted you."

"Does this mean Ìyá-Ilé will help me?"

"Go, Abidèmi."

She waves me on, her kofia framing her face like a halo. Folding my body, I curtsy my thanks.

There's no use hesitating or asking what she means. Ayaba has never steered me wrong, no matter what it cost her. She came for me, when no one else would, and acted as my guide. That alone is enough to give her my trust without restraint.

I step into the cave without looking back. The air is damp, the smell of rotted fruit thick in my nostrils. Still I walk on, trailing my fingers against the glowing orbs that coat the walls, watching them change colors as I brush against their slippery surfaces. They bloom verdant greens and sunny yellows, lighting my way into the darkness. A few spark a deep violet as I reach the narrow mouth at the bottom of the cave, and I duck past the hanging tendrils of vines obscuring the way. Cave walls fall away to reveal an expanse that stretches miles high, a starlit night sky gleaming through a narrow hollow at the very top.

I am on a ledge with nothing beneath but a raging sea, rushing water lapping hungrily at the walls hemming it in. As I inch my way out, the orbs in the expanse walls come alive, winking on their variegated lights, a storm of color like skies that blanket the mountains north of Nordgren during Winter Harvest. Then the orbs draw themselves out, spilling into the air, curled tendrils fanning out like sun rays, propelling them as they swim.

I take a step back, and the rock where my foot was gives way, crashing into water below. The water sings its triumph, sending up a spray as it receives the rock in its waiting arms. Mummy taught me to think of the Spirit Realm as a vast house with many rooms, each living and breathing, shifting and changing in its own time. But even though I've spent time in Benin Forest with the Aziza, made brief visits to other Oluso in the Spirit Realm, I have never seen anything as breathtaking as this.

"You're not familiar with elèsè?"

I turn to find a tall man with thick white dreads standing on the precipice of one of the razor-thin juts of rock connecting my ledge to the wall. He takes a step forward and the moonlight illuminates skin the rich amber of garri, and a wide set of eyes that mirror my own. If nothing else, the jagged half spear in his hands marks him as my father, Iron Blood Osèzèlé.

"I've never seen them, no," I answer. I once told Nana that I saw him as a mere betrayer, someone I no longer needed to know anything about, but my traitorous heart leaps in my chest, lapping up my father's presence like a hungry dog.

He skips onto another outcropping, no easy feat since the rock he's balancing on looks as though it could shatter in a heartbeat. "They're living stone, one with this cave. They sense emotions and respond to them."

"They're beautiful."

He sniffs, watching me with a curiosity reserved for a wild horse or stray dog. "I thought your mother would've shown you more. Prepared you."

Clenching my jaw, I rein in that misplaced joy, molding it into spite. "She did her best caring for me alone. She had only eight name days to teach me anything before she was murdered."

He raises a hand as though to touch me, but I flinch and he draws back, closing his empty hand into a fist. "Yetundé always knew how to make the best out of a bad situation. Even when that situation was family. Her mother was not an easy person."

"What do you want?" I say finally. "Why did you call me here?"

All this talk of family reminds me that Nana is trapped, wasting away from poison while my absent father reminisces about the mate he abandoned. The Oluso are at odds, wondering if their newfound freedoms will be ripped away from them or if they should risk their spirit bonds, the very thing that makes them who they are, on a bloody revolution. The K'inu have resurfaced to wreak havoc on an already distressed kingdom.

"I wanted to give you your birthright. Properly this time." He taps his spine. "I warned you that the iron is demanding. I see it's already wrought its mark. If I'd had time to teach you—"

"But you didn't, did you?" I shout. I'm tired of his riddles. The only thing I've ever received from this man is magic and the knowledge that he taught the Sorensons ironwork—he chose his vengeance over my mother and me.

He sighs, brushing a hand through his thick hair. Even now his scarred face is youthful, belying the moonlight tresses adorning his face.

If I had passed by him on the streets of Benin, I would have thought him a man of thirty-five, no more.

"Another time, I will explain. For now, your anger is your greatest weapon . . . and your downfall. Your will is the blade that sharpens the iron, but control—a sound mind—is what will chase away the spirits that desire to engrave their mark on you."

I sneer. "If you want to teach me control, it's a bit late. I've killed."

To my surprise, he smiles. "So you have; that can be remedied. But only if you find your way back."

"In words I can understand?"

He slashes at the spired rocks underpinning the ledge and they sever all at once, crumbling into the waiting sea. The ledge trembles and I dive for the cave mouth, grabbing on to a hanging rock before the shelf gives way, tumbling into the depths below.

"Are you trying to kill me?" I scream. My fingers are slipping, the rock gnawing cuts into my palms but I hang on, struggling to pull my torso up.

Osèzèlé's voice tickles my ear. "The first lesson in control is fear."

He slams the blunt end of the spear across my fingers and I let go.

Tucking my arms into my chest, I try to control my fall, angle my body so I land somewhere near rock. But no amount of planning prepares me for the icy waters that crash into me, robbing my lungs of air. I slap my hands together, try to wriggle forward as Jonas taught me, but the current is too fast, knocking me out of form every time I think I'm ready to kick my legs. I claw at the water desperately, but it continues its assault, tossing me about until my body grows heavy and I open my mouth, swallowing the salty water.

Black spots fill my vision, and now my eyes are drifting closed. The fire in me is dying, quelling to a smolder, and all I can think about is the people I'm leaving behind. Of Nana, who wakes me every day with a smile and lovingly braids my hair. Of Will, who laughs so hard he has to hold his sides and totes Haru around, letting her tug at his beard. Of Baba, who grunts his approval. Of Colin and his warm hands, his smirk, the defiant look always lurking in his hazel eyes, and the secret smile he saves for me, one corner of his mouth twitching after the other. Of Jonas, whose day-bright eyes linger on me, tinkling with wonder and delight every time our gazes meet, of the touch of his skin on mine and the song of our hearts together. Of all the Oluso I've met over the years and their shining, tearful faces. Of all the pain I've carried in me like a scythe, letting it rip me anew every time I meet an Oluso in danger.

Then I'm flying out of the water, sputtering as air tears into my lungs, forcing me to breathe. Soft tendrils curl around my neck, green light emanating from the bulbous orb attached to my shoulder. I cough, spitting salty water, and the elèsè shudders as the coughs rack my body. We're hovering above the sea now, held in midair by forces I don't understand but have no desire to question.

"Ìyá-Ilé has spoken. You are ready," Osèzèlé announces.

"What?" I cough through salt-cracked lips. "That was a test? Now?"

"Everything is a test, daughter." He chuckles, and now I glimpse the metal tooth hiding in a full row of pearly ones. "Iya makes her own decisions. But she has judged your heart and found it worthy."

"You nearly killed me," I protest.

"I did not. Your fear did. But it saved you too."

Ofen muoria zeh bho odoto ede. Muolen bhu udu, uki ayere egue ya okhun agbon.

Fear is the weight that pulls you into the water's depths. But if you hold it in the correct room in your heart, it becomes a reminder of your place in this world, of the lives and bonds tied to yours.

He tosses me the spear in his hands and I clutch at it with my clammy fingers. It shrinks, curling into a pendant that fits my palm, its clear surface reflecting the light of the elèsè.

"This will lead you to Ren, your next guide. Find her and you'll find me."

"I don't need you; I need Iya."

"And you will have her," he says simply. "But . . . a word of warning: Iya will only grant one request. If you seek to reclaim your spirit bonds, garner enough power to defeat the evil trickling into your realm, you must ask for that and only that. If you ask for something else, your bonds will be lost forever."

I still. I can't heal Nana and Will, then, not if I want my magic back. Dread surges in me like a tidal wave, threatening to swallow me whole.

"You're certain of that?" I blurt, grasping for options, hope—anything to keep the abyss of despair from overtaking me. "I can't ask Iya for more than one thing?"

"I am living proof," Osèzèlé answers. "In my youth, I made a bargain with Iya. Later, I begged her for something else, but she did not deign to respond." He flashes a wistful smile. "One day, I might tell you what I begged her for."

I clench my fists at my sides, holding back the urge to scream. I should have known the spirits would not give freely—not without sacrifice. If this first test is any indication, the road to Ìyá-Ilé is perilous, full of trials that might break me, and I don't have time for that, not now. This all but confirms it—I need Ekwensi's help. He alone has the means to shift the tides of fate. With his army, I can push the Council out of power and force them to give up Mari. We can defeat the K'inu before the Council employs them in another attack. I just need to get to him alive, and everything will fall into place.

My father's words bring me out of my anxious stupor. "The choice is yours, young one, whatever path you walk. Iya will not force you into her arms. Know that."

He turns to go, but I dart forward, grabbing his shoulder. The air around his skin ripples like water disturbed by a pebble. I snatch my hand back, remembering Ayaba's words too late.

"I—I just wanted to ask . . . did you love my mother?"

The question has dogged me since the day I became old enough to understand the village children's jokes about Mummy and me. Even as I voice it now, my heart aches, and I watch my father with guarded eyes, each moment of silence a festering wound.

He softens, his eyes taking on a faraway look, his mouth bearing the ghost of a smile. "I still do, even now." His face shutters, a scowl eclipsing that soft look. "But I owed her more than love."

The waters beneath us begin to chatter and roil. Bubbles rise, peeling from the surface of the waves like pearls breaking from clams, color warping on their smooth, fragile bodies.

"Leave now!" Osèzèlé shouts as bubbles cluster around me, swelling into a shape.

A boy fades into existence, moonlight casting his earthy skin with a bluish tinge. His dark hair is loosely braided at the top but cascades into unbounded feather-white locks that run down his back. In his hand is a spear, what mine would look like if the two halves were whole. When the bubbles settle, bursting against his skin, he opens sugary-brown eyes that are entirely my own.

I take in the sight of him, shock running through me like a current. Ayaba's words from our time in Benin Forest hit me again.

A moon born with a smothered sun.

This is my brother, the twin I should have had, the other baby that didn't survive.

"Sister," the boy says, eyes bright with excitement. "Is that really you?"

He reaches for me, and my heart constricts as though a fist has closed over it, pain crushing the air from my lungs. The elèsè lets out a shrill noise, the sound stabbing my ears like shattered glass, and suddenly I understand that it's lamenting, crying because of what is happening to me.

"Release her," Osèzèlé demands. "Do it now, Ayodélé!"

The boy draws back, but the crushed feeling does not dissipate. I claw at my chest, struggling to breathe. The elèsè springs away from me, and now I'm falling, speeding again toward the waters. Just before I hit that icy wall again, the elèsè spreads its lower body out, slapping onto my nose and mouth. Warmth hums through me like a song and I melt into the air, coming into my body as it's stitched into another place. I open my eyes to find Jonas hovering over me, his hands stroking my face.

"Welcome back," he whispers, but he is shaking, tears gathered in the corners of his eyes.

"What happened?" I croak. My throat is raw, as though I've been screaming for hours.

He flashes my gilded hairpin, the deer horns adorning it stained red, and now I notice the wound in his shoulder, blood blooming from his pale skin like roses sprouting in snow.

"You stopped moving and I thought you were in the Spirit Realm, but . . ."

"But?" I ask. I try to ease myself up, but my arms jerk back to the bed, held in place by shackles that loop back to the bedposts. I flex my legs, feeling similar weights trapping them in place, pinning me to the bed like arrows studding a tree.

"What in Olorun's name—"

Jonas waves a hand and the shackles fall off, ringing as they strike the ground. "You attacked me," he explains, shame burning his neck a deep pink.

No doubt he's thinking of the stories I've told him, of watching the king's soldiers put Oluso in shackles every time the raids began. Of the nightmares that have haunted me since I was a child, before I knew I had iron magic—that I would one day wake in chains, iron suffocating the embers of my spirit.

He swallows. "It was a temporary solution. You weren't yourself."

"What happened?"

"You ascended to the Spirit Realm. Then you opened your eyes, came after me."

"I did this?" I whisper, touching his chest. The wound is deep, an eye-shaped crater with flayed skin bunched around it like a flimsy curtain. He hisses, and I pull away instantly.

"I'm sorry."

"It's all right." He sinks back, shoulders loosening as he settles on the edge of the bed.

Scrambling onto unsteady feet, I gather the blankets over my chest. "We need to rub bitter leaf in the wound before it starts to fester. My kit is just outside the kitchens."

He catches me by the wrist as I flutter past. "Don't."

"What—"

"This section of the castle is closed off. No one is to enter or leave. Except me."

Understanding dawns as a blush stains his pale cheeks.

"I'm a prisoner then," I say.

He shakes his head furiously, pulling me softly back onto the bed. "You're not. You can still go up to see Nana. But this is the only way I could think to protect you. I may trust my father not to be foolish, but Ayn is another story. She might come after you while you're weak."

"And you think a few closed-off rooms will stop her?" I ask, anger gathering to me like a cloak. For the second time today, Jonas has managed to surprise me. And I'm not sure if my anger is born from the loss of control I feel, the fear that my fate is in the hands of others, or the itchy feeling this surprise creates in my belly, the certainty that there are many sides to my mate I have yet to see.

"I'm leaving my personal guard behind. They've sworn blood oaths to protect you. And before you say they don't believe in the spirits, I hold their families' lives in my hands."

The personal guards of an Eingardian royal are deadly not just because they're the best soldiers but also because, from the time they are selected, their families are forced to live apart from them, secured in a special part of the castle like hostages. It's a system that served Alistair Sorenson well, made certain that loyalty was a foregone conclusion. It's frightening to hear Jonas invoke him now, but I don't remark on that.

"You'll have no one to watch your back," I say, swallowing past the lump in my throat.

"I'll have Mina and Mikhail. That is more than enough," he adds.

It seems Jonas has thought of everything.

His eyes are locked on me, searching for a sign as though my body is a scrying pool reflecting the fate of the world. He clasps and unclasps his fingers, and I know that he aches to draw me in, bridge this chasm between us, but sharing warmth won't be enough to quell the icy pool of anger filling my heart.

But I draw my fury back, slipping it between my ribs like a dagger. I won't leave my fate in anyone's hands, but he has no need to know that yet.

"All right. Let me try healing your injury then," I say, breaking the silence.

He cracks a nervous smile. "I may be poor at using your magic, but I can do this much at least." He splays a hand over the wound, and green fire sparks at his fingers, the healing magic knitting his skin together a direct consequence of our bond. I grit my teeth against the wave of resentment and longing that curls in my belly.

"Did you find anything in the Spirit Realm?"

I lie, the words slipping off my tongue like honey: "Ìyá-Ilé will help us. Once Will arrives, we can complete the bonding ceremony. Try healing Nana again."

He frowns. "Didn't Baba say that wouldn't work?"

"Baba was wrong. Ayaba appeared to me in the Spirit Realm and showed me how to get to Iya."

"And the K'inu?"

"Iya will help with that too. You were right, we just needed time."

He lets out a sigh of relief. "Then we have a path forward."

I nod, not trusting myself to speak. Later, when he finds out what I've done, he will be angry, but in time he will see I had no choice. I don't know what happened to my body while I was in the Spirit Realm, but it's clear I'm out of control. Something is stirring within me and there's no way to know what will come next, what chaos will unfold at my hands. And since the spirits want to speak in riddles, it's time for me to take a new road, act before the dangers lurking consume us all.

Jonas studies me for a moment, and I wait, willing my face into a calm mask. Then he reaches for me, and I crawl into his arms, taking refuge from the storm of the world. There are so many questions, worries that fly through my mind like bats, screeching their displeasure. But I lean against the shelter of Jonas's arms, breathing in his earthen scent, knowing that this may be the last time I welcome its lingering kiss on my skin.

Golden light twines with swelling purple clouds, the sun's rays piercing through the crosshatched slats in the window to the left of our bed. Time passes differently in the Spirit Realm, and it's clear now that I've lost more than a few hours.

Jonas presses a kiss to the top of my head. "I have to go soon," he murmurs.

"I know."

He takes my chin in his hand, the gold flecks from the sun's rays brightening his ice-blue eyes. "When I get back, we'll settle everything. Nana, the Council, us."

I hold his gaze, committing his smiling face to memory. "We will," I promise. Those words may very well be a lie, but for a brief moment I believe them. Despite the anger gnawing at me, I want to believe in a world where things could be as Jonas wishes them to be, a world where we can solve the problems between us with determination and love alone.

He leans in for a kiss, and this time, I wrap my arms around his neck, pressing myself against him as though I could meld us together, kissing him with the desperation of a hungry ghost clinging to life. We stay there for a while, exchanging small kisses, stoking the fires we ignited last night. Then sounds of the castle awakening cut through our cocoon; boots from marching soldiers gathering in the courtyard; the soft whispers of attendants cleaning the wider room leading into our bedroom.

We break apart with a sigh. Then Jonas is off, throwing on clothes, grabbing his scabbard before an attendant knocks at the door. He leaves me with a smile, and I return it.

Once he crosses out of the solar, I spring into action, pulling on a long-sleeved blouse and jerkin trousers. Grabbing my satchel from under the bed, I stuff food from our morning platter in it, shoving meatpies and agidi wrapped in plantain leaves into the extra clothes in my pack. The ofada rice mixed with crayfish that sits in a wooden bowl I scoop into an extra leaf and bundle tightly, ignoring the alluring scent of locust beans and stewed peppers. Then I place the letter I scrawled hurriedly last night on the desk a few steps away.

I scramble across the room, then skid to a halt at the door. The groove Dara's ax made stares back at me, fierce and angry as a battle scar. Taking a moment, I lay my head against the strong, solid wood and breathe in the òwón's honeyed scent. This door was Jonas's first gift to me, a promise of hope—a belief that this place could one day become my home, that Oluso and Aje would find a way to consider each other. Now I see that this door was little more than a compromise, another shackle keeping me tethered to an impossible dream.

Whipping around, I take off my father's ring and place it on top of the letter. I owe Jonas this, at the very least, a remembrance that I loved him.

I charge through the door, pretending not to notice when the royal guards stir from their posts, gazes trailing me. Instead, I make a show of gathering up the sheets in my arms, stuffing the satchel I packed deeper into the cloth. Then I waddle toward the privy at the end of the narrow corridor. For once, having disrespectful attendants is a blessing. There is no one to follow me in, insist on helping me bathe.

I slip into the damp room, folding into the steam rising from the heated pool at its heart. Then I dart behind the furnace, wedging my hand into the crevice between the iron and the stone, pulling the lever hidden there. The wall in front of me gives way, illuminating uneven moss-covered steps crowded against the wall like rotted teeth. Bloody handprints mark the wall, a grotesque map that leads up to Nana's wing at the west end of the castle.

Ducking into the low passage, I begin my ascent into darkness. I can't risk summoning a wind spirit to light my way, not when the act might incapacitate me. Soon, when I absolutely must, I can bear the pain of using my magic to secure our escape. For now, my wits are my best weapon.

The passage ends in a cobwebbed storeroom. Stealing out of it, I sprint down the corridor, slowing only when I glimpse an approaching attendant.

"Yemé's Day sings for broken hearts," he says, bowing low.

"May your tears be filled with purpose," I respond, returning the greeting of the day.

I soldier on, barely managing to maintain a neutral pace until he is out of sight. The door that awaits me is similar to the one I left behind, its warm copper tone beckoning me closer in welcome.

I scoff. I've been a fool. If I were anyone else, another Oluso without the power of iron, this door would be a death sentence separating me and Nana. At the betrothal, I accused Jonas of failing to see the intricate ways Eingard itself is hostile to Oluso, but I am also guilty of the same. I have been blind, exiled from my people by only the promise of a better life— exiled by iron, the blood that keeps me safe in these walls and the rest of my people out. But I refuse to submit anymore.

Reaching for the handle, I wrench open the door. It's time to take charge of my fate.

TESTING

EDWINA DOZES, HEAD TILTING TOWARD HER CHEST, ARMS FOLDED OVER the basin of warm water she's been using to clean Nana. As I cross the threshold into the room, the feather ward attached to the frame bathes me in its golden glow, offering a welcome. I open the window overlooking Nana's bed, letting the sun's molten fingers caress her body. The veinlike bitna markings ceased to grow overnight, ending in rough circles, ink blots dotting the parchment of her skin.

As I press my finger to one Nana opens her eyes and I jump.

"You're awake." I cover her hand with mine, warming her cold fingers.

She cracks open chapped lips ringed with the moss green of Baba Sylvanus's tincture. "Water."

I scramble for the cup sitting on the cabinet across, pouring in dregs of honeyed water from the pewter flagon nearby. I press the cup to Nana's lips, tilting it up slightly, and she laps it like a freshly born kitten, tasting the world for the first time.

"How long?" she asks, squinting drowsy eyes.

"It's Crow Hour. You've been asleep for half a day."

She darts her tongue out, moistening her lips. "I mean, how long do I have?"

The relief that surged in me settles into anxiety. "Baba thought three days last night."

"So two and a half at worst." She nods, the jewels still adorning her braided hair glittering in the sun like starlight. There's a legend of an Oluso who traded her life to an eloko to save her Aje lover, fading into the sky soon after. At springtime, when the stars align in the shape of a woman's head, we hold the Chuno Festival in celebration, living out the joy that unknown Oluso never knew. Before we changed the laws, parents would take their children to watch okri perform, teaching them over meals of sticky buns and spun sugar that the Oluso have always existed to smoothen the path of Aje lives. I have always hated that story.

"Ìyá-Ilé will help heal you. Baba went to fetch Will."

I despise lying to Nana, but I doubt she would approve an alliance with Ekwensi, even if it meant finding Mari faster and saving her and Will's lives.

Nana's slim brows quirk into a neat line. "Ìyá-Ilé? The Mother Tree?"

I untuck the pendant Osèzèlé gave me from the pocket of my trousers. "I'll explain later. We need to leave now."

"Wait. Where did you get that?" She inspects the pendant, a strange smile blossoming on her lips, bringing life into those hollowed cheeks. "Just when I thought I had no vision for you . . . the ancestors surprise me again."

"What is it?"

"I've had the same dream since I've been here."

She grips my hand and an image of a woman appears in my mind. The woman is slender, dressed in a stained blue skirt that swallows up most of her body, a reed growing against swelling waters. On her head is a hui-cheok, the flared black crown woven with precious stones that Gomae empresses wear, and in the center of that is a fold in the shape of my pendant. All around her, the room burns, smoke misting her golden face like a veil. But she makes no move to escape, only lifting a dagger to the floor-length braid hanging over her shoulder, severing it at the nape of her neck. Newly shorn, she throws her hui-cheok and braid into the waiting flames and takes a seat as blood-red embers spark new flames at her feet.

Nana drops my hand as a wave of pain overtakes her, shaking like a leaf in a monsoon. I slap her back lightly as she coughs, hacking as though something is storming its way up her throat.

"Baba said the bitna affects magic. You shouldn't use it for now."

"It can," she says after another sip of water. "Bitna dries up your spirit reserves, forces you to use your life in exchange for magic."

"Then why did you show me that?" I protest, panic flaring.

She throws her legs over the side of the cot. "So you'd recognize Ren just in case."

I frown. "How did you know—"

"Empress Ren is the woman who raised my mother."

"The Mad Queen?" I spit, recalling now the stories of the former Empress of Gomae—the one who gave birth to her first and only child nearly two years after living in solitude, out of the presence of men. After passing the baby to a nurse, she set her entire palace on fire and perished.

"My mother would slap you for saying that."

Edwina stirs, and the basin jumps to the floor like a displaced cat, skittering and spewing water on stone. I barely have time to motion to her when footsteps pound toward the door.

"Everything all right in there?" a woman shouts.

"S'fine," Edwina mutters, wiping drool from her chin. "Just a small accident."

Nana throws an arm across my neck and I heave her up, threading an arm underneath her shoulder. She sags against me like rotting wood hanging onto the threads of a flooded house and we shuffle for the window, her ceremonial socks smearing the water around.

"Do you need help? I'm coming in," the woman responds.

I shake my head at Edwina and she rushes to the door as it swings open. "No, don't—"

Baba's feather flashes crimson as the woman pokes her head in, doe-brown eyes taking in the scene. It's Martine, one of the new maids the Council assigned to me. "Hey. You're not supposed to be—"

Whatever she wants to say is lost as the feather rips from the frame and slaps itself onto her fair skin. She barely has a moment to scream before hairy spindled legs protrude from multiple sides of the feather and it scurries over her body, draping her in a cocooning web. She tries to shuffle back, but the web wraps around her ankle and then there's a sharp crack, like rocks smashing into glass. She howls, blood staining the web a darker gray.

More attendants crowd into the corridor, the guards bobbing behind them.

I kick the basin at Edwina, and she catches on immediately, falling to her knees in dramatic anguish even as the bowl skids past her. Then I toss the feather Baba gave me out the window with my free hand, counting three breaths before it explodes in a flare of orange flame, and a massive feather the size of a baby gwylfin takes its place.

The first guard reaches Martine as I push Nana safely onto the feather. The second guard shimmies just under the reach of the feather spider ensnaring Martine and dives for me. I jump off the window ledge, grabbing on to the feather's edge. Nana tries to help me up, but I jostle her back, scissoring a leg onto the hard scale of the gwylfin feather as a flaming arrow races by my shoulder.

"They're escaping," a soldier shouts from the turret to the east, golden hair flashing as she waves a torch.

"Dèmi, tell me you planned—"

"Hang on tight!" I scream, splaying my fingers against the feather's quill. Pain rips through me immediately, like talons puncturing skin, but the wind spirits obey, gathering the air to us like water building into a wave. We blast off, the wind buffeting our cheeks and slapping at our clothes, shooting toward the wall west of the castle, away from the clamor of soldiers rushing into the courtyard.

As we cross the west wall, speeding closer to the outer stables, the pain in my back builds to a scorching heat and I bite my lip until I draw blood. We spin out of control, whipping this way and that as I struggle to keep my swollen, wind-struck eyes open. As we near the hull of the great oak tree that shades the outer stables, I toss my body over Nana's before the feather dips, skimming the timber of the stable walls and sending up sparks before capsizing and dumping us into the dirt.

Dragging myself to my hands and knees, I shake my head, trying to clear the flashes of color bursting across my vision like fireworks. Nana rears up from a pile of hay, straw streaking through her hair, and I offer a silent prayer to Olorun for making Oluso bodies stronger than the average person's.

"What was *that*?" Nana thunders, the bitna veins on her face popping like leeches swelling with blood.

"I can't"—I stop, suck in air to my screaming lungs—"I can't control my magic. I killed one of the assassins."

Nana's glare creases into a worried frown. "You need to be with Jonas, then. You'll unravel faster away from him."

"Too late for that." I crawl to her side, pouring the last of my strength into pulling her up. "The Council claims Ekwensi destroyed an Eingardian city, so Markham banished the Oluso. Jonas is escorting them to Yusa right now."

"So, I take it they'll disapprove of us leaving as we did," Nana says dryly.

"In a fashion."

The pendant knocks against my chest, catching sunlight. Colors swirl on its surface and a ribbon of silver wafts out of it like an aroma, a trail leading somewhere.

I stuff it back under my blouse. Ekwensi was rumored to be in Gaeyak-Orin. So we ride southwest. Lurching upright, I half drag Nana to the leeward side of the stables, searching for the esin kéké that is supposed to be there, awaiting our arrival. But there's no sign of the horse-drawn wooden carriage or the grandchild of Edwina's Mikhail entrusted it to.

"Thunder fire him," I curse, wishing misfortune on the delinquent grandson.

"Dèmi!" Nana chides.

"What?"

Beyond the stables, yew trees cluster into a grove, waving branches like crooked fingers beckoning us in. On the right side of it is a ridge, burying the shadowed grove like a jewel in the earth, secreting it from passing onlookers. I tug Nana to the mouth of the grove.

"Edwina warned us he was a wastrel."

Nana opens her mouth to respond, but just then a cry rings from the grove, stopping us in our tracks. There in the shaded bower of a tree Elodie looms over another woman like a goddess demanding worship. The woman's face is flushed a seedy red against Elodie's supporting arm, but I recognize Cariadhe, the head maid assigned to me by the Council a few months ago. Elodie's other hand is lodged in Cariadhe's skirts, thrusting up and down with the practiced ease of a boatman steering a vessel. We watch as Cariadhe arches against the purple flowers twisting up the bower, crying out in shrill, breathy gasps like a nervous foal.

"You do like to misbehave, don't you Cari?" Elodie whispers before nipping Cariadhe's earlobe.

Cariadhe whinnies, eyes fluttering closed as she strains forward, rocking with every movement of Elodie's hand.

Heat creeps up my cheeks as I realize what is happening. I edge back, trying to turn Nana, when my foot crushes a twig. Elodie swivels as it snaps, a rosy blush staining her porcelain cheeks. Cariadhe gasps and ducks low, frantically arranging her skirts.

"Who's there?" Elodie takes a step before catching sight of me. "Ah."

I offer her a nod. "We're taking a stroll. Fresh air. We'll go the other way." Then I search the grove for another path, evading the pointed look she's giving me.

"There is only one path. Which you don't know because you're not from here." She shakes out a glove, slipping it onto her hand as she speaks, with all the calm of an accomplished hostess entertaining guests. "I can direct you to where you need to go if you'll tell me where that is."

I grit my teeth, reaching for any excuse that will save me the trouble of a fight. No doubt Elodie's already heard of Markham's decree and knows that Nana and I shouldn't be here. I weigh picking a full fight, tying them to the tree she and Cariadhe were just at. Or I could intimidate them, scare them just enough to buy ourselves time to escape.

"I didn't take her for your lover," Elodie starts, nodding at Nana. "But you never know where people's tastes lie. I find the uptight girls more interesting." Cariadhe sniffs and Elodie shoots her a winning smile. "No offense to you, Cari. *You* are especially delicious." Cariadhe's answering blush laces her neck like a collar.

The idea of a fight wins out. I unwind myself from Nana, placing her gingerly against the bark of a sloping yew. Then I draw my bone blade and take a step toward Elodie. My back is still screaming, each step sending fresh pinpricks up my spine, but I can't back down here. Elodie could rally the whole Council after us. I need to make certain that doesn't happen.

"Oh, no need for that," Elodie purrs. "I can help you."

"Help me with what?"

She rolls her eyes as though I'm a small child insisting on staying up to watch the festival lights. "I didn't take you for one who liked games, Dèmi."

"I'm not," I say, arching my back foot and drawing in the front so it rests parallel to the blade I'm holding across my body. "Make this easy for me. Both of you sit still while I fasten you to that tree. Or I can give you new beauty marks to show off to your friends. Which will it be?"

To my surprise she grins and pulls out a rapier from the scabbard buried under her waistcoat. "Do you know what I like more than uptight girls?" she asks, twirling the weapon about like a quill pen. When I don't respond, she shrugs and pulls it back, hinging it like a crossbow bolt ready to fire. "Feisty ones. They taste the sweetest."

She launches at me. I sidestep the first swipe, kicking her back leg as I shift away. She lands on her knees. Out of the corner of my eye, I catch Cariadhe scrambling on her hands and knees for the mouth of the clearing. Then Elodie is up in a flash, lashing at me again. When I hop back this time, she feints forward, grabbing a fistful of my blouse. I slam my elbow into her arm and she lets go.

"That one hurt."

"I don't want to hurt you," I breathe.

"Too late." She lunges again, stabbing toward my ribs. I knock her away with my bone blade, pressing her off balance. The force of the blow coupled with the pain reverberating through my body is too much, and I stagger a bit. "You're leaving without a word," she shouts, breathing hard now. "And I thought we were becoming friends."

"I don't know what you're talking about."

Springing forward, I grab her elbow and aim a well-placed kick to her side. I need to end this fight before I lose too much stamina. No doubt the guards will be headed this way soon, and we have no more time to lose. She grunts and stumbles back. I step in as she redoubles, hooking the elaborate hilt of her blade with mine and knocking it out of her hands.

Cariadhe jumps up from the dirt, gathering her skirts as she breaks into a run.

"Shit."

Shoving Elodie to the ground, I break for Nana, jerking her to her feet. "We need to go."

"Wait!" Elodie shouts. "I can promise you both safe passage out of here. All you need to do is take me along."

I ignore her, throwing Nana's arm over my shoulder. This is merely a diversion tactic, a barefaced effort to keep me from escaping.

Elodie darts in my way, spreading her arms. "You should never turn your back on an opponent, you know."

"Move," I growl. "The next time I put my hands on you, you'll lose more than your weapon."

She shuffles aside, blowing at the curled blond tendril escaping her pristine, Council-approved chignon.

I take a few steps toward the thick foliage deeper in the clearing, clenching my jaw as I shoulder Nana's weight. The pain from earlier is receding now, trickling out like water through the cracks in a dam. Without the pain seizing my attention, I can think, weigh our options—but right now it feels as though we have none.

"You won't get very far!" Elodie yells after us. "They'll set the dogs after you, and they'll take you back."

A horn blows in the distance accompanied by a cacophony of barks, as though her words are a spell summoning the guards nearer. Cariadhe must have reached them by now, warned them of where we are. Damn.

I stumble on the roots of a particularly large oak tree and nearly go down. Nana hisses as she twists with me, body half-bent.

"Maybe she can offer us something," Nana mutters as I shift us upright. I shoot her a grimace. Elodie is the last person I want coming with us. Taking an Aje along on a dangerous journey is foolish enough, but an Eingardian Aje who is the daughter of one of the most powerful people in the Council? Criminal.

"I can," Elodie quips, trailing after us. "The way I see it, I have something you need, and you have something I need."

"And what is that?" I snap, not bothering to hide my annoyance. "What could you have that we could possibly need?"

The barking is louder now, merging with the thundering flurry of horse hooves.

Elodie fishes out a handkerchief from her waistcoat, waving it like a flag. Azure flame leaks from the black-and-white checkered cloth, a remnant of an Oluso's sign I know all too well. My heart thunders to a gallop.

"He said you'd understand if I showed this to you. Something about the first gift you gave him?"

Nana gasps, and I know the sight of that handkerchief is stirring up the same things for her—worry, doubt, and love bubbling like a pot threatening to overflow.

I reach for it, but Elodie yanks it away. "Not until you promise to take me with you."

"You're serious?" I ask, swiping at the sweat dripping down my face. She grins. "Absolutely."

"Why do you want to come?" I don't quite understand what she wants, and despite my urgency, I won't just take her out of expediency. "You don't know even where we're going," I press. Then I pause, wrinkling my nose at her outfit; an elaborate waistcoat the rosy color of the touch-and-die flowers that litter the valleys surrounding Ikolé; a silk blouse; rich emerald skirts that cinch at her waist, emphasizing its shape; and a red ribbon looped through the knot of her chignon, a mark of House Ayn. "You're not dressed for a journey either. People will take one look at you and know you're no village girl."

She flashes me a grin before hiking up her skirts, revealing leather breeches and high, calfskin boots. "I can travel light when I need to." She yanks the ribbon from her hair, letting it fall into a cloud around her face. "All you need to know is I want a life I can imagine for myself. Not what my mother wants for me." She fastens the ribbon to her wrist. "Imagine betrothing me to Jonas when I've stolen kisses from girls since I was old enough to want them."

I blush, remembering her with Cariadhe, grateful for the rich brown of my skin that keeps my cheeks from appearing as heated as my face feels.

"We don't have time to stop on this journey," Nana offers. "We're leaving Eingard."

"I know," she says, green eyes twinkling. "It's precisely why I need to go with you."

I narrow my eyes. "How do we know this isn't a trap? What's to stop me from beating you where you stand and taking that handkerchief?" This woman is nothing like the flighty social butterfly I've avoided for the last several months.

She smirks. "You can beat me, yes. But I can fight back, long enough for someone to come with more than just a knife." She thrusts the handkerchief at me. "Or you can trust that I have my reasons, and we can stop wasting time we don't have." The barking sounds overhead, swimming down the ridge sloping away from the edge of the grove like flames panting after wood, fiery tongues licking destruction in their wake.

"You can come," I blurt, ignoring the alarm bells ringing in my mind. "Now, give me that."

She tosses the handkerchief at me and I snatch it from the air, wrapping its soft chill against my heated fingers. I place it against the Oluso mark on my wrist, and suddenly there's a spark, a flicker of blue light. Nana weaves back on shaky legs, gripping the bark of a tree.

The air creases as a shadow the same shade of blue stitches into it. As the color brightens, a man steps through the haze, materializing tawny skin crowned with curly brown hair and dancing hazel eyes that hold a mischievous smile. As he lengthens, towering over me by a head, the winged clasp on his ear, twin to the one in my satchel, catches an errant ray of sunlight.

"Hello, lovely. Miss me?"

I want to run into his arms and squeeze tight, touch his skin and make certain he is real. I want to laugh and release the coil of fear and worry that has tangled up inside me since the moment he left to join Ekwensi. Instead, I ram a fist at Colin's face, startling when he catches my clenched fist, pulling me to him as the moon draws a tide. He lowers his face to mine, his sweet breath tickling my cheeks as he whispers, "I deserved that and more, but let's get out of here first?"

He lets go of me, and I shiver at the ghost of his touch that lingers. His voice is even deeper than I remember, his shoulders broader and tight. But there's an alertness in his body, a tension that belies the easy grace in his steps, like an arrow notched in the snare of a bowstring.

He throws an arm under Nana's shoulder. She smiles at him like a flower blooming under the cover of moonlight, coming alive after the scorch of the midday sun. As I move to join them, my traitorous body sings with joy, each step back to him lighter than the last.

"I'm coming with you, remember?" Elodie huffs, slipping by me. She twines a hand round Colin's waist with a familiarity that unsettles me. "You can't leave me here."

Two dogs appear at the mouth of the clearing, nosing at the ground. Behind them, I catch slivers of iron and the purple fabric of the guards' capes through the dense fronds of yew leaves. I grab Colin's collar, closing Nana off from sight.

"Let's go."

"As you wish."

We fold into the air, clutching each other as the fabric of the world shifts. Somewhere, a dog howls, but the sound stretches farther and farther away, ringing like a distant bell. Then we're flying, hurtling through a burst of color and light, cool air pressing light kisses over my skin. We settle with a thud, exploding onto a patch of scrubby grass, eyes facing the cloud-bitten blue swell of sky.

"Landings have been tricky," Colin explains as he sits up, working to untangle Elodie's hand from the inner sleeve of his robe.

I say nothing, wrenching myself to my feet and dusting off my clothes. Nana waves me away when I hold out a hand, preferring to stretch out on the grass, so I move away, squinting against the sky.

We're nestled behind a low stone wall overlooking a valley. A stream cuts through the rolling green, water sluicing in between piled stones, trickling into a small pond. Children wade in that pond, skirts and trousers tucked high, skipping stones across the water. Beyond them, stone and wood buildings spring out of the valley side like olu that litter the forests, slim white bodies sprouting from rot. Their sloping red roofs with lined patterns even resemble the circular olu caps, cresting toward the sun while stretching their edges wide. In the center of the valley are a cluster of buildings, stacked together like parcels. And all around us, another wall stretches like a mountain, its shadowed outline dwarfing the valley below, curling around the city like a sea serpent guarding its precious eggs.

"Where are we?"

"Nyzchow," Elodie announces, beating at her skirts. "Though why you'd want to come here is beyond me. Every soldier the Council can spare is on the way here. My mother announced that last night."

I shoot Colin a panicked glance. "Get us out of here. Somewhere else."

He raises his hands as though in surrender. "Can't. That jump took all the stamina I had."

Panic stretches into fear, and my words come out in a rush, like steam escaping a boiling pot. "Why would you bring us here?" I snap. A thought materializes then. Nyzchow is right next to Wellstown. Colin was also in Lleyria, right after the kokulu attack. "Wait," I start, "did you and Ekwensi actually—"

"I had nothing to do with Wellstown," Colin answers calmly. His voice rumbles with certainty, the low timbre of it making me squirm. "And I didn't bring us here." He pulls back his sleeve, and I gaze past the familiar tattoos knotting his muscles to where his finger taps at his wrist. Blue lines ring them like leeches feasting on blood, undulating and curving. In the center of those lines is a red flower, petals folded as though hiding its beauty from my sight.

"What is this? What do you mean *you* didn't—"

"I went through a ritual to stabilize my magic. Ekwensi controls it now."

BRIGHTER

"WHAT DID YOU DO?"

The question sounds accusatory even to my ears. I mean to ask what it means for Ekwensi to control Colin's magic, why he does, what is going on—but somehow, I can't get the words out. If Ekwensi controls Colin's magic, then Ekwensi brought us here. I should be overjoyed, having reached my goal, but I feel cornered, caught in a tangle I can't see my way out of.

I look at Colin, take in the calm look on his face, the unflinching way he meets my gaze even though the rings on his wrist keep stretching, pulsing against that flowered center like a living organ. His hazel eyes are dull, beaten copper in place of the molten gold I know so well, and I see now that this Colin, with his tense movements and an easy, placid smile is a shadow of the man I know.

I narrow my eyes. "Where did we first meet?"

I know Colin better than the skin on the back of my hand, and I don't think I could be fooled by a Shadow-walking Ekwensi, but it never hurts to be sure.

His lips twist into a wry smile. "Am I so changed?"

"Where did we meet, Col?" I insist.

He steps forward, and I have to catch myself before I stumble back. He tucks an errant braid behind my ear before taking my hand and placing it on a scar running down the inside of his left arm. "You gave me this, remember? For stealing. Then you stitched me back up with a hot needle and only a cup of agbo for comfort."

I let out the breath trapped in my chest as I trace my fingers along that familiar knot of flesh, feeling the comfort of this well-trodden path, a map that holds so many memories. I remember being nine again on my first trip to the Benin Market with Baba, seeing a boy feed akara into his sleeves as he flitted along the market stalls. I did nothing, just watched until he tucked a familiar piece of cloth, the brocade we'd come to the market to buy for Nana, under the flap of his robes. Though I couldn't begrudge him a quick meal of fried buns bursting with fish, I drew the line at stealing Nana's name-day present.

Trailing my fingers down, I bring them to rest against that pulsing heartbeat on his wrist. He winces but stays still. "What do you mean Ekwensi controls your magic?"

"I mean that sometimes my magic responds to him rather than me. I intended to get somewhere nearer to Oyo, but we're here instead. You don't have to worry otherwise."

"And Wellstown?" I ask, searching his face. "You were there?"

He clenches his jaw, but his eyes are brighter now, sparking with fury. "As I said, I didn't hurt anyone in Wellstown. I couldn't have. You know me. As far as I know, neither did Ekwensi."

Elodie pops up at my side and I draw back, only aware now of how close Colin and I were to each other. "Sorry to interrupt, but we need to get moving before we get caught."

She points a finger at the mountainous wall, where spires rise along its turrets, lances in the hands of sentries swarming together like bees gathering to a beehive.

Colin utters a curse as he throws off his cloak, draping it over my shoulders. Then he scoops Nana up and tucks her into his chest. "There's a place we meet. Follow my sign. Baby gwylfin rules."

A corner of my mouth twitches. There's no doubt this is Colin. The Colin I know is deathly afraid of gwylfins but lets me tease him mercilessly about it. The Colin I know suffered through a gwylfin ride last year when we worked together to kidnap Jonas. I smile at him. "Baby gwylfin rules."

Elodie cocks her head. "What in seven bogs are gwylfin—"

"Split up!" Colin barks, charging downhill.

I take off, jetting to the left. Elodie calls after me and gives chase, and I realize too late she can't track Colin, but I don't slow until I reach the stream. The children nearby steal glances at me, but I wave at Elodie like we're playing a game and shout in the best Ceorn accent I can muster, "I win! You're too slow!"

Years of hiding in plain sight have taught me that anyone can be an informant, even the innocent child sitting on the street. The key is to convince people you're part of the landscape, a tree swaying in the breeze rather than the rare bird chirping in the branches.

The children mutter amongst themselves, words tumbling over one another like birds fighting over a worm.

"She's brown as an acorn," one says.

"Judith's mum is like that. And she always gives me and Tobin sweets. She's nice," comes another.

"Think she's Judith's sister?" a third wonders.

An older child, the red of her cheeks matching the deep auburn of her hair shushes them. "It's not polite to stare."

Elodie comes huffing to a stop. "You run so fast," she gasps, fanning herself with her hands.

"She's probably a comara," another child mutters. "You know, they swallow you up if you hang about too late at night." He wriggles his fingers in my direction.

"In the daytime?" the first child exclaims. "No way."

Elodie raises an eyebrow. "If she's a comara, I'm a síntèan." She flashes him a grim smile. "I'm lily pale, you see. You should be more afraid I'll draw the marrow from your bones to color my skin."

The children gasp, and I nudge Elodie. "Hey, quit scaring them."

She shrugs nonchalantly. "Maybe they'll think twice before saying awful things."

There's a tug on my cloak, a little girl the spitting image of the auburn-haired one looks up at me, one seashell-pink hand outstretched. "I want a sweet. Can I have one?"

An idea occurs to me then. Nestling a hand into my satchel, I fish out some sugar cane strips and fold them into the little girl's hands.

"Ta!" she gurgles before running back to her friends.

"Hey, you have to thank her properly," the older girl cries, but the younger ones flock to the girl, begging her to open her hands. "I'm sorry," she says, nodding at me and Elodie. "She's young."

"It's fine," I answer. "Just remember, you didn't see us."

Elodie winks. "We wouldn't want our mothers finding out we were skipping lessons."

The girl gapes. "You go to school when you're that old?"

Elodie freezes, and I grab her arm before she can respond, shuffling her downhill.

"Did she just call me—"

"Let it go," I quip, laughing a little now.

"Just like you let their comments go?"

I shrug. "Used to it. This is inner Eingard. Not bigger cities like Wyldewood or Porto Pischu. The children here don't know any better. With the right teaching, they can still learn."

She sniffs indignantly. "You know they still tell children bread falls from trees?"

I stifle a smile.

We reach the first ring of houses and I hustle through the streets, tracking the trail of azure magic that threads through the air, remnants of Colin's Oluso sign that act as a compass. I keep my head low, dodging citizens as they race through the streets, each nosing toward their destination as though they can escape the grasp of time. A few people notice Elodie as we pass by, lifting their faces like dogs drawn to the scent of food, but I pull her along, increasing the speed of my steps until we're in an alley the space of two bodies. Hanging above us is a weather-beaten piece of driftwood with the word "Taryn's" carved into it. A brightly painted door sits under that sign, the red springing from the cracked white walls like an open wound. The door swings open as we approach and Colin beckons us in.

"The city is under curfew," he pronounces as we step inside. "We can't leave until they change guards in a few hours."

"We don't have a few hours," I mutter, falling into step with him.

"We'll have to take the time unless you want to get caught. Nellie will warn us when it's time."

He nods at the fair-skinned woman perched at the edge of a bar, pouring a liquid into a thick mug. She nods back, but I don't perceive any trace of magic from her, just a vibrant butterfly tattoo gracing her neck.

I place a hand on Colin's arm. "She's Aje," I say in a hush.

He smirks. "I know. Ekwensi recruited her himself."

My heart thrums in anticipation. "Where is Ekwensi?"

"You'll see soon."

The bottles stuffed in the shelves shudder like chattering teeth, the scent of mulled berries mixed with cinnamon and wheat kissing my nostrils as Colin leads us through the dark room. We swerve around low tables and people lying around in a drunken stupor, faces slack like cloth wrung dry of moisture.

Then he ducks against the low ceiling, taking a step into a sunken room not unlike the first, only this one is a corridor with several identical doors. He leads us to the bigger door at the end, and once we step through, he places a pail at the door and turns the key, locking us in.

There is a bed pushed up against a boarded window and a simple, low table stinking of mildew next to it.

"You"—he nods at Elodie—"get out." He wrenches open a door to a connecting room without another exit leading out.

Elodie crosses her arms. "What happened to common hospitality, Nicolás, my dear?"

Nicolás? They're on close enough terms that she uses his given name?

Suddenly, I'm unsettled, discomfort prickling at my skin like hot needles stabbing into flesh.

"I won't ask twice. You've had your fun giving Dèmi the wrong impression," Colin says, whipping Elodie around. She twists into him like they're dancing.

"And what might that impression be?" I ask, crossing my arms.

"Nothing of consequence," he answers, dropping her arm.

She pouts. "You're no fun." Then she sashays into the next room, stopping to blow me a kiss before disappearing into the dark.

Colin moves the table to her door, the scrape of its legs against the floor like knives clashing. I grit my teeth against the onslaught of sound.

"Nana?" I ask when he's finished.

"Lying down. She's tired."

He nods toward an identical door on the other side of the room.

"She's poisoned. We don't have much time to waste."

"I know."

"Where is Ekwensi?" I ask again. "I was hoping he could help."

He clasps his hands in front, considering me. "Why do you want to know?"

"I'm here to pledge myself to him," I blurt.

He raises his eyebrows, blinks. "Come again?"

"I'm here to join Ekwensi. I need his help. Where is he?"

Colin groans. "Elodie, *of course*." He scrubs a hand across his cheek. "Ekwensi isn't here. He's half a day's ride away in Gaeyak-Orin."

"Then why are we here?" I cry.

"My magic malfunctioned," he says, attempting a smile. "I didn't have enough for a jump that far." He scrunches his eyes shut, opens them. "And Elodie mentioned you were looking for Ekwensi. That you offered his head to the Council."

"Wait, Elodie told you what—" I stop, as I realize what he's telling me. Elodie has been reporting on my actions to Colin. Her desperation in the grove makes sense now—she's a spy. And if Colin believed I was out to kill Ekwensi, he's here to waylay me.

"You don't trust me," I say, backpedaling.

"Dèmi, wait," he starts, holding out his hands as though to calm a frightened animal. "Don't jump to conclusions. I just wanted a chance to talk to you."

"You wanted to test me!" I shout, scrambling back into the table. Throbbing pain spreads through my foot, sudden and overwhelming as a flood. I hop on the other foot, cradling my injured toes.

Colin reaches for me, but I swat him away. The pain somehow is sobering. "Explain from over there."

In a way, I realize I'm not being fair, that I'm exhausted, body scream- ing against the day's abuses. It hasn't been long since I leapt from Nana's window, but even with the pain from using my magic, I put one foot in front of the other while thinking only of one thing—getting to Ekwensi.

But now we're here, and Colin is asking me to wait. With him. And as much as I've wished for this moment with Colin, turned at every laugh that resembled his, scoured the streets looking for a hint of honey-brown hair the shade of his, I can't take the time after all to do this with him—to unravel the buried hurt that lingers between us like an abyss. I mustn't. Not with Nana running out of time. Not with Ekwensi half a day away. Not when talking to Colin feels like digging a knife into my chest and carving it out. Yet I have to. I have to fight through this breach between us. I need him to trust me enough to lead me to Ekwensi. But I also need my friend back.

"Why?" I say finally. "Why did you leave me behind? Why haven't I heard from you until now?"

"Dèmi, I know you're angry," he starts with a sigh.

"You don't know *anything*," I snarl. "You can't. You haven't been there this past year."

He smirks. "And whose fault was that? I gave you a choice."

"Not a fair one. You stand there with that stupid smile, as if this is funny. But I was honest. I needed *time*."

He makes a noise halfway between a groan and a sigh. "Like it or not, you *did* make a choice. I did too. We have to live with that."

"That's what you call Porto Pischu? Living with it? I saw the carnage, Col. I was there."

His shoulders slump as he deflates. "That was different."

"Do you know what happened to the Oluso after that?" I press. "The Council wanted curfews, and passes for Oluso to go into different cities."

His eyes widen in surprise. "I didn't know—"

"Of course you didn't!" I charge. "What was it you said before you left?" I pause, pretend to think. "Right, you wanted freedom. But maybe it was just an excuse to vent your anger. Maybe you needed a reason to abandon our oaths. Abandon me." I spit the words, hurling them like knives intended to wound, and I know once those last words leave my lips that I have hit my mark.

Any embarrassment vanishes, and Colin flares like a lesser deity whose rest has been disturbed, vengeful and imposing. "I didn't abandon anyone, and everything that happened in Porto Pischu was just." He takes a step toward me, looming like a tree unsettled by the wake of a dust storm. "You didn't choose me. You thought it'd be better to play Eingardian Queen—ah, but wait—you're not even that, are you? From what I've heard, the Council can't even be bothered to look you in the eye. So, tell me, was it worth it? Sacrificing your freedom for love? Especially when that love isn't even real?"

I snap my head as though I've been slapped, and now I want to twist the knife deeper, cut at him with my tongue until my fury cools to a slow burn. "You don't know the first thing about love. Or freedom. You chose Ekwensi. And he did *that* to you." I stab my finger toward his wrist. "And now we're stuck here for Olorun-knows-how-long while Nana is dying."

"He did it to save me!" he shouts, voice thick with anger. "I was dying and he saved me." He stops and takes a breath, chest heaving.

Worry smothers my fury like snow blanketing scorched earth. "What?"

He scrubs his hand against his face. "When I left you, I wasn't stable. You know that. All those flare-ups, remember?"

I think of the times Colin would tense before trying to teleport, fearing he would lose a piece of himself, and of all those moments magic poured from his skin like a furnace, threatening to devour everything in sight.

"I remember," I say, softening. "Are you all right now?"

"What do you think?"

We hold each other's gaze.

Everything about him is the same, but different. His brown hair, once curled and braided into thick tendrils that framed his face, now hangs loose past his shoulders and almost to his waist. Black spirals peek out of his collar, his tattoos still in place, but there are new markings that stretch down his chest, visible through the open button at the top of his shirt. He wears his same nonchalant smile, but it's belied by the hungry look in his eyes, as though he's drowning and I am the air his lungs so desperately crave. I feel like I am peering at the surface of a stream, catching a shadowed reflection that refuses to hold still, the image shifting with every movement of the light.

I go to him and he catches me up, twining his arms around my waist. I let his full weight sink into me, breathing the salty scent of his skin, pressing my hands against the knot of scars and muscle that is his back.

Thoughts explode through my mind like pebbles flung against glass, each one vying to leave a bigger mark, but one wins out over them all.

Colin is here in my arms and he's safe. He's alive.

"I thought I'd never see you again," I whisper, surprised at the wetness on my cheeks, the choking lilt of my voice.

He presses a kiss to my hair. "I left without thinking of how we'd get in contact." He pulls back, stroking the tears from my cheeks. "I'm so used to just popping in front of you, you know? And it's not exactly easy sneaking into that castle."

I laugh, thinking of just a year ago, when we walked around like two halves of a whole, a shell carrying a precious turtle, a song echoing from the lips of a flute.

"You should have come by anyway," I say, flicking the moon symbol hanging from the end of his earring.

"I tried."

He takes my arm and leads me to the bed. We sit, backs pressed to the wall, fingers laced. Eingardians have different rules around proximity and reserve touching like this for lovers, but in Oyo at least, touch is merely another language, bodies coming together like threads painting a picture, reminding us of our shared humanity.

"I came for the Weavers Festival," he says. "You were on the balcony, tending to your flowers. I thought of opening the door, but then . . ."

His words die away, but I remember the sudden taste of the sea on my skin while I hid in the alcove Jonas built me a month before. I'd been frustrated with my Council lessons, wanting instead to walk amongst the throngs of people below and dance, silks whirling, the way I would in Oyo. But just as I stood in search of that taste, Jonas clambered over the balcony wall, aided by a shaky use of my wind magic, and offered me a garland he'd woven from the cloth he'd snuck out to buy. I pulled him down to me then and kissed him until the hollow in my chest flooded with his warmth.

I swallow, taking a moment before saying, "I would've welcomed you. There were other chances."

He lets his head fall against mine. "Not likely. My father's been looking for me. Elodie's helped a lot with that actually."

I stiffen. It's strange to hear that Colin has gotten close to someone else, especially someone I distrust. "I didn't realize you two were close."

He shrugs. "Ekwensi trusts her, so I do too. Desperate situations make interesting bed partners."

The hairs on my arms rise. Ekwensi has been keeping track of me through Elodie, making good on the promise he made that we would meet again. I feel like a fly caught in a spider's web, squirming against sticky threads that pull me tight, sealing me to their desired fate.

But Colin doesn't seem to notice, continuing on. "Also I couldn't do anything once the chaining took effect—I can only use limited amounts of magic. And sometimes it does something strange, like what happened today."

"Chaining?"

"It's an ancient ritual. It ties two people together and grants you power, like mates do. Ekwensi knows things about the Spirit Realm you couldn't even dream of." He lowers his voice even further than the throaty whisper he's been speaking in. "You remember that woman from Lokoja? Sanaa?"

I will never forget the anguish that played over Sanaa's face when her lover, Etera, took a blow meant for me and died. I see her even now, pain stretching her honeyed face into a silent scream, arms reaching past her swelling belly for a ghost that will never kiss her fingers.

"She went with Nana and Will after everything that happened," I say quietly.

"Ekwensi found her again. She joined us. Apparently she has a rare Oluso bloodline, magic that allows her to connect with the spirits more deeply. He's been using that. I'm not exactly sure what for."

I raise an eyebrow. "He's recruiting far and wide then. Sanaa was in Benin last I heard."

He shrugs, brushing my shoulder with his. "Ekwensi has done a lot of things, but he's helped people too. So many Oluso would still be in chains if not for him. People come to him, not the other way around."

"So what happened in Wellstown? And Balman Keep a few months ago?" I pause, softening my tone. "What happened in Porto Pischu?"

He shifts to face me, letting go of my hand, and I curl my fingers, trying to fend off the sudden chill in them. "Ekwensi has done a lot of things," he says, his voice heavy, like there's a storm inside of him waiting to break. "He's killed. And asked us to kill for him. I—"

He stops, looking down at his wrists, and it dawns on me that there are a few reasons why Colin would give someone else control of his magic.

"Did he force you to—"

"No," he interrupts. "There was a man in Porto Pischu. A merchant. When we liberated the okris he had, he ran off with one. A girl, maybe nine. He was trying to sell her as an asewó."

I clench my teeth as bile fills my throat, trying to fight the bloodlust that rises in me like a wave, every word from him stirring it further. I can just imagine how frightened that little girl was, hearing her master offer her as a pleasure slave. This is why I came in search of Ekwensi. The governor of Porto Pischu knew of the laws protecting Oluso, and she still allowed the okri trade to happen. The laws are not enough—not when those in power are corrupt from the root.

"I went after him. He tried to hold the girl hostage. Was going to cut her throat." He stretches a finger and ice coats it like a second skin, lengthening into a vicious claw. "I killed him. Pierced his skull with one of these."

I let out a breath and the taste of blood fills my mouth, ripe and bittersweet. When I speak again, my words fall like a hammer, resolute and final. "You did well." I press my tongue into the wound I bit in my cheek and let the moment sit.

He sinks his head against mine, his breath tickling my face as he confesses. "You didn't see it, Dèmi. I tore his innards out. I couldn't stop myself. I wanted every trace of his evil gone." He smiles, his eyes empty of mirth, fathomless pools that draw me in. "The girl ran away after that. She was afraid. Of me.

"But I couldn't stop myself after that," he says, shuddering. "My magic exploded."

"The ice storm," I whisper.

"It was a massacre." He closes his eyes as another tremor over-takes him.

Pressing my hand against his cheek, I trace a fresh scar on his chin that mars his otherwise smooth skin. "You tried your best to help. Yes, maybe you went too far, but Col, I get it. Every day living with this, holding back when they try to erase us, feels like dying."

He nestles his head against my hand. "So you won't condemn me?" He quirks his lips into a wry smile. "The Dèmi I know would tell me I had a choice."

I drop my hand and untie the ribbon of my cloak, shrugging it off. Then, pulling my braids away from my neck, I expose the skin at the top of my back and tug the leather jerkin I'm wearing away from my blouse. I know Baba told me not to show anyone my mark, but this is Colin after all. I can trust him to keep my secrets.

"You can't tell anyone about this," I say in a low hush.

He rears back, tawny cheeks darkening to a furious red. "Dèmi, I'm not the kind of man to boast about bed matters, but I don't think now is the time—"

"Focus, please. This is clearly not the time," I say, giving him a level look. "I murdered an assassin last night." I bend forward, letting his eyes catch the spread of silver-veined branches reaching for my neck. He reaches out to touch me and I shudder as his fingers kiss my skin.

"So this . . ."

"This is the mark of breaking the oath. I'm dying."

He wrenches my blouse back up, as though to erase what he's just seen. "You won't die," he says resolutely. "Ekwensi can help you. No—he *will* help you."

I nod. "I'm counting on it. I can't go back, not after Wellstown. The Council will see my escape as an act of war."

"Who cares about the damnèd Council?"

"They still control the kingdom. They write the laws."

"But they don't have to." He brightens like an eloko who has closed a deal, hazel eyes sparking with unholy light. "We can change everything with Ekwensi; you'll see."

"I hope so. But we need to move quickly, and we need to do it as cleanly as possible. We target the Council, seize control that way."

"And Jonas?" he asks quietly, fixing me with an assessing gaze. "Is that precious mate of yours going to aid us or stand against us?"

I sigh, lowering my head. I don't want to think of Jonas now, to imagine us on opposing sides of a war. But that is a reality my mate might choose once he comes back to the castle and discovers I've sided with the enemy. "It's not so simple."

Colin's expression darkens, his brows pulling together like a thundercloud. "Right. Jonas. He wouldn't be so keen to fight for our freedom. No, he prefers offering you as a neat and tidy sacrifice and calling it a fair compromise. Blood and bones are much dirtier than pretty words and promises you can break at any moment."

"It's not like that," I mutter, wrapping my arms around myself. But Colin's words are a battering ram, piercing the wall I've been building around my mind since last night. All the feelings I've chosen to run from, tucking them away like neatly pressed letters addressed to no one, war in my chest like hungry ghosts come to collect their due.

"How do you feel being locked up in that castle, waiting for them to see you?" he jeers. "You chose him and shackles are what he gifted you. Maybe they're not made of iron, but they constrain you nevertheless. Meanwhile, the Oluso die in the streets while you look down from your tower."

I spring on him, shoving him against the wall so hard that there's a dull thud. Keeping my clenched fist inches from his eye, I shout, "Take that back! I have suffered at the hands of the Ajes, done everything to endure that place, all for the Oluso. You don't know the first thing about what I've done."

He lifts the corner of his mouth in a bitter smile. "All for the Oluso, right? Just for us? Nothing more."

I slam my fist into the wall. We're breathing hard, anger simmering like a calabash left on an open flame, the heat threatening to shatter its body.

Then Colin's eyes drop to my lips and I realize that I'm straddling him, with not even a fist's worth of space between our faces. He leans in, closing the gap between us, and I shut my eyes. For a brief moment, I wonder what it would be like to lose myself here instead, and forget the feelings Jonas stirred in me, the impossible dreams we wove together like flower crowns hanging at the mercy of a breeze. I sense Colin drawing nearer, and my heart stammers into a beat. But the rhythm is discordant, nothing like the comfort of Jonas's heart. I roll away and spring to my feet.

Silence hangs in the air like icy rain, bringing us to our senses. Colin sinks against the wall with a sigh. "That was uncalled-for, sorry."

I don't ask what he means—nor do I believe he's in any way sorry; I merely nod. The thought of Jonas sits between us like a specter, but I'm not ready to face any of it now. If the spirits smile on me, it will take a day for Jonas to discover I'm gone, and I hope he holds only precious memories of me then.

"Wellstown was a mistake," Colin starts, moving beyond his accusation—and our near-kiss. "We received word that Oluso on the way to our camp had gone missing there. We arrived and, soon after, the kokulu attacked. They burned the city to the ground in minutes."

"And Lleyria?" I ask. "What were you doing there?"

He considers a moment, his eyes stormy pools. Then he sighs. "I was looking for you. I heard you were out there. That things had been strange in the city."

I sense that there's more, but I'm not sure I will get it out of him now. "We need to deal with the K'inu."

His face goes blank, and he cocks his head at me. "The K'inu?" he asks.

"They're the spirits that control the kokulu. Devouring spirits."

He nods. "Ekwensi would be the person to ask, then. We've encountered the kokulu during our travels. He always knows how to deal with them."

I lick my lips, then add, "But first priority is Nana." I flash the pendant hanging from my neck at him. "The spirits asked me to find Ìyá-Ilé using this. But you know how they are, their tests would take too long. I'm hoping Ekwensi can figure out where in the bloody realms Mari is. She sent the assassins after us."

"Search is over, then." A smile cracks across Colin's face, the satisfied look of a cat pressing its paw against the neck of its prey.

"What?"

"I know exactly where she is."

BLUFFS

Elodie taps her fan against my cheek, and I hiss, swatting it away.

"You need to look down," she says, rapping my fingers with the lacquered fan shell. "Eye contact would get you flogged in noble houses. No one will buy that you're a servant."

"I'll do fine enough for the guards." I stalk past her, busy myself with arranging the hay in the back of the carriage, making it smooth enough for Nana to lie comfortably in. If I keep busy, I won't be tempted to smack Elodie for spying on me all this time.

"I like pretty things." Elodie says, unbidden. She hops onto the carriage edge, and sits sprawled across the narrow opening. "It's how I met Nicolás. We had a mutual admiration for a barmaid, so we tried to see who would win her first. I've been an asset to the cause ever since."

"I never asked you," I say, crossing my arms.

She shrugs, the sun catching the loose tendril of hair hanging from her braid, polishing it a burnished gold. "You didn't have to. Question's been on your face this whole time, distracting me. I can read women quite well, you know."

Considering that Colin and I have been hard at work for the past hour, stripping the carriage enough for it to pass as a noble's trading cart while Elodie just tumbled in from a midday nap, I doubt her words.

But I take the bait, leaning forward until I loom over her. "Then tell me, what am I thinking now?"

She holds my gaze, lips curving into a brazen smile. "Some version of how much you'd like to beat my arse, but I'd hazard that our plan won't work without my pretty face. Like it or not, you need me."

I'm still not sure about that—she helped us get out of the castle, yes. But now? Going forward? There's no guarantee this plan of hers will work, and I might end up committing my second murder if I have to suffer her any longer.

Before I can respond, though, Colin comes down, pulling Nana out of the shadowed covering of the bar's back room. I go to help, ignoring the triumphant smirk on Elodie's face. Bored nobles will be the least of our problems if we don't leave this city soon.

We set Nana in the carriage and Colin leads in a foal born of Baba Sylvanus's feather, then shrouds himself and Nana with the hay. Elodie and I take our places at the front, and I wait while she straightens the feathered hat she borrowed from the bar hostess. The city bells ring once, a shrill, ominous note announcing the start of Bear Hour. I pull the reins and the horses burst into a gallop, knocking the small mirror out of Elodie's hands.

"Hey. Your mistress wasn't ready," she chastises in a high, amused voice.

"My mistress will be first to die if any of this goes wrong," I respond with the same sweet tone.

She sighs. We ride in silence save for the thundering of horse hooves accompanied by the gasps of onlookers who startle as though we are Death himself, charging toward them with open arms. This discordant music rolls to a stop at the obsidian gate stitched into the base of that mountainous wall. Rather than the host of soldiers gathered before, there are only four guarding the door to the city.

The first on the right, a young man with wheat-gold hair and a wide forehead, swaggers over.

"And where might you be going?" he asks, gaze trained entirely on Elodie.

"I am Lady Phenalia of Drowan House in Eingard. I've come to collect the foal I purchased. My mother's name day is tomorrow, and my servant disappeared when I sent him over to bring it back."

The guard draws his mouth into a sympathetic smile. "Servants can be so unreliable. But I can't let you through without a pass. Governor's orders." His eyes flicker at me, then back to Elodie. "We've had a few issues lately. Foreigners causing trouble."

I hold my breath, not daring to move.

"Really?" She leans forward conspiratorially, catching his arm. "My servant girl has been with me for years, but if not for that, I wouldn't trust just anyone. I would never want to do something that would put our people in harm's way."

She shifts a little closer, letting him glimpse the swell of her breasts against her slightly opened blouse. "I really am late returning to the capital. Is there any quick way we could get that pass?"

The paired guard he abandoned, a woman with dark-brown hair and ruddy skin, answers her. "You'd need to visit the local council, madam. Or if you can't wait until tomorrow, we'll need to search your carriage."

I grip the reins tighter, trying not to squirm. This plan was meant to get us out of Nyzchow with minimal resistance, but if they require a search, a fight is unavoidable. I let my eyes roam, checking the turrets above us and the surrounding barricades for any extra guards. No one. Good. We'll make this quick then. I've rested enough that I could take on one guard, maybe two. Colin can handle the rest.

"I'd prefer you take me at my word," Elodie says icily. She cracks her fan toward the back of the carriage. "You see the horse, no? What more do you need?"

The woman steps forward, resolute. "If you please, madam, it's only for your safety. You don't seem like an ordinary noblewoman, and your servant keeps looking around. How do we know you're not under duress?" She jabs a finger at me. "Is this woman by any chance threatening you?"

I bare my teeth in a snarl. I can almost hear Elodie's gloating, *See, I told you to look down*, ringing in my head, but I don't look away, staring straight at the female guard, daring her to try me. If we're going to have a fight, I might as well enjoy myself.

The other two guards shuttle forward, the iron from their protruding sword hilts glinting off the glossy darkness of the gate like mami wata tendrils emerging from brackish water. The obsidian gate in Nyzchow is no doubt from Berréa, forged from the tears of Mount Y'cayonogo. Though many Eingardians no longer believe in the old ways, they no doubt still hold the belief that obsidian wards off vengeful spirits. I am more than happy to show them what a vengeful spirit looks like today.

Elodie stretches to her full height, smoothing her long skirts, every inch a goddess passing judgment on her worshippers. "There's no need for this. But if you insist on stopping us, I insist on having you accompany me to the local council, and after they confirm my identity, to my mother's keep, where you will summarily be punished."

The male guard backs up, lowering himself into a bow. "That's not necessary, madam. Is it, Ygritte?" he mutters, tugging at the elbow of the female guard.

Ygritte huffs, red spreading over her skin like a rash, then she nods to another guard, a younger woman who watches us all like a mouse in the midst of hungry hawks.

The younger woman and her paired guard waste no time opening the gate.

"Thank you," Elodie says. "I'll grant you a boon and forget this ever happened."

I drive out, keeping my gaze forward as the gates shut behind us. Once we're past the first hill, I signal the horses to go faster.

"I told you so," Elodie singsongs.

I grit my teeth. She was right after all.

"How did you know they'd let us through?" I ask. "They could easily have fought."

She smiles, rosy lips quirking. "I didn't. But Mother raises songbirds. You've seen them at Council meetings. She carries them in her hands from the moment they are old enough to leave the nest."

"Songbirds?" What is she going on about?

"Songbirds love to fly. They're like hawks, born with a taste for the wide world. But Mother's songbirds never fly off, even when she opens her hands." Her smile deepens, the cut of her mouth like a scythe bent on reaping. "Make others believe that the world is in the palm of your hands, and you'll always have what you need. That's what she taught me."

Then, because she can't just leave it alone, she adds, "And if you would have just done as I told you, our exit would have ventured even smoother."

Cold breeze buffets my face as we crawl up another hill, and I shiver against the sudden chill. For the first time since we left Château Nordgren, I'm glad Elodie is on our side even as her very being needles at me. Something tells me she would make a more frightening enemy than Lady Ayn.

I sit back and we drive on in silence.

PART II

THE CITY OF SHARDS

TRESPASS

WE COME UPON GAEYAK-ORIN LIKE A KNIFE HUNGRY FOR A PLACE TO bury its head, desperate and insistent. The city sits in deep slumber, eerily quiet for a hub in the midst of all four regions. But when we pass through the lonely arch that welcomes all visitors, I linger at that golden-framed opening like a dying soul crossing from one world to the next, terrified of what is to come.

The City of Shards is splayed open like a palm frond, a thick stem of a river separating two banks. The left bank boasts high and colorful buildings pressed together like sweets in a tin, each competing to be the brightest and most beautiful. They hang at the edge of the riverbank like cups placed at the border of a table, threatening to spill. Footpaths carve narrow gaps between, each secured with thick rope ringed with paper talismans. The right bank, in contrast, is a well-tended lady reclining in the embrace of her lover: white walls ringed with flowers, roofs lacquered in black and gold spread against the onslaught of the midday sun. Balconies jut from every building like open arms, waiting for someone to step onto them. The vines tangled around their balustrades hang down like tendrils of hair concealing a secret.

"You're in luck," Colin says, leaping onto the coach seat between Elodie and me. I jump, startled.

"Gaeyak-Orin is unregulated, so it draws a lot of people," he continues, taking the reins. "Ekwensi comes here from time to time to recruit. But our target has been here a while."

"Who?" Elodie asks at the same time as I blurt, "You're certain?"

We've been on this journey together for half a day, and she's clearly been working with Colin, but still, I hesitate before responding, "We're looking for Mari."

Elodie quirks a well-manicured brow. "Ah."

"She has something I need. I—" I stop with a hiss as the pendant bites into the skin of my left breast, the sudden heat of it like a scorching kiss. I drag it out with a curse. The pink color has deepened to a rose, meaning the signal is stronger—we are nearing Ìyá-Ilé—but the magic threading through its crystal body points beyond the City of Shards, winding over the river toward the cliffs that gather at the vestiges of the city, and disappearing into the fog blanketing them. It's almost as though the spirits are warning me, offering me a choice: I can choose to follow the path, work to find Ìyá-Ilé, or I can descend into the City of Shards and hunt Mari.

Colin places a hand on my shoulder, startling me out of my reverie. His brows are drawn together in concern, and I realize now that we've stopped.

"Do you still want to?" he asks, his voice low and soft, as though we two are the only people here and all that matters is my answer.

"I need the talisman," I say simply, but the words burn on my tongue like hot coals, branding me a liar. I need a talisman to cure Nana and Will. But just as much, I want to see the look on Mari's face when I catch her out. I want to hear her plead for the mercy she never gave my mother or Nana. I want to cast off an ounce of this pain, these voices that have clawed at me since I left that dungeon in the castle, telling me that my foolish dreams of peace have failed the Oluso—that I am the one to blame. It is said that Olokun, the ancestral spirit that cracked herself open to birth the deep waters of Ifé, watches over this city, promising a drowning death to all who do evil. But even the threat of being swallowed by the river is not enough to dull the anger raging inside me.

"Then we will. We'll get her, no matter what it takes," Colin promises. His hazel eyes spark with understanding, those earthen-and-gold mirrors reflecting the agony and guilt engulfing me. We agreed in Nyzchow to discuss the things that have happened while we've been apart another time. But here, in this moment, I understand for the first time the weight Colin must have been carrying all these months, the darkness that has plagued him like a rot, sinking its diseased claws deeper into his heart with each thing he's had to do.

"Ekwensi will make it so," he affirms.

I run my teeth over my lip. Right. Ekwensi first. I need his help if I'm to get to Mari at all.

"No need to show off," Elodie says, her voice high and amused. "Dèmi could take my aunt on without your help, Master Brooding."

He groans in annoyance. "I told you to stop calling me that."

"You don't like it? What should I call you then? Nicky? Nico? Coco? What was the name you gave the barmaid—"

"Shut up."

They bicker with the ease of siblings, stopping only when we cross a lower platform that opens the dirt road to a forked path. The rotting sign advises in five different languages that the left is "Mi'hayla: The city where men dare not sleep" and the right "Su'maila: The city of masks and roses." Except the Yoruba word on the right-hand sign is "iboju," the word the okosun would use for masks that present wayward spirits with a grinning human face. My skin puckers into gooseflesh. Another warning—this city is dangerous.

"We need to take a detour, make sure no one is following us," Colin announces. He tugs the reins toward the right and the horses set off in a canter. A wooden bridge awaits us at the end of the path, and once we're on it, trying to ignore the way it sways in the high, tottering winds, I glimpse people walking the well-paved streets of the Su'mailan district.

We enter without hassle, gliding in as smoothly as a tongue running against teeth. The townspeople barely acknowledge us as we pass, only a few staring pointedly at our cart as we rattle along. Though we could not hear much when we entered the main arch, the city is swelling with people; there are all kinds of faces here, every shade from a starry, moonlit darkness to a cloudy pale; people shouting, talking, and singing in languages that blend together like a song or war, like cats in alley streets. Children dart by market stalls, slipping sweets and sugar-cane strips into their sleeves with practiced ease. One woman threatens another with her hairpin, stroking its curved end against the other's cheek. A man watches our cart, one leg pressed forward like a deer in full sight of a predator, ready to dart in front of it. But as we near him, he catches the look on Colin's face and pulls back like a chastened child. Behind him, a group of scarred old women squatting around a table complain and cackle as one throws a winning hand of cards.

But though the city seems alive, like a vein pulsing against skin, I can't shake the feeling that it is a pit hiding in plain sight, waiting for us to fall in. Something is missing. Quite a few Oluso signs wink at me, but the bearers continue about their business like they have nothing else to look forward to. An Oluso man lies with his head cradled in an Aje's lap, looking at the younger man as though he were the sky itself.

"There are no Eingardian soldiers here," Colin says, as though he can hear my thoughts. "They tried to enforce the border laws, stop people from mixing, so the Lovers did away with them a few months ago."

"The Lovers?"

Before he can answer, the wind shifts. I duck as an arrow flies overhead, embedding itself into the wood paneling behind me.

"Shit." Colin yanks on the reins, and we swerve onto another street. "I should have known they'd be watching the bridges."

"Who?" I demand.

"I don't want to find out, thanks," Elodie quips, diving for the box wall just under the bench.

A rider explodes from a nearby alleyway, torso turned toward us, legs braced against her horse's stirrups as she nocks an arrow into the longbow in her hands.

"Get to the river," Colin commands, tossing me the reins.

He draws the knotted whip from his belt, striking the arrow now racing toward us. Then he leaps onto the carriage roof, lashing at an attacker who vaults down from a nearby balcony, grabbing onto the side of the carriage.

"Which way?" I shout.

"West."

"This is why I find no enjoyment in men," Elodie mutters. "They never explain anything."

Another rider cuts ahead of us twirling a copper whip mace. Offering a prayer to the spirits to protect Nana from splitting her head against the carriage walls, I urge the horses onto a market street as the rider gives chase. Colin goes down with the sudden turn, grabbing on to the bar crossing the carriage roof as he tries to hang on.

"Just two more streets!" he calls out. "Help will meet us at the river."

"Clear the way!" I scream as we thunder down the street. But people stop what they're doing to watch, crowding like rats enticed by the promise of food. I veer into a narrower lane to avoid the gawking onlookers who stand seemingly unconcerned about the carriage hurtling toward them.

Merchants abandon their wares, diving out of the way as we speed past. Chickens follow suit, their hasty retreat sending a rain of feathers that stick to my hair and cloud my eyes. I swipe one off my face just in time to see a cart full of paw paw in the middle of the road. Leaning forward, I steer the horses to the left of it. The back carriage careens in the opposite direction, knocking several green fruits onto the bench.

Elodie snatches one, cradling it. "Before you say anything, I am starving."

"Help me find the river and you can have all the custard fruit you want," I grit out.

Another rider pulls up alongside us, jabbing their spear at me. Elodie jerks forward, thrusting the fruit out like a makeshift shield. The spear impales the paw paw, splitting it open, and a piece comes away in her hands.

"It's my lucky day," she gloats, lifting the pulpy yellow flesh to her lips.

"That luck will run out if we get caught," I bark.

A foot soldier latches onto the side of the driver's bench, swinging a club at Elodie's arm. She dodges, dropping the fruit, then elbows him in the eye. He crashes onto the street, and she claps her hands, dusting off the sticky custard resin.

"These idiots can't even let me enjoy a meal in peace."

"Left turn!" Colin yells, kicking another enemy climbing up the side.

We curve into an alleyway, and now I see the river burbling past the ledge capping the street. The other half of Gaeyak-Orin lies beyond it, colorful buildings swelling over us like balloons rising into the sky.

Dropping the reins to my waist, I click at the horses and we roar to a stop.

Colin tumbles down, tossing a mottled pebble into the water. He surveys the street, then jerks his head at a squat building caked with damp and quick-growing moss. "Help me get Nana inside. We don't have much time."

I don't argue. Wrenching the carriage doors open, I scoop Nana up from her hay-encrusted slumber. Her skin is clammy, her face tight with exhaustion, but her eyes are open. One of Baba's brown-and-white feathers sits where the foal once was, the smoldering orange flames from it the only whispers of magic left.

"I take it we're not to Iya yet," she says, flashing me a wan smile. "The spirits should offer us a less bumpy road next time."

"We're almost where we need to be," I answer, shoving her into Colin's arms. Hopefully Nana will forgive me this deception, understand that I had no choice. The path to Iya may be nearby, but there's no telling how far it stretches, how long we'd need to travel before we get there, and Nana is down to two days.

Foot soldiers round the corner, dressed in thick leather gauntlets and sleek black chest plates that hug them like a second skin. Every one of them sports reddened eyes. As they near us, the sickly sweet aroma of koko fills my nostrils.

"Colin," I warn as he darts out of the building. "What's the plan?"

Taking on a few Aje guards without magic is one thing. Fighting a host of frenzied koko users in a narrow alleyway when I can't use my magic is another.

Pulling a ribbon off his wrist, he ties back his hair. "We delay until help arrives."

Elodie hops off the carriage ledge. "I'm in. Need to work off my hunger."

"Colin," I repeat, drawing my blade as the thugs advance, "what is going on?"

He cracks his knuckles, hazel eyes singing with excitement. "Gaeyak-Orin is a haven for criminals. Ta'atia and Oyéré run this city."

"The Lovers?"

"Yes. Except they're no longer together."

"So, what? All visitors are greeted like this?"

"No. I . . . I might have made some enemies last time I was here."

"Of course."

He shrugs. "It was unavoidable. Ta'atia granted Ekwensi safe haven. That makes us the natural enemy of Oyéré's Dogs."

The only woman in the group of thugs saunters forward, a slim pipe hanging between her parted lips. "You're in the wrong territory."

"Last I heard, the entrance to the city is a communal space," Colin retorts.

"Was," the woman declares. "Mother—Ta'atia didn't pay her dues."

"Mother?" he echoes. He cocks his head, his expression bright with recognition. "I've seen you before. You're one of Ta'atia's little handmaidens."

"Was," she repeats again. She produces long needles from her vest, flipping them up like cards. "That's exactly why I left. I wanted to grow up."

I groan as I recognize the weapons Fox Bead and Silver wielded just the day before. "Let me guess: Mari is in league with Oyéré?"

Colin grins. "I knew you would catch on. Word is Oyéré invited Mari into her bed."

Elodie wrinkles her nose. "Wouldn't advise it. It's hard seeing two women at once. Trust me, I've tried."

The woman flings her needles at us.

"Those are poisoned!" I shout, dropping low.

Colin spins, dodging a few, then he cracks his whip, knocking more to the ground. Elodie recovers a fallen needle, hurling it at another attacker. It plunges into his throat and he drops immediately.

"I've had practice," she says when she catches me gawking.

The other thugs burst into action, whirling maces with barbed, hungry ends. Two charge Colin, but I jump into the fray, kicking an assailant in the face as he goes for Colin's back.

A window in the decaying building next to us slides open and an elderly man peeps through the curtains. "Fifteen lira on the boy!" he shouts.

That's enough money to feed a family for several years. And he wants to waste it all on a bet?

An answering window flies open in the high building behind. "No takes. Twelve on the girl dying. The pale one. The other one looks hungry."

"I heard that!" Elodie calls, dodging a swipe of her assailant's claws.

I smash my fist against another attacker's elbow, knocking him back as Colin slams his whip into the man's knees. More people gather in the street behind, watching the fight with interest.

A child runs between them bellowing, "Oyéré's Dogs take on new-comers! Five hundred kobo to join the pot! Payout at Snake Hour!"

"Are they . . . betting?" I shout as I dance past one man swinging his mace at my chest.

Colin traps the mace in his whip's teeth, yanking it from the man's hands. "Reminds you of home, doesn't it? Nothing like a Benin market street fight. I'm glad Eingard hasn't spoiled you."

"Shut up." The man goes for a punch, but I feint to the side and Colin steps in, cracking him with a blow of his own.

"Ten on the Dogs!" I hear.

Colin scoffs. "How are we the underdogs in this fight?"

I stumble as another assailant kicks my knee, but Colin throws a steadying arm around my waist. When the man lunges again, I rock back and Colin lifts me, allowing me to lodge two well-aimed kicks at the man's chest. The man catapults to the ground as Colin places me on my feet. I grin. I'd missed this: the chance brawls Colin and I found ourselves in from time to time in Oyo, the way we worked together like ice spreading over water. Sweat runs down my neck, and my body screams its exhaustion, but my blood pumps against my ears, howling for more.

"I've missed you," Colin admits, his lips widening into a grin that matches my own.

Suddenly water sweeps into the alley, sloshing at our feet. There's a churning sound like water heating to a fearsome boil. We turn to see the river swelling, clawing onto the street ledge like a desperate hand searching for purchase during an arduous climb.

The horses rear up in fright and bolt to the end of the alley, dragging the carriage along. I dart after them, desperate to survive this impending flood, but Colin snatches me by the hand.

"This is our help," he declares.

The waters rise, splitting across the sky above us like fireworks. The thugs scramble to get away, but curtains of water rain down, sealing off all points of escape. Elodie gains the upper hand against her female assailant, catching the woman's arm and twisting it behind her back. She shoves her against the wet stones as four women emerge from the borders of the water cage, clad in silk blouses that hang above their navels and splay open in slits below their necks and at their shoulders. Their matching baggy trousers flap in the wind, and from them they each pull a coil of something resembling a ball of yarn.

"A hundred on Ta'atia's Handmaidens," someone screams above the din of flowing water.

"What in Olorun's name—" I start.

Colin chuckles. "I've missed that too. You never say 'ten shits' or 'bastard born of an eloko's spit.' It's always something invoking the spirits."

A handmaiden surges forward, throwing her ball. Dark loops of thread spit out like ink from a mami wata, cutting through the wood of a lantern post before biting into the arm of one of the assailants still standing. He screams, an unholy, wretched sound, as his arm flesh sags away, revealing the gleam of bone beneath.

Cursing, another thug rushes us, iron mace swinging, but another handmaiden whips her thread at him. The tendrils fasten around his neck, jerking him back just steps away from me. I scramble back as his eyes bulge, the smell of blood and rotted flesh spilling into the air around my face. The crowd watches in delight—whooping as blood gushes from the fallen man's neck in a waterfall.

The female foot soldier begins to tremble, terror etched onto her sun-kissed face. "Mother," she pleads, "we can talk this out."

"Save the explanation," a third handmaiden responds.

Another attacker lunges toward Elodie, the blade in his hand a blur. A host of threads cleave through his wrist, but it slices on, heading for Elodie's back. Clenching my teeth, I stretch my hand forth, but Colin is faster. Ice laces over the threads and they still, hanging over Elodie like naked tree branches bereft of leaves to hide their shame. It's an advanced technique, achieved with more control and stamina than I've ever known Colin to have; it's why he always failed at crafting things with Will.

Obviously, things have changed.

"My magic is back," he says, answering my surprised look. "I told you, chaining works. It could for you too."

I don't respond as Elodie stands, placing her foot on her assailant's back, unfazed. "Thanks for that."

The thread-wielding women step forward.

"Still causing trouble I see," one taunts, brown eyes shining above the rosy square of cloth concealing her nose and mouth. Her dusky skin is only a shade or two lighter than mine, but she speaks in fluid Ceorn. "It's a good thing Mother could help, is it not?"

Colin lowers his head in a bow. "We thank her for her mercy. We'll pay homage at her quarters."

"You are to leave the city before the wolf howls at the moon," a hand-maiden quips. There is no hint of malice in her pale face, but her blue eyes blaze like burning coals, daring us to argue. Her matching cloth waves as she turns around, no doubt assured we'll heed the command to leave the city.

"I thought you were allies," I blurt.

"Of a fashion," Colin asserts, frowning. "Do we no longer enjoy safe passage in these lands?" he calls after the handmaiden. "What of my master?"

A third answers him, ripping a square of chrysanthemum-yellow fabric from her sleeve and throwing it over. "Ekwensi and our mistress have come to an understanding. If you wish to come along, you must abide by it."

She nods at the woman Elodie is pinning down. "We will take the traitor. In exchange, you will not break our laws or trespass while you remain. It is as my sister said: Wolf Hour, no longer."

"What if we need more time?" I ask. If Mari is involved with one of the leaders in this region, going after her might be complicated, even with Ekwensi's help.

"Pray you do not," she answers, her long black hair falling like a curtain as she walks away.

The crowd disperses like ants pouring out of rotten fruit, disappointed and listless. The bet-collecting boy throws a bag at the man in the decaying house and he snatches it before slamming his window closed. Bodies lie in the street like animal droppings rotting in the midday heat. Only the fourth handmaiden remains.

She regards us for a quiet moment, a scar running through her eye like a misplaced smile.

"Ekwensi has made his bargain," she says. "Do you require something else of my mistress?"

Her voice is rich and leathery, and as she speaks my heart settles into a calm, easy rhythm as though by magic. The violet Oluso sign on her exposed navel glitters like a jewel.

Colin's scowl shifts into a smile. "I wish to ask your mistress the time." I quirk an eyebrow at him, but he doesn't spare me a glance.

He continues, "I hear that Ta'atia can always predict when the tides will favor the city, so I wish to ask what time would be best to set sail."

"Are you certain?"

He bows with a flourish. "As certain as a weary traveler wishing to be on his way can be."

"The tides are quite lovely now," the woman says, crossing her arms. "What keeps you in my city?"

My city.

I take a second look at the woman. She seems relaxed, tangling a finger absentmindedly through a lock of hair. But as I peer closer, she shifts ever so slightly, mirroring my movements. This woman is no simple soldier.

"We need time to find someone," I blurt as my mind fills with a growing certainty. "Tall woman, dark-haired, a scar on her face like so." I draw my finger from my nose to the curve of my mouth. "Can you help us, Ta'atia?"

The woman stills, regarding me a moment. The cloth mask on her face shifts almost as though she is smiling, but she merely answers, "You're exactly as I've heard, aren't you, Dèmi? Always sniffing out trouble."

She darts past before I can answer, leaping at the wall and catapulting onto the waves that undulate and babble like a child begging attention from its mother. "Follow me, omodé. Perhaps we can come to an arrangement." Her accent is different now, distinctly not Oyo-born though she pronounced the Yoruba word for children flawlessly.

"How do you know me?" I ask.

Ta'atia whistles. "Come, we have little time to lose. I will answer your questions in due time."

"This invitation includes me, yes?" Elodie asks, getting to her feet. She flashes Ta'atia a winning smile, the same one she uses to keep the court ladies enthralled. Ta'atia merely stares, unblinking. Elodie's smile widens. "Would you consider taking on a new apprentice? I'd like to learn better fighting techniques. Mother's bodyguards are too soft with me."

"The invitation is for all of you." Ta'atia stops, sniffing the air. West of us, dust gathers like the stirrings of a Harmattan storm. She frowns. "More are coming. We don't have much time."

"No need to ask me twice," Colin says. He disappears into the moss-eaten building and reappears with Nana perched on his back. Elodie plucks the assailant's pipe from a nearby pool of blood.

"What?" she asks when she catches my pointed look. "I think she'll need it, don't you?"

I nod grudgingly. Advanced koko users can no longer live without the drug fueling their waking moments, even as it shrivels their livers and curdles the blood in their veins. The captured woman's ruddy face was already haggard at the end of the fight, no doubt as a result of a hasty withdrawal. Without the drug in hand, she is as good as dead.

"Thought so." Elodie nods. She pockets the pipe.

I turn to survey the carnage beyond, pushing back a roiling wave of nausea as the stench of blood and urine greets my nostrils.

"What about them?" I ask, pointing at the fallen fighters. "We can't leave their bodies in the streets."

"They will find their way soon enough. The people will bury them after the rites are said."

Blood has stopped erupting from the foot soldiers' corpses, urine and feces now staining the lower halves of their bodies. Though I have fought many times and grown up a constant companion to death, being this close to these decaying bodies is enough to make my heart swell with grief.

Closing my fingers around my pendant, I offer a silent prayer for the men gathered here. They were all Ajes bent on killing us, but it does not stop me from hungering for a world where blood no longer fertilizes the earth like daily rain.

Ki a ri emi yin ninu okunkun oru,	*May your souls be found in the dark of the night,*
K'ikun nyin ki o kun b'o ti de opin re,	*May your bellies be full as you meet your end,*
Ki enyin sa kuro ninu aijinile,	*May you run from the shallows,*
Ki e si rì li apa ibuduro.	*And sink in the arms of the waiting deep.*

Colin touches my shoulder as I finish the last words, his nearness an instant balm of comfort. I lean against him, shuddering against the chill settling over my skin.

Just then, there's a flicker of light, like sun reflecting through shards of glass. Shadowed forms take shape and hold that light, their gossamer wings shimmering as they wisp from the air itself, their faces all differing in hue save for the white-gold eyes that announce them as otherworldly creatures. The Aziza do not spare me a glance, though I recognize many from the time I spent in Benin Forest. Instead, they throng over the bodies of the fallen men, their expressions molded by that same weariness I saw reflected in Ayaba's face. As we watch, they lift their arms to the sky and begin a song, one that leaves my ears as quickly as it arrived but leaves my heart aching nonetheless.

"Hurry up!" Elodie yells. "What are you standing there for?"

I turn away, the sanctity of the moment lost. Ajes can't see the Aziza unless they come to the halls of the Spirit Realm. To Elodie, who has lived a life of courtly intrigue and bloody machinations, this battlefield is yet another happening, a familiar dance with steps that do not change.

I'm glad, though, when I move to the riverbank, that Colin is still watching, transfixed. I wonder how many of these singing-aways he's witnessed after months with Ekwensi, seeing countless bodies litter the ground like pebbles. No doubt, once we take the kingdom back from the Council, I will stand as he does, listening to the Aziza sing, in hopes of hanging on to the last threads of my humanity. But at least then the Aziza will be safe too.

I wait until the final note of the Aziza song finishes.

Then as they splay their fingers over the men's bodies, threading out glittering essences that resemble dandelion seeds, I step into the waiting waves.

BRIGADE

As soon as my boot touches the water, the world shifts, dissolving into a cool wetness that laps at my skin.

Suddenly we're standing in a layered courtyard framed by vaulted ceilings and curved archways that surge like arrowheads between slim pillars decorated with colorful patterns.

"A mirage," Colin explains, catching my confused expression.

Ta'atia sits at the edge of a fountain in the middle of the courtyard, stroking a hand through the water.

"Welcome, my friends."

She waves and chairs scrape across the patterned tile floor, depositing themselves in front of us.

"Have a seat. My children will serve refreshments."

She snaps her fingers. Women dressed in the same slim wrap trousers and blouses appear like shadows from the archways, carrying heaping trays of food. They place them on the table beyond the fountain, arranging them like offerings before the ancestors, smoke still curling from a few.

I want to tell her we don't have time for this, ask her where Ekwensi is, but I'm also loath to make an enemy of this woman. Colin places Nana gently in a chair and she sinks in, resting.

The handmaidens appear, carrying the captured foot soldier between them.

"Mother," the soldier pants, falling to her knees. "I—I never thought I'd see you again."

Ta'atia tuts, rising to her feet. "You look a bit too wasted, Annika. Oyéré never gave you limits, did she?"

Annika rakes her fingers over her cheeks, collapsing into a fit of sobs. "I hurt so much, Mother. The koko is sweet, but when it's done, it's like a knife in my belly. I smoke and smoke and still there isn't enough to fill me."

Ta'atia gathers the sobbing Annika to her chest, stroking her limp brown hair. "It is well, my child. All will be well." She nods at one of the women behind her, and the woman produces an embroidered satchel. Ta'atia presses the satchel to Annika's nose and the soldier tenses, her legs shaking in a spasm. Then all at once she stills.

Two women come forward and gather her up, carrying her into an adjoining room.

"What did you do to her?" I ask.

"It's abon powder," Nana answers. We all look at her. "Mint crushed with peppers and the remnants of an elu bug. It will ease her pain for a little while, give her sweet dreams."

I raise an eyebrow.

She shrugs. "My sister used to take it. When she had fitful dreams."

"You are well informed, daughter of Tenjun," Ta'atia says.

"You know my father?" Nana asks with a frown.

"Okun mọ gbogbo."

The sea knows all.

Ta'atia walks over to the table, pouring tea into some cups. "I grew up near the rivers here, excepting a short time away. I know many things and people."

Nana smiles, a small quirk in the corner of her mouth. "My father has always loved the sea. Even more than his own children."

"Ah, but Tenjun loves battle even more, does he not?"

Nana's smile deepens. "True."

"Come, you all look so stiff waiting over there," Ta'atia says, balancing four teacups in her arms. "Drink with an old woman. It won't be long before our guests learn of your presence."

"Guests?" Colin asks, narrowing his eyes. "Where is Ekwensi?"

Nana freezes. "What do you mean by that?" She turns her bewildered gaze on me. "Dèmi, what is going on?"

I swallow, unsure of what to say. Colin looks between the two of us. "You didn't tell her?"

Footsteps thunder overhead, and I'm saved from answering by the faces that gather on the second-level balconies surrounding us. One of them, a dark-haired, lightly tanned woman catches my attention. In her arms is a young girl with curled ringlets, golden skin like the rays of a setting sun, and wide, dark eyes—Ekwensi's daughter.

The girl whips back to her mother, little fingers moving fast in a series of hand signs. There's no question—Samira and Malala are here.

"You're here!" a young woman screams, waving her arms. Her tan skin shines brightly under the daylight streaming through square slits in the ceiling.

"Why are you here, Adaeze?" Colin asks, his expression darkening. "All of you. What is going on?"

"You thought we'd go to Ismar'yana," another woman answers. She peers over the railing, and though her face is now thin, I still recognize Ga Eun's slim nose, short hair, and the Oluso mark winking from behind her ear. Her eyes are unfocused, not looking at anything in particular, but she turns her head, squinting.

"Is that Dèmi?"

Last I'd seen these women, they went off with the Oluso from the arena to join Ekwensi. I stagger back, looking round at all the faces gathered on the balcony. There are over a hundred, maybe a hundred and fifty, and I recognize many from the arena. This is Ekwensi's army.

"Dèmi," Nana says in a hush. "I trust you'll give me an explanation later."

I offer her a quick nod, but she merely purses her lips and looks away. Fear clutches my heart, squeezing until I find it hard to breathe, but I try to will it away. Nana will understand when I save her, I assure myself. She'll understand everything then.

"It seems you've been kept in the dark," Ta'atia says, holding out a cup of tea. "Why don't we sit awhile and catch up? There is much I can share that might . . . shed some light on the situation?"

One of her handmaidens, a pale-skinned woman with long, dark hair hanging in a braid, clears her throat.

Ta'atia laughs, the fabric of her mask rippling. "You must forgive Li'uoa. She always warns me to keep my secrets."

"It is wise advice," Ga Eun says. Her words are matter-of-fact, but there is a certain air that makes them sound more menacing.

"You forget your place," Ta'atia says quietly. She places her cup down gingerly, but there is deliberation in the action—danger. "You are in *my* home. I am your ally, yes, but I choose who I share my time with. Is that clear?"

"Completely."

The ceiling peels back like an eyelid, opening to let in the sky. Light streams in, temporarily blinding us, then there's a flash of white as a kokulu descends, its mouth open in a screech.

Throwing my body to the side, I roll upright and whip out my bone blade, ready to fight. But no one else seems to be bothered by this monstrous invasion, and I watch as the kokulu weaves between the low pillars, scraping the floor with its long tail, then swerves to a halt at the fountain, depositing the man on its back onto the floor.

Ekwensi lands on his feet, steadying himself with the long cane in his hands. His face is worn, fresh lines in it like the grooves of an iroko tree. His hair is longer now, thick coils hanging over his ears and temples. When he catches sight of me, he smiles, his wide grin like the look of a hungry jackal.

"I promised you we'd meet again," he says simply.

"You nearly killed me last time," I sneer, displaying a bravado I don't feel. I may be here to ask for his help, but I can't show Ekwensi my weaknesses. This man is a predator, and I have no intention of being devoured.

He puts a hand up in acknowledgment. "Circumstances were rough. I meant you no harm. It takes a while to master magic you've long forgotten."

The kokulu rattles its tail, shaking as though in laughter, and I notice now that its eyes are huge dark orbs rather than blue. It is a mere transformation—a falsehood. I let out a breath, but I don't let go of my weapon.

Ekwensi acknowledges Colin and Elodie with a nod. "Welcome back, my friends."

"Why is everyone here?" Colin asks, jaw clenched tight.

"Are you so unhappy to see them?" Ekwensi answers. He takes a step forward, leaning on his cane, and the kokulu draws in its tail as he passes.

"But you—" Colin starts, then he swallows, lowering his voice. "You said nothing of this move to me, Baba. Is it not dangerous to have everyone here?"

Ekwensi grins wider, but there is no mirth there. "You say nothing of your jaunts to me and I find no issue with it. I suppose you succeeded in fetching Abidèmi from Nordgren this time. Well done."

This time? I glare at Colin, but he doesn't take his attention off Ekwensi.

"That was all me," Elodie declares, snagging one of the teacups out of Ta'atia's hands before flopping into another chair. "I helped her out of a situation. She owes me."

"I owe you nothing," I seethe. Despite her help in the city, I still haven't forgotten she's been spying on me. I wonder what else she's kept Ekwensi apprised of.

She shrugs and takes a sip of her tea. "Mm. Is this cardamom? Delicious."

Ekwensi doesn't seem to even hear us. "I wanted to consult you but there was no time, Nicolás," he says to Colin. He touches his cheek. "Do not doubt this; your thoughts matter. You are important to us." His voice is warm, swelling with patience and pride, the voice of a father speaking to his son.

Colin's shoulders unknot, his expression settling into as serene a look as I've seen him wear since we met again.

Looking like someone who isn't himself.

"What are you doing to him?" I cry.

Ekwensi raises an eyebrow. "Providing him with the answers he asked for?"

"I'm all right," Colin says, flashing me a half smile.

I study his face, looking for signs of magic, but his expression is merely bright, focused.

Ta'atia chuckles. "So, it isn't only me who finds it hard to trust you, Tobias."

"Our relationship doesn't require trust," Ekwensi answers, taking a seat in one of the cushioned chairs Ta'atia offered us. "Merely a contract."

"One that I *trust* you'll hold to?" the warlord asks.

"Certainly." Ekwensi leans back, crossing his legs, as comfortable as a king surveying his court. The false kokulu angles itself behind him, wrapping its tail around a pillar. "I made a tactical decision to withdraw us here. After Wellstown, I didn't trust that we'd be safe in separate locations." He drums his fingers against the arm of his chair, turning his attention to Elodie. "Somehow you failed to forewarn me they would take Wellstown. They burned down their own city, used sixteen of our people as kindling. They got their nobles out in time though. I met a soldier on the streets, looking to see if he'd missed one."

I whip around to face her. "You knew?"

She sighs. "Hazard of the job." She takes another sip of tea before adding, "My mother insisted I prepare for *someone's* betrothal. I didn't have time to send a missive."

Clenching my fists at my sides, I lower my blade. This confirms it—the Council summoned the kokulu to Wellstown. They planned that city's destruction. I can still see the darkness in Markham's face. What were his exact words?

One life is enough to pay for thousands.

Yes. The Council belonged to Alistair Sorenson, after all. Even his ghost. They would destroy a city, murder their own people, if it meant that they would have the means to harm the Oluso.

Another thought burns through my head like a hot stone.

"Did you know about the plans for the betrothal?" I demand. "The assassination?"

Elodie wafts her tea, nodding at Ta'atia. "This is definitely cardamom, yes?"

"Awin," Ta'atia answers. "It's native to my mother's region."

I look at her, startled. Awin grows in spriggy bushes near Ikolé, the village I grew up in for the first eight years of my life. It makes sense now that Ta'atia speaks Yoruba. But now is not the time to investigate shared experiences.

"Elodie," I call again.

Elodie inclines her head. "I have no idea what that is, but it sounds nice."

Ekwensi tuts. "It's tamarind in Ceorn. You Eingardian nobles never pay much attention to other regions' languages, do you?"

"Everyone shut up about the stinking tea! You knew about this, didn't you?" I ask, rounding on him. Hot panic razors through me. If Ekwensi knew and didn't warn me, does he want me dead too? Have I only run from one danger into the arms of the next?

He sighs, rubbing the handle of his cane, a silvered antelope head. "If I wanted you dead, Abidèmi, you wouldn't be here. I would have killed you long ago."

He speaks the words so simply, as though he is doing nothing other than discussing the weather. A chill runs up my spine, but I push away the fear gripping my heart, reminding myself that this is precisely why I came. Ekwensi is dangerous—strong enough to help me overthrow the Council and cunning enough to figure out how to achieve his goal no matter the cost.

So I lift my chin, leash my anger. I need to speak in a way he understands, show him I am worthy of his help. "Why didn't you warn me then?" I ask.

His gaze latches onto me, eyes shifting as though he knows what I'm doing. "I *did* warn you," he responds. "You forget, I was beholden to that Council for over ten years. I know how they operate. I know they were not to be trusted."

"Then work with *me*," I declare. "Ally with me to destroy the Council and all they stand for. The Council has gained new knowledge—you saw for yourself that they used the kokulu to attack Wellstown. They've allied themselves to devouring spirits. If we joined forces, we could—".

"We?" Ekwensi leans forward, fingers choking that antelope head. "When did this become a 'we'?"

Colin speaks up: "Dèmi has come to join us."

I feel Nana's eyes burning holes in my back, but I don't turn to look at her.

Ekwensi throws his head back and laughs, the sound ringing in my ears like a warning bell. The Oluso on the balconies stir like hawkers in the marketplace, each shouting for their voices to be heard.

"It's a trap!"

"She's one of them."

"No, she killed the former king. We were there."

"She only defeated Sorenson. It was Master Ekwensi who liberated us."

Ekwensi slams his cane twice. The room falls silent at once. He turns that intense gaze back toward me. "Tell me, Abidèmi, why are you truly here?"

I straighten, present my blade as though I'm giving a gift. "I'm here to make you an offer. I will join you, fight alongside you to overthrow the Council and make the Oluso safe."

"And in exchange?"

I don't dare steal a glance at Nana as I answer. "In exchange, I require your assistance on some urgent private matters."

The room erupts again in hushed whispers, but Ekwensi does not acknowledge them.

"I heard about the unfortunate happenings during your betrothal," he says, getting to his feet. "*All* the unfortunate happenings."

I stiffen, suddenly conscious of the welts on my back. I'm not sure if he's referring to my broken spirit bonds or the fact that Jonas and I failed to complete the bonding ceremony. Still, he could be lying, testing me.

"Where are you getting information?" I ask.

He wiggles his fingers, imitating a spider's creeping. "Word travels. I hear things on my walks. I've taken a few back to Château Nordgren."

Skin-walking. No doubt he's still using Malala's magic to keep track of the goings-on in Nordgren.

"Then you know I am sincere," I insist. "You know I left it all behind to join you. The Council tried to kill me—"

"*I know* I don't trust you," Ekwensi interrupts.

"Trust?" I scoff. "Why would we need trust?"

"Trust is necessary in war."

"You and I have never operated on trust, only bargains. We trusted we would honor those, and nothing more." *And just barely that*, I think. I jerk my head toward Ta'atia. "Do you two have trust? Trust is a luxury when a situation calls for action."

Ta'atia chuckles again. "She makes a fair point."

Ekwensi takes a step toward me. It takes all I have not to move back. "And what would you bargain with? What can you offer me?"

"Dèmi is Fèni-Ogun," Colin blurts. "She can help us be more effective in our attacks, reduce our casualties by removing their weapons and iron shields—"

Ekwensi holds up a hand, cutting him off.

"Abidèmi is not one of us," he pronounces. "I have no reason to work with her."

I shake my head in disbelief. I've traveled so far, gone through so much just for this. I can't back down now, not when the Council has a new weapon to terrorize the Oluso and Nana is a mere two days from death.

"The Oluso are in danger," I challenge. "What happened in Wellstown happened in Lleyria. It will happen again, and the losses could be worse. We don't have time to sit and consider. We need to help each other."

"I don't trust you. Need I remind you that we parted on less than amicable circumstances?"

"And whose fault was that?" I bark, losing a hold on my composure. He was the one who nearly killed me after I risked my life to defeat Alistair Sorenson. "You betrayed me."

He cocks his head. "And how did I betray you? By freeing you from those dungeons? Telling you about Osèzèlé? Tell me, Abidèmi, did I not give you everything you asked for and more?"

"You *lied* to me," I growl. His words curl around my ears like flowers, kissing my skin with their rightness. I almost believe that Ekwensi didn't betray me after all, that he's not using his magic to compel me right now.

"You were never going to work with the Eingardians," I accuse. "You wanted me to weaken Alistair Sorenson so you could kill him and be the hero. You wanted the Oluso to give up on them. You used me."

"Dèmi," Colin says, touching my arm gently. "The Eingardians were never going to work with us. All Ekwensi did was show us what we'd been too naïve to see."

"But they worked with me," I counter. "I didn't need trust to force them to act. We've passed laws, freed people."

"And how many of those people were suddenly banished from Nordgren last night?" Ekwensi snaps, slamming his cane against the floor. "What of the sixteen souls we lost just yesterday?"

Colin shifts, blocking me from view, back tense as though he is on guard. "Sir, to be fair, Dèmi had nothing to do with—"

"She had everything to do with it!" Ekwensi roars, stalking past him. He pins me with an imperious gaze. "Answer me this: why do some noble Ajes so removed from their magic histories suddenly know how to summon ancient creatures? How would they know to make deals with devouring spirits like the K'inu?"

The question has slumbered in the back of my mind, waiting like a poisoned adder to strike my heart.

I get a flash of Jonas's face just then, his reassuring smile as the Council dismissed me from their secret meeting. I shake my head furiously. Jonas knows even less about the ancient ways than I do.

Right?

"That's not possible," I say aloud. There has to be another explanation, something I don't yet know. In the last year, Jonas and I have shared a bond, and I have seen many of his deepest thoughts. Though I haven't always wanted to look, though he might choose the Council once he realizes I left to join Ekwensi, I can't believe the man who shared my bed just this morning, who was desperate enough to risk everything for my safety, could do something like this. I won't believe it.

Ekwensi straightens, his eyes never leaving my face. "What isn't possible? That you spent the last year trusting your enemies? Or that your precious mate might be involved?" He grins again. "Come now, Abidèmi, discernment was never your strong suit."

His words are like needles burrowing into my skin, reminding me that everything I've worked for has come to nothing. I curl my hands into fists, trying not to let the guilt and sorrow churning inside overwhelm me.

He circles me now. "Tell me, how was it? Working with that Council you couldn't trust? Fearing their covert attacks, all the ways they undermined you? I showed you my power, gave you an opportunity to join me, but you claimed to know better."

"I was wrong," I admit. "But what matters now is who wins this war. So, let me be your partner in this fight. You need me, and I need you."

Ekwensi lets out another bark of laughter and the sound ricochets off the walls, echoing through the room. "Oh my dear girl, you walked in here with no intention of being honest. I am aware your spirit bonds were broken. You can't use your magic as freely, am I correct?"

I grit my teeth, but he does not wait for my answer. "Your guardian here is in danger." He nods at Nana. "You also think to use me to be rid of the bitna curse. Did I miss anything?"

"I am still powerful," I insist, struggling to keep hold on the hope quickly deflating in my chest. "I can be of use."

"You are desperate," he pronounces. Then he sweeps away from me, heading to the table. "People make mistakes during times of desperation. I do not seek to be one of them."

Ripping my pendant out of my blouse, I bluff, "I don't *have* to join you. I have options. But I came here of my own will to choose you. Help me, and with the power I receive, we can transform this world into one of peace."

It's not entirely a lie. With the help of the spirits, I could get my spirit bonds repaired, stabilize my magic. But there's no telling how long it would take—and even if I'm back in time to overthrow the Council before they strike again, I will lose Nana in the process. Everything depends on Ekwensi believing me, and this is the only way he will bargain.

He pours himself a cup of tea from the porcelain kettle sitting on the table, then he brings the cup to his nose, breathing in. Every eye is on us, but he doesn't seem to care, taking his sweet time before entertaining a sip.

Drawing the cup away from his lips, he nods at Elodie. "There *is* cardamom in this. Good nose." She beams.

"Ekwensi!" I shout.

He turns with that jackal grin. "Let me guess, the spirits promised you their help. But it required going on an arduous journey. One you might not even survive."

I frown as his smile stretches wider. "You forget, Abidèmi. I once served the spirits with great attention. I know them well. They're always long-winded in their lessons. Insistent on things like growth and love." He wrinkles his nose. "As if they also give up the capacity for anger, destruction, and chaos alongside all those things. Hypocrites."

"The spirits never betrayed us," I retort, wanting to strike at him just once. "They gave us the capacity for creation. Destruction is just another face of it. We are the ones tasked with controlling ourselves."

He raises both eyebrows. "Good to see you still believe in the old mores. But your presence here tells me you don't much care for their nonsense. I don't believe you have anything to offer me."

"You won't help?" I say quietly, trying to keep my voice from trembling. "Even if it means our people suffer?"

"The Oluso suffer just as much under siege from the kokulu as they do from the Ajes. I don't see why joining hands with you will make them suffer less. The suffering will continue until we are free."

"So fight with me for that freedom," I urge, banging my fist to my chest. "Let me undo the wrong I've done. Help me, and I will never forget this." I can't lose here. Not after turning down the spirits, not after dragging Nana here. I have to succeed, even if it means being beholden to Ekwensi.

"Dèmi has fought for us in her own way," Colin declares. "Should that not count for something?"

"What do I always say, Nicolás?" Ekwensi asks, rising to his feet once more.

Colin looks down as though stricken. "Trust is lifeblood in the battle for survival," he mutters.

Ekwensi claps his shoulder. "Thank you." He lifts his arms like a ringmaster putting on a show. "Trust is our lifeblood. So, Abidèmi, how do I ask the kunkun to put their lives in your hands?"

"The kunkun?" I ask.

The false kokulu jerks up and screeches, revealing a lolling tongue rather than any rows of teeth. Bone shifts into red-brown skin reminiscent of the loamy soil decorating Old Maiduguri. Its sharp head melts into a shock of plaited copper hair laid down in rows over an angular face, and its wings turn into muscled arms ringed with triangular tattoos. The transformed kokulu stretches, shoulder bones jutting back impossibly far.

"You've spent too much time in that form, Danou," Ekwensi chides. "You'll soon forget you're human."

Danou bows over one arm, flashing a pulsing ring on his wrist similar to the ones Colin has from his chaining. "It's all in service of the kunkun." He straightens, beating his chest. "Kunkun!" he shouts.

"Kunkun!" the watchers on the balcony roar back.

"Kunkun!" Danou repeats again.

"Kunkun!" they echo, rolling a hand into a fist and placing that hand across their necks as though practicing to drag knives across their own throats. The air is thick with electricity, an energy that tingles on my skin.

Colin answers me, his eyes lighting with a fire I didn't realize I'd missed until this moment. "It's short for kuro ninu okunkun."

Out of darkness.

A fitting name for Oluso who have been told all their lives to accept darkness and despair as their fate.

"I will vouch for Dèmi," Colin announces. "I know her better than anyone else. She's here for the right reasons."

"Of course you would vouch for her!" Adaeze yells. "You're still hoping to bed her. Don't think we all can't see it."

Colin flushes, tawny cheeks darkening. "Take that back. I wouldn't risk our freedom for mere lovemaking."

"Hm, but maybe you think you'll get more out of this one," Danou says, sizing me up. "I could see the vision, maybe if she—"

"Try finishing that sentence," Colin barks, taking a menacing step toward Danou. "I'll strangle you with your own tongue."

The other man lifts his hands in surrender.

"The Council is our common enemy," I start, seizing on the opening. "Even now they harness the power of the kokulu to destroy us. Yet they blame us for this evil."

"*You* are our enemy." Adaeze leaps over the railing, the Oluso mark on her shoulder blazing as red as a falling comet. "You spent all this time fighting for *laws*," she spits.

I swallow before nodding. "I did."

"Laws are just words. Except when they're enforced by swords." She eyes me disdainfully. "Why did you bother? There were laws in place when the Eingardians took over our village. Laws that prevented someone from kidnapping a four-year-old girl and forcibly putting a child into that same girl when she had only seen sixteen name days." She slams her fist into her chest. "They didn't protect me. So how could yours be any different? Tell me the child I lost would have been safer under your laws."

"You lost the child?" I mutter.

She edges up to me, her face a hard mask. "That's not the only thing I lost."

Guilt pierces me like a spear gutting my belly. When I met her, Ga Eun, and Samira in those dungeons last year, they were pregnant, forcibly inseminated by Eingardian soldiers in a bid for Alistair Sorenson to keep power. Adaeze's child would've been half-Eingardian, like Will, but that wouldn't matter to the Ajes who fear the Oluso. She's right. There are no easy answers. Laws have no power without the people believing in them, holding them as sacred as their own lives. The only law in wartime is life or death, spoken in the language of blood.

Still, I plead, "There are some people who believe in those laws. People who have stopped mistreating Oluso. People who are on our side. If I didn't believe that, I wouldn't have tried."

"Dèmi is telling the truth," Colin says. He addresses the balcony. "We didn't find any enslaved Oluso in Yusa. People in Wyldewood helped us when we first escaped. Why do you think that is?"

"Yusa is a small place," Ga Eun counters. "They are right to fear laws. Wyldewood was kind to us, yes. But what of places like Yomo, where the okri market is growing? Or Sadok, the village that sold me? There are twelve girls on a ship from Sadok right now, headed for Ala'Ker. We all know they'll end up being more than housemaids. Word is the new regional governor of Ala'Ker has a preference for Oluso who can transform in bed."

Colin flinches. As retribution for Colin's involvement with Ekwensi, the Eingardian Council reduced his father Lord Kairen's influence, appointing new regional heads to key cities in Berréa like Ala'Ker, Uru'Legba and Ke'redu.

"But with the laws, we could arrest him. Push for a new governor of Ala'Ker," I insist.

"How long will that take?" Adaeze asks, crossing her arms. "How many of us have to suffer before you act?"

"I acted then!" I shout, anger filling me now. "I defeated Alistair Sorenson. I fought to become your queen."

"And what a queen you've been," Adaeze scoffs. "Letting the Council manipulate you."

I want to scream. In the years since I lost Mummy, while I still lived in Benin with Will, Nana, and Colin, all I could think about was survival. Then, once Ekwensi threw my world off its axis, I began to believe I could do more than protect the people I cared about. I began to think there was more to life than just making it day to day. When I defeated Alistair Sorenson, I felt as though I could call on the winds and ride their waves into the clouds without looking back—I was free. But then I woke in that lonely solar and found that the world did not change just because I did. The Council still ruled, and though I had the blood of Queen Folaké and Afèni in my veins, I knew nothing about ruling a kingdom, let alone which traditions and laws were just for all of us. I spent the last several months alone studying from dawn to dusk, learning the things I'd missed. But though I've given myself like a sacrifice for the Oluso, none of it is enough. Not the laws I've tried to pass or the way I've fought the Council. Not even the fact that I'm here.

Nana convulses into a fit, breaths unspooling into labored gasps. I dash to her, argument forgotten. "Breathe," I beg, rubbing her back. "Breathe, Nana." Her skin is cold, but she is sweating so much.

Ta'atia snaps her fingers and Li'uoa steps forward, moving to Nana. She squints, examining her. "Her body's water is running low."

"Meaning?"

"Her time is dwindling. She's not long for this world. A little less than two days, perhaps."

I wipe the sweat from Nana's brow as fear closes around my heart like a fist. I have lost. I'm going to lose her too. Colin puts an arm around me, whispering in my ear, "It's all right. I'll help you, even if he won't."

"Tobias," Ta'atia says, setting her cup aside. "Need I remind you that your time in my home is limited as well? Wolf Hour approaches without delay, and you have yet to share with me how you intend to make good on our agreement."

"Gull Hour has yet to start," Ekwensi responds. "There is still time."

"You won't begrudge me if I asked for further proof then? A guarantee?" Ta'atia asks, crossing her arms. "Perhaps a daughter to keep me company while I await your delivery." She looks pointedly at Malala.

Ekwensi freezes, and a charged look passes between them.

"I'd prefer not to renegotiate the terms of our agreement," he says finally, speaking through clenched teeth. "What do you want?"

"Give the girl an opportunity, in the same way I gave you one. That is all I ask."

I look up, startled. Why would Ta'atia want to help me?

Ekwensi twists the head of his cane, wringing the antelope's neck. "And if I refuse? If I consider this a breach of our agreement?"

"You are well within your rights to refuse," Ta'atia states, fingering a curl of her hair. "Though it is funny you'd do so, considering I aided you without a guarantee." Her words sound so light, but the edgy look in her eyes is anything but.

He sighs. "An opportunity then. I can grant that at least."

She brushes past him, offering me a hand. "Come, Dèmi, come enjoy a feast at my table."

"Why would you help me?" I ask. I see no reason for Ta'atia's sudden favor, and every reason for her to leave me to Ekwensi's devices. "What could you benefit?"

She places her fingers under her mask and trills. I shudder as a memory springs up in my mind like a shoot breaking though frost. This is the diduo's cry—the signal Mummy and I always used.

"I owe your mother a life debt," Ta'atia explains. "I'd like to pay it this way. And whether or not you and Tobias come to an agreement, I will still help you. That is what I can do beyond assuring you won't be forced into anything. What do you say, young one? Feast at my table?"

Taking her hand, I rise, hope surging in my breast. All is not lost.

"Why don't we do this?" Ekwensi says, settling back onto his would-be throne. "Convince the kunkun that you should be allowed to join us, and I will ally with you. I will also save your guardian no matter the cost. We can discuss the finer terms of our agreement then."

"You'll help me?" I repeat. Then, narrowing my eyes, I add, "What exactly will that help entail?"

He sighs again, a world of patience in the sound. "This is precisely why I spoke of trust."

"Perhaps we should make time to eat," Ta'atia says, yawning as though she's witnessed all this before. "The food is cold."

"An excellent suggestion," Ekwensi agrees He stretches a hand out toward the table. "Please. Let's discuss our disagreements over some food."

Adaeze's voice rings out, each word a gauntlet thrown. "The kunkun will not feast with you. Not until you have proven yourself to us. We'll host an ija. You will attend, show us you are worthy of our help."

An ija—a brawl of one against many.

I bare my teeth. "Is that an invitation or a threat?"

She lifts her chin, towering over me. "We'll find out, won't we?"

I look up at the wider balcony. Beyond the arena where Alistair Sorenson tried to kill us, I have never before seen so many Oluso. The eyes staring back at me are full of all kinds of emotion; fear that I know better than the skin on the back of my hand; anger that dogs my every step; confusion at what the future might bring. But there is something else here, too, something I haven't felt in months except in those quiet moments when Jonas and I are alone, speaking to each other in hushed tones about impossibilities we'd like to make real—hope. I see it, in the defiant looks cast at me, the way some of the Oluso hold their heads higher than the proudest courtiers. I see it in little Malala, who stands tall, holding her mother's hand tight. Whether we go to war together or I find a way to garner the Oluso peace another way, it would be a waste to leave the embers of hope in this room to fizzle into nothing but despair and darkness. It's time for me to stoke that fire, ignite the hope once smothered by pain and disappointment, move beyond mere dreams of peace. It's time to try something new.

"Bring on the ija!" I thunder. "I am more than ready to meet the challenge."

TERMS

"You're not fighting anyone," Ta'atia announces. "Not without some food in your belly."

She whistles and three handmaidens slip into the room from the connecting passages. "Take Tenjun's daughter to my personal rooms. Give her a tincture of abon for the pain, and burn the sandalwood incense. We must restore her strength."

I pull Nana to me, shaking my head. "I'm not going anywhere without her."

"My personal rooms are magically protected," Ta'atia reassures me. "No one will be able to enter unless I give permission. Not even my handmaidens."

Colin takes Nana from me, scooping her into his arms. She seems so small, cocooned against him like a newborn baby, unwise to the evils of the world. "I'll take her; don't worry, Dèmi."

Still, I place an insistent hand on his arm. "If anything happens to her . . ."

He grins. "You'll rip my throat out and feed it to me. I know."

They disappear into the passage, following the handmaidens, and my heart squeezes tight, as though a part of me has just been severed.

"When is this ija?" I ask Ekwensi. "How soon can you give me the aid I seek?"

Nana has only two days. I can't afford to languish here, waiting for aid that may never come. I need a guarantee.

Ekwensi smirks. "We are disciplined here. The kunkun meet at Gull

Hour every day. It's typically a time for remembrance and meditation, but you will have your ija then."

"And once that is over?"

He whips his cane into the crook of his elbow. "Convince the kunkun of your worthiness, and I will aid you immediately after." His eyes glitter as he adds, "I can eliminate the curse caster tonight."

He knows, then, or he's at least guessed, that I want to kill Mari.

Ta'atia crosses her arms. "Whatever you do, so long as it's in my city, it must be completed by Wolf Hour."

"Of course," Ekwensi says, smiling that jackal smile. "It will be as you say."

Wolf Hour. Just half a day and Nana will be freed from her curse. This nightmare is nearly over. Then there's the Council to reckon with next, the Oluso to save. But even if attacking the Council leads to bloody war and I die in the midst of all that assured chaos, at least Will and Nana will be safe. Haru will not be orphaned. That is enough.

But Ekwensi is not finished. He bows low. "Thank you, Ta'atia, for your friendship to the kunkun. We could not have escaped Wellstown without your cooperation."

Ta'atia picks up one of the knives on the table, stabbing a rolled date covered in sugar. "I'm glad I could be of assistance. I trust you will return the favor soon. Wolf Hour approaches."

Another look passes between them. He nods. "Undoubtedly."

He whips around, tossing a pouch at a still-seated Elodie. She snatches it, jingling it before whistling. "This is enough to buy an entire new season of clothes. Or weapons. I hear the Gomae girls use hairpins as weapons these days."

"The price of selling people out? Reporting on their every move?" I jeer. I'm still angry she knew of the danger awaiting me and Jonas and did nothing.

Elodie takes out a gold coin, biting it before flipping it into the air. "Everybody has a price. Informants should never work for free, should they?" She flounces out of the chair without waiting for a response, heading straight for the food.

I glower after her, annoyed that a part of me was hoping she'd apologize, admit that her attempts to gain my friendship was more than mere pretense.

Malala sticks her head in between the railings. "Baba," she calls, "are you staying long this time?"

Ekwensi's jackal smile morphs into a wide grin of genuine warmth. His eyes soften as he reaches his arms up. "Come here, my dear. Baba has stories to tell you."

Malala darts away from the balcony, disappearing from sight, and all the Oluso around her part, clearing the way. Then all I hear are quick footsteps like stones skipping across water, and suddenly she is leaping past the railing, arms spread wide like an eagle soaring on the wind.

Ekwensi catches her, twirling her around, and it is frightening how quickly he changes. Gone is the sarcastic, confident, calculating man who assessed me a moment ago with cool eyes, and in his place is a middle-aged man who is throwing a young child onto his shoulders and holding her aloft as though she is queen of the world. This is Tobias Ekwensi the father.

I swallow, suddenly aware of the hollow in my chest, the longing that keeps my eyes tied to Ekwensi and his daughter as they flit about the room, laughing. I will never have a moment with my father like this because of all the choices he made. I shove Iya's crystal into my collar, putting it out of sight. If I can solve this problem on my own and save Nana, then I have no need to see Osèzèlé's spirit again, worry myself into sleepless nights wondering why he did the things he did.

Colin reappears, rising out of the connecting passage, and his gaze falls on Ekwensi and Malala like a treasure hunter sniffing out fine cowrie shells. His expression darkens, no doubt thinking of Lord Kairen.

Ekwensi and his daughter disappear down one of the low archways and only then does the energy in the room shift, dying into a steady rhythm. The Oluso on the balcony disperse, some disappearing into the upper archways, others settling into cushions, chattering to one another while stealing glances at me. A few slip out of view and reappear on the lower floor, reaching for some of the food on the table.

Danou reaches for one of the doughy pasties on a tray and Ta'atia smacks his hand away. "Not you. You ate sixteen meatpies alone yesterday. Li'uoa saw you."

Though all the attention was on us a moment before, none of the other Oluso are meeting my eyes now.

Ta'atia hands me a bowl of pepper soup. The smell of hearty broth simmering with peppers, freshly caught fish, onion, and a mix of spices sets my stomach grumbling.

"Eat," she commands. "There's even garden-egg stew and yam if you'd like some. I have matters in the city to attend to." She turns on her heel, but I'm not ready to let her go.

"You knew my mother," I say. "How? Were you friends in Ikolé?"

Ta'atia's mask ruffles in what I assume is another mysterious smile. "Spirits willing, I will tell you that tale another time. For now, ask Li'uoa if you need anything." She nods at the pale handmaiden standing a few feet away.

I dip my head toward Li'uoa and she returns my bow.

The air trembles, and suddenly, Ta'atia is gone, leaving only a faint trace of dew behind.

I eat quickly, swallowing morsels of food as though the plate might disappear. I hadn't realized I was so famished, but it makes sense, considering the last meal I had in preparation for the betrothal was a bowl of griej.

A memory seizes me then, Jonas laughing when I told him I'd pledged to eat the wheat porridge if only to spite Lady Ayn and prove I was just as worthy as Eingardian brides.

"Plotting rebellion already I see," Colin taunts, taking the seat next to me. I shove all thoughts of Jonas away, burying them in my heart like a dirty secret.

"Only if you're ready to burn everything with me," I shoot back.

His plate is loaded with coconut fried rice and two thick slices of yam slathered in banga. I swipe a little of the banga, unearthing a little bit of rice, then I lick the deliciously thick palm-nut soup off my finger, moaning all the while.

Colin's neck and cheeks darken with a cloud of red. "I take it you were really hungry," he says, not meeting my eyes.

"Ravenous." I drag over some more offerings; meat pies partly covered by a cloth, akara buns that cluster together like baby chicks, a pot of thick yellow custard that is quickly developing a skin on top.

"Don't let me stop you then."

"I won't, thanks."

I make a show of heaping my plate, then once the last of the Oluso are gone, I lower my voice and lean closer to Colin. "Tell me about the ija," I whisper softly. "What are they planning?"

He shifts away, reaching for a glass of water that he gulps down in one go. Then he answers, "I'm not exactly sure. I'm not in charge of the planning for these things, but it will be a fair fight. The kunkun despise unfairness because of what we've suffered."

I nod, trying to find a way to push out the next words, give voice to the discomfort I feel. "The other Oluso don't like me, do they? They think I betrayed them by choosing to rule."

He sighs. "Not exactly. When the Council announced that we'd have an Oluso queen, people rejoiced. But there's been no news since then, and though the new laws are in place, things are getting worse in certain areas. Then there have been rumors . . ."

I turn to face him. "What rumors?"

"That you're not becoming queen after all. That you sacrificed the Oluso in exchange for the Eingardian Ajes to guarantee your safety."

"That's not—"

"Some people wonder if you're even Oluso at all," he says, chuckling. "Olodos, every last one of them." He threads his fingers through mine. "I'm just glad to have you back."

"What should I do? How do I win them over?"

He cradles my cheek, staring into my eyes. "Listen to them. Maybe you'll find something you need. And maybe you can convince them of who you really are—the Dèmi I know."

Maybe I can figure out that myself.

"I'm about to eat the last of the garden egg if that's all right," a woman says.

Colin and I spring apart. The pot lid by his elbow clatters to the floor, ringing loudly through the room like city bells warning of a coming storm.

The woman at the end of the table jumps, the beads in her hair clinking together. She looks down at the baby nursing at her breast, but the child does not stir from its focus, kneading its little fist against her chest as though it can push the milk down faster.

"Didn't see you there, sorry," Colin says.

"It's all right," the woman responds. She turns her wide-eyed gaze to me, and I recognize her heart-shaped face with skin a shade darker than golden biwa fruit. It's Sanaa, the woman Ekwensi wanted rescued in Lokoja, the one whose betrothed, Etera, risked his life, and his position as an alagbede, a trusted Aje blacksmith, to protect.

"I'm glad that you're here, Dèmi," she says, offering me a weary smile. "I never got to say thank you."

"She didn't save you for your thanks," Colin blurts.

"Colin." I shoot him a withering look. "I can speak for myself, thanks." I don't know what is eating at him, but I refuse to be unkind to this woman. The baby at her breast presses its head farther in and Sanaa hisses, hooking her finger into the child's mouth.

"Don't bite Mummy, Tuléa. Be a good boy."

Tuléa wails, pawing at her other breast. His sun-kissed face and dark hair are a faithful copy of his father's. Sanaa flashes me an apologetic look, freeing her other breast from her wrap. "Sorry, he's always hungry."

Colin turns away. "I'll wait by the stairs," he says quickly before dashing through an archway.

"Colin!" I call after him but he doesn't turn back. Scrubbing a hand through my hair, I face Sanaa once more. "Sorry about that. He's just tired."

"It's all right," Sanaa says. "He doesn't like being around me." She looks around before lowering her voice. "But I'm glad you're here. You are the one of the few who understands what it's like to love an Aje."

I stiffen. As far as the world is concerned, Jonas is an Aje prince. Though that might soon change with his exploits at our betrothal last night, the Council will not rush to announce his status as an Oluso.

No wonder the Oluso here hold resentment for me.

"Etera was more than my betrothed," she continues. "He and his family took me in when I was just a baby." She strokes her son's dark head. "They found me, when I was no bigger than Tuléa, in a funny little boat—the kind palm wine tappers use—on the shores of Lokoja. I didn't have anything on me, just a lock of hair tied with a ribbon."

"So Ajes were kind to you from the start," I say.

"They took care of me, protected an Oluso baby, even though they knew it would be hard. Etera was everything to me." She pauses, trembling a little now. "You know as well as I do, that not all the Ajes despise us. Many fear us, yes, but some find ways to live with us. Just look at this city."

I don't know what to say, so I merely nod. It is true some Ajes live side by side with Oluso. Even in Ikolé, though the village elders betrayed Mummy and the children were often cruel to me, there were a few Ajes who never did us harm, even helped us every now and then. In Benin, we could count on people like Gideon, who fancied Amara, or Mama Seita, who ran the needle shop next to Nana's stall. Mikhail has always been one of our staunchest supporters in the guard, and, since we changed the kingdom's laws, there are many people on the streets of Wyldewood who look at me with welcome and curiosity rather than fear. Just as Oluso differ in gifts, Ajes differ in their responses to us.

They just didn't seem to have any power, not enough to truly change our lives.

"I understand that Ajes don't all hate us," I respond finally. "But I think everyone understands that, yes? Does it seem like the other members of the kunkun don't?"

She shakes her head frantically. "No. It's not that the others hate the Ajes. Some do, but many of us just want to find a way to move forward." Tuléa lays his hand against her chest and she rubs a finger against his tiny palm.

"It's just hard, every day, living on the run, being afraid of everything." Her eyes are heavy with tears now. "It's hard looking around, not being sure if the Aje you'll meet is your ally or your enemy." She sniffs.

"I'm doing everything I can to help Ekwensi. I even let the spirits pass through me—"

"What spirits?" I ask, narrowing my eyes.

She seizes up. "It's not important." Pulling a hand out of her pocket, she shoves something at me. "I came to give you this. I've had a sense for weeks that I had to give this to someone, and that feeling came back when I saw you."

I look down to find a finely braided silken knot of dark hair tied with a red ribbon and a beaded ornament. "It's what I was found with. I think of it as my charm of fortune. I added a lock of my own hair to it." She stuffs it into my hand. "Take it as thanks. I have no need of it anymore."

"I couldn't possibly take this," I say. "This must be so precious to you."

She wrenches herself away as though she might think better of giving me this offered gift. "No. Without you, Tuléa and I . . ."

She breaks off in a sob but before I can comfort her, another woman rushes in, pale hands fluttering as she gathers Sanaa up. Edith, Jonas' old nursemaid. She rubs Sanaa's back while glaring at me.

It is strange to see her here, protecting another Oluso from me, the Oluso whose life she once endangered. What was it Lord Kairen said?

War makes for strange bedfellows.

The city bells ring suddenly, five counts to announce that Gull Hour has arrived. It's time for the ija.

INTERMEDIARY

STUFFING SANAA'S GIFT INTO MY BELT, I HURRY THROUGH THE ARCHWAY Colin disappeared into, running up the steps two at a time. Colin is seated at the top on the second level, speaking in hushed tones to the air.

"Colin," I call.

His eyes widen as he catches sight of me and he shakes his head as though waking from a trance.

"Are you all right?" I ask, offering him a hand.

He springs to his feet. "Fine. Trying to remember something." He nods toward the lower end of the steps. "Are you done? With her, I mean?"

I cross my arms. "Care to tell me what that was about?"

"It's her," he says. "She's the one helping Ekwensi commune with spirits."

"That's not enough reason to be rude."

"You're right," he says, almost mechanically. "I'm sorry." He stalks into the next room and I dog his heels.

"Col, what's happening?"

He shakes his head. "Nothing."

I tug at his sleeve, but he keeps moving. "We mustn't be late," he says. "The kunkun might hold that against you."

Colin quickens his steps, rushing down the corridor as though something is chasing him. There are sounds beyond us, a swell of footsteps and voices, the whistles of chairs across the tile floor and the clinking of porcelain cups announcing that we'll soon be in full view of the other Oluso. Whatever is eating at Colin, I need to know now before others can guess at what is happening.

Speeding up, I throw myself in front of him and spread my arms. He grinds to a halt and I take one of his hands.

"Whatever it is Col, tell me. You know I would never let you carry your pain alone." I step closer, meeting his clouded, stormy gaze. "What happened? Why are you so afraid of Sanaa?"

His mouth draws into a thin line. Then, blowing out a breath, he says, "Every time I see her, I dream of my dead mother."

"What?" I exclaim, taken aback. "Does Sanaa look like Eyani?"

"No," he says quickly.

Colin's mother, Eyani Al'Hia, was a well-known warlord, the Scourge of T'Lapis, whose reputation was so fearsome even Alistair Sorenson feared invading Berréa. She raised Colin to be strong, training him from birth in all manner of fighting techniques before he was old enough to speak.

He tightens his grip on my hand. "Mother . . . I see her in the moments before she died of father's poison. She tells me she's sorry. She wishes she had done better." He lifts a corner of his mouth in a half smile. "Funny, right? Saying that after it's too late."

"No, not funny at all."

I envelop him in a hug. I don't understand what is happening to him, but I want to reassure him somehow. And then there's the ija that awaits me, a test that will determine whether Nana is saved and I have a future fighting for the Oluso. I lay my head against Colin's chest, realizing now that I need this reprieve just as much as he does.

He hesitates a moment, then his arms snake around me, holding me tight. We stand there for a few heartbeats, resting together, and once again I wish for the easy days when we were two children playing in the marketplace, wondering who could run the fastest. Even then, the fear of being found out as Oluso cast its shadow over the airy lightness of those days. But now it feels like nothing awaits us but war and darkness, and I don't know how to stop it.

"Dèmi," Colin starts, pulling away. "Can I tell you something?" He stops, licking his lips, but that does nothing to soften the dark intensity on his face. "Something that might frighten you?"

"You can tell *me*," Adaeze quips, sauntering up to us. She shoots us a withering look. "I wondered what was taking so long. Turns out you were too busy lovemaking."

Heat flushes up my neck. "That's not what is happening here," I start.

Colin groans. "We're coming. We were just—"

"Catching up?" she finishes. "That's what Tenioluwa said when Jin Tae joined us. She's due in six moons now. Just announced. Be sure to congratulate them on the good news."

Colin's ears turn a fierce red. "I thought . . . I really wasn't . . . I mean I was only . . ."

"Bind them!" Adaeze shouts, leaping back.

Several members of the kunkun burst in from the shadowed landing, rushing us. Colin barely has a moment to turn before Danou wraps bear-transformed paws around him. Another Oluso touches their shoulders and all three disappear. Hands grab me, twisting my arms behind my back, crushing me to the marble floor.

"The harder you fight, the more painful this will be," Adaeze whispers, her breath slithering into my ear.

Colored vines appear, lashing around me like a python bent on suffocating its prey. I try to move my wrist, and more vines appear, binding me tighter. Then light chokes my vision, and I squeeze my eyes shut.

When I open them again, I'm standing in a consuming darkness, ankles tethered to the floor.

"What is this?" I shout, struggling against the bindings gnawing into my wrists. The vines tighten in response, and I swallow a groan of pain. "Seems you're too afraid I'll win if I'm unbound."

Something slams into my back, knocking the breath out of me.

Adaeze's voice dances behind me. "You're not in a position to question us."

"It's a test!" Colin screams. His voice echoes through my body, and I can't tell where it's coming from. "Whatever you do, don't try to hit her. Use your magic to absorb the blows."

"What do you mean use my magic? I—"

Another blow explodes against my ribs, so fierce that I double over. My heart is racing, my lungs screaming for relief. My magic leaps in response, clawing desperately at my skin.

Colin's voice comes again, louder and angrier. "At least tell her the rules!"

A hand brushes my shoulder, and I whirl, snapping at my attacker with my teeth. Danou's voice visits me next. "Whoa, whoa. This is a test we give to the kunkun's strongest fighters."

"Some test," I seethe, wincing against the pain tearing through my chest.

"The Eingardians have always tortured us," he says. "Everyone here has gone through it at one time."

"So you intend to torture me as the Eingardians would? That's how you get people to join you?"

He sighs, but the sound comes from my left. I pivot again, trying to place where he is. "No," he answers. "Since they hold us in iron chains, we developed a way to keep ourselves intact and alive. We call it lilé, or sealing. You'll have to learn it if you desire to be one of us."

"When you're in danger," Colin cries, "your magic flows out, tries to save you. Try anticipating the blows, using your magic in areas where you might be hit. Think of it like a shield."

"But my spirit bonds are broken," I protest. "How can I—"

"All our spirit bonds are broken," Adaeze interrupts. The wind in front of me shifts, and I brace myself as I sense something driving at my knee. "It's better to learn by doing."

Just before the weapon rams into my knee, I feel it—a frisson of concentrated magic coating the skin there.

Then pain explodes through my joints, and I bite my lip hard, drawing blood.

"You're so done when I get over there," Colin rages. "Even for an ija, this is too much."

Adaeze merely sniffs. "That one was for Ga Eun."

"Where is Ga Eun?" someone asks.

"She's not feeling well," another answers.

"Isn't Colin next in command then?" a third asks. "Should we let him down?"

"If you hurt Dèmi any more," Colin warns, "you'll all find out what pain means."

"I've already felt unimaginable pain," Adaeze mutters. "The promise of more means nothing."

The air is charged again, and I sense the weapon hurtling toward my belly. Hunching slightly, I feel for the winds charging against me, and I think of a shield, stronger than a turtle's shell, covering my belly.

When the weapon strikes me, I feel its wooden body, the small ridges cutting through its thick shape, but I feel no pain. The rod bounces off me, and I exhale in relief.

"Colin said you were quick," Danou compliments. "Please excuse me then." The wind currents behind my legs warp subtly, and I imagine a shield there again, but this time, I think of my magic as a wall covering my whole back.

The rod flips at the last minute, ramming toward my lower waist, but again it ricochets off me. I've done it.

The darkness tears away from my eyes, revealing the crowd gathered on cushions around a hearth, all watching me like crows gathered on a tree branch awaiting the first sign of chaos. There are many Oluso here, hailing from all over the Kingdom of Ifé. An older woman to the far right of the circle studies me, the gold rings studding her eyebrows, lips, ears and nose moving in tandem as she leans forward. Those rings mark her as a high noble hailing from west Berréa, someone I wouldn't have expected in Ekwensi's camp. Next to her, a boy no older than sixteen name days glares at me through the green ribbon of paint unfurling over his dark eyes, a sign given to orphans born on Sayaji Island, the site of Afèni's last battle with the kokulu.

Danou touches my forehead and the vines restraining me melt away. "Congratulations," he says, grinning. "You've passed."

He backs away, and the vines lashing Colin to the ceiling melt. He drops into a crouch, then dives at Danou, wrapping a muscular arm around his neck. "Told you I would repay you for this, you son of a gutter horse. Nobody hurts Dèmi and gets away with it."

Adaeze ignores them, offering me a proud smile. "I knew I didn't read you wrongly. Well done." She threads her arm through mine, her earlier hostility gone. "Stick with me, Dèmi. These men think they're clever. They always say they want friendship even when they wind up in your bed." She tuts. "Let me help you, my sister. We always end our battles and rituals with iranti. It helps cleanse our minds and bring our emotions to calm. You can sit next to me."

Iranti, a remembrance ceremony for the dead.

I shudder against the sudden chill gripping my skin, but I follow her as she breaks the circle. Pain radiates through me with each step, but I clench my teeth and keep it at bay. I suspect enduring the pain is part of this. Besides, iron bloods can't easily be healed by other Oluso, not without stealing a bit of their lives.

She pulls me to a seat by the sea of flames, then looks out to the Oluso gathered. "Iranti is a time for remembrance, yes, but it also a time for healing." She pierces me with her sharp gaze. "If there's anything you're holding back, anyone you've lost, now is the time to share it."

I look away, rubbing my bruised wrists.

Danou taps Colin's arm. "Care to start us, second-in-command?" he rasps.

Colin drops his arm at this, discomfort evident on his face.

Danou clears his throat, his voice cutting through the silence. "Kunkun!"

"Kunkun!" the others echo back.

He produces a piece of paper from his pocket, holding it up for everyone to see.

I read the words: Haniff Olaitan.

Tossing the paper into the copper bowl in our midst, Danou selects a stone from the array lying next to the bowl, placing it on top of the paper.

"Haniff was a herder not much older than me. His ancestors hailed from east Berréa and lower Oyo." There are nods and murmurs in response. "Haniff was Ariabhe, but . . ." Danou pauses, breaking into a grin, "his healing only ever seemed to work on animals." A few Oluso laugh. "In fact, I would always ask him when he'd stop healing cows and help the rest of us." Some more laughter.

"But when I asked Haniff to join us, especially since he could help heal those of us who transform, he left his little village in Saku to come make history." Danou's smile disappears. The kunkun go still.

"And he did. He made sure Ga Eun and I got out of Wellstown alive."

He picks up the gourd on the other side of the bowl and pours some of its contents into the bowl. The scent of tombo tangles over my nostrils.

He sits back down and the Sayaji-born boy holds up another piece of paper. "This one is for my sisters, Eniko and Kilem. We had no family name. They kept me alive, even though they were children themselves." He crushes the paper in his fist before throwing it into the bowl. "They would have joined us if they'd made it past Wellstown."

He shoots me a look as though he could burn me with his gaze, and I stare right back. "If you want to fight, too, let me know," I growl. "Don't blame me for what I never did."

"Do you have something to say?" Colin asks, taking a seat next to me.

The boy looks between us, jaw clenched, face pinched as though he is ready to explode. Then another young man gets up, putting a hand on the boy's shoulder. At his touch, the boy curls up like a burning piece of paper and sits down without giving me another look.

"I want to go next," a woman says. She is short, dressed in a simple wrapper tucked under her armpits. But it is the chalk marks streaked across her golden face that draw my attention. These are the marks of someone from Bia-Hyang, the place my father grew up in.

Adaeze looks to Danou, who shrugs. "You may proceed, Shatu," Adaeze says finally.

Shatu walks into the circle, holding out a piece of paper. I straighten as she locks eyes with me and marches over. She kneels in front of me and offers me her paper. It's blank.

"I know it pains you to be here today," she begins, "to hear of all the losses that we carry. I know also that many of us have blamed you unfairly, looked for a sacrificial lamb to bear our faults." She presses the paper into my hand. "I come to ask you for something else."

"What is this?" Colin says, edging closer.

"It is true the Oluso have suffered," she says. "That we have been hunted like animals. But it also true that we were warned."

"Not this again," Danou mutters.

Adaeze reaches out to Shatu, touching her lightly on the shoulder. "It's enough. Go back. You'll frighten Dèmi."

Shatu clutches my hands tighter. Her dark eyes are full of terror, a darkness so consuming I cannot look away. "I have seen it," she whispers, "the dreams of the past. What the Oluso did to the Fèni-Ogun. In Bia-Hyang we say, Aigbokhaebho—you cannot destroy the history of a people." She lets go of my hands, her voice devolving into a loud wail. "We Oluso tore the Fèni-Ogun apart with our own hands—"

"Shatu!" Adaeze shouts, getting to her feet, but Shatu is folding, rocking back and forth like a frightened child.

Danou stalks over, grabbing at her, but she springs up, seizing him by the arm and flinging him across the room. The other Oluso scramble back in fear. I get to my feet, blood rushing in my ears, everything in me screaming that I should run. Colin pushes me behind him just as Shatu swerves back to me. Her eyes are stark white, a fathomless sea that calls to me.

"Child," she whispers, in a voice that sounds as ancient as the cliffs that gave rise to this city. "Do not forget us, daughter of Osèzèlé."

She reaches out a hand and the paper in my fist catches fire, its heat stinging my palm. I hiss, flinging it away, and it lands perfectly in the ijadé bowl.

Shatu takes shaky steps toward me, her body jerking like a dancing puppet.

"Stay back," Colin yells, dragging out his whip.

Shatu waves a hand and he flies back, knocking into the wall.

I turn, trying to go to him, but my limbs will not move, my body fixed to the spot.

"Do not let them bury us . . ." Shatu rasps, "in shallow graves." She reaches out to touch my face, her fingers crawling like worms against my flesh. Suddenly I am engulfed by a devouring grief, a sadness that seems to radiate from my very bones.

I can't breathe.

"Make them remember. Free us."

Ekwensi appears behind her, blue flame dancing against his skin. He strikes Shatu on the side of her head. She slumps, and he catches her, placing her carefully on the ground. I suck in a gulp of air, drawing in the smoke and tombo choking the air in the room. The bowl of names is burning, set alight by the fire on Shatu's empty paper.

Colin stumbles over, a stream of blood trickling from a nasty cut on his forehead. "Are you all right?" he asks, pressing his fingers to my face. My throat feels tight. My words swell against my tongue, clawing at me like a creature buried alive.

"It seems things have gotten out of hand," Ekwensi says.

"Shatu was talking about the iron-bloods again," Adaeze says, rubbing the prickled flesh on her arms. "She went berserk and started howling like a rabid dog." She shoots me an apologetic look, genuinely cowed. "I'm sorry. I was the one who asked for this."

But Shatu's words are echoing through my mind.

"Didn't you hear what Shatu said?" I whisper, a chill growing in my heart despite the sweltering heat in the room.

She sighs. "Shatu should never have brought the iron-bloods up. It does no good to rehash history. All it will do is divide the Oluso. The Fèni-Ogun are long gone."

"Almost," Colin says, glaring at her.

Her eyes widen as she realizes what he means. She throws me an apologetic look. "Sorry. It's so easy to forget, you being the last iron-blood and all . . ." She knocks her fist against her mouth. "Sorry."

I nearly correct her, mention that Jonas is iron-blood too, but my mind is still paralyzed by disbelief, struggling to make sense of the situation before me. Even Colin does not seem to have noticed anything strange. Still, I tug his sleeve and ask.

"Did you hear anything else?"

He frowns, the skin between his brows puckering tight. "I don't understand."

"Did *you* hear anything?" Ekwensi asks. He watches us, eyes heavy with a sort of bemusement. But I see the edge to his jaw, the way he stills as though waiting for a revelation.

I shake my head instinctively. "No—I just wasn't sure. I thought she was trying to frighten me into leaving."

Whatever just happened, I can't reveal it carelessly—especially not to Ekwensi.

He considers me for a moment more, then gets to his feet slowly.

"We should talk to Ta'atia. Perhaps something in the food caused Shatu to have fits."

He claps his hands. A few Oluso come running. They gather up Shatu and haul her away as we look on. Adaeze trails after them, stealing glances back at me.

"Did you hear anything after all?" Ekwensi presses, lowering his voice. "Or . . . is it the madness? It is not uncommon to experience illusions after losing your spirit bonds." His lips curve in a sad smile. "Trust me, I know."

I still, not daring to breathe. I want to tell him he's wrong, that I am not imagining things no one else can hear. Even Colin watches me, concern heavy on his face. The other Oluso look over, their frightened stares like hooks stabbing into my flesh. Suddenly my chest feels tight, and for a brief moment, Ekwensi's words ring with an air of truth.

But the memory of the voice that came from Shatu dances around in my mind like a childhood rhyme. I don't know where, but I'm certain I've heard that voice before. I still feel too, that sadness in my bones, an ache buried deep within me.

Ekwensi flexes his withered right hand, the orange Oluso mark on it gleaming as brightly as the now extinguished flame. "I once believed breaking our spirit bonds meant we had no choice but to lose ourselves and our minds. Now I know there's another path—chaining."

I lick my lips. "And if I don't desire that path?"

He shrugs. "The offer remains. You can always change your mind. Now that you've passed the ija, it is time to discuss our terms. Come when you are ready." He walks away without a backward glance, his cane clacking alongside him, its steady taps like drumbeats spurring on the rhythm of war.

"Are you all right?" Colin asks. He bends to examine me, the silvery moon at the end of his ear cuff brushing against my cheek. The pieces come together in my mind then.

Rivers of blood await you, sleeping moon.

I'm certain now—the voice from Shatu's lips was like the voice from the young girl in Lleyria.

That was the voice of a K'inu.

EXCHANGE

Sucking in a breath, I dart after Ekwensi, chasing his quickly disappearing figure. My mind is racing, thoughts colliding like rocks caught in a Harmattan storm. I have so many questions, but I need to focus on what's most pressing now—saving Nana's life. Later, I'll ask Ekwensi about the K'inu carefully, use this as leverage if I must.

"Wait!" Colin calls after me, but I disappear into the adjoining passage slowing only once I catch up to Ekwensi.

"I'm ready now!" I shout. My voice echoes off the walls, swimming back to me in discordant waves that sound eerily like screeches.

He places a hand on my shoulder and we fade out of the corridor just as Colin catches up to us, stitching into a low-ceilinged chamber with light streaming in from voluminous windows. Colin is there, too, at Ekwensi's elbow.

"Now we assign your final task," Ekwensi starts, lounging on the chaise at the far end. "Once it's completed, I will accede to your requests and aid your guardian."

Colin and I raise our voices in tandem. "What?"

"That wasn't the deal," I add.

He leans back against the headrest, lacing his fingers. "I told you to convince the kunkun that you were worthy of joining us. You forget. *I* am also a member of the kunkun. My opinion matters as well."

Anger bubbles inside me, threatening to spill out in curses and unchecked fists. I should have known better. Ekwensi has always spoken in half-truths, weaving veiled meanings into his words as easily as a fisherman casts a net. This was yet another game.

Colin places a restraining hand on my arm. "Baba," he implores, "Dèmi proved herself willing to take blows for the kunkun. I also vouched for her. What else do you need?"

"I need assurance," Ekwensi says simply. "An unwavering belief that Abidèmi is committed to our cause and nothing else. Her actions last year, her failure to kill Alistair, did not convince me she cannot be swayed."

I shut my eyes, suppressing a groan. I'm tired of having my motives and actions questioned over and over by everyone around me.

"What would you have me do?" I grit out.

Ekwensi's jackal smile returns. "A simple retrieval. I need an item. You get it for me, and we'll be in alignment. I will have Mari killed, save your guardian's life. You will join the kunkun as a general, and once we've destroyed those fools in Eingard—cut off the head of the snake—we can discuss governmental options, figure out what is best for all."

I cock my head slightly. "Just like that? An item is all you need from me?"

"Guaranteed success is what I need," Ekwensi answers. "My informant tells me the item is in an iron cage. Our enemies planned to prevent any Oluso intervention."

"Your informant?" I ask.

He snaps his fingers. The shadow under the door undulates, and the door swings open.

Elodie falls into the room, cheeks blooming red. She dusts herself off, ever the noblewoman. "Well then," she says, "thanks for deciding to include me in the fun."

Ekwensi chuckles. "I told you before, just knock. No need to skulk around."

She flashes him a nonchalant smile. "It's the thrill, you see. Unmatched."

"You've got to be yabbing me," Colin mutters. "What is she doing here?"

"Elodie will be your guide to the Gardens," Ekwensi answers, rising to his feet. "There you will retrieve Ta'atia's shell and return it here before

Wolf Hour approaches. Succeed in this, and I'll make good on all our agreements."

"The Gardens? Mari and Oyéré's hideout?" Colin sputters. "You want to send Dèmi in there alone? How would Elodie even know the way?"

"I've maps copied from my mother's letters," Elodie supplies, moving to perch on the arm of the chaise. "My mother is Mari's spy on the Council, in case that wasn't obvious."

"You can't send Dèmi in there alone," Colin insists. "She's still injured from the ija. Let me go with her."

Ekwensi shakes his head. "This is a test for Abidèmi alone. It does not involve you."

"I volunteer to go."

"You are not needed, Nicolás."

"It doesn't matter. I'm going."

"Not if I restrain your magic," Ekwensi challenges, rising to his feet. The two lock stares.

"Ta'atia's shell," I repeat, breaking the charged silence. "Is that the agreement she made with you?"

"Of a fashion," Ekwensi answers simply.

"And what would you have done without an iron-blood to solve your problems?" I jeer. "I get the feeling Ta'atia does not bargain easily."

Perhaps I can negotiate with this, too, force Ekwensi to give me more favorable terms.

He cuts his eyes at me. "I would have found a way," he pronounces. "I always do. Any obstacle that is treated as absolute is a sure defeat. I don't accept defeat so easily." His voice is relaxed, amused even, but there is a thread underneath that breathes malice.

A shiver licks up my spine, but I lift my chin, stand like the queen Mummy always impelled me to be. "I don't either," I say. "So let's make a different deal. I'll give you information I have about the K'inu. In exchange, you cancel this mission."

His smile falters, then his expression settles into calm repose. But there is a hint of something in his eyes—fear. The realization calms my stormy heart. Even if I can't trust him entirely, his desire to possess information, especially about a threat like the K'inu, could push him to help me, give up this game he's playing.

But after a breath, he answers, "Impossible."

My heart drops. "What's impossible?" I query. "Don't you want to know what I know? This could be critical in the fight against the K'inu."

"No deal."

I frown. "Why not?"

He grips the head of his cane tight. "If you truly intend to work with me, you'll complete this mission and secure my alliance with Ta'atia. For now, I won't make amendments to our deal on the offer of something unproven. You could be bluffing for all I know."

I rake my fingernails across my palms, trying to hide my frustration. "If the information is real, what will you give me?"

He waves a hand and the daylight streaming through the windows east of us turns darker than a starless sky. I turn around, but the room, as well as Colin and Elodie, are gone, replaced with an endless darkness.

"Just a bit of shadow magic. I'd prefer to have our conversation in private," he explains. Now, what do you know about the K'inu?"

"You haven't promised me anything."

He sighs. "Convince me to cancel this mission. Talk."

I don't need further prompting. "I spoke to a K'inu in Lleyria a few days ago."

His fingers tighten on his cane. "It actually spoke to you?"

"It possessed a young child."

"They've become more powerful," he mutters. "What unfortunate timing."

"Don't you want to know what the K'inu told me?"

His lips quirk with the ghost of a smile. "If I did, would you tell me?"

I mirror his smile. "Cancel the mission. Give me help now."

"No. Think, once we become allies, you'll have to share whatever you know anyway."

"We exchange information then," I spit. "The K'inu are moving *now*. Maybe something I tell you can be of immediate help." This is a gamble, but I have no choice. If Ekwensi won't give me a better trade, it might be worth it to find some things out on my own, make sense of why the K'inu reached out to me without anyone knowing I'm hearing the voice of the enemy.

To my surprise, he throws his head back, laughing as though I've said something ridiculous.

Heat flushes up my neck, embarrassment sparking into anger. "I don't have to tell you anything," I growl.

"You misunderstand me," he says, wiping a tear from his eye. "I'm impressed. The Abidèmi of a few months ago did not know how to bargain. Now here she is, giving commands. You've grown."

Pride swells in my breast, cresting like an eagle taking flight. I smother it. "You mock me."

"If I truly did, I wouldn't grant you a moment of my time." He takes a step closer, dark eyes gleaming. "Now, how about we make a true bargain? There *is* something I want to know. And I'm willing to exchange that information for the answers you seek."

I narrow my eyes. "What do you want to know?"

"In the arena, when you awakened your iron magic, what did you see?"

The question is not anything I expected. Just then a breeze whispers against my neck and the chill in my skin grows sharper. Something tells me that I should hold on to the truth, hide it away from his prying eyes. But I can't leave this place without answers, not when people, Oluso and Aje alike, will suffer from the K'inu's attacks. Not when I'm starting to fear that their presence has something to do with me after all.

"I'll answer two questions you ask me in exchange for just this. Honestly," he offers.

"*Truthfully*," I counter. "Swear to the spirits."

He thrusts out a hand, snatching the end of the bone blade strapped to my waist. I jerk back and he hisses, raising a hand covered in blood.

"As the spirits watching us bear witness, I, Tobias Ekwensi, swear to answer two questions Abidèmi Adenekan asks me, truthfully."

I nod my satisfaction. "My questions first—what do you know about the K'inu?"

"Be more specific."

I pause a moment, considering what I know. Then I ask, "How did the K'inu first enter the Physical Realm?"

He hums appreciatively. "Good question. Before the Great War, there was no record of the K'inu. The royal okosuns sang of how the kokulu appeared like burning clouds over Bia-Hyang. They swooped down from the heavens and began destroying everything in sight. That, of course, began the Great War."

Bia-Hyang is the mountain village just north of Sayaji Island and west of Manapané. It is also where my father, Iron Blood Osèzèlé, grew up, secreted away from those who would harm him. I swallow against the lump in my throat, remembering Shatu's words. Somehow, I doubt this is mere coincidence.

"Do you know—" I start.

"I would take a moment if I were you," Ekwensi interrupts, eyes dancing with amusement. "Wouldn't want to waste the question."

He's right. I know there is more here, a thread that could weave an entire landscape if I just had the other pieces to put it all together. But I don't know enough of anything just yet.

I bite my lip hard. I should have asked a better question.

"I will ask my question now," Ekwensi declares. "Then you still have a question left. You have the upper hand." He taps his fingers against the head of his cane, streaking blood all over the silvered antelope head. "Tell me—what did you see when your iron magic was awakened?"

Taking a breath, I answer, "I saw my father. He spoke to me and gave me a spear."

His fingers still. "Is that all?"

I lick my lips. "I asked him where I could find him. He said to look between the river and the path."

His eyes cloud for a brief moment, then he nods. "Thank you."

"Why do you want to know?"

He jerks his head toward me like a shark sensing blood in the water. "Am I to understand this as your second question?"

I made a mistake with my first question, but there is something about the way he reacted a moment ago that makes me certain the clues I'm searching for are buried in this man's mind.

I lift my chin, refusing to back down. "It is."

"Your father disappeared after conducting the transformation ritual in Benin Palace. I had hoped he was still alive—that he could help our cause right now. We could use a seasoned Fèni-Ogun right now. But your revelation tells me he's not in a place I can reach."

"Where is he then?" I ask. "What does it mean to be between the river and the path?"

He flashes me his jackal smile. "That is a third question. What are you willing to give me in exchange?"

"I can tell you what the K'inu in Lleyria told me."

"No," he says flatly. "I can already guess that it wasn't anything good. You're not the first person the K'inu have spoken to."

I frown at this. "There was someone else?"

"Ask Tenjun's daughter." He grins. "Consider that a bonus answer."

It takes a moment for me to make sense of his words. What does Nana have to do with the K'inu?

He offers me a slight bow. "And now, we return to the matter at hand—the retrieval." He lifts a hand before I can muster a protest. Light pierces through the dark walls shrouding us, a hundred brilliant suns erupting in our faces. We are in the room again, Colin and Elodie awaiting us.

"I have nothing to give you," Ekwensi announces, casting me a piteous smile. "Perhaps, after you return from this mission, we can negotiate."

I frown, confused.

Colin sighs, touching my arm. "Let it go, Dèmi. He never budges when he's like this."

Ekwensi winks, and I understand now that Colin and Elodie were locked in time, unable to perceive that Ekwensi and I disappeared.

Ekwensi produces two red orbs that resemble marbled candies, holding them out to me and Elodie. "These will change your appearance, ensure your safety while you're in enemy territory. All you need to do is take the shell from the shelf Oyéré keeps it on, and bring it back. Keep the shell away from water."

Elodie snags one, popping it into her mouth. Her face begins to widen, her pert lips growing fuller, and her skin sprouts pockmarks. Her hair is now a muddy shade, running down her scalp in three long braids. Her noblewoman's garb has been transformed into the close-fitted black-and-red uniform of the thugs that attacked us earlier. She shakes her head, coughing. "That was quite spicy."

Ekwensi lifts an eyebrow. "Good to know. You now have the appearance of one of Oyéré's soldiers. The change will last so long as you don't touch iron. Any questions?"

"No," I say. I'll have to use my magic then to open the iron cage, but of course he didn't think to mention that. "I'm clear," I confirm.

"There's not one for me?" Colin bristles.

Ekwensi rises to his feet, slowly. "I already told you you're not going. In fact, you are not to set foot out of this place, Nicolás. Am I clear?"

"Is that an order?" Colin challenges, stepping up to him.

Ekwensi sighs and pats Colin's shoulder. "I will not order you, no. But whatever you do is at your own risk. I have no transformation magic for you."

The city bells ring, six ominous clangs that reverberate through our bodies. Halfway through Gull Hour now. Five hours until we leave the city—enough time to save Nana's life, move forward with a new army at my back.

Ekwensi transfers his gaze to me. "You may see Mari when you get there. But remember this, do not divert from your goal. Prove you're committed to this cause, that you're willing to sacrifice anything for it, and you will emerge the victor."

He hands me the remaining red orb. And with that, he wisps into smoke.

EBBING

THE MOMENT I STEP OUT OF THE ROOM, TA'ATIA IS THERE, AN ARROW jutting from her shoulder like a flag, her face cloth clinging in bloodied tatters to her cheeks. "The capital guards just left Nyzchow. They're riding for Gaeyak-Orin."

Colin flinches. "What?"

"Come with me," she commands, taking my arm. "You"—she jerks her chin at Elodie—"tell Tobias what I've discovered. Now."

Elodie crosses her now-broadened arms, no doubt emboldened by her disguise. "Those were not my orders," she responds in her newly deepened voice.

Ta'atia releases me, drawing a slender, razor-sharp shell dagger with yellow and pink streaks fanning out at its tip. She moves in, looming over Elodie. "A little magic can't fool my eyes. While you are in my home, you will heed my orders. Is that clear?"

Elodie backs away. "Absolutely." She spins on her heel and scurries off.

"Come," Ta'atia repeats, pulling me in the opposite direction.

"Wait." I place a hand on her arm. "I have to go to the Gardens, retrieve something for you before we leave the city—"

"I know," she interrupts. "I heard Tobias's plans."

I widen my eyes in surprise. "What? How?"

She rips off her face mask, revealing a too-wide smile, and a neck ringed with scars, old wounds scattered across her skin like love bites. "I am the owner of this house, the ruler of Mi'hayla. Nothing happens here without my notice. Now, hurry, you must speak with your guardian before you leave. I will help you if you promise to do that. Will you?"

I nod quickly.

"Wonderful." She beams, her lips drawing like a tightly strung bow. "I suspect you'll need my help. Men like Tobias always require contingency plans. When you are finished, I will send you to the Gardens myself. You have less time than Wolf Hour, but the guards should not reach here for some hours yet."

We race along, zigzagging through a series of low-ceilinged rooms connected by corridors. Then we enter a courtyard teeming with vegetation that crawls up the supporting pillars and trees swelling with fruits— juicy red ones shaped like gourds, plump mangoes bigger than a man's head, and tendrils of tamarinds that slip from branches like silkworms. In the center of it all is a pool full of bubbling water that rivals even the sky with its color.

Ta'atia leads us past this to a room overlooking the fruit-filled courtyard, weaving around the long chaises scattered about like sentinels. She stops at a set of double doors.

"These are my private quarters," she supplies. "Once we enter, no one can come in without my express permission."

She opens the door. The room, if it can be called that, is carpeted with lush grass that slicks against my ankles. Bright plants in reds, greens, golds, pinks, and blues grow from the muddy walls, their barbed tentacles coalescing around hard rings in the shape of an eye. The ceiling is an expanse of the night sky, complete with distant stars and a fingernail moon. An enormous gray shell stuffed with a thick mattress and heavy blankets sits under that moon, its glossy exterior shining like the surface of a pearl. Nana sleeps in the middle of that shell, bundled under a trove of blankets like buried treasure.

"Is this a portion of the Spirit Realm?" I ask.

Ta'atia nods as Li'uoa springs up from the marbled wall of the deep pool a few feet from the bed, rushing to examine the arrow in Ta'atia's shoulder, but the warlord waves her toward Nana.

"Wake her."

"She's been having visions. Her fits may return if I do—" Li'uoa protests.

"Wait, why—" I start.

"Wake her," Ta'atia repeats. "You will understand shortly."

Li'uoa nods, hurrying to Nana's side. She spreads long fingers over Nana's cheek, trailing them up to her forehead, and a faint pink aura appears at her fingertips.

"I come from a long line of Madsens," Ta'atia explains. "My mother was convinced our powers would be stronger if we stayed near water. Hence the pool."

"You're one of us?" Colin asks, eyes widening in surprise. I know what he's thinking. Madsen Oluso with affinity for water are common. Madsen Oluso who can form mirages are a near impossibility.

"My mother soon tired of the sea," Ta'atia continues. The lines around her eyes crinkle as she speaks, her cheekbones jutting out as she flashes a wistful smile. "It unsettled her stomach, and sometimes, when we spent too long by it—her mind. I came up with this as a compromise."

"Where is your mother now?" I ask softly. Maybe it is because she knew my mother and the pain in her voice reminds me of the hole in my heart every time I think of Mummy, but I suddenly want to know more about this woman.

"She disappeared a long time ago. Right after the Great War. She said she needed to find something she'd lost, but she would be back to fetch me. She never returned. Or, if she did, perhaps she missed me altogether. Visiting Aje merchants sold me up the river as okri."

I rub my clammy palms against my elbows, curling my arms around myself. I want to believe that Ta'atia's mother was prevented from return-ing to her child rather than abandoning her altogether, but there are some Oluso who leave their children behind out of choice, fearing that they can't protect their young ones whose magic hasn't awakened yet. It was a more common practice at the end of the Great War, when the power of the Oluso declined as a direct consequence of their betrayal of the Fèni-Ogun. The Ajes grew in power once they realized the Oluso now feared iron, and started to make moves to remove the Oluso from power once and for all.

Something tells me Ta'atia's mother abandoned her fledgling child.

Ta'atia's eyes spark with a sadness that seems to envelop the whole room. "Sometimes, I wonder if that is why I can never leave this place. I'm still waiting."

The room is silent, as though we are all holding a collective breath, giving space for Ta'atia's sorrow to be.

Then Nana stirs, chest rising and falling in a more pronounced fashion. Li'uoa presses her forehead to Nana's.

I take a step forward, but Ta'atia touches my arm. "The dreaming is a delicate process to extract a person from. Wait."

"The dreaming?" Colin asks.

"It's what we use for our injured. It calms the mind, gives them only things they wish to see."

She claps an arm around my shoulder, her eyes bright once more. "It was your mother who found and freed me nineteen years ago. Because of her, I have my own children now. Girls who had no one to turn to. I have no need to revisit the pain of the past."

If only it were that easy.

"It is for this reason, I implore you to speak with your guardian, bid her farewell before you leave on this journey. We must never take our partings for granted."

Nana springs up just then, clutching her chest. "Dèmi," she gasps through short, stuttering breaths. "Dèmi, something is wrong."

I dart over to her, taking her hands in mine. Her eyes are black marbles, the white swallowed up by the poison. Her hands are cold and waxy, as though there is no life in them at all. "Breathe, Nana. Please."

She sucks in another breath, and I glimpse her blackened tongue. "Will—Haru—they're dying."

"That's not possible—we have more time," I say, desperately wishing the words were true. There should be two days left still. Why is she getting worse?

"You did something," Colin says, staring at Li'uoa. "You hurt her."

"Don't be ridiculous," Li'uoa says. She turns away, stalking to the pool of water.

Nana screams, thrashing against me, and I let go. She rakes her hands over her chest as though she can claw out her heart.

I look to Ta'atia. "What is happening?"

Li'uoa thrusts her fingers into the pool. The water begins to churn, and steam whistles up from the surface. A watery orb erupts from the depths, flying towards Nana.

I swipe at the orb, but it evades me, splitting into smaller pieces and flying past. It knits itself together in front of Nana's face.

But now images shine on its fragile surface: Will sits lashed against a ship mast, blond hair blowing with the sea winds, black veins spreading from his eyes like sun rays. In his arms is an unmoving Haru. Her little face is expressionless, pale-gold skin now a wintry blue.

Nana stills, black tears running down her cheeks. "My baby," she cries. "No, please no."

We watch transfixed as Will rips off the bracelet on his wrist, freeing a flashing blue bead from the middle of it. He crushes the bead between his fingers, blowing the powdery remnants onto Haru's face.

In an instant, Haru opens her eyes, her mouth curling into a wail. Baba Sylvanus takes her from Will and bounces her against his hip.

"Your child is safe for now," Li'uoa reassures Nana. "Your mate was wise to give her some of his life. But the poison will work faster on her. Every time it tries to steal her life, you will feel it."

"Why is Haru ill?" I cry. "I don't understand."

Ta'atia explains. "Bitna affects family lines. There's a reason it's called a curse. It's not just parents who sicken but their children as well."

She gestures to Li'uoa, who is glaring at an apologetic Colin. "Come. Give these two a quick moment. Time is of the essence."

She shuffles them out of the room, leaving Nana and me alone.

Nana seems thinner than before, her soft cheeks whittled down like leftover tallow from a candle. Her back is bent, shoulders sagging as though the weight of life itself is crushing her.

I want to throw my head back and howl. I did this to her. This is my fault.

"Dèmi," she calls.

I clasp her hand in mine. "I'm here."

She pushes against me, swinging her legs onto the floor.

"Nana, I'm not sure it's a good idea to stand," I argue.

"I choose to stand," she snaps, jerking onto wobbly feet. Once she's upright, she breaks away from me, taking a stumbling step toward a pillar. I reach out to catch her, bracing my hands against her shoulders.

She takes a deep, shuddering breath. "Were we not on the way to Iya?" she asks after what feels like an eternity but I know is a mere breath.

"We were," I begin, but the lie feels heavy on my tongue. Taking a deep breath, I amend my words. "We weren't, no. I'm sorry."

Her pupilless, poison-filled eyes widen—bright, luminous orbs seemingly devoid of emotion, but when she speaks, I hear the betrayal and hurt thick in her voice. "You deceived me. You left me open to danger. I'm dying—Will is dying. Haru—" She breaks off, closing her eyes.

"I'm sorry," I plead. "But you won't die. I swear it. I promise I'll save you. This will be over in just a few hours."

She wrenches away from me, stepping back, and I can tell by the tremor in her arms how much the motion cost her. "Why?" she asks again. "How could you do this?"

My heart twists in anguish, hot shame filling my belly. "I couldn't lose you," I blurt, falling to my knees. "I couldn't do it. Mummy died, and all I had was you and Will and . . ." I pause, choking down the tears gathering in my throat. "The Council—Mari, she did this. She was going to take you from me. I couldn't let her win."

"Then why not seek Iya?" Nana cries. She seems even paler than before, her golden skin shining with sweat. Yet she edges against the pillar behind her, trying to stand tall. "Why engage in all this . . . deception?"

"It would have taken too long," I sob. "Two days is all we have. The spirits do not care for time as we do. They don't know what it is to lose as we do."

"So you chose for me. You decided it was better to gamble with my life."

I thrust Ekwensi's bead towards her. "I'm going to save you right now. All I need to do is get something for Ekwensi. If I succeed—when I succeed—Ekwensi will kill Mari. Your curse will be over."

She shakes her head, staring as though I am a stranger. "All this time . . . I could have been with my family. Held Haru again. Instead, I'm here with you—"

She breaks off, falling into a fit of quick, breathy gasps. I close my eyes against the tears clouding my vision. A part of me wants to remind her that I am—was—part of that family. That I needed her too. But I was wrong. I see that now, now that it's too late.

Colin raps at the door. "Dèmi, it's time. Ekwensi is headed this way."

Swiping a hand across my face, I stagger to my feet. "I have to go. I'm sorry."

"Wait."

Her cry stops me as I move to open the door. "Tell me just one thing. You could have left me to die. If it took too long, so be it. But you didn't even try to get to Iya. Why?"

"Iya would have made me choose," I say quietly, trying not to let my sorrow overwhelm me. "She only grants one request, and only to those she calls." I turn to face her, flashing her a wistful, tear-filled smile. "I know that I need my magic back, that I need to save the Oluso. But I can't imagine a world without you in it. I don't know how I would breathe. I can't even remember my mother's face. Don't ask me to lose you too."

Nana is silent, but her expression says it all. Her eyes swell with tears, her mouth trembles as she looks at me.

"I'm sorry," I say again. Then I leave the room, shutting the door behind me.

I march straight to Ta'atia, swiping at my tears. "Promise me you'll keep her safe," I demand.

"You saw those plants on the walls, yes?" she answers. "Those are amadu, sea guardians. Just like the elèsè are cave guardians." I remember the tentacled creatures that helped me when I visited my father in the Spirit Realm.

"If anyone unrecognized by me tries to enter the room, the amadu release a poison that will kill the intruder instantly. Nana alone will emerge unharmed. If that doesn't assure you, perhaps this will." She pauses, ripping the arrow out of her shoulder. The iron tip is viciously curved, encrusted with blue liquid. I stare, shocked. I have never seen an Oluso withstand the touch of iron for so long.

"I will let no harm come to your guardian," Ta'atia declares. "You have this as my solemn promise."

"Thank you," I say, breathing a sigh of relief. Her pledge, more than anything, lessens the fear squeezing my lungs.

"A word of warning: do not touch the waters outside." Her eyes grow as dark and hard as an obsidian blade. "When I was with you, you had free rein, but the river in the city is the lifeblood of a particular spirit. If you touch it, it has the power to grant your heart's desire, but it might just eat your heart in exchange."

Footsteps sound out then, and Li'uoa reappears, a transformed Elodie in tow. "Time to go."

Ta'atia lowers her voice to a whisper. "This is the help I can give. If you're in danger, draw some blood with the shell you find." Then she draws back. "Good luck," she says, loud enough for Elodie to hear. "We'll make a handmaiden of you yet."

"I'd love to be a handmaiden," Elodie mutters.

Li'uoa ushers us into the fruit-filled courtyard, and we sidestep mangoes and prickly bushes with torch ginger flowers hanging off, their petals dangling open like bloody mouths overfilled with flesh.

When we come to the bubbling pool, she places a hand against my temple and I flinch at the icy touch of her skin against mine.

"You're headed to the Gardens. The waters will take you where you need to go. The rest is up to you."

Elodie peers at the pool, studying it. "What does that even mean?"

"Precisely what I said." Li'uoa sniffs.

I tug at Colin's arm, pulling him aside. "I need you to stay here, watch over Nana."

Colin groans. "Dèmi, you can't be serious—"

"I am. You protect Nana while I can't. If she's in danger, take her to Baba. I will get what I need from Mari and come back."

He studies me, and I lift my chin, holding my back straight. Mummy's words brush my ears again.

Eluó òr mudiàn nosèn ghè odumah bhé èlo. *The hare stands tall under the gaze of the lion.*

I need to project power, strength, even though the fear that grips my heart is enough to sink me. I have to believe I can save Nana. Then there's a part of me, the part that burns with the memory of what happened in the betrothal hall, reminding me that killing Mari is an alternative to completing this mission. But I silence that part. I've caused enough trouble. It's time to face the consequences. I have to carry through this mission for more than just Nana. This mission is a chance to free the Oluso once and for all, so families can never be torn apart like this again.

"Promise me you will run at the first sign of danger," Colin concedes.

I smile. "I promise I'll be careful."

"That's not what I said—"

"I know."

He sighs. "Just focus on getting the shell. Mari is no easy opponent."

"Neither am I."

"She's survived like a snake all this time, killing Oluso, wriggling into every hole. You need to be extra careful." He grips my hand. "Promise me."

Sighing, I nod.

He folds a small glass bead into my hands, the deep blue of it resembling the threads of his magic. "If you're in trouble, crush this. I'll come, even if I have to fight to get you out." He brings my hand to his lips, brushing a kiss over my fingers. "Good to have you back. Don't make me lose you again."

I flick his cheek. "You stay alive until I see you next."

Li'uoa clears her throat, and I pull my hand from Colin's grasp.

Li'uoa steps back and I stand over the water, looking down into its depths. The pool is surprisingly deep, its crisp blue waters reflecting the burning-red sun as it sinks toward the earth in a fiery kiss. In the richness of that surface, I catch a glimpse of someone behind me—a blue-skinned omioja with a slim nose and jagged teeth longer than any omioja's I've ever seen. The omioja raises a hand and I turn to find Li'uoa's hand in the same position. She shoves me into the water.

I tumble into the pool, a rush of warm water seeping into my nostrils. I gasp, struggling to breathe, and kick my feet toward the light above my head, but something is pulling me down and away.

I sink.

My chest is burning, my mouth and nose clogged with water. My eyes are stinging, but I squint against the black depths, holding on to the sliver of light now sinking farther away. The world seems to be an endless stream of blue half-darkness, the water's soft yet forceful fingers ferrying me along. Then I burst out into the air, colors spiraling across my vision until I hit the ground with a thud.

I lie there, staring at the impossibility of the gold-trimmed sky. Red clouds gather like rust, the silver-white streaks of lightning passing through them sharp enough to split a tree. There is a scuffling, no doubt the wind stirring the pebbles on the ground. The air is pregnant with the scent of water tangling with the earth—it is only a matter of time before the rain comes. I need to hurry.

Sucking in a breath, I roll gingerly to my feet and take stock of my surroundings. I am standing on a footpath, a small puddle at my feet. A moment later, Elodie appears, slamming into the dirt.

She rubs her back, groaning. "Did she really have to push me like that?"

"Something tells me her strength isn't the same as ours," I answer, offering Elodie a hand. Omioja strength is ten times an Oluso's, but Elodie has no way of knowing that. Li'uoa probably thought she was touching us lightly. I wonder briefly, how Ta'atia convinced an omioja to work with her after all.

At the end of the path is a foothill, dressed in wildflowers and mixed patches of brown and green shrubbery. A tunnel peers out through the dense foliage creeping over its base, letters and images etched into its stone walls. I shudder as I stare into its promised darkness, reminded of the okè giga, the stern-faced mountain spirits rumored to sleep throughout the land, waiting for Ìyá-Ilé to rise again. The crystal lying against my chest hums briefly as though in confirmation. I take it out, but there is no color in it—a fluke.

Pushing Ekwensi's bead onto my tongue, I wait as the bead burns its way down my throat. Then the world shifts—suddenly I can see from a much higher vantage point, and my hands are paler than ash.

"Shango fire you," I curse, and a male voice booms out. "Now I have to speak flawless Ceorn."

Elodie erupts into a bout of laughter. "Oh, you should see yourself." She tangles her fingers into my now-wispy blond hair, drawing it like a curtain closer to my face. "You are a little cute though."

I shrug her off. "What's the plan? Where do we find the shell?"

"My mother's letters only mentioned it being in Oyéré and Mari's shared bedroom. It's some kind of magical tool."

I nod, then turn to face the tunnel. "This is going to be dangerous. Once we enter, I can't guarantee your safety."

Her smile only deepens. "I can handle myself." Without another word, she sprints off, breaking for the tunnel.

A vulture hanging on top of the hill takes off, black and white feathers spilling as it catches air. I watch its ascent, then, as it soars into the horizon, I run after Elodie.

THIEVERY

WE WALK IN SILENCE, THE SOUND OF OUR BOOTS SLOSHING AGAINST THE thin stream of water coating the ground echoing through the cavern. As we get farther in and the dim light from the opening fades away, the smell of oil smothers the air like a blanket. I take a torch hanging from the damp walls and dip it in the stream at our feet before striking it against the wall. The torch flame sprouts into being with a hiss, illuminating the slick brown-and-red liquid swimming atop the receding swell of murky water, clinging to our feet like kwasho bugs gathering in the summertime. I lift the torch higher, lighting the path forward, where more liquid swells and bubbles like a boiling ofada stew. But this is no fermented palm oil and locust-bean delight. There's enough oil here to burn us alive.

Elodie jumps, an anxious expression breaking through her usually confident facade. "Hold that thing higher. I'd prefer not to be turned to ashes."

I lower it slightly just to annoy her, but I creep closer to the wall, hanging on to the drier bits of stone that peek out as we wade into the stew. We come to a split, three paths like gaping mouths in the darkness, promising to devour us. They're all fairly identical except the left-most path boasts a tangle of vines with trumpet flowers that swell through, their pouting lips dripping bits of nectar.

"This way," Elodie says, pointing at the flowers.

We are immediately rewarded with sounds that prick our ears like knives, moans and bouts of laughter that bounce off the tunnel walls like ghosts in search of a mortal body. The tunnel opens to a hollowed outcropping that stretches wide and far, forming a smooth ring that travels several feet deep. I crouch to my belly, crawling to the edge of the wooden platform secured to the cavern wall as Elodie hangs back at the tunnel. There are several of these, six feet apart, ringing the cavern like teeth in the mouth of an elèsè. Between these platforms are rope ladders, and farther below, where the platforms furrow into full ledges, people spread out around a fire, faces obscured by a haze of smoke that curls around them.

Only when I stretch a little farther do I understand why this place is called the Gardens. Deep in the heart of the cavern, five levels down, a sea of red flowers sways in the cool cavern air, petals fluttering like young maidens' dresses at festival time. People weave around the flowers as though they fear waking a sleeping child, stopping only to coax a few swanning above the rest into pouches tied to their waists. The harvesters with fuller baskets of koko tie their bounty to ropes hanging down from the platforms above, and iron bells tethered to the levers at the other end of that rope set off in chorus, their shrill and steady cries echoing throughout the cavern. A group of people come running immediately, like starved dogs at the scent of food, nearly knocking each other off the upper platform as they rush to the levers.

"What is that awful noise?" Elodie says, startling me into a lurch.

"Shh!"

I edge back, careful to keep my movements small. There's not much room to hide in a place like this, only a few crevices, natural formations in the cave walls that offer the embrace of shadow. Once we descend from this first platform, everyone will be able to see where—and who—we are. We have to be careful, deliberate with everything we do.

"What are we waiting for?" Elodie asks.

I bristle, annoyed. "If you haven't noticed, there's not an easy way to get down there. We need to map out where we're going."

She continues, unfazed. "Annika said Mari and Oyéré shack up on the third level. We only need to go that far."

I quirk an eyebrow. "Annika? The woman we captured? How did you get her to tell you anything?"

She grins. "I told you already: I have a way with women. The koko pipe helped too. You know—"

Her next words are swallowed by the sound of boots splashing against the oil in the main tunnel behind us. People are coming and there's nowhere to hide.

I pull her along, stepping over some abandoned weapons. "This way."

We dart over to one of the platforms, reaching the attached woven basket held up by twin ropes just as a voice swims out from the mouth of the cavern.

"Moloi!" a guard calls, waving. I'm not sure if he means me or Elodie.

"Wave at him," I mutter, lifting my hand in a semi-wave.

The guard cocks his head, then bounds over, torch in hand. He thrusts the light in front of our faces, getting close to us. "Ah," he says, squinting. "Dragzby is here too. Duma nu'meir!"

I recognize the Ashkenayi phrase for *good harvest* and respond in kind.

He grins. "Haven't seen you in days. Thought you two had run off together. Katsa will be glad you're back!"

"Where is Katsa?" Elodie replies, fluttering her eyelashes at him.

He tuts at her. "No, no, Moloi," he says. "I know better than to fall for that. I'm not getting in the middle of you two's relationship with Katsa. I don't know why you three decided to be together, but you'll have to work it out."

I blink, trying to keep my eyes from widening. "Yes," I bluster. "Can you steer this thing so we can get down to . . . er . . . Katsa?"

He chuckles, clapping me on the back. "Always a jokester, Dragzby." Then he leans closer, whispering in my ear. "The others left their posts for the party on level seven, so I'll let this slide just once. Next time, though, just use the ladders and don't look down."

I quirk my lips in a half smile. "Thank you."

He claps my back again in answer, then he opens the wooden basket. "Hop in. I'll send you down."

Elodie and I scramble into the basket. The stench of koko clings to the reedy material, and its splintered ends scratch at my neck, forcing me into a near hug with Elodie.

"What level?" the guard asks.

"Three, please," Elodie responds.

"I thought you patrolled level four," he says, scratching his balding head. I open my mouth, trying to think up an excuse, but he brightens. "Ah, you're trying to surprise Katsa then? Good luck."

I bite back a scream as the basket drops, careening into the abyss. My heart stutters in panic and I jostle against it, feeling the mockery of the cool cavern air as I fall. Then the basket stops, seizing in midair.

Elodie whoops, "That was amazing!"

"Shh!" I press a finger against her lips.

The platform awaiting us is full of guards, distributed in different pockets along the cavern walls like mushrooms. Some are hunched over games of dice and cards, barks of laughter punctuated by cries of frustration. Others are slumped against the walls, heads lolling as they sleep. A few are patrolling, pacing back and forth in the same routine, and even then, most hold koko pipes between their lips.

"The room is supposed to be the biggest cave," Elodie whispers, breath tickling my finger. I yank back my hand immediately and she hooks an arm around my waist. "Don't forget, we're lovers. You have to prepare to act the part."

Smirking, I lean down, let my lips hover close to hers. Her gaze drops to my mouth, and she flicks out her tongue, moistening her lower lip. I put a hand around her neck, and jerk her head to the side, pointing out the well-lit cavern only a few paces away.

"Remember what Ekwensi said," I taunt. "Focus."

She snorts, clambering out of the basket. "You can't satisfy me anyway."

Giggling, I follow suit.

Six guards cluster in front of Mari and Oyéré's cave, watching two scorpions fight. A few look up as we approach but only one keeps track of us, the others returning to their fun.

The lone guard slides out of the group, coming to meet us. "Hey, Dragzby. I thought you'd be on level seven," she says, running a hand over her freshly shorn hair. "Didn't you hear? Some gang leader sent us wine for weeks. Lined up at the entrance this evening."

My gut tells me that wine supplier is Ekwensi. I just smile and nod.

The guard lifts an eyebrow. "Not feeling talkative today?"

Elodie saves me. "He's a bit down. We've had work on the surface for a few days."

The woman nods. "Say no more. It's better down here by far." She lights her pipe, offering it to me with a tilt of her head.

"I'm on sentry duty," I respond, pushing it away.

The woman shoots me a quizzical look, and Elodie steps in, lowering her voice. "He's missing Katsa, so we were hoping to get to her."

The guard's puzzled frown turns into a piteous smile. She nods at a nearby cave where two bodies writhe, the sound of moans echoing off the walls.

"Katsa has moved on." She coughs. "I would too."

Elodie pouts, then she nods at Oyéré's cave. "We came down to get something for the mistress. Mind if we go in really quickly, Nadine?"

I bite the inside of my cheek, burying my surprise. Of course Elodie would know the guards' names—she probably extracted that from Annika as well.

The woman eyes us again, then Elodie flicks out a lighter, putting it under the woman's pipe. Sweet smoke chokes the air between our faces as the koko powder goes up in flames.

I hold my breath, trying my best not to turn away.

The woman waves the smoke away after a moment. "Why not?" she says. "It's a celebration day. We're moving to the capital soon anyway."

Elodie beams, her false mouth stretching wide. "Thank you."

We slink into the cave as Nadine returns to the scorpion watchers. The cavern room is simple. Two tables—one fairly long, some leather-backed chairs, and a large bed smothered with pillows. A recessed shelf runs along the cave wall, sitting above one of the tables, and right in the corner of it is an iron cage with a conch inside. The shell is the size of both my palms put together, with a worn exterior as though it has been bandied through the storms of life.

"Look out for me," I whisper to Elodie.

Then I creep forward, getting close to the cage. Taking a steadying breath, I stretch my fingers, tugging gently at the threads of my magic. I can't afford to lose control here and get us caught.

The iron creaks as it stretches, two bars inching apart. As it warps, fresh pain knifes through my back. I hiss, trying to hold on. The stationed guards erupt into cheers, drowning the noise.

"Hey, Moloi, come see this!" Nadine calls, looking up.

Elodie scurries over, blocking me from sight. "What's happening?"

My heart thunders at the sudden interruption. The iron wrenches violently apart, letting out a squeal.

Nadine lifts her head again. "What was that?"

Elodie stumbles, falling into Nadine's arms. "Sorry," she says. "Two left feet."

Nadine lets out a throaty laugh. "And here I thought you were trying to proposition me."

Slipping a hand through the wreckage of the cage, I grab the spire of the conch. It's heavy, with deep ridges that fit the pads of my fingers. I stuff it into the hidden pocket of my cloak, but the spire sticks out a little, nudging against my belly.

It's done. Nana, Will, and Haru will be freed with this. I can finally leave this city, work toward freedom with the Oluso.

I rush to the cavern mouth, clearing my throat, when I spot Elodie with Nadine against a wall. Elodie presses another kiss against the guard's neck, then she kisses her fingers. "I shall return, my dear."

Nadine gifts her a dreamy, flustered smile.

"Do you always have to seduce them?" I ask as we take long strides toward the ladders sticking out from the cliff face, just a pace away from breaking into a run.

"It's the easiest way to get information," she sniffs. "People respond to arousal. Sex or fear, it's all the same thing."

We reach the ladders, but before I can climb, she puts a hand on my shoulder. "Nadine says they have another stash, on the first level. It's a hole in the wall, literally. Mari and Oyéré put some things in there in view of everyone and check it every day. If anything goes missing, the whole camp is punished."

"Why are you telling me this?" I say, casting a look about. "We have what we came for."

She shrugs. "Just thought there might be something fun there."

An idea occurs to me then, gnawing at me like a fire ant determined to clear the way for a nest. What if the talisman is in this stash? I could use it to heal Nana, make certain Ekwensi can't renege on his end of the deal. It could be my guarantee.

I pinch my arm. No. I have to stay focused on the goal. All I have to do is get this shell back to Ta'atia.

I start to climb, cognizant of the way the wood creaks as my weight sags onto it. Elodie follows after me, and soon we're on the first level again.

I scan the platform. The first guard is nowhere to be found, no doubt drinking in the depths with the others. Pausing a moment, I search for a nook, a split in the dark walls that might house a stash. There's a small spot, a slit in the gray stone shaped like the reptilian eye of a gwylfin, wide enough for the two of us to shove ourselves into, if we're careful.

"You see it too?" Elodie asks. "What if we just peeked? We don't have to take anything. The exit is right there."

Curiosity nibbles at me, urging me forward.

Sighing, I acquiesce. "We're only looking. No touching."

She nods. "Of course." Then she grins wide. "Unless there's treasure to steal. I like lovely things, don't you?"

"This way," I say, snatching Elodie's arm.

Pressing myself flat against the wall, I tread as quietly as I can over the wooden boards. Elodie stumbles after me, stepping on a rotting plank, and it squeals against her boot, a whine so loud that a woman on the fourth platform looks out. I stop, my breath caught in my throat, the pounding of my heart filling my ears.

A man curls his arm against the woman's shoulder and she turns away. I tug Elodie's arm and skirt another rotted plank, fingers slipping into that small groove. There in the split, are three threadbare sacks. A faint silver aura emanates from one—magic.

My heart thrums in my chest. Here is my leverage, the talisman that could free Nana, spur her to forgive me. But somehow I can't bring myself to pick it up.

"Success." Elodie pumps her fist, snatching up one of the bags. She rips open the mouth to reveal several jewels, cowrie shells, and gold coins.

She stuffs the bag into her cloak and reaches for the one with the silvered aura. I block her hand.

"What?"

"Not that one," I answer. "That one is mine."

Then I take the pouch and rip it open, my fingers brushing against a cold smoothness. The talisman is a small plaque with carved welts that curl into the fine, expressive script of Goma-dori, Nana's native language. Joy swells in my chest. Finally.

Then footsteps erupt from the mouth of the cave, so many that it sounds as though the water itself is chattering from cold.

Slipping the talisman in my cloak pocket, I leap into the groove, yanking Elodie to me and keeping my arms tight on her shoulders as she slots into the embrace of the cave wall. We stand, bodies pressed together tighter than the fit on an Eingardian court-approved corset—only a fist's separation between our faces, breathing hard. If we're caught by this treasure trove, we might end up delayed, reaping a punishment that would reveal our identities.

The footsteps ring out of the tunnel.

"Did we entertain any visitors while I was gone?" a woman shouts. Her voice is loud and assured, smoother than the leather of a newly crafted scabbard, a voice that has haunted my waking moments and stalked me in nightmares for months. Mari.

"No one, my lady," someone calls from the platform directly below.

"What did Annika send a message for then?" Mari mutters, stepping onto the edge of the platform.

She's dressed in a dark-red coat littered with spines that wave in salute as she moves, exposing the fitted breastplate vest and trousers beneath. She looks relaxed, a smile playing on her pale lips, the scar running from her eye to the edge of her mouth softened in the pale-orange glow of the torches studding the cavern walls like precious stones. But the array of weapons hanging from her belt like trophies gathered during a hunt tell a different story. The pouch bulging against her hip is stained with red deeper than the ruby richness of the koko flowers below. She takes an-other step, one foot toeing the edge of the platform, and the pouch drips fresh liquid that pitter-patters to the ground like rain, forming a puddle.

Some of the liquid drips onto the quills studding her coat, and to my surprise, they let out a low shriek and stretch away, huddling together like children taking shelter in a rainstorm. Bile fills my mouth and my stomach churns with grief as I realize what I'm looking at. Mari is wearing the hide of a shuku shuku, prized for its resistance to all elements, a living memory of the sacred animal designed to protect the Oluso it sheds its hide for. I bite the inside of my already bruised cheek, trying to contain the rage roaring in me like a furnace.

"Bisi reported a nest of rats at the east end, my love," another woman says, twining her arms around Mari's waist.

This woman is tall, with honeyed brown skin that peeks out from a patchwork of leather and furs, and wavy dark hair shaved on one side that curls into a wave framing her slim face. This must be Oyéré.

"You believe the men we lost today were killed by rodents? Or are you admitting you've given these fools too much free rein?" Mari asks, voice lowered in a dangerous whisper. "I won't have them killing each other when my back is turned."

Oyéré throws her hands up, a gold medallion thrumming against her ample chest. There is no doubt now that she is the one Fox Bead spoke of.

"They cannot control themselves," she says. "The drug is too much. My best warriors behave like bulls in the arena. All they see, want, or smell is koko. It's a wonder Annika survived the rot as long as she did. Perhaps one of them put her out of her misery."

Elodie cranes her neck, twisting to get a better look, and I shove her back, notching my hand against the curve of her neck.

"If I knew secret missions would get you looking my way, I would have tried them long ago," she whispers, smirking at me. "Then again, you were always so tangled up with Jonas. He's not here with you now though, is he?"

I bare my teeth, wishing the cave walls would split and swallow me up. This is not the time for her foolery.

Mari turns, seizing the other woman's chin. "You've had a lot to say lately. Tell me, Oyéré, do you wish to escape our partnership? Go back to the woman who abandoned you with your tail between your legs?"

Oyéré stares back, meeting Mari's flinty gaze with a fiery one of her own. Then after a moment, she lowers her eyes and mutters, "I just fear if this will work. If we can't control what the drug does to them, can we do anything after all?"

"You leave those worries to me," Mari responds. She shifts slightly, turning her body toward us, and I burrow farther into the crevice, not daring to breathe. Elodie follows suit, but her ribbon comes loose, whipping off her wrist and dancing into the cool cavern air.

"You are right, my love," Mari says. She lunges forward, sliding to a stop at the mouth of the crevice. "We have rats."

"I can explain, Mistress," I sputter. "We noticed someone else here earlier, and we were just checking that everything is intact."

She lets out a noise of appreciation. "Hm. Very good." Then she trails her finger down my cheek, snatching at a hunk of my braids. "Come now, Dèmi, do you think I no longer remember your face?"

I lift my hand, but my pale skin is gone—faded to brown. I've shifted back.

Shit.

Surging forward, I throw a punch, but Mari is already ducking out of the way, unsheathing her blade as I stumble into a pivot. Elodie pushes off the wall, slamming her shoulder into Mari's waist as Oyéré drops her torch, diving to catch her lover before she tumbles off the edge of the platform.

"Run!" I scream. But instead Elodie darts closer, aiming a kick at Oyéré's stomach. Oyéré catches her by the leg, hurling Elodie off the ground and flinging her over the chasm.

"No!" I leap forward, arms outstretched, sending a ball of wind that folds around Elodie like a web, drawing her back toward the platform. My back flares immediately, pain surging as my skin puckers into another welt. Mari rushes me again, this time with a curved copper blade that blazes orange in the light of the torches, and there's barely any time to dodge before it bites into my forearm. I cry out and stagger back, dropping my arms. Elodie falls, and for a moment I'm sure I failed, but she crashes onto the platform, scrambling for purchase like a fish returned to the sea. There are shouts from below as soldiers abandon their pipes, emerging from clouds of smoke like ghouls, scurrying up rope ladders in haste to get to us.

"Nowhere to run, little girl," Mari snarls. "This time you and I finish what we started."

Oyéré yanks Elodie up by the hair and I look around, searching for an opening, anything that could get us out of this mess. Nothing. I curse myself, hissing as the wound in my arm burns anew. I press my fingers against the ripped flesh, trying in vain to keep blood from spilling out. I can't heal myself on a whim, burn through more magic when I'm untethered. There's no telling when my magic will disobey me, spiral out of my control, and I need to get us out of this cave. I should have never have stopped for the talisman, or better yet, I should have forced Ekwensi to retrieve it for me once I returned with the shell. But here I am again, nowhere closer to what I need.

Then my eyes land on Oyéré's abandoned torch, its flames waving like a mischievous child. An idea takes root, spreading through my mind like poisonous blooms through clear water.

"All right," I say. My heart is pounding, my limbs sagging with the weight of the day's events. But I draw my feet apart, lower my arms as though in surrender. "You win."

Mari narrows her eyes. "You think me foolish? You forget—I saw you in the arena. I know what you're really like." She smiles, something like pride shining in her eyes. "You may not have Yetu's gift for strategy, but you have her strength—tenacity. I loved that most about her."

I bite my lip, holding in the anger that explodes at the sound of my mother's pet name on Mari's lips. I want to tear that smile off her face, turn that light radiating from her eyes into shadowed fear. I want to see her weak and bleeding, the way she left Nana. Instead, I concentrate, letting the wind wisp about my fingers, imagining a string wrapping around the wooden body of that torch. The wind spirits bubble up from the ground, coalescing into a thick plank instead. My back screams, muscles spasming as though there are several knives piercing me at once.

I buckle, sinking to my knees and putting my hands on my head. I don't know how much more of this pain I can endure.

"You win," I rasp, keeping my eyes on Mari.

"Thank you," she crows. "I am more merciful to those who surrender."

I rock back, willing that plank to move and slam the torch into the waiting tunnel. Instead the plank morphs into a ball that knocks into the torch. The torch tumbles away from the soldier standing nearest it. My head is pounding now, my vision blurring.

Please, Oya, I pray, calling on the premier spirit of the wind. *Let that torch make it!*

Oyéré comes to Mari's side, leaving Elodie to the care of soldiers who crowd around her like hyenas panting over the last piece of meat. One of the soldiers brushes Elodie's cheek with his sword and her appearance reverts back.

"Yetu?" Oyéré asks.

Mari shrugs off Oyéré's heavy stare. "No one."

"My mother!" I shout, clenching my fist. The torch flies into the air, protruding from the dark of the tunnel like a discerning eye.

Thank you, Oya.

A soldier catches sight of the torch and gasps, diving for it. I unfurl my fingers, imploring the torch to spin, but it merely wobbles, then clatters to the ground. More soldiers turn at the commotion, gasps becoming shouts. The pain is so much now that I can hardly speak.

"I may not have my mother's gift for strategy," I gasp, "but I am her child. And there's something every child learns early—" Twisting my mouth into a shaky smile, I slap my hands together. The torch spins then jumps, descending into the oil-soaked liquid like lightning dropping from the sky.

"Don't play with fire."

Flames erupt as the torch hits the ground, sparking a cloud of heat and smoke that smothers the air. Soldiers scatter, leaping for the safety of rope ladders; others race towards barrels sitting on the end of the platform. Oyéré pulls off her cloak, beating at the flames before they can swim farther in and spread to the wider pool of oil deeper in the tunnel.

Elodie staggers to her feet, covering her mouth and nose as she wades through the smoke.

Ripping the conch from my cloak, I drag it against my palm, crying out as it bites into me. Then I toss it to Elodie, praying she makes it out. "Go!"

This is our best chance. With luck, Ta'atia will make good on her promise and come to help me. But at least if the shell makes it back, Ekwensi will save Nana. That's all I can hope for now.

I turn as something strikes my cheek, sending a shower of sparks across my vision. Blood fills my mouth, choking me as pain sings through my jaw. Mari appears through the smoke like a vision, the hilt of her blade stained with fresh blood.

"You always choose the difficult path," she rages, slamming her fist into my ribs. I fly back, crashing into the cavern wall, its ridged fingers tearing at my skin as air screams from my lungs. "Must you be broken before you understand?"

The wind shifts as she bears down on me again, but my head is ringing, darkness warring with the glare of flames consuming my vision. I clutch at the wall, fighting to steady myself, but my body is heavy, every ragged breath a knife puncturing my chest. My iron magic is screaming, clawing against my skin like an animal desperate for freedom. All I can do is close my eyes and perform lilé, envisioning my body covered by a mountain of shields. My magic spreads in a layer over my skin, and though Mari's blows rain down on me like an avalanche, brutal and unrelenting, I feel nothing.

My vision clears as Mari nears me once more, the flames between us bending away as the quills on her cloak breeze by them. "Look at you," she says, dragging me up by my chin. "All this wasted potential. Fighting for people who will never acknowledge your sacrifices. I feel almost sorry for you."

"That's why you tried to kill me?"

She grins. "If I wanted you dead, I wouldn't have used poison."

"How kind of you. I'm shaking with gratitude."

"Don't you wonder why I didn't have you killed? Why your life means anything to me? You *need* me, so why can't you accept it?"

I spit, lobbing a mix of blood and saliva in her eye. "You should wonder why *your* life means anything to me."

She backhands me and I slam into the wall, pain splitting my skull.

A few soldiers succeed in breaking open one of the barrels, and water gushes out, flooding the platform. The fire only grows, expanding into a blaze that engulfs everything. There is a fire in my chest now, too, burning everything inside me. I am going to die.

Then I catch a glimpse of flyaway golden hair as Elodie disappears into the embrace of the tunnel. Cursing, Oyéré bolts in after her. The shock of cold water against my skin makes me wince, shocking me into alertness. I crawl, getting to my knees as the water cascades around me. Elodie is out. It's now or never.

"This is for my mother!" I scream.

Pushing off my heel, I charge forward, head lowered. Mari barely has a moment before I collide with her, shoving with all my might until we catapult off the edge, feet falling away from the hard surety of the ground.

We fall, spinning toward the blood-red sea below, but I don't let go of her arms, clutching her to me with all my might. It's better we die here together, that the world be rid of her evil, even if it costs me everything. This way, too, Nana will be free, and the Oluso will have struck a heavy blow against the enemy.

Moments from smashing into the koko-covered abyss, I close my eyes. The memories of the people I've loved and lost flash through my mind—Mummy, Nana, Will, Colin—Jonas. I wish for the barest of moments that I could see him smile at me again, dawn eyes sparkling with joy when I walk into the room.

Then something loops around my waist, stopping me in midair. I open my eyes to find we are encased in a bubble, water sluicing over us like a mother caressing her children's cheeks. The bubble reverses course, flying toward the roof of the cave.

Oyéré stands at the platform's edge, holding out the glowing conch with one hand. Her other hand is busy curving a knife over Elodie's throat like a satisfied grin.

"I'm sorry," Elodie says. "Couldn't run fast enough."

We've failed. Nana is as good as dead. I want to rage, but I am spent, numb as we float towards the platform, wobbling a bit as the water falls away like an oversized cloak. Mari falls through, hitting the ground with a satisfying thud, but the water ferries me safely down, depositing me on shaky feet before burrowing into the hollow of the shell.

Oyéré abandons Elodie, rushing to her side as Mari lifts her head, blood spilling from her nose. It's probably broken again. Good.

Then something snatches at my ankle, yanking me to the ground. I thrash, clawing at the white residue swallowing my leg, cementing me to the ground with every motion. Soldiers crowd in, carrying white sheets that gleam like freshly shined pearls, and slick and slip over their fingers like oil. I throw my arms up as they fling the sheets at me, but the material swims over my skin, hardening into a cocoon as it unfolds.

"You should've listened while I was being kind," Mari says. Then she slams her fist into my eye and the world melts away, eaten up in a wave of darkness.

TUMBLING

I COME TO, BURIED IN THE DARK, WRAPPED IN A THICK COCOON SUSPENDED over a dying fire. My arms are trapped at my sides, my eye stinging from Mari's blow. My knees are bent beneath me, but my stomach is thankfully no longer churning.

"It's oruka," Nadine offers, lighting her koko pipe a few feet away. "The more you struggle, the tighter it binds. You might suffocate if you're not careful."

Now I recall the beaten rubber sheets spread out in the fields of Ikolé, the excitement with which Mama Seyi, our local rubber tapper, spoke of secret Ashkenayan techniques that would make the white gold drip faster from trees and harden like calabashes.

"Where am I?" I ask.

The female guard tosses me a piteous look. "At the end of your life."

Then she walks away.

My head dangles awkwardly out of the cocoon, my neck muscles knotting with each moment I remain aloft. At first I wait, thinking someone will come for me, but as time passes, shadows inching over the wall as the fire quiets to a smolder, I wriggle, tangling myself in the ropes holding me enough to tuck my head against them.

There are a few rattan stools shoved in the corner, keeping company with cracked mugs and slim pipes on plates stuffed to the brim with white powder. I count the legs on those stools, then the pipes and mugs, over and over again, trying to keep my mind from descending into the frenzy lurking in its depths.

Mari will come. There's no way she'll leave me here. Or Colin will once he realizes I'm not back. There will be time to get Nana help. The spirits won't abandon me. Maybe Elodie will escape. Everything is not lost yet.

I string the thoughts together like soldiers gathering on front lines, each waging a battle against the fear that threatens to unravel me. Then when my head grows heavy and I lose count of the number of stool legs, I close my eyes again and think of the people I love. Jonas's soft smile as he peers down at me during a dancing lesson, the strength of his hand at my back as we move together, cutting through the room. Colin's laughter as a moth lands on my nose and I jump into his arms in fear. Nana's steady gaze as she hands me my first knife and guides my fingers to its tip. The warmth of her skin as she teaches me to feel its weight, and use that to judge how far I need to throw. The sound of Mummy's voice as she braids my hair, her song curling over me like a blanket, soothing the chill from my skin.

Ọjọ iwaju jẹ imọlẹ, ọmọ mi,
  ọkan mi,
Awọn owo ni awọn ẹiyẹ,
isokuso fun iṣẹju kan,
mimi lati mu ara wọn
  lẹẹkansi,
Ṣugbọn nigbati ayọ ba de,
Awọn ẹmi yoo jo,
Ati awọn afẹfẹ pe awọn
  oromodie kekere wọnyẹn,
Ki o si fun wọn ni iyẹ lati fo kuro
	The future is bright, my child,
	  my heart,
	Sorrows are birds,
	Perching for a moment,
	A breath to catch themselves
	  again,
	But when joy comes,
	The spirits will dance,
	And winds call up those little
	  chicks,
	And give them wings to fly away

I hum the tune, letting tears bead on my cheeks, missing the comfort of that voice. Then suddenly the tune grows louder, the words rushing against my ears. I open my eyes to find Mari singing, her rough voice swelling into the sweet melody, every word nearly perfect save for the words for joy and spirits that take on a decided Ceornian lilt.

I stare transfixed, dumbfounded as she finishes, brushing a finger against an errant tear hanging from her eyelash.

"Don't look at me like that, girl," she says, sitting down. "That song was mine before it was yours. Yetu sang it to me at night when we were children."

I suck in a ragged breath, surprised at the ache that blossoms in my chest, the hunger that sweetens every word. This is a portrait of my mother, pieces from the life she had before me, gathered like a child's collection of shells.

Mari continues, my silence all the consent she needs. "Camilla may be my cousin, but my branch of the family was poor. Beast workers, fit only for the slaughterhouse and fields. I was included in the maid selection for the royal family because my mother was an Ayn. A lowly girl who ran away with the first man to look her way. But I came to Castle Benin with nothing. Not even a cup."

She throws a handful of broken sticks and leaves on the dying fire, then she crouches, blowing a piece of kindling to sparks. I wait, not daring to breathe. A tiny flame yawns out of the carnage, and she coaxes it, feeding it smaller pieces of wood. Finally, the silence is too much for me to bear and I ask, words tumbling out, "What happened?"

She settles onto one of the rattan stools. "Yetu chose me from a selection of a hundred and two girls. Many had the finest lineages and came from wealthy families. But she walked up and slipped her fingers into mine." Her voice lowers into a trembling whisper as she imitates my mother's rich voice. "*You and I belong to each other now, Mari-Elaen. I will treat you as you treat me. I will wash your feet, and trek along with you. I will sup where you sup, and make my bed where you rest your head.*"

The fire climbs higher, straining for her fingers. She leans away and the shuku-shuku cloak falls away, leaving her exposed. "No one told me the handmaid's oath could be so intimate. I fell for your mother right there."

Then you killed *her*, I want to scream, but the words cling to the roof of my mouth, refusing to whistle out. Not until I hear more about Mummy.

"A noblewoman's handmaid is her shadow. A royal's? Her armor. I trained every day: tasting poisons lest someone put any in Yetu's food; combat, in case there was need to protect my lady; I learned about the spirits, the creatures lurking in the forests too. I bathed with her, to keep those who would desire her at bay. Slept in the same bed, so that even nightmares could never dream of ensnaring her." She smiled, a touch fondly, a touch bitterly. "Alistair envied me."

I can see it so clearly in my mind's eye, two little girls clinging to each other like tree roots in the swell of a flood, every memory tangling them further until no one knows where one ends and the other begins.

Mari gets to her feet, pacing as she speaks, each word laying out a familiar path she's clearly lost herself down before. "Every birthmark, blemish, muscle, curve—I knew them all." Her lips crest into the ghost of a smile. "When we came of age, Queen Folaké started to worry about marriage proposals, people lining up with claims that they were your mother's rightful mate. Alistair would go on rampages, swearing to kill them all." She turns to me, her eyes burning with intense delight. "But I was the one whose arms she slept in. I taught her to kiss. When she begged for more, I gave her that as well. Everything she ever asked for, I provided. Yetu was born with everything she could ever want, but I made her understand what it was to need. She needed me."

"So you betrayed her," I say, unearthing my voice, letting it carry all the pain and anger that has eaten at me for years. "You let Alistair Sorenson into Benin. You forced her to watch as her people were conquered—"

"She betrayed me first!" Mari shouts. Her face is red, the light in her eyes smothered in an instant. "She taught me to want. I didn't want anything, anyone, before I had her. Then she took it all away. I loved since then—I had Alistair. But it wasn't enough."

A chill rises in my bones despite the swelling heat. Mari's words bear down on my neck like an ax, threatening to tear me apart. She may think she's unburdening her heart, confessing her undying love, but all I hear is greed, a wanton possession. Mummy always told me love was a seed buried in the soil of people's hearts, a gift that would grow and change with time. Love could blossom like a flower under the care of someone's warmth, or wither to chaff in the hardened soil of fear and hate. Mari may have loved my mother once, but it is all too clear that that love meant becoming like the frosted flowers sold in the Eingardian marketplace, polished jewels perpetually on display. One small shift and it would shatter, never to be put together again.

I remember now the feelings Jonas stirred in me, love that felt like a soft rain, tickling my skin, watering me when I had nothing left to give. And sometimes, when I felt as though the winds besetting us would carry me away, a rope knotted around my waist, tethering me in the face of the coming storm. I close my eyes, pushing away the memory. Jonas is gone. I gave him up for good reason.

"I had to tear out my own heart," Mari whispers. She stomps on a pipe, crushing it underfoot, and I flinch. My thoughts are jumbled, scattered like pebbles kicked on a path. Why is she telling me all this? Why now? The curiosity that gripped me earlier is gone, dread rising in its place like a warning.

I need to get away from her. Every movement births a fresh round of pain, but I wriggle my fingers, try to retain feeling in my muscles so I am ready to run if I ever find my way out. Just then my fingers brush against the glass bead Colin gave me. I strain for it, nudging my finger against the taut fabric of my pocket. The oruka tightens, crushing my fingers against my leg. I bite my lip hard to suppress a cry. The motion swings me slightly against the hooks, but Mari does not notice.

She stands frozen, trapped in a nightmare that will not end. "It started slowly at first. Yetu wanted to try different foods, take lessons apart from the ones we had together. She'd sneak out of bed at night, hide from me."

I barely hear what Mari is muttering now, all my focus on what my fingers can feel. I hook the bead with my middle finger, dragging it closer to my waiting palm. The oruka fights me, constricting with each movement, squeezing until I feel as though I might vomit. But still I push— just a little further.

"Then she asked to go on a sojourn of her own, visit other regions to learn more about their terrain. She came back with Osèzèlé, claiming he was her mate. She gave me up, denied Alistair as her betrothed—all for a common, dirty *meascan*."

The mention of my father causes me to still. Rage reigns over caution, and I can't keep a retort from darting off my tongue. "You know nothing about my father. It was my mother's right to choose who she wanted."

"No, it *wasn't*." Mari whirls, stalking toward me, each word thundering like drum beats announcing a war, loud and fast. "She *promised* me.

'I will sup where you sup, and make my bed where you rest your head.' *Her* words. I left my home for her! The least she could have done was shared herself with both of us. We would have been happy, the three of us."

"So you destroyed her then!" I shout, my voice echoing off the cave walls. "Hunted her down. Took every happiness from her and let her die in the street." The bead rolls into the crevice between my finger and my palm, and all I need to do is squeeze, crush it, and summon Colin to this place. But in that moment, my anger consumes me, bloodlust surging like a wave. Magic rushes into my body, urging me to spark, ignite a flame that will burn everything. It's the same feeling that visited me in Lleyria and the betrothal hall, the part of me that hungers for destruction, to rage and thrash until the pain in my heart melts away. Tears threaten to spill from my eyes, but I hold them at bay, surrendering myself to fury.

Mari seizes my chin, and my fingers falter, the bead dropping through them and rolling into the cocoon. "Stop testing me," she hisses. "Don't forget—it's my kindness keeping you alive. I should have killed you long ago."

"Do it then," I snarl. "End it. Kill me."

I press my fingers against the cocoon, willing my magic to my fingertips. Now that her shuku-shuku cloak is off, her iron breastplate taunts me. All this time, I've held myself together like shards of an amo ikoko cast into a kiln, swept away my anger and pain while the fires of hope swore to forge me anew. But now I am tired of living like an ornament, a clay pot fashioned for an ancestral shrine no one will ever sweep. I want to be free of this pain that has clung to me like a shadow for as long as I can remember. Nana's curse will be broken once Mari is dead. The spirits may never welcome me again, but so be it.

My magic bubbles up, prowling at my fingertips like a caged beast. If I release it now, in this state, I will probably die here. But then, so might Mari. Just a little more and I can end this nightmare.

She draws her other hand up, trailing a finger along my face. "I can't," she admits in a quiet voice. "You're all I have left of her. How can a mother harm her own child?"

I stiffen, and my magic sputters, sinking away. "You're not my mother!" I yell, wishing my gaze were enough to set her aflame. "You took my mother from me, remember? And you hurt Nana, the only other mother I've ever had."

"Beg me to save her then," she says, straightening. "If you ask nicely, I just might come with you." She draws a pouch out of her sleeve, shaking out the recovered talisman and a small, iron ring. I curse inwardly. Of course, that must have been the cool metal I touched; the iron that got me caught.

"Come with you where?" Oyéré calls from beyond us. She bustles in, pushing Elodie in front of her. Elodie stumbles on tethered, unsteady feet, landing next to the fire.

"I thought the plan was to kill the girl," the city mother says. "A sacrifice of sorts."

I narrow my eyes. I knew Mari's words were too good to be true.

Mari sighs, rubbing her temples. "I told you I wasn't to be disturbed."

Oyéré crosses her arms. "You took too long. Explain."

"Are the others in place for tonight?"

"You asked me that at Pig Hour, and I confirmed. Now, tell me why you made the girl an offer you told me nothing about."

"Must I tell you everything?" Mari snaps.

"Yes!" Oyéré lifts her chin, defiance shining in her face. "You promised equal partnership. I've had enough with secrecy. At least with Ta'atia, it made sense."

Mari's mouth curls into a sneer. "And here I thought you resented being told *meascan* business was too much for you to comprehend."

"Oluso is the term we use here, my love." Oyéré sniffs. "Please keep that in mind. I don't want Baba Alaji picking a fight with you in an alleyway. You might win, but he always takes a pound of flesh." She rubs a strangely bent finger, obviously broken and improperly set. "Now, what is the plan for the girl?"

A spark jumps from the flames, landing near Elodie's face, and she writhes, her cuffed hands scraping the ground behind her back. Oyéré drags her up by the collar and places her by the wall, pulling the gag from her mouth. "Comfortable?"

Elodie nods, gulping in a breath. She darts a look at me, but lowers her head just as quickly. I wonder how she escaped being bound in this same kind of cocoon.

"Good." Oyéré turns back to us. "My love, you are running out of time to come up with an excuse."

Mari knots her hand in Oyéré's hair, a flustered blush staining her cheeks. "Fine. There is supposedly a *meas*—" She stops, correcting herself. "An Oluso power. One manifested by people like her father. The power of resurrection."

I jerk back, fear striking my heart. The cocoon tightens in response, squeezing the air from my lungs. Resurrection is one of the forbidden lines an Oluso can never cross. Awǫn ti o pè awǫn èmi pada ji ounjé lati ęnu awǫn èmi.

They that call back souls steal food from the mouths of the spirits.

"We can't sacrifice the girl until we march into Eingard," Mari continues. "I need a place where the soul we're searching for has great resonance. Alistair lived most of his life in that castle. He died there."

It is clear Mari studied the ways of the Oluso with Mummy, but I never thought her capable of this. I have learned the ancient ways all my life and I have never heard of an iron-blood power like this until now. The confidence in her voice tells me that if she performs the resurrection ritual, my death is certain. Whether she succeeds does not matter. The spirits demand a price for rousing their anger. Always.

"Why bother bringing him back to life?" Oyéré asks. "We have everything we need to take the kingdom. An army, money from koko. What could a dead king gift us?"

Mari curls an arm around her waist. "The thing you have always desired, my dear. Legitimacy." She pulls her into a kiss.

My heart is pounding in my chest, my stomach knotting as I consider what I've just heard. Mari's army might just be enough to overtake the kingdom. Ekwensi would certainly not stop her—no, he would let the rival factions of the Council fight it out and take on whichever opponent was left.

There is no comfort in that, though. Once Mari sacrifices me, Alistair Sorenson might come back, yet another evil the Oluso will need to deal with. The freedom I've been fighting for seems so far away now, a child's dream of peace. Ekwensi warned me to keep my eyes on the goal. I see now what my foolishness has cost. The Ajes might use me as a pawn, a magical tool to be exploited and discarded, but the Oluso will suffer all the same.

"What of the kokulu?" Elodie says, clearing her throat. "Surely you've heard the reports from Mother. How do you intend to send them back to where they came from?" She licks her cracked lips, working her mouth into a courtly smile. "Don't you think you might need Oluso help? Why don't we see if there's a way we can all win?"

Mari smiles. "You still have such a smooth tongue. Use it to think of what to say when I return you to your mother. I'm sure she'd love to know how you wound up here. I doubt she'll be pleased."

Elodie's expression darkens. Then she smiles, every suggestion of distress wiped away like a trick of the light. "Nothing pleases Mother. Not even me."

There is nothing I can do but listen, horror carving my insides. Then I see the handle of Oyéré's blade sticking out of her belt. I am drained, my body aching in so many places. Heat clings to me like a second skin, threatening to smother me in its embrace, and my magic feels so far away, drawing apart from me like tides swelling out to sea. But I grasp for the feel of it, channel what I find at that dagger hilt, willing it to move with all my might.

I shut my eyes, calling for the spirits—anyone—to help me. Nothing.

Then Iya's crystal throbs against my chest.

The dagger rattles, flying out of its sheath before Oyéré can catch it. It dives straight for Mari, reaching for her throat, but Oyéré counters with its twin, knocking it aside. Mari dashes at me before I can try again, grabbing a pipe from the ground. Oyéré slashes across the ropes holding me up and I fall, head slamming against the rock. Blood gushes down my forehead, dripping over my bruised eye. But I am already in so much pain, reduced to a throbbing mass that breathes.

"You are such a stupid little girl, aren't you?" Mari spits.

"I'm not the stupid one. What makes you think I'll help you?" I pant. My head hurts so badly, and all I want to do is shut my eyes, but I can't give in, let her have the last word. I need to hang on, keep my dwindling hope alive.

"My dear, you have no choice."

And with that, Mari blows on the pipe. A cloud of white powder scatters over me like snow and the world is enveloped in its light.

PART III

THE SPIRIT REALM

TOU

I WAKE IN A PIT OF SWEAT, SMOKE PAWING AT MY FACE AND TIGHTLY BOUND body like unwanted hands. The cloying smell of koko rides the air, forcing its heat against my nostrils. I cough and try to rock back, get myself up, but my arms will not move.

In the haze, I see Elodie sitting a few feet away, shouting at someone, a shadow beyond the smoke. When I croak her name, she turns, eyes full of fear, then the darkness swims up again, pulling me into its depths.

The second time I wake, everything is a wash of color. Cave walls split into waves that dance across my vision, the burning orange of a torch transforms into a golden-winged serpent that swims over the curve of my ear, whispering of a world beyond, a life that awaits after this one. I jerk, feeling its scales nip at my skin, knowing the koko has entered my mind, infecting everything with its poison.

"I am not a mere illusion," the serpent insists, drawing high above my nose. Its long whiskers dance in the air, two horns flaring like wings from its elongated head. "I will come for you if you wish it. But tell me this: are you the child of my blood?"

I open my mouth to speak, but no sound arises. The rubber sheets draw tighter, crushing me. I close my eyes and fall.

When I open them again, it is dark, the moon bathing me in her silvery glow. Cold wind blows against my cheeks, cooling my burning skin. I stretch my arms out and hop to my feet, marveling at the way my body moves, the feeling of that suffocating cocoon fading in an instant. The dark swells with music, the sound of laughter ringing from a distance, but I am calm even as the laughter grows to cackling brays.

Better to wander lost in the Spirit Realm than lie in that drugged haze, knowing I have thrown away Nana's life for my foolishness. At least here my body is whole, unencumbered.

"You're late," Osèzèlé declares.

I turn. A thicket of trees looms before me, black streaks stealing along their ash-white bodies like handprints. My father emerges from those trees, a brace of thorns crowning his head. His brown eyes burn tiger gold just like Ayaba's.

"I'm borrowing this form to speak to you," he explains. "You're not close enough to Iya for me to appear before you properly. You strayed from the path."

Shame burns through me, but I stand my ground. "I didn't know if I'd make it. My guardian is dying. Her child nearly died!"

"So you thought to ally with one who has long lost his way and kill the one who cursed her?" He says the words calmly, but there is a tightness to them, the faint scent of disapproval.

"I had to try," I say. "I don't care if you understand. You don't get to appear in front of me after nearly nineteen years of nothing and play Baba. At least Ekwensi is there for his child, despite everything."

To my surprise his lips quirk in a soft smile. "You're just like Yetu. Enough fire to burn a kingdom down."

A smile steals onto my face. To others who didn't know her well, Mummy seemed calm, her words and expressions as peaceful as a flowing stream. But I knew of her hidden depths, the strength in her frame, the fire that burned in her heart.

He sighs. "But that's not what I'm here for. The next thing you must learn is resolve."

He whips his gleaming spear overhead, spinning it in an arc. Then he beckons me with his other hand. "Come. Take this from me."

I raise an eyebrow. "You want to fight me? I'm stuck in a drug-fueled stupor and you fight me rather than help me?"

He dashes forward, striking at my side with the back end of his spear. Springing off my heel, I block the blow with my forearm, hissing as the cold metal slams against my flesh.

"This *is* help," he says before pivoting on his heel and bringing the spear round to stab at my thigh.

The spear hits its mark this time and I scream as the blade rips through my skin. My muscles tense, fire burning through my leg. He dances back, spinning the spear like a well-practiced acrobat. "This will continue until you take it from me."

He jumps at me again, but this time I press my weight onto my uninjured foot, swerving away from him, then I bring my bone blade up to meet the wicked end of his spear. He knocks me back easily and I barely recover in time to parry his next crushing blow.

"You are undisciplined," he breathes, hacking at me. "Unruly." A second blow. "Inefficient." He sweeps the back end of his spear overhead, slamming it into my shoulder. I collapse onto the forest floor. He stands over me like an ancestral spirit passing judgment. "Suffering will teach you to stop making these foolish mistakes."

I scoff, incredulous. "Haven't I suffered enough?"

He sighs. "I told you, your anger is a useful weapon, but you must control it. You mustn't let your rage cloud your judgment."

Blood rushes to my head, anger and humiliation causing my skin to grow hot. "What about you?" I shout, holding my smarting shoulder. It hurts to even move my arm, and the pain radiating from my clavicle tells me the bone is likely broken. "You taught Alistair Sorenson's people how to craft iron because you were angry. You exiled the Oluso to a life of pain and misery."

My father stills, his fingers tightening on his spear. When he speaks again, his voice is heavy, full of sorrow that makes my heart ache. "It is difficult, learning you are alone in the world, that your people fell at the hands of those you would call brethren. I made mistakes. My anger blinded me to the truth of what I had. Including the blessing of your mother's love."

He sighs and I settle back, suddenly ashamed.

"But I learned that every action comes with a price," he says, lifting his chin. "I chose to save those I could in Benin rather than enact my vengeance. And for that I paid the toll of failing to be there for you as a father." He lifts his spear, drawing his foot back in an attack stance. "Consider my actions as my amends."

I get to my feet, heart pounding in my chest. But it is not the threat of battle that has me filled with excitement. "You turned fifty-thousand Oluso into Ajes. How?"

My father smiles. "You are a young woman now. No longer a child. Come to Iya and I will teach you the hidden gift of the Fèni-Ogun, the power of resurrection." He charges forward, spear held over his head. But this time I am ready.

Touching my betrothal bracelet, I call on my iron magic, gritting my teeth as pain overtakes me. The bracelet morphs into five toothy knives, their jagged edges cut like unforgiving smiles. Another spasm of pain ripples through my back, but I clench my teeth and hold firm even though my fingers are now trembling.

He thrusts his spear at me, and two of my knives fly forward, clashing with the spear mouth. Then, before he can recover, I twist my hand and another knife slices through his left forearm. Startled, he loosens his hold on the spear and I lunge, snatching at it. He tightens his grip, but just before he pulls the spear out of reach, my other knives drive into his back and his eyes widen in surprise. I rip the spear from his hands.

"Got it."

He nods his approval, wincing a little. "Obilu. *Well done.*"

The spear melts into a silvery liquid that runs over my fingers. A few of those liquid pearls latch onto the crystal fastened around my neck, and the light within it grows.

"Iya's flame is reignited. Stay on the path this time, no matter what happens," my father says.

He smiles, the blood spilling from his mouth staining his teeth red. "Remember," he says, reaching a hand out to brush my cheek. "Sharpen the iron or it will sharpen you."

He fades into the night, scattering like butterflies perched on a tree.

"There you are."

I look up to find a boy watching me, the dark of his face framed by the half-white locks that fall like a canopy past his shoulders. The boy who interrupted my time with Osèzèlé earlier—my twin brother, Délé.

I shudder, a chill running down my spine. "What are you doing here?" I ask.

"Why? Are you afraid of me?"

"I—"

He disappears, and I stumble forward, searching the moonlit spot where he last stood.

An arm slips around my neck. "You're right to fear me, sister," Délé whispers. I hear him with my whole body. Suddenly I cannot move. I open my mouth to scream, but my lips will not part, the scream in my throat buried.

"Not to worry. I'm much worse than you fear."

He stabs a hand into my back and I collapse, eyes snapping shut.

———

I WAKE, GASPING IN LUNGFULS OF AIR, HEAT GATHERING OVER MY SKIN like rain, pummeling me from all sides. I blink away the haze clouding my vision and suddenly I'm staring into a pair of icy-blue eyes, the fury in them searing my skin anew. Jonas sits me up, his hands a cooling balm against my scorching skin, and immediately my heart races, singing to a rhythm only he knows. My cocoon lies in a heap around us, caked bits of white littering the ground like broken stone in a graveyard.

"Are you injured?" he asks. His voice is strained, worn as a frayed string.

I lick my parched lips, force sound through my dry throat. "Just my head, but I'm not bleeding anymore . . . I think. Everything hurts."

What I really want to say is how? How is he here? How did he find me? How can he sit there looking at me as though I am the only thing that matters after everything I've done? There's something else I'm forgetting; a name that sits on my tongue, begging to be spoken out loud; a face that mirrors mine. But I can't remember what it is—who I'm looking for.

Jonas lets out a breath, searching me with that unrelenting gaze, and I look away, scanning the platform for Mari and her soldiers. It is surprisingly empty, save for a few dust-covered bodies littered around the dying fire.

"Where is everyone? Elodie?"

"Mari took her to the surface. Turf war."

I straighten at this. "Turf war?"

"You'll see when we get aboveground." He strokes a finger under my swollen eye and I flinch, jerking back. He sighs. "This will hurt, but I imagine the pain you're feeling is worse." Placing his other hand on my chest, he pours silver-blue flames onto my skin. I scream as the healing magic razors through my abused flesh, shoving my bones back into their rightful places. But the magic is soothing, too, a familiar warmth warding away the chill.

He yanks his hand away abruptly, breathing hard. "Let's go."

I shudder, feeling the immediate loss of his warmth. My eye is still smarting. I snort, marveling that though he seems so changed, so stern, the day apart didn't give him mastery of my healing magic.

He darts to the mouth of the platform and looks out. I drink in the sight of him; the discreet black cloak draped over a cross-body plate and fitted leather trousers he usually reserves for reconnaissance missions; the way his hair is tangled, streaked with bits of bark and leaves as though he's rolled around on the forest floor; the water dripping off his pale skin, making pitter-pat noises like rain—it's clear he's been on the road for some time. My heart swells with love, my fingers itching with the need to pull those leaves from his hair and run my hands over his skin. But another part of me is reminded that there's a breach of trust between us, a chasm we have yet to cross.

So I ask, "What about the Oluso you were escorting?"

"The Oluso are in good hands. I tasked Mina and Mikhail with getting them the rest of the way to Yusa," he says.

He darts back to me, and now I see that his jaw is tight, a dam straining against a raging sea. "As for how I found you . . ." he says. "Apologies if it's something you'd rather forget, but we're mates, remember?"

Guilt rends my heart like claws, but I nudge it away, shaking my head. "I shut you out."

He smiles, but there is no lightness in his eyes, just anger and love warring in those icy depths. "Remember what Nana told us after my uncle died? A bond between two iron-bloods is unique. You may have pushed me out of your mind, but that didn't stop it from sending me memories, flashes of what was happening to you. So, I turned around once we got to Porto Pischu. Started tracking your sign."

I close my eyes, stifling a groan. The pair bond. I thought it was unfinished, a flame without a hearth to grow in, but somehow we performed enough of the ceremony for our lives to be entwined. A warmth settles in my belly, something akin to hope sprouting its petals. Then I open my eyes as I realize what he's just confessed.

"You could see my memories?"

"Bits of them. Feel things you felt too." He slips an arm under my legs, cradling my back with the other. I sag against him, annoyed at the relief that blankets me like a coat. He strides onto the platform, stepping over the bodies in our way.

"You know, then, that Colin is here," I whisper, willing my voice to come out evenly. "That Ekwensi believes the Council has found a way to control the K'inu."

"Among other things. I also know that Mari has lost her mind and wants to resurrect my dead uncle. And Lady Ayn could not be trusted—no surprise there." He stops at a rope ladder and sets me against the wall, placing my hands on his shoulders. "Hold on tight," he warns. "I know you're dying to get as far away from me as you can, but help me at least get you out of here."

Using his shoulders as a support, I tuck my legs around his waist and latch my arms around his neck. We're eye to eye, a space of a breath between our faces. "I wasn't running away from you," I mutter.

"Definitely fooled me, then. I told you to wait for me." He draws his hands over my hips, pulling me in more securely, then he starts his ascent. I rock forward with the movement, pressing against his neck, the rich, comforting scent of his skin licking my nose.

"I couldn't wait. You have to see that. Nana didn't have the time. I had to act."

"So you ran off to join Ekwensi? You trusted him to solve your problems more than you trusted me, your mate, to understand," he responds. His voice is matter-of-fact, even, but I hear the storm of hurt and anger behind those tightly delivered words.

"I had no choice!" I shout. My voice echoes off the cavern walls, distorting into something menacing and ominous.

He laughs dryly, a low rumble that starts in his belly and travels up, rocking his chest against mine. "You always have a choice, oko mi. All this was a choice."

"The Oluso are in danger," I cry. "I don't even know if Nana is dead or alive." I'm breathing hard, each swell of my chest causing flares of pain—another incompletely healed injury.

"I needed someone who wouldn't be too cautious," I continue, "too afraid to do the wrong thing even if it brings us more peace. I needed someone who wasn't afraid to fight."

His control severs as neatly as a tendon. "And what have I been doing all this time?" He swings us onto the next platform and stops climbing, focusing his attention on me. "Don't you realize, Dèmi, that I came here after you? That the Council will consider me collateral damage?"

He brushes a hand against my cheek. "You ask for action now, but I have fought alongside you. I know what seeing death costs you. I've held you at night when you unravel. I've felt the pain and grief you carry in you like a knife. All I wanted was to keep that grief from killing you. There is no peace for me, no change, no world if you're dead." He presses my clenched fist to my heart. "Any change that means sacrificing you, killing you, isn't worth it. You have to live to make this world better."

I blink away the tears gathering in my eyes. "No, I don't. The Oluso don't care if I'm alive. They just need change. They need peace now."

He places his forehead against mine, closing his eyes against his tears. "When are you going to understand, oko mi—change can only be better and lasting with the right people to keep it going? What if you change the world, but there isn't anyone to keep believing that change is needed? What do you do then?"

"I don't know," I say, burying my face in his neck. "At least Ekwensi has vision. He's wanted this change for even longer than I have."

The truth hits me then like a wayward stone. I failed Ekwensi's test. I'm on my own now, and I'm out of options.

Jonas relents with a sigh. "That remains to be seen. But let's not do this here. We need to get to the surface."

He starts climbing again. There are more bodies on the next platform, piled in a heap like burial stones. I squint at them, but I find no trace of blood, just the same fine black dust covering them like dirt, fluttering into little clouds as they breathe through open mouths.

"How did you—"

"Ta'atia's invention. They'll sleep the day away."

I lift my head, nearly knocking into his jaw as we clamber toward another platform. "You know Ta'atia?"

"We're allies. Have been for years."

"Years?" I narrow my eyes, an ugly feeling spearing through my heart like ice. "Why didn't I know this?"

He bounds up the last ledge, setting me down at the mouth of the tunnel. He takes the waiting torch off the wall, peering into the dark before beckoning me closer.

"It's clear, let's go."

"Jonas."

He keeps walking. I dart after him, frantically trying to keep in step. "Jonas, what aren't you telling me?"

He clenches his fist. "Dèmi, I can't do this with you right now."

"Do what? *Talk* to me?"

He sighs again, then he turns on his heel, stalking toward me. I glare up at him, waiting for the words to fall from his lips, bracing myself for another betrayal, but he just yanks me to him with his free hand and kisses me. I shudder as his tongue comes crashing into my mouth, teasing mine out, and his fingers flex against my cheek, cooling my burning skin. My heart thuds in my chest, and suddenly images flood my mind, bursting through my defenses like a wave.

I see a youthful Jonas, no hint of stubble on his cheeks, on his first visit to Gaeyak-Orin. I feel his fear as bandits attack his convoy, and anger as they strike down some of his guards. Then, as he charges into the fray, his exhilaration and triumph as he conjures flame and seizes all the weapons flying about with his magic. Everyone falls back, revealing two women at the center standing back to back, Ta'atia and Oyéré.

He breaks the kiss, and I gasp, my lips trembling with the remembrance of his touch. He trails his hand down from behind my head, cradling my cheek. "Dèmi, there are a lot of things you don't know about me, because you've been too afraid to connect. When I gave you my heart, I let you into my mind. And I understand that you've been alone your whole life, so this is new for you, but for once I wish you'd give me the same trust I give you."

"I do trust you," I say weakly. "I never would have stayed so long with you if I didn't."

But even as I speak the words, my thoughts brand me a liar. I may have trusted Jonas well enough to live in Eingard the last year and pledge a betrothal, but there's a part of me that has always held back, waiting like the spring of a trap for something to go wrong and bring us crashing down. And every time he sought to try again, to give the Council another chance to prove themselves, that spring frayed more and more, bringing my spirit closer to gnawing teeth dipped in sorrow and disappointment. I may have defended him to Ekwensi, but there was a part of me that wondered whether I was a fool after all.

He smiles slightly, lifting one corner of his mouth. "If that trust is all there is, we have a lot more things to work through."

I bristle. "What does that mean?" The words sting, especially with everything I've gone through to earn someone else's trust.

A horn blows in the distance, its wail echoing through the cavern. Jonas picks up the torch and grabs my hand. "It means we have to go. Come on."

He tears down the tunnel, pulling me along, and I stumble into a run, teetering as we splash through the thick oil.

"What's going on?" I ask again. "Where are we headed?"

"The Council guards have flooded the city. Ta'atia sent me to get you out."

I blink. Ta'atia did not betray me then, even though she didn't appear to rescue me. "Did she say anything about Nana? Where is she?"

"She's with Ta'atia's general," he gasps. "Let's hurry. We need to get out of this city."

"We can't leave the city before I get the talisman from Mari," I protest. "I made a deal with Ekwensi, but I failed. I don't have a choice."

We slide through to the adjoining tunnel, spotting the distant silvery light at the entrance looming like a hungry moon.

"Why not head towards Ìyá-Ilé?" he asks. "There's no way Mari will give up that talisman."

"I'm not sure we'll make it," I admit. "Nana has lost enough time as it is. What if I fail? What if Nana dies because of me?"

"That won't happen. I won't let that happen."

"How can you be certain?" I retort. "Why do you get to decide that?"

"Not *me*," he growls. "*Us*. It was always going to be *us* making sure that didn't happen."

I am about to reply when we burst through the opening, fresh air slapping our faces. Gaeyak-Orin is awash with darkness, the night settling over the city like a bruise. Plumes of smoke rise in the distance, fiery sparks that glitter like stars piercing the night sky, but I also hear the sound of crickets searching for mates, feel the cool breeze dancing around my skin in welcome. I suck air into my greedy lungs, marveling at the lightness that envelops me. The horn sounds again, louder and insistent, its cries cutting through the quiet of the grove we're in.

"That's Ta'atia," Jonas says, the heat once again gone from his voice. "We need to hurry."

He leaps onto the waiting horse tethered to a lantern post, a kola nut–colored steed that always bucked every time it caught sight of me, and offers me a hand.

"I'm not going back to Eingard," I say, stumbling back on shaking legs. It is as though I have just emerged from a grave, my body learning what it is to live again. "Whatever happens here, after I get the talisman, or I find Iya and heal Nana, I'm leaving."

He nods. "I'll help you, no matter what you decide."

"I also won't compromise, whether I have allies or not. The Council must be stopped. They are the enemy."

His face hardens, but he nods once more. "They became the enemy the day they attempted to murder you in front of me. I don't care what resources or titles or power they hold, they all have to go."

I nod, but I make no move to take his hand.

He vaults down, seizing me by the waist. "Someday, I'll tell our children how stubborn their mother is and why I love her for it, but let's not make today a tale for them, hm?"

I freeze, the thought of children turning my blood cold. I have always loved babies, spent years accompanying Mummy to birth after birth. Every child we pulled into the world was brighter than the stars, wizened faces brimming with memories of the Spirit Realm that fell away like second skin as they swam into our world. When they opened their eyes for the first time, or gripped my fingers with their little hands, I held my tears in, thanking the spirits that I had a chance to see life blossom before me like the dawning of a new day. But in the years since Mummy passed, I've watched families with a mournful heart, and the laughter of children became daggers that traced along my skin, gifting me fresh wounds when they mocked me for what I am. Since then, I have never dreamt of children of my own, never wanted to give a child the inheritance of hatred and hurt that clouds an Oluso life like a blight. And now, my sundered Oluso bonds have guaranteed me an early grave.

Jonas sighs, no doubt reading my thoughts, then he puts us both onto the horse, his hands tight on my waist. "We can talk about children another time."

I barely have time to grab on to the saddle horn when he whistles and clicks his heels against the horse's side. We thunder down the streets, wind whipping at our cheeks as we race toward the gathering smoke.

TEMPEST

THE RIVER DIVIDING THE CITY OF SHARDS IS ABLAZE, ORANGE FLAME sliding over dark water like an ill-fitting dress. Shadowed figures hang over that tempest, balancing on thick metal threads that loop across buildings on either side, cast like statues in a golden shimmer from the inferno below. We turn from the riverbank, jumping over abandoned fruit carts and dodging people running through the streets, but I look back over Jonas's shoulder as one of those golden figures skimming across the threads makes a leap, her white garments floating on the night breeze. She flies towards a waiting thread looped around the edge of a balcony, but too late she sees the soldier clad in red, sawing at the thread. As her feet grace the rope, skating over its surface like a bird trying to find purchase on the ground, the soldier's blade whistles down in a final blow, severing her lifeline. She hurtles toward the burning waters with a wordless scream.

I lurch, nearly falling off the horse, but Jonas pulls me firmly in. My heart is pounding, my mind screaming with the agony of being too far away to do anything, too spent from my time in Mari's hideout to save that falling woman.

"Oyéré has gone too far this time," Jonas mutters darkly. "There's no going back from this. Ta'atia won't let this slide."

"Why are they warring?" I ask.

He grips my waist more tightly as we leap over a closed gate. "Gaeyak-Orin has always been a safe haven for people from all regions. But the Council has stationed more soldiers here in recent years. So Ta'atia drove them out by using water magic to cut down the fish supply."

I remember Lord Islington's complaints from the Council meeting. Omioja have affinity with all sea creatures. It's not hard to believe that Li'uoa warned the fish away from entering the city. That or whatever lurks in these waters devoured them.

"After that, Oyéré wanted Ta'atia to use her magic to do more. Threaten the Council with loss of access to the salt mines and fisheries. Expand the borders and carve Gaeyak-Orin into an independent state. Protect the region by taking a seat on the Council and moving to Nordgren."

"Ta'atia disagreed, didn't she?" I pause, remembering the way she spoke of her mother, the desperation in her voice when she confessed she was bound to this city. "She didn't want to leave Gaeyak-Orin."

He snorts, the action pushing his chest more firmly into my back. "You've only known her for a short while and you already know what she's like. She told Oyéré that Gaeyak-Orin was her home and refused to explain any further. That, amongst other things, made them fall apart; that's all I know."

I think of how difficult the last year has been, the loneliness that has dogged me since I started living in Eingard. I think too of Ta'atia's proud expression when she spoke of her handmaidens. "It wasn't enough to trust that Ta'atia might have her reasons?"

"Shouldn't she share those with Oyéré then? Give her a choice?"

"You sound like you think Ta'atia made the wrong choice."

He shakes his head, his hair brushing against my neck. "No. I only thought Oyéré's plan might work. Help break up the Council's power."

"What if there's no choice," I say, clenching my jaw. "Life can be cruel. People say they love each other, but that love lasts as long as their desires are met. Sometimes those desires are impossible. What then?"

He leans closer, his breath tickling my neck. "Then you ask the one you love to fight for the impossible with you. Like I am doing right now."

I bite back a retort, focusing on the road ahead.

We clamber down narrow streets, dodging broken pots and idols strewn about like remnants of a bloody war. The streets are mostly empty of people save for one or two stragglers who startle as they catch sight of us, as though we are hungry ghosts set on devouring them.

As we emerge from a maze of adjoining alleys, I glimpse the golden threads, traces of Nana's Oluso sign twining with the blue of Colin's. They swim in the direction of the cliffs at the edge of the city, splintering only as they reach the fog that stretches its fingers over those cliffs like a jealous lover. The light from Iya's crystal deepens to a dusky rose, the magic trail emanating from it pointing toward that path.

"This way!" I shout, but Jonas is already spurring the horse in that direction.

We burst into the open square, where the riverbank curves into the bottom of the cliffs. A gaggle of soldiers are locked in battle with Ta'atia's handmaidens, wooden batons and swords clashing with metal threads that coil and whip like angry snakes.

Ta'atia spins through the maze of bodies, lashing her threads around a soldier's neck when they attempt to strike her. Then, lurching forward, she flings the soldier into the waiting river and glides to a stop in front of us.

"I thought you would never come. Thank the spirits you are safe," she says, the scar gracing her left eye drawing back as though in greeting. Her hair is much longer than earlier in the day, nearly sweeping the ground as she moves. "The shell registered you were in danger, but all I could do was send magic to give you immediate help. Something interfered when I tried bringing you back to my home."

So Ta'atia sent the water from the shell after all—she saved my life. I can't think of what to say, how I could possibly thank her. But as I open my mouth, Jonas vaults to the ground.

"Took longer to retrieve my mate than I thought," he says. "Where are the others?"

She wrinkles her nose. "Manners, boy. I excused your brusqueness when Dèmi was in danger. It's tiresome now. I'm old enough to be your mother, if not your grandmother."

"My apologies," he blurts, cheeks flushing.

She spits in her hand and offers it to him. He copies her and they clasp hands.

"The body's water is the most precious," she says, catching the curious look I throw at her. She nods toward the cliffs. "I sent your friends up with Li'uoa. Oyéré and her lover went barking after them. Li'uoa will protect them as long as she can."

I spring from the saddle. "We have to help them."

"I would hurry. My children report that the capital guards are minutes from reaching this part of the city."

"Ekwensi?" Jonas asks.

She chuckles, her eyes empty of mirth. "Tobias is gone."

Something like disappointment rises in my breast, but I ignore it. Ekwensi told me he would leave with or without me. I had one task to complete and I failed.

"He promised to find a way to help me escape this city," Ta'atia continues. "But it's only right that I can't leave. In his defense, I tasked him with something difficult. I should have kept my shell instead of entrusting it to Oyéré in the first place."

Guilt sits like a stone in my belly. I am the reason Ta'atia lost her chance at freedom. She places a hand on my shoulder, her cool touch like a jolt of electricity through my skin.

"I am sorry I could not tell you more about Yetundé. But I'm glad I could help you." She grins at Jonas, flashing misshapen teeth. "The spirits have a sense of humor giving you this nran buruku as your mate. It's good. With her at your side, you'll never get too much of a big head."

Jonas raises an eyebrow, no doubt trying to remember whether *hellcat* is an insult or an endearment in Yoruba. I smile in spite of my worry.

"I'm half Oyo-born," she says, the brown flecks in her green eyes dancing. "What's the point if I can't yab someone in Yoruba every now and then?"

The city bells come alive, releasing a single somber note. Wolf Hour is here.

"There's a storm coming," Ta'atia declares. "I tried to prepare our people for it all day, but no one would listen. The spirit that stirs these waters is on its way home."

"What does that mean?" Jonas asks.

"Stay away from the sea if you want to remain intact."

A soldier breaks from the skirmish behind, charging with a lance. I step forward, drawing my bone blade, but Ta'atia spins in a flash, lashing her threads around the weapon and flinging it away. She kicks the offending soldier in the face, turning back to us as the woman collapses.

"They think I've gone soft because I'm old." She claps my shoulder. "My dear, never let age dictate what you can and can't do." She taps the Oluso sign on her belly. "People see us and make judgments enough. Don't let gray hairs become a shackle too."

Ta'atia's Handmaidens throw the remaining offenders into the river. Another horn wail fills the air, this time descending from the cliff, raining down on us like messages delivered from the spirits. A new batch of soldiers pours in from the streets behind, purple-and-gold uniforms flashing as they run toward us. The capital guards are here.

Ta'atia lifts her arms and leaps, surging like a blade thirsting for a bite of flesh. She lands, slamming her fingers together as her back foot joins the front, and the fog obscuring the way rips apart in an instant, carving a path up the looming cliffside. The whispers of Colin's and Nana's Oluso threads linger in the darkness like a faded aroma.

"Go. I'll come after I deal with them." She scowls as the soldiers advance. "This is what I get for taking a human youngling as a lover."

Her brown skin falls away like scales, revealing a purplish blue that shimmers under the moon. Her dark hair ripples away from her head, weaving like tendrils. I gasp. Now I understand why Ta'atia would have a water spirit as a lieutenant.

Ta'atia is okun-omo, the forbidden offspring of an omioja and an Oluso.

"Thank you, Ta'atia," Jonas calls as he tugs me forward.

Yet I linger a moment, watching as her arms lengthen and spiny grooves grow at her elbows. Then, just as twin horns elongate from either side of her neck, Jonas pulls me again and I run up the cliffside, digging my feet against rocks that bite through my worn deerskin boots.

I focus on the climb ahead and the fading, flickering trails leading to Nana and Colin. But as we scramble onto the final rock shelf, I dart a quick look behind. Water flies up from the river, weaving around Ta'atia like a silk robe, and she glides forward, her hair hardening into silvered spears. Then the fog rushes in, obscuring her from sight, and I press on as the air fills with screams.

We scramble toward the far side of the cliff, stopping as we reach the shelf where Mari and Oyéré stand with a host of soldiers gathered at their backs. In their midst is a giant bubble, with Nana, Colin, Elodie, and Li'uoa trapped inside. Soldiers hack at the bubble to no avail, blades sending up a shower of sparks every time they strike its glassy surface.

Li'uoa's arms are raised, but she trembles visibly as a soldier rams her blade into the center of the bubble. A crack emanates from the blade tip, fault lines spreading over the bubble's smooth surface like marbled veins lining gemstones.

I spring forward, but Jonas catches my shoulder, jerking me back. "They don't know we're here yet. We need to use that to our advantage."

"We don't have time for that," I argue. "Colin's magic isn't reliable. The others won't be able to defend themselves."

"Li'uoa is with them," he whispers harshly. "You're in no state for a prolonged fight, so stop wasting your energy and help me figure out our next move."

Clenching my fists, I back away. Jonas is right. It is as my father said—I need to build resolve, look for ways to solve my problems without resorting to anger and immediate action.

We huddle behind a boulder. From here, we can still see the entire shelf, but we're far enough away from the closest soldier that we can talk without fear of being heard.

"What do you propose we do?"

"There's a path." He points to a dark ribbon of rock winding up the shelf, the farthest edge of cliff worn down by sea air and errant sprays of water. Jagged rocks stud its face like unruly teeth, obscuring the path from view of the main shelf. "We climb that way, get closer to the others. Even if we have to fight, it'll be easier if we're together. We can buy some time until Ta'atia can help."

"Let's go," I say, scrambling onto unsteady feet.

He tugs at my arm, holding me in place, then he presses his hand over my eye. I barely have time to wince before the world is awash in green flame. The throbbing in my eye dissipates instantly, the biting chill in my skin lessening to a whispering cold.

"Thought you said we shouldn't waste energy," I mutter when he pulls his hand away, cursing myself for missing the warmth of his palm, the kiss of his fingers against my cheeks.

"The more I saw that wounded eye, the more I thought of ways to kill Mari. Trust me, it was more productive to heal you." He speaks so calmly, but his words drip with rage. Gone is the impish levity he employs at court, the polite shield he uses to mask his words and feelings. A part of me is giddy, my heart thundering at the idea that he's enraged on my behalf, but then I remember the way he spoke in that dungeon, how he implored me to trust the Council once more, and that giddy feeling disappears like smoke. What's broken between us cannot be fixed by a moment of ruthlessness and simple explanations.

He slips his hand into mine, breaking me out of my reverie. "Come on. We're running out of time."

Keeping to the shadows, we clamber downhill, feeling our way through the mist until we reach that first spiked tooth. The path is uneven, gray rock sloping every which way, expansive enough in some areas that we can both fit and hide from the raging sea below but worn to a sliver—a foot's dance—in others.

I start up first, careful to avoid the slippery green moss crawling along the rock face, and Jonas follows.

Everything in me tells me I should run, rush as quickly as I can back to the main shelf. But I take my time, keeping one hand on the cliff face, stepping lightly on each bit gingerly before pushing my full weight down. Jonas catches me as an errant piece of rock gives way and I stumble back.

The sea's bellow is thunderous, water stirring with a hunger so stark that it slams against the cliff face, slapping us with its greedy, salt-ringed fingers. Above us, voices duel, straining to be heard, but the words dissolve into the winds cutting against the cliff. I soldier on, letting my heartbeats mark the time, reminding myself as doubt and worry nip at my heels, urging me to go faster, that all is not lost.

There's a break in the path, a gap between the final crest and the saltwater-slicked piece of stone we're clinging to. I stop with a curse,

Jonas nearly crashing into me. A few feet ahead, at the tail of the waiting ledge, is a slender spire of rock reaching up to the sky like a hand.

I reach for my magic, searching for that familiar pull in my chest, but I can't seem to grasp the threads, spark anything to my waiting fingers. Clenching my teeth, I try again, willing the wind spirits to answer. Since waking from my koko induced slumber, there's been a pit gnawing in my belly, an absence that has haunted me. My magic is out of reach, buried deep like the tree spirits that hide during winter, waiting for the promise of spring. My heart seizes with dread. Then there's a whistle like iron scraping steel, the call of a blade piercing its target. We're out of time.

"We need to jump!" I yell, scrambling back a few paces. "My magic isn't responding."

Jonas throws an arm in front of me. "Whoa, let me try. I'm your mate, remember?"

"Then do something now! The others are in danger!"

Jonas has the tact to not say "I know." He slaps his hands together, closing his eyes. The crease between his brows deepens as he concentrates, and as he draws his hands apart, fingers spread wide, a few wind spirits appear, flickering like fireflies. The wind gathers around him, licking over my skin, but I know before some of it wrests away from us, screeching at the cliff, that it's not enough. Jonas has tried for months to master my magic, but though he's improved marginally in healing, the wind spirits do not feel the need to obey him.

"Son of a vulture eater," he curses. "Let me try again."

There are shouts now, screams piercing the air that need no words to make their message known.

"Too late."

Whipping out my bone blade, I burst into a run. Jonas's shout carries on the wind like an arrow chasing me, but I don't stop. There's no time to lose. Nana and Colin are in danger, and my foolishness has brought them closer to their deaths.

My feet slide against the rock, but I push on, leaping just as my foot brushes the edge. I fly for a moment, tasting salt and tang, like the handspun sweets Goma merchants give out during festival days. Then I stumble onto the waiting ledge, grasping at air before I slip and slam into the ground. I roll backwards, rocks tearing my trousers and cutting my cheek. The gray skies mock me as I flip between their gaze and the ground, thunderclaps booming like laughter in my ringing ears. Then, just as my feet sink past the bottom of the ledge, I bring my arm up and stab my bone blade into the ground. I lurch to a stop, body halfway dangling into the waiting abyss.

"Hang on!" Jonas yells.

My chest is burning, each gasp for air loosening my wet grip on my blade. Then there's a rattling, and I dart a look at the sky, half expecting the glinting, beady eyes of a kokulu. Instead, a chain alight with Jonas's flame flings itself over the spire to my right, coiling around it like a snake. Jonas catapults after it, landing near the spire, and now I see that the other end of the chain is wrapped around his waist. He reaches back, inching toward me.

"Give me your hand."

My arms are burning, my fingers aching as they struggle to keep hold of my blade. I want to reach out and take his hand, but something tells me that once I do, I'll fall.

"Dèmi. Please. Give me your hand," Jonas pleads. His blue eyes are as stormy as the sea, his face tight with concentration. Still, I make no move to take his outstretched hand. "I won't let you fall."

You've heard all this before, a voice whispers, slithering against my ear. *Promises. But the Aje never keep their promises, do they?*

I swallow, trying to keep myself from heaving. This must be the remnants of my drug-filled stupor, or worse—the madness from breaking my spirit bonds.

"Dèmi!" Jonas cries again. The screams above us intensify, drowning him out. My fingers are slipping.

I am no mad dream, or pitiful drug, but the spirit that rules these waters. What will it be, daughter of Oya? Olorun will always welcome you home if you seek to make your bed in my arms.

My heart seizes. This is what Ta'atia warned me of—the spirit that runs through Gaeyak-Orin.

Jonas takes two steps farther, and now the chain is at its limit, groaning as it struggles to hold his weight. "Trust me for once, damn it," he snaps.

He reaches for me, bending at the waist. "I'd rather fall with you than let you die alone."

For the last several months I've been losing myself, trying to remember the person I was before I came to Eingard. I thought I could handle the Council's politics, having struggled through worse survival games in Oyo, but every insult, every frightened stare, every Council scheme has been a knife driving into me, pushing me further into the pit of despair. Yet every time I've been on the verge of succumbing, I've looked into Jonas's eyes and seen myself reflected. Those eyes are burning now, begging me to fight.

Pushing away that niggling voice, I rip a hand off my blade, grasping for Jonas's. Our fingers kiss in a light caress before a spray of water hits us, knocking me back. Jonas dives for me, uncaring as the chain snaps at his waist, grabbing my wrist before I disappear past the ledge. He wraps his body around me as we plunge through the gap, turning us in midair so my body hangs over his. I barely have time to scream when he stretches a hand upward and the wind spirits gather to us like bees seeking flowers. We float up, speeding toward the ledge, and his chain lashes onto his waist as we land on solid ground.

"How did you—" I start.

"Baba said our bond would grow the more we trusted each other," he says, gasping. "Also, I figured having skin-to-skin contact would strengthen my hold on your magic like it did in the betrothal hall."

I frown. "That was a gamble."

He shrugs, lips pulling into a smile. "So is loving you."

Heat rushes into my cheeks, but there's no time to respond because just then bodies come flying off the top of the cliff. The soldiers drop into the sea below, red-and-black tunics bobbing like flotsam on the tempestuous waves.

We race up the summit, breaking onto the shelf as Li'uoa tosses another soldier off the cliff, her dark hair hooked around the woman's throat. Another soldier runs as a tendril of her hair chases them, scuttling down the side of the cliff. More soldiers close in, holding up shields with one hand, their swords pincered toward her with the other, forming a crown around her waist.

Colin glances up, shoulders loosening with relief as he catches sight of me. "Took you long enough," he says with a teasing grin. "I fought Ekwensi to stay and wait for you."

His smile melts as Jonas presses in behind me, but all my attention is on Nana. She is hunched, eyes closed, chest rising and falling at a rapid pace. Her golden skin has whittled to a pale blue, the bitna veins on her skin seemingly sharper and more severe in the moonlight. I press my fingers against the bubble's surface, hovering by her cheek, but she does not open her eyes. Her promised three days have run down to two and it's all my fault. I don't even want to think about how Will and Haru must be faring.

Elodie whirls. "Auri, is that you?"

Jonas puts a finger to his lips but several pairs of eyes settle onto us, Mari's and Oyéré's amongst them. Oyéré at least has the grace to look sheepish when she spies Jonas.

"So much for surprises," Jonas mutters.

"You didn't like my proposal then," Mari says. Her expression is calm, but I don't miss the way her fingers tighten on the hilt of her blade.

"What proposal?" Colin asks, frowning.

"I could save your guardian now," Mari says, taking a step forward. "All you have to do is trust me. Without my help, you will never be able to help her. What good is your freedom if everyone you love is dead?"

I scoff. It's ridiculous that she's bringing up trust when she nearly killed me in that cave. "The same trick won't work on me twice," I declare. To Colin, I respond, "Mari believes that iron-bloods can bring back the dead. She wants to sacrifice me."

Mari moves closer. "Perhaps you need a little more convincing."

Jonas draws his sword. "Stay where you are."

She flashes him a mirthless smile, her eyes burning like coals. "You have no authority here, princeling. The worst thing Alistair ever did was raise you with his particular swill of arrogance." She smirks. "Funnily enough, your meascan blood isn't pure enough to bring him back. All that energy wasted raising his precious heir, and for what?"

Jonas bares his teeth. "I made a mistake showing you mercy."

"If asking me to rot in a dungeon was mercy, I shudder to think of your kindness. But no need for all this. You soon won't matter after all."

"Don't bet on your little rebellion with Lady Ayn," he says, narrowing his eyes. "Half the Council is loyal to me."

I lift an eyebrow. At last count, we had only recruited three Council members, but now is not the time to challenge Jonas's statement.

"Half. Exactly," Mari concedes. "The others are merely biding their time, waiting to see who will win, your father included." She whips her sword around as though testing the weight, and it whistles as it slices through the thick cliff winds. "If I bring Alistair back, show them a path to defeating the evil plaguing their lands, who do you think they'll side with?"

More soldiers flood uphill, purple-and-gold uniforms puffing like spiny alaféfé raring to spit poison. They halt at the shelf's edge, faces twisting in confusion as they catch sight of Jonas. Yet they kneel.

"My liege," they cry.

"I thought we were here to support Captain Mari," a vanguard whispers.

"We are," someone answers. "The prince isn't supposed to be here."

Mari addresses them. "Good soldiers, what you see before you is mere illusion. Your prince is halfway across the kingdom, driving the vile meascans back to where they came from. This man is an impostor."

"Lies!" I yell, but the soldiers are already muttering amongst themselves, voices thrumming with uncertainty. Ìyá-Ilé's crystal blinks against my chest, dusky rose shifting to the rich hues of efo tete, the heart-shaped plant rumored to gift immortality. The trail unspooling from it runs toward the sea. We have to go. I have to get us out of here.

Jonas lifts both hands, as though the gesture is enough to allay their fears. "I am no illusion!" he shouts against the onslaught of the wind. "I am Jonas Aurelius Sorenson, son of Markham Denarius Sorenson and heir to Alistair. I may not know your names, but I have trained with you at Aensyled and Ellaria. You may even have accompanied me on one of my tours through the kingdom. Rest assured, I am real—"

A soldier breaks from the crowd, throwing a rock that hits Jonas in the chest.

"My prince isn't some dirty meascan!" she shouts. "He's on our side. You're an impostor."

Jonas flinches, and I can tell that her words hurt worse than the blow he just received. This is the reality he hasn't wanted to see—that even though we've worked to change how the world sees the Oluso, there are still some who cling to their hatred.

Some soldiers jeer their agreement while others argue back.

"But what if that's our prince? Our first captain was in the betrothal hall. She said—"

"No way, he's riding for Yusa."

"Could be 'im. 'E's got strange since meeting that meascan temptress."

"The Oluso aren't half-bad actually. A couple helped my pregnant wife give birth."

"Enough!" Mari shouts, raising her sword. "You were tasked with fighting for me. Obey your orders."

Half the soldiers shuffle forward, breaking ranks to gather behind her while the other half remains still, looking between Mari and us.

"I don't understand who to believe!" a soldier cries.

"Then follow me," Mari snaps. "Trust in the order that was set out for you. Quit using your foolish mind to make decisions."

I want to rip out her throat. Instead, I clutch Ìyá-Ilé's crystal and edge toward Colin. "Can you get us across the sea?"

"To the Three Sisters villages?" Colin answers.

"I think so."

He whistles, and Li'uoa turns. "We're ready."

Li'uoa swings a tendril of hair, knocking all the soldiers in front of her away. Then her hair speeds toward us like a lance, piercing the bubble. It melts, frothing like an overfull mug of tombo, then disappears, leaving behind traces of shimmering dust.

Colin catches Nana before her head can hit the ground, folding her against him. "Let's go."

"Don't let them escape!" Mari calls, beckoning the soldiers forward.

A few brave souls charge, bearing down on us, but some of the opposing faction who haven't yet joined Mari clash with them, iron singing a symphony of destruction. Another group of soldiers joins the fray, but Jonas waves a hand and their weapons still in midair, refusing to move.

"You see it now!" someone shouts. "Our prince is one of them!"

The soldiers fighting for us look at one another.

"I'll settle this myself!"

Mari lurches toward us, but Li'uoa snares her by the arm. She slashes her blade at Li'uoa's dark locks, but it ricochets off, landing a few feet away. Li'uoa's ropes her hair around Mari's waist, yanking her into the air. The soldiers back away in fear.

Oyéré rushes at Li'uoa. "Let her go," she cries. "Ta'atia promised not to harm what is mine."

Li'uoa growls, the slits in her neck flaring as she speaks, "Ta'atia said no harm was to come to *you*. She said nothing of the humans you betrayed her with."

I pull Jonas by the arm, slipping my other hand into the crook of Colin's elbow. Elodie scrambles to Jonas's side, putting an arm around his waist.

"Thank you, Auri," she whispers, laying her head against his chest. He stiffens, flicking a glance at me, but does not push her away. His expression is one of such discomfort that I'm tempted to laugh. It's clear he doesn't know she prefers women. But now is no time for laughter.

Colin's magic flares, a rich sapphire haze that engulfs us all, but there is no stirring in my belly, no flutter of magic against my skin. I close my eyes, blink them open to find we are still in the same place.

"What is happening?"

He scowls. "Let me try again."

Oyéré charges Li'uoa with a cry, hacking at her exposed chest.

I start forward but Li'uoa waves me away. "Go while you still have a chance. I'll be fine."

She barely has a moment to dodge before Oyéré is on her again, swinging her ax at her shoulder. This time Oyéré's blade hits true, and Li'uoa hisses, inky blood spilling from her shoulder. Before Oyéré can strike her again, she shakes Mari and the soldiers loose and tethers her hair strands together like a wall, blocking the blow.

Colin's magic roars to life once more, bathing us in its glow, and now I sense the tug of his magic, a whispering invitation calling me to somewhere beyond.

Oyéré raises her blade again, but Li'uoa curls a tendril of her hair around her throat. "You betray us still, fighting with those who would harm us."

"You hurt me first," Oyéré gasps, clawing at the braid tightening around her neck. "Always hiding. Secrets."

"Why couldn't you trust Ta'atia?" Li'uoa shouts. "Even now she loves you." She points at the conch fastened to Oyéré's waist. "What did you think that was? She gave you her soul."

Oyéré kicks her foot out, connecting with Li'uoa's belly. Li'uoa doubles over, releasing her.

"I don't need the love of someone who can't trust me," Oyéré says.

The words are a punch to my already bruised ego, but then the world begins to fold before my eyes, sounds collapsing into a dull roar. Any moment now we'll flit through the air like leaves stirred up in a night wind. Everything in me screams that I should break the sanctity of this circle, move forward and help Li'uoa, but I clamp my eyes closed and push away the dread eating at my gut. This is the resolve my father preached. I need to stay focused.

For a moment, the world is cloaked in silence. Then my ears fill with keening, a hoarse cry that splits the skies like a scythe. I fling my eyes open.

Ta'atia hovers at the precipice, water flowing around her skin like a cloak, hair combing through the skies like bereft fingers. I once thought Elodie resembled Oya's turn as Yenu, the spirit of Death, but Ta'atia is every bit as imposing now. Her mouth is open, the scream from her throat cutting through my body until I feel a warm wetness pouring from my ears. But it is the figure a few feet away that commands my gaze.

Li'uoa is clutching at her belly, midnight streaks of blood spilling from her gut. Standing before her is Oyéré, her stained blade still in hand, her face warped in shock.

I break from the circle, rushing to her, but Jonas seizes me by the arm. "Don't."

Mari vaults over, plunging her blade into Li'uoa's back.

Ta'atia descends like a comet tearing through the skies, flying at Mari, water rushing after her like a tail.

Oyéré dives in front of Mari just as Ta'atia reaches out, the water stretching into vicious claws that pierce through Oyéré in several places. Oyéré falls with a gurgle and Ta'atia's crying grows louder as she realizes what she's done. The shell tied to Oyéré's waist comes loose, flying a few feet away.

The wind picks up speed, waves thrashing as water stirs into the air, as though an invisible hand is at work at the potter's wheel, shaping it into an earthen pot. We huddle together, crouching as the wind cuts at us. Soldiers run helter-skelter, searching for places to hide, but some run at the cliff's edge, their eyes lit with unholy light. I try to stand, but the wind bears down on me and I am powerless as they jump off the cliff like baby birds learning to fly, arms bent like broken wings.

Ta'atia's screams ride higher on the wind.

"We're not dying here!" Colin shouts, magic leaping over his skin. He is burning, but a layer of ice stretches from his feet, mounting into a thin wall that sits between us and the sea.

Suddenly water rises over the cliff, fingers grasping at the shelf, bursting through the ice wall and sweeping the soldiers who fell to Ta'atia's cries into its depths.

"Run!" I scream. The others rush to obey, Colin throwing Nana over his shoulder, but another wave comes through, slamming into us. I nearly collapse, but Jonas pulls me to my feet, dragging me out of its reach. We run into an alcove, a small lean-to formed by two boulders pressed against each other like cupped hands. I glimpse a shadow of dark hair as Mari disappears into the mist hugging the side of the cliff, taking my last chance at getting the talisman with her.

Elodie is shivering, her creamy skin turned a raw shade of pink like a freshly peeled fruit. "I don't want to die," she sobs.

"No one is dying!" I shout, but fear makes the words wobble off my tongue.

Colin splays his fingers, calling up a tiny flame. "Shit," he says. "Now is not the time for this nonsense to be happening."

"Tell me again how chaining helps if Ekwensi just takes your magic," I growl.

Colin scowls. "He used it to get the kunkun to safety, but I thought I'd have enough."

The waters are rising again, rushing toward us like hounds closing in on their quarry, and the wind whips with hunger, clamoring for sacrifices. We're out of options now—except one. Closing my fingers around the crystal dangling from my neck, I pray.

Please, Ìyá-Ilé, I beg. If you want me to find you, help us. Show us light in the midst of this darkness.

All my life, I thought I understood want. A hunger so stark it pushed you to do impossible things. I realize now that I've been remiss, shielded from true hunger by the comfort of my magic, unforgiving as it is. Perhaps this is what it is to be Aje, to live at the mercy of the world, afraid of the shadows of night, waiting for the comfort of the sun singing into the sky to chase away your bad dreams. Everything before me is a living nightmare, a world in which my loved ones will die by my hands, and now more than ever I would give anything to reverse that fate, even if it meant my spirit would never find its home again.

The crystal burns hot against my fingers. I hiss as I open my hand.

Ta'atia's shell rattles a few feet away.

Come, a voice whispers, the same one that haunted me as Jonas and I struggled across the cliff path—the spirit of the river. *Pay the price and I will aid you.*

I rise to my feet, an ache stirring in my bones. I know that I could ignore it, shut my ears to the hunger the voice awakens in me. But I have to take this gamble—find a way to save the people I love.

Turning on my heel, I dash past Jonas, heading straight into the storm. The sea is calling and I must obey.

Ta'atia is quiet now, an island marooned by Li'uoa's and Oyéré's bodies, but she looks up as I thunder past, her eyes leaking inky tears. Footsteps gather behind me, Jonas's and Colin's cries chasing me. But I don't look back. Once I reach the cliff's edge, I spread my arms and jump.

BORNE

I PLUNGE TOWARD THE DEPTHS, MOUTH FILLING WITH SALT AND WIND. But just before I slip into the grave of those icy waters, a ribbon of white threaded with blue slices through the gray like lightning. I slam into a steely body, sucking in a breath as needles pierce my skin. I raise my head, peering closely at the glowing scales, rougher than a gwylfin's hide, kissing my fingers.

"Welcome, child of Oya," the voice says, but this time it is loud, reverberating through my whole body like a ripple through a river. "Hold on tight," it commands.

I snatch at a raised fin, the curved, needle-sharp protrusion nearest my face, wincing as blood stains my palm. Then we're off, rocketing into the sky like a shooting star. We glide up the side of the cliff, the wind lashing at our backs. We pass the summit, a curtain of water hanging over it like a hand, cutting off my view of the main shelf. The wind seems to call my name, but before I can figure out whose voice is chasing me, we turn, darting toward the moon.

Gaeyak-Orin lies beyond, the City of Shards aglow with little fires that burn like incense candles in the darkness, prayers for the many souls that passed from the Physical Realm this night alone. As we burst through a cloud, cool air settling over me like a robe, I force my wind-swollen eyes open from their squint and flatten myself against the creature's slippery body.

The creature stops, its whole body rumbling, and I realize that it is laughing.

"I know the Oluso are made of sturdier stuff than this," it says.

"My daughter's mother, in fact, once gathered me into a net like I was a mere eel. How could I not love her?"

"Who are you?"

I ask the question loudly, hoping my voice is filled with all the courage I don't feel. We are so far off the ground, and without my magic I am like a baby freshly born, at the mercy of the world's cruelty.

The creature whips its head back to me, nearly shaking me off. I clamp my thighs around its length, digging my heels in. Its scaly face is wide and long, not unlike a fish, but its mouth protrudes into a long snout bigger than any gwlyfin's. On the top of its head are seven horns that weave across each other, the mottled white of them rivaling even the biggest kudu's. Its marbled blue eyes glint like freshwater pearls as it faces me, the light in them winking with a brightness that could outshine any star.

"You people have worshipped me since my father saw it fit to birth this land. I gave you the waters that clothe your skin, yet you do not know my name?" It huffs, its whiskers stroking my face as it does, a spray of mist coming from its slitted nostrils.

"Olokun?" I say, a feeling of certainty deepening in my mind the moment I say the name. I can't quite believe it could be the spirit Ta'atia mentioned, because it feels too impossible to comprehend. Olokun is the ruler of the deep, the keeper of secrets and twin to Yemaya, who rules the waters of the Spirit Realm. Every idol carving in Ikolé showed Olokun as a woman whose tresses stretched beyond her legs and eyes gleamed like mirrors. But the voice warming my icy skin is rough and deep, closer to the timbre of Baba Sylvanus's voice than any woman's I've ever heard.

And yet I'm *sure* I'm riding Olokun. I shudder, thinking of the power this spirit possesses.

The creature twists its mouth, revealing a row of sickle-shaped teeth, and I think that might be a smile. "Good to see you have not lost your wits."

"But I thought you were—" I swallow, thinking of how to explain without disrespect. "Your voice does not resemble a woman's."

"Don't be so foolish, child. You should know by now—we spirits are unbound by the constraints you humans place yourselves in. I am what I choose to be. Once I admired the skin of a serpent who dared creep into my bed. How glittering his scales. So I took it for my own. You may address me as you would him. Poor thing needs a remembrance."

He jerks his head around and we plummet from the sky.

I scream as we catapult downward, clinging to Olokun's fin until my fingers grow slippery with blood. We knock into a sudden gust and my legs fly away from his body, whipping like a flag behind me as I strain to keep my chest anchored to his scales. Just as my fingers lose their grip, and the wind rips me away from the icy warmth of Olokun's body, his tail curls around me like a vine, spiked ends leaving fresh welts in my skin and tears in my already-tattered clothes. We whistle through the water curtain surrounding the cliff and stop before ice statues arranged on the cliff's edge like trophies decorating a hunter's mantelpiece. I realize in horror that these are my friends.

"What have you done?" I ask as he deposits me on the ground.

"Saved them."

He flicks his tail over the statues and they melt in an instant. Colin thaws first, darting for me as soon as he's freed. He scoops me up, burying his face in my neck. A salty wetness burns the open cut on my cheek and I realize he's crying.

"I thought I lost you," he whispers.

"Touching," Olokun murmurs, whiskers dancing. "I'd forgotten how you Oluso cling to each other like oju-oro. So sticky."

Jonas takes a step toward me, his burning gaze setting my heart thundering, but Elodie clings to him, peeking at Olokun from the safety of his back.

"It talks?" she whispers.

Olokun does not acknowledge them, turning instead to Nana, who stretches as though she's just awoken from a long nap. "Tenjun's last child. You are far away from home, young one."

Nana smiles, a genuine expression that brightens her bitna-stained face. "Don't pretend you didn't laugh at my father's expense, Sei. If you wanted to help him, you would have sunk my boat when I left home."

"You *know* Olokun?" I ask, peeling out of Colin's hold.

I know Nana came from a fishing village, one of the Three Sisters across the sea. But beyond knowing who her father is, and meeting him once on an expedition with Baba, I know very little about the life she had before she came to Benin. Like Mummy, Nana shed her past life like an ill-fitting cocoon, embracing her new life with Will as though there had been nothing before.

"Sei watches over the Daiying Sea in addition to the Benin one. My father made us start the day with a morning swim, no matter how injured we were. I drowned in his bathing hole at least once a week."

I swallow, remembering General Tenjun's face, the calm way he watched me when Baba presented me to him at twelve. He didn't say much, just exchanged pleasantries with Baba over a meal of honey-blossom cakes and zobo. But when I spilled the scalding hibiscus tea on the edge of his cloak while serving him, he didn't even glance at me, just patted his robes as though I was merely a fly he had to swat rather than a child worthy of his attention. I wouldn't put it past him to fail to act when his children suffer, thinking it better to harden them, sharpen them to cut down life's obstacles, but the experience left a bitter taste in my mouth nonetheless.

"Spirit of the waters," Jonas says. "Thank you for watching over us."

He bows, curling his knee and sinking near the ground in the traditional way I taught him. My heart swells with pride.

Olokun surges toward him like a knife. Elodie backs away, but Jonas stands unmoving while Olokun swirls around him like a powder, inhaling deeply. "An Aje? But you have the scent of an Oluso on you as well." He presses his snout against Jonas's shoulder, teeth flashing like daggers. "Warring spirits, how interesting."

It takes all that I have to keep from getting between them. I know better than to offend a premier spirit.

"Sei, why are you here?" Nana asks. "What do you want?"

Olokun huffs, releasing another cloud of mist. "You've grown impatient. How bothersome." He flicks his tail at me, caressing my face with those spines. Colin pulls me behind him, squaring up as though expecting a fight.

"The child called for me, asked me to save you all. I promised to grant her wish."

"You don't grant wishes," Nana says, growing even paler.

Olokun laughs, tail swishing as he speaks. "You do remember that—good. I am no wish granter, but one who lives for bargains."

"What did you promise him?" Colin whispers.

I shake my head. "Nothing. I just asked the spirits for help."

"Nothing . . . *yet*. I answered," Olokun says, slithering next to me. "Saved you all from certain death. You are an Oluso raised to understand the statutes. Tell me, what is the price of a life debt?"

I swallow, fear stilling my voice. Mummy always warned me that the spirits came in different hues. Some, like Ayaba, could be kind, helpful to Oluso who knew how to ask. Others were exacting, seeing the Oluso as little more than upstart children Olorun himself had abandoned.

Nana darts between us. "This child is meant for something else. You are in error here, Sei."

"Am I?"

Colin steps up, whip drawn taut in his hands. "You are."

Jonas folds me behind his back, his thoughts brushing my mind as soon as our fingers kiss.

If he tries to take you, run. Don't look back. Leave us behind and go.

Olokun laughs again, a roar that drowns out the very winds, mocking us. "Such foolish children." He rears up, his majestic head blocking out the moon, every inch the fearsome sea serpent. "Test me if you will, and I will show you why I am called the spirit of the waters."

"Father," Ta'atia calls from behind us. "You returned." She shuffles nearer, carrying Oyéré's body with the care a child would have for a broken doll. Dangling from her neck is an ornate shell, the elemental form the omioja take when they die. That's all that's left of Li'uoa.

Father?

I blink, everything falling into place. Ta'atia could not leave Gaeyak-Orin while her father's spirit wandered elsewhere. She has been bound to this place, rotting away while her lover chose another in despair.

Olokun sighs, whipping away from us, and the tension in the air dissipates like steam whistling out of a pot. He stretches a lanky arm, curling a claw against Ta'atia's cheek, tracing the tear streak running down it.

"What's wrong now, omo kékéré?"

I let my mouth drift open in shock. His voice is soft, almost warm as he calls her the affectionate term most Oyo mothers reserve for their newborns. The imposing spirit that threatened us a moment before is nowhere to be found.

Ta'atia presents him Oyéré's body like a worshipper bearing an offering. "She's dead, Father. I killed her."

"That was wise of you, my child," Olokun says, nuzzling his snout against her head. "It is a difficult thing to love humans. An Oluso is trouble enough, but the Aje are even more fragile—unwieldy. You are wise to leave her behind."

Ta'atia's hopeful expression withers, her brown face growing as ashen as the moonflowers that stud the rivers, folding under the glare of the sun. "You will not save her?" she says, voice flat.

Olokun presses a claw against the scar running across Ta'atia's eye, and I'm startled by how well they fit together, like two pieces of a puzzle. "The rules apply to even you, omo mi. If you wish to save this Aje, you must give something in return."

Nana inches closer to me, Elodie in her wake. I lift an eyebrow but she shakes her head. Ta'atia lifts her gaze at the sudden movement, then she lays Oyéré down. When she speaks again, she is looking straight at me, determination shining from her eyes.

I brace myself, heart in my throat.

"It is as you say, Baba. I will give you something. But I beg one thing of you as your child. You must listen to what I say and grant what I ask without complaint. Can you do this?"

Olokun huffs another breath, a fine mist dusting Ta'atia's face, then he settles onto the ground, stretching like a lizard basking in the sun. "So long as we abide by the spirit rules, and you do not wager your life for this Aje, I will grant you what you ask."

She nods. "Thank you." She points to me. "First, answer this child's query. You owe her a life debt. Her mother was the Oluso that saved me from those who wished to gain immortality by consuming my flesh."

Olokun cuts his gaze back to me, marbled eyes gleaming with unholy light. "Very well," he says. "I will not take her life. She is free to leave as she wishes." Only the tightening of his jaw, the barest flash of his teeth, gives away his annoyance.

"Not just freedom," Nana says. "Safe passage to Ildok. *Everyone intact and alive.*"

He snorts, but Nana crosses her arms, and finally he says, "Done. You forget the mercy I showed you. That sister of yours was dead before I took her in my arms."

I stiffen, darting a look at Nana, but she keeps her gaze firmly on Olokun.

"For safe passage, I'll charge my usual fare." He grins, the cut of his mouth stretching back like a hook, revealing further rows of deadly teeth. "But the price is higher since there are five of you." He cocks his head, considering. "How about . . . half a lifespan? Will that do?"

"I'm not giving up my life for anyone," Elodie says.

"You can't be serious!" Colin shouts. "We can find another way across."

"If we travel by horse and wade through the marshes, we can reach Ildok in a day and a half," Jonas adds.

A day and a half would be far too long, wearing the thread of Nana's life down to its ends, but I don't voice that. There's got to be another way. Perhaps Colin's magic will work the next time we try.

"Half a lifespan from only one person." Nana declares. "Me."

"No—" I shout just as Olokun answers.

"Done."

He flicks his paper-thin tongue between his teeth, latching onto Nana's exposed wrist like a leech. I draw my blade, swiping at his tongue, anything to get him to stop and take me instead. Before this moment, I could not fathom raising my blade against a spirit, but Nana cannot afford to lose any of her lifespan, and my life is already forfeit, doomed to flutter out like a poorly tended candle.

My blade clashes with his tongue, squealing as though it's hit stone, the force enough to knock me onto my back. He reels it back in but I am too slow to stop the purpling bruise he paints onto Nana's skin.

"I thought you were a wise child," he growls. "You're fortunate I do not devour you for your foolishness."

"She didn't mean it," Jonas says, coming to my side.

Olokun cuts back to Nana. "And you. You've only given me a day. I asked for half your lifespan. You cheated."

"I wouldn't dare," she answers triumphantly.

"Why?" I cry, grabbing her hands, pleading. "You're losing time as it is, you don't have any more to give!"

"Because *I* choose to," she says simply, her face a forbidding mask. "I decide what and who I want to give my life for—not you."

The words are a knife driving into my heart. I drop her hands and back away. I was the one who forced Nana into this position. I took away her choice, and now she has one day of life left. There's no way to tell, either, whether this will affect Will and Haru as well.

"Family strife," Olokun rumbles. He circles me, sniffing. "How delicious." He flicks his tongue through his sickle teeth, wriggling it a fingertip's breadth from my nose. "Tell me, child, is there something else you wish for? I'm willing to grant it, so long as you pay the *price*."

"Father!" Ta'atia calls again, diverting his attention. She is kneeling before Oyéré's body, and in her hands is Li'uoa's shell. "Deal with me first."

"You can't mean to sacrifice your sister's spirit for this Aje's," he growls, jetting over to her.

She shakes her head. "Li'uoa was blood of my blood and bone of my bone. She never begrudged me my human mother. I want only to share her last will. Then I will tell you my wish."

"Go on."

She touches Li'uoa's shell and the white-pink curves transform back into the pale-faced human body capped with flowing black hair. Only now, without the face mask, we can all see that Li'uoa's human face is nearly identical to Nana's.

Nana gasps. "You used Miri's body. You promised me you would take care of her!"

"I did take care of her," Olokun sniffs. "She had the honor of becoming my child's human shell."

I remember Li'uoa stroking Nana's face gently, the tenderness in her expression when she woke her from the Dreaming. I wonder if a part of her held on to Miri's memories, knew that Nana was her human shell's precious sister, and cared for us for that reason.

"Li'uoa asked that she be born again as ijapà," Ta'atia says. "She wants to feel the love of a family from her very birth."

Olokun snarls, whiskers crossing like blades. "Absolutely not. My child will not be anything that can be caught and killed."

He's right. Turtle soup is a delicacy all over Ifé, the most popular variation containing stewed meat from baby turtles.

Ta'atia forges on, ignoring his disapproval. "My last request is that you grant Oyéré back her life. But you must take mine in return."

"I already told you—"

"My human life," she says, stroking her fingers over Olokun's snout as though soothing a wild thing. "My human half always reminded you of Mother. How she left us. It is as you've always said—it holds me back. Makes me weaker than I should be. So cut it out of my body, give that to Oyéré. I will do as you wish and make my bed in the sea."

"Then you leave Oyéré behind," Jonas says, clenching his fist. "How will she feel when she wakes to find you gone?"

Ta'atia smiles with all the joy of a young child inhaling sweets, the shadows of sadness and pain long stolen from her face. "It will be as she wished. She will be free."

"You may not change your mind," Olokun says. "You cannot speak those words lightly."

"There's no need to," Ta'atia says, pulling off her veil. Her mouth is far too wide, as though it was carved into her face with a sharpened knife.

Or a claw, I think to myself.

Olokun cruises into the air, arms working in sync, then he zigzags into a dance, flying some distance away. Ta'atia's hair flies free and she spreads her arms like a mother welcoming her child home.

"What do we do?" Elodie asks.

"Just wait," Nana says. She moves to stand by me, taking my hand. "Everybody get in a circle. Hold on tight."

Olokun curls up like a spring then catapults in our direction, his body a quicksilver arrow in the wind. He passes through us like a ghost, threading a chill through our bodies, then he pierces Oyéré's heart.

My eyes grow heavy as the world collapses around me. My body lifts into the air, lighter than a feather, and if not for the weight of Jonas's and Nana's fingers ringing my hands, I would believe that I were not a person at all, just a speck of dust. But as the wind gathers over my skin and the smell of honey-blossom cakes fills my nostrils, I open my eyes wide, trying to catch a glimpse of the place we're leaving behind.

All I see is a young child emerging from a pile of ash, her midnight skin resplendent in the moonlight. She wears Ta'atia's heavy brow and dimpled cheeks, but her mouth is less severe, quirked in a smile. She waves to me. Then she, on wobbly, childish feet stumbles to the cliff and dives. Olokun catches her, and she hangs on tight, whistling away on his back. As we fade out of existence, Oyéré sits up, blinking against the ash covering her face like a cloud. She scrambles, looking around as though she's lost something.

I close my eyes, leaving behind that lonely figure.

BLOOD

WE STEAL UPON ILDOK AS IT ROUSES FROM SLEEP, THE BLUSH OF THE SKY against the green-and-gold terraced hills warning that Rabbit Hour is upon us. We wade through the muddy path streaking between terraces, avoiding budding rice shoots that duck away like children playing hide-and-seek. Every now and then, we fall into the streams hemming the paddies, the coppery glow of the morning sky across their surfaces like blood drowning our ankles. Elodie jumps once when a fish hiding in that stream wriggles against her boot, but beyond a curse, she does not utter a word of complaint, hurrying through the marsh as though Olokun might change his mind and come after us.

Houses appear, sloping wooden roofs sitting atop thatched walls, rustling in the sticky, humid air like fisherman hats, gathered onto tall stilts that squat above waters the color of a periwinkle snail. Smoke crawls into the sky from a few, and as we pass behind one, a kettle whistles, squalling like an infant woken too soon.

"Not far now," Nana says, picking up the pace.

"Sure you don't want me to carry you?" Colin asks. Nana doesn't even turn, charging ahead though each step causes her unimaginable pain. It makes sense—Will and Haru await us at the end of this trek. For her that's enough reason to push through.

"I'll take you up on that offer if you don't mind," Elodie says, wrinkling her nose as she steps in another puddle. "Where are we going again?"

"General Tenjun's," Jonas answers. "We need to regroup, figure out how to get Dèmi to Iya."

"And this Iya is another monster or—"

"We?" Colin scoffs, his voice drowning out Elodie's. "Last I heard you were all for law and compromise. Now it's 'we'?"

"Colin," I warn.

"*We're* all fighting for Oluso freedom," Jonas retorts. "So, yes, it's we. I'm prepared to do anything necessary."

Colin's eyes take on a dangerous glint. "Anything? Even bleed for that freedom?"

"If we lose track of Nana and end up lost, I'll bleed both of you," I growl, pushing ahead. "Save your anger for the coming war. We need to get to Master Tenjun's."

Elodie catches up to me, her face bright with amusement. "I heard Tenjun could cut a single strand of hair with only a swipe of his fingers. Do you think he'd demonstrate if I asked?"

"*Master* Tenjun will cut off more if you're not careful," I mutter darkly. General Tenjun isn't one to entertain what he perceives as disrespect, even from Eingardian nobles.

She grins. "Challenge accepted."

I don't bother responding. Better to let her find out.

We speed up, chasing after Nana as she wends her way through her former hometown with the surety of a fish returning to its birthplace. Soon we scramble onto scrubby dirt paths, darting away from the harbor beyond those stilt houses. Giant Eingardian ships festooned with purple-and-gold flags stud the shoreline like barnacles, the crash of water against their wooden bodies unsettling sleeker junkets lined up like sleeping pallets. A junket with fluttering blue sails pulls into the low dock, and the patrolling Eingardian guards fall upon the boat like ants scavenging for their next meal, rifling through its cargo against the cries of its sailor.

I bristle. "Why is Eingard in control of the border? Isn't this in violation of Tenjun's treaty?"

Colin shoots me a quizzical look. "You didn't know? The Council decreed that all regions harboring free Oluso had to double their tributes to make up for lost revenue."

Jonas shakes his head, incredulous. "I never authorized any such thing."

Colin scoffs. "Then you're a fool who can't read treachery in your own ministers, or they've managed to hide this even from you."

"At the very least, my father wouldn't—" Jonas starts, then stops, forehead puckering, as though he's just remembered something. "He would," he finishes simply. "We signed an agreement a few weeks ago to send aid ships to the other three regions. This must have been what he meant by 'aid.'"

"*A good ruler must learn to compromise*," I parrot. "Isn't that Markham's motto?"

Elodie sidles next to him. "My mother led the charge on this. I acted as witness to the decree along with Lord Kairen."

Colin frowns. "My father knew?"

She nods. His mouth sinks into a flat line, brows drawing together into a scowl. He walks faster, shuffling ahead until his back looms like an impenetrable wall between us.

I rush forward, but Jonas tugs at the hood of my cloak, holding me back. "Leave him. He needs some time to think."

"How would you know?" I seethe. "You don't know him like I do."

The words ring out like fire-tipped arrows, quick and bent on destruction. The rage I thought I'd controlled in Gaeyak-Orin returned at the sight of those ships, building in my chest like a heap of burning coals.

Everything has been a mirage, a war fought with smoke and mirrors. We spent so long dancing around the Council's unreasonable demands, fighting for compromises, only to find that our blades were dulled from the start—they had no intention of working with us. But what hurts worse is, all this time, I've believed in Jonas's vision, suffered in hopes of freeing the Oluso. Yet now it seems that all we've done is live idly, dreams of love blinding us to the chains binding our feet. And though I know he isn't entirely to blame, that I made this choice to wait and hope, I can't forgive anything right now.

Jonas drops his hand as though he's been burned. I forge on before I think better of my anger and apologize, leaving him with Elodie.

I fall into step beside Colin as Nana turns, leading us onto a wide road. The street is clear, with not even a lizard in sight. Buildings the color of bone run alongside us, leaning against their wooden rafters and beams like weary soldiers seeking reprieve. Papered windows adorned with letters or pressed-flower patterns hint at shadows beyond, but save for the strong smell of tallow mixed with the piercing odor of whale skin and dried fish, nothing lies in wait.

"He sent me a letter asking me to come home," Colin offers.

I don't need to ask who *he* is. In a way, it's strange to be able to conjure up an image of Lord Kairen when he has been a nameless specter hanging over Colin for so long, an oft-salted wound that refuses to heal. I just nod, waiting for Colin to continue.

"He said he regretted everything. Trying to kill me, rushing into another marriage, joining the Council. He told me he still grieves my mother." He reaches for the scabbard strapped to his back, muscles beneath his navel winking at me as the motion makes his shirt ride up just a little. I avert my eyes as he thrusts something under my nose. It's a paddle with several faces carved in the body and two spikes jutting from its sides like horns, a wooden ceremonial sword inscribed with a family's history.

"It's my mother's acama," he says, using the Berréan term for what I know as an idun. "With it, I can return to T'Lapis, be recognized as it's heir." He pauses, shooting me a wry smile. "I'd be a prince of sorts, if that's something you're into."

I swallow against the sudden lump in my throat, my pulse quickening against my collarbone. We wade up stone steps at the end of the street, the clack of our boots against the stone disguising the way my heart drums in my chest. There are more houses peeking over high walls with slanted roofs and curved eaves that tip up at the end in a smile. Wisteria trees cry in the sticky heat, littering the path with lavender flowers that flutter like butterflies in the slight breeze up hill.

I clear my throat. "Did you accept his proposal?"

He sighs, the sound lingering between us like a rift.

"All right then, I suppose princehood isn't appealing to you." I glare at him, and he quirks his mouth in answer.

"I used the acama to visit the Berréan elders." His eyes spark now, ablaze with purpose. "The kunkun now have a stronghold north of Ismar'yana. It's where Ekwensi took the others. People fear the desert, so we're safe. My father knows nothing of it."

Then his lips draw into a thin line, flame extinguished. "I should have known better than to trust the esteemed Lord Kairen. No doubt he needs something. My father has never done anything that didn't involve self-interest."

There is raw hurt in his voice, a nakedness that betrays the hope he's buried deep inside. I want to tell him to forget his father, to reassure him that he has me, and Will, Nana, Haru, and Baba—that we are his family. But that family is dying, and there's no time for comforting sentimentality, not until we're all safe.

Still, I understand the pain he feels. After all, it's the same thing that keeps Nana ahead of us, retracing her steps as though she is a wayward child hurrying home for a meal rather than a prodigal daughter banished to an unknown fate. The same wellspring of curiosity and grief that lingers in my chest like a cold every time anyone offers me a glimpse of what my parents were like.

Slipping my hand into his, I give Colin's fingers a squeeze. Elodie makes a noise behind us, and I know Jonas must have noticed as well, but I don't care. Colin is my *friend*, and if it bothers the Eingardians' sensibilities, that's something *they're* going to have to deal with. I don't have time to explain Oyo-born standards of intimacy, not when we have lives to save and a war to wage. Not when those Eingardian ships are so close inland, hovering like salivating beasts.

Nana ventures into a circular recess in an adjacent wall, stopping at the bronze gate at the center. There are two statues on either side, creatures that resemble the form Olokun appeared in, with orbs in their mouths.

Ìyá-Ilé's crystal warms against my skin, the deep rose darkening to a near crimson. There are some characters inlaid vertically in the door, and a wooden plaque to the side in Orchean, the main language spoken in Goma. I cannot read Orchean; Nana only taught me basic shapes to get by, but I know the plaque spells out her discarded family name. The characters I have better luck with, having studied Goma-dori under Nana's care.

To catch a tiger, you must go to a tiger den.

Murmuring the words as though they're a spell, Nana backpedals, running full-force at the door. Right before she collides with it, she leaps onto a statue, dislodging its orb, and springs to the gate's apex, flinging onto the other side. A dog barks. And with its cries come other voices, hushed whispers that swell together in frenzy. Feet tap out staccato beats, and moments later the gate creaks, swinging back on rusted hinges.

A small boy peers through the slit of an opening, his mop of curly brown hair hanging heavy over his acorn-like face. I push back the urge to stare, but I know with growing certainty that I have seen him before.

"The master asks that you wait," he says in a voice much bigger than his wiry frame. "He'll send for you when he is ready. The house is not prepared to receive visitors."

"You're Elu's son," I say. "What are you doing here?"

He glances at us, realization dawning on his face, then he looks around before adding, "Wait here without making noise, then knock once you hear the chimes for Crow Hour. Someone will open the gate for you then."

With that, he slams the gate shut.

"He can't be serious," Elodie says. "It's bad manners to turn away a guest. We haven't had anything to eat in over half a day."

"No one asked you to come on this journey," I snap.

"Rude." She settles against the wall, using her cloak as a pillow. "You wouldn't have gotten far without my help."

I hate that she's right.

"Can we afford to wait that long?" Jonas asks.

"I don't know," I say. And I hate that even more.

Colin stalks to the gate. "We don't have time for this."

I catch his arm. "We can't afford to offend General Tenjun. Crow Hour is not far off."

In Goma, perceived disrespect is enough to get you banished from a home or community events. For elder Oluso like General Tenjun who fought during Alistair's Betrayal, it is an act of war. Though we're bringing Nana home to get her help, he could find fault with us simply for the trivial act of waking him when he's not ready.

"It will offend him more if we brought home his daughter's corpse. I say we go in."

I look to Jonas. He shrugs. "You wanted action, right?"

Sighing, I nod. We have to go in, customs be damned.

"Rules were made to be bent," Elodie contributes, stretching leisurely. "You can't worry about hurting people's feelings when there's something you want."

I stifle a laugh. I don't know why I expected anything different. Her very presence here is evidence she does as she wants when she wants. It's both frightening and strangely admirable.

Jonas clasps his fingers, holding them out in front of him. "You jump, and I'll boost?"

Elodie wags a finger. "I won't be doing any of that. Too much work."

Colin flicks a tendril of her hair as he moves back, getting some distance. "No need, princess. Only one of us needs to open the gate. He meant me."

I cross my arms. "Or me."

He flushes, embarrassed. "Yes—sorry." Then he sprints toward the gate, leaping off Jonas's hands as a support. A breath later, we hear a low thud, followed by a string of curses.

The gate whistles open and Colin appears with an elderly man in tow.

The man takes in our tattered clothes and dirty faces. "The master welcomes you in," he sniffs, turning his back to us.

I wonder now if he was there the entire time, if this was another test. If so—we've failed handsomely. But I don't much care at the moment. We're running out of time.

We thread after the man like ducklings following their mother. The sun creeps past the clouds, its heated glare banishing shadows, but the air is still wrapped with the dewy kiss of a new day. Soon we are in a courtyard, broken up by patches of manicured bushes and well-tended trees. Young boys sweeping look up as we pass, the white rags on their heads bobbing together into a sea of foam as they cluster to gawk at us. Elodie gawks right back, unperturbed.

Other servants bustle about with arms full of cloth or steaming trays of food, their Oluso markings peeking out from sleeves and hems. But there are some who have no markings at all, Ajes who weave through the throng as though they're merely part of the landscape.

"You allow mixing here?" I ask, the question spilling out of me like water from an overfilled well.

Once Alistair Sorenson came to power, the Gomae elite brokered an uneasy truce with Eingard by employing a system of banishment and tribute. Gomae Oluso identified at birth live in designated Gomae nokha—Oluso clans run by specific magical families. The nokha rarely allows people to leave. So, it's strange to see so many Ajes here, living and working in a house with Oluso.

"Our master has allowed it since Lady Nana left the house for her marriage." Our guide pauses to let out a polite cough. "Lady Hanae thought it best to help prepare for when Lady Nana and her consort returned. These Ajes were poor folk living in town or on the outskirts. They willingly joined our nokha once we opened up our home."

I raise an eyebrow. From what I know, Nana's parents never so much as intimated this. Beyond communicating their disapproval of her marriage with Will, they haven't replied to her letters often since she left. Still, it's nice to see both Oluso and Ajes going about their regular days as though there is nothing to fear.

Jonas catches my eye, and I don't need to read his thoughts to know what he's thinking—this is the Ifé we've been dreaming of, one where everyone lives together in harmony.

"Is no one afraid an Oluso might . . . lose control?" Elodie asks.

The old man sniffs his disapproval. "Life is beyond your control, young one. There is a risk in everything. But our Ajes believed enough in our restraint to trust us. We do not take that lightly."

She hums appreciatively. "Good to know."

A small girl darts across, chasing a flying piece of parchment. Jonas catches it and she bows, flashing the okri tattoo marring her dusky cheek. The other part of the Gomae truce forces nokha to give up a few Oluso every year to Aje nobility, as well as treasured gifts of jade, embroidered cloth, and jewels. In return, the Gomae Ajes offer a protection of sorts—as long as Gomae Oluso keep strict social codes and reside in their nokhas, they are not hunted the way the Oyo Oluso are ruthlessly hunted.

Our guide turns on the girl, snapping his fingers, and she scampers off.

"Apologies, esteemed guests. She is a new arrival."

"You take okri from other places?" I ask, frowning.

Our guide pulls down his sleeve, revealing a mark similar to the girl's on his wrist. "Master Tenjun pays extra tribute to relocate abandoned okri." He purses his lips, and I suspect that's the closest to a smile I'll get from him. "The local lords know better than to demand okri from this nokha. We have never paid the due in twenty years."

We reach a low bridge overlooking a pond filled with speckle-bellied fish that whip between lotus flowers. A brilliantly painted pavilion lies beyond, under an arbor of camellia trees. As we near it, a man rises, tapping his rod against a low stone. He is half-turned, but I would recognize his craggy face and his slim nose anywhere. Seven and a half name days have passed, but General Tenjun is the same.

The Oluso spread in neat lines on the raised dais behind him call up their magic in unison, a riot of flames bursting from their fingers. There are at least a hundred faces, but I make out in particular fifteen we saved last year in Lokoja. At the front is Elu's son, his slim frame doused with a magenta flame that spreads out over him like a peacock's coat.

"Hold it, Haroun," General Tenjun says. "Feel the pit in your belly. That is the hunger inside you. Tap into that."

Little Haroun tries, but his magic flickers.

"Think of all the things you want to do," General Tenjun instructs. "The desires that are unfulfilled. Hold on to those. Now . . . take hold of everyone. Without turning your back."

Haroun shifts his feet apart, stretching his fingers toward the shadows falling onto the pavilion. Almost immediately, his magic flares, and the two Oluso closest to him freeze. I watch, breath stopped as he curls his fingers and the arms of the Oluso swing to the slim blades at their waists, as though controlled by an unseen force.

Haroun's skin beads with sweat as the flames surrounding him dim again, burning down to an aura.

General Tenjun speaks again, his voice a war drum, rousing his soldiers to action. "Think of your mother. What did she suffer? Your aunt. How did she die?"

I stiffen. "Master Tenjun—" I call.

"Will you let them be forgotten?" he bellows.

Haroun's flames explode, pluming into the sky, and suddenly every Oluso on the platform shifts, hands drawing to the blades at their waists, perfectly in unison.

"What in the seven hells?" Elodie exclaims, ducking into the pavilion. "Can you all do things like that?"

Haroun startles, and the Oluso rattle to a stop. Haroun collapses onto his back, breathing hard, and people around him bend to his aid.

General Tenjun cracks his rod against the bench, whirling to face us. "First you clamor at my gates before a reasonable hour. Now you interrupt training?"

"If you please, sir," Jonas begins.

Pressing my hand against his back, I push him into a bow, then follow suit, hoping the others will do the same. "Forgive us, Master Tenjun. We don't mean to disturb, but we come seeking aid."

"Abidèmi, do I look as though I have lost my eyesight?" he asks.

"No, Master. But we would not demand help at this hour were the need not great."

"How great is your need?"

Switching to Goma-dori, I add, "The wolves are at our door and our blood is drunk by wild beasts."

He pauses a breath, then answers almost reluctantly, "Then I will carve you a pot to hide in. Rise." He moves closer, peering at our faces, lingering for a moment on Jonas's before focusing on me. "Is this all of you?"

I frown. He must not have seen Nana yet.

He sweeps past, taking my silence as an answer. "Come."

We rush after him as he all but flies through the walkway adjoining the pavilion. Pulling open the sliding door leading into the house interior, he discards his slippers just outside, and I copy him, flinging off my wet, marsh filled boots. The others take a moment to remove their shoes while I follow him, shuffling onto the lacquered wooden floor that squeaks. He stalks down a long corridor, passing more doors woven with flawless seams of paper. Then he swerves to a stop near a circular opening reminiscent of the pattern at the gate.

Beyond is a low table with some scrolls neatly arranged on the desk. A large stone wheel and a slab of ink keep the papers company. The room is sparsely furnished save for paintings that show the beauty of the Goma landscape and a few that depict battles fought in times past. A slightly raised seat lingers behind the table and several cushions are scattered on the floor on the other side.

He indicates the cushions. "Wait here."

"You expect us to sit—" Elodie starts.

He turns on his heel, rushing away.

Then he stops, listening, poised like a lion on the verge of securing its prey. Whipping around, he stalks to a door at the end of the hall with a paper-thin partition embroidered with the riotous pink patterns of the camellias outside. I dart after him before I think too much, fearful of what I might find.

Squaring his shoulders as though preparing to go to battle, he slides the door open.

Nana sits on a blanket on the floor. Will is at her side, cradling a sleeping Haru whose little hands ball tight near her face, the bitna veins puffing against her round, heavy cheeks. Another woman lingers near, waterfall hair obscuring her face. Catching sight of her father, Nana jerks up, pressing her face to the ground, but the woman pulls her back.

"Keep still, Little Bird," she clucks. "Your injuries will only get worse."

She dabs at the cuts on Nana's hands while Will offers a low bow.

Tenjun clears his throat.

"She is my daughter," the woman says, peering at a particularly deep gash splitting Nana's thumb. "I am allowed to welcome her at any time, even if you choose not to."

"I didn't say a word, Hanae." Tenjun sniffs.

"You didn't have to. You called me by my name."

He flinches. In Goma, it is customary to refer to people by family relations just as we do in Oyo. Once a family has children, naming relations are even more important, seen as a sign of respect for the hard work of producing children and a way to remind everyone of their place in the unspoken order of things. In Berréa, children's family names even follow the lines of their mothers.

"Sejin-ama," he amends. "I thought you would at least call me once she arrived."

"I didn't see the need to. You didn't carry her as I did, *Tenjun*."

He opens his mouth, but his wife is not done. She rises, and I nearly gasp. Her slim eyebrows, high cheekbones, and expressive eyes declare her Nana's mother. It is as though the spirits carved them at the same time, thought better of making them sisters, and bound them together as mother and daughter instead.

Hanae's soft voice fills the room in a flood of quiet fury. "I walked for hours with her, soothed her when she cried. Every time she woke with fits, I poured medicine down her throat and begged the spirits for mercy." She stops, voice breaking. "I made a mistake. I gave her to you and let you break her because I was afraid. But I won't do that anymore. I refuse whatever you *think* you want."

I know Nana is a last-born child, brought into this world after two difficult pregnancies that nearly killed Hanae. The two children before her were birthed safely but did not live to see their twelfth day naming ceremonies. With her eldest brother dying during a battle-drill accident when she was young, and her sister passing away, there are but three remnants of the initial seven Hanae Ryu suffered to birth.

The general darts a look at us from the corner of his eye, but Hanae turns back to Nana, waving us away like an empress dismissing her court. "We're long past demanding respect, Tenjun. Ataya can tend to our guests on my behalf. Get them out of here."

"Ama," Nana says, getting to her knees. "I didn't mean to cause a fight."

Her mother wrestles her back to the ground. "Sit, Little Bird. This is between your father and me. Children need not interfere."

"If my mother protected me with half this energy—" Elodie whispers. Jonas puts a finger to his lips. It's pointless, though—I firmly believe Elodie incapable of silence, and can only imagine what next will come out of her mouth at the absolute wrong time.

"We are very grateful for the help you have given us so far," Will says, a stricken look marring his already-weary face.

"Willard, close your mouth before I close it for you," Hanae threatens.

Will snaps his mouth shut.

"I came with Nana," I say, speaking up. "We brought her from Nordgren. I'm her ward, Dèmi. These are my friends—"

"You left my daughter bleeding at the main gate," Hanae accuses.

"We were told to wait by a younger attendant," Colin explains. "Nana got over the wall by herself. She must have gotten injured in the fall."

Hanae throws another murderous look Tenjun's way, and his mountainous face slackens, the tips of his ears going pink.

"I only meant to keep them waiting a short while—" he starts.

"I don't know why I'm surprised," she seethes, "Playing games with our children's lives is your specialty. What would you have said if she died at that gate?"

"It's nice to see that you two are still happily married," Baba Sylvanus chirps from behind us. Elodie jumps, nearly knocking into the door. He brushes by her, handing me a steaming bowl of golden liquid that reeks of the sharp, minty smell of camphor. "I was beginning to worry. Tenjun, you've been sulking all day, refusing to see your cute grandchild. I thought your marriage bed might have gotten cold."

Tenjun throws Baba a withering glare. "If you weren't my elder . . ."

"You'd beat me within an inch of my life? Try it." He beckons to me and I trail after him, walking gingerly to keep the scalding liquid from spilling.

"Baba," I interrupt. "We don't have much time." I fish out the necklace hidden under my blouse, careful to balance the bowl in my hand. "Nana has a day left. The spirits have shown us the path to Ìyá-Ilé. We need to find Empress Ren immediately."

Hanae's gaze settles onto me like a torch. "You're looking for my surrogate mother?"

"She's the guide who will get us to Iya."

She gathers her skirts, racing to the door. "Ataya," she screams. "Ataya!"

A blue bird with a snowy plume flies down the corridor, perching at Hanae's feet. There's a flare of color, and an old woman wearing a white head rag materializes like smoke. Elodie shrieks, backing away.

"Bring my box of ornaments and ready the horses. We ride for Aerin-Cho," Hanae commands. The old woman bows before disappearing in a shower of feathers.

Tenjun lumbers over, the shadows in his mountainous face deepening. "That woman is dead. You can't be thinking of performing that ritual—"

She whirls to face him, glaring. "I can do whatever I please. My daughter is back and I will not lose her again." She points a finger at a sleeping Haru. "My grandchild is here before my eyes. You want me to live a half life not knowing them? I would rather die."

"You will if you succeed."

"Then so be it."

"Whatever we're doing, we must do it immediately," Baba says, inspecting the veins under Nana's collarbone. They meld into a river of shadow over the ibante covering her breasts. "The medicine is useless at this rate. The poison has entered her heart."

I drop the bowl with a clang, sending a spray of scalding liquid spilling onto my skin. The liquid burns, and I hiss. Haru wakes squalling and Will gathers her to his chest, soothing her. Hanae crumples, falling on her bunched skirts, and Tenjun rushes to her side.

"You don't have to save me," Nana says in a quiet voice. She shares a look with Will and he nods. "You don't have to save either of us. Give what's left of our lives to Haru. Save her."

"You can't be serious—" Tenjun starts.

"I am more than serious, Father," she answers, a smile growing on her face. "I know I disappointed you when I ran away, and I'm shamelessly asking you the impossible now, but just do this for me. This is all I ask of you."

"Nana, there's still time," I plead. "We can find a way."

"I can get us to Aerin-Cho," Colin says. "Or I can try. My magic is really back this time, I feel it."

Nana looks to Jonas. "Can you take care of our girl? Make sure she gets to Iya? That she doesn't blame herself for this?"

He gives a silent nod.

"No! Stop this talk. I won't let you die!" I scream. "I'm not giving up."

General Tenjun straightens, his eyes flashing at me. "How certain are you that you can find Iya?"

"I'll find her even if it costs me my life," I promise.

"Your life is not just your own, Dèmi," Will cautions, looking at Jonas.

"Even if you manage to find Iya, she will only grant one request," Nana counters. "You cannot use yours to save my life. You must use it to win the coming war."

"Then how do you expect me to save Haru?"

Hanae kneels by me. "Plead with Iya. Ìyá-Ilé is our mother. Surely, she will have mercy on a child whose life has just begun."

"I should have gone to her before, shouldn't I?" I say, despair gnawing at my heart. "I should have trusted and hoped I'd get there in time and begged."

Nana shakes her head. "There was no way to know you'd get there in time. You did what you thought you had to do." She takes my hand. "Now, do this. Promise me you'll go to Iya. Haru will have more time. Go to Iya for her and for all other Oluso children who will suffer if the Council wins. Go for me."

"Please don't leave me," I beg. "Please let me find a way."

"Dèmi." Nana brushes a hand against my cheek. The look in her eyes is tender, loving. "You have to let me go."

"I can't," I sob. "This is my fault."

"No, it isn't. You asked me before if I saw anything about you. I didn't. Not until last night in Gaeyak-Orin." She brings my hands together, pressing her forehead to mine. "I saw you rising into the clouds, brighter than the moon itself. I saw you holding your own against an army."

"No!" I shout, wrenching away from her. "You can't do this. You told me visions could change."

She places a hand on my quivering shoulder. "Iya only calls one person at a time. It is for her own reasons. Just as she has called you to her, I believe she has called Will and me to meet our fate."

"You can't," I cry. "Please don't."

Colin turns away, fists clenched. No doubt he's struggling just as much. Will and Nana were parents to him too.

Will comes over, hemming me in. "The Council is gathering its forces, planning an invasion. You saw the ships on the border. You ran from soldiers in Gaeyak-Orin. The war is here, you have to see that."

"I know it's here," I argue. "But why does it mean I have to lose you?"

His squeezes my shoulder. "You have to fight for more than just us. You have to fight for the Oluso. This is what it means to rule. You have to be responsible for your people."

"I don't want to rule. I just want the people I love to be safe. Why can't that be enough?"

This is the truth I buried in my heart for so long, telling myself I was struggling only with the Council's ill treatment. This is the thorn that pricks me every time I see myself reflected in Jonas's eyes, every time he urges me forward, holding up a mirror in an effort to convince me of my own glory. This is the fear I haven't wanted to face—the part that believes I would never be good enough to rule, that the Eingardians were right after all and my hands are mere tools of destruction set to push the Oluso into chaos and misery.

Jonas speaks up, his voice tender yet firm. "It is enough. But we have to make the world we desire, sustain it so the people we love can truly be free. You said you wanted action—this is it. Go get your magic back so we can repel the forces that would steal our freedom."

I smash my fist into the floor, hissing when my fingers crumple against the hard wood. He's right, but I hate every single word. It is so much easier to run, to fear that I might fall.

My father's voice whispers in my ear, *Fear is the weight that pulls you into the water's depths* . . .

I laugh, the noise high and unnatural, a guttural cry that sparks from the deepest part of me. My body trembles, quaking as I laugh, but I cannot stop myself, only let the cries rip from me until my laughter becomes wrenching sobs that tear from my heaving body. Jonas wraps his arms around me, pulling me into the hollow of his chest.

"She's definitely lost her mind," Elodie whispers.

"What is wrong with you?" Colin yanks her back, steering her into the corridor. "Stay over here."

Nana sighs, then reaches for her mother's hand. "We're ready."

Will goes to her side, taking her other hand as Hanae places Haru in her arms.

"You won't change your mind?" Tenjun asks. "You accept this fate?"

Nana smiles. "The moment I met Will, I had a vision of us dying young."

"But you left anyway," Tenjun chokes out.

"I saw, too, that we would be happy. Joyful. I had to take that chance."

Will brings her hands to his mouth, kissing them. "It was absolutely worth it for me."

Tenjun lets out a shuddering breath. "We're doing this then." He peels back his outer robe, revealing a muscled torso knotted with scars. Hanae touches his shoulder gently as he unties the taba around his waist, handing her the belt. An orange-gold Oluso mark lies over his navel. "I'm ready."

Ataya flutters in, carrying an ornate box fashioned of rosewood and onyx stone. Hanae opens it, revealing several compartments: Hairpins of varying lengths tangle with necklaces to form a golden field on the left end; the right end boasting a river of silver combs adorned with a myriad of gems that swim along their polished surfaces; in the middle, a cluster of jade stones form a ring. In the midst of those stones are two sets of double rings. Hanae plucks these out, taking both to Nana and Will.

She gestures for her daughter's hand, placing the lavender-colored pair of rings on her left ring finger. Then she places the darker green pair on Will's right hand. "These are the rings I would have gifted you upon your marriage."

"Ama," Nana says, tears swelling in her eyes. "I can't take this. We can't take these."

"I know what you did for us," Hanae says, patting her hand. "Miri could not live under the weight those spirits gifted her."

Nana's eyes widen. Hanae leans close, whispering something in her ear. Then Hanae guides her to her feet, beckoning Will to follow. As we look on, she arranges both of them on either side of Tenjun. Finally, she places Haru in her grandfather's arms.

Tenjun pats Haru's cheek, his expression melting into a tear-streaked smile. "She's so light," he admits.

"You would have known that if you weren't such a stubborn old tortoise," Hanae clucks. She pulls off the jade stone necklace from around her throat, a small, white piece with an eye-shaped hole in the center, and places it on Haru's neck. The baby wriggles in her sleep, letting out a small yawn.

Tenjun pats her back one more time, then settles as Hanae arranges herself behind him. She pulls out the wooden hairpin that holds his hair, laying her hands against his temples as he relaxes against her. Hanae begins to hum, and suddenly I feel a chill creeping up my skin. The air in the room grows frigid as her steady voice rings louder and louder. My mind swells with her song, and my heart settles into a rhythmic beat. It is as though time itself has stopped.

Tenjun takes a deep breath, exhaling an amber colored smoke that spreads from his nostrils, clouding over his face. The smoke billows out in a steady stream, draping over Haru then curling its fingers against Will and Nana's faces and hands.

"What's happening?" Jonas whispers.

"Spirit transference," Baba answers quietly. "The giver exchanges a portion of their life to lengthen another's."

"Why couldn't we do this for Nana?" I ask.

"It's a difficult technique. Possible only between family members and mates." He stops as Tenjun opens his eyes, then he adds. "There's also a debilitating side effect."

Nana's gaze falls onto me, her eyes piercing through the smoke. "Promise me you'll find Iya."

Swallowing, I nod. "I promise."

She smiles before closing her eyes.

Hanae stops humming. The cloud of amber dissipates all at once. Nana and Will stand frozen, a fine sheen of gold dusting their faces, molded statues fit for ancestral shrines. Haru still sleeps peacefully, cheeks rosier despite the bitna scars still staining them.

Tenjun rocks back, the lines in his craggy face deeper than before, his dark hair turned a shock of ash white. He hands Haru to Hanae, who cradles her gently to her breast. When he speaks again, his voice is lower, raspier. "I have given what I can. Now you must find Iya."

INTENT

THE SCREEN DOOR FLIES OPEN AS ATTENDANTS BUSTLE IN, HELPING GENERAL
Tenjun to his feet and moving to carry the statues of Nana and Will.

"Take them to the family shrine," Tenjun orders.

But I lower my head into a bow. "Please give me room to say goodbye."
I barely breathe the words, my heart twisting from the anguish of losing
both Nana and Will at once. I know I need to find Iya, but I want—need a
moment here with them. "I want to be alone."

General Tenjun sighs but seems to understand. "We'll be in my study."

Then he and the others sweep out. Jonas gets to his feet as the last of
the attendants crosses the threshold. "We'll be here, when you're ready."

Colin lingers a moment more, then he follows Jonas out, and together
they pull the door shut.

I sit in silence, staring at Will and Nana's immortalized faces. They
look oddly peaceful, gazes still locked on each other even after death.
I want to cry, to throw myself about this room and rage, but there's nothing
left in me—nothing but sorrow nestled deeply in my bones.

An attendant flings the screen door back, slinking in half-bent.

"I want to be alone," I repeat, not bothering to look at her.

She sets a food tray down, rice covered in a plantain leaf, a perfectly
cut and skinned sliver of mackerel, and a thick, chilled soup with floating
red beans. My stomach rumbles at the sight, but I ignore it.

"For the offering," she explains, eyes never leaving the ground.

I nod. "Thank you." Then I remember that offerings can only be
made three days after a passing.

"Wait—"

I turn to find the attendant staring. Her eyes are voluminous dark orbs, her freckled cheeks are trembling, vibrating as though something hides behind them.

Placing my hand on the hilt of my bone blade, I ask, "Who are you?"

The attendant grins, then her face recedes, peeling back like an orange skin. Ekwensi's broad face appears like a crocodile emerging from the surface of the deep. Then his body follows, rising out of the attendant's shell until he stands in the room.

But I've had enough. "Why are you here?" I spit. "I failed your test. What more could you possibly want?"

He looks toward the statues of Nana and Will. "I've come to pay my respects." Throwing aside his cane, he kneels, bowing until his forehead kisses the ground. Then he repeats the motion twice more. I am shocked, bewildered, especially since he sent me on a mission that nearly took my life and cost me an opportunity to save Nana.

Darting over, I drag him by the arm. "You don't get to do that. You don't get to steal this moment."

He scowls, seemingly troubled. "It was never my intention to."

I snatch his collar. "Why are you here?"

He sighs, then he gets to his feet. "I need"—he stops, shakes his head—"the kunkun need your help. We need you in our army."

I sneer. "You're unbelievable. You said you didn't trust me, that you had no need for me. You left me behind."

"I was wrong," he says simply. "We were attacked by a convoy of soldiers pouring into Berréa. They had the kokulu to help them. I lost a few members of the kunkun. So I reconsidered."

"You *reconsidered?*" I shout, stabbing a finger at his chest. "You waltz in here after you went on about trust, and all it took was one attack to make you reconsider?"

His eyes spark with anger, and he tightens his grip on that silvered antelope head, strangling it. "I'll admit it—I'm not perfect. But I'm here to beg for your help this time. Join us; we need you."

"What can you offer me?" I taunt. "I don't need you anymore. I have General Tenjun and Baba and—"

He sneers. "Those fools?" He taps his cane as he leans close. "Tell me, Abidèmi, do you really believe they will fight with the force you need? Those two are too afraid for their precious spirit bonds to do what is needed. Isn't that why you came to me in the first place?" He edges even closer. "Would you have been in the predicament you were in had they urged you to slaughter the Council in the first place? I believe Sylvanus would tell you something like this—O ko ja éjò kan ninu ogba rè laibikita iwon."

You do not raise a snake in your garden, no matter the size.

I flinch, shame gnawing at my belly. "I was wrong."

"Really?"

"I never should have considered you an option," I say, crossing my arms. I feel so impossibly small, so inadequate next to him, but he doesn't need to know that. "You're just here because you realize you don't have the power you need. You hate feeling powerless."

He straightens to full height, flashing me a mirthless smile. "You are correct. What can I say? In my line of work, powerlessness is instant death. But there is one thing you still need to consider." He pulls back his sleeve, showing off those chaining marks. "I alone have the power to help you strike at the Council's heart with impunity. I can free you to take the actions that will make our people safe once and for all. *That* is worth more than two old generals discussing strategies to subdue an Eingard that has progressed far beyond their time."

"That technique is unreliable," I jeer. "Colin never has his magic when he needs it."

"Ah, but he's free to take lives knowing he won't bear the crushing weight of the spirits' judgment." He flicks a look at Iya's crystal hanging against my chest. "The way I see it, you're not even free to make your own decisions, are you? The spirits have you obeying their whims even now."

"Iya will help me, unlike you."

"*If* you prove yourself to her," he counters. "You despise me for making you prove your loyalty, but spirits do the same as I did. They measure everything out in their turn."

I'm reminded of Olokun, the way he ruthlessly took his daughter's human life, the speed with which he accepted Nana's sacrifice. Still, I don't want to let Ekwensi win.

"At least the spirits don't hide who they are," I seethe. "They don't pretend to care for people then discard them. Do you even care about the members of the kunkun? Or are they just a means to an end to get you the power you seek?"

He stills, then steps toward me, twisting the head of his cane. The silvered antelope handle gives way to reveal a blade, its sleek white body like a hardened piece of moonlight.

"Do you know, Dèmi, why I invited you into my camp? Why I wanted you to see the kunkun?"

I swallow past the lump in my throat, my eyes on that blade. "You wanted me to see what the other Oluso are suffering, how things have really been."

He makes an appreciative noise like a teacher whose student has done something wise for the first time.

"I wanted you to see your fellow Oluso, yes, but I also wanted you to understand this." He swings his blade at me, and I leap back. Just then, he disappears from sight and I barely have time to turn before I feel a hand grab my neck. The point of his blade digs against my back. The metallic scent of blood fills my nostrils.

I lurch forward, trying to break away, but his fingers are an iron clasp on my throat. His voice is oddly soothing, like the murmurs of a father to his crying child.

"Opportunities belong to those who make them. Not the strongest or the wisest or even the most deserving. If you want something, you must find a way to make it happen."

He lets go and I stumble forward, breathing hard.

"Commit that lesson to heart. I am prepared to do what it takes to free our people. That is the ultimate care. It's why I want to work with you. Trust me or not—I don't have to prove myself any more to you. In the meantime, kindly refrain from testing my patience further." He snaps the blade back into the cane, and it screams, bone whistling against metal. "If you change your mind, you know where to find me."

The door rattles open, but Ekwensi is already gone, the unconscious attendant the only sign he was here.

Colin and Jonas stand in the doorway, their hurried breaths making it clear they scrambled over.

"You cried out," Jonas explains, reaching for me. "What happened?"

Shuddering, I lean against him. "Ekwensi."

"Here?" Jonas spins, searching the room.

"No—he's gone now."

"What did he do to you?" Colin asks, jaw clenched. "If he hurt you, I'll kill him. I don't care if he's the leader of the kunkun."

I can still feel the burn of Ekwensi's hand against my throat, the promise that his fingers could crush me if they wished. But I can't bring myself to speak of this—not now.

"Nothing," I croak, lying smoothly. "He just frightened me showing up is all. I'm ready to strategize."

Colin's hazel eyes narrow as he scours my face, searching as though he missed something. But after a moment, he nods. "General Tenjun just received a missive—the Council is holding a funeral for Jonas in three days, inviting all the regional dignitaries. They claim he died in Gaeyak-Orin. They probably plan to unleash the kokulu there. We need to leave shortly."

With that, he disappears into the passageway.

Jonas strokes a hand against my bruised neck, and I feel a soothing, magical warmth. My throat feels better instantly.

He tips up my chin, inspecting me. "You know your lip trembles when you lie, don't you?"

"I didn't—" I start.

He kisses my forehead. "Come. We have to discuss things with Tenjun on the road."

We turn into the passageway to find Colin still lurking against the screen door. He offers me a wry smile. "Good that someone else can read your tells. Now you have to work harder to hide your pain."

He turns away before I can answer, heading to the study.

Jonas lets out a low whistle. "The sky must be turning. I think he just complimented me."

General Tenjun's voice rings out like a punch. "I won't be marching my soldiers anywhere. I can get you to Aerin-Cho to see Iya, yes, but I draw the line there."

"Then we will fail," Baba pronounces.

We hurry to the door. Tenjun and Baba are seated on opposing sides of a table, locking stares over a map spread between them. Elodie, blessedly, is nowhere to be found.

"You want to bury your head in the sand," Colin accuses. "Make a cowardly treaty like you did with Eingard years ago."

Tenjun slams down his teacup, and the porcelain cries out as it strikes the wood. "You failed to raise this boy properly, Sylvanus. He seems to think this is a marketplace he can hawk about instead of an elder's home."

Baba's sigh tells me this isn't the first time he's had to get between them. "To be fair, my friend, he just lost two people who treated him like their own."

"And I lost my daughter," Tenjun protests. "Don't ask me to throw away more people in a needless war."

"Your daughter gave her life so we could win that war," I say, stepping into the light of the four lanterns illuminating General Tenjun's office.

"She gave her life so her daughter might survive," he counters. "My granddaughter needs stability, not an aged grandfather running off to fight."

Jonas settles onto a cushion, pulling me down to sit next to him. "Let's consider what we know together, shall we? Perhaps then we can arrive at an agreement?"

"I'm considering the general still thinks he can bargain with the same people employing the K'inu to murder us. You should tell him that's not a wise idea," Colin grits out.

General Tenjun quirks a brow. "Is that confirmed? That they are in league with the K'inu?"

Jonas nods. "Dèmi and I met a K'inu in Lleyria. It spoke to her."

General Tenjun and Baba exchange a look.

"Maybe it'd be better to make a deal with the K'inu," Colin says. "Maybe there's something they want. We could win them to our side, stop them attacking."

"They're evil spirits," Jonas says.

Colin's brow furrows. "The K'inu are powerful. I still don't understand why they would let Ajes control them."

Baba sighs. "The K'inu have been known to have an affinity for certain kinds of people."

I swallow, remembering Ekwensi's tale. The kokulu were first sighted over Bia-Hyang. The K'inu are tied to the Fèni-Ogun. I'm sure of it.

General Tenjun taps his fingers against the body of his teacup, the pitter-patter of the motion like rain knocking against the windows. "The K'inu were not always thought of as evil spirits. Once, they were lingering regrets. Souls that couldn't ascend easily into the Spirit Realm—troubled souls even the Aziza did not come for."

"They're not necessarily evil then," Colin mutters.

I can still feel the voice of the K'inu that spoke to me at Ta'atia's. The immense sadness that threatened to drown me.

Free us.

"How do you know this?" I ask. "Ekwensi says the royal okosuns didn't know where the K'inu came from."

General Tenjun's fingers cease their movement.

Baba puts down the teacup in his hand. "No need to discuss that, Tenjun. You've suffered enough for one night. I will tell them what they need to know." He turns to me, his mouth drawn tight. "I never told you how I came to know your father. As a youth, before he left for Eingard, he trained with me. But I met him when he was a baby. Afèni took him from the arms of a kokulu."

I rise to my knees, bracing myself against the table. "*What?*"

Baba sighs. "It is as the songs say. The kokulu appeared out of thin air and destroyed everything in their sight. For three years, they waged war, snatching Oluso and Aje alike. They even attacked Benin Palace. Afèni sought the help of the ancestral spirits. With their help, she turned the tides of the Great War."

He shifts his teacup to a floating mound just west of Bia- Hyang— Sayaji Island. "Afèni tracked the last kokulu here and discovered it was protecting your father. Before she destroyed it, it begged her to help Osèzèlé."

General Tenjun pours more tea into Baba's cup, the rush of liquid filling the cup like an accusation in my ears. "We believe the K'inu are spirits of the Fèni-Ogun, the iron-bloods who were unjustly murdered before Afèni's reign."

I dig my fingernails into the hard wood. Deep inside, I already knew. The kokulu first appeared above an iron-blood village, and if they are indeed wrongfully murdered spirits, the iron-bloods slaughtered by their Oluso brethren are prime candidates. The K'inu have also spoken to me twice when they are not known to speak to anyone.

Jonas puts a hand on mine, but I stare blankly at the map, unable to summon the words to express the anguish crushing my heart. Now I understand the ache I felt hearing that K'inu voice, the sense of never-ending loss. Beyond me and Jonas, the iron-bloods are no more. Their history, culture, ancestral knowledge is all lost—wiped off the face of the earth like an unwelcome smudge.

"So, Jonas could be the one controlling the K'inu," Colin says, eyeing us.

"Or someone else." Tenjun lowers his voice. "We never found Os-èzèlé's body."

I jerk to my feet, fists clenched. "My father is dead," I declare. "You may blame him for teaching the Ajes ironcraft, but don't blame him for this. He is the reason I defeated Alistair Sorenson. He awakened my iron magic when I needed it most."

Tenjun looks away, his expression a little sheepish. "It is only one theory."

"You're still forgetting the possible culprit among us," Colin says, his eyes still on Jonas.

I rub a hand against my forehead. "Part of the bond between mates is reading each other's minds, Col. I doubt Jonas could hide a scheme like that from me."

He blushes, his ears and neck growing a darker shade. "He can see all your thoughts?"

"Yes. Unless I keep him out. And even then, some of his leak into my mind and vice versa."

"There is another possibility," Baba says, turning to Jonas. "You can't think of anyone we might have missed in your list of forebears? Someone who might have been an iron-blood?"

Jonas shakes his head. "There is no one. I didn't even understand the concept until my uncle Fred noticed my powers near my sixth name day. He was surprised. My family has been Aje for four generations."

"So what does this mean?" I ask, holding up Iya's crystal. "My father has been guiding me, leading me on the path to Ìyá-Ilé. Why would he do that if he wanted the Oluso punished?"

Baba nods. "I also believe Osèzèlé is on our side. He transformed the descendants of the Oluso in the capital when he could have let every one of them fall into bondage. Which means we're still missing key information."

"How can you be so sure that the K'inu are what you say?" Colin asks suddenly, zeroing in on Tenjun. "Where are you getting your information?"

Baba flashes him a warning look, but Colin does not even flinch.

I turn my gaze to Tenjun, whose fingers are tapping again. Ekwensi mentioned the K'inu talking to someone else related to Nana.

Tenjun sighs. "Nineteen years ago, before Alistair's War, the K'inu visited a Cloren Oluso in dreams."

"After they'd been vanquished?" Jonas asks, leaning forward.

Tenjun nods. "It told her of the child it once had, a child who had fallen to the bottom of a well while its mother was at the market."

He pauses as Baba hands him another cup of tea, then he continues. "We went to the well in question and found the remains of a child fitting the description the Oluso gave. After that we held a burial ceremony, and we watched the K'inu and its child as the Aziza sung them away."

"Could that Oluso help us now?" Colin asks, hope swelling in his voice. "They could talk to the K'inu, find out what they really want or if they're working with the Council."

Steam curls around General Tenjun's face like a shroud, obscuring his features. When he speaks again, there is no mistaking the sadness in his voice. "The Oluso can no longer help. She's dead."

My heart sinks as I realize who he's talking about, why he knows this story so well. *We*, he said. Miri, the sister Nana missed, the one whose powers could not protect her from an early death.

"Is there someone else?" Colin asks. "Someone from the same family?" I cut my eyes at him, shaking my head slightly, but he doesn't catch the hint. "We need to figure out what the K'inu intend to do before they unleash the kokulu again," he adds.

"Maybe all they want is rest," I say, remembering Shatu's words. "To find peace in the next world."

General Tenjun drinks the tea in one gulp. I wince as he sets the cup down, steam still rising from the clay, but when he answers his voice is controlled. "My daughter Miri was one of the greatest Clorens to live. The K'inu killed her even though she helped them. They must have, otherwise she wouldn't have drowned. She was a strong swimmer."

I shudder, recalling Nana's conversation with Olokun. Her sister was already dead when she released her body into the sea. Something else must have happened.

"It doesn't matter to me if the K'inu were wronged," Tenjun says finally. "They cost me my child. For that, they, or anyone who works with them"—he darts a suspicious look at Jonas—"are my enemy."

"So tell us your plan to defeat them," Baba says, pouring Tenjun another cup of tea. "You asked me to entrust the Lokoja Oluso to you, but you've been a bit secretive, my friend."

General Tenjun leans back in his seat, clasping his hands against his belly. "I gave a demonstration earlier. There is a strong Basaari in my ranks, a boy I know you are familiar with." He nods at me. "I thank Olorun for sending you to Lokoja last season. That boy's shadow magic could be the key. Haroun can hold hundreds in his thrall now. Imagine how we could change the battlefield if he could control thousands."

"Shadow magic can defeat the kokulu?" I ask.

"It can hold them in place long enough for us to fight back."

"Haroun is just one boy," Jonas says, his expression pinched. "It's a lot to expect him to hold several kokulu on his own. Dèmi and I fought one kokulu with nearly three hundred guards, and we almost lost."

"Haroun will only be fighting the kokulu that attack us," Tenjun says matter-of-factly.

Jonas's forehead knots into a frown. "So you're determined not to bring your forces to Eingard?"

"They are an Eingardian problem. I don't wish to waste our resources on chasing specters when the Council continues to push its way into Goma." Tenjun slams his cup down again. "Our soldiers are training for the day your Council sets its sights on finishing the conquest of our region. Oyo went down because of Osèzèlé's actions—apologies"—he nods at me—"but Goma will not fall as simply. We have to be a bastion for all the Oluso here."

"This is madness!" Jonas shouts, getting to his feet. "The kokulu are attacking Eingard now, but it is only a matter of time before they're at your door. Dèmi, tell them what that thing told you."

Four pairs of eyes fall on me, and I square my shoulders. "The K'inu that attacked us in Lleyria knew I was descended from Afèni. *Rivers of blood await you, sleeping moon.* Those were its exact words."

Colin scrubs a hand through his hair. "Maybe it was the remnant from Afèni's time, someone she wronged," he says. "Perhaps it mistook you for her."

I shake my head. "That K'inu looked at me like it knew me. It knew who my father was."

"The Oyo Oluso, and you, Abidèmi, will always have a home in Gomae lands I have influence in," Tenjun says. "But until we see the promise of this new kingdom you and this *boy* have proposed to build, we will refrain from any hasty pledges of alliance."

I scrub my hand over my eyes. One step forward, two steps back. Ekwensi was right. I don't have an army, not even a coalition of soldiers, but at least I have the path to Iya, a way forward.

Baba whistles between his teeth. "You've made your choice, Tenjun. I only hope you don't live to regret it."

"Tell me you haven't heard the reports, Sylvanus? Or seen the Ashkenayi pouring into our cities by way of Berréa? Not to mention that Tobias is lying in wait, searching for a weak spot to exploit."

"Ekwensi does not wish to fight you," Colin says, bristling. "He's liberating other Oluso who aren't yet freed."

"And leaving bodies in his wake, including our own," Tenjun counters.

"You're leaving more to die—"

"The Ashkenayi are Mari's doing," I interrupt, speaking up before Colin has a chance to say anything else. "You recall Captain Mari? Alistair Sorenson's right hand? She's using koko to strengthen her ranks. She's been plotting a rebellion with help from members of the Council. She's also trying to resurrect Alistair Sorenson."

"What?" Baba gets to his feet. "How would she—" He stops, chewing furiously on the chewing stick hanging from his mouth. "A blood sacrifice. How does she know to do this?"

I shake my head. "I don't know. But if she succeeds, the campaign the Eingardians waged against Oyo would be mere child's play. This time, they'll take Goma and Berréa with help from the Ashkenayi. And if they work with the K'inu—"

"We're completely fucked," Colin finishes. "We're running around like chickens with our heads cut off while they're executing a master plan."

"So, let's stop playing into their hands," Jonas says. He pushes aside the teapot, pointing to the smaller Eingardian cities on the map beneath it. "I've been building a network—lesser nobles, lords, and regional leaders who would come to our aid if I asked. If we showed them we were on their side, and we'd fight the kokulu on their behalf, they would help us." He turns to General Tenjun, pleading. "Give us a chance. If we marshal our forces together, we can defeat the evils in our way—be they the K'inu or the Council."

Baba whistles again. "What is the saying, Tenjun? Ikpakpaègbé éwi olè okpa éwi mhò."

The tortoise only has its shell.

It is a story every young Oluso learns. The tortoise went out to bring food to the spirits, but he met a leopard on his way. He ran from the leopard only to fall into the lion's pit. He crawled out from the lion's pit and swam into the river, only for a crocodile to corner him. Finally, before the crocodile crushed his head, he remembered his shell and dove in.

The message is simple: All the world is chaos, and troubles will meet us wherever we are, but we must remember what we have, and use that to quell our troubles.

"We'll see about that." He pours a final cup of tea, tipping the pot until just the dregs are dripping out, then offers the cup to Jonas. "Save my granddaughter and I will reconsider your proposal."

Jonas takes the cup, throwing the contents back in one gulp.

"You're lucky," Baba says fondly. "In my day, you had to drink ogogoro. All this tea nonsense is making our young ones soft."

I wrinkle my nose. Ogogoro is the cleanest distilled form of tombo, so bitter and acidic that it is rumored to strip iron. It is also the most popular drink during wartime, with soldiers drowning themselves in ogogoro barrels in hopes that they can abrade their minds of the horrors of war.

"If he drank that swill, he wouldn't be able to walk for a day, never mind saving anyone," I say.

Baba winks, a cheeky smile stretching across his face. "Ah, but he would have our respect." He turns to Colin. "Did you not pledge once to drink ogogoro if I betrothed you and Dèmi?"

I stiffen, heat filling my face. Besides being popular during wartime, ogogoro is also drunk during weddings, a sign that the groom is serious about wedding the bride. If the Council had approved honoring Oyo traditions, Jonas would have had to drink rice wine, tombo, and ogogoro, three drinks varying in strength, and hold his bearings long enough to get through the first part of our marriage ceremony—all to prove himself worthy of me.

Colin looks at me, then away before responding. "We need to move. We can talk of personal matters another time."

General Tenjun chuckles, a hearty laugh that sends the mustache above his lip flying. "The youth are still so passionate. The boy does not want to discuss it, Sylvanus. He's shut you out."

"Would that they would devote half that passion to training, our problems would be solved," Baba says, sighing. "Now, we are to send them off, yes?"

Tenjun rings the bell hanging off his seat, and a bird flies in. This one is black all over with a white and red plume that crests high. It hops down next to Tenjun's seat then disappears in a cloud of smoke, revealing the disapproving servant who led us into General Tenjun's home.

"What have you found?"

The servant bows, clasping his arms parallel with his ears. "Your

Eminence, this humble servant, Zetian, has conversed with the palace forest spirits. They report Ren's spirit will wander at Fox Hour, at the dawning of the Harvest Festival. Lady Hanae need not attempt a ritual summons."

"And how would our friends find her spirit?"

"All of us with the sight will take to the skies in watch. Ataya, Nexar, and I will be the signal bearers." He nods at me. "For our guests, the spirits spoke of a mask the Aziza queen gave them."

Shoving my hand in my pocket, I pull out the deer mask Ayaba gave me. "I can use this?"

"With it, you can see Lady Ren without needing a Cloren's sight."

"And the guards?" Tenjun asks. "We don't need trouble from them."

Zetian's mouth curls into an assured grin. I blink, surprised. "It is an auspicious day. Aerin-Cho is alight with laughter and dancing. The guards will long to visit the festival stalls, or they could be enticed into a game of jigo."

Tenjun reaches his hand out, and Zetian straightens, handing him a small embroidered pouch. He slides it toward me. "There is a mirror inside, attached to my soul essence. When it is completely dark, it means you are out of time. My granddaughter is dead, and our ties are severed. You will no longer be welcomed in this house."

"You can't be serious," Colin protests.

Baba puts a hand on his arm, but Tenjun says, "I am talking about the death of my family. Of course I'm serious." He stares down Colin, who has the presence of mind to actually stand down.

Tenjun continues. "Use this as motivation. Do not fail me. Come back, and you can have an army with which to fight the Council."

"I will," I answer, scooping up the pouch. It is light in my hands, as though it were a mere trinket rather than an indication that Haru's life is in my hands.

Jonas gets to his feet. "We won't fail you."

"See that you don't," Tenjun says. With that, he gets up and leaves the room without a second glance.

BRIDGE

My scalp itches, the jeweled combs Hanae stuck in my hair rubbing against it every time the carriage lurches over a hill, but I don't move to rearrange them, cognizant of the two men hemming me in. Jonas clasps his fingers together, his shoulder kissing my half-exposed arm, and my heart sets off in a gallop, my skin tingling at his nearness. Then Colin crosses his legs, and his foot brushes against the slit in the silk fabric hanging over my thigh. I sit higher, pressing my back against the carriage cushions, hoping the makeup Hanae powdered onto my cheeks is enough to hide my panic.

"Say the word if you feel like sitting in *my* lap," Elodie says, stretching along the cushion across from us. The layered silk dress Hanae lent her wrinkles as she presses her feet to the carriage wall, but she doesn't seem to care.

"I'm all right, thanks," I say. Colin's magic is still not back, courtesy of Ekwensi, so I'm just stuck in this situation for now.

She shrugs, pushing the dark wig covering her blond hair a little out of place. "Suit yourself. Just seems more comfortable on my side than over there."

"We're going to Aerin-Cho with purpose, Elodie, not for a holiday," Jonas says quietly.

"This is why she finds him more interesting, you know." She nods at Colin, whose head is pressed against the small window on the left side of the carriage, seemingly asleep. "He knows how to have a good time. When was the last time you forgot your duty, Auri?"

A ghost of a smile ripples across Colin's face. Not asleep after all.

I scowl. "He's shirking his duty joining us in the fight against the Council. As are you. That duty is what's keeping me from throwing you out of this carriage at the moment."

She grins, lips curling in a triumphant smile. "That's better. Not so nervy now, are you?"

I'm not sure pissed off is better than nervous, but at least it's different. I reach across the carriage in answer, ripping open the thin curtain covering the window. A cool breeze brushes its fingers against my face, and my magic sings in response. Outside, lush, green mountains stack next to each other like turtles, swimming against the cerulean sea of sky above us. The sun peeks over the shoulder of one of those turtlebacks, blinking a sleepy eye at us as we roll toward the city below. Iya's crystal hums against my chest, the thread of red light streaming from it shifting into an encompassing black.

We approach the main arch leading into Aerin-Cho, and Ataya calls the carriages to a stop. While she flutters out of Lady Hanae's carriage to exchange greetings with the smartly dressed Gomae guards standing outside the gate, I peer at the city awaiting us. The city is a riot of color, bathed in the golden-red light of the sun like a bride dressed for her wedding day. Ribbons and cloth of every color hang from arches and beams, fluttering in the cool breeze like ornaments. Buildings set in wood, stone, and clay layer on top of one another like patterns on a hand-crafted gown, each jockeying to catch my eye. Then beyond the main causeway, a round bridge rises aboveground like a wedding ring, clasping the shadow of the river beneath it.

For a moment, I am overcome with grief, thinking of how Nana often described this city, her wish that one day I would get to visit it—one day when we were free.

Jonas pops up next to me, startling me out of my grief. A guard looks over at the sudden movement. Ataya stuffs a handful of clacking coins into the pocket of the guard's uniform. The guard nods her thanks and settles back into her post, her blue vest puffing like a peacock's feathers.

"You can't be seen, remember?" I hiss, pushing Jonas back.

Light skin is not rare in Goma, where people range from ash to golden to rich midnight. Light hair, as well, is not entirely uncommon;

a few children every year are born with ash-blond hair even lighter than an Eingardian's. But blue eyes are very rare, an immediate sign that the bearer is definitely from another region, as most Gomae have brown eyes. Dark hair, blue eyes, and earthy skin could mark you as Berréan or Oyoan. You could still walk the markets of Aerin-Cho with lighter skin and lighter hair. But the likelihood you would be stopped and asked to give your family name, is much higher. And anyone who stops Jonas will definitely be able to tell he is no Gomae half-caste.

Jonas settles onto his cushion. "I just wanted to see what you were looking at." He taps a finger against his leg—the sign he's lying. No doubt he sensed my turbulent emotions and tried to offer comfort in his own way.

"Save the curiosity for when we're not being scrutinized?" I chide, keeping up the pretense.

The carriage lurches to life and I snatch at the collar of his traditional side-pinned shirt to keep myself from falling, bringing our faces just a breath apart.

"Thank you," I say, hastily drawing away from him.

He leans back with a smile. "Any time."

Golden-haired trees bearing swelling orange fruits adorn the main causeway, the sickly sweet smell of baby vomit kissing our nostrils as we rattle past the city gates. The curtains on both sides are decidedly closed, but as we move forward the breeze flings them open at different points, bringing us flashes of the world beyond. People racing through the streets carrying food and conversing; market stalls with criers who lob promises like common pebbles—prayers that will heal any injury, a lodestone that will protect its user through any storm, a mirror that will show a future lover. Then there are the young maidens dressed in flowery clothing that waves with the breeze, little children who dart between the passersby like monkeys making mischief in the trees.

The carriage rolls to a stop in front of a severe gray-and-gold gate guarded by five blue-robed soldiers on either side.

Lady Hanae appears at our window. "Ataya will take you to the markets. Once we spot her, I will send our signal. Don't get too distracted."

"We won't fail you," I answer.

She raps the side of the carriage twice. Ataya sets off with us in tow, leaving Lady Hanae behind with Zetian. I watch as she presses a soldier's arm gently, speaking to him in the high tones of Orchean, the main language spoken in Aerin-Cho. The guard's dark cheeks flush, his eyes brightening with a smile. Good. She will have no trouble getting in.

"What's the signal supposed to be again?" Elodie asks, yawning.

"A flaming bird," Colin responds, sitting up now.

"Ah."

I know Hanae wanted our signal to stand out against the fireworks and that Zetian had done this before as General Tenjun's page during wartime. Secretly, I wonder though what Zetian had said when Hanae asked to light him on fire. Had he been annoyed? Justified in his instant dislike of us? I am curious and also hoping I never have to know the answer.

The carriages come to a stop and we file out of the top entrance squinting like moles seeing sunlight for the first time.

The Harvest Festival is a time of contradictions in Goma. A time to honor and remember the dead as well as celebrate the newness of life. Then again, a harvest is just that—reaping the bounties of the fields and seabeds but leaving them dry and empty. Our bellies might be full, but the ground and swells starve for a little while in return. It is a season of give and take, a balance that must be honored in full. Including tonight.

People carry lanterns in different shapes, heading to the river that runs through the city to give them up as offerings for the dead. Then, on the stage behind us, young women crowned with white blossoms sway in light silk to music strummed on a long-bodied string instrument resembling a yomkwo.

I frown, trying to remember the Gomae name of the instrument Nana taught me—gaya?—geuma?

We wander past the stage to swelling market stalls bursting with scents; the oily sweetness of glass-thin noodles piled high on wooden plates battling the soft fragrance of neatly pressed, colorful rice cakes; the savory richness of thin fried rolls stuffed full of onions and minced meat; and crisp yet doughy cakes bursting with potatoes rolled in chutney.

Elodie stands too close to a merchant's basin, admiring eggs cooking in a roiling brown liquid, and I have to pull her away before the merchant's ladle cracks into her back.

"I just want to try one. I've never seen food like this in Eingard."

"We do have food like this, El," Jonas says. "In Porto Pischu, and Aelwyn. You just never visit those cities."

"Imagine what Mother would think if I went to those mixed-region cities. Or somewhere even crazier like Benin." She rolls her eyes, placing a dramatic hand against her forehead. *"My poor Elodie, besmirched by the impure thoughts of those bush people!"* she exclaims.

Colin produces a skewer of whirlwind-shaped potatoes and a flattened honey cake from his sleeve.

I shoot him a questioning look. "Didn't see you pay for those. Old habits die hard, shabi?"

He laughs. "There's enough for tonight. Don't think they'll miss any."

"It's more about not bringing attention to us."

"It would only bring attention if they caught me. And I don't get caught."

"What about that time when you were nine? And eleven? And fifteen—"

"I was a child then," he says indignantly.

"Ah, yes—and you're so grown-up now," Jonas mutters, and I can't help but laugh.

We pass a stall manned by two darker-skinned men wearing long patterned brocade coats paired with white silk trousers that billow in the breeze.

"Care for some tea?" one calls to me.

The other pours a cup of a thick, rich brown liquid, shoving it into my hands before I can say no.

"The spirits be with you, young one," he whispers before backing away. I glimpse the white Oluso mark winking at me just above the high collar hiding his neck.

There have been a few Oluso about, racing across the edge of my vision like fish slipping into the dark waters of a stream, hoping to blend in between the reeds. I know, too, that though Aerin-Cho is not as unfriendly to Oluso as Benin, the people here are prone to turn a blind eye when Oluso are being dragged away. It's most likely why Ataya paid the guards so much, beyond making sure they didn't look too closely at Jonas and Elodie.

Elodie pouts. "I would like some."

But the men are seated again, laughing and talking as though no one else is there.

"Better luck next time," Colin says with a smirk.

She stalks off to a stall a few feet away, admiring the way a light-haired Gomae merchant weaves rice skin into little eggshells while an Oyo merchant singing in Tiv, another language spoken by a few closer to Manapané, fills the eggshells with fish mixed with tamarind, ginger, and peppers.

"How much for one of those?" Elodie asks.

The Oyo merchant seizes up, narrowing her eyes. Jonas slides in front of her, blocking Elodie from sight. "My sister is a little silly, she likes to imitate the guards at the harbors," he says in slightly accented Tiv.

The merchant smiles, and her partner, the Gomae man next to her, pushes a few eggshell cakes our way.

Jonas offers a small bow and we scamper away, holding our warm bounty in sweaty hands like children caught misbehaving.

We double back to the stage. "You can't just slip into Ceorn like that," I huff, trying to catch my breath.

"Ceorn is the only language I can speak," Elodie says, staring as though I've grown two heads. "If they can understand me, what's the problem?"

"The problem, El," Jonas answers, "is exactly that. Ceorn is the language of Eingard. Our region has spent twenty years chipping into this one. People may understand you, but we're in Gomae lands. Ceorn is not respected. All of your status and privilege means nothing here—actually, it only makes them distrust us."

She shrugs in lieu of answer, directing her attention back to the stage. Another set of young women are dancing now, their silk shirts cut over their bellies, long skirts flying in the wind as they whirl. The bells on their ankles rattle and sing as they point their arms this way and that, glorying in the dance. Some beat colorful wooden sticks together to keep the rhythm, their beats getting louder as the crowd cheers.

My heart twists, and I wonder for a brief moment what it would be like to live like them, to have a golden garland plaited through my hair, my head held high, no fear that those around me might change their minds about my existence at any moment and devour me like wolves after a long winter. Instead, I stand here cloaked in grief, wishing for something that could never be.

"They are certainly gorgeous." Elodie slings her arm around my shoulder. "Why don't you dress more like that? Your skin's about the same shade—you could make it work."

"Back off," I say, untangling myself from her. Behind us, Jonas and Colin converse in hushed tones, but they don't look up, each absorbed in what the other is saying.

She giggles. "I can see the envy all over your face. If you want to dance, just do it. What's holding you back?"

"You don't understand," I snap. Shame burns my throat, mocking me for being so easily read. So I fashion my words into daggers. "I know this is thrilling for you, but there are real lives at stake, people who will suffer if we don't do what we came here for."

"I work with Ekwensi," she says cheerily. "I do understand."

"No, you don't." I clench my jaw. "You don't know anything. You're not Oluso. You don't have to live in constant fear of being killed, or worse."

She blinks owlishly. "I never said I was anything else. I just said I understood. I may not know what it's like to live in constant fear. In fact—I admit it, I *don't* know. But all I'm saying is you can't actually live like that all the time. You have to let go sometimes. You know, *live*. If all you know is fear, what are you even supposed to do if you win? How can you give people hope when all you know is despair?"

I open my mouth to say something, anything, then I slam it closed. The words she spoke feel like fresh air dispelling the fog that hangs over me. I want to tell her she is wrong, but I start to think about everything I've felt since I started this journey. All I have known is an unassailable fear driving me forward like a whip cutting into a horse, the fear that my failure will doom everyone I love. I have never once thought of what I'd do if that fear ever left me—how I'd put one foot in front of the other—and that thought scares me.

"Think about it," she says, winking. "I'm off to inspect those outfits. Some of those girls have belly rings. I've always wanted to know what it'd be like to kiss one!"

She flies off before I can say anything else, leaving me alone.

I watch as fireworks whistle across the sky, covering Aerin-Cho in a shower of sparks. One blazes the violet color the kokulu give off, and immediately I shift in a stance, already on my guard. But seconds swell into minutes and nothing happens. No bone-white figures tear the sky like meteors bent on destruction. This festival is safe, normal, and I don't know what to do with that.

Then Colin tugs at my sleeve, pointing toward a lone dancer in the courtyard just below the stage. The dancer wears a carved mask with a drawn chin and bulging eyes. We watch as they dance, leaping and shaking in the air like a kite, touching the ground only on one foot at a time like the seasoned masquerade dancers who come out during festival time in Oyo. People clap and sing, some holding their awestruck children in front of them like kangas hoarding precious pearls. Others whisper to each other, telling the story the dancer can only parse out in movement.

My heart clenches with the sudden hunger for home. To dance and sing with the Egbabonelimwin while the shekeres rattle and the bata drums stir my blood. I want to run the dusty streets of Benin without the burden that sits so heavily on my shoulders, reminding me that each carefree step is paid for with the blood of others, that shackles are my only inheritance for the crime of being born Oluso.

Colin gives my hand a squeeze. "I'll be back," he says before melting into the crowd.

"I asked for a masquerade, you know," Jonas reveals, appearing beside me. "For our betrothal."

"Oh?" I answer, maintaining a blank expression.

"The Council didn't approve, of course." He stops, giving a little laugh. "But if we had made it through that night—"

If the Council hadn't attempted to assassinate us, I think.

"I was going to ask you to look down from our balcony."

I turn at this. "You smuggled a troupe in?"

He grins. "The ones you talked about the most. From Ikolé."

I shake my head, disbelieving. "They would never dance for just anyone. That group of Egbabos are descended from the royal line. They only perform with the okosun out of respect."

"I offered them money at first. Enough riches to pass down two generations."

"And what did they say?"

He laughs again. "They spat in my face. Told me that all the blood money in the world couldn't buy them. That they would only dance for those fitting of their glory."

"So, how did you convince them?" I ask, curiosity getting the better of me. Jonas is here now, yes, but I think there are still things we need to iron out, things I need to hear to heal the hurt in my heart.

He reaches for me, stroking a hand against my cheek, and I still, not daring to breathe. "I asked them to dance for a queen they could be proud of, for an Oluso who refused to let hatred become her grave." He pauses, peering down at me through long lashes. When he speaks again, his voice is whisper-soft, caressing my cheeks as he leans in. "I asked them to dance for the woman I love more than life itself, the woman I know I'd hurt by asking her to live so far away from all the things she knew and loved. I got on my knees and begged them to give me a chance."

"Is that what you're doing right now?" I whisper, eyes flicking to his lips. "Begging for another chance?"

"Is it too unreasonable to ask?"

I lift my gaze, meet his. "No."

He kisses me, softly at first, a kiss that stirs the embers in my loins, making me hunger for more. Then he deepens the kiss, twining a hand around my waist and pressing me to him. We're out in the open, but I don't even care. Every touch of his skin is a burst of color eroding the darkness ensnaring me.

Then someone bumps into us, knocking me off balance, and I come to my senses, putting a hand between Jonas and me.

"No. Not now," I breathe, shaking my head.

I don't want to hurt Jonas, to burn the bridge he's trying to build between us, but I know that I need time, to sort the feelings warring in my heart and focus on something other than the fear that there will always be hurdles to cross, battles to fight to protect the love we have. And if I let the truth gnaw at me long enough, I will have to admit a deeper fear— that I may never be able to trust enough to sustain any kind of love.

He inhales, shuddering as he does. "You're right. Not the time. But we should talk after all this, yes?"

Colin reappears then, thrusting a meat skewer in front of me. "You might as well eat while we wait," he says without batting an eyelash.

I flush, grateful for the change, even knowing that he must have seen Jonas and me a moment ago—knowing it might have hurt him just a bit.

"They had a few Oyoan stalls over there," he says, shrugging in another direction. "Thought you might want a taste of home."

"Thank you," I say, sniffing at the skewer. The scent of scotch-bonnet peppers and peanuts fills my nostrils.

Jonas smiles. "Good idea on the suya."

"I know a hungry Dèmi when I see one," Colin quips. He offers me his arm. "Elodie is busy pestering Ataya with all sorts of questions. What say you we go rescue an old woman?"

"Sure."

Jonas seems flustered, but he only nods. "I'll keep a watch out for the signal. Not long now."

Colin leads me to the stage, where Elodie jumps up and down like an excited puppy, the wig on her head in danger of flying off.

"Be careful with that, it's a bit spicy," Colin says as I bring the suya to my mouth.

I scoff. "I may have lived outside of Oyo for a year, but there's nothing wrong with my tongue."

He laughs. "Whatever you say."

I sink my teeth into the suya defiantly, nearly piercing my mouth with the wooden skewer. The pepper stings my tongue, and my eyes water. Suddenly I am struck by the urge to laugh until my belly aches. Instead, I open my mouth and all that rises is a sob, desperate and unrestrained.

Colin pulls me against his chest, rubbing my eyes with the hem of his flowing robes. "I told you to be careful. You never know how time and your surroundings change you," he mutters.

He hugs me to him, holding my shoulders as I quake, crying in a way I haven't allowed myself to in a year. When I am finished, spent like the survivor of a shipwreck emerging onto a distant shoreline, I settle back and he tips my chin up.

"I know you're scared, but we'll get through this. We will be free."

I flash him a half smile. "Thank you." He always seems to know exactly what I need to hear.

He slips his fingers through mine. "Know that I will do *whatever* it takes to keep you safe. Never doubt that."

A firework explodes in that moment, illuminating his tawny face, and I'm struck by his raw beauty. There is strength and fierceness in the way he looks at me, a defiance in the way he holds his full lips, but there is a sadness in his eyes, an ache that calls out to me from those hazel depths, asking me if I'm willing to sink and never breathe air again.

A bird flits overhead then, its black feathers blazing with red flames that rip across the darkened sky like a knife.

It's time.

TRIBUTE

Slipping my mask on, I follow that blazing trail and turn into a side street. I sprint, racing down another as soft, white forms appear out of the darkness, ghostly apparitions that flicker like lanterns behind paper shades. I flick a look to each one as I pass, hoping to find a woman dressed in traditional royal Gomae garb, but my initial search is not fruitful.

Colin follows above, leaping between rooftops, and I mark my position from the sound of his feet thudding against the clay tiles.

Jonas catches up to me as we burst back out into the main market. "Elodie attracted the attention of some guards," he breathes. "We need to blend in."

"I just wanted to try fermented rice wine." Elodie huffs, hands on her knees from running.

Ataya twitters in bird form, hopping up and down on Jonas's shoulder. Then she soars into the clouds, disappearing from sight.

"I don't suppose we could call the forest spirits here, decode what she said?" Colin asks.

"She's fetching Lady Hanae," I answer.

Jonas lifts an eyebrow. "You understand bird-speak now?"

I tap the antlers of the mask half covering my face, and he mouths his acknowledgment. "Ah."

Colin jerks a finger toward five approaching guards, each wearing the rich azure and purple signifying Goma. "We can't afford a fight. Violence scares off visiting spirits, remember?"

Elodie rolls her eyes. "Lady Hanae only repeated it multiple times." She straightens. "I suppose this means we split up?"

I shake my head. "We need to blend in. Not trying to end up in Gomae prison when your mother is starting a war. No offense."

She grins. "None taken. If it makes you feel better, every day with Mother is war, even in her own household."

The guards catch sight of us, and now they rush forward, giving chase. "Stop!"

We disappear into a maze of backstreets, breaking out onto one that slopes downhill. Zetian streaks overhead again, and Colin shouts, "This way!"

He leaps across another roof, knocking down a string of lanterns that fall onto our path and roll toward the riverbank. Just then, I spy a lone figure standing on the bridge, arrayed in full skirts, a silken overcoat that retains a hint of color, and a hui-cheok that towers above her head—Empress Ren.

I stop in my tracks, announcing to the others, "She's here. On the bridge."

Jonas comes to my side. "Now what?"

"We join the crowd, appear as mourners. Remember what she said—we cannot appear to perceive her, only give an offering."

"Speaking of offerings"—he looks to Elodie—"any luck there?"

Elodie grins, producing a stoppered clay pot and a bag of honey cakes from the hidden pockets of her inner sleeve. "I didn't know how much to pay for these, so I took what they wouldn't notice."

Jonas's eyes go wide. "El—you stole these? Wait, is that why the guards were chasing you?"

She rubs her neck, not the least bit cowed. "What? I got the job done, didn't I?"

Putting a hand to my mouth, I stifle a laugh. It seems like Colin isn't the only quick-fingered one.

She slides out a toothy iron dagger that gleams under the high moon. "Got this too." She flips it in the air, then catches it. "Can't wait to try it."

Lady Hanae appears just then, bustling around the corner with Ataya on her shoulder. She hands us sections of a waxed cord tied at her waist. "Bind yourselves so we do not lose each other. Bridges are symbols of joining but also of parting, and we have to cross the bridge once before giving her tribute."

We lash ourselves to one another, leaving just an arm's worth of space between our bodies. Lady Hanae nods, satisfied. "Let's go."

The smell of incense tangles with oil and salt as we gather into the procession lined up at the bridge. All around us, people chatter, clashing and clinking like rocks gathered in a stream. Some carry lanterns with names inscribed on the paper coverings; others hold candles attached to lotus-blossom leaves meant to ride the river like little boats. The Oyo-born in the throng sing songs of remembrance, dancing their way along as though they are headed to a feast. The Gomae watch with excitement and trepidation, some dancing in their own way, others contributing poems that meld effortlessly with the songs piercing the night air.

I sing quietly to one of the songs, one about a woman who gives the last morsel of food she has to her child and turns into a bird, promising to teach her child to fly in the next life. To my surprise, Jonas mouths the words too, careful to keep his deep voice from swelling above the tide of voices.

"I didn't know you knew that one," I say once the drums announce the final note.

"You've sung it a few times this year alone."

I merely nod in response. This year I have seen too many Oluso bodies, sung that song of remembrance so those who hear it might find comfort, an assurance that this life of heartbreak is not all that is left for their spirits to experience.

The line begins to move and everything falls into hushed silence. People split into three paths, some dropping their leaf boats onto the west side of the river, others releasing lanterns from the east side. We stay in the middle, shuffling forward, eyes fixed on getting to the other side of the bridge. I sense Empress Ren's presence as we pass her by, lingering in the midst of that chaos, but I ignore the temptation to turn and look.

We reach the other side of the bridge, but before I can turn, a chill rises up my back. I spin on my heel. Empress Ren stands in front of me, a hairsbreadth from my face. She places a hand on my arm, and the world loses all color, flashing into a devouring gray.

I appear in the carcass of a room.

White cloth sits, ghostly pale in the moonlight, on charred remnants of what once might have been furniture. Beyond is a sea of black, a pit of broken wood, dirt and ash dusting what was once a floor. Water drips from the half-burnt ceiling, drumming an insistent pit-pat-pat rhythm that promises our shoes will be caked with mud.

Lady Hanae pats Ataya's feathers. "Telling me to use the cord was wise," she praises.

"Where are we?" Elodie asks.

Colin scans the surroundings. "There was a fire here, wherever it is."

Jonas points to the gold inlay in the lacquered wood pillar. "This is too fine to be just anywhere. I think we're in a palace."

"Ren's palace," Hanae confirms. "I grew up here."

She puts down her lantern and takes out our offerings.

"My adopted mother fostered us when we were young. We were all girls from influential families who had been orphaned early." She pauses, arranging our offerings in a circle. "People joked that Ren must like young women. But the truth was that she saw us, knew how vulnerable we were to greedy relatives who might marry us off for dowries or prey on us. So she took us in."

"What happened to her?" I ask.

She tears the honey cakes.

"She wanted a child of her own. It was all she asked the spirits for." She unstoppers the rice wine, pouring it on the cakes in a straight line.

"She used to have these dreams of walking in the Spirit Realm, talking with various spirits. Then she told us one day that she had a dream where she swallowed the moon."

"A conception dream," I mutter, chills running down my spine. The K'inu's voice whispers against my ear again. *Rivers of blood await you, sleeping moon.* "She got pregnant."

"How? She didn't have a consort," Jonas says.

"All those walks in the Spirit Realm," Colin answers, his expression twisted into a peculiar look. "She may have run into a spirit that could give her a child."

Elodie whistles. "There are things like that? Share the secret. I do want to have children someday."

Colin shakes his head. "I don't think you'd like that method. Falling in love with spirits is a difficult thing."

I swallow, thinking of Ta'atia.

"She gave birth to a baby girl," Hanae continues.

"A moon," I add.

She nods. "A powerful Cloren." Hanae's mouth curls into a wistful smile. "She was so bright. Rich skin like winter chestnuts and Ren's stormy eyes."

"Where is the child now?" Jonas asks.

"Let's find out." Hanae closes her hand over the lantern flame and the room falls into darkness.

A sudden wind whistles through the charred remnants of paper hanging over the windows.

"I don't like this," Elodie whispers, clutching my arm.

Suddenly Iya's crystal glows, glittering like an obsidian shard. Empress Ren appears in front of me, holding out her hand. "Give it to me," she whispers.

"What?"

She points to my ogbene, and I open my waist pouch. Inside, beyond a few stray coins, and bits of plantain leaf, is the lock of hair Sanaa gave me. I stare at it, recognizing the pattern on the ornament dangling from it—it's the same as the red-and-black pattern on Empress Ren's robes.

"Sanaa," I mutter.

"My daughter," Ren confirms, reaching for the braid. As our fingers meet, my skin grows clammy and cold and the world curls like rumpled fabric.

More apparitions arrive, faded outlines that go about their business as though we are the unseen.

A young Empress Ren stands before a mirror carrying her crying baby girl. She kisses her child on the forehead, nuzzling her nose against the colored beads plaited through the girl's braided hair. Then hands reach through the dark of that mirror, and Ren pushes her daughter into them, sobbing as those hands ferry her away.

Voices surround us, piercing the chill of the room.

"Break the door!"

"I can't—"

"Burn it down," another voice commands. "That witch in there must still respect fire."

Ghostly flames roar to life around us.

Elodie tightens her grip on my arm, her face paling. "I didn't come here to die!" she shouts.

"Just hold on—"

Ren spins, staring right at me. She smiles and severs her long braid at the nape. It's the scene from Nana's vision.

Cool air brushes my back and I turn to see a slit in the air, a ripple of silver cutting through the fabric of the world. A ghostly Ren jets up as the flames grow higher, running into that ripped seam.

"Follow her into the mirror city," Hanae commands, rising to her feet.

I've heard of mirror cities before, spirit dwellings tied to places in the Physical Realm much like the forests of Ifé are tied to the Spirit Realm. But mirror cities are no place for tree spirits to frolic and Aziza to weave with wind spirits through the sky. The dead, the spirits who refuse to pass into the next world or find their rest in the arms of Olorun, walk through them, fashioning an echo of the lives they once had. People, both Aje and Oluso, fall into mirror cities from time to time, so getting to one is not the issue. Leaving is the difficult part.

"I am not going into whatever that is," Elodie says. "Sea beasts are exciting, but I draw the line at ghosts."

"This is the only way out of here," Hanae urges. "The old palace is shut up. No one will think to rescue us from here."

Colin leans closer to Elodie. "Would you rather go into a ghost city or be buried alive here?"

Elodie shudders. "Fine, let's go."

"A word of caution—don't touch anything when we enter," Hanae warns. "The dead don't take kindly to theft."

Elodie tilts her head like a dog who's just caught the scent of meat. "What could be worth stealing?"

"Let's not find out," Jonas says firmly.

We step into the seam.

Cold whispers against my skin as my body slips away, as though it is nothing but a shell curled around my very essence.

We appear on a road the color of slate. The street is an exact copy of the one we marched down in Aerin-Cho, but here there are no people milling about, pulsing with life like a beating heart. The same food stalls lie in wait, the aroma of their wares pungent and enticing, but there is a sharpness to the smell, the kind that clings to our clothes as we wander down the street. The rice cakes are brighter in color, the cuts of meat and potatoes bigger. Steam arises from the bubbling stew Elodie once craved, but when I wave my hand over the pot, cold air snatches at my fingers.

"This isn't as bad as I thought," Elodie says, reaching for the ladle rising out of the pot.

I smack her fingers just before they brush the ladle. "Leave it."

"The food here is for the spirits," Hanae explains. "They're partaking of life still. Don't rob them of that."

Elodie scowls, rubbing her smarting fingers. "There's no one here."

Hanae shakes her head. "You're just not looking in the right places."

The wind rustles against chimes fastened to an awning, and I catch a blur from the corner of my eye, a silvered gray form that gathers shape and billows away again like smoke streaming from a blown-out candle. The cord connecting us unravels and falls to the ground.

The hairs on my arm rise. "We need to go."

The sky thunders as though in agreement, swelling clouds promising rain. Downhill, a pillar of light shoots up from the bridge in the middle of the city. Taking off down the empty street, I chase that light as though there are wolves nipping at my heels.

"Dèmi, wait!" Jonas calls, but I don't stop.

Colin keeps pace, pulling ahead with me. Jonas and Elodie trailing just behind, and Lady Hanae rounds out the pack, surprisingly fast in sandal-clad feet.

We race onto a side street with ancestral shrines in wooden groves lining the entire street like market wares on display. Crisp paper bearing the inked faces and names of dead loved ones curl like crooked fingers inviting us to look. They sit next to an abundance of riches—gold and jade piled carelessly amongst swelling offerings of food that threaten to overwhelm the long-legged tables bearing them.

I slow, still moving quickly but without the speed that might offend the watching spirits, tell them that I care nothing for their last remembrances. Then Colin stops, his eye drawn to a painting of a long-haired man with a stubborn chin, the fierce look in his eyes burning through the very paper.

"What is it?" I whisper as though those images could rise from their inky graves and engrave themselves as flesh and blood upon the world again.

"Nothing. It's no one."

He hastens away and I steal another glance at the paper. The long, slim nose and wide forehead are identical to Colin's. My stomach churns—it's a drawing of a young Lord Kairen. Yet his image being here could only mean one thing—he's dead.

"Colin!" I shout, rushing after him, but he's already turned onto the next street.

"What's wrong?" Jonas asks, catching up to me. "Was that—"

"Lord Kairen? I can't be sure."

Sucking in a breath, I push myself to get to Colin faster. Mirror cities may reflect the worlds they are tied to, but it only takes a moment for someone wandering one to become lost, find themselves in an unfamiliar place. And once they do, the spirits who wander that city might decide to keep that person as entertainment, watch them waste away within reach of food they can never eat, and clothing that will never warm their chilled bones. Now that we're no longer all linked, Colin is in danger.

"Colin!"

I shout his name just as he reaches the riverbank. He turns around as a shadow rises from the surface of the river, and I yank him back as it lunges at him. The waters bubble where the shadow was, but whatever lay in wait does not return.

"You can't go off by yourself!" I cry, knocking my fist against his chest. "We have to get to Iya intact."

"I'm sorry," he mumbles.

Throwing my arms around his waist, I pull him into a hug, reminding him I am here. He stills in my embrace before hugging me back. The pillar of light, the path to Ìyá-Ilé is just before us. But somehow, I know that if I let this moment go, brush Colin's feelings aside for now, something in him will break, growing crooked like a bone set wrong, and no amount of trying to fix it in the future will work.

"I saw your father," I reassure him. "I promise I saw him alive and well in Nordgren two days ago."

He clutches my fingers like they are a lifeline. "Are you certain?"

"I'm sure. I saw him too," Jonas huffs, catching up to us.

"I rode out this way on Ruko's Day," he adds. "It's Gura's Day now. So unless something happened in the last two days, your father is well and safe."

The sky roars, thunderclouds sparking. Hanae arrives, dragging a red-faced Elodie along.

"Caught her trying to take something else," Hanae reports.

"I was merely curious," Elodie retorts. "I wanted to see if the dagger was similar to the one I just bought."

Jonas pinches the skin between his eyebrows. "We don't have time for this. We need to go in."

"Welcome, daughter of Oya." A masked figure arises from the pillar of light.

The woman is tall, furs covering every inch of her body excepting her face, which is sealed with a drooping wooden mask. Snakelike horns arise from the head of her mask, and when she cocks her head, the red-and-gold-stained mask rattles as though its neck is merely a stalk bearing the heavy weight of a flower. She steps closer, the water rippling against her silk-slippered feet, and the rain itself parts around her, forming a dome that shields her from the drizzle.

Hanae bends immediately, folding her arms at the waist. "Lady Yaki, servant of Oya, ruler of the Egun Sea of Souls, I salute you."

I follow suit, dropping to my knees in a proper dubalè, the way we would in Oyo, but Yaki holds up a hand.

"We have no need for formalities. We are family, are we not?"

She pulls off her mask, and I glimpse then the golden face from Nana's vision. Empress Ren may have been presumed dead for almost twenty years, but her face is the same as when she sat in her quarters surrounded by the flames.

"Ama!" Hanae shouts. She rushes into the rain, arms wide open.

Empress Ren reaches for her and the moment their fingers touch, Hanae rises high like a phoenix reborn. Then Hanae drifts down like a feather in the wind, wonder brightening her tear-streaked face.

"You saved my daughter, Sanaa, from certain death. For that reason, though you strayed from the path, I pleaded with Iya to be your guide," Ren announces. She reaches out to me. "I will send you to Iya for my final voyage."

"Final voyage?" Hanae asks.

Ren nods, producing the lock of hair from her cloak. "I am at peace, now that I have a bit of my child's essence with me. It is time for me to be released from service." She reaches out a hand to me. "We must hurry. Ìyá-Ilé awaits you. We must get to court before the ruling spirits tire of hearings for today."

I frown. "You mean to bring us before the Court of Spirits?"

The Court of Spirits are the premier spirits who rule the Spirit Realm under Olorun and Iya. But though Olorun fashioned the Spirit and Physical Realms and Iya, the Mother of All, gave it life, they rarely preside over the court themselves, leaving judgments to the premier spirits to sort according to their whims. Before Olokun, I had never met a premier spirit, but if the rest are anything like him, I fear going before them at all, especially with broken spirit bonds.

"The premier spirits are concerned with the chaos of the Physical Realm. They've demanded that all new souls pay their respects before finding their way through the Spirit Realm."

"What do they mean by paying our respects?" Colin asks, brows drawn together.

Ren waves a hand and a boat appears upon the water, long and sleek like the husk of an irisi. The inside of her barge even contains the same firm yellow grooves that appear in the cocoa bean, makeshift seats that promise us we won't be escaping them so easily.

"To cross into the Spirit Realm from here, I must take your mortal bodies. That is the first step."

Elodie's eyes widen. "You want to kill us?"

"It is necessary, yes," Ren responds with a sigh. "To have a sustained presence in the Spirit Realm, enough to appear before the premier spirits, you must give up your bodies. If you wish to abstain, I will send you back to the Physical Realm. You only need to let me know."

"What will happen to our bodies?" Jonas asks.

"They will lie in a sacred grove in the Physical Realm. I will return you to them when you are ready."

"Can we lose them? Die while we're away in the Spirit Realm?" Colin asks, his jaw tight.

Ren nods. "You can. But once you go to the Court of Spirits, they will provide you with spirit anchors, other souls that will help you remember who you are. That should hold your mortal bodies in place until your spirits are ready to return. The choice is yours."

"I'm staying behind," Elodie declares. "Send me back. My arm is starting to hurt anyway."

"What about your arm?" I ask. "If something is wrong, you'd need to ask the Spirits to look at it."

She shakes her head. "Not interested. I'd rather lose an arm than risk my life."

Hanae speaks up. "I, too, will stay behind. I can keep watch over the young ones' bodies."

Ren smiles. "Ever the mother, Hanae. I wish you had gotten to raise my little one."

"What happened to the baby, Ama?"

Ren's smile remains, but the crinkles around her eyes unfold until I'm sure I'm seeing a practiced expression, a mask she puts on for performance. "Her father took charge of her as was his right. He sent her to a home where she would be loved."

She plucks a glistening, gold-tipped feather. "Your Miri as well I ferried into a new life, one where she will never be so saddened as to reject her own again."

I hitch a breath. This must be the truth Hanae thanked Nana for hiding—Miri took her own life.

Hanae cradles the feather to her breast, no doubt thinking of her lost daughters. Ren folds away, leaving Hanae to her grief.

"And you, daughter of Oya," she starts, settling onto me, "what do you wish to do?"

I don't bother taking a moment to consider. Our lives are already forfeit if I cannot restore my spirit bonds, help lead the battle against the Council. We have so little time as it is.

Squaring my shoulders, I thrust out my hand, clasping Ren's waiting one. "I will go."

"Me too," Colin answers.

When I look at him, he grins. "Did you think I'd let you die alone? What do you take me for?"

"Wherever Dèmi goes, so will I," Jonas says. He looks at me, the surety brimming in those dawn-blue eyes. "It's the pledge I made to you. I'm not leaving you behind."

"Well, you certainly inspire loyalty," Ren says.

I flush as she whips around, spreading her furs like an eagle opening its wings.

The world dissolves, darkness swanning over me like a blanket, and when the light hits me again, I'm sitting in the hull of the irisi, stuffed in one of those grooves like a cacao bean. Jonas and Colin sit behind and to the right of me.

Elodie and Hanae now stand on the shores of a shaded grove behind, curled under golden-leafed trees that scatter their bounty over the waters. Next to them, laid out like stones gathered along a riverbed, are our physical bodies. In the distance, I see the walls of Aerin-Cho, its proud blue flag waving in the wind.

"I do not know what else the spirits will ask of you," Ren says as we drift away from those shores, pulled forward as though by an invisible hand. "I only know that whatever tribute is requested, you must pay it. Knowing this, do you still wish to go?"

I turn to Jonas and Colin. They sit like trees, steady and upright, but I glimpse also the fear and resolve carved in their faces. When our eyes meet, they each give me a look, mirrored gazes full of longing and hope.

Rubbing my clammy hands against my dress, I peer into the gray of the horizon. Living means nothing if I can't protect my loved ones. So, into the arms of death we go.

"We're going," I say firmly. "Take us to Ìyá-Ilé."

Ren slips on her mask and we set sail.

BROTHER

WE COME UPON THE SPIRIT REALM'S SHORES LIKE BIRDS RETURNING home to nest, hearts stirring with longing when we glimpse the distant salt flats sitting beneath a blanket of cerulean sky. As we pull closer, the clouds part around us like waves, beckoning us in. There in the midst of that stark white that seems to go on forever, is Ayaba.

She flits over before Ren can call the boat to a stop, gossamer wings reflecting the light hugging the clouds, throwing silvered light on our faces.

"Abidèmi, you arrive later than asked," she says. Her voice is calm, but the look in her tiger-bright eyes tells a different story.

Shame spears my belly, and I have the urge to hide away from her scrutinizing gaze. I feel as though she could peer beyond the veneer of the unkempt silk clothes Hanae lent me and see the extra leaves that knotted on my back after I changed course to join Ekwensi.

"I'm sorry," I whisper.

"She's here now, isn't she?" Ren tuts. "I thought you adopted this one, Ayaba. You frighten her too easily."

Ayaba does not deign to give a response, turning her attention instead to Jonas and Colin as they climb out of the boat. The valley between her brows deepens.

"I see you've brought death and despair with you."

I groan remembering the words she spoke over me in Benin Forest last year: *One will bring you death, the other despair.*

"I see you haven't changed," Colin answers.

This time, it's Jonas who hits him between the shoulder blades, causing him to stumble into a haphazard bow while Jonas dips in a proper one. "Greetings to you, Olá rè. Thank you for guiding us."

Ayaba lifts a corner of her mouth in the barest hint of a smile while Colin glares at Jonas. "Strong spirits. You'll need them if you're to survive the court."

She glides away, the sleeves of her gown billowing in the breeze.

As I get to my feet, the ground beneath me shifts and my nostrils burn with the strong smell of salt. Ren reaches out an arm to steady me.

"Be careful. I've had a few travelers disappear into pits that opened out of nowhere." She lowers her voice, but her next words echo through the shores like a saworo drum issuing a challenge. "Elegua's sense of humor has only gotten worse."

I stiffen at the mention of the premier spirit of the pathways. Olokun may have been a challenge to navigate, and Shango, the spirit of thunder and fire, is rumored to have a short temper. But it is Elegua's capricious nature I fear the most. When Olorun spun the Oluso from dust and breath, Elegua gifted the power of teleportation to those of Madsen blood. Though the ability is one of the strongest, every Madsen fears losing themselves or a piece of their bodies while teleporting. Elegua's gifts reflect his two-sided nature, and if we're to survive here, we need to make certain we don't run afoul of him.

"I thought Eshu was the trickiest one," Jonas says, drawing near me. "Is Elegua trickier than Eshu?"

"Eshu is another of Elegua's forms. A different side to him," Ren explains. Her mask remains firmly in place, but the anger and sadness coloring her words come through like a knife tearing into flesh. "You'll see," she says simply.

We hasten after her, digging our feet into the treacherous salty earth. Palm trees taller than mountains await, bodies hunched like pregnant women gathering at a birthing hut, fronds waving as we approach. Then, just as our feet break past the last reaches of salt onto the loamy red clay that awaits, palm nuts fall from those trees, hitting the ground with earsplitting thuds.

We run, dodging skull-sized shells as they crack open, spraying palm oil richer than the molten gold of the sun blazing at our backs.

Past the grove, there is a smudge against the gathered clouds, a figure waiting on a rug that stretches beyond. As we break from the last swath of ashen-bodied palms, that smudge solidifies into features and I slip in a pool of broken palm nuts, drenching my ankles and skirt in their rich orange blood.

The face looking back at me is one I would know anywhere. His midnight skin is even more glorious, glowing as though imbued with moonlight. His braided hair is whiter now, the dark piece of it receded to just the patch on top of his head. His face is painted with black, red, and white, but no amount of chalk is enough to deny the wide brown eyes, twin to my own, staring back at me.

"You came, sister," Délé says, and suddenly his voice stirs a memory hanging at the edge of my mind: him stabbing a hand into my chest in the Spirit Realm as I languished in Mari's hideout.

Jonas edges in front, blocking me from sight as he lifts me from the carnage of palm oil. Colin takes a menacing step toward my brother.

"Who are you calling your sister?" he asks, voice tight. But there is something else in there beyond surprise—recognition.

"I told you we'd meet again soon, omo Éyani," Délé answers. He smiles, the canines of his shining white teeth flashing at us. "Welcome to my home."

Son of Éyani. How does my twin brother know Colin?

Colin tenses, his hand moving to the handle of his blade.

Ren steps between them. "Ìyá-Ilé has called for your sister. The court awaits her. Please let us pass."

Délé throws his head back and laughs. His laughter thunders through the forest surrounding us, and black birds appear on the tree branches, beady eyes watching us with interest.

"You act like I am here to devour my little sister, Ren," Délé says, wiping a tear from his eye. "We all know that the story was the other way around. I came out first but she smothered my light."

"She did no such thing," Ayaba retorts, materializing behind him. "Your spirit had already lost its will to live when your sister was born. I sang you away myself." She smiles, amusement flickering in her otherworldly eyes. "In Oyo custom, you would be the younger twin, no?—a mere servant sent out to see the world before your queen could arrive."

A smile blooms on my face before I can stop it, and Délé's burning gaze travels to me again. "You're right," he says. "She is my elder. I am merely here to welcome her. Nothing more, nothing less."

"How can I trust you?" I ask. I remember the pain that filled me, both in Nordgren and Mari's hideout. Both times I felt on the verge of death.

He puts a hand over his heart, his face twisting in a wounded expression. But when he speaks, his words are mocking, bordering on laughter. "My dear sister, what reason would I have to harm you?"

"Whatever grudge you bear, Iya has called her," Ren says, tapping her foot impatiently. "Now, we have to go before *he* becomes impatient."

"Ah," Délé says with a triumphant smile. "But *he* sent me. Elegua asked that I give you all a brief tour. The three of you already have spirit anchors. Your souls will remain intact; you have my word."

"Who are our anchors?" I ask.

"That is for the spirits to reveal."

"I don't need a tour," I declare. I have the sense that my brother means to draw me in, ensnare me in the Spirit Realm, but there are people I left behind to get here, mere days before the Council attacks the Oluso again. I don't have time to quibble and argue—I must see Iya.

He stiffens, then his lips curl into a sneer. "Remember, this was *your* choice."

"What of my role?" Ren asks, frowning.

He shrugs. "He asked you to visit his chambers. He's missed you while you've been away."

She flushes, her face a tangle of hatred and fascination. "Fine. But inform him today was my last voyage," she declares.

Taking off her mask, she thrusts it at Jonas. "Take this. If you need my help, put it on." She turns to me, flashing a warm smile. "I am forever grateful to you, Dèmi." Pulling her furs around her, she dissolves in a flash of light.

"I trust you won't lead them astray," Ayaba says, looking hard at Délé.

"I wouldn't dream of it," he singsongs.

"Dèmi is a child of the Aziza," she warns. "Her success is ours. Her failure dooms us all."

He shoots her a wry smile. "How nice, to be somebody's child."

Ayaba sighs. "Go on, then." With that, she disappears.

"Excellent." Délé rubs his hands together. "Now, sister, don't be shy. I know your friend here." He nods at Colin. "We're comrades of a sort?"

"We're *nothing* of the sort," Colin barks.

Délé laughs. "Introduce me to your other friend," he says, nodding at Jonas. "Who might this be?"

I say nothing, studying the smiling boy in front of me. When I first heard that I'd been a twin, I had wondered what the other baby would be like, what our lives could have been if war and Alistair Sorenson hadn't forced my mother to give birth in hiding with only Mama Aladé at her side. Now I half expect my twin brother to rip off his skin and reveal the grinning face of an eloko beneath. But still, there is a part of me that yearns to know what his life has been all these years in the Spirit Realm.

"You won't do me the courtesy of an introduction?" Délé says, twisting his mouth. "I'm hurt. It's almost like you consider me an enemy."

Jonas reaches out a hand. "I'm Jonas of Eingard. Dèmi's mate."

Délé's eyes gleam as he clasps Jonas's hand with both of his. "A mate? How exciting. Fully bonded, I hope?"

I frown. "Why do you ask?"

He lifts his hands in mock surrender. "Only for your protection. Mates can be lost here, you see. It helps to have bonds to tie you back together again."

A rattle sounds and I look to the sky, waiting for a kokulu to swoop out of the trees. Délé straightens, pulling an iron half spear just like mine from the air. My chest tightens.

"We're summoned then." He sweeps a hand toward the waiting rug. "Please, after you."

As soon as my feet touch the thick cloth, patterns stitch themselves around me like fire burning through grass, an invisible hand weaving color into the pale gold of the rug. In the space before me is an elephant standing taller than the herd she shepherds. Beyond her a mami wata reaches its tentacles toward a waiting moon, the waters below it reflecting a fiery-headed omioja. To the right are two ashen figures hugging each other, and I know before I see their red eyes that those figures are Amina and Rollo, the okri children I saved last year. These are events from my life.

"How nice it is to have a destiny," Délé says, gliding past me. The images disappear as his bare feet touch the rug. "How nice to be living."

"Dèmi didn't ask to survive," Colin says. "It just happened that way."

Délé tuts. "My friend, you will soon learn that coincidences are for the foolish. Come." He walks briskly away.

"How do you know him?" Jonas asks Colin.

"I don't," Colin answers, clenching his jaw. "I just saw him once."

"Where?" I ask. "In a dream? A vision? Where?"

He flinches, then in a low voice he asks, "If I said I would tell you later, could you wait? Trust me?"

I study him, unsure of what to say. For many years, Colin has been a mirror, a face I could look into and know exactly what I'd find. Now his eyes are to the ground, and I am painfully aware of the wall that sits between us; not just the time we've been apart but the things he's had to do for Ekwensi that changed him. He shifts under my scrutiny, digging his toe at the rug, and an image appears behind him—an armored woman charging into battle on horseback, her swelling belly the only part uncovered as her blade meets an enemy's. Éyani Al'hia, Colin's mother.

Maybe it is that image, the desperation clear on her face as she rides into battle, the look I'd seen on Mummy's face so many times, or that I know, deep down, Colin and I are the same—children born carrying the weight of those who bled to give them a chance at life, that I declare, "I'll wait."

A voice of warning bubbles up in my mind like the first stirrings of a storm, but I push it away, repeating my answer with certainty. "I trust you. Just tell me before this causes any issues."

Even now, I know that Colin shares the same fear—that nothing we do will ever be enough to protect the ones we love. He wouldn't hide anything from me if he thought it might truly harm me.

His smile is small, a quirk of the mouth, but it is as though the sun has broken through the clouds. "Thank you."

I nod. "Let's go."

"We should hurry, before the spirits come looking for us," Jonas says, taking off in front. Patterns trail him like a shadow, rearranging as we get closer.

But I catch snatches of a few. A baby lying on a bed with only a thorny crown for company. A child with a spear through his heart.

As we reach my brother, my patterns reappear in the rug. But this time, next to the elephant is a boy standing on a path underneath a burning sun. As I step nearer, though, I notice two things—the sun is the long-fanged, whiskered serpent that visited me while I was deep in my koko-fueled haze, and it is also the boy's shadow.

"I've heard the living are quick, but you took so long I nearly told Elegua you'd forfeited your audience," Délé says.

He drums the end of his spear twice on the first step of a marbled flight of stairs before us, and color radiates from the place he touched, the cool marble melting away, leaving nothing behind but an endless sky, a sea of blue interrupted only by drifting clouds.

"Meeting the premier spirits is a matter of faith," he says, stepping into that sky. "I recommend that you don't look down."

"No way am I climbing into the clouds," Colin says. "Bring those stairs back."

My brother chuckles and jumps away, his feet dancing along the gathered clouds.

"Come on, Col," I say, taking his arm.

He shakes his head at me. "Dèmi, gwylfins are one thing but do you expect me—"

"To put aside your fears for a moment and help us get to Iya?" Jonas says. "Yes, I do."

He sidles over, grabbing Colin's other arm. "Let's go."

Colin groans. We step into that sky together, moving quickly until we reach the point where my brother watches with amusement.

Délé draws back, slashing his spear into the clouds, and a set of gates appear. The gates are several feet high, carved faces with open mouths and unseeing eyes peering out at us from a patchwork of gold and bronze. They open to reveal a courtyard housing a building more majestic than any I have ever seen. The building is simple, cream-white walls studded with carvings in stone, brass, and gold, capped with red clay tiles that slope sharply at the ends. The carvings move and shift as though they are living, breathing things—a boy transforms into a copper-headed lion in one, and a diduo spreads its wings over the plains in another. When the diduo opens its mouth, I can almost hear its triumphant cry upon the wind. But the most striking thing about the building is the iroko tree that juts up from its heart.

The tree is tall, with rich brown branches that spread into the sky like those eagles' wings. Some of the branches are heavy with golden leaves, and others with leaves the color of blood. A few here and there are bare, frost snaking over their thin bodies. But the tree's central branches are ripe with leaves greener than I have ever seen and round glass fruit with blue flames in their centers. This is Ìyá-Ilé, the Mother Tree that poured her lifeblood into Ifé.

"Welcome to the Court of Spirits," Délé announces.

The carvings in the wall turn, eyes settling onto us. Suddenly, the lion boy bursts from his frame, bronzed teeth gleaming as he charges us. I drop Colin's arm, reaching for the bone blade strapped to my hip. But just as my fingers reach it, the lion boy skids on heavy paws and tumbles onto his back, rolling around like an oversized dog ready to play. Jonas lets go of his blade with a sigh of relief and Colin puts together a string of curses in High Berréan.

"Iké, you're not serious," Délé chides, scratching the lion-boy's belly. "Call the others. They're next in line for an audience with the court."

The lion boy whimpers, then he rolls upright, letting out a roar that pierces the entire courtyard. More and more carvings pour out of the walls, spirits that watch us with curious eyes as Délé leads the way into the front gate.

"These are koriko, lesser spirits," he explains. "They're denizens of the Spirit Realm and the Iya Palace guardians."

The diduo settles onto Délé's shoulder, cocking its head at me. "Yes, Agidi, that's really her," he says. He scratches the tuft of brown feathers under the bird's beak and the diduo nuzzles against his fingers, trilling happily. The sound brings tears to my eyes, the memory of practicing that trill with Mummy swimming up in my mind.

"Agidi was Mother's in her youth," Délé explains.

Mummy told me often of the diduo she raised, the tiny treasure she cared for until she fled Château Nordgren to escape my father and Alistair Sorenson. After Alistair's conquest, all the diduo, as symbols of the royal family of Oyo, were caught and killed.

"This is Mummy's bird?" I ask, reaching out a finger.

Délé strokes her tufts. "One and the same. She's been with me since I came here. I suppose Agidi's soul sensed I would be living in the Spirit Realm alone, so she took care of me, nurtured me."

I frown. "You were alone? What of Osèzèlé?"

"Father?" Délé laughs, the sound as hollow as the calabash sitting outside the main gate. "Father was still alive when I passed. He came a few moons later, but no—I was sent here as a new soul alone. Mother had to stay with you. I had no one to guide or care for me."

My heart wrenches, guilt and sorrow twisting like a knife in my breast as I think of Délé arriving in the Spirit Realm alone. This is my brother, the family I've longed for all this time, but all I've done is treat him with fear and suspicion.

"The ancestral spirits in your family line then?" Jonas asks. "What of them?"

Délé throws his head back and laughs again. Agidi jumps off his shoulder, flapping her wings by his head. "Sorry," he says to the diduo, "I'm not trying to be rude. It's just so funny."

He wipes an errant tear. "You don't know, do you? Afèni exchanged the lives of all but one of her immediate descendants for power to defeat the kokulu. And she failed. Our ancestral line is sealed. We can't access anyone in our maternal lineage beyond Queen Folaké."

I shake my head in disbelief. Ancestral severance is a serious punishment. Despite the fact that Ajes are born of Oluso who committed acts of murder, Olorun did not see fit to cut off their ancestral lines. The Spirit Realm is meant to be a home where all souls can rest, find their places with those who came before. For those who choose to journey to the next world, it is a place to nurture their world-weary spirits before they can pass into the next life. To be cut off from one's ancestral line is to die a second death, to lose the wealth of history and tradition that is our birthright.

"Afèni defeated the kokulu," I sputter. "She succeeded. Why would the spirits—" I stop as the pieces come together. The K'inu control the kokulu. With them around, the kokulu would never experience true defeat. Afèni dealt with only the outcome, not the root cause. She *had* failed.

Jonas places a steadying hand on my shoulder, but even the warmth of his touch is not enough to chase away the chill gathering in my heart.

Colin balls his hands into fists. "How could she do that? Throw away all of you for her ambition?"

Délé regards me with something akin to pity. "I struggled with this too, sister, when they told me." Agidi trills at him and he nods. "There is Queen Folaké, our grandmother's spirit. But you know she never approved of Mother's choice of mate. Father's people are gone too. No one has seen an iron-blood since they all perished before the Great War."

"Is Mummy here?" I ask, hope swelling in my heart. My brother hasn't mentioned her yet.

Délé's face twists, all the brightness winking out of it like a light. He turns away, drawing near to the main gate. "She's not here."

"She's not?" I frown. "How is that possible?"

"It's time for your audience. Leave your questions until later."

He walks briskly away, but I chase after him, trying to keep my panic at bay.

"Wait, explain please, now."

He tuts. "Remember, dear sister, you asked for your audience. You didn't want a tour."

"Is Mummy at least all right?" I blurt. *Please*, I beg the spirits silently. *Please let me see my mother again.* It doesn't matter that our ancestral rights have been stolen from us. Just as long as Mummy is here and safe.

"She's all right," Délé says finally, eyes clouding with emotion. "Now, let's go."

I leave it—for now. Once I've found Iya and we're all safe from the Council, I will push, find out more, but for now, I have to accept this, even though it hurts so painfully.

We delve into the inner courtyard beyond the gate. The inside of Iya Palace is larger than the building appears, with ceilings that would take at least three of Jonas to reach and giant, forbidding doors fastened with wooden beams alternating with smaller open rooms. The courtyard is full of carvings like the ones that decorate the palace walls; bronzed statues tangled with each other, caught in what seems to be a wrestling match or a dalliance between lovers; gleaming brass and copper heads with eyes that twinkle as though they hold the secrets of the world; weapons cast in iron, copper, and gold that stud the walls like trophies. The marbled floor gleams as we rush down the torchlit corridor, turning our shadows into monstrous shapes that stalk after us.

Then a lion roars in the distance and drumbeats chase the sound, drowning us in a symphony that reverberates through our bodies like a beating heart.

"What is that?" I cry.

My brother flashes me a wide grin. "That is the Court of Spirits."

TRADITION

WE RACE DOWN THE CORRIDOR, THE MARBLED FLOOR THRUMMING WITH that rhythm, spurring us on. Doors slam shut as we run by, as if they, too, are answering a summons. As we arrive at the gilded doors outfitting the ancestral court, the drums rally into a crescendo and cease.

Twelve women guard the ancestral court. Each is dressed in sleek woven wraps, their muscled bellies peeking from a gap in their wrap cloths, showing off skin varying from the rich ebony of an overripe kola nut to the doughy paleness of a pounded yam. The decorations on their spears are equally variegated, one sporting a red silk binding over the body of her spear while another favors a series of painted scales reminiscent of a gwylfin's hide.

Délé saunters past them and I take a breath before following suit. Each guard lowers her spear as we pass, the colored tattoos on their cheeks lighting up as they do. They trail us into a room swallowed up by cushions and draped in lush fabrics that hang from every pillar. The air is thick with the heady scent of honey and palm wine, and kola nuts rattle in their wooden dishes as we walk past, chattering like spectators in the marketplace.

At the center of the room is a bronze chair in the shape of a hand, its fingers reaching toward the circle of sky peeking through an open hole in the roof. The room is otherwise empty, save for our party and the guards following us.

A woman's laughter fills the room, tinkling like the sweet pitter-patter of an udu drum. I jump.

"You owe me money, Oshosi," she sings.

The air shimmers as a slender woman appears atop a nest of cushions, kicking her feet behind her like an excited child listening to a story. She rolls up, the beads in her plaited hair clicking as she lifts her head. She is beautiful, with rich brown skin that shines in the gold dress that spills over her like a waterfall, and deeper gold-brown eyes that remind me of a hawk.

"She looks nothing like Afèni," she pronounces, her gaze drinking me in.

"I never said she looked like Afèni," a man growls, appearing beside her. "I said she reeked of her spirit." He steps into the light, revealing deep scars gouged into his ochre skin, crisscrossed lines over his wide cheeks marking him a seasoned warrior. This must be Oshosi, the premier spirit of the fields, whose magic of transformation lives in Igbagbo Oluso like Baba Sylvanus.

I curtsy, offering my blade in both hands in a sign of respect. "I salute you, Great Hunter."

Jonas falls to his knees a breath later echoing the same cry. The female warriors behind us lift their spears, adding their voices,

"A gbọ ọ, ọmọ awọn aaye. A dupè lọwọ rè, Hunter Nla." *We hear you, son of fields. We salute you, Great Hunter.*

Only Colin remains standing, a defiant look on his face. I cut my eyes at him, silently willing him to behave.

Oshosi chuckles, his large body shaking with the movement. "This is what I'm talking about. This is the respect we are due."

He adjusts the sleeve of the blue-and-gold agbada hanging half off his shoulder so it covers more of his scarred chest. "I see you are still fearless, omo Éyani."

"I see you are still shameless," Colin answers, baring his teeth.

I nearly fall out of my curtsy. Yet another spirit Colin knows. Why hasn't he mentioned any of this before?

Oshosi whistles. "We'll see how long you keep that up." He waves the udamalore in his hand, the glass beads on the ceremonial sword rattling against the ivory carvings pressed into the wooden frame. "Jagunjagun, fall in!"

The female warriors rush to circle us. The one closest to me with a gull tattoo gleaming red against her brown cheek shoots me a pitying look. I tighten my grip on my bone blade. In all my lessons with Mummy, she always painted the ancestral spirits as fair rulers who often walked the line between justice and retribution.

I remember what Mummy told me about the ancestral spirits now.

Dèmi, the ancestral spirits are bound by covenants we do not understand. But they, too, cannot do as they please. There is one law that governs their ranks—Awọn ọmọ Olorun jẹ ọkan ti Olorun.

Olorun's children are Olorun's heart.

The warrior with the fox tattoo pushes her spear closer and I tense. My mother may have believed in the benevolence of the spirits, but I also know the spirits refused to interfere in the Great War, letting the other Oluso massacre the iron-bloods. Only after the Fèni-Ogun were nearly extinct did they give the remaining Oluso the curse of remembrance— the iron that shackles our gifts and engraves its will on our flesh. I am fortunate enough, with my iron magic awakened, to no longer suffer the burn of iron, but every time I see it I remember the anguish I carried in me like a knife for years, the pain every Oluso still bears. I can't let my guard down. Not now.

Délé lifts his hands as if to hold the warriors at bay. "We come in peace, Oshosi."

Oshosi crosses his arms. "Do you know why I despise seeing your face?"

Délé laughs. "Because mine is more handsome than yours?"

A boy's voice answers from behind us, a soft, sweet tone that stirs the very air. "Because your face reminds him of mine."

Oshosi groans.

I dare not look up because Oshosi hasn't asked us to rise, but small feet appear before me, the golden anklets decorating them jangling against the red-and-black cloth swishing against the floor. A boy springs his face underneath mine, and I fall back, startled.

"Got you," he says, chuckling.

Délé laughs along, and I shudder as a chill rises up my back. The timbre of their voices are eerily similar, and I notice now that the chalk on Délé's face is patterned after the red, black, and white adorning this boy's robes.

"Orunmila is coming," the gold-clad woman sings. "I would change faces if I were you, Eshu."

"Ever the darling, aren't you, Oshun?" Eshu blows her a kiss, and Oshosi's groan deepens into a growl.

As Eshu's fingers leave his face, his forehead grows wider, his owl-like eyes settling over chiseled amber cheeks and a full mouth. He straightens, dusting off his agbada, suddenly three feet taller and broad shouldered and I can't stop myself from staring at his mesmerizing, tender face.

"Like what you see?"

He grabs me by the chin, fingers biting into my cheeks, his hold threatening to crush my jaw.

Jonas jumps to his feet, propriety forgotten. "Let her go!"

Colin lurches forward, snatching at Eshu's hand, but the premier spirit flicks a finger and the ground opens up, swallowing Jonas and Colin until half their bodies are sticking out. So much for fair and be-nevolent ancestral spirits.

"Don't try me," he warns, yanking me toward him.

It takes all I have not to cry out, but I keep my eyes fixed on his, showing him I'm not afraid. This is what I have to endure to see Iya, what I must bear to free us once and for all. He will not frighten me into cowardice. My magic bursts out of me in a wave, wind spirits gathering around us like locusts in a swarm.

Eshu smiles, revealing pearly teeth with pointed ends. "You think to test me, little dove? Do you know who I am?"

"I meant no harm," I grit out. "My magic acted on its own."

"Who am I?" Eshu roars, speaking over me.

"Ìyá-Ilé called her," Délé interjects, his voice high. "You have to hear her out first, arakunrin."

Eshu's hold only tightens on my face when Délé calls him his elder brother.

I swallow, tensing as the action draws my face further into Eshu's palm. My iron magic sings through me now, humming with the promise of retaliation, but I shove it back. "You are Elegua, spirit of the pathways," I choke out.

"You're also the wrong end of a horse—" Colin starts. Jonas clamps his hand over Colin's mouth, but the rest of his words make it through.

"Who saw it fit to give curse-like gifts."

Elegua's laugh echoes through the room, making the kola nuts shiver in their bowls. "If I had known I'd get some amusement like this, I would have welcomed you all sooner."

"Leave them be," Oshun says, walking over. "She is beloved of Oya, no matter her deeds. Do you want Oya to send gales after your children again?"

"That's even more reason to do this."

He rips the bone blade from my hand. Then he howls as the blade blazes orange against his fingers, flinging it to the floor. "Do you think a trifle such as this will keep me from passing my will?"

He takes a spear from the hands of one of the watching warriors and I scramble for my blade. Ancestral spirits or no, I won't go down without a fight.

Jonas's voice brushes against my mind.

Don't back down, oko mi. Even from here, I will fight with you.

"That's enough for me, brother," Oshosi says, waving his udamalore. The warriors fall back. "Oya is already angry with you, but you want to borrow trouble from Ogun too? This one is Osèzèlé's child."

Elegua shrugs. "Our egbon never come anyway."

"Never mind our elders. He's angry Ren is going," Oshun says, smiling widely. "I should send her a vision of what you're doing now—I'm sure it would make her feel better about leaving."

He tosses the spear away immediately, dropping it as though it's just stung him. Then he plops onto the bronze hand-shaped throne. I keep my fingers tight against my blade. There's no telling what he'll do next.

"That was low of you, Oshun," he says.

Oshun flounces onto another set of cushions. "You weren't saying that when I convinced Ren to stay last time."

The curtains by her stir as two figures appear behind them. The first, with dreaded black hair and midnight skin catches her by the waist, throwing her in the air. She laughs as she lands in his arms, the thick red and gold beads in his hair clinking against hers as she leans forward to kiss him. The golden two-headed ax strapped to his back shifts as he pulls her closer in.

Oshosi cracks a kola nut in his fist, letting the shards fall onto the ground as the second figure swans out. The second man is shorter, a tawny-skinned, bespectacled elder bedecked in a jaunty green cap and flowing green-and-gold robes. He surveys the room, stopping at the sight of Jonas and Colin trapped in the floor.

"Elegua, before I count to three."

"I had good reason, Orunmila." Elegua pouts, rising.

Orunmila starts. "One, two—"

Elegua waves a hand. Jonas and Colin shoot out of the floor, landing unceremoniously on their backs. I rush to help them up.

"I asked you to report to me once Abidèmi arrived!" Orunmila shouts. I look up at this. The spirit continues, wagging his finger at Elegua. "Instead, you behave worse than Shango!"

The man tangled with Oshun breaks their kiss to stare at us. "What are you calling my name for now?"

"Nothing, my love," Oshun says, tugging him onto a cushion. "Ren's twenty years are up, so Elegua is acting out."

"It's not that—" Elegua protests, his cheeks flushed. "This olodo put my daughter—Ren's daughter—in danger. And now she's here to beg our help!"

I freeze—Sanaa is Elegua's daughter?

Before I can ask anything, Orunmila swans over, offering a hand. His smile is kindly, his wrinkled face not unlike Baba Sylvanus's. The moment his hand brushes mine, warmth rushes into me, and the cut Elegua opened on my cheek heals instantly.

"Welcome, Abidèmi, daughter of Yetundé and Osèzèlé, child born of Afèni's flame. I have long waited for the day you would return to us."

He touches Jonas on the shoulder. "Welcome, Jonas, flower of first frost. We recognize your lineage once again."

Jonas looks to me, but I shake my head, equally confused.

Orunmila steps back, opening his arms, this time looking at Colin. "Welcome back, our brave omo Éyani."

I gasp as Colin rushes to him, burying his face in the elderly man's shoulder. "Everything is a mess, Baba."

Orunmila pats Colin's back. "Then we will restore balance to the world."

"Why do you know the ancestral spirits?" I ask, awestruck.

"Omo Éyani is a child of the pathways," Orunmila explains. "It is only fitting that we would encounter him as he journeyed between."

Colin touches the back of his neck, throwing me a sheepish look. "They've gotten me out of a few scrapes."

The action draws down his sleeve, and Orunmila takes his hand, inspecting his ringed wrist.

"You gave control over your magic to another?" he asks, placing a finger to the flower in the center of those rings.

"Someone I trust," Colin says, pulling his hand away. "Don't worry too much, Baba."

Orunmila just sighs. "You are a child of Elegua's blood. I cannot interfere in your fate even if I desired to."

I frown. "Is something wrong with that mark?"

Orunmila shakes his head. "Not necessarily. Chaining can be a good thing. It just depends on the conditions of the bond."

"Time is fast spent, egbon," Shango says. "We should begin."

Orunmila turns to Elegua. "It is your turn to choose the trial. But I don't trust you to be fair. Appoint someone to choose the trial for you."

Elegua's lips quirk in a smile. "I thought you'd never ask." He snaps his fingers and my brother stumbles out of the shadow of a pillar, running over.

"It is only fitting that you, as Dèmi's anchor, decide her fate. What trial must she face to meet Iya?"

"*He* is my anchor?" I ask, disbelieving.

The lines in Délé's face tighten as he speaks. "I am what tethers you to this world, dear sister." His mouth stretches in a wide grin. "And I have the perfect trial for you. You will fight a musin blindfolded. Your companions will be bound."

I stiffen. The musin are unruly spirits born of souls lost in the Spirit

Realm, those whose essences have no chance of being reborn. They grow in power as their souls waste away, and their hunger for life, their desire to absorb life from the spirits they encounter, makes them the most ferocious beings in the Spirit Realm.

"That's not fair!" Colin yells. "An unruly spirit could kill her in one touch. How does she avoid that blindfolded?"

Orunmila nods. "Ayodélé, that trial is a bit harsh on your sister. Why don't we choose another?"

"You always tell me that we all must prove ourselves worthy of the power Olorun gave us," Délé counters. "My sister was gifted with the power of the Fèni-Ogun and the Ariabhe. Taking down one unruly spirit should not be impossible."

"I thought he might choose the alayo rooms—unravel her mind with her memories," Elegua says, humming his approval. "This is easier in a way."

"A blindfolded fight, yes?" I say, displaying a bravery I don't feel. "Any other conditions?"

Jonas speaks up then, pleading, "Let me fight with her. Her spirit bonds were sundered. She cannot fight alone."

"We know well what happened," Oshun answers. "We feel the loss of every Oluso's spirit bonds. Were you fully bonded mates, we would have no choice but to honor your request—you two would fight as one—but you are not."

"There is a way for you to help," Elegua says. He slinks closer with all the confidence of a fox approaching a hen. "Give up what is left of your bond, and I will grant you the power to fight at her side."

My heart twists as the words reach my ears, the ache in my chest threatening to pull me apart. The thought of surrendering my bond to Jonas, severing the connection between us, is too much to bear.

I clench my hands into fists. "No deal."

Elegua ignores me. "The two of you can fight as one for the duration of your trial. But in exchange, your connection will be severed."

Délé bristles. "That wasn't what I asked for, arakunrin—"

"I'll do it," Jonas interrupts. "I'll give up the bond. Just let me fight with her."

"No." I grab his arm, turning him to face me. "You want to give us up? Is this what you meant by proving yourself to me?"

"I can't let you die!" he shouts. He pauses, taking a steadying breath. "This is the better option—with two of us, we have a better chance of handling any surprises."

"Our love will die," I declare.

He places his hands on my shoulders. "Our love can live without a bond. There's more to us than just magic, I know it. We fight this thing together, we survive together. If we die, we died trying. Together."

"This isn't only your decision to make," I spit.

"No, it's not." He stares into my eyes, looking at me as though we are the only two in this room. "Which is why I need you to say yes. Trust me. Believe in us. We can beat this—together."

I lick my lips. "How do we know we can trust him?"

"I assure you I mean everything I just said. My egbon here are my witnesses," Elegua answers. "You will fight together as mates"—he nods at my brother—"under the conditions that Ayodélé devises."

"And what conditions are those?" Colin asks, voice low and menacing. "The blindfold is already plenty."

Elegua throws his head back, bursting into a throaty laugh that rings in my ears like a warning bell. Shango elbows him, and only then does he stop.

"You are fortunate I am even giving you this chance," he snaps.

"And we'll take it," Jonas responds, looking to me. "Yes?"

I can't breathe. For the last year I have nurtured this spirit bond, held it like a lifeline keeping me from drowning in life's storms. Every time I dealt with hostility in Eingard or fear and anguish sunk their unforgiving claws into me, I reached for that thread pulsing between us, tangible proof we could grow together and birth something like love. I've resented it, too, being beholden to someone else, knowing one look from Jonas is enough to split me open, peel back the protective shell of anger and fear that has held me together for so long. But now, all I hear is the echo of Jonas's words, the resolution in his voice. I know he wants me to trust him, but it feels as though he is giving us up with no guarantee that we'll find our way back to each other. But I need to survive this fight, make it to Iya at any cost—even if it costs my heart.

"Okay."

He folds my hands in his, bringing them to his lips. "I promised you, oko mi, that I wouldn't waver. This is me honoring that. If giving up our bond means you'll get to Iya, then I would do it a thousand times, even if it means I might become nothing to you. But I don't think that would ever happen. There's too much else between us."

"You might die in this fight," I croak, swallowing past the lump in my throat. "With my magic as it is, what if I can't heal you? How can you trust me?"

"Easy," he says, smiling. "I make the choice each time, oko mi. Every day, I trust you."

I study him, relishing the way the gold flecks in those cerulean sky eyes twinkle like sun rays piercing through clouds after a storm. Everything, from the gentle pressure in his hands to the soft smile on his lips and the reckless thrum of his heart singing with mine, tells me what I've been afraid to look at for so long—he loves and trusts me, even if there is no guarantee that I might do the same.

"All right," I repeat. "Let's do it."

Orunmila clears his throat. "I appreciate the bravery and affection you're all showing at the moment, but we must commence with the trial."

"I'll fight with her also," Colin declares, stepping up to Elegua. "Tell me what I must do."

"You will do no such thing," Orunmila answers.

"Why not?"

Orunmila pulls off his spectacles with a sigh blowing on the lenses. When he looks up, his golden eyes are burning bright. "Éyani is the sole reason the K'inu haven't entirely overrun the Physical Realm. I'd like to keep her happy, wouldn't you?"

Colin's expression darkens instantly.

"What do the K'inu have to do with Colin's mother?" I ask.

This time it is Délé's turn to laugh. "Didn't he tell you, dear sister? Éyani Al'Hia is one of their generals."

I turn to Colin, but he does not meet my gaze. Now I understand Délé's cryptic words upon our arrival, Colin's relief that the K'inu were not necessarily evil. His mother Éyani was murdered by his father, poisoned by wine that Colin himself delivered as a young child. If the K'inu are wandering spirits born of lingering regrets, Éyani Al'Hia would be a perfect candidate to join their ranks.

"Col," I say in a low voice, "is this true?"

Colin doesn't answer.

I feel like an utter fool.

"You've been helping the Council all this time?" Jonas asks, forehead knotting into a scowl. "How is that possible?"

Colin snaps his head up. "I haven't. My mother has been appearing to me in dreams for the last few months. In every dream she turns into a kokulu."

"Why were you in Lleyria?" I demand. "I think we deserve to know."

He sighs. "My mother told me about it. She told me she saw you, that she was afraid her brethren would do something to hurt you."

I frown. "How? She's never met me."

He swallows before answering. "You've always been in my dreams. She recognized you from there."

I look away, unsure of how to respond.

"You didn't think to tell us?" Jonas demands. "To trust us?"

"I didn't know what to make of it," Colin retorts. He darts a quick look at me before adding, "Everyone is afraid of the K'inu. I didn't want you to find out like this."

"Why are they doing the Council's bidding?" Jonas asks. "Do you know that at least?"

Colin shakes his head. "I don't. My mother only tells me of the things she regrets, the dreams she has of our future together."

My heart aches. If Mummy ever appeared to me in a dream, I would hold on to it no matter what came of it. I can't imagine what it's been like for Colin to carry this secret, worry that revealing it will bring harm to the people he loves.

An errant thought drops into my mind like a coin falling into a stream.

"Does Ekwensi know?"

Colin's gaze returns to me, and I glimpse so many emotions crossing his face in one breath. Shame, anguish, anger, resolution.

Finally he says, "Ekwensi has been supportive. He was there when I felt abandoned."

I wince. That is answer enough.

"I only told him after Wellstown," he adds quickly. "He told me to bury it. That people would accuse me of the kokulu attacks."

"And I'm one of those people?"

It is his turn to wince. "That's not what I mean."

"I understand," I say quietly. It hurts to know that there is still a rift between us, that Colin hasn't fully forgiven me for choosing to stay in Eingard.

"It's not because I don't trust you," he insists. "I just didn't want you to feel like I was no longer the person you knew. I've—we've changed—"

"We should begin the trial," Orunmila interrupts. "The faster we do, the sooner you can resolve your personal issues outside the ancestral court."

"Or die," Elegua adds. Délé laughs at that.

Colin slams a fist into the pillar behind him, then he hisses, shaking his bloodied hand.

Oshun tuts. "I thought Shango was the only fool."

"Hey!" Shango crosses his arms. "I've gotten better at communicating."

She pats his shoulder. "You have, darling. I'm just surprised when I meet people that remind me of past you."

Oshosi chuckles. "You used to set fire to furniture rather than ask for help getting a splinter out of your hand."

"I did not!" Shango cries, but even as he says the words, flames spark at his fingertips.

I narrow my eyes. "You all knew the K'inu were ravaging the Physical Realm."

"We are ancestral spirits," Oshun says, twirling a braid on her finger. "If we didn't know, who would?"

"You refuse to do anything about it?" Jonas asks.

Orunmila laces his fingers together, holding them out as though they are a barrier that will protect him. "We cannot act as freely as humanity does. It is not our way. Tradition dictates we must maintain the balance. But that is why you're here to see Iya. She, as our mother, may make a different choice." He turns to Oshosi. "If we are done deciding, we must get moving."

Oshosi waves his udamalore, and the air folds. Pillars and fabric give way to a raised stone altar surrounded by statues. Orunmila takes a seat in the lap of the statue of a bronzed woman whose spread palms have eyes embedded in them. Oshosi lays his back against a panther in mid-jump while Oshun perches on a wave cresting high against some cliffs. Shango leaps onto the horse-drawn chariot beside her, leaning against the fiery mane of the horse on the right. The women warriors take their places around the altar, their tattoos all aglow.

"Beyond guarding our halls, the Jagun Jagun are keepers of time," Oshosi says. "If you break the rules set out during the trial, they will stop your time permanently."

Each Jagun Jagun tattoo corresponds to certain hours. Behind me is Crow, and to my left, Snake. Rabbit faces me head-on, spear slightly tipped as though challenging me to test her.

"Will you tell us the rules *now*?" Colin asks, stepping nearer to me.

Elegua leans against the palm of his throne, kicking his feet. "Ah, yes—" He nods at Délé. "Go on, aburo."

My brother beams, no doubt wishing he were actually Elegua's younger brother than my twin. "The rules are simple, sister," he says. "Find a way to destroy the musin's heart, and in doing so, give it peace. You may use magic or items you brought into the arena."

He knocks his spear twice on the ground and shackles shoot out of the stone, latching onto Jonas's ankles and waist.

"This isn't what we agreed to," Jonas protests.

Elegua grins. "We agreed that you would fight with Dèmi as her fully bonded mate. And you will. You will experience every blow, every wound, just as she would. You may also aid her with your magic or your voice if you wish. Trust that this fight will be as real for you as it is for her."

He waves a hand and Colin turns translucent.

"What is this?" Colin cries.

"Just a little precaution, in case you forget this fight is meant for those two alone."

I scan the room for further surprises. We should have known better than to trust Elegua. Orunmila casts him a scornful glance, but Elegua does not even look concerned.

Orunmila sighs. "Let us commence."

"Not so fast. I believe we forgot the stakes," Elegua says with a grin. "If you win, you will see Iya."

"Get an audience with Iya," Orunmila amends.

"Yes, yes, an audience. But if you lose—" His grin widens.

Délé speaks up. "I get to keep your body, sister."

A chill races up my spine. "What does that mean?"

"You'll stay here in the Spirit Realm while I take your place below. You will die."

"Do you accept?"

BRAVERY

YOU WILL DIE.

The words echo in my head like a trumpet, but I can't bring myself to say anything. Hasn't this always been the path? I knew, from the moment I first took Ekwensi's hand, that I would either succeed in doing something to help the Oluso or I would die in the effort. A year ago, all I could think about was what would happen if I did nothing. Now, nothing has changed. I will move forward, no matter the cost. Desecrating my body, refusing me final rest, is a mere insult compared to all I've suffered.

"She can't accept," Colin says. "You can't just make up rules to suit your whims."

Délé turns to Elegua, who shrugs. "I gave you power to decide, aburo. Do as you see fit."

"Baba." Colin turns to Orunmila. "Tell them they can't do this."

Orunmila sighs, leaning back in his throne. "Délé, explain to me why you seek to possess your sister's body."

I wait. Spirits are incapable of lying before the elder ancestral spirits, so whatever my brother admits, it has to be the truth as he knows it.

My brother answers earnestly. "The K'inu are the family who raised me. They looked after me while my father could not. Éyani was my mother when I had none to guide me."

"The K'inu are not destroying the Physical Realm for no reason," my brother continues, words falling off his tongue like well-rehearsed lines in a masquerade. "They only seek restitution from those who have wronged us."

"But you're working with the Council," Jonas says. "Inciting war."

He lifts his hands, the chains binding his wrists rattling as he talks. "Almost everyone is a descendant of the Oluso who betrayed the iron-bloods. Do you intend to kill every person?"

Délé bristles, his voice dripping with undisguised venom. "*You* are the last person I want to hear that from, oloté."

I frown. Why would he call Jonas a traitor?

"The K'inu desire only the life that is owed them," my brother goes on. He turns to Colin. "You understand. Éyani was murdered, robbed of her illustrious life. Should someone not be held responsible for that?"

Orunmila taps his staff against the floor. "Enough!" He nods at Elegua. "Appoint one of us to oversee the trial. This foolish pup seeks murder."

Délé kneels, pleading. "The K'inu want a ceremony, a way to recognize the lives that were stolen from them. I am not one of you, egbon. I am a mere initiate. I have no reason to lie."

Oshun sweeps out of her seat, anklets tinkling as she steps onto the altar. "Say we believe you, Ayodélé. Why not teach your sister how to appease their anger? Why choose this path?"

My brother presses his head lower to the ground. "I want to repay the kindness they have shown me with my own hands. I will use my sister's body to conduct these rites and appease their anger. Nothing more and nothing less. It is said the river only finds peace in the sea. You, as the spirit of the rivers, know this well. Let me show my brethren the peace they've longed for."

"I don't believe you," I say. I still remember the sadness the K'inu showed me in Gaeyak-Orin, and I can believe that some of them want peace. But there is something about my brother's answers that sets my teeth on edge.

Shango leans in, running a finger down the body of his ax. "You doubt the word of the spirits? You think we can be fooled by lies?"

"No, egbon," I answer. "I trust *you* all." I can't afford to offend the spirits, not now.

"Then it's done. Let the trial commence." He nods to Orunmila. "I know firsthand what it is to feel you owe. Father stopped Yemoja from taking my life after I accidentally burned her children. He granted me another chance. So should this child have one."

He stands abruptly, flinging his ax towards Oshun. She whirls, catching its handle as the blade dances by her neck, then she brings it down, striking the altar.

The ground begins to shake, Jonas's chains rattling against the stone. I throw my arms around his waist, holding on tight as the tremors ripple through us.

Oshun and Délé disappear from the altar, flashing onto the edge; Oshun perches on the arm of Shango's throne while Délé takes his place behind Elegua like a dutiful shadow.

Colin reaches for my wrist, but his fingers pass through me, leaving a tingle on my skin.

"Son of a gutter horse," he curses. "I can't help you."

"More like ten gutter horses," Jonas mutters, his gaze trained on the spot where Oshun once stood.

I turn. Standing a few feet away is a beast fouler than a nightmare. It is tall, standing on hind legs that resemble the end of a horse, with long, lanky hair hanging over what appears to be a mottled human face lit up by twin violet flames in its eye sockets. Its arms are scaled, its talons as sharp as execution blades. But the most fearsome thing about it is its torso—a hollowed chest with flayed skin hanging over rows of interlocking teeth as long as rib bones.

"What in Olorun's name is this abomination?" I whisper.

The beast opens its cavernous, decaying mouth and shrieks. A glob of blue liquid flies out, and the stone it falls onto sizzles as it rots away, leaving only a trail of azure smoke.

"I wouldn't insult a musin if I were you," Elegua warns. "They may be blind, but they're very sensitive about their appearances."

The musin sinks low, and the teeth in its chest open like a flower basking in the sun's rays. Buried in its ribs is a burning violet flame, the musin's heart.

Oshosi waves his udamalore. "Jagun Jagun! Clear the way."

The Jagun Jagun flip their spears, stabbing them into the ground. A golden sheen unfolds over the altar, its thickness not unlike the sticky membrane I've rubbed off of newborn babes. Jagged currents ripple across the barrier, lightning sparks promising a swift retribution. There is no escape.

"The path is clear!" the warriors shout.

"You may begin," Oshosi says, taking a seat.

"Wait!" Elegua produces a ribbon of violet silk. "Let's not forget the blindfold. We are in pursuit of fairness after all."

"How can you call that fair?" Colin protests. "Musin are plenty deadly even without a blindfold."

Elegua snaps his fingers and Colin's mouth stitches closed, blue thread webbing diagonally over his lips. "That's more like it."

Orunmila glares at him and he shrugs. "I want to watch this trial in peace. I'll remove it when we're done."

He appears behind me, trailing the silk against my face. As soon as the fabric touches my skin, it crawls over my eyes and cements itself there. The world swells as dark as the night sky, leaving only faint traces of light hinting beyond that darkness.

Panic swallows me whole, and I stretch my hands out, reaching for something, anything. I fought blindfolded with the kunkun, but those were people rather than beasts that could liquefy my bones.

There is a rush of metal dragging along the ground and suddenly I feel the warmth of Jonas's hand gripping mine.

"Trust me, oko mi."

Now there are hoofbeats, the easy canter of a predator sensing its prey.

The skin on my arms prickles.

"I can't," I whisper. "I can't—I can't see anything."

"Listen to me," Jonas whispers, squeezing my hand. "Remember what it feels like to be in my mind."

The hoofbeats are getting louder, closer.

My heart pounds in my ears, fear twisting my stomach into knots.

"I don't know," I confess. "I don't know how."

"Settle down," Jonas commands. "Listen for my voice. Think of memories we've shared. A memory you want to see through my eyes. Come on."

Sucking in a breath, I quiet my mind, reaching for the hum of the bond that sings between us. I touch it, flow along with it as the air slices over my face and hoofbeats turn to wild, triumphant screeches.

I remember.

... ANOTHER SNOW-BURIED DAY IN EINGARD.

I sit in the window of our solar, staring out at the white world. My cheeks are cold, my breath frosting the glass as I exhale. Though I am wrapped in three layers, it feels as though my bones are made of ice. I set down the leather-bound book languishing in my hands—*A History of Eingardian Songs and Minor Lore.* My head hurts. My eyes sting from reading and memorizing all morning. The air is so dry that my nostrils threaten to bleed. I am tired of sitting here. Waiting.

"You'll turn into ash if you keep staring like that," Jonas says. He— no, I enter the room. There are flowers tucked into the waistband of my trousers, hidden just out of sight. I carry a tray of well-salted salmon— this morning's catch—sitting next to a bowl of periwinkle stew. The steam rising from the bowl warms my face, and I smile thinking of how the woman in front of me will look when she lifts the wooden spoon to her lips and tastes the chewy, tangy flesh of the small sea snails, the ones I visited over forty Oyo merchants for.

She turns to me, her face nearly swallowed by the furs clinging to her neck and the woolen hat pressed over her coils. Her brown skin is so bright against the soft white fur, but her expression is flat, the smiling eyes I'm used to as worn as burnished copper shields.

I know she's missing home again, wondering when the snow will stop falling in Nordgren. If it could stop falling. I know she longs for the warmth of the Oyo sun on her skin, and the bustle and noise of the Benin marketplace. She says she's gotten used to the Eingardian day winking away by the end of Bear Hour, but sometimes I catch her staring into the sunless sky, rubbing her arms as though for comfort.

"Are you finished for the day?" she says.

"Rara mo jà dé." *No, I snuck out.*

I speak the words in Yoruba although my mind goes over them in

Ceorn again. This is one of the few things I can do for her, show her I love her in the language she understands best.

She rewards me with a fleeting smile. My heart tightens in my chest.

"The almighty Council fell for your trickery?" she lobs back in Yoruba.

"They had to. I dismissed them as their king. Royal headache."

She snorts.

I set the tray in front of her, pushing yet another history book aside. The book falls with a thud and I kick it away. It slides to the hearth, knocking into the bowls I scoured with ash only that morning. My mate loves this too, knowing I respect her enough to clean our bowls as she would, thank the Spirits for the life of the food they granted us.

She looks down at the stew now, her eyes widening as she realizes what it is.

She gasps. "Jonas, how?"

I reach for her, stroking my fingers across her soft cheeks. "Didn't you say you were craving it?"

"But how did you get it?" She flashes me a real smile, showing off the tiny space between her top two teeth.

"I have my ways," I say, drawing her in. Then I press my lips against hers, tasting her softness, stroking my fingers against her neck. She returns the kiss with just as much fire, the feel of her like molten gold running through my fingers.

We draw apart. "I don't want the stew to get cold," I whisper, enjoying the sight of our frosted breath tangling together. "But when we get closer to Harvest, I will take you to Aeynsled to see the seals."

She laughs, her voice lighter than the sound of bells. "There's an Eingardian song in the book. About taking your lover to see the seals."

Come away with me
My love
My heart
Come dance among the seas
The seals they wait
To play and bark
And gather with the breeze

Let's wait under
The setting sun
And watch for
The moonrise
Today let's bind
Our hearts as one
And flow along with time

I sing the words softly, tugging her to stand with me. Then, as I whisper the last words, I kiss her forehead and rub my hand along her back. *Soon, I promise myself. Soon, she won't be trapped like an ornament in this castle. Soon, we will do as we please. We just need time.*

I close my eyes, relishing the scent of her skin . . .

———

I OPEN MY EYES. THE MUSIN IS CHARGING, ITS HEAD AND TORSO LOWERED like a bull. It leaps into the air, flying straight at us. My body stands next to me, arms frozen in the air.

"Shit."

Jonas's thought drops into my head: *Use my vision. But don't forget to control your body.*

I imagine bending my knees to keep them from buckling. My body obeys.

Good. Now, do what you need to do.

I reach for my magic, begging the spirits not to fail me. The pain in my back flares, stilling my breath, but the wind spirits obey, forming a wall just as the musin drops over Jonas and me. The musin screeches again, swiping at the wind wall cutting the arena in half, but I pour more and more magic out of my fingertips, willing the wall to stay firm.

The musin turns around, cantering in the opposite direction. But I keep my hands up, watching through Jonas's eyes for any signs of deviating movement. It stops, bending its torso back, and the teeth in its chest splay open. Smoke floods out, leaking into the air like a fragrance. It sweeps into my wind wall, melding with it.

The stench of rotted flesh crawls over my skin as the smoke stings my nose. My magic recedes and my wind wall shatters.

"Dèmi," Jonas coughs as the sound of hoofbeats drown out the buzz of the barrier overhead.

"I'm on it," I say, gripping my bone blade tight.

The musin swipes at me. I leap back, but the tips of its talons catch me, ripping my blouse. A fire erupts in my belly; then, just as quickly, it disappears.

Jonas cries out, and I look down with his eyes. There is blood on his shirt, claw marks in the exact same spot the musin cut me.

Elegua's laugh drifts through the smoke. "You wanted to experience the battle as her full mate. How is it so far?"

The musin strikes at me again, but this time I spin on my back foot, turning in a circle. Using my momentum, I stab at its rump and it rears up as my bone blade plunges into its flesh.

"I wouldn't do that if I were you," Elegua calls gleefully.

"Hold your noise, brother," Orunmila rebukes.

The musin bucks, dragging me into the air. I let go, falling onto my back. My blade remains trapped in the musin's hide. Folding my arms, I roll out of the way as it stomps the ground around it, moving in a circle. I get to my feet as understanding dawns.

The musin cannot see. Which means there must be a way it's finding me.

The musin stops near the center of the arena. Then it opens its teeth again, and azure liquid spews out like rain.

I trip on a loose stone in my haste to get away. Some of the spittle falls on my legs, eating into my trousers. Jonas gasps in pain, and I look down to see fresh burns staring up at me from the holes newly etched into his trousers.

"Sorry," I whisper.

"It's fine," he says through gritted teeth. "I can handle this much."

Bracing for the pain, I touch the bracelet on my arm, trying to summon my iron magic. The musin turns, lifting its nose into the air, then it paws the ground and charges in my direction. I fold, crossing my arms in front of myself, thinking of an iron shield in front of my body like the kunkun taught me. The musin crashes into me, but my iron magic leaps to my skin, absorbing the blow. I exhale, grateful. All that torture was not for nothing.

The musin's hoof comes up then, striking my rib. I fly back, smashing into the stone, my chest ablaze with pain. My ribs creak as I try to stand, blood spilling from my mouth.

"Focus," Jonas rasps, coughing up more blood.

More azure smoke seeps out of the musin's chest, clouding around my body. I inhale, struggling to breathe as it rushes into my mouth, stuffing my throat. The spark of magic at my fingertips dies and I stagger back in panic.

I look through Jonas's eyes, but all I see is a fleeting shadow, my body buried in a haze of smoke.

Elegua's voice pierces through the haze. "You are weak. Pitiful. Imagine a child of Oya and Ogun's blood moving like this."

"Shut your mouth unless you want to summon them here," Oshosi warns. "You won't escape with just a gale storm this time."

The hoofbeats come again, thundering in my ears. I scramble, turning around, but I can't tell where I am or what is around me. Panic turns into gut-wrenching dread and I breathe in short spurts, trying to muster up my courage.

"Get down!" Jonas shouts as the smoke clears.

I drop to the floor. The air above me whistles, releasing a sudden breeze that tickles my cheeks. I see through Jonas's eyes that the musin jumped over my head. But the musin keeps running, driving at the barrier. Then, at the last moment it halts, nostrils flaring as it sniffs the air again. It's not my scent—it would have been tracking me far more easily if that were the case. *That's it.*

Magic.

The musin can only sense my magic.

The sound of metal scraping stone eats at my ears, and I wince. Something slams into my side and I fall to my knees.

"Pick it up!" Jonas shouts. "If you can't use your magic, tap into mine."

"Don't use your magic!" I scream. "It'll come after you."

Elegua's furious voice rises overhead. "That is a breach of the rules."

"In what way?" Oshun answers. "You did say they could fight as full mates. Full mates have access to each other's magic."

The musin turns, zeroing in on Jonas. Then it rushes at him, and I run at it, gripping the spear his magic constructed for me like a lance. We collide, my spear impaling its rump and it lurches back, flinging me and my spear to the ground a few feet away. The pouch holding Silver and Fox Bead's bracelets slides out of my pocket.

I lie there, pain bursting through my skull, the faint auras of light beyond my blindfold winking like dying stars. The musin pounces, ripping through what's left of the lower half of my blouse. It sinks its talons into the pit of my stomach. I scream as pain fills my senses, a raging fire burning every part of me. The musin stabs me with its other hand, ripping into my torso. Its chest opens wide, teeth flaring as though ready to devour me. The spear slips from my trembling hands.

"No!"

Jonas is screaming now, chains rattling as he clutches his belly, but he holds up the pouch of beads with one hand, shaking them like a baby's rattle. The musin turns it head, sensing the life magic in those beads. As soon as he has the musin's attention, Jonas drops the pouch, stretching a hand out toward me.

The spear flies into my fingers, the kiss of cold iron bringing me to my senses. Pouring out the last of my strength, I bring my spear up, driving it into the musin's chest. My fingers are slick with blood, but I shove the spear with all my might, impaling the violet flame in the center of its body.

The musin throws back its head in a scream. It jerks away from me, raking its talon over its chest, and I'm sure we've both made killing blows.

The flesh of my torso knits back together, the sting of pain melting away in mere breaths. I scramble up on bloody hands as the musin yanks the spear from its chest. But this time it tears past me, speeding toward Jonas, who lies bleeding, struggling to keep his eyes open.

A sudden burst of energy floods me, and I leap forward, calling the discarded spear to me. The musin raises its forelegs. The world winks bright and dark all at once as Jonas's eyes flutter.

Stepping on my bone blade still jutting from its side, I land on the musin's back and stab the beast in its spine and out through its chest as the world goes dark.

It screams a final time, then all I can hear is the sound of my body smacking into the stone. The blindfold falls and I blink against the flare of colors assaulting my eyes. A moth lies in a pool of blood, purple and gray patterned wings fluttering against sticky blue liquid seeping between the altar stones.

Jonas's eyes are closed, his skin pale against the bloody mess of his stomach. I scramble to him.

"No, no, no," I cry, pressing my hands over his stomach. I call on my magic, pleading with the spirits, but nothing happens.

The barrier melts away, and Colin races to us, threads falling from his mouth like dead skin.

"Hold on, please," he says, dragging me back. His skin feels real against mine, solid.

"He's dying!" I cry. "My magic isn't working."

Colin pulls up Jonas's eyelid. Then he looks to Orunmila. "Do something, Baba."

Orunmila rises, but Elegua puts a hand out. "The trial has not been concluded. She technically had help. We need to issue a new one."

"You approved her getting help from her mate," Orunmila counters.

"I see you are still up to your tricks," a woman's voice announces. A white-haired woman with skin like mine and sharp brown eyes materializes atop the giant efon statue next to Elegua's throne. Grabbing onto one of the animal's curved horns, she swings down, the forest-green dress she's wearing rippling behind her like a cape billowing in the wind. If the machete strapped to her hip or the bones gathered at her waist like a belt don't reveal who she is, the sparks of lightning crackling at her feet and the horned circlet adorning her coily hair mark her as Oya, the premier spirit of the wind.

The one who grants me my powers.

I lower myself to the ground, hope swelling in my breast. "I greet you, Mother of the Wind, Keeper of the River of Souls. Please help your humble servant."

I don't have any choice now but to beg Oya for help. Though the other spirits must remain neutral, she, at least, as the Mother of all Ariabhe Oluso, has incentive to help me.

"Rise, Abidèmi. It is not your humility I seek today. It is your fighting spirit."

Oya lifts a hand and Jonas's skin burns with a white flame. His torso seals up, smooth skin folding over muscle until there is not a speck of blood to be seen.

"Good to see you could make it, sister," Elegua says, flashing her a bright—albeit clearly false—smile. "No marital troubles with Ogun today, I hope?"

The fingers on Elegua's throne morph into talons, curling back against his face and neck. A man with skin the color of rust emerges from the shadows behind Elegua, his hand outstretched.

"It seems you have a short memory, Elegua. I warned you not to disrespect my wife."

Elegua swallows, the tip of a talon grazing his throat. "I thought we agreed to keep things civil, Ogun. I had reason to quibble with my dear sister."

Ogun relaxes into a simple-looking chair with a forge beneath it. The fires in the forge blaze a deadly orange as he places his feet atop it. "You are fortunate I am in a good mood."

Jonas opens his eyes and sits up, sucking air into his lungs.

"Thank you," I say, bowing again. "Thank you."

Jonas reaches for me, dragging me into the circle of his arms. "I thought I'd lost you." He inhales again, pulling me closer as though he could breathe me in. "Don't ever do that again. Ever."

"You were the one who nearly died," I cry.

"I had to watch you be disemboweled." He rests his head in the crook of my neck. "Never do that to me again, oko mi. I couldn't bear it. Just the thought of you dying . . ." He breaks off with a shudder.

"I thought you removed their bond," Shango says, amusement heavy in his voice.

"I did," Elegua snaps. "Humans keep such lingering attachments."

I pull back, trying to read Jonas's thoughts. Nothing comes back but silence. My heart tightens, suddenly aching. There is no more song between us, no bone-deep rhythm. It is as though I've forgotten something that flits just out of my reach. Yet I still feel warmth looking at him.

Colin offers him a hand. "Glad you're not dead."

Jonas smiles as he gets to his feet. "Thanks."

"My children won the day," Ogun crows.

I start to lower myself into another bow, but he puts out a hand. "Stand tall, child of Osèzèlé. You have proven worthy of my blood." He nods at Jonas. "Five lifetimes have passed, but it is good to see my line return in you, Jonas. See you do not follow the foolishness of your forebears."

Jonas jerks to attention. "I don't understand. Who in my family had magic?"

Ogun sighs. "The children come unschooled these days. They lack knowledge of their own ancestry."

Oya pats him on the arm. "That isn't their fault. Life has been cruel. Remember what Iya taught us when we were children—Itan je okùn kan ni ọwọ akoko."

History is but a thread in the hands of time.

"Threads weave in and out of cloth. They are lost and rediscovered. But without them, we have no guide with which to find our paths."

Oshun folds a hand against her cheek. "I wish you would give half your wisdom to Yemoja. She's getting on my nerves, refusing to come back from the realm she's fallen into."

Shango barks out a laugh. "She's enjoying being a goddess. Imagine— the people worship two moons, but they're both just her."

Oshosi groans. "Don't remind me. She got Obatala to go with her. He is some sort of sun creature. Everything revolves around him."

"As I was saying," Ogun interrupts, clearing his throat, "your forebear, young man, was a fool with little parallel. Croiden Aurelius Schulson. I gave him the gift of my blood and he used it to frighten his brethren."

I make a mental note to ask Baba about the name when we return to the Physical Realm.

Ogun waves a hand. "But that is not what you're here for. You may go see Iya."

Elegua gets to his feet, sighing. "I will take them to Mother."

Oya flicks a finger and Elegua is snatched into the air, dangling from his collar. "Not so fast. I will clear the way. You stay where I can see you, naughty boy."

She snaps her fingers and Ren appears in a whirl of fur, pulling back the animal-skin veil on her head. Elegua stills, staring forlornly at her, but she does not even glance at him.

"You called?"

"Send the other two for cleansing before the ceremony tonight. Abidèmi is going to Iya."

"Why can't we go together?" Colin asks.

Oya smiles. "Wonderful to see you in good health, omo Éyani. Irreverent as ever."

Colin flushes.

Oya leaps off her efon and glides over. "Iya called for only Abidèmi."

"As her mate, could I—" Jonas starts.

She holds up a hand. "Dèmi has no mate at present."

"Can't you make a tiny exception?" Colin pleads.

Oya crosses her arms. "I made plenty of exceptions for you and Éyani. But there will be no special treatment here. This is Iya, our mother. We don't play games with her."

I quirk an eyebrow at Colin, confused. He opens his mouth, then closes it with a sigh. He nods.

Oya pats him on the shoulder. "Good."

The air fizzles, pinching in different places, and we find ourselves in the cushioned room. This time, however, there is a glass door where Elegua's seat once stood. The ancestral spirits and my brother are gone. My brother's spear alone lies on the floor—a challenge. Nothing is over for him, I see.

Ren beckons me to the door. There is a shadowed recess in it fitting the shape of my crystal. "Wait here."

She backs away, tugging at Jonas's and Colin's sleeves. "This way, let's go."

Jonas and Colin look to me, worry on their faces. I wave them on. "Go. I'll be fine."

I watch until they leave the room. The crystal lying against my chest shifts from onyx to amber. Taking a deep breath, I push it into the door.

INHERITANCE

Ìyá-Ilé is even more beautiful up close. Gold and silver veins thread her branches like skeins of precious metals bleeding through the earth. As I step closer, the glass fruits underneath the varied leaves brighten, the flame in them taking on the color of the leaves they dance under. Then there are tiny flowers studding her bark and branches, blue and violet buds that come open as though in welcome.

"Welcome, daughter," Osèzèlé says, stepping out from behind Iya's trunk. My father is smiling, holding his arms out as though he expects me to run to him. After a moment's silence, he drops them.

"Too soon for that, I see."

"I've met you three times in my life."

His lips quirk with a sad smile. "I wish it could have been more."

I lift three fingers. "The first time, you handed me a weapon that saved my life." One finger ticks down. "The second time, you drowned me."

"A test to make you strong."

"The third time, you beat me bloody."

"To remind you to walk the path. That is why Iya brought me here now, granted me the opportunity to be her vessel."

He tosses me the spear in his hand and I catch it without flinching. He nods his appreciation. "Tell me, could you have won against the musin as you were before?"

"I don't know."

"I *do* know. Let me tell you this—few have managed to stand where you are right now. Even the greatest warriors fail the tests of the spirits. Afèni failed."

"She saved your life," I challenge.

"She did. And that was her saving grace. If she hadn't, there would be no you to right her mistakes. To heal many of our foolish mistakes."

I curl my lip in a smirk. "Sounds like you're speaking from personal experience."

"I am. My test was simple." He points to a bare branch holding only one fruit. "I was to inherit the means to resurrect my people. If I passed, the spirits would give the iron-bloods a resting place. If I failed, well . . . you understand in part some of my failures. You were born during the war after all."

I narrow my eyes. "You mean the spirits told you to share the secret of ironcraft with the Eingardians?"

He shakes his head. "No. The spirits protected me in their own way. They made sure I grew up, that I met the right people at the right times." His lips curve in a wistful smile. "I met your mother even though I ran from their guidance. That was the mercy of the spirits."

I ran from their guidance too, I think.

I cross my arms, hugging myself. "What are you saying?"

"I am saying I wanted vengeance. I couldn't understand why my people were hunted within an inch of their lives. Before the K'inu ever spoke to you, they visited me in dreams and memories." He slams his fist against his chest. "Every waking moment, I endured the torment of knowing my people were murdered, cast away like chaff. I wanted the feeling to end."

I swallow, thinking of the K'inu I met in Gaeyak-Orin, the immense sadness it filled me with. What would it be like to endure that every day? To see all life as pain and suffering?

"I ran to Eingard with the idea that I would tip the scales. The Ajes were already attacking the Oluso, but I believed that if I found a way to give them more power, my ancestors would be satisfied. In my foolishness, I gave away some of our secrets to the Eingardians."

That smile returns again, his eyes crinkling with it this time. "I also met my end—your mother. Yetundé's love healed what a lifetime of reflection could not. I began to regret my actions. I wanted so badly to fix everything."

"So why didn't you? Why did you leave my pregnant mother to fend for herself?"

I try to soften the words, but there is anger still simmering in my heart, an ache reminding me that my father still failed us.

He scrubs a hand across his face. "I didn't. I made yet another mistake."

He opens his palm and two ghostly figures appear. A woman carrying a young child. Her face is bright, her pale cheeks flushed as she carries a young boy. The little boy tugs at her long brown hair and she chatters to him while bouncing him on her hip. The boy's dawn eyes twinkle as he laughs back at his mother. I would know that face anywhere—Jonas.

"The little prince liked to follow me around. I think he found me fascinating. It's interesting to see how much he's grown." My father gives me a knowing look. "How much you've grown with him."

I lick my lips. "We're not mates anymore."

He nods. "That, too, I consider the Spirits' little joke. Imagine pairing the descendant of the man who first broke the oaths of the iron-blood with the descendant of the woman who set out to heal it."

"What do you mean?"

My father sits against Ìyá-Ilé's bark and pats the spot next to him. "Come. Our time together will be short. But I want to make the most of it."

I hesitate, my heart clenching tight. This is a moment I could never have dreamed of, a want I didn't even know I had. But I don't have time for sentiment. "I must return to the Physical Realm," I announce. "War is on the horizon."

"I'm here to give you what you need to win that war." My father offers his hand to me. "For years I have waited, between the river and the path, neither dying nor being reborn, just so I could be here for you. Please—come sit by your old man, Abidèmi. Just for a little while, let me make your name a lie."

Abidèmi, a girl born without a father.

Taking a breath, I trudge over to him and perch on the roots of the tree. Then I say quietly, "Mummy didn't mean that, you know. She named me that way because she hoped you would come back and change it. She still loved you."

He smiles softly. "I know. When I find your mother, I won't ever let her go, even in the next life."

"You still don't know where she is?"

"I have my suspicions, but I will come to that soon. First, let me finish this tale."

He spreads his hands once more and the apparitions jump off his palm, racing to the dirt near our feet. They grow a little in size, and now there are three figures. The third is a face I will never forget, red-gold hair crowning a hauntingly beautiful face—Alistair Sorenson. But this figure of Sorenson is younger, smooth-faced compared to the man I grew to fear. I watch as the young Alistair happens upon Jonas's mother, Arianne, and Jonas. I know how this story ends. With Arianne in the years-long sleep she's been in and my father framed for her injury.

"I ran to Eingard not because I wanted to cause generations of harm to the Oluso," my father starts. "But because the Eingardian ruler five generations before had been descended from the Fèni-Ogun. I hoped I would find more of my kind."

My breath hitches in my throat. "The man the spirits were talking about."

"Croiden Aurelius Schulson, the first iron-blood to break our oath. He feared the Ajes outnumbered the Oluso, and so he sought to join their ranks, find a way to control them. He killed an entire village. And once he started the chain of violence, it was hard to stop it."

Everything comes together like threads weaving a tapestry. "He was the reason the other Oluso began to fear iron-bloods."

My father nods. "Honestly, it was likely a matter of time. The other Oluso had always been wary of our kind. Croiden only showed them the worst of what we were capable of. But they used it as an excuse for atrocity."

"So, they killed the iron-bloods, and the unjustly killed became the K'inu who hunted the Aje and the Oluso in turn."

My father sighs. "The cycle of violence is tiring. The villain you strike down today may disappear. But in his child's eyes, you are the monster. And so it continues." He gives me another sad smile, glancing pointedly at my back. Fox Bead and Silver's beads are once again in my pocket, a heavy weight I will no doubt carry all my life.

I bristle. "Then what are we to do?" I say, words flying out like thrown stones. "How are we to settle things? You haven't been alive for a long time. Do you know what the Ajes have done to us since? How they've murdered and enslaved us?"

"You forget I grew up in a town where I was the only Oluso," my father answers. His voice is calm, but there is an edge to it, a bitterness that is hard to ignore. "Bia-Hyang was once a Fèni-Ogun haven, but I had to watch as the Ajes looted our relics, built their stone houses over the remnants of our mud homes. The village boys loved to walk the cemeteries at night pissing on graves—my people's graves."

I lower my gaze, wanting to hit myself in the mouth. I should never have assumed he didn't know what this pain was like, hadn't lived through it as I have. But I don't know what to do with what he's telling me. If nothing has changed from one generation to the next, how can we hope for anything at all? If our tangled histories are a spinning wheel, crushing all of us under its weight, perhaps we are doomed to repeat the atrocities of our elders—to kill and be killed, hunt and be hunted in turn.

He blows out a breath. "So don't tell me I don't understand how far this madness has descended. It was my inheritance." He gets to his feet. "Now I am tasked with giving you yours."

The ghostly apparitions exchange a series of words. An argument. Arianne puts young Jonas down, but now Alistair has his sword drawn. I wait, not daring to breathe as I anticipate the blow that will send Arianne into her years-long slumber. But to my surprise, Alistair stabs his blade into *Jonas's* heart.

I let out a cry as Arianne drops, clutching her dying child to her breast.

Then a fourth figure comes running in—a man with silver dreads and skin the sun gold of cassava porridge. My father places his sword on Jonas's chest and my heart thrums. Then he places a hand on Arianne's and mutters a few words. He stabs down into Jonas's heart, and a flower appears at the tip of his blade, a crescent moon shimmering under it—an Oluso mark. Arianne collapses in a heap and my father gets to his feet as guards in full livery appear on the scene. The figures melt away, fading like smoke.

"You are the reason Jonas is Oluso," I whisper, awestruck.

My father straightens, his eyes burning with an otherworldly brightness. When he speaks again, his voice fills the expanse around us. Only now it is not just his voice but hundreds, thousands of voices raining on my ears like thunder called from the sky.

"It is the gift of the Fèni-Ogun that they be the vessels of resurrection. For centuries past and for centuries to come, we have guarded this magic from those who sought to destroy it. That symbol on your back is a reminder of that—the weight of our bonds."

He puts his hands together and a flower blossoms in his palm, its golden glow as bright as the light of the sun. Then he folds his hands together and the flower collapses into a bright pellet, a seed.

"Just as one is made, so too, can it be unmade."

I swallow. This must be how he transformed the Benin Oluso.

"It is your birthright, Abidèmi, to carry this forward. Do you accept this gift, though it might cost you everything?"

I look into my father's eyes. They are the same warm brown as those in my own face. But in his, I sense more eyes looking back at me, the weight of ancestors past, the promise of descendants to come.

Taking a breath, I get to my feet and answer. "I accept."

I don't know how yet, but I know this gift is an important part of what I still need to do.

My father reaches out a hand and I take it. The earth beneath me begins to tremble, and suddenly I feel something pierce my chest. I grit my teeth and steel my belly, willing myself to keep standing. My father drops my hand and the pain evaporates.

I stand, breathing hard, and he clasps my shoulder. "Well done."

"You didn't tell me," I gasp, "that this could kill me."

He smiles. "If I had, would you have accepted it?"

I grin despite the queasiness in my stomach. "You have a point."

"The power of resurrection will cost something each time. To unmake a bond, you must pay a blood sacrifice. But to make a bond, it will cost the spirit itself." He frowns. "Arianne begged me to save her child, so I sent her to this place."

He points to another lone fruit hanging under an awning of red-and-gold leaves. "She is at peace."

"Her body is still alive," I say.

My father looks at me, the lines etched into his forehead making him seem older than he is. "It is not. When her son crossed over to the Spirit Realm, she passed on here. Her soul has been his anchor since that day in Eingard."

I gasp, a hand flying to my lips. Jonas's mother is dead.

"I am sorry to give you this news. Comfort your friend. No doubt life will be bleaker without the promise of his mother waking one day."

The leaves rustle as a whisper passes through them, the golden leaves brushing against the green. My father looks up, nodding as though he hears something.

"Iya reminds that resurrection need not be a single act. You may tie people together with a resurrection or untie them. But the effects are more permanent."

I frown, trepidation filling my heart. "What do you mean?"

"It is a simple concept. Take Oluso mates. Oluso can choose to be with their mates or with someone else. If they choose their mates, the threads of their lives intertwine and a new path in life is born. If they do not, the seed that bonds two Oluso shrivels and dies. A new one between the Oluso and their chosen partner arises."

"So just now, when Elegua undid my pair bond with Jonas, he unraveled the threads between us?"

My father nods. "He severed the threads between you in this world. Since the action is permanent, it will take an act of totality to restore them. If you continue on with him, you may find that your threads find their way back to each other, but they have just as much a chance of coming apart. It will take a commitment of a lifetime, working together every day, to stay together."

"And if I redo the bond?" I ask quietly. "What then?"

"To truly heal it, you must tangle your threads in every world." My father's eyes dance as he speaks. "It's a purer version of the Oluso commitment ceremony. You pledge to be together in all worlds, and you consummate the union. Your mother and I did that." His smile grows even wider, and in his face I glimpse the young man he once was. "I promised that I would find her in all our lives. Even if she was born my enemy, or with a body like mine. In every form, in every lifetime, I am hers and she is mine."

Tears prickle at my eyelids, and I sniff, holding them at bay. "How do you know you won't regret that choice?"

My father throws his head back, laughing with abandon. "It doesn't matter if I regret it," he says finally. "Loving your mother, even for a short time, was everything I needed. I'm still waiting for her even now."

The wind picks up speed again and the branches sway with it. My father looks up as a fruit falls from the tree. Its flame is bright gold rather than the blue of the others. He leaps to catch it, then presents it to me.

"This ancestral fruit just arrived. It belongs to the child your guardians sacrificed for. Her life is not yet ripe for Ìyá-Ilé to receive her. Take it to the Physical Realm, and the curse on her life will end."

I take Haru's fruit with trembling hands. It is as light and polished as a precious stone. It shrinks in my hands, now no bigger than my thumb, then it flies into the crystal hanging from my neck, embedding into it like a seed.

My father sighs. "And now our time is fast spent." He puts his hands on my shoulders, looking at me as though he is committing my face to memory. "Goodbye, my dear daughter. Perhaps in my next life I will be so lucky as to have you as a child."

I snatch his hand, clinging to him. "Let's stay here a moment longer." I have to return now, but I want just a breath, a moment to be with my father.

He strokes a hand through my hair. "My little girl grew up lovely," he says. Then he folds his arms around me, pulling me into a hug. I put my arms around him, suddenly at a loss for words.

"Don't burn like your foolish father. Leave the pain of the past behind and bloom."

"What of my broken spirit bonds? Will this power heal them?"

"Iya has one more test for you, if you are willing to face it. There, she will heal your bonds. You have only to wait. It won't be long."

"One more test?" I cry. "I don't have any more time."

"Trust Iya," he says, pulling away. "She will aid you when the time is right."

The fruits on Ìyá-Ilé's branches shake in the breeze, tinkling like bells.

"One more thing," my father says. "The K'inu desire recompense—the lives that were stolen from them. For this, they have found new methods to live again."

I nod, thinking of the girl in Lleyria. "They're possessing people now."

"Yes, but there is a way to make the possession permanent." He looks hard at me.

This must be what my brother meant, why he wanted my body so badly. I shudder.

"Whatever you do, protect the power I've just gifted you. The K'inu must never gain the power of resurrection. Do what you must to protect this power at all costs."

"I will."

My father steps back. "Thank you, Dèmi. For more than you'll ever know."

I stand there a moment, unsure of what to do. I don't want to say goodbye, to leave this peaceful bower. And yet I know I have to go, to fight the chaos in the world awaiting me.

"Baba," I whisper, "will I ever see you again?"

My father's eyes shine with unshed tears. "I will always love you, my daughter. Imẹ hoẹmoẹn ẹ."

Swallowing hard, I leave before the tears run down my face.

As I step through the door that leads out of Iya's courtyard, the whisper of my father's voice follows me.

My dear one, my child. It is well.

BID

I ENTER INTO A FEAST.

The room on the other side has shifted once again. A grassy meadow studded with wildflowers and short, sloping grasses sits under a twilit sky. Koriko mill about, dancing and laughing, chasing each other into the forbidding trees that hem the meadow. A low stream burbles on the other side, its surface reflecting the rose-gold ribbons of cloud unfurling against the violet dress of the sky. Just by the stream, the ancestral spirits sit at a long, wooden table, dwarfed by enormous chairs made of tree roots snaking up from the ground.

"You're done with Mother then," Oya says, appearing at my side. Her flowing green dress is now matched by a crown of hydrangeas plaited through her hair. She threads an arm through mine. "Come. Walk with me a moment. It's not every day I get to see a child of my blood."

"Time is fast spent, egbon," I answer, bowing low. "A war awaits me." I can't afford to get pulled into anything else. Time moves differently in the Spirit Realm, so three days may already have passed in what is a few hours here. Everything hinges on our return.

She quirks an eyebrow. "You cannot leave without a guide to steer you home. The River of Souls is treacherous when you sail unguided."

I straighten. "When can we leave?"

"I sent Ren on a small errand. You may leave when she returns."

I pat my pockets, feeling for the pouch containing Tenjun's mirror. I curse, realizing now it's with our other belongings.

Oya's eyes glow. "A mere two days have passed in your world. Ren will return before the third." She pulls me along, clearly considering the matter closed. "I don't think you resemble Afèni. My brother, Oshosi, is wrong. But I do think you seem so much like her. You're given to action rather than contemplation. You run when it might be wise to walk."

I open my mouth in a retort, but she throws me a knowing look. I say nothing.

"I have watched you all your life. I watch all my children. I know what drives you." She draws me to the stream.

"This stream flows from my River of Souls. Oriomi. Waters of destiny. Tell me, child, what do you see?"

I look. I am a hazy shadow over golden waters, an island interrupting its flow.

"I see a shadow."

She laughs. "You can't see yourself clearly because you do not look. You fear you are monstrous."

Her words are like a knife peeling off my skin. "I don't believe that." I say the words like a magic spell, breathy and quiet, as though they'll be enough to make my lies become truth.

She pushes me into the stream. Little fish brush against my fingers as I scramble up. Then an image appears in the water and my breath catches in my throat. A woman stands on a high hill with the moon looming behind her like a crown. In her hand is a jagged half spear, and on her face are the markings of a warrior. Gold tears leak from her brown eyes. The face is undoubtedly mine.

"You have always had a destiny, my child. But you don't believe in such things. You love so deeply, but you fear the only way to prove that love is sacrifice. You believe that if you run hard enough, fight even harder, endure all the pain this world has to give, you will be worth something."

Oya snatches at my chin, drawing me up. "But you are already worthy in my eyes. You are seen. You must understand that."

"Then why is everything so hard?" I demand, tears filling my eyes. "Why have the ancestral spirits turned a blind eye to our suffering? Why do you test us when all we need is your help?"

Oya sighs, a world in the sound. "We do not test you, not truly. We are bound by covenants as you are."

"You demanded Afèni's lineage as sacrifice. Her children."

"I did not." she casts a quick glance at the table. "My husband, on the other hand, wanted her to feel the sorrow he had. His children, the Fèni-Ogun, were ripped apart. He wanted her to feel that pain, to understand."

She turns back to me. "If Afèni had succeeded, we would have released her children's souls to the Spirit Realm. But she failed." Her mouth curves in a wry smile. "Still, she earned herself a chance at redemption with the mere act of saving Osèzèlé. Without that, you wouldn't have been born. Funny, isn't it? How a single kindness can change everything?"

Ogun bellows from the table, "Oya, let's go. It's time."

Oya grips my hand tight. "This is all the wisdom I can give you— sometimes the peace you gain is in recognizing your inherent worth, the thing no one can take away."

With that, the spirit of the wind bows her head slightly and glides away.

One of the koriko take her place, the lion-boy from earlier, Iké. The tufts of hair gracing his ears reminds me of Chi Chi, the forest child I met in Ikolé.

"Lady Ren has returned. She'll take you back soon."

I nod my thanks and he scampers off, leaping at something in the grass.

I watch the stream at my feet. I am grateful for a moment to breathe, to think on all the things I've heard today. I don't yet know what Oya's words mean, but I am comforted by them nonetheless.

A hand grazes my shoulder and I meet Colin's searching gaze.

"Hey."

"Hey," I reply. I look behind him, expecting Jonas.

He drops his hand. "Our princeling isn't here. Headache. He needed to lie down."

I frown. "Oh."

"Ren says he might have spirit sickness. Or something might be wrong with his anchor. She went to check."

I snap my head up. "His anchor is dead. It was his mother."

The skin between Colin's eyes puckers as he frowns. "How do you know that?"

"My father. He was the vessel Iya used to speak to me."

His eyes spark with sudden intensity. "Did he tell you anything else? Anything about the K'inu?"

I know he's thinking of his mother, wondering what the spirits will do to her and the other K'inu. How would he react if I told him about the possessions?

He scrubs a hand over his eyes. "Actually, don't answer that. Iya's revelations were for you alone. Only tell me something if you're all right with me knowing it."

I pause before asking, "What if there was a way for the K'inu to live again?"

His eyes widen. "You mean to bring them back to life?"

"In a fashion. They would live in other people's bodies."

"What happens to the people they possess?"

"I don't know."

He pulls me to him. "It would cost your life, wouldn't it?" He searches my face as though it is a scrying bowl that holds answers. "This is why Iya asked you to go alone. Is this the answer she gave? Is this her test?"

I shake my head. "My father warned me about it. I can never let myself fall under their control."

He nods grimly. "I won't let any of them near you, even if it is my mother. I want her back but not at the cost of you. Never you."

My cheeks flush hot, and I pull away softly, suddenly aware of the burning intensity of his gaze.

"We still have to help them. My father said I had to find a way to make the K'inu hear me."

"What does that mean?"

"I don't know."

We stand in silence while Colin traces his foot against the banks of the stream. Finally he whispers, "I'm sorry. For lying to you, for not telling you what was happening with me."

He flashes me a wistful smile, his hazel eyes glistening. "I accused you of becoming someone else. But the truth is that I have." He sucks in a breath before continuing. "I've been afraid, Dèmi. When I went off to join Ekwensi, I thought everything would be simple. That all we needed was direction for our hunger. That we would be free if we demanded our freedom by force."

He stares into the abyss of those still waters. "But even though we've been fighting for a year, even though I've done things—" He breaks off, curling his hands into fists. "There are even more of us in chains than before. And now the K'inu are working with those hyenas in the Council. I don't know how we can win."

I slip my hand into his. I understand the confusion he feels, the churning in his heart that will not cease. It is the same deadly mixture of fear and hope and dread that has gotten me up every day, caused me to throw myself into something, anything, that could help the Oluso cause.

"Just wait and see, Col," I whisper. "We're going to be free."

I inhale, feeling the magic my father imparted rise against my skin. With this power, I can change the tides, steer the fate of Ifé in a different direction. With the power of resurrection, maybe there could be more Oluso, enough that the Ajes won't be able to hunt us so easily.

Suddenly, Colin brings my fingers to his lips. My breath hitches as his lips scorch my skin.

"I may never get to do this again, so I'm confessing now," he says, hazel eyes ablaze with that fire that threatens to consume me. "I love you."

I lick my lips. "I have—"

"You have Jonas, I know," he finishes. "But I had to say it."

I stare at him, and for a moment his face is deadly serious. Then his lips widen into a grin . . . and yet I feel it's just as serious, and equally devastating. "I wanted to believe magic was all you two had, but seeing you fight together . . ." He takes a breath, then lifts a hand to my cheek. I shudder, pulse jumping as he trails his fingers over my skin. "What I wanted to say is when I left to join Ekwensi, I thought about you—every moment. I dreamt of you, only you."

He twines his fingers with mine. "I wanted you to regret my absence." He drags up our clasped hands, pressing them against his chest, and I feel his heart racing through the thin fabric of his robe. "I wanted you to choose me, want me, crave me."

I swallow hard, heart twisting in anguish. While he longed for me, I was building a life with Jonas. But there is still a part of me going over all our memories together—the moments of joy and passion, the fights, missed points of connection, a part that sees what we could have been. A part that whispers, *"In another life, perhaps . . ."*

"I don't know what happens once we get to the Physical Realm," he continues, "whether I'll even survive, but know this"—he leans in, lips just a breath from mine—"I will always love you." Then he brushes his lips against my fist in a gossamer kiss.

"I will fight for you, no matter the cost."

I can't breathe. I feel the heat of his skin against mine, the sincerity in his words, but though my heart aches, I know it doesn't beat the same way it does for Jonas.

Elegua appears then, shooting out of thin air like a weed in a well-kept garden. Colin and I leap apart.

"Oya asked me to apologize." Elegua sniffs. Then he clears his throat. "Actually, Ren told me what you did, giving her a piece of Sanaa. Thank you."

"You're welcome," I say quickly. Now I notice Sanaa's expressive eyes are Elegua's.

His haughty mouth tucks into a wistful smile. "It was foolish of me, loving a human, thinking I could be good father. Look at what I gave my Oluso children."

"So you know," Colin mutters.

I don't bother reminding him to be respectful. Risking limbs every time while teleporting as Madsen Oluso do is a curse. Plus, Elegua nearly killed me and Jonas earlier.

"But I chose correctly," Elegua says, speaking more to himself now. "The Spirit Realm is no place for a baby. It was better to send her away."

The air pinches, and Ren appears in a flurry of fur.

"My love—" Elegua starts.

But she only has eyes for me. "They're killing him," she gasps. "Your mate."

My heart drums a battle cry. "Where?"

Her eyes shift from brown to red. "The alayo rooms. He is wearing my mask, but I can't go to where he is. Hurry. There's not much of him left."

Elegua lets out a curse. "Ayodélé, that foolish boy. They feed on your deepest desires, and destroy you." He points at my feet. "I'll send you directly there."

The ground opens up and I fall into the earth.

ETERNITY

I stand in front of our hut in Ikolé. The door is open, the smell of roasted pumpkin-seed soup and goat meat greeting my nostrils. I step in as a warm breeze kisses my skin.

Mummy looks up, her fingers caught mid-weave on the cloth she is making. "I told you not to stay too late at Mama Aladé's," she chides. She puts down the cloth in her hands and opens her arms wide. "Come here, my darling."

She is the same as I remember: rich, soft brown skin, braided hair in a crown adorning her heart-shaped face. She smiles, warmth radiating from her eyes. I run to her. I throw my arms around her and she runs her hands along my back.

"Oh my dear, I missed you," she whispers.

"Mummy," I cry. My throat is tight, my tongue thick with buried words. This is my mother. The woman who gave up everything for me. The woman who loved me more than life itself. The woman I've been missing for so long.

Or was it long?

"Where have you been, Mummy?" I ask. But now my voice is small, shell-like. I am eight again in my mother's arms.

"I didn't go anywhere, my love."

She pulls back, stroking her fingers along my face. They're cold despite the warmth of the room. I frown.

"I missed you while you were away," she says. "I know you love playing with the other children, but don't forget Mama is always waiting for you at home."

"I don't like them," I blurt. Just the other day, Seyi tried to force a frog down my throat. No one in this village likes us. They think the magic in my blood is a serpent biding its time.

I open my mouth to tell Mummy so, but I can't remember what I am supposed to say.

"You don't like the little boys and girls?" Mummy asks, looking concerned.

The air around her shifts as someone appears behind her. A young boy with startling blue eyes.

I gasp, getting to my feet. Mummy tightens her grip on my arm. The boy disappears, flickering out like the lantern on the wall.

"What's wrong, Abidèmi?"

I stiffen. My mother never calls me Abidèmi unless she's angry.

"Mummy," I whisper, stealing a glance at her, "did I do something wrong?"

"Oh, my dear. You have done nothing wrong." She pulls me to her, her hands like chains on my small wrists. I flinch, but she does not let go.

"Stay with Mummy. Can you do just that? I'm making your favorite—goat meat and egusi."

She smiles, but her eyes are cold, bright marbles in her still-youthful face.

She will never age past this.

The thought drops into my mind like a leaf falling onto a stream, and now everything seems wrong. The walls of our hut melt, turning into white, bubbling liquid.

Mummy snatches at my face. "Look at me, my darling. Focus on me."

"No." I wriggle away, suddenly afraid.

My hands are getting bigger, arms lengthening. And when I step back, I see higher than I did before. The window above my cot shatters into pieces.

"Stay with Mummy, Abidèmi!" my mother shrieks.

But now her face is peeling like the walls.

"You're not my mother," I declare.

Everything collapses into a fine black dust that falls around me like snow.

I am in a room lit only by a bleeding moon. I peer into the darkness. There, a few feet away, is a raised pillar covered in vines. The dust swirls into a winged shape and bursts away, flying toward the pillar.

Jonas lies beneath it, vines snaking from his pale skin like leeches feasting. Drawing my bone blade, I run to him, then start hacking at the vines. My blade just glides over their steely bodies. One vine detaches, swimming toward me, and I bring my blade up, striking at its spiny teeth. The vine screams as my bone blade pierces its mouth, and shrivels like a larva, morphing into more black dust.

More vines slink away from Jonas, swirling around me. I dive at him, scrambling onto his body. Then, as the vines shoot toward us, I call on my magic, imagining a barrier. A thin membrane forms over me and Jonas. The vines slam their bodies against it, screaming their discontent.

"Wake up, Jonas, please," I beg, shaking him.

He does not move.

Pushing aside Ren's mask, I peel back one of his eyelids. His pupils are wide, dancing as though he's dreaming. I touch his cheek and my body shakes as a frisson of energy passes into my skin.

I slump against him.

I'm standing in a courtyard. The sky is gray, the air thick with frost. Curling my arms around myself, I rub my chilled skin. A woman saunters down the path ahead, chattering to the young child on her hip. He smiles at her with piercing blue eyes. Jonas and Arianne. We're in the memory of the day Jonas became an Oluso.

"Jonas!" I shout, running after them. "She's not real. None of this is real."

He turns to me and the dream crumbles around us as our eyes meet.

Now I'm in the Eingardian royal court.

Another me sits on the throne, holding a golden scepter. An older Jonas rises from the silver throne to the right. He lifts the hand of my twin to his lips.

"Jonas!" I cry. "None of this is real. Wake up."

He turns, but my twin draws his face into both hands. "Look at me," she orders. "Focus on me."

I step closer. "Jonas, ask her what my name is."

My twin smirks. "Dèmi, of course. I know my own name."

Jonas looks between us, confused.

I try again.

"Jonas, what is the nickname you gave me? Can she answer that?"

"Omo mi," my twin answers triumphantly.

"Nice try," I say, returning a smirk of my own. "But I hate *baby* as a nickname. Jonas calls me—"

"Oko mi," he answers, turning to me.

I reach a hand out, smiling. "Yes. It's me. I am real. But this is all a dream."

His eyes go wide. "It can't be. Mother woke up after we married."

A rosy-cheeked Arianne waves from the end of the dais.

"She's not real, Jonas." Swallowing, I add, "Your mother is dead."

He backs away.

"Who is dead?" the false Arianne asks.

My twin wraps her arms around Jonas's waist.

"Why do you insist on listening to this rubbish?" she chides, snaking a hand into his hair. "That thing over there is not real."

"Jonas," I plead. "It's me, Dèmi. It's your oko mi. Your mate. Remember the time we walked in the market and you bought me an entire cart of honey-stewed apples?"

I smile as the memory springs to my mind. "I hadn't had them before, but you thought I'd want another one after trying the first."

He swallows, and I can see his eyes sparking, remembering.

My twin spins in front of him. "Remember kudu sledding with me for the first time?"

I snort. "Of course he doesn't. We couldn't get Council approval to leave Nordgren for the first two months."

Jonas breaks from her, eyes glistening with unshed tears. "If you are real, then my mother is dead, isn't she?"

I give him a solemn nod. The ceiling crumbles, bits of plaster caving into the room. Twin me jumps back.

"If you are real, then our kingdom is not at peace," Jonas continues.

"Correct," I say, stepping up to the dais.

The court around us flickers, both Oluso and Aje disappearing from sight.

"If you are real, then we are not together," he says finally. "We are strangers, you and I. We severed our ties. You won't ever sing me songs when I am ill or heal my wounds."

I reach him, wrapping my arms around his neck. He searches my face, and I think of something else just then—the time we lay outside of Old Maiduguri a year before, watching the stars, reveling that we were both Oluso after all.

"Incorrect," I declare.

Then I lift myself on my heels and kiss him.

Twin me screams, and the dream dies into darkness.

We come to as the barrier protecting us fades.

"This way," I cry, tugging Jonas off the pillar.

He staggers to his feet, chasing after me. We run toward a small square of light underneath the blood moon.

The black dust shapes into a hand that flies after us. Just as it reaches Jonas's collar, I jump through the square of light and yank him along.

We fall into a bedroom.

Elegua exhales. "I was afraid I'd have to come rescue you."

"Thank you," I say, bowing.

Jonas trembles suddenly, nearly falling. I slip underneath his arm, steadying him.

Elegua's forehead puckers in a sudden frown. "Your friend doesn't look so good."

"His anchor died," Ren explains.

"I need to get him out of here," I say. "Can we go back to the Physical Realm now?"

Ren shakes her head. "We can't take him back until his essence stabilizes. Otherwise, he'll be lost in the River of Souls."

"How long will that take?" I cry.

"An hour," she responds. "Not long."

I swallow. An hour here means more below. We're pushing things so close.

"Is there nothing else we can do?" I ask.

Elegua smirks. "He'd be more stable with a bonded mate. Unfortunately for both of you, that bond is severed."

"This is your problem," Ren hisses. "You always meddle with happy people. Force them to prove themselves." She stabs a finger at Elegua's chest. "You can't face me, so you make others suffer."

They lock eyes and suddenly I feel we need to leave.

Elegua flushes. Then he snaps his fingers and the adjacent door swings open. "There is a bed in there. Go rest. One hour, no more."

A bed awaits us, accompanied only by a small lamp and a skein on a low table. I help Jonas over.

He pinches the skin between his brows. "Sorry, for all this."

"It's all right." I busy myself with removing his boots, trying not to think about what Elegua said.

"Délé tricked me. He said you were in danger."

I stop studying the pattern on the down blanket covering him. "You went with him to the alayo rooms because you thought I was in danger?"

He licks his lips. "I went with him to a door. I think those rooms shift." He swallows again. "I'm thirstier than a desert whale."

Grabbing the skein, I sniff at its contents. No odor. "Drink some water," I say, reaching behind his back to help him up.

He inhales the liquid, some dribbling down his throat. I am suddenly thirsty.

He fans himself. "This is why it's difficult being from Eingard. You're too warm everywhere you go."

Shoving him back into the bed, I unbutton his top without another word. He studies me before admitting, "I don't feel our song anymore. But that doesn't mean I don't still care for you." He lifts a shaking hand to my cheek. "In fact, I think it confirms what I've known for a long time."

"What's that?" I ask, licking my lips. We haven't had a chance to talk since surviving the musin. If we're here for a moment, I want to know what he's thinking.

"I never needed the bond to fall in love with you. I would have fallen for you anyway. When we were young, you were the friend that saved me."

A smile tugs on his lips. "But when I saw you again, I felt this pull, and I know that it was the bond but—" He takes my hand. "Dèmi, have you met yourself?"

My mind is racing, heart pounding like I'm in the midst of a fight. "What do you mean?"

"You stormed into Benin Palace and you dragged me out of it. Then you proceeded to save everyone you came across. No one was too small for you to help. Too unimportant."

I swallow, suddenly self-conscious. "I've heard I do that a lot, rush into things."

He laughs, his voice tinkling like a bell. "You do. But it's because you care. You had every reason to hate me, but you accepted me as Oluso without question."

I shrug at that. There are few who could have accepted that an enemy Aje prince was one of us, but stranger things in life happened.

"When I asked you to be mine, to walk the hard path of taming the court, you said yes." He pauses, sighing. "It's good we're no longer mates. I was a terrible one, not knowing when you were hurt. Unable to always protect you." His mouth twists in a grim smile. "The spirits have a sense of humor. I severed the bond between us, but nothing has changed. Seems I spent the last year falling madly in love with you."

My breath hitches in my throat. He can't mean anything he's saying. It's not possible.

I shake my head. "I haven't always been nice to you."

"You have been kind, honest, telling me where my faults are, showing me the places where I fail the Oluso even though I mean well—that is all kindness." He tugs at my hand, slips something into my palm. "That is love."

I look down. In my hand is a ring, similar in pattern to the one I left behind; two gwylfins racing toward each other, scaled bodies intertwining. But whereas my father's ring is made of iron, this ring is forged of iron and wood, and in the heart-shaped space between the gwylfins' neck, is a gem the color of my eyes.

I stare at him, transfixed. "How?"

He grins weakly. "I had this made immediately after I asked you to be with me. I've waited all this time to give it to you. I wanted it to be a symbol of our future together, our hope."

I want to cry. Instead, I ask the question I've been afraid to know the answer to. "How do you see me, really? What am I to you?"

My heart races, pulse quickening as I wait.

"You are a blessing," he says, his voice suddenly low, intimate. "I could have gone my whole life without knowing you. I could have still become compassionate without you." He threads his fingers with mine, bringing our joined hands to his chest. "But having you as my mate, more than my equal, the queen of my heart—I see you as the brightest star in the night sky. I could have missed seeing you if I didn't know how to look. But life is sweeter, brighter and better, with you here. You could shine your brightness on someone else, and I would still be in awe at how beautifully you shine. I would still love you."

I swallow against the sudden lump in my throat. "You don't need me to be perfect? Flawless?" I ask quietly.

He laughs. "Spirits no. I would be even more unworthy of you then."

I slide onto the bed, moving nearer to him. In the last year, I have had a chance to get to know this man, to see all of his sides and flaws, to hear his heart. When we severed our bonds, I feared that everything would change. But what frightens me more now, is the fear that I'll miss this.

"You don't regret this? Us?" I ask.

His gaze flicks down to my lips, then up to my eyes again. "Never."

Placing my hands on his shoulders, I drag my lips to his in a fiery kiss.

We taste each other at first, tongues dancing. Then he pulls me firmly into his lap, and our tongues clash, sparring like swords locked in a duel. His hands roam from my back to my blouse and then he is tugging at my hem, pulling it over my head.

I let him pull it off and sit unmoving as his eyes sweep down me and back again. I shudder. I have never felt so seen, so thoroughly desired.

"Spirits, I want you." His voice is thick and breathy, his hand still gripping my shirt. "You're sure about this?"

I straddle him, wrapping my legs around his waist and rocking my hips against the hot length of him raised like a flag between us.

"I'm old enough to know what I want," I say before pulling the top ribbon of my ibante. It falls to the bed in a heap and my breasts spill free.

He groans. "You're going to be the death of me."

He surges forward, snaking one arm around my back and stroking my breast with the other. Then he kisses me again, nibbling my lower lip while softly twisting my nipple.

I moan, and his kisses grow more frenzied, frantic. He leaves my mouth to suck on my neck, then he strokes my other breast while I grow hot and heavy in his arms. I rake my teeth against the top of his ear as he sinks against me. And when he moans, I plunge my fingers between us and unknot his trousers. He rips himself away, peeling off his trousers and knickers in one fell swoop.

I stare at the full length of him as he unbuttons the cuffs of his shirt and climbs over me.

"I want to be yours. Bond or no bond," he whispers, tangling a hand in my hair. I wriggle my hips out of my trousers, leaving only my underwear on. Then I lift my hips, grinding against him.

"You are mine," I declare. "Let's do it again, the ceremony."

He leans back, sitting on his knees. "Are you certain?"

I shove up, pulling him into a deep kiss.

When we break apart for air, I whisper against his lips. "I will run at every beckon."

He smiles, warmth filling his dawn eyes. "I will run at every beckon," he repeats.

"I will heed every word."

This time our voices tangle together, inextricable.

"I am one in this circle."

Silver-blue flame leaps from his skin, lacing along mine.

"I choose this winding road."

Green flame ignites against my skin, and I tighten, bracing myself for an onslaught of pain, but nothing comes.

"My spirit shall not waver . . ."

I place a finger to his lips. "Not just this life. Every lifetime."

He nods, kissing my palm.

Taking a breath, we finish together.

". . . in every lifetime and the next."

Magic flares between us, swirling around our joined bodies, then it pierces our hearts and suddenly I can feel his every breath, the desire flooding him.

I kiss him again as our hearts beat as one.

He cradles my head, then attacks my neck, sucking and licking me. I run my palm down his chest, squeezing his cock with my other hand. He hisses his delight and tugs me in for another scorching kiss.

As I pull back for air, he trails his tongue down to my breast, twirling his tongue around my tip. I arch my back, feeling the tightening in my loins, and he slides his fingers against my undergarments then, tugging at the string holding them together. They slide off my hips as lightly as a feather drifting to the ground.

He slips his fingers into my wet folds, thrusting them hard into me. My hips throb with need. I writhe, feeling every inch of his fingers as they plunge in and out of me. Then he sucks at my other breast, nipping at my pert peak every time I moan.

"Jonas," I beg, "please."

He nips at me again, slipping another finger into my folds. I tremble at his touch.

Every inch of me is on fire. I want nothing more than to climb on top of him and sink down on his length, riding him until we quench the thirst in our bodies.

"Please," I cry, lips parting in a breathy whisper.

He shudders. "You unmake me."

Then he slides his fingers out of me and pulls me into his lap, palming my bottom. I grind my hips against his length and he bucks, straining against me.

Still, he looks me in the eye, blue eyes clouded with desire, and I shudder at the intensity of his gaze.

"Once we do this, there's no going back," he says, trying to speak in what I know to be his diplomatic voice. The one he uses when he's trying to make concessions with unruly members of the court. "Even so, do you still want to?"

I yank him to me in answer, sucking on his lower lip. Then I shove him back and climb on top of him, lacing my fingers with his. His eyes widen as I move down, pushing onto his thick length. He gives a hiss of delight, shutting his eyes as though he can't believe what is happening. I clench at the sudden tension in my hips, the feel of him inside me. Then I throw my head back and rock, savoring the way our bodies writhe together.

He jerks his head up, leaning back on his elbows. "Yes, Dèmi, please, oko mi."

My loins are throbbing, my belly tightening as he drives deeper and deeper into me. When I think I might shatter, he pulls me to him, biting hard on my neck. I rake my fingers against his shoulders, trying to get more of him. He runs his hands over my navel, sliding one down to the place where we are joined. Then he works his fingers against the nub at the apex of my loins.

I cry out as pleasure fills my senses, making me want to scream. He places a hand on my lower back, pushing me deeper onto him while he rocks his hips upward.

"I am yours and you are mine," he gasps. "In this world and the next. In every world under every sky. All you have to do is live."

We rock harder against each other, hands laced, two hearts beating a rhythm that only we know. Our rhythm gets faster and faster until I am breathless and on the edge.

"Dèmi!" Jonas screams as he floods me with his release.

I roll my hips against his one more time, then I throw my head back as my body tightens.

I shatter.

PART IV

WAR

TREACHERY

JONAS STROKES HIS HAND ALONG MY BACK AND I SHUDDER AT HIS TOUCH. My hips are sore, my muscles aching. The area between my legs is still wet and throbbing. He slips his fingers against it, teasing me.

Muttering a curse, I try to roll off him, but he presses his hand against my lower back. "Just a few breaths more, oko mi," he whispers. "I want to enjoy the feel of you. It's nice this is finally not a dream."

Heat flushes up my neck and ears. "You've dreamt about this? About me?"

He chuckles and his chest rumbles beneath me. "Almost every night since I met you in Benin Palace. I've had to sleep next to you without touching you like this for months. It's been torture."

I bury my face against his chest, tugging at the ring now hanging from a cord around my neck—his ring. "You men are all the same. Nothing in your mind but making love."

He laughs as he hardens against me. "I'd like to think there's more to me than just that, but I'd like to do it again right now if you'll have me."

I shove him away. "We did it twice already."

Ren pounds on the door. "Come to the gates. Time to go."

I spring from the bed, taking the blanket with me. The biting cold of the ground sets my mind racing as I scramble, looking for my clothes.

Jonas blinks owlishly at me. "What's happening?"

My heart quickens. "Two human days have passed. We have to hurry. We can't lose any more time."

We dress hastily, throwing on our wrinkled, journey-worn clothes. Then we are out of the room, running in search of Ren and the others.

The Jagun Jagun greet us at the end of the corridor, slanting their spears in a salute. The one with the Crow tattoo points toward the central room leading to the outside.

"The spirits await you."

We burst through the main doors, entering the outside courtyard just in time to glimpse my brother kneeling before Ogun and Orunmila. Ren and Colin stand behind them, their arms full of belongings.

"Took you long enough," Ren shouts when she catches sight of me. She runs up and tugs at my blouse. I look down and spot the purpling bruise right under my collarbone. "I trust the night was restorative," she mutters.

I blush, rubbing my hand against my neck. She shoves my bag in my hands and I take out Nana's mirror then, flicking it open. The shadow has only halfway filled the glass. I breathe a sigh of relief and slip the mirror back in my pocket.

Colin comes up to me, his hazel eyes dancing with excitement.

"He finally got caught," he says, nodding at Délé. "For trying to kill our princeling in the alayo rooms." He slips an arm around my shoulder. "How was guard duty? Isn't watching over a prince a handful?"

Heat inflames my cheeks once more. No doubt Colin thinks I was merely guarding Jonas.

Jonas appears, throwing his arm around us both. "Group hug?"

"To celebrate you being saved by the spirits?" Colin shakes him off with a smirk. "In your dreams."

"You are banned from leaving the shores until further notice," Ogun is saying to my brother. "If you attempt to enter the Physical Realm, we will know it."

Orunmila sighs. "Délé, I know things have been hard for you. But I don't understand why you must make them even harder."

My brother stares at the ground, hands clasped together. "If you would allow it, let me apologize to Dèmi myself."

The spirits exchange a look, then they turn to me. I give a small nod. In a way I can understand every thing Délé has done. If I thought that someone was born to rob me of every thing I ever desired, I would be resentful.

Délé approaches me gingerly. Jonas and Colin move to stand beside me, but I step away from them, meeting my brother halfway.

"I'm sorry," he says tersely. "But I had my reasons." He darts a look at the spirits behind. "What I did was foolish, I know. But the K'inu are family to me. They are my everything."

I nod. "I understand that."

"I want them to have peace. But they won't until you seal them again."

I frown. "I don't understand."

He studies me, eyes wide with disbelief. "You don't know, do you?"

"What don't I know?"

"Ogun's blood and bones," he curses.

"Watch your tongue, young man," Ogun snaps.

"The lives of the K'inu are tied to the iron-bloods," my brother explains. "When you awakened your iron magic, you unsealed them. It's your fault they are lost in the Physical Realm."

"Is this true?" I demand of Ogun.

The premier spirit of iron sighs. "Yes. My children were meant to protect one another."

Suddenly Délé throws his arms around me, resting his head in the crook of my neck. "Goodbye, sister. I *will* miss you. Until we meet again."

He draws away just as quickly, his finger snagging at the edge of my pocket, dislodging the mirror. Lifting his hands, he backs away as Jonas and Colin step in.

"I'm leaving. See you again soon."

He disappears, leaving only a trail of black dust. But his words echo in my mind like a town crier's horn, reminding me I am responsible for the carnage the K'inu have wrought.

"It's my fault for letting Eshu raise that child," Orunmila says. "I took pity on him for losing his own."

Ogun chuckles. "You have only just discovered that now?"

Ren kisses the tips of her fingers, inclining her hands toward the ancestral spirits in a gesture of farewell. "Until we meet again, egbon."

She slips on her mask. The world around us changes in an instant. Stony ground shifts to ribbons of salt. Gray clouds suddenly hang over the sun. We stand in the irisi, the slim boat rocking gently as it pulls away from the ancestral shores.

Ren moves to the head of the boat, oar in hand. "This part of the journey will be quick, but I recommend you sit."

I obey, folding my arms and legs in. A vulture swoops over the salt shores, chasing us. Its fleshy head paints a bloody streak against the sky, black wings slicing through the air like an ink pen scrawling on paper. My heart leaps in my chest and suddenly I am frozen to the spot, fear gnawing at my insides.

Jonas touches my shoulder. "What's wrong?"

"Don't worry. We'll get back soon," Colin says, brushing lightly against my back.

The vulture turns in a wide arc, hissing at the sky, then it disappears into the arms of a cloud. The wind rises just then, and with it a wave grows, sweeping toward us like an ax head. The waters churn as the wave shoves us forward at greater speed, a devouring gray that threatens to capsize the boat.

"Hang on!" Ren shouts, striking at the waves with her oar.

I lower my head, bracing my hands against the wooden hull of the boat. Jonas and Colin fold as well, hemming me in on either side.

But the wave is only growing, dwarfing us with its shadow. The winds are picking up speed. I squint, forcing my eyes to stay open against the onslaught of seawater thrashing against our faces. Ren lifts her oar high like a priestess holding a ceremonial scepter.

"I can stop it!" Colin shouts, stretching a hand toward the wave.

Ren smacks her oar against his hand. "This is Oya's blessing. We must ride the winds."

The wave crashes down, slamming into our bodies with the force of a bull spurred by the sight of blood. We fall into its depths, and I flail my arms about as water rushes into my mouth and nose.

My lungs burn as I struggle to breathe, then the burning fades, and I sink against something solid, earthen.

I gasp in cool air, flicking my eyes open. I am in a field, overlooking the high terraces of Ildok. My skin is clammy, cool sweat running down my chest, but my back is warm. I ease up, trying to sit properly, but my arms and legs are bound, skin rubbing against a tight, rubbery substance. I am trapped in the oruka again. My stomach drops.

"We're tied together," Jonas says, his voice drifting over my shoulder. That explains the warmth.

"What are the chances one of your people did this?" Colin hisses from the other side of us. He sits lashed to the golden-haired tree we are under, iron chains binding his wrists and ankles, Ren next to him.

"Low actually," Mari says, crossing into the field from a lower bank. "I am my own person."

A garrison of soldiers close in behind her, worker bees gathering around their queen. One shoves Hanae as she waddles forward on iron-bound feet. There's a gash on her forehead and one of her eyes is swollen shut.

Fury rises up in me, blood rushing in my ears. "What have you done?" I cry.

"I've prepared a welcome feast," Mari says. "Welcome back to the world of the living." Mari grabs Hanae by the hair. "Before you think to use magic, recognize this—I *will* kill her."

I bare my teeth, defiant. Hanae's eyes don't betray a trace of fear. Instead, she asks, "Were you successful?"

I incline my head in a small nod. Since we're back in time, the ancestral fruit will remove Haru's curse. Nana and Will's sacrifice was not in vain.

She lifts her chin. "We thank the heavens for a sign of mercy."

Mari yanks her back, twisting her arm too. "My mercy is what you should be begging for."

"How did you find us?" Jonas asks.

She knocks Hanae to the ground and steps aside. Elodie emerges from the web of soldiers, clad in armor bearing her family's colors. "I told you, I'm a good little informant."

I close my eyes, open them. But Elodie is staring back at me, a calm expression on her face.

"What happened to wanting your own life?" I snarl.

"I am living it." She lifts a hand and a soldier presents her the dagger she stole from the marketplace. She taps the tip of the blade with her hand, testing it. "See, I was raised to obey one rule—"

She whips around, slashing at the soldier who gave her the blade. The young soldier staggers as a red smile opens at her throat. She coughs and sputters, then collapses like a felled tree. Mari beams like a proud parent.

"Power is the only law. Whoever has it, has everything."

Colin sneers, his eyes swelling with barely restrained rage. "So you joined the kunkun because you thought we had it."

She smiles. "Actually, no. I joined because it was exciting—at first, anyway. Ekwensi wanted me to smuggle my mother's letters out of her room. I did so for a fee." She beckons to another soldier and he flinches before coming forward. She cleans her blade against his tunic, leaving a bloody smudge like a kiss mark on the gold of his uniform.

"I learned subterfuge under Ekwensi's careful tutelage. Then, in time, he introduced me to the Oluso women in the east wing."

A chill rises in my skin. Ga Eun, Adaeze, and Samira spent so many days underneath Château Nordgren, believing they were doomed to have their bodies stolen, to be forced to bear Eingardian Oluso children who would one day grow to despise and hate them.

"You knew what my uncle was doing?" Jonas asks. I can't see his face, but I hear the cold fury in his voice.

"I knew everything, Auri. That was my power—knowledge."

She points the dagger in my direction. "How did you think I knew where to show up when you were escaping? Or find you all those times I appeared in front of you at odd moments?" She twirls the dagger this way and that like a baton. "Cariadhe was a useful foal in my stable. But if I thought she might be a danger to me—" She breaks off, slashing the dagger through the air.

I can't believe what I'm seeing, that this is the true face of the laughing girl in Aerin-Cho who begged for food and kisses from random maidens.

"Our capture in Gaeyak-Orin," I say as a picture grows in my mind. "You came to make sure I failed."

"Guilty," Elodie sings. "I had to act especially well during that one.

Oyéré nearly actually killed me, but then, she didn't know the plan or my face."

"You spied for Ekwensi. You spent time with the kunkun," Colin yells. "How could you help Sanaa with her baby while scheming behind her back?"

She shrugs. "Ekwensi keeps secrets all the time. I don't see why mine were any different."

"Then why did you come with me?" I ask, searching her face. "Why start this journey?"

"Every Oluso I've met has been radiant. Especially you." She steps closer, her voice wistful. "I remember the first time I saw you at Auri's coronation. So brilliant, jewel-like. You shone in a room full of enemies. All of the court ladies envied you." Her lips twist in a small smile. "You're not my type if that's what you're thinking. Bit too serious for me."

"Good to know," I say.

"You dazzled me, if you must know, like a diamond." She peels back the shoulder of her overcoat, revealing skin the color of gray ash, the dead certainty of stone imitating a once-living arm. Her petrified fingers grip another gleaming dagger.

I gasp. She stole from the mirror city after all—this is her punishment.

"But diamonds dazzle until they cut," she continues. "We think of them as the finest gems, but they are dangerous weapons. Just like all of you."

"Because you made us that way," Colin roars. "You hunted us until we had no choice. But when we fight back, you use it as an excuse to murder us."

"As you can see, I need no excuse to murder. But in the case of the Oluso, it is the way of life," she says, stepping closer. "People think the strongest animal is the powerful one. But true power is formless. It conforms to whatever shape it needs to survive."

She bends, leaning in until she is a breath away from my face. "Just look at you. The power you hold in one finger is enough to make the sturdiest iron chains quake. But the threat of killing one woman has you in those very chains."

"You'll do more than quake when I'm finished with you," I seethe.

She pouts. "How sad. I really thought we could be friends."

"El," Jonas pleads, "it's not too late to back out of this. Whatever it is, it isn't you. I know you. You're someone who cares deeply about others."

She laughs, a bitter, strangled thing that sends a chill up my spine. "Are you really telling me who I am, Auri? You who have always had options?" She presses her dagger to his throat and he stiffens against me. "You have never had to be powerless, Auri. Not one day."

"The power you crave, do you really believe Mari will let you have it?" I ask.

"I will have what I require."

Jonas scoffs, the action pressing his throat against the blade. I tense as it bites into his flesh, but he does not flinch. "My uncle beat me bloody in the name of preparing me for the crown. He left me with nothing—not a Council that would heed my commands or any real power of my own. Just a title. So don't pretend I've had everything handed to me and you're the only victim in the world."

She scoffs. "Your point?"

He lowers his voice, darting a look at Mari who stands several feet away, giving orders to the soldiers. "My uncle and Mari were birds of a feather. Whatever she promised you, do you think she will honor it?"

Elodie is silent a moment. Her expression is calm, a nice courtly mask, but now I see a slight furrow in her brow, glimpse the barest whisper of uncertainty.

"What do you really want?" I ask.

"For everything to stay as it's supposed to be," she blurts. She lowers her blade, getting to her knees. "That those of us without magic are not left at the mercy of reckless gods."

"If we were as reckless and deadly as you claim," Colin whispers, "you would be dead where you stand."

"You've been with us, Elodie," I say softly. "You know we are not the monsters your mother believes us to be."

"It's not too late," Jonas adds. "We are fighting for a better future for both Aje and Oluso. We can't achieve that if we're all at each other's throats."

Her lips are pursed as though she is weighing our words, listening.

"Leave them, Elodie. It's time," Mari calls. "We secure our fate with this."

Elodie's eyes go wide. She stands abruptly, backing away from us. "Know this—I understand that the Oluso have suffered. But I am an Aje. I have no wish to have everything I know burned to the ground. Your suffering is the sacrifice that guarantees our peace."

Her words are knives flaying my skin. I want to scream. All this time we've pleaded, begged her to see us as we are, and still she would rather choose war. The memories of the past several days, the quiet moments we've shared, none of it means anything in the face of her fear.

Reaching for my bond with Jonas, I pull some of his iron magic into me. The bracelet on my wrist morphs into a blade that slices through the thick skin of the oruka. I launch myself up on shaky legs as the guard standing over Hanae puts his blade to her neck.

"I wouldn't try anything if I were you," Elodie says, and there's no fear in her voice. She turns her back to us, shouting to Mari, "I'm ready."

Ready for what?

Mari puts two fingers between her teeth and whistles. The soldiers at the rear drag up more people, attendants from Tenjun's compound still wearing those white hair rags, pushing them into a circle, where they huddle like a herd of baby dik-diks, wide-eyed and afraid. My heart sinks in my chest.

"How did you—" I sputter.

"We made a stop at our dear Master Tenjun's before coming," Elodie explains. "The time in his compound proved useful for identifying weak spots." She points in the distance. Smoke curls into the sky from Tenjun's home, hanging over it like a burial shroud.

I shake my head. It's impossible. Tenjun was—is—a master fighter. He could not be bested so easily. Then again, he always wanted to fight without causing harm.

Elodie saunters over to the circle of Gomae hostages. "I knew once I met the women in the east dungeon that real power existed beyond what I could dream of." She steps over to one of the hostages, an elderly Aje woman who blinks at us with clouded, unseeing eyes. "You should ask Ga Eun to transform for you sometime. Powerful stuff."

"Elodie," I beg. "Don't."

Jonas touches the iron binding Colin and his chains fall off.

"Sin-ama!" Elodie calls out. Old Mother.

"What is it?" the elderly woman asks in Goma-dori.

"I am just giving you medicine." Elodie replies in perfect Goma-dori. "Lie back. This won't hurt."

She slashes the woman's throat and the elder crumples like a straw doll, head folding into her chest. The guards fall on the other Gomae then, dragging their swords along their throats. The people fall like dandelion stalks, broken and lifeless. The smell of blood and urine clouds the air, seeping into my nostrils like poison.

"No!" I scream, leaping forward. The chains that bound Colin rattle and squeal as they swim into the air.

Mari shoves her foot into Hanae's back. "Control yourself before I control you."

Dark clouds appear overhead, unfurling against the midday sky like the shadows riding the surface of the deep. Spheres of violet flame burn against those clouds like floating lanterns, dancing between darts of lightning streaking through. The kokulu are coming.

"What have you done?" I choke out.

"This is only the beginning," Mari says. "My soldiers are marching, setting out to purge the evil in this land. Your flying friends here seem to appear when many people die at once. They've been very helpful to us lately."

Thunder crackles through the sky and the rattling begins.

"That's how you did it," Colin says, his eyes blazing with anger. "You killed the Oluso and the kokulu came out of that. You planned the destruction of Wellstown."

Mari cocks her head, her face bright with unmistakable glee. "That's not the only thing I planned. A rumor has gone around lately, have you heard it? The people believe the Oluso bring evil spirits with them. They fear what is to come. Their prince was making laws to protect those who would threaten their safety."

"You've murdered our people to bring about war!" Jonas yells.

"I've done much worse, dear prince. But you're wrong: I've brought about war to bring peace." She steps away from Hanae and I see my chance then. Lowering my hands to my sides, I stretch my fingers toward the bonds on Hanae's wrists. The bonds begin to curl away from her skin.

"Eingard was just the start," Mari says. "People of every region will hunt and sacrifice every Oluso to stop these things from coming after them."

"But you'll only be making more of the kokulu. People will realize they've been tricked."

"At least the Oluso will be dead. Then we can focus on the kokulu."

It's a logic that's both so twisted and so sound that I can't help but marvel at its brilliance, cursing myself all the while for not killing this woman when I had the chance.

Hanae's wrist bonds shrivel and she curls her body inward, inching her feet toward me to escape the notice of the guard standing above her. I set to work on her ankles.

Jonas clenches his fists, his voice tight with fury. "You have no idea the calamity you've brought on us all."

Mari laughs. "I have *some* idea. But not to worry. I'm going to give the people the safety and security they crave. I will become their hero."

The anklets on Hanae dissolve. She edges up, drawing something from her robe—a blue snake with a snowy streak running down its head—Ataya. She nods to me and sets Ataya in the grass.

"You're trifling with power you can't control," Colin warns. "The K'inu will hunt you in turn. You're foolish to think you have power over them."

"And you're foolish to think I'm so stupid that I'm unaware of the risk they pose. Rest assured, I know a way to stop them when the time is right." Mari's eyes cut to me. "After all, they first appeared when she fought Alistair in the arena. Something tells me they'll disappear if she dies."

My brother's words return to me. The lives of the K'inu are tied to iron-bloods. Mari is right.

The violet flames descend then, streaking toward us like shooting stars. Elodie looks up, transfixed by the dazzling light. The soldiers at Mari's back mutter amongst themselves, some clearly frightened.

A sudden jolt of pain pierces my skull. I place my hands on my head as a wave of fury and sadness bursts through the walls of my mind.

Jonas grabs my arm to steady me. "You all right?"

I can't answer though—the pain is too much.

The violet flames fall on the dead bodies like flies hanging over a corpse. The soldiers backpedal, frightened, and Hanae shoots up then, darting toward us.

"I'll get help!" she shouts.

There is a haze of rose-colored flame, then a blue flying serpent with a snowy-white plume swoops in front of her. Elodie whirls around, snatching a handful of Hanae's robe as she tries to hop onto Ataya's back. But Hanae digs in her heels.

Gritting my teeth against the pain, I lurch forward, striking at her. But Mari dives at me. I step back just in time to meet her blade with mine, but she bears down on me, knocking me back. The mirror falls from my pocket.

"Not . . . letting . . . you . . . go," Elodie screeches, snatching at Ataya's tail.

Jonas slashes at her with his sword, and she collapses, screaming as the blade meets the pale flesh above her petrified skin, severing the dead limb. Ataya whistles into the air, headed for the burning compound.

Mari shouts to the soldiers, "Archers, shoot that thing down!"

The soldiers obey, drawing their bows and sending a hail of arrows into the sky. Jonas stretches a hand, silver-blue flame spilling from his fingers. The arrows stop midflight, clattering to the ground. But the soldiers nock more arrows and soon Ataya is dancing between those iron shadows, wings flapping desperately as she crests into the sky.

Jonas sends a wave of wind, trying to knock away the arrows, and Mari rushes me again.

I meet her blow head-on, then another burst of pain explodes through my skull, and I fall to my knees. Colin's whip cracks out, wrapping around Mari's surging blade, holding her in place.

I scramble upright, fingers finding the mirror. It falls open in my palm. The glass is completely shadowed, darkness staring up at me under the light of the midday sun.

Haru is dead. Will and Nana's sacrifice was for nothing.

I shake my head in disbelief. I shake the mirror again, but the clouded surface does not change. A sob erupts from my throat.

Then Colin's scream rips me from my grief.

"The arrows!" he shouts.

I look up. Another wave of arrows seizes the sky, and one buries itself in Ataya's wing. They close in as she and Hanae plummet, and with them, my last shred of hope.

I open my mouth in a silent scream.

The kokulu erupt from the violet flames, screeching as their bony wings spear the wind, their knifelike jaws as cavernous as open graves.

Mari curses and she doubles back, yanking a dazed Elodie along. "We took too long. This one is lost. Run."

I fall to my knees as the kokulu open their mouths, teeth spilling out of their maws like rain. Some snatch at the soldiers, ripping them from the safety of the ground.

"We need to go!" Jonas yells, pulling me up.

"Everyone is dead!" I scream, shoving the mirror at his chest.

"We're not," Jonas says as Colin darts over, throwing an arm around my waist. "Hold on tight!" he shouts as magic explodes onto his skin.

A kokulu slams its tail through a running soldier's back, cleaving him in two. His legs dangle from the creature's claws, waving like a surrendering flag.

I watch the carnage as the world folds around me. Screeches grow distant and the glare of the sun becomes a mere memory on my skin, but the stench of blood and the sight of Ataya falling linger in my mind.

We flash onto the road. The gates to Tenjun's compound are agape, the broken family plaque hanging like loose skin. Smoke clouds our nostrils and faces as we stare into the abyss. Beyond us, bodies litter the courtyard, consumed by a fire that rages unabated.

Our army is gone. Everything is lost.

Snatching at Colin's arm, I command, "Take me to him, now."

"Wait—" Colin starts, but his magic responds, ripping out of the smoke.

We crash onto a dirt floor.

"Nice of you to return," Ekwensi says. He is seated at a table just before us, an amused smile on his face. "My dear prince, it is good to see you living. All of the capital is rife with news of your death."

Jonas's hand flies to his sword hilt, but Colin puts a hand on his arm. "Don't."

"Why did you bring us here?" Jonas cries.

"I asked for it," I whisper. "We can't go back. We failed."

We failed.

The words are a fire burning everything inside of me.

Marching up to Ekwensi, I hold my wrists out. "I want to bury them alive. Chain me."

Everything in me is numb, buried under a sea of grief. But there is the flame that burns inside, a fiery rage that promises destruction, and I'm tired of fighting it.

Ekwensi's smile drops. "Are you certain? You have to do this of your own will."

"Oko mi, consider—" Jonas starts.

"I'm certain. This is freedom."

TIME

THE HEAT OF THE MIDDAY SUN BURNS OUR FACES AND NECKS AS WE STALK toward the mud houses gathered like hunched children poring over sweets in the marketplace. As we pass by each, Ekwensi blows on a slim reed pipe and members of the kunkun filter out like hibernating animals woken out of season.

Jonas keeps trying to catch my eye, but I keep my gaze forward, pinned on the golden sands surrounding the kunkun hideout. This is Ismar'yana, the southernmost city of Berréa, the humble place Lord Kairen arose from. It is said that this part of Berréa was once lush land, but the greed of the people tilling it caused the sands to rise up and swallow them whole. And now there is not much beyond the sands that swell like rice in water, promising to cloud our view if we dare wade into it. Still, I keep staring at that landscape, hoping to find something there, something that will make sense of the burning inside of me.

Jonas darts in front of me, blocking my view of a scrubby plant with foxtail fronds weaving in the heat. "Are you sure you won't regret this?"

I lift my chin, defiant. "I regret not doing it before now. We should have fought back, killed those who hunted us."

Colin puts a hand on Jonas's arm. "It is her choice what she does. You have no right to interfere."

To my surprise, Jonas merely says, "You're right. I just want to be certain that Dèmi is doing this of her own free will—because she's thought it through, and not out of anger and grief. But also, whatever she chooses, I will support it."

"Does this mean you'll agree to be chained as well?" Ekwensi asks, sliding his pipe into the front pocket of his vest. The air is thick with heat and still he is dressed in an immaculate silk shirt, full vest and trousers that don't betray a single wrinkle.

"No, it does not," Jonas says quickly.

Thirty members of the kunkun are gathered now, studying as they await Ekwensi's orders.

"I need four blowers, two wave bearers, one shifter, and"—Ekwensi nods at Sanaa, who is at the head of the crowd—"our resident priestess, of course, to predict the sand shifts."

Several Oluso step out from the group, and the others crowd them, laying out netted shirts and puffy trousers for their use. Ekwensi nods at us. "Our destination is known to be a bit treacherous. This will protect you."

A few kunkun head over, arms full of more of the protective clothing. On the top of the layered pile are red clay face masks with horns protruding from just above the eyebrows and diagonal slits for eyes.

"The desert spirits become rowdy as the sun sets. They stay away from only things they fear. Their curiosity is worse than an eloko's. With these, you will resemble nwadu, and that should keep them at bay."

"Nwadu?" Jonas asks.

"Desert plants that can cut the flesh of all things, including spirits," Colin answers.

Jonas lets out a hum of appreciation.

We dress quickly. I strip off my grime-covered leather trousers without a second thought, grateful for the cool kiss of the light cotton trousers that billow against my legs. The netted shirt is equally soft against my skin, the gel sac in each layer of the netting making me feel as though water is pouring off me.

"It's wara-wara cloth," Colin says. "We stuff ice pellets into jelly, then the Angma Oluso who can channel hand flames help us fuse it all to the linens." He grins, tugging at the hem of my shirt and pointing at a small blue streak on the end. "I made this one."

When I don't smile back, his grin disappears, replaced with a determined look. "We'll make them pay, Dèmi. I swear. We will be free." He squeezes my shoulder, and I nod. This is all I can manage for now.

"Today, my brethren, our numbers grow!" Ekwensi yells.

I slip on my nwadu mask. It fits immediately to my face, squashing my nose and making it hard to breathe. But after a moment, it shifts on my skin and adjusts.

"We enter the depths of the sacred fire heart as a scattered band of rebels. But we will emerge from it as conquerors."

Conqueror—perhaps that is what I should have aimed for all along.

The kunkun cheer as the Oluso standing near Ekwensi place their palms against the earth and the ground beneath us rises into a platform. I spread my feet, bracing myself as the platform settles. The Oluso trace their feet along it and stone pillars rise from different points, each with a ring our hands can fit through. Sanaa goes to the central pillar and places her hands in it. Danou hops on, moving to stand guard at her rear.

Four others climb onto each corner, their Oluso marks aglow as they stretch their fingers to harness the wind. The wind spirits gather in their hands, shifting into billowing sails that erupt from the center of the platform, turning it into a makeshift skiff. Then another two seat themselves at the very ends, drawing water bubbles from the dry air. They funnel the water into waiting skeins held by the other Oluso. Once those are full, they tuck their legs into the skiff like lions stretching in the sun, waiting for prey to appear.

"It is time," Ekwensi announces. He settles in next to Sanaa, then beckons us toward the rings at the front, just in front of the sails. I take my place there, Jonas and Colin following suit.

The Oluso who raised the skiff jump off. Taking a steadying breath, I push my hands into the rings just as the Oluso in the corners send handfuls of wind into the sails. We race into the desert, sand and hot air blowing into our faces. The wind nips at our backs, spurring us on to an uncertain future.

We glide through the sands, whipping past spiny tusi plants with bright-pink flowers growing on their ends. From the corner of my eye, I spy faint outlines of towns and villages hidden deep in the sands, the air around them grainy and dark, as though they are mirages after all. We fly over dunes and crash into valleys that drag us near sand pools that threaten to bury us. Every now and then, I catch threads of blue and white weaving across the sands, streams and lakes hidden like buried treasures in the desert, but we don't stop for anything. Not even for the karani that swim across our path, their protruding fins spearing the sands as they race towards unsuspecting prey. Right as the sun burns the bright flame of copper, Mount Y'cayonogo appears, a sloping dark mountain with tufts of green dotting the obsidian surface.

I have heard all my life of Y'cayonogo's Heart, the red and molten gold that bubbles up and runs down the volcano's sides every year, reducing everything it touches to a fine ash that rains down from it like snow. Still it is fearsome to look up at Y'cayonogo now, see her craggy, unforgiving face and know I must prove myself worthy by rising to meet her.

"Brace yourselves!" Ekwensi calls, throwing an arm around Sanaa.

All the other Oluso obey, wrapping their legs around their pillars and pushing their arms through the rings until they are through to their elbows. I copy them, wincing as the pillar ring shrinks around my elbows. We speed toward Y'cayonogo's base with no sign of stopping, and I clench my teeth, bracing for impact. Surely Ekwensi has a plan.

"Now, Danou!" Ekwensi cries.

The young man, still untethered, runs to the side of the skiff and leaps. As his body hits the air, he morphs; his arms meld into scaly midnight wings capped with a protruding horn and legs become powerful thighs with massive paws reminiscent of a leopard's. His tawny face curls into the sleek, feline head of a panther. I stare in awe. This is the danamétokun, the winged black leopard that once flew the skies of Ifé, the first spirit companions of Igbagbo Oluso that taught them to transform.

Danou launches upward, his growls greeting the still, ominous air. Then, just before the end of the platform strikes the base of Y'cayonogo, the Ariabhe Oluso stretch their arms and the winds grow into a gale, seizing us into the air.

I squint, holding tight to the pillars as the wind cuts across my face. My thighs burn from holding on and my muscles scream for release, but still I hang on, pressing my elbows against my pillar ring.

The wind dies. But now there is something underneath, shooting us forward. Danou's midnight wings stretch out on either side of us, horned tips swimming in and out of view like oars. We speed against the chilled air slapping our faces, hurtling toward the clouds crowning Y'cayonogo's summit.

As we burst through the clouds, the air blankets our skin with a layer of heat. We circle over the high walls of Y'cayonogo's crater, staring down at the molten gold that roils in the midst of that crater like an all-seeing eye. I stare awestruck as Danou flies us to a craggy shelf at the east end of the crater. He closes his wings, allowing the skiff to slide off his wide back. We touch down with a jolt, teeth clacking as we slam into the ground.

"Secure them," Ekwensi calls out as Danou changes back into human form.

The other Oluso spring from their positions, rushing to help us out of our rings. I gently nudge away the hands of the female Madsen Oluso who tries to help me and slip onto the crater floor myself. Ekwensi helps Sanaa down, lifting her gently at the waist as she comes forward.

The air is thick, the heat in it nearly unbearable, but I step closer to that heat, marveling at its sheer power, its ability to shape worlds.

"What do we do now?" Jonas asks.

"*You* do nothing," Ekwensi answers, moving to my side.

"Are you sure about this test for her?" Colin asks, his voice stiff with worry.

"Chaining is a test of faith," Ekwensi says. "She is of Afèni's line. She must partake of the heart to fully engage in the process."

"What must I do?" I ask, clenching my hands into fists. I could turn back now, but something is propelling me forward. I wasted so much time trying to compromise, time I could have used to hone my power, kill the Council and Mari and all those who oppress the Oluso. Now there's none left.

I will not hide from who I am again.

Colin's eyes widen with fear. "For my test, I had to drink mami wata poison. I was bedridden for a few days, and only after that did the magic work."

I swallow, my words suddenly heavy in my throat. "Do you expect me to drink the lava? We don't have days for me to recover from severe burns."

Ekwensi places a hand on my shoulder. "Your test is much simpler. You must bathe in Y'cayonogo's Heart."

"You want her to jump into a volcano?" Jonas shouts, incredulous. "How is that in any way simpler?" His hand flies to his hilt. "If you wanted a fight, all you had to do was ask."

"You may not understand this because of your upbringing," Ekwensi says, his tone betraying a slight annoyance. "Y'cayonogo is a sacred place. People have received visions here, strengthened their bonds with the spirits. Éyani Al'Hia perfected her magic here. A mere volcano would have burned us to ash for standing so close, but Y'cayonogo is merciful. She does not kill for sport. It is not her nature." He looks to me now. "And Dèmi agreed to come here. Did you not, Dèmi?"

I nod. Ekwensi is right. It is time to enter those flames, let them shape me as they would the earth, become free of the fears my spirit bonds have held me in for so long.

"I'm going."

Jonas puts a hand on my arm. "You can still do this differently. If you want to."

"I don't. This is the way."

For far too long the Council has hunted us with impunity, turned us into sacrifices on the altar of their hate. Refusing to break them as they have broken us, to let them feel a sliver of our pain, is no longer an option. I shudder, remembering the lifeless faces of the people Mari and Elodie murdered, the burning bodies. The Ajes will use their deaths as reasons to justify our murder. I have to act.

"Begin the ceremony," I tell Ekwensi.

He and Sanaa take positions on either end of the crater's mouth. Ekwensi begins chanting in his native tongue as Sanaa stretches her hands out, palms up as though she is waiting for a revelation. It strikes me now how much she looks like Ren and Elegua, how unmistakable the resemblance is. I don't know what happened to Ren after we returned to the Physical Realm, but I make a promise to myself to tell Sanaa of her mother.

The Oluso mark on Sanaa's cheek glows a blazing purple, and suddenly she throws her head back, her pupils fading to a fathomless white.

"Abidèmi Adenekan," Ekwensi thunders. "The Fiery Mother awaits you. Come and be carved by her spirit."

Sucking in a breath, I take a step forward.

"Don't do this, oko mi," Jonas begs, darting in front of me.

Colin shoves him away. "I know this is hard to see, but we don't have a choice. You need to respect her wishes. Dèmi knows what she's doing."

"What if this breaks her?" Jonas fires back. "What then?"

"We have never been whole. That is what you don't understand," Colin says. He squeezes my hand, giving me a wistful smile. "Even if you are broken, you will never face ruin alone."

My heart aches, my eyes threatening to spill the tears creeping up my throat. But I can't weep now. Not when there are so many people counting on me. Not when failure here means the kingdom will only get worse. Not when I've already failed and let the people I love die. I don't have time to mourn or second-guess—only act.

Twisting on my heel, I dart between Jonas and Colin, racing for the crater's mouth. There are footfalls behind me, voices clashing, but I push on, each strike of my foot against the rocks a drumbeat urging me on. As I reach the jagged peak of the crater's mouth, I leap, arms wide like a bird learning to fly.

I want to close my eyes, but the heat presses into my eyelids, forcing them open. There's no time to think before my feet slip into Y'cayonogo's Heart, the shock of pain discordantly like ice stabbing into my bones. I flail wildly, but soon every inch of my skin is burning with endless pain that tears at my core.

I want to cry out, but my screams are buried in my throat. I close my eyes and sink, knowing I have failed.

Then cool air blows on my skin and my eyes flicker open. I am lying in a shallow pool of water, its chill soaking into my body. I jerk up and look around. Everyone else is gone. The bloody sun that hung over Y'cayonogo is nowhere to be seen. Instead, I sit underneath a buoyant moon, her silver glow pouring over me like rain.

The sky begins to shift, golds and reds gathering over that midnight sky, announcing the breaking of the day. But still the moon does not leave her triumphant place, instead swallowing the sun as it threatens to swim into the sky. Red-golds become ribbons of orange-pink, those ribbons un-spool into the swelling blue of dawn, that dawn melts into the steady light of day, and that day falls into night. The cycle continues over and over again, the lights above me changing, the celestial bodies dancing as they brighten in the sky, but the moon remains, refusing to give up her throne.

Then, finally, the air grows colder and I fall into the blue half-darkness of twilight.

"It is never easy seeing it," a woman says from behind me.

I turn. An elderly woman stands clad in full armor, a red Oluso mark burning on her neck. Her long white hair scattered in thick coils around her rich brown face is the same silver as the moon bathing us. The hodge-podge leather and copper armor stitched over her skin does not hide the pride with which she carries her thick frame.

"Who are you?" I ask.

She smiles, the corners of her eyes meeting in a kiss. "I am bone of your bone and flesh of your flesh. I am the one called Afèni, daughter of Empress Yomi."

I stiffen, worry flooding my mind. "Am I dead?"

She lets out a low chuckle. "No, you're not dead. Actually, I shouldn't be here. But the spirits took mercy on me. I did a lot of questionable things in my lifetime, but they seem to find a few things I did laudable."

"You sacrificed our ancestral line. Left future generations to fend for themselves," I remind her.

She smiles. "That I did and more. I committed many crimes in my lifetime. Took the people I loved for granted, ignored relationships that mattered. I pursued justice—at least what I thought of as justice—for all of those I believed needed my help, and shunned those who were starved for the simplest of things. I died with my regrets." She steps closer. "But I don't want that for you."

I narrow my eyes. "What do you even know about me?"

"I know that you are out of balance. You carry a weight that should never have been your burden to bear."

She points to the moon above us. "Consider this sight. Look at how the moon lives. She watches time go by, and her children spin their lives out to the thinnest threads."

"The spirits sent you here to talk to me about the moon?" I scoff.

She hisses, whirling on me. "I know Yetundé didn't raise you to be disrespectful like this. In my day, we would have lashed any impertinent children with koboko. I may be dead, but it doesn't mean I can't teach you a thing or two."

I stagger back, my mind focused on the first words she uttered. "You know where my mother is?"

Her annoyance morphs to amusement so quickly I have to blink. She grins, a twinkle in her eyes. "I know more than that, my child. Now, listen carefully." She turns back to face the moon.

"The moon bides her time. She reflects the shine of the stars, and the dying of the sun in turn. But the only way she can live is to maintain balance. The sun cannot be allowed to shine when it is not day, and the stars cannot be seen to shine when night is tucked away. Each is equally precious."

I understand instinctively what she is trying to say. I am the moon, and the Aje and Oluso are the sun and the stars. Still, I want to make her say it, explain with her own mouth what she is asking me to do.

"If you're trying to change my mind, a riddle isn't going to help."

"Imagine an Oyo-born girl not liking riddles," she mutters to herself. Then she says, "There is a way for both Oluso and Aje to live. There is a way to break the cycle of pain, the wheel forged by our giving in to our baser natures."

She breaks off with a guilty look. "I cannot tell you more. The spirits have changed your fate already by allowing me to meet you like this. Riddles will have to be enough."

Her words stir up a warmth in me, something wholly different from the fires raging in my heart, the bud of hope I thought long dead. Still, I push that feeling back, not daring to give it air to breathe.

"How?" I challenge. "Balance is not a good enough answer. They outnumber us twentyfold. They kill us like we're ants. I doubt they consider balance when they murder us." I let my disdain slip into my words. "But you want us to show them mercy?"

She sighs. "Of course you're as stubborn as me."

I shrug. "I am descended from you."

A distant tune echoes, its rhythmic whirring like the sound of a pestle skating the surface of a copper bowl.

"Son of a custard lover," Afèni curses. I stifle a laugh. That's an insult I'll need to share with Colin.

"I'm running out of time, so listen up," she says. "Flames burn. Fires shape. But in time, they extinguish. What's left after that but ash?"

I cross my arms. "So what is your solution?"

"You must learn to act as the moon does. Reflect what you wish to see, and rest. Your strength is in your power to decide what you reflect."

I frown. "You want me to do nothing and hope that they do nothing?"

She starts to fade, her body melting into glimmering sparks that light up the darkness. "One more thing: Remember, the moon draws the tempestuous waves. Not the other way around. There are many voices that will demand their due. But you must find a way to seal them up. Don't let them steal your hope."

My mind is racing, my thoughts darting about as I try to make sense of what she's saying. She obviously means the K'inu, but I don't understand quite yet why she is telling me this.

"My only wish is for you to do what I never could—thrive." She whispers these words, but they echo through the crater as her body fades.

"Wait!" I scream. But she is gone.

The moon above me darkens, a rust creeping into it until it is bloody and full. I shudder, remembering the alayo rooms.

Then the voices begin, filling the crater like the hum of a thousand spiritual chants, tearing at the walls of my mind.

He wouldn't listen when I said no.
 She took my children and she burned them alive.
  They promised us riches and a place to live, but they built their
  cities on our bones and turned our joy to ash.
 He sent me wine that would kill me and I left my little one behind.
 She buried me inside the well before I could take my first breaths.

I clench my eyes shut, falling to the ground as voices and memories flood me all at once, sweeping through my mind with all the force of a whirlwind. Oluso laughing as they walked under the midday sun, a rich night sky. Ajes dancing in festivals, arms thrown out in abandon.

Babies squalling as they take their first breaths, lovers meeting in the covered brush, a child's smile as their Oluso mark unfolds against their skin. Then fires burning, eating people as they run, the smell of charred flesh heavy in the air. Waves clawing against the hulls of boats, pulling travelers into their depths. Soldiers cackling as they drag people into the streets with iron chains that burn their flesh. A Fèni-Ogun child lying dead in their mother's arms. An elderly man's hand crushed as people run through the streets, eyes wide with fear, the magic brimming against their skin like mere fireworks as swords, spears, knives, shadows, thunder rip them apart inch by inch until nothing remains but a river of blood.

I open my mouth in a wail, but nothing stops the sadness and grief that barrages my mind, a never-ending flood of pain. I scream.

Cool hands kiss my face and I open my eyes to see Jonas and Colin hovering over me, their voices thick with concern. I am in the crater again, sitting on the ledge by the skiff.

"Are you all right?" Colin asks.

"Breathe, oko mi," Jonas says, tears misting his eyes.

Ekwensi wears his jackal smile. "The ceremony is complete. Well done."

His pupils reappear, blossoming like the dark flowers the omioja use to send off their dead. I look down to find that my wrists are covered with the same thick, pulsing rings as Colin's, the flower in the midst of them resting over my pulse.

But now I know what Ekwensi did not say, what he hid from me. These voices and memories, they can only be from one place.

"The K'inu—" I croak. "You sacrificed me to the K'inu."

He laughs now, high and free, like a child with nothing to do but be a child. "I told you, didn't I? I am not afraid to do what it takes for us to win. This is how we win. With the power of resurrection."

DESPAIR

THE VOICES AND MEMORIES BEGIN AGAIN, FLOODING MY MIND LIKE STONES flung at my body, each taking a piece of me. I fold, throwing my arms around my knees, curling up like a sleepy child as my mind unravels with voices that will not let me go. Somewhere in the distance, the Oluso's voices knot in anguish. I am vaguely aware of Colin's angry shouts as he rushes at Ekwensi, of Jonas's arms wrapping around me and the cool relief of his touch.

I close my eyes as the pain fades for a brief moment.

Then it returns in full force, along with the weight of all the memories.

The flame inside me is fully alive now, stoked by the fires of grief, misery, and vengeance.

I burn.

BATTLE

WHEN I COME TO, I AM IN A BED. THE FLOOD IN MY MIND HAS SLOWED TO a trickle. The voices and memories are gone, but the feeling of despair remains, settled in my bones like a snake coiled into its nest.

Jonas sits up in the chair at my bedside, his warm hands flying to my chilled face. "Can you see me? Do you know who I am?" he asks.

My throat is raw, but I push the words out. "Jonas. My mate."

He heaves a sigh of relief. Then as I ease myself onto my elbows, he puts his arms underneath my shoulders and helps me up. Colin stirs at the end of the bed as my thighs shift the blanket away from him.

His clouded eyes sharpen as he realizes I am awake. He jerks from his seat, kneeling next to Jonas. There is a purpling bruise at the edge of his mouth.

"I'm sorry," he whispers. "I didn't know. I should have known, but I assumed—"

"Ekwensi deceived us all," Jonas explains. "Most of the Oluso who are chained don't remember what happened in their ceremonies. We've asked. No one knows Ekwensi has been binding them to the K'inu."

"Except Sanaa," Colin adds.

"Those were the spirits she was talking about," I mutter to myself. "Ekwensi used her as a vessel to reach the K'inu."

"I didn't remember my binding," Colin says, his hand balling into a fist. "I didn't recall anything until after I saw what happened to you. I've been dreaming, trying to find my mother and ask for answers."

"Did you . . . meet . . . her?" I whisper. There is an image in my mind of a tall, broad-shouldered woman with the same tattoo markings as

Colin's and heartbreaking hazel eyes that seem to hold all the sadness in the world.

"Nothing so far," he says, shaking his head. "But I'll keep trying. We've a bit of time left before we leave."

Those words bring me to my senses, and I sit up fully, blinking against the sudden glare of the lantern at my bedside. "Where are we going?"

Jonas produces a piece of wrinkled paper, smoothing it out for me to see. On it is a sketch of his face, along with an official announcement stamped with the Royal Council's seal.

"Your funeral," I gasp, "The next planned attack."

He nods. "The capital is in danger."

"But Ekwensi sacrificed us to the K'inu," I cry, shaking my head. "We cannot help him."

Jonas and Colin exchange a look. Finally Jonas answers, "We don't have a choice. Ekwensi used Colin's magic to bring us here. He intends to use it again to get us to Nordgren within the hour. He controls you both now."

"Control," I mutter. "The K'inu are how he's tethering us. We have to obey or we suffer pain."

"Our kunkun spies reported that Mari's soldiers are marching their way to the capital," Colin adds.

"The villagers aren't closing their gates to foreign soldiers?"

He shakes his head. "The rumors have spread that Oluso are to blame for the kokulu. And Mari's soldiers helped evacuate a few villages that were mysteriously attacked by the kokulu. Those villages were all in their direct path, of course."

My head is pounding, but everything is coming together now, drawing together in my mind like pieces of a puzzle.

"She's attracting the kokulu by massacring people, then riding in to save the day."

Jonas nods. "The funeral procession begins at Fox Hour with the Council giving a speech. Mari's soldiers will be at the capital by then. We're certain that they'll unleash the kokulu in the main square."

"And Ekwensi will let them," I say, letting out a breath. It all makes sense now. Just as the Council has been stoking the fires of hatred in hopes of war, Ekwensi has bided his time, waiting for an opportunity to win sympathetic people to his cause.

Colin grimaces. "Ekwensi doesn't control all of them. He was nearly killed by a few in Wellstown."

"The K'inu are the unpredictable element in all of this," Jonas agrees.

"They're even more powerful with my magic," I say.

Both men shoot me questioning glances. I tell them what my father shared with me in Ìyá-Ilé's courtyard.

Jonas's mouth puckers into a frown. "So the K'inu want to be reborn using your magic?"

I nod grimly. "It's a similar concept to chaining. With my magic, they can engrave themselves on the human bodies they possess."

"But what is the price of such a ceremony?" Colin asks. His brows are knitted together in thought. "Osèzèlé said there had to be a physical or spiritual price. Who pays that?"

We fall silent, turning over the idea in our minds. There is no easy answer.

Pressing my back into the cool of the mud wall, I lace my hands across my chest and think. Everything is chaos. Ekwensi is unpredictable, the Council is setting up another brutal war, we have few allies beyond the kunkun, and the K'inu have access to my magic and my mind.

A voice tickles my ear and I flinch, expecting the barrage of memories and pain to begin again, but it is a whisper of Afèni's wizened voice, a flutter that presses against my skin like a tender touch.

The moon draws the tempestuous waves.

If I am the moon, and the K'inu are the waves, there has to be a way for me to direct them, bend them to my will instead of having theirs rule mine.

Shuffling to the edge of the bed, I throw my legs over the side. Both men reach out to steady me, but I brush them off.

"Take me to Ekwensi. We need to hear his reasons once and for all."

A knock sounds on the door. Before any of us can react, the door swings open and Adaeze bursts in, eyes frantic.

"Dèmi, we need your help. It's Ga Eun."

I dart over to her. "What happened? Where is she?"

She whips around rushing into the main courtyard. A few Oluso stand outside a slightly larger mud house at the courtyard's edge, their arms full of glittering scales. We push past them, the smell of burning flesh greeting our nostrils before the door is even opened.

The hut looks smaller on the inside, stuffed to the brim with clay pots that surround the low cot shoved in the corner. But it is the hut's inhabitant that sucks all the air and space out of the room. A full-size gwylfin lies on the floor, its slitted eyes half-closed. Its back is raw and bleeding, reddened flesh flashing where gray scales should be. Samira is seated at the hearth next to it, its long neck nestled in her lap. She strokes it softly as another Oluso, the pierced older woman, applies a sticky salve to its ridged belly.

"What in Olorun's name—" I start.

The gwylfin's eyes flash open, reddened slits glaring at us. Its tail flicks out, the fanned ends waving like wagging tongues. I jump to the side just as it slams its tail next to the spot where I stood, cracking open a pot. It roars in pain, horns scraping against Samira's hands.

"Ga Eun, she can help you," Adaeze pleads.

I stagger back in surprise. Now I notice that the gwylfin's scales are a slate gray rather than the rich periwinkle gray of the sentient ancient creatures Chi Chi introduced us to.

"I promise I'm not your enemy," I say, putting my hands out.

"Bora shouldn't see her mother like this," Adaeze adds.

The gwylfin huffs, a stream of hot air threading through its snout, then it closes its eyes. Gray scales melt into seashell skin and the gwylfin's horns morph into Ga Eun's small ears. She is naked, her thin arms threaded around Samira's neck. Her back is a raw mass of wounds, some fresh and oozing, others scabbed over with thick, ugly purple flakes.

Colin's voice thunders behind me as he confronts the Oluso outside.

"This is where you were getting the scales?"

"She asked us to do it," one answers.

"What are the scales for?" Jonas asks.

The second Oluso answers. "This is the best protection from iron. With these, we last longer in a fight."

I scoot over to Ga Eun as Adaeze stalks to the door, her face knotted in anger.

"You nearly killed her!" she screams. "What will you do if she dies?"

Ga Eun's skin is cold. Her eyes flutter open as I brush my hands against her back.

"Hold on," I say quickly. "I'll heal you."

I don't know how my magic has changed after the chaining, but still, I have to try. Placing my fingers over the oozing flesh, I brace myself and pour green fire over those wounds. The magic streams from me effortlessly, and Ga Eun's flesh knits back together, smooth skin appearing under my fingers.

There is no tightening in my back, no knotted welt springing up like a boil. But a few images flash through my mind; a young child hiding in the remains of a well; a woman running as a crowd of villagers give chase, the torches in their hands illuminating the Oluso mark on the back of her neck.

I tense, falling back as a wave of melancholy rises in me again. The elder woman next to us throws a thin blanket over Ga Eun as I back away. Jonas slips in through the door and pulls me to the side.

"Are you all right?" he asks, voice heavy with concern.

Adaeze is still shouting, snarling in the other Oluso's face while Colin holds her back. "Take your dirty scales and get out of here before I dust you, Ralek."

"We weren't trying to kill her," Ralek answers.

"Hush, Adaeze," Ga Eun says, fluttering open her eyes. "I asked them to do it."

Adaeze turns, breaking from Colin's grasp to dive at Ga Eun. "Then I should be yelling at you!" Still, she throws her arms around her. "Don't ever do that to me again. I wasn't even sure you were breathing."

Ga Eun eases up, pushing against Adaeze's arms. "I'm all right now."

She nods at the female Oluso standing by Ralek. "Go, Sumi. There's not much time to weave the vests."

Sumi and Ralek rush off like thieves fearing discovery. Colin slips into the room, slamming the door closed.

"I thought you asked the gwylfins for help. That is what you told me."

His expression is dark, his voice trembling as he speaks. "But you—you were skinning yourself all this time?"

Ga Eun's face flushes an angry red. "What did you expect me to do? I've been useless since we started out."

"You lost a child!" he shouts.

"I can no longer fight!" she screams back, every word a clap of thunder. "My flesh is a small price to pay for our freedom. At least I can give that. You of all people should understand—this is our only chance."

I rock back on my heels, the ache in me growing. I assumed Ga Eun had borne her child.

Ga Eun's eyes flash to me then. "You have to fight for us. No matter what you think Tobias is doing, you have to help us. You can't hide behind laws or intentions anymore."

I clench my hands into fists, anger flaring at the mention of Ekwensi's name—this is the hidden cost of revolution, the truth he'd rather not face. Still, I reassure her. "I'm going along with the others to the capital."

She nods. Then, after a moment's hesitation, she says, "The baby was born sickly. The kunkun were on the move. We couldn't get to an Ariabhe in time. I got to name her at least."

Tears prickle in my eyes, but I merely nod. I don't have time to weep, not when Mari's forces are gathering at the capital. Not when Oluso lives and the lives of innocent Ajes who are none the wiser are at stake. Not when I've already lost everything.

The door swings open. Ekwensi looms in the doorway, blocking out the light. He is dressed in a crimson coat bearing the Ashkenayi emblem, twin snakes devouring an eagle. Underneath, a vest comprised of glittering scales peeks through over long dark trousers.

His gaze lands on me. "I hope you've had time to recover and get used to things. We leave soon." He nods at Jonas. "I assume I won't have to drag you along, since you follow Abidèmi wherever she goes."

"That's all you have to say?" I start. "Nothing about what you've done to me—to all of us?"

Colin bares his teeth. "I trusted you, and you deceived us."

"Come now," Ekwensi says, his jackal smile firmly in place. "You of all people understand that everything comes with a price. I've granted you access to magic you wouldn't have been able to keep, magic without restriction."

"But not control," Jonas adds. "Never control. You don't trust those you are fighting with, do you?"

Ekwensi's smile disappears. "The nature of chaining magic requires a soul contract. Would you rather I left your lover here to suffer the consequences of her broken spirit bonds? Live that pain?"

I narrow my eyes at him, and he lets out a bitter laugh. "You forget. I was once onyoshi. I am familiar with the pain of broken spirit bonds."

He turns to Colin now. "Who was the one who begged me for help?"

"Your help meant losing my magic at inopportune times!" Colin yells.

Ekwensi scowls. "I thought you were willing to do whatever it took to be free. Do you regret those words? This contract allowed you to see your mother again. Do you regret that too?"

Colin stares, eyes sparking with emotion, then he lowers his gaze. "I don't. I don't regret it."

Ekwensi nods. "I'll take that as agreement then. We're handing out supplies. See that you get yours."

He stands there a moment, and I realize that he's waiting for us to leave. There's so much I want to ask, but I can tell by the tightening in his jaw that Ekwensi will tell us nothing more. Not until he's ready.

If at all.

I shuffle into the courtyard, Jonas and Colin following along. As I pass by, Ekwensi's face softens into a genuine look of worry.

"Uncle," Ga Eun cries, lifting her arms.

He embraces her, rubbing her back as she bursts into tears.

The older woman closes the door, shutting us out.

The main courtyard is awash in a flurry of activity. Members of the kunkun run about, passing out staffs and blades made of copper and obsidian. Some shrug on Ashkenayi-crimson coats over leather armor. Others help their fellow Oluso into scaly vests like one Ekwensi wears.

"I'd prefer to skip out on wearing one of those," Jonas says.

"You won't need it. The tomé vests are meant to repel iron's effects as well as iron itself," Colin says. His expression is still dark, his mouth twisted in a scowl, but I can see the pride flashing in his eyes. "We got the idea after finding some shed gwylfin skin once. Ga Eun volunteered to talk to them and ask for more, but they must have declined."

I nod. The gwylfins, like the forest spirits, abhor getting tangled in humanity's squabbles. They are saddened by the loss of life, and I suspect they believe that aiding humans is only the first step to humanity making continual demands of them while threatening their survival.

Danou comes over to us, his arms full of uniforms. "Glad to hear you're joining us." He shoves the pile at us. "Suit up quickly."

We dress quickly, throwing on Ashkenayi coats and checking our weapons. Within moments, Ekwensi makes his way back to the crowd of kunkun in the courtyard.

They line up, ordering themselves by height. Jonas, Colin, and I stand off to the side, unsure of where to go. Ekwensi ignores us, coming to stand in front of the kunkun. He crosses his arms behind his back.

"Today we go to the city of Nordgren, a capital that once revered the Oluso as their finest artisans. Those Oluso are long dead, killed at the hands of their brother Ajes who envied the gifts the spirits granted us all."

He twists the head of his cane and draws out his blade, the bone singing against the silver of the sheath.

"Today, the Royal Council, under the guise of mourning, is launching an attack on its own people. Why, you ask? They seek to blame us, to give the Ajes a reason to cry for the blood of every Oluso who has ever graced this land."

The kunkun cry out in protest. Ekwensi nods.

"I know. I know, brethren. The Ajes kill us as they will, but there is no consequence for their wickedness. They desire the eradication of our people, and the spirits trap us with ancestral bonds."

The kunkun stamp their feet, rhythmic steps that make the ground tremble with their weight. Ekwensi rises slightly into the air, hovering off the ground.

"But today, brethren, we will be free. We will turn the Council's plans on their head. We will fight, not for the glory of war but for the peace we have been denied." He lifts his hands to the sky, and lightning crackles across the clouds. "And when we win, the Ajes will see that our reign is benevolent, our demands reasonable, and our ways just."

The kunkun stir up now, whistling and cheering.

"Freedom. Justice. Peace," they cry in every language spoken across Ifé.

My heart is soaring, and I find myself opening my mouth, mouthing the same words in Yoruba. Ominira. Idajọ. Alaafia.

Those are the things I have wanted all my life. A life where Oluso and Aje can live in peace. A life where Oluso are not hunted or shunned for their gifts, and where Ajes do not fear living in community with us.

But there is another part of me that shies away. A part that wonders whether those words mean the same thing to Ekwensi. Whether this fight will unleash more horrors and suffering instead of ushering in a new age.

Ekwensi lands and taps his cane against the ground. As the silver strikes the earth, blue flames spring from it, racing into a circle that engulfs all of us.

"Let's unveil a new world!" Ekwensi shouts.

The kunkun throw their hands across their throats in salute. The cool desert air fades as we are swept into another place.

It is time for war.

ENTRENCHED

WE APPEAR IN A DELL COVERED IN THICK FROST. EKWENSI RAPS HIS CANE against the ground twice and the kunkun split wordlessly into two groups. Colin, Jonas, and I hang on the edge.

Ekwensi nods to Sumi, the girl who took Ga Eun's scales. "Go to the castle, ensure the Council members make it to the square. Every last one."

Sumi cracks her knuckles. "Alive?" she asks.

"For now."

Her group of twenty closes around her. They fizzle into the night air, leaving only a whisper of red flame.

"She's a nobleman's daughter too," Colin explains. "Her father fell in love with his Oluso slave."

I clench my hands into fists. "It's not love when you own a person, when their life depends on your every whim."

"Sumi's father's wife beat her mother to death while she was chained. I'd say she agrees."

Ekwensi turns to us.

"You lot will come with me. Our goal is twofold: Subdue any and all ruling Council members. Defend against the kokulu attack. Use any means necessary."

Colin stiffens, and Ekwensi adds, "Excepting Lord Kairen. He, of course, will be spared."

"He wears an earring just like Colin's," Danou calls to the remainder of the group.

"Do we kill the Council members?" Ralek asks.

Ekwensi shakes his head. "Wait for my signal."

He cuts his eyes at me now. "Your time will come. The vengeance in your heart will be satisfied, I guarantee it."

"How do you presume to know what I want?" I snap.

"Because I have been as you are—desperate. You want peace, do you not?" He swipes a hand over his face and his dark skin fades to a broad, scarred face with freckles sprinkled across ruddy cheeks. "Watch and see the peace we'll create."

"Is there nothing for me to do?" Jonas asks.

Ekwensi flashes him an amused smile. "It's strange, isn't it? That we don't seem to need you? Your whole life people have revolved around you. But no more."

His smile drops like an ill-fitting mask. "Whether you choose to fight with or against us doesn't matter. I would advise you, though: the life of the woman you love is in my hands. So do your best not to get in our way."

Jonas gives him an even brighter smile. "Duly noted."

We wade through the trees scattered across the low valley and emerge on the main road. People, carriages, and horses throng toward the iron city gates. We swim into the ocean of people, dispersing amongst a group of Eingardians that take up space in the middle, their brown cloaks waving in the bitter, chilled winds.

A woman ahead of me wears the white of Gomae mourners, while a couple riding a donkey to my right boast the patterned gold of Oyo-born. I even catch flashes of violet and black, the colors favored by Berréans, as we flood toward the city gates.

Members of the kunkun hold hands, steeling themselves as they prepare to enter the iron gates. There are only a few guards stationed at the entrance to Nordgren, another sign that something is wrong. The battlements of the city walls are abandoned, mourning cloth draped over them, obscuring the proud purple-and-gold pennants that used to fly freely.

The capital city is alive, the hum of people bustling about like a frantic heartbeat. People brush against each other in the streets, squeezing past like caterpillars burrowing into hedges. Merchants seated at stalls lining the main street call out as we pass by, hawking spun-glass candies, thick meat pies, and hot tombo for sale.

Voices are everywhere; hushed conversations between people standing in doorways, loud chatter from the crowd swelling around us, shouts from children weaving through the hum of the throng, and then—the ones that waft around my head like a lingering aroma, regaling me with secrets and lies and truths that no one else will ever remember.

I try to keep them at bay, but they seem to grow with each step I take into Nordgren, their noise building into a thunderous din. After a few more steps, I clap my hands over my ears and stop. But people march on, knocking me about, and I drift between bodies like flotsam caught on the waves.

Then Colin snatches me from the crowd, pulling me into an alley. He holds my face between his palms. "Dèmi, look at me," he pleads.

I focus on those hazel eyes, try to sink into their golden depths.

"Breathe," he commands.

I obey, taking quick, short breaths. After a few moments, the voices fade.

Jonas appears beside me, pulling off the thick hood concealing his face. "It's still happening, isn't it?" he asks.

I nod, not trusting myself to speak past the bile clawing its way up my throat.

"Is there no way I can take some of it, pull them into my mind?"

Colin eyes him. "How would you do that?"

I shake my head before Jonas can say anything else. "He's iron-blood as well," I croak by way of explanation. "But I think it's just me they want."

Jonas blows out a breath. "All right. Tell us when it gets bad, please."

I nod again.

He points to the adjoining alley. "If we follow this side street, we can get to the main square and be in place without encountering too many people."

Colin drops his hands from my face and takes my hand. "Lead the way."

Jonas looks at our joined hands, then he gives my shoulder a reassuring squeeze and charges ahead.

I didn't change my mind.

I send the thought to him as we follow him through a maze of alleyways and side streets. I smile as his response unfurls in my mind like a gentle touch, a brushing of fingers.

In every lifetime, I know. Was trying not to clog your mind with more voices.

Thank you for that.

His answer sends heat flushing up my cheeks: *He can hold your hand, but I still get to sleep next to you.*

We push into the main street, hovering at the back of a crowd that churns around a raised platform like water bubbling in a cauldron. Soldiers stand, hands on their hilts at the edges of the platform. Several members of the kunkun, distinguishable only by the blue streak woven into the high collars of their mourning cloaks, revolve around the platform like sharks scenting blood.

The city's bells ring, each discordant boom like a fist cracking against bone. The crowd's voices increase with every strike, but when the ninth and final bell signals the start of Fox Hour, the crowd falls silent like sleepers under a magic spell.

A trumpet sounds a flourish, and more join in, wailing as an eight-horse carriage clambers down the strip of purple carpet tracing all the way from the gates of Château Nordgren to the waiting platform.

The horses pull to a stop, and the coachman leaps down, opening the gilded iron door of the carriage.

The crowd's voices rise again as Markham and Lady Ayn emerge from the carriage. Markham sports a black tunic with golden epaulets and long breeches that tuck into his leather boots. Lady Ayn is resplendent in a sweeping gown with a high, feathering collar the same shade and black gems that stud her fingers and ears, and hang from an elaborate necklace hugging her throat. Jonas stiffens next to me.

"I said it, didn't I?" a man close to us whispers. His thick beard waves as he sniffs. "King's in bed with the nobles. His son was the one cared about us. Not him."

The woman with him nods, the red scarf tied around her hair bobbing with the motion. "Just look at them. Crowlike. Birds of a feather. Bad omens."

The man behind them scoffs. "His son was carrying all for them meascans. Not protecting us."

Thick Beard shakes his head. "You've got that job at the milliner's now, don't you? They're not allowed to force meascan slaves to weave the threads. The laws that passed for the meascans helped us too."

Another flourish sounds, swallowing the second man's response.

The kunkun press closer to the stage, excepting one who slips away from the crowd.

"Who is that?" I ask, pointing at the tall figure as it disappears into the alleyway across.

Colin shrugs. "They might have gotten different orders from Ekwensi."

Markham and Ayn ascend the platform, her hand hovering above his. A few other Council members trickle after them, lining up in seats at the back of the platform. Their expressions are mirrors, fear and trepidation playing across their faces. Only Lord Kairen seems relaxed, arms crossed as though he is merely watching a masquerade.

Markham and Ayn move to the front. Now that they are closer, I see that Markham's face is gaunt, dark shadows under his eyes. Ayn beams at the crowd, her darkly painted lips cutting a garish smile across her pale face.

A soldier passes her a zela, and she holds the long horn to her lips, speaking into it as she would a lover. Her voice echoes through the main square.

"People of Eingard, friends, dignitaries, passersby, we welcome you into our humble capital."

She waits a beat, but the crowd is silent.

"Did she think we'd be impressed?" Thick Beard says.

Red Scarf hushes him.

"I know you are all so pleased to enjoy all the wondrous things the capital has to offer," Ayn continues. "It is sad that these enjoyments must come at such a difficult time for us all. As a Council member, I want to share how much my heart aches with you, the great people of this kingdom, the hands and feet that make our glorious age of abundance and enlightenment possible."

Now it is the woman's turn to scoff. "Abundance? Who is she talking about?"

"Four days ago, we received word that our beloved prince, Jonas Aurelius Sorenson, went to be with his valiant ancestors."

"That's probably the nicest thing she's ever said about me," Jonas quips.

"That you're dead?" Colin snorts.

"That I was beloved."

The crowd bursts into murmurs, and Ayn holds up a hand. "I know this is troubling for you all. Our prince was well loved and known to have a good heart." She pauses, her eyes sparking like an eloko falling in with unsuspecting travelers. "One might even say his heart was too good. And that good heart betrayed him in recent times. His choice to take a meascan queen—"

"This is a waste of our time!" someone in the crowd shouts.

"You royals are all the same!"

"We were promised food," another cries.

"That's more like it," Jonas says. "I was starting to worry that she actually cared."

Ayn snaps her fingers and more guards pour in from main street, surrounding the perimeter. Markham remains unmoved, his gaze pinned to the sky as though it holds answers. The crowd devolves into a swell of whispers.

"What is the point if she was going to force us to listen?" Thick Beard complains.

"As I was saying," Ayn continues. "Our prince made some unfortunate choices. The most dangerous of these was passing laws to protect those who are our natural-born enemies—the meascans that seek to steal you from the safety of your homes and bathe in your children's blood."

"It's always the same drivel," Colin mutters. "Why would we want to bathe in blood? Riddle me that."

A woman in the crowd steps up, her fiery hair waving as she shouts, "The Oluso saved my family when the capital's doctors left us for dead."

The middle-aged woman at her side adds her voice: "The ones in our village have never done us any harm. They are the only ones that play with my children."

"I've heard our prince was one of them too!" someone else shouts. "My sister seen him using magic in the castle!"

Ayn throws the guards a pointed look, and a few wade into the crowd, pushing toward the hecklers.

"Meascans destroyed Wellstown," comes another voice. "Those flying beasties come with them."

"I saw the same in Lleyria," another chimes in. "They're curses!"

Ayn seizes on this. "That gentleman is right. Wellstown's destruction is the direct fault of the meascans. You've heard the whisperings in the last few days. Let me also tell you this: our beloved prince died at meascan hands."

"She's gotten better at speaking to crowds, I'll give her that," Jonas says. "Looks like it's my turn," he starts, tugging at his hood.

Just then, a rattling sounds in my mind and the voices stir up again like hornets. I clutch Jonas's arm and he settles back. Violet flames spark into being, small explosions in the sky that have the crowd looking up. The crowd's whispers roar into an awful din, myriad voices jostling for supremacy.

"It's the beasts!"

"I'm not dying here!"

"Are those for the celebration?"

"I swear those notices promised food!"

A few people break from the crowd, and the kunkun rise up in their places, getting even closer to the stage.

Ayn lifts the zela to her lips, but there's a slight tremor to her otherwise stalwart voice. "Behold the danger I warn you about. The meascans have sent flying creatures to attack us while we mourn."

A convoy of soldiers flow in from the direction of the city gates, marching toward the stage. A strangely subdued Oyéré leads the charge. The crowd parts like water split against the rocks and a figure emerges from the sea of red cutting through the thickness of the mourners' cloaks.

Mari's face has a fresh scar over her right eyebrow, but she is beautiful nonetheless. The wolf heads on her shoulder braces gleam as she turns beneath the light of the torches festooned around the stage, rising onto that platform like the sun singing into the sky.

"Am I terribly late?" she asks, taking Ayn's hand.

Her cousin flashes a triumphant smile. "You always knew how to make an entrance."

Markham's expression knots with confusion. The other Council members rise out of their seats. Ayn simply hands Mari the zela and steps back.

"People of Eingard," Mari starts. "Loyal subjects from tribute regions, you may remember me as the companion of our late king, Alistair. But I wish you to know me as I am—Mari Strumblud."

Markham's ghostly face pales even further. "You—" He thrusts a finger at Ayn. "What is the meaning of this?"

Ayn beams. "I did what you were too cowardly to do. I saw an opportunity and acted."

The crowd is buzzing, murmurs building in a wave, but Mari continues on, ignoring the commotion.

"Since our king's passing, there have been many falsehoods, including a belief that I am a traitor to this great kingdom. So I came out of mourning for my king with one goal in mind—to prove my loyalty to you all."

Markham and Ayn's voices clash like dueling swords, rising and falling. The violet flames spark even larger, drifting toward the city square like snow.

My heart pounds in my chest, adrenaline flooding me. We have been witness to this farce long enough. It is time to prove to the city once and for all who the Oluso really are.

"Our kingdom is in grave danger!" Mari shouts. "But know this: I am here to fight for you." She nods at the soldiers and a few raise pennants, waving them against the stirring winds. "In mere moments, you will be forced to run for your lives. My soldiers are here to take you to safety. See that you obey them."

Bone-white forms split from the violet flames like shoots rupturing the body of a seed. The kokulu screech as they emerge, their jeweled eyes even more cold and unforgiving against the blanket of frost covering the city.

The crowd disperses instantly. People run in all directions like chickens with their heads cut off, screaming as they cut into back streets and alleys. Many head for the soldiers as the kokulu swoop down, spilling teeth from their maws. Some fall in their haste to get away, curling into themselves as they are trampled underfoot.

A child sinks in the midst of the chaos, and I lurch forward, snatching her up just as more people thunder past. The little girl sobs and Colin takes her from me.

"Where are your parents?" he asks, shouting over the clamor of the stampede.

She wails even harder and he curses as he pats her back.

The kunkun catapult into action, throwing off their cloaks. Two Madsen Oluso standing back-to-back send out a giant water bubble that settles over the market square like a shield.

Soldiers race to the stage, lifting body-length iron shields. They close over Mari, Markham, and Lady Ayn, blocking them from sight. The other Council members flee, running for the carriages lining the royal carpet. The kunkun give chase, snatching them up before they can reach the safety of their iron-welded carriage doors. Lord Kairen alone is rooted in one spot on the stage, watching in awe.

I run for the edge of the bubble, Jonas and Colin following in my wake. "This way!" I shout at people fleeing. "There's safety in the square."

Kokulu teeth drive into the surrounding buildings, violet flames burning through as if the stone and brick were mere straw. The people nearby stagger and fall as they scramble to get away. Three kunkun run after us, hurling ice shards at the sky. One of the shards finds its mark, piercing a kokulu through the underside of its jaw all the way into the soft spot in its head. The kokulu screeches as falls to the ground in a blazing heap, violet flame consuming everything it touches. Steam erupts from its bony body, and there in the ashes is another young child, a boy whose lifeless eyes are fixed on the sky—Namiz'en.

I run to him just as a kokulu tooth cuts into a woman's neck, and she stands still in the midst of the chaos, frozen in time.

I touch the boy's chilled flesh, and immediately flashes of memory erupt in my mind. Namiz'en swimming happily in a creek, the red uniforms of soldiers that swarmed the trees, dragging him from the water. Hot tears as he stood next to his fellow refugees, pleading with the sky. The soldiers' blades as they tore into his flesh. The stench of urine as he disobeyed his mother for the last time and peed all over himself.

Jonas is shouting in my ear. "Stay with me, Dèmi. Come on."

I look up to find his dawn eyes tight with worry. "Get up, please. You have to keep moving."

Pushing the memories aside, I surge to my feet. He's right. Those who have become K'inu are already dead. I need to fight for the living.

More people have fallen in just that brief moment, and now an elderly man rushes down the street, stumbling as a kokulu cuts toward him like a knife. Just as its claws grab for his shoulders, an Angma Oluso rushes over, flames sparking at his fingertips. He hurls a ball of flame at the kokulu and the creature swivels around, diving at him now.

Jonas delves into the fray, unsheathing his sword as the kokulu sinks its claws into the other Angma Oluso's shoulder. The young man screams, then Jonas is there, cleaving the kokulu's hind leg off.

Calling on the wind spirits, I envision a spear. My magic erupts like a spring and a burning spear of white flame appears in my hand. I throw it at the kokulu as it plunges toward Jonas again. The spear drives through the middle of the creature's head and it slams into the ground.

"I thought it was over for me," the Angma Oluso says, clutching his bleeding arm.

"Then why did you jump in?" I ask.

"In Ker'edu, they teach us to respect our elders, you know."

I spread my fingers over his shoulder, and the flesh knots back together.

I swallow. It's so easy to wield my magic now, after chaining myself to Ekwensi and the K'inu. A part of me wonders if I should have done this long before, given over control in exchange for freedom—power. Enough power to force the Ajes to leave us alone.

A kokulu rips by, piercing through the belly of a running child with its tail. I squash my thoughts, pulling my bone blade from my belt and running at the kokulu head-on as it whips the boy into the air.

"Dèmi!"

Jonas's shout falls on deaf ears. I slam my blade into the kokulu's tail and the creature screeches, flicking its knifelike head towards me as the end of its tail and the boy come tumbling to the ground.

"It's different fighting someone who can fight back, isn't it?" I spit.

The kokulu surges toward me like an arrow. I spin around, poised to run, but soon bony claws shred through the rough cloth on my back and pierce my skin like a knife bursting through overripe fruit.

The pain is instant, an icy fire making kindling of my bones. My knees buckle and I open my mouth to scream, but all that comes out is a gasp. The kokulu snakes its neck around me, peering into my face with those cold, glittering eyes.

Jonas runs for me, crying out as the kokulu pushes its claw in further, tearing into the muscle of my left shoulder.

Then a haze of blue flame cuts off my vision of Jonas, and Colin is there, driving a copper blade through the soft spot on the kokulu's head. My ears ring with the kokulu's screams as its claw slips out of my back. It crumples, folding into a burning heap.

"Can't leave you alone for a moment, can I?" Colin says. But his voice trembles as he speaks the words.

"I'm fine," I gasp. "It bloody hurts, but I can fix it."

Jonas rounds on us, peeling away the mess of cloth and blood and skin clinging to my back. "Son of a—" he breaks off with a growl, then says in a clipped, barely restrained voice. "Why couldn't you just wait?"

I nod at the child who is still curled on the ground, the remains of the kokulu tail burning through the hole in his belly. "If I waited any longer, there would be less of that child left to save."

He hooks a hand underneath my shoulder, pulling me up. "For once try worrying about if there'll be enough of *you* to save."

Colin snorts. "Say it again. Maybe if we both keep screaming it, she'll start caring about her life."

I shoot him a deadly glare.

A kokulu catapults by us just then, and Jonas yanks me out of the way, whipping me behind him. The creature races past and slams into the ground, where it erupts into flame. There's an ice shard lodged in its forehead like a crown jewel. All around us, more kokulu are being driven back by storms of ice shards and iron swords.

"We're winning," I say, frowning. Something feels wrong. A few kokulu are capable of razing a whole city. But more than twenty lie burning in the square. How are they losing this fight?

"We have a problem," Colin says, pointing his blade toward the city gates. People stand in the middle of the street, unmoving. Violet flames blaze across their necks like collars.

Dread twists my stomach into knots. Of course. The K'inu wouldn't lose a fight so easily. "They're possessed," I say. "We can't purge the K'inu inside of them without killing them too."

The wall of shields comes down, revealing Mari and Ayn standing over a bleeding Markham. Jonas lets out an anguished cry and drops my arm, running for the stage.

"Shit."

Splaying my fingers over my ruined shoulder, I will the flesh to knot back together. I need to help Jonas win this fight. My magic sparks at my fingertips and dies.

Frowning, I try again, tugging on the well of magic roaring through my chest. Nothing.

The links on my wrists throb as though in answer. I am powerless.

"No, no—" I cry.

Another flourish sounds. Soldiers flood through the city gates, their red uniforms clustering in what seems to be a never-ending sea. More rise on the battlements, purple-and-gold uniforms flapping in the wind as they nock arrows to their bows and aim at the people scattering below.

"Run!" I scream.

We dart for the safety of the bubble just as a hail of arrows rains down, striking both dead bodies and frightened people. A few of the possessed fall like bricks in a pile, crumpling into the dirt.

The fleeing people race after us, cowering as they fall into the bubble. The invading soldiers drive their way through the crowds, swords swinging like scythes during harvest, mowing down everyone in their path.

"How much do you want to bet they blame all this bloodshed on us?" Colin asks me.

But my eyes are on the stage, watching Jonas as he approaches Mari and Ayn, brandishing his sword. Oyéré leaps up, cutting him off. She dives at him with her curved blade as he brings his up to meet hers.

The kunkun drag the other Council members off the side of the stage. "Surrender," they shout, "or we will kill them!"

Mari just laughs, her body shaking with the movement. "Hack their throats for all I care. They're of no further use."

A soldier rams into one of the Oluso maintaining the shield, stabbing her in the stomach. His blade ricochets off her tomé vest, but she startles and the shield flickers out of existence. Her fellow Oluso punches the soldier in the face, then spins to kick another as even more close in on them.

I leap forward, kicking a soldier in the back as he bears down on a member of the kunkun. My shoulder burns, and I nearly bite my tongue from the pain. Colin tackles another, lifting him by the waist and throwing him over his shoulder.

"You were better off being dead," Mari taunts. "But thank you for gathering my enemies for me. It makes everything much easier."

"Close the city gates!" I yell. "Or they'll overwhelm us with numbers alone."

"Killing Mari is faster," Colin says. "No commander, useless army."

Oyéré slashes at Jonas's knee then, catching him in the thigh. I hiss in pain as my leg throbs in the exact same spot.

Colin pulls me to his chest, using his momentum to kick the soldier rushing at me.

"I thought the bond was gone!" he shouts.

I clutch his arm, blinking as dark spots cloud my vision. My head is pounding, more voices seeping into me like smoke filling my ears, but I hold fast to the walls of my mind, willing it all away.

"Is it starting again?" he asks.

"Yes."

Blue flame erupts from his hands and a ribbon of ice spreads over the ground around us, cutting us off from the fights happening nearby.

He squeezes my hands tight. "Breathe. Focus on the sound of my voice." I stagger against him and he snarls, "Where the hell is Ekwensi?"

I am the moon. They are the waves.

I repeat the words in my head over and over again until the pain subsides. Jonas knocks Oyéré off the platform and runs to his father's prone form. Ayn backs away, scurrying to the corner where Lord Kairen cowers.

"There's no use doing all this!" Mari yells. "We've already won. Whether you kill those fools or not, the people will remember what happened today. They will despise you even more."

Lord Kairen rises from behind his chair, and now I glimpse the knife winking from his sleeve. He pulls it out, the white of it flashing like a smile as he stabs it into Lady Ayn's chest.

"On the contrary," he says, turning to Mari. "You've failed to realize the kind of situation you are in."

Kairen's tawny face peels back to reveal Ekwensi's grinning one. Colin sucks in a breath, staggering back. The painting in the mirror city comes back like a faraway dream, the sketch of a young Lord Kairen. Colin was right. His father is dead.

INVINCIBLE

"Colin," I say carefully, "Ekwensi could just be skin-walking again."

There are enemies all around, I can't have him losing his cool. But Colin is already stalking toward the stage, the blue flame emanating from his skin flaring like a wildfire threatening to burn everything in its path. Mari steps back and her soldiers close in around her.

I stumble after him, cursing. The spirits must be laughing at our expense. I know the pain of losing a parent, even if they were someone you were never quite sure loved you the same way you wanted to love them. I am Osèzèlé's daughter, after all. But I also know that Colin's grief and the explosion of magic that would come with it could destroy everything in this square.

"Colin," I plead.

But he is snatching Ekwensi's collar, looming over the older man.

"You killed my father?" he thunders.

Ekwensi sighs. "A necessity for the cause, young one. I needed access to the Council, to learn their schemes. It was the only way."

"It was the easiest way!" I shout, stopping just behind Colin. "You knew Kairen was trying to reconcile with his son."

For once, Ekwensi looks ashamed.

"How could you?" Colin demands, jaw trembling. There are tears brimming in his eyes, and he looks at Ekwensi with all the hope and disbelief of a beloved child rejected by their father.

Swallowing, I place a hand on Colin's back. It's clear Ekwensi meant more to him than even I knew. It was only natural, finding a father in someone who had seen his potential. To those of us orphaned by the cycle of war and hatred, parents and guardians were idols to be worshipped, fantastical beings who could have abandoned us in the bid for survival but chose to fight for us anyway.

Jonas looks up from his own father then, all color drained from his face. Even he could not abandon Markham in the end.

"How could you?" Colin asks again. His voice is whisper-soft, but I hear the anguish in it, so loud and raw that my heart twinges with grief.

Ekwensi's mask of confidence is gone, replaced with a bewildered look, like a spirit who has lost its last worshipper. "I did only what was necessary," he entreats, squeezing Colin's shoulder. "Your father was dying, a wasting sickness from poison—all I did was hasten his end—"

"You poisoned my father?"

Ekwensi's eyes go wide with shock. His words spill out like tumbling bricks, falling from his lips all at once. "No! When I saw him again, Ferdinand was already suffering. He could not even keep down a bowl of rice—"

Colin smashes a fist into Ekwensi's jaw. The older man's head cracks back like a warning shot.

"Colin!"

I snatch his arm before he can repeat the blow and nearly fall with the motion. My skin is hot, my neck beading with sweat. The rings on my wrists pulse faster and faster, like lungs working to swallow up air. The well of magic burns inside me like a hot stone, threatening to devour me whole. Still, I hold fast to Colin's arm.

"Please," I beg. "Now is not the time. This is what they want." I dart a quick look at Mari, who watches the scene with interest. "They want us to fight and kill each other. Not now."

All is silent as the kunkun turn their attention back to the stage. Even the guards stop fighting to watch.

Colin drops his hand from Ekwensi's collar, staring at his bloody hand as though he can't quite believe it's his. Ekwensi straightens his head slowly, wiping the blood that is now leaking from his lips. His eyes are hard, all semblance of vulnerability gone. "Consider that your debt paid. You *will not* strike me again."

Mari smirks. "Didn't take you long to turn on each other, did it?"

Jonas gets to his feet, sliding his sword from its sheath. "I'd worry more about your own life. The penalty for murdering a ruler is execution."

"Even if you manage to kill me," Mari says, stepping away from her guard, "you'll never make it out of this city alive." She cocks her head toward more approaching soldiers, another sea of red rushing into the city square. Elodie leads the charge, riding in like a conqueror on an iron-clad horse at least four times her size. She grins as she catches sight of me, offering a cheeky little wave as she draws her horse to a halt. There is an iron circlet woven through her golden curls, and her fitted battle dress bears the emblem of House Ayn, an openmouthed wolf with a sparrow in its jaws.

The surviving mourners press closer to the stage, hiding children and loved ones behind them as though it were enough to survive this. There's no way out. Either we kill Mari, Elodie, and their army, or we wait to be slaughtered.

"Thought you'd gotten rid of me, did you?" Elodie quips, touching the knotted stub of her right arm.

"I'm sorry," Jonas responds. "But I had to stop you." He gentles his tone, appealing now. "All the Oluso want is to be left alone. Oluso and Aje have lived in peace before. We can do it again."

"Peace is relative," she counters. She nods at a member of the kunkun, a child who is holding up a small magical barrier over three other kunkun, along with a few cowering Aje children.

"Just look what that thing, that child, can do right now," Elodie says, leaping off her horse. "Imagine what would happen if it decided to murder everyone in that pathetic barrier in a fit of anger. Would anyone be able to stop it?"

"We do not murder!" I yell, anger and betrayal thick in my voice. "Not without a price. Our spirit bonds prevent that."

She tuts, wagging her knife at me like an errant finger. "I've worked with Ekwensi. I know that's not exactly true."

"You cannot begin a reign with bloodshed," Jonas pleads. "Have you learned nothing from watching my uncle? There are others who will oppose your rule. They'll fight to keep you from the throne."

"They'll lose," Mari answers.

"The people will never forget this. They will call you usurpers. They will remember the blood you spilled today."

Mari whistles and the guards flanking her surround the stage, cutting us off. "Alistair taught me this: murder affects memory. People desire to forget the horrors they've seen. They'd rather obey a tyrant and tell themselves all is well than admit they might be instruments of evil."

Colin steps away from Ekwensi. "So what do you intend to do? Kill every last person here? Do you think we'll go down without a fight?"

Mari's smile widens. "I know you won't. In fact, I know you'll do just enough that anyone lucky enough to survive this will spread the word from city to city and generation to generation. The meascans are murderers. They're animals that seek to devour us. They brought a plague of monsters upon our heads. It's kill or be killed."

I turn to Ekwensi. He promised us retribution and freedom, a master plan to end this farce. But all he's doing is standing like a shadow, pinning me with that solemn, resolute gaze. I realize now that he's waiting for something—for me.

The voices still linger in the back of my mind, thrashing against me like fish fighting to get back to the sea.

Finish it! they beg. *End our suffering.*

The K'inu are ready, to consume those in their thrall, to take over this entire city if they must. All I have to do is set them free.

"You'll never stop hunting us, will you?" I say, almost to myself. "We'll never be human to you, never something worth protecting."

Something inside of me is loose, a devouring emptiness where my heart used to be. In this moment, all I want is to carve Mari's head from her body, end the nightmare that has plagued me since the day I first saw her face. But she is not the only one. I know in my bones that even if I took Mari's life today, condemned myself to a lifetime of pain and madness, it would not be enough. Not to soothe the hollowness inside of me, the wound that will never heal. Not to bring back the people I have lost, the life I could have had. Not to save the Oluso.

There will always be someone who believes we are not worthy of life, a new evil that will work to smother us until we are nothing but dust.

"So be it," I say, clenching my fists.

My pulse quickens. The rings on my wrists stop throbbing. Suddenly, all I feel is a piercing chill, a thousand frost needles burrowing into my skin. A dull roar engulfs my ears, a rushing noise like a tidal wave embracing a city.

Elodie sighs. "If it makes you feel any better, I don't hate you. You were actually fun to talk to"—she breaks off, cheeks flushing—"a bit like a friend. If we'd met under different circumstances . . . we could have had some laughs."

The storm of magic in my breast expands, a writhing, uncontrollable thing that yearns to unfurl itself, combust. I surrender to it.

Jonas gasps, clutching his chest. "Dèmi," he says, staggering toward me. "Your eyes."

I catch my reflection in his blade. My eyes are burning a jewel blue—just like a kokulu's.

A noise cleaves the air, a splintering like nails clawing against wood. All around us, the possessed, still burning like straw dolls, begin to move. Their eyes are sharp jewels twin to mine, reflecting nothing but the violet flame suffusing their bodies. As they creep closer, the flames explode into small cinders that race like scurrying mice, searching for more bodies to burn.

"What in the seven bogs—" Elodie begins.

Ekwensi's pursed lips give way to a smile. "I warned you, did I not? That retribution was coming. For all those who have hunted the Oluso. This is it." He spreads his arms wide, his voice carrying over the din. "All those who stand with us will be spared. Those who stand against us will become kindling, seeds for the world that is to come."

The flames from the possessed reach some soldiers, leaping onto their red coats and setting them ablaze. The soldiers beat at their garments, some dropping to the ground to roll on the stones, but they keep burning. Many cease moving, their eyes turning that same hard shade of blue.

The crowd huddled by the stage begins to beg and plead. "We are with you!" they shout. "We will hunt the Oluso no more." Some attempt to clamber onto the stage but they are knocked back by Mari's guards, who beat at them with swords and batons.

Colin hisses in pain, clutching at his wrists. Other members of the kunkun follow suit, dropping their weapons as they hold their burning wrists.

"Wait!" Elodie screams, wading into the crowd, trying to fight her way to the stage.

"Kill the girl," Mari commands, yanking a sword from the belt of the guard at her side. She lunges forward, swinging at me, but Jonas is there slamming his blade against hers. She presses hard against his injured shoulder, and I feel the burn of pain in my own torn muscles.

Closing my eyes, I push the pain aside, focusing instead on the breadth of the power inside of me, the sun igniting in my chest. Even with my eyes closed, I can sense everything around me—the wide expanse of the stormy skies, the rough polish of the cobblestones in the city square, the metallic, smoky scent of blood and ash that lingers like a fog, leeching into everything it touches.

"On your left!" Jonas screams. But I am already spinning. The soldier grits her teeth as she drives her spear up at me, but violet flame springs from my ruined shoulder like a gwylfin wing unfurling. The woman does not stand a chance. The fire leaps onto her skin with all the greed of a starved beast. Her spear clatters to the ground as she burns, the unholy flame turning the whites of her eyes into an abyss.

Another wing erupts from my right shoulder as Colin falls to the ground, writhing as bony wings sprout from his back. The kunkun at the bottom of the stage collapse into a similar state, their screams morphing into screeches that pierce the sky.

Now the townspeople begin to run, screaming and yelling as they scramble away from the stage. The soldiers, fearing the flames surrounding their fallen colleague, follow suit, scattering into the streets. Even swaths of the red army edge back, barking commands at those too frozen to the spot to move. Their voices are so distant to my ears, dull whispers of sound and fury. My hair begins to dance around my face, each braid alive with flame that glistens as bright as any star. Then a flood of heat spreads over my legs and I feel myself expanding—becoming.

"Dèmi!" Jonas screams my name again, kicking Mari in the chest then slashing a cut through her arm. His voice alone is an explosion in my head, a nail lodging into the walls of my mind.

But then the voices of the K'inu—the whispers of my brethren, meld in my mind in a hissing murmur. I open my mouth and free the flood of their thoughts.

"The time has come."

My—their—voice echoes, sinking into everything around and beyond us. It is a hollow cry, a wail hungry enough to send forest creatures from their burrows and wake children from their beds. Their voice seeps into the earth, into the hidden cracks and nooks and the very bed of the sea.

"For so long you have damned us, murdered us for sport and greed. You have failed to see the light in us. You have killed our spirits, disturbed our bones, and denied us rest. Now we will build our houses in your bones and live once more in your flesh. We will take as you have, until your spirits fade into nothingness. We will consume you."

Magic thrums through my entire body. Every inch of me is aflame, burning with possibility. I am more than a remnant of once-proud bloodlines, more than a fugitive broken by a cruel world, I am—we are—infinite, immortal, invincible.

Our heart pounds in my chest. We place a flame-doused wing against it, and it speeds up. The power of resurrection is here, dangling like ripened fruit sagging on a vine, all we need to do is reach in and pluck it out. Once this traitorous human heart is out, we will be as we were made to be, more fearsome than the Fèni-Ogun of old who called up iron skeins from the heart of the Earth herself and forged kingdoms of copper and gold. We will have vengeance for all the pain we have endured and emerge victorious from the burial shroud of injustice. We will live.

Our brethren await, their beating hearts in the flames searching for bodies. All we must do is take out this heart, burn it alive, and everything denied us will return. We can rage and ravage the land and find the home that was denied us in the Spirit Realm.

"Dèmi."

A man approaches us, reaching out his hands. He's young, broad-shouldered, and full of vitality. He moves with the surety of one who commands, yet he comes to us with an air of supplication, kneeling at our feet. We—no, this vessel we inhabit, this frail human woman—begins to weep. We see through her eyes this man as a grinning boy, twinkling blue eyes full of mischief. Then the boy hardened into a man, with burdened shoulders and a heavy crown. Finally, we see the man now, laying his weapons down, begging us—this vessel—to remember, calling that name like it means something. The timbre of his voice echoes in our mind.

"Dèmi, please."

We want to laugh, mock this man. The vessel we inhabit weeps for him, but we know what he cannot. The vessel is nothing more than endless flame now. She is lost, buried deep behind the suffering she endured for so long, nothing more than the fuel that keeps us going. The only spark of her left is this human heart.

But now this heart is trembling, turning into a wild thing we cannot tame. It is running fast, galloping as though it can escape us.

Another man stumbles to his feet. His wings are glorious, sharp things that curve around him like sea serpents guarding a treasure. One eye is our brother's, bright and beautiful as the sky. But his other eye is the gold of a harvest season, stubbornly refusing to change. He is fighting us, hanging onto his spirit, defiant.

"Abidèmi, get your arse out of that creature before I drag you out!" he screams. "You're not allowed to run away."

Our human vessel's heart leaps again. Our mouth opens though it is not our will. "Colin . . . you know better . . . than to call me that."

The defiant man smirks, though we know that his spirit is locked in a battle with our brother's. "You were the one who taught me hope. You don't get to run away when yours is dead. Fight, damn you. Fight it, fight them like you always did with me—for me."

We take a step forward, flexing a wing. We need to move before the vessel resists us, crush these men's souls and consume their bodies.

A shrill whistle pierces the sky. We clap our wings over our ears. But the noise only grows until we can no longer shut it out.

Dark creatures streak over our sky, their mouths open in challenge. When they speak, an inferno greener than forest leaves bursts forth, falling onto our brethren like stormy rain. We scream with our brethren as their bodies crumble, and we fold as we feel their souls, their essences being dragged away, back to the Spirit Realm.

"No!"

We take to the sky, shooting toward the creatures that dare interrupt our plans. But they tear at the air around us, barraging us in waves until we can no longer keep our vessel's eyes open enough to see the sky. We look with our mind's eye instead. They dance around us, sweeping past us so quickly, but we recognize them all the same. We have called them by many names—a'ur, sutat, ngwerya, yong, lokhe, drakkon—but our souls murmur the one name that makes us quiver, sets our vessel's heart beating even faster—gwylfin, protectors of the Earth.

"This is not your fight!" we rage. "We will not harm the Earth as she stands. We only seek to live."

As though in mockery, a building in the city below crumbles as one of our brethren slams into its side as she struggles to fight the soul of the Oluso vessel she's consuming. Our servant, Ekwensi, rushes to help her, pulling her from the wreckage.

"You do not know what you seek."

The largest of the gwylfins sweeps around to face us, her ridged plume helmed by a creature with elephant ears and bird feathers growing from her scalp, a child of the forest.

"Chi Chi," our vessel whispers. But our voice thunders all the same.

"You're still in there then, auntie Dèmi," the girl answers with a chuckle. "Good. You promised me human sweets."

Our vessel has the audacity to smile.

The gwylfin speaks again without opening its maw, its voice drowning us in its intensity: "You are lost children, souls abandoned to the hatred and malice that first took your lives. You have languished long in the darkness, but now it is time to be free. Give up your vengeance and we will fight with you. Give us your rage and we will build a world your souls can rest in."

"And if we do not?" we answer defiantly.

Our human vessel is starting to uncurl, to swim past the layers of pain and sorrow we've buried her in. We dig our wing into our vessel's shoulder, tearing muscle and drawing blood. Our vessel's soul thrashes as another wave of agony hits.

"Then you will be purified by force, burned until nothing remains of your souls. Not even your malice can save you then."

The gwylfin opens her mouth this time, revealing a mouth full of emerald flame.

We shudder, jerking away. "Why do you deny us our victory?" we cry. "Where is our justice? Where is the payment for all we have endured?"

Another gwylfin rises up like a mountain cresting above clouds. On its back are two elderly men, one dark-haired, one not. Our vessel gasps in air, nearly choking herself.

"Baba . . . Tenjun . . . how?"

"Dèmi," one man calls. "I didn't raise you as a weapon. I didn't nearly die so you could terrorize the capital city. Take hold of yourself and come out of this."

Our vessel's heart clenches tight, beating with renewed vigor. Her soul is flaring brighter, like a moon in her fullness, drawing us into her light.

Below, our brethren are beginning to lose, their essences burned away by the gwylfin fire. Then Oluso vessels are breaking down, bony wings shattering into dust as the humans reclaim their minds. We are losing.

The air before us peels back and a woman emerges from it like a seed. Her gossamer wings are blinding, illuminating her burnished skin. Her white-gold eyes are spears holding us in place, full of judgment and pity.

"I did not make you my child for you to run from the world, Abidèmi," Ayaba cries. "Open your eyes, and face yourself. Build on the ashes of your pain."

"And then what?" We—I howl. "What is left after all this suffering?"

The Aziza queen seizes us—me—by the shoulders. "Without the Oluso, our realms will perish. The forest spirits depend on that protection. The water spirits will fade without it. The wind itself will cease. Do as you were born to do—build hope from sorrow. Craft beauty from carnage. Fight for your people!"

We howl as our vessel breaks through another layer of the binding we placed on her soul. We flood her with memories of pain, memories of all the sorrows that have eaten away at her life. "There is nothing to fight for!" we scream. "Only debts that can never be repaid. How can we live when all we know is hunger? When those that hurt us never see our need to live?"

The soldiers below crawl out of their hiding places like ants, surging toward the stage as our brethren fall to the ground, falling upon mourners and the few Oluso vessels still in control of their bodies.

We scoff, "You see, they war even without us. They murder and they kill. Why not give them to us? Let us consume them and use their bodies to be born again."

Ayaba puts a hand to our face and now we see that her eyes swell with tears. "Even if you are tired of fighting, my child, fight for yourself. Don't forget that you deserve to live. These spirits fear letting go, being reborn into another life, but you are yet living. Live, my child. Live."

Now our vessel's soul roars, and she struggles against us, willing us out of her mind.

We fold our wings around ourselves and plummet. As we fall, we see snatches of another army arrayed in blue and gold charging into the sea of red, magic swirling about their bodies like fireflies in a darkened night.

As the wind rushes against our ears and the sky floods our skin with brief, cool kisses, we remember, for a brief moment, the taste of human life, the joy of freedom.

We know then that if we stab our fingers into this vessel's chest, rip out this beating heart, our vessel will die, and we will never taste life like this again.

So we close our eyes, curl our wings around ourselves one last time, and fall.

"Dèmi!" Jonas's voice bursts into my consciousness. "Hang on!"

I open my eyes. I am speeding toward the ground, mere seconds from slamming into the earth, shattering in her embrace. I reach for my magic, anything to save myself, but nothing sparks.

The world is a wash of light and sound, a patchwork of color stitching into the devouring gray that awaits me.

Drawing my legs in, I try to ball myself tight, keep my bones from splintering. Then a gust of wind rips into me like a hook, seizing my body in midair. I hang upside down but I can still make out a grinning Jonas as he stares up at me, his outstretched hand lit up with my magic.

"All that practice and failure came in handy," he says breathlessly. He crooks a finger and the wind twists around me until I stumble into a landing on the stage. Then he launches at me, pulling me into a tight embrace as I shake, not quite sure of what just happened.

"Thank you," I whisper, burrowing my face into the warmth of his neck. It feels good to rely on someone like this—to trust.

Colin's mouth tugs up in a half grin as he struggles to a seated position. "I guess your fool of a mate is good for something."

Jonas returns Colin's grin good-naturedly, and for the barest of moments I can imagine what it would be like if these two had grown up together, if they'd had a chance at least to be friends.

Then Colin's eyes lock with mine. We hold each other's gaze, and even without the ghost of a smile tugging at Colin's lips, I know that he is thinking, just as I am, of how grateful we are to be alive, to have each other.

"We survived," he says finally.

I give him a shaky smile. "We live."

Jonas shifts, leaning back so he can support more of my weight, and I slip forward, flopping onto his chest. I flush. I didn't realize how much I had been leaning on him for support.

"Sorry, sorry," he apologizes.

But the moment is lost. Colin breaks away first, ratcheting to his feet. "The fight's not over. We should help the kunkun, get people to safety."

"Where is Ekwensi?" I ask, scouring the city square.

"I don't know," Colin answers. "The K'inu possession made it impossible to stay fully conscious."

I frown. There's no way Ekwensi would leave in the midst of all this, especially after what it took to bring us here. Something is wrong. Nearby, members of the kunkun begin to rouse, holding their heads as though they have woken from a bad dream.

Beyond the stage, Mari's army is locked in battle with the Oluso clad in blue and gold. General Tenjun is in their midst, using a magically crafted staff to knock three soldiers back at once. Some Igbagbo Oluso behind him slam their assailants with their bare fists, sending electric currents through their bodies. The Ashkenayi army keeps applying brute force and keeps being rebuffed. It is like watching puppets without a puppet master, marionettes who can't seem to do anything but dangle limply.

Elodie is fighting back-to-back with Mari, keeping another woman at bay with her blade. To my surprise, Oyéré is the woman in question, swinging her curved blade with all the ease of a reaper come to harvest as Elodie struggles to fend her off. Oyéré's eyes remain locked only on Mari.

Perhaps Ta'atia's sacrifice was not forgotten after all.

Catching sight of me, a few soldiers rush toward us, but vines sprout from the cobblestones and snake around their ankles and waists, dragging them to the ground. Two wooden posts in the square twist into human shapes, flowers and feathers streaming from the long curls adorning sleek, chiseled faces. It's Adé and Obi, Chi Chi's tree-spirit parents.

I smile for the first time in days. Leave it to tree spirits to accompany their child to a war as though it is nothing more than an afternoon's excursion.

The tides are turning in our favor—but only for a moment.

A helmeted commander manning the city walls puts a horn to his lips, blowing out a call. More soldiers pour through the city gates, flocking toward us like vultures setting upon the carcass of a great beast.

Mari lifts her blade and screams, "To me, my soldiers! Your master is here." She is still bleeding from the wound Jonas opened in her arm, but she hacks at the Oluso soldier to her right. It is only the soldier's quick summoning of an ice shield that saves their neck.

"She's going to get away," I say, surging to my feet. I stop, wincing. Everything hurts. My muscles are too tight and my skin too brittle, chafing against the rough cloth clinging to it. My magic is a dull hum under my skin. With all the days of fighting and the K'inu possession just now, I am no better than a husk, a hollowed shell with all its treasure ripped out. I can't fight, not in this state.

"I don't think so," Colin says, appearing at my side. I'm not sure if the words are a caution or a reflection on what happens next.

Oyéré breaks through Elodie's defenses then, backhanding the younger woman across the face with the flat of her blade. Elodie goes flying, slamming into a wall of new soldiers. Oyéré charges Mari, ramming her blade into Mari's side.

Mari grunts, then she smashes her forehead into Oyéré's. The warlord staggers back, and in that moment, Mari snatches at a running child, a wailing girl no older than five.

"Stay back," Mari sputters, flecks of blood and spit flying everywhere. "Stay where you are or I'll cut her throat."

"That is Ilona's daughter!" Elodie yells, scrambling to her feet. "She is a noble child. One of us. You cannot harm her."

Mari smiles, revealing bloodstained teeth. "I told you, dear niece. No one is untouchable. You have to be prepared to kill anyone standing in your way."

The Oluso near her back away, giving her a wide berth.

"No!" I shout. "Don't let her get away with this."

But the Oluso ignore me, looking to Tenjun instead for answers.

"That's right, shove off," Mari rasps. "Before I carve your names into this girl's flesh." She edges back, one arm hooked around the girl's waist as the child continues to kick and scream, trying not to trip over the bodies and debris littering the ground like common pebbles.

"I'll stop her," Jonas says, silver-blue flame flashing at his fingertips. An iron spear half buried in one of the bodies begins to rattle as Mari passes by.

"Sure you won't hit the girl?" I ask.

"I'll try."

General Tenjun raises his fist. "Now, Haroun."

Darkness falls over the city square, a creeping darkness of shadows lengthening and growing until they form a monstrous forest, dark branches cutting off the light.

All the soldiers cease fighting, their bodies frozen as though encased in ice; even Tenjun is a resolute statue. Mari is trapped mid-jerk, her eyes moving frantically from side to side like a flag in surrender. The girl she kidnapped is suspended in midair like an acrobat, arms splayed in opposite directions.

My body is frozen too, but I catch a shape from the corner of my eye—Haroun standing on the ruins of a nearby platform, his arms and legs burning with red-gold shadow magic. He shifts, kicking a foot out and spinning. A number of the soldiers in the square mimic his movements like jerky marionettes. There are thousands of bodies in this square, all prey to Haroun's power. He has mastered it after all.

He snaps his fingers and certain parts of the landscape come to life once more. The chill in my muscles recedes and I start to move, amazed at how light my body feels.

Then my back burns and a crippling pain engulfs my chest, so immediate and crushing I can hardly scream. I look down in disbelief, searching for the knife in my chest. Instead, I find fingers erupting from my skin like thorns, curled around my frantically beating heart.

"Got you, Little Bird," Ekwensi whispers against my ear. "Thank you for your sacrifice."

TITHE

"You."

I barely choke out the word. Blood rushes against my tongue and teeth, filling my mouth with the sharp and bitter taste of iron.

"Me," Ekwensi answers.

"Why?" Jonas gasps. He's on his knees, hand clutching his chest. He can feel this too; my lungs as they shudder, begging for air; the pain splitting my bones, searing into my very flesh; the frantic, swallow-like beats of my dying heart.

"I need the power of resurrection. There is no other way," Ekwensi says. The skin on his forehead sags as he frowns, turning him ancient, something more than the power-hungry villain ripping out my heart.

"You bastard!" Colin screams, charging us. But Ekwensi snaps his fingers and the rings on Colin's wrists pulse. He falls to his knees, screaming in agony.

"I'm sorry," Ekwensi whispers. He tightens his grasp on my heart.

The air around us rips like a torn seam. Ekwensi yanks his hand from my chest and jumps into the chasm that opened.

I struggle to my knees as air rushes back into my lungs. My heart clenches like a fist, sending another wave of piercing pain through my bones. I cough, blood spraying from my lips. I'm dying.

The world moves as though in slow motion. Tenjun is turning toward me now, catching on to the situation. High above, a gwylfin descends, streaking for me like a shooting star, mouth wide in an open scream. But the world is going quiet, nothing in my ears save a small ringing sound.

"Get her through here!"

The voice breaks through the silence. My vision is blurring, but I rock back on my heels, staring up at what looks like a cracked reflection of my brother's face.

Délé stares at me from the portal Ekwensi created. "Come on!" he shouts, his eyes wide with fear. "You have to come through if you don't want to die."

"I thought . . ." I pause, coughing up more blood, ". . . you wanted me . . . dead . . . so you . . . live . . ."

My brother drags a hand across his eye, and I swear if not for my blurry vision I would have thought he was crying. "I tampered with your mirror so you'd give up hope," he admits. "But you didn't. You can't die yet. You have to free the K'inu. You can. I saw it just now. Quick, before Ekwensi uses them further."

He pushes his hand through the portal, and his fingers crumble into dust as they push into the Physical Realm. The dust from his fingers flutters out, spreading over Jonas and Colin like dandelion seeds. They ratchet to their feet, suddenly restored.

Jonas darts for me, scooping me to his chest. "You can't die, oko mi, I won't let you," he sobs.

"Get her through the portal!" Colin yells, shoving at his back.

We tumble into the portal, falling into a darkness that seems to stretch out forever. I close my eyes as we plummet, sinking into the feeling of my body racing through the air. There is no wind here, no sun, no light, just emptiness and sorrow—regret.

Open your eyes.

The command is a whisper in my mind, but the voice seems to come from within and through me. I flick my eyes open.

We stand in the room where the Spirits lounged, facing the door to Ìyá-Ilé's. My father waits before those gates, a spear in his hand. He takes one look at me and turns away, his face twisting into a murderous rage. His dreads spread out, dancing in the air like snakes, golden threads of magic crackling over his skin in sharp currents.

"Open this door!" he screams at Iya's gates. "Give me that coward."

The voice that spoke to me reverberates through the entire room, as loud and piercing as a warning bell.

I alone decide who to welcome. I alone hold judgment.

My father stabs his spear at the door, then takes to beating it with his fists. "You cannot do this!" he shouts, each word accompanying a new blow. "He hunted my children for his gain. Let me deal with him at least."

Iya's voice is warm yet unsympathetic. *You may not enter. The mercy I have shown you is enough. Now, bring me my child.*

My father slams his fist against the door, then he lays his head against it, his back shaking as he sobs.

"Baba, you have to let her go," Délé says. His skin is fading, growing translucent.

"What is happening?" I choke out.

"I broke the rules, went to Physical Realm. My essence is fading," my brother answers, mouth set in a grim line.

"No!" I cry.

"Forget about me. I'll be reborn." My brother turns to Jonas. "You must take my sister through Iya's gates. Iya has called her for a final test."

"A test?" Colin sputters. "I thought you were going to save her!"

"This is saving her. Iya waits on the other side of those doors."

I shudder despite the warmth suddenly flooding my skin. I'm not sure whether to smile or scream. It seems ridiculous. I am dying, and yet Iya awaits me behind these doors for a test. Leave it to the Spirits to choose their own time to do anything at all.

"I will go," I croak, tugging at Jonas's collar. His sky-colored eyes are darker now, fear-stricken.

"What if it doesn't work?" he says, shaking his head. "I can't lose you."

"You will lose her if you don't get going," my brother says. He nudges our father, pressing him lightly on the shoulder. "Baba, move away from the door."

Osèzèlé looks as though he wants to protest, then he takes one final look at me and nods. "He's right. You have to face this."

"Then I'm going with her," Colin declares. "Surely, Iya wouldn't expect a gravely injured woman to complete a spirit test on her own, would she?"

He offers this statement to the room, shouting so his voice carries through the arches.

"I'm going too," Jonas adds. "It's my right as her mate."

So be it, Iya answers.

The gates fly open in a burst like vulture wings as they embrace the sky. Beyond them is Ìyá-Ilé, the Mother Tree, but her branches are now completely bare, save for the golden stars that swell from their ends like rotting fruit. There are darker shapes still, clinging to her robust body, elongated circles that crawl up her bark like boils sprouting from infected skin.

Jonas carries me over the threshold, Colin falling into step beside him. As we pass through, the pain seeps out of my body like smoke winding from flame. I suck in a breath, relish the feeling of my lungs filling with air. Then Jonas moves us closer to Ìyá-Ilé and I come face-to-face with one of the bulging shapes protruding from her bark. There are sturdy teeth tucked under chapped, cracked lips, and glassy eyes like colored marbles, the horror in them perpetually on display. They're people. I stop breathing.

The doors slam shut behind us.

Under Iya's leaves is a stone altar, raised to about my waist height. On it, Malala lies still, eyes closed and arms folded. Her chest rises and falls steadily, her chubby cheeks growing as she smiles while dreaming. Ekwensi kneels beside her, a knife in his hands. Olorun is nowhere to be found.

Welcome, my children, Iya says. Her voice is a whispering caress, a fluttering thing that tickles my skin.

I have called you for a simple test. A tithe.

Her branches stir, shaking as though in a thick breeze, and one of the star fruits falls to the ground, splitting upon the earth. Ekwensi dashes for it, but the dirt opens like a mouth and swallows the remains of the fruit. His fingers clutch at nothing.

I told you, Tobias, to gain what you seek, you must give me what is most precious to you.

Ekwensi sags, hunching by Malala once more.

I tighten my fingers on Jonas's shoulder as I take in the scene before me. "You want him to kill his child."

He must pay the price for the power he seeks! Iya booms. *Why do my children always hunger for what was never theirs? If you seek the power of the spirits, you must live as a spirit does—loyal to nothing but the laws of the Spirit Realm.*

Pushing against Jonas, I begin easing myself down.

"It's not safe," he protests.

"No one can take life in Iya's presence except if she allows it," Colin reassures him.

"I still don't trust him."

"Neither do I," I add, stepping toward Ekwensi.

"I am dying," Ekwensi declares without turning from his vigil. "The K'inu gave me magic, but they fed on my life-force and the life-force of those unborn."

Everything comes together suddenly like puzzle pieces slotting into place. "Those unborn," I mutter, remembering Ayaba's words, Ga Eun's grief. "You mean the lives of the spirits. The forest spirits like the Aziza, other unborn Oluso. That's why our children are dying—you sacrificed them all for power."

Ekwensi looks up at the star fruit dangling out of his reach. "I promised the K'inu new life. One found me, you know, after your father transformed the Oluso in the capital all those years ago. It was a wayward spirit, a K'inu born of an Aje, funnily enough. It promised me freedom, and an end to my pain if I would give myself as its host." He stops, stroking his daughter's face. She stirs slightly but does not wake.

"And you believed it?" Jonas asks, wending closer.

Ekwensi shoots him a menacing glance. "My village was destroyed when your uncle marched his forces into the Oyo region. So many of us dead. My magic began to leave me because I chose to fight back, keep you Eingardians from trying to murder our people."

Jonas lowers his head, cowed. "I'm sorry for that."

Ekwensi gets to his feet now, studying the fruit hanging from Iya's branches. "The K'inu didn't ask anything of me at first. They just gave. Enough magic for me to keep myself from being brutalized the same way my brethren were. They cared for me when I had no one."

"So you became their vessel," Colin says. His lips are set in a wistful smile, as though he understands. "You chained yourself to them, did everything they asked."

Ekwensi nods. "It was the only way. Chaining is a soul bond, much like the power of resurrection. But it's one that requires consistent sacrifice, another soul to carry the weight. I could either serve the K'inu, let them devour me, or fall prey to the purge Alistair Sorenson was waging on the land. I had no choice."

I stand at a loss for words. Even with everything that's happened, I can understand. If I had witnessed my loved ones dying around me, and the only person to reach their hand out to save me was evil incarnate, I would have willingly taken that hand. There really was no choice in that moment, not for Ekwensi. But after that, there were countless moments, a million choices he actually had. Actions that he chose of his own will.

Steeling my jaw, I turn back to him. "You promised them the power of resurrection when it wasn't yours to give."

He swallows. "For years, I had to bide my time and wait. I knew Yetundé had birthed children, that her children might inherit Osèzèlé's power as iron-bloods. I knew they—you—were the key I needed."

"So you approached me first, asked me to kidnap Jonas."

He nods. "I needed to test what magic you had. And I knew that Alistair could not help but seek to possess you. You were the spitting image of the woman he once coveted more than life itself. I needed to draw you out of hiding, force you to choose a side. Show you that you had to fight for yourself."

I sneer, angered that I feel a pang of pity, even respect. "You wanted my power. I was happy in Benin for the first time in my life. I had people who loved me. I was—"

"You weren't living," Colin interrupts, shaking his head. "I was there with you, Dèmi. You weren't happy. Not really. Not while all the Oluso were suffering."

I open my mouth to protest, then I admit it. "Fine. It wasn't enough. But why couldn't he have told me about my power?" I stab a finger at Ekwensi. "Why couldn't he have told me about my father and everything that came before? Why couldn't he have given me a chance to fight for us on my own terms?"

Ekwensi straightens. "People never know what they're willing to do, how far they will go, unless they're forced to act. I even forced you into that cave to see if it would draw the power out of you." He whips out his knife, the action so hasty he nicks his fingers and draws blood. He does not even flinch. "You mean to tell me you would have been ready to wage war, to spill blood, to save your people?"

"I would have liked to be given the choice!" I yell. I yank open my ripped blouse, showing off the scarred flesh where Ekwensi's fingers tore out my heart. "It didn't have to come to this."

He smiles, a wry, halfhearted thing. "And what have you done with that choice so far? The Oluso are still at the mercy of the Ajes in the capital. How have you saved them?"

"I've fought beside them. I intend to keep fighting."

"That's not enough!"

Ekwensi leaps at me gripping my shoulders so tightly I flinch. "Use your power. Restore the Oluso bloodlines. Change the tides of this war."

"And who pays the sacrifice?" I ask, studying his frantic gaze. "Whose souls are given in exchange to awaken our dormant brethren?"

Jonas shoves Ekwensi away from me. "All you're asking for is more bloodshed, Ekwensi. The new Oluso won't know how to control their powers. They would hurt friend and foe."

Ekwensi staggers toward Colin, pleading. "You must see the wisdom in my words. Without numbers, we will fall. The Ajes will never tire of killing us. If I could control her power, I would be able to free us once and for all. We could rule the way we were born to. We could be the benevolence this land needs."

Colin frowns, looking away from his former mentor, the man who once treated him like the son he never got to be. Our gazes meet, and although his steady gaze tells me he's with me, I see the anguish in his eyes, the way his body is still turned toward Ekwensi. He's considering those words, turning them over like a well-worn lucky coin.

"Bringing the K'inu back won't save us," I say in as soft a voice as I can manage. "They possessed the chained Oluso the first chance they got. They're just as angry at us as they are at the Ajes."

"All they want is to live!" Ekwensi screams, whirling on me. "We robbed them of their lives in the first place. Our foolish forebears stamped out the Fèni-Ogun out of fear."

"I am still living!" I scream back. "I am their direct descendant and yet you sought to kill me!"

He drags a hand over his face, clawing at his skin. "It is the only way," he mutters, as though we are not there at all. "I am doing what is right. Losing a few of our own is only fair. We need their power. With the power of resurrection, I could restore our bloodlines, make more Oluso, change our fate altogether. We could finally fight back in bigger numbers. We could win."

I inhale, steel myself. "Sacrifice her then," I say, nodding at Malala's sleeping form. "Rip out your daughter's heart like you did mine."

Pulling my bone blade from my belt, I thrust it at him. "Finish it. End our suffering here. If this power will give you everything you seek, do what Iya asked of you."

He stares, incredulous. His lips tremble as he tries to speak. I step closer, shoving the blade hilt at him. "Come!" I shout, filling my words with every bit of the rage that has burned inside of me for so long. "Kill her. Just like you would have killed me."

Ekwensi's gaze travels between his daughter's face and mine. Then he backs slowly away, shoulders bowing in. "I can't do it," he says. He looks at me, eyes filled with unshed tears, and suddenly he seems so young, a boy horrified by the first sight of blood in war.

"I can't hurt her," he whispers finally. He bends, leaning his cheek against Malala's. "I'm sorry, dear one. I'm sorry."

As he speaks, his skin begins to dissolve like seafoam melting on the wind. I stagger into Jonas's firm embrace. Ekwensi's mouth melts into nothing, but his eyes remain open, his voice carrying onto a wind that races through the courtyard.

"All I wanted was for us to be free," he mutters. "When . . . will we ever . . . be free?"

Then he is gone, his cloak the only remainder hanging over Malala's sleeping form. In a moment, she too fades away, leaving nothing but a shower of sparks where she once lay.

My child has fallen, consumed by those he gave his life to, Iya thunders.

I turn to her, regard those glowing star fruits waving in the wind.

"I thought you were a benevolent spirit!" I shout. "You could have freed him! Instead, you made a test of him killing his child. What kind of Mother Spirit are you?"

Jonas puts a hand on my arm, but I shake him off. Colin's eyes have darkened, and he stands apart, staring at the place where Ekwensi disintegrated.

There is still so much rage inside of me, howling like a windstorm that will never cease, more now that Ekwensi is simply gone. With every breath I take, the sadness and never-ending grief of the K'inu also fills my body. For so long, I have done the will of the Spirits, kept myself from violence because I believed that they saw our suffering. But now Iya has called me here for a test while my loved ones are dying below. Now the only man who was brave enough to do more than cower and survive is nothing but ashes and wind. Now I am tired of hope itself. I want more than answers.

Iya answers me all the same, her voice as sweet as a mother singing a lullaby. *I can do many things, but I do not rule my children in absolute. If I did, I would have no children, only creations to live within the confines I give them.*

"So you turn a blind eye while people suffer?" I challenge. "You leave them to their fate?"

The wind rustles through the trees. Ìyá-Ilé is sighing.

With every child, every soul I have nurtured, I have always let them be ruled by their own will. Look at the children trapped in my bark—I do not even suffer them the rewards of their deeds. I gave my children spirits to guide them, and guardians to protect them from the harsh nature of the world herself. Am I to blame if my children kill their spirits out of fear and burn their guardians to dust?

I laugh, letting out the bubble of frustration and rage trapped in my chest. Jonas reaches for me again. "Oko mi," he says softly.

But I keep laughing until tears are running from my eyes and all I want is to slam my fist into Iya's bark over and over again. She is right. There is no one else to blame for everything we have suffered. The struggle we face is a never-ending cycle of will and pride and chaos. Once, one struck another down in a quest for domination. So the first Aje was born, spirit broken. Then again, the Olusos' fear of the Fèni-Ogun led to the destruction that birthed the K'inu. All my life, all I have known is the fear of the Ajes who seek to eradicate us. And when we're all gone? I'm certain there will be someone else made a scapegoat, someone hunted within an inch of their lives, all to sate human pride and ill-begotten fear. The blood that soaks the earth, choking the seeds before they can blossom into flowers, will never run dry.

Then Afèni's words come back to me, blanketing my ears like a warm cloak in winter: *The moon reflects the shine of the stars and the dying sun. She maintains balance.*

I cease. I know what I must do.

Whipping myself upright, I rush toward the empty altar, knocking past both Jonas and Colin.

"Tell me," I call up at Iya's branches. "What is my test?"

Her voice coats the air like a frosty wind: *For the power you seek, you must give up what you fear to lose the most. Your life is my ransom for this debt.*

"You can't be serious," Colin barks at the same time as Jonas shouts, "No!"

But I need power more than anything right now, more than my own life.

I call out to Iya, "My life will be enough for what I wish?"

Pay the price, and you will have all that you seek.

Jonas seizes me, cupping my face in his hands. He glares, dawn eyes sparking like treacherous black ice. "Don't you dare do this," he growls. "Don't you dare make this decision for both of us. Again."

I reach up to touch his cheek, relish the softness that greets my fingers. "It's the only way."

He shakes his head. "No, it's not. We haven't even sorted through our options."

"We could offer something else," Colin argues, appearing behind him. "Like we did with Olokun. Give Iya each a portion of our lives."

I smile at him, not bothering to hold back the tears welling in my eyes. "You know that won't be enough."

He drags a hand through his hair, then he slams his boot against the dirt, driving up a shower of dust. "You want to die? Fine. What then? How will that fix anything? How are you sure the spirits will even uphold their end of the bargain?"

Careful, Iya warns. *I honored your wish by allowing you in here. Don't make me regret my choice.*

Jonas closes his eyes, opens them, clearly wishing all this away. "What is this about?" he pleads. "Explain to me why I should let you die."

"We will never be free while the Ajes refuse to see us as people. The Ajes will never see us that way because they need us. Without us, there is no them. There is no hierarchy, no free labor, no bodies at the bottom for them to use as pillars. They can only be everything good and right if we are evil things to be vanquished." I pause, a rueful smile stealing onto my lips. "After all, every hero needs a monster."

Colin sinks to his knees, gripping the hem of my cloak. "Dèmi, please, please let's get out of here. Anything but this."

I pull away, stepping back from both of them. "It has to be this way." Lifting my hands, I face Iya. "I am ready."

Jonas dives for me, but Iya's roots shoot up just then, curling around him like vines overtaking a wall. When he reaches for his sword, another root ensnares the hilt, flinging it away. Colin doesn't even make it to standing before Iya's roots wrap around his waist and bind his wrists behind his back.

"This isn't fair!" he screams. "You can't force her to do this!"

A tangle of roots emerge in answer, twisting and locking together until they form a small raised pillar.

Dropping my cloak, I stride to the platform.

Now is the time, my child, Iya whispers in my ear. *The power you seek is only as strong as the worth of your sacrifice.*

I step onto the pillar and the roots grow over my legs, cementing me in place. The boils on Iya's bark begin to glow with golden light, and a few of them recede, folding neatly into rich bark. Three more star fruits unfurl on Iya's branches, shimmering like stardust. I see things as I hadn't before. The trapped people are not kept perpetually in anguish, cursed never to live again. They are seeds, given new life though their former lives were mired in darkness.

Jonas's voice is like an explosion in my mind: *Don't do this, oko mi. There has to be another way.*

I'm sorry. I mouth the words as I take one last look at him and turn away.

One of the star fruits drops off the tree, shattering as it crashes into the dirt. But instead of the ground opening to receive it, each jagged piece of fruit glows brightly, like scattered sunlight lacing through tree branches. Then a piece transforms into a hand as rich and earthy as the soil beneath it. Another piece follows suit. Yet another melts into a heart-shaped face that makes my heart seize in my chest.

"Mummy," I cry.

The pieces of my mother come together, swimming into existence like a tapestry unfolding until she is standing just a few feet away, her hands gripping a bow with its arrow trained on my chest.

Behind me, there are anguished cries, screams that threaten to overwhelm my ears, Jonas and Colin begging me to turn back. But all I see is the woman in front of me.

"Mummy," I call again, choking back tears. Her gaze is warm, loving as she considers me. I smile, wondering how I could have forgotten the majesty of that face, the focused intensity that could only be my mother's.

"My dear darling," my mother says, her voice as airy as the wind kissing my skin, warming me with its touch. "It is time to come home. Lay your burden down and rest."

I exhale, fury truly extinguished now. My mother is right. It's time to let go and fall. If nothing else, I must thank Iya for this, for granting me the wish I've longed after for eleven desperate years.

Lowering my head, I wait. My magic stirs like a gwylfin hastily awakened, restless and ready for action. It roars up, burning my skin, urging me to fight, but I stand as still as I can manage.

"Look at me, my darling," Mummy's voice calls. "Chin up like a warrior. The ancestors await you."

I obey, locking eyes with her just as she lets the arrow fly. The silvered blur races toward me, promising a speedy death. But just as it reaches me, I close my eyes and grab onto the ring gracing my neck—Jonas's ring. For one moment, I hold on to the life we might have had, the love, the joy and hope—the future. Then, letting my hand fall, I surrender, wishing with all my heart for the power to wield my resurrection magic as I wish.

Then the arrow strikes my chest, driving into me with a force so immediate, I cannot breathe. I slump, clutching at my throat as the pain rips air from my lungs. But then my heart leaps, beating with an intensity that shouldn't be possible.

I reach down, feeling for the hole in my chest but touching flesh and scarred skin and Jonas's ring and nothing else.

I open my eyes, dart a look up. Jonas stands before me, grasping at the iron arrow impaling him. Blood drips from his pale mouth, but his eyes are twinkling with warmth.

"I love you," he whispers.

BINDING

"No!"

I erupt, reaching for him, straining against the vines trapping my feet. They disintegrate into dust right as Jonas collapses. I catch him, easing his torso against mine, careful not to disturb the arrow protruding from his chest. Colin, freed from his bonds, catches up to me and helps me ease him down.

"Why?" I cry, wiping the blood from Jonas's lips, pushing the hair out of his face so I can place my fingers on the pulse at the base of his neck.

"Couldn't . . ." he starts, breathing in short, hungered gasps, ". . . couldn't let . . . you die . . ."

I lay his head against my lap, pull his fingers away from the arrow. "I won't let *you* die," I sob. "Please, no."

"This way . . . you're free . . ." he mutters, smiling at me. His eyes are still shining, dawn eyes so bright I swear they hold the sky itself. But the golden flecks, the bursts of daylight framing his irises are darkening, fading as he struggles to keep his eyes open.

"Stay with me, Jonas, please," I beg. I gesture frantically to Colin. "Help me!"

He kneels by my side. Then, bracing our hands against the dirt, we yank the arrow out of Jonas's chest. He howls as we pull it through, muscles stiffening as his body rises with the arrow. Then it's out, and I lay my fingers against his chest, tugging frantically at my magic.

"Don't," he whispers, ". . . I will . . . take too much . . ."

"I don't care!" I scream, drawing magic into my fingertips. White flames erupt on his skin, engulfing him like a funeral pyre, but the wound remains a muddy crimson crater in his chest, weeping blood like rain.

"The world needs you . . . let me . . . go . . . oko mi," he whispers.

"I can't," I weep, choking back a sob. Colin just watches, stricken.

The magic is draining out of me fast, but I don't care. It doesn't matter what it costs to heal an iron-blood. Jonas is my mate, the man I love, the man I chose when I could just, for once in my life, choose just for me. The man who chose me, gave up everything to save me, just as I have saved others for so long. I can't let him die.

"Mummy, save him!" I shout, looking around for the ghost of my mother. But she is gone yet again, the fragmented shards of fruit on the ground the only sign she was ever there.

"Iya!" I yell, anger surging. "This isn't what we agreed to. Save him. Take me."

Iya's answer is as relaxed as before. *Well done. The life of a mate is as your own. This is a worthy sacrifice.*

"I don't care to make a sacrifice," I blubber, tears choking my voice. "This isn't what I chose. Just bring him back to me."

The power of resurrection is in your hands. You may do with it as you see fit—so long as you pay the price.

I want to scream, but I have no strength left for that. To keep Jonas's soul from leaving, I need a soul sacrifice, and I have nothing left to give but my own. To think that I was so willing to die a moment ago, for the power to end this war on my own, but now I am faced with the reality that Jonas will die alone while I descend to end the war, and the thought itself is unbearable.

He stirs, eyelids fluttering closed, inhaling a shallow breath. His skin is chilled despite the magical heat I'm pouring into him. He's dying. And I can't stop it. Not if I want freedom for the Oluso. To win this war, I have to give up my heart. I have no choice.

"Please," I beg, knowing that every moment is pulling him farther from me, that the spirits will not relent. Everything comes with a price, I have always known this. But I can't bring myself to let go of Jonas.

Colin threads his arms around my back and folds his fingers over mine, his skin alight with a blue aura. "I promised I'd never make you cry," he says, mouth tucked in a half smile.

Too late I realize what this means.

"Colin, no—" I yell, trying to knock him away, but he leans forward, pushing his weight over me and Jonas. The aura bathing his skin shifts like sand in a hourglass, pouring over Jonas in a flood.

The skin under my fingers grows warmer. Jonas bolts upright, sucking in air as Colin slumps back against me, his bronzed skin colder than ice. Jonas looks to me, incredulous, but I am already turning, folding Colin gently onto the ground.

His aura is gone, his soul essence transferred, given away to keep Jonas alive. Only a little spark remains in those earth-and-gold eyes, a whisper of a flame.

"Why?" I whisper, leaning down, pressing my cheek against his. "Why couldn't you leave it alone?"

He inhales shakily, then mutters, ". . . told you I'd make you happier than he ever could." He breaks off, coughing weakly, and my heart wrenches tight, the tears in me welling to an overflow.

Jonas crouches close, gripping Colin's free hand. "Thank you," he says, words spilling out in a breathless huff.

Colin blinks slowly up at Jonas, fading faster now. " . . . Don't leave her alone. She hides her tears when she's alone."

I cry now, salt tears dripping onto Colin's face, mixing with the rich scent of dew and spring that still clings to his skin.

"This is enough, right?" he gasps, forcing trembling words out like punches into the air. "You'll honor this sacrifice, won't you, Iya?"

Iya's voice sweeps over us like a crashing wave: *A sacrifice of the heart willingly given is a sacrifice honored.*

Colin's lips twitch in the ghost of a smirk. "It'd better be," he mutters. "No more wiliness from you spirits."

My mind is racing, thoughts spinning and colliding like shooting stars at a loss for their destination. "We won't let you go like this," I say, brushing my fingers against his forehead, tracing the scar on his brow, an injury he got protecting me when we were no bigger than mischievous children who had only seen twelve name days. "I'll find a way to come back for you, resurrect you. I promise—"

"Don't," he says, a tear running down his cheek. "I'm tired . . . of fighting . . ."

A ghostly figure wisps out of the air, a tall woman with long, thick braids and an intricate spiral tattoo weaving around her left eye like a sea serpent. I gasp. Her sun-loved skin is now a pale gray, not unlike the apparitions we glimpsed in the mirror city, but it's clear, even without examining the maze of tattoos spread over her skin, honors granted to a Berréan chieftain, who she is.

Colin sighs, the sound akin to a shudder. "You've finally come . . . here to see your wayward son off as he dies . . ."

The spirit of Éyani Al Hia watches, eyes tight with sorrow, mouth curled in a wordless cry.

"It's okay, Mother," Colin tuts. "I lived well."

He turns from her, pressing a hand against my wet cheek, holding on with all the strength he has left. "Come visit me every now and then . . . it might get lonely . . . even with Mother . . . and the spirits lack a sense of humor . . ."

The time has come, Iya thunders. *I can hold you here no longer. You must go. Save my children below. All of them.*

The clouds overhead rush in all at once, the sky flashing into a darkened abyss. There is a flash as lightning strikes the ground just an arm's distance from us, leaving a pit that everything begins to sink into.

"Dèmi," Jonas warns, reaching for me. But I can't move, can't leave Colin alone in this place.

The star fruits begin to fall as the winds pick up speed, cutting through the air with the fury of a hurricane.

"Dèmi," Jonas calls again, pulling me up.

I shake my head, muttering now, "I can't—we can't—"

"Finish it," Colin whispers. "Make this worth it. Go." His eyes flutter closed.

"No!" I jerk toward him again, but Jonas drags me away.

"We have to go. Now."

Lightning splits the sky again, this time near our feet. The ground yawns, a chasm opening like a hungry mouth, waiting to devour us. Iya's swaying branches fall, cracking under the strain of the cutting winds. Water rushes up from Iya's roots, raging into a flood. It swells over Colin's body, embracing him like a lover.

Darting forward, I try to hold on to him, keep his body from being buried under the waves, but when my fingers touch his skin, his body turns to water, and my fingers pass through. The ground beneath my feet gives way.

Before the ground rushes away from us and the sky disappears, I look back. Colin stands not far off, his aura now silvered and ghostly, his arm thrown around Éyani's shoulders. She looks proudly down at him, and for once, he is smiling, beaming like there's no tomorrow.

Jonas wraps his arms around me as we tumble into the abyss.

TIES

WE FALL FOR WHAT FEELS LIKE AN IMPOSSIBLE AMOUNT OF TIME, EYES smarting as the wind bats us through the air. Then we tumble through the seam Délé opened up and find ourselves standing on the platform in the city once more. The battlefield is as we left it.

Haroun still stands on the pillar, straining to control the shadows of those before him.

Tenjun spots us immediately. "What happened?" he cries, rushing forward.

"We were in the Spirit Realm," Jonas explains.

"And? Did they offer any help?"

Jonas looks to me, and I nod. "I know how to end this war."

Anozie touches down then, the mother gwylfin's tail slicing through a frozen battalion of soldiers, knocking them over. Baba leaps from her back, running to me. He envelops me in a hug just as I blurt, "We don't have much time. I need to conduct a ritual to set things right before Haroun loses control."

He pulls away, nodding. "Where's Colin?"

"He's dead."

I turn away before he can see me cry. I can't mourn, not until I see this through.

Calling on the wind spirits, I rise into the air, aiming for Haroun. He startles when I appear next to him. Blood drips from his nostrils as the strain of using so much magic eats at him.

"Release them all!" I shout over the force of the wind billowing about me.

His brows draw together in a frown. "They will kill us once I do."

"Release them, trust me."

Whirling around, I look out at the entire city. There are so many people here, so much life lived in the confines of this space. I close my eyes, imagining a vine growing from a sprout, that sprout twisting into a tree. My magic flares, heat flooding into my skin as my heart roars into a gallop. The power of resurrection sits in my gut like a honey blossom ripe for picking. I reach for it, let it explode through me, fill me until I am burning alive. It is time.

Flinging my eyes open, I peer at the people below. I'm not so far up that I can't see, yet every person seems scarcely more than miniature figures, brushstrokes in an elaborate portrait. But I can now perceive the threads between them, the invisible wisping strings that twine around their hearts.

Reaching my hands out, I feel for those strings, calling them to me, then I encourage them to grow, to spread and twist until the land is covered and every heart bound up to the same coil of thread—Oluso lives, Aje lives, I hold them all. The life of the land itself, its rocks, streams, forests, creatures and guardian spirits, I gather last, cupping them in my palm. Then I open my mouth and the golden flames of resurrection burst out of me, catching on those threads, devouring each one.

The people below come alive. They stagger out of their frozen states, clutching at their chests. Those possessed by the K'inu fall to their knees as the K'inu spirits leave their bodies in bursts, burning K'inu teeth exploding out of them like comets. The teeth disintegrate, their violet color fading to the smooth gray of an ancestral spirit, and the now-gray orbs flare before disappearing. The rings on my wrists follow suit, and the voices in my head recede like distant screams drowned out by a storm. The K'inu have finally found peace. They can be reborn.

I look at the people below—my people. When I speak, my voice echoes across the land, spreading into every corner like rain soaking the earth. "People of Ifé, I have come, as a messenger of the Great Spirits, as an appointed ruler of this land, to give you the freedom you so desperately seek. From this moment forward your lives will bear out the weight of your actions. You will live, not as spirit-bound and spirit-broken, but as one people, bound for all the ages."

The people respond in myriad ways; soldiers reaching for their bows, working in arrows to shoot me down; townsfolk arguing about who I am or what I mean; others cowering, bowing as though to appease a rageful deity.

As the arrows fly toward me, the gwylfins take to the sky, blowing a haze of frost from their nostrils that paralyzes the arrows. They fall back to earth, shattering like mirrors. The wind spirits whip around me, winking and dancing like fireflies on a hot summer's night, forming a protective ball. The gwylfins join them, circling me like sentries protecting their queen, the fans on their tails spread wide, screeching and roaring in triumph.

"Those who seek destruction," I shout, "will reap destruction! Those who seek goodness will meet only joy and bounty. This is your warning. Your lives are no longer yours alone. The very lands you inhabit will no longer bend to your will. From now on, you learn to live as one, or die."

Then the inferno of magic pouring through me ceases like a flame extinguished, but there is no more pain, no new leaf sprouting on my back. The wind spirits disappear and I fall, speeding toward the earth like a remnant of a dying star. It is done. I—we—are finally free.

Suddenly Jonas is there, plucking me from the sky, holding me tight against the scaled, leathery skin of a gwylfin's back. We drift downward like feathers gracing the night wind.

But the fighting has not ended. Mari is screaming for her soldiers, urging them forward. Her pale face is nearly blue with chill, her raven hair matted with blood and dirt. She nurses her wounded arm, holding it limply against her side while darting nervous eyes around the square, swinging her sword wildly at anyone who dares approach her. The girl she held as hostage is now in Tenjun's arms, secreted under his cloak. Gone is the tyrant who plagued my dreams.

"I will still win," Mari declares as the gwylfin deposits us on the ground. "I have enough soldiers to overwhelm your forces."

"For the sake of your soldiers' lives, I would surrender now," Jonas cautions.

Mari sneers. "You think your little display did anything? My soldiers aren't afraid of a little magic. They've dealt with it all before."

My magic has exhausted me, drained me so deeply I can hardly stand. Still I declare, "The blood you spill will be answered."

She spits, a wad of blood and saliva landing near me. "Before the day is done, I will bathe in your blood."

A young woman appears behind Mari, slamming her staff into Mari's side. It's Sumi, the member of the kunkun who rounded up the Council members. Mari buckles, falling forward. Sumi brings her staff down again. Mari catches herself, rolling out of the way just in time. Sumi pivots, circling her, and Mari scrambles to her feet, mirroring her steps. Oyéré joins the fight, swiping at Mari with her blade, but Mari leaps back in time.

"You traitor!" she shrieks.

"You killed Ta'atia. That was the one thing you were never supposed to do!" Oyéré screams.

Sensing an opening, Sumi charges in, sweeping her staff toward Mari's feet, but Mari is prepared. She drops her sword, catching the staff, and before Sumi can shake her off, she yanks it, drawing Sumi in.

Oyéré stabs at Mari's arm, but Mari pivots on her heel, shoving Sumi ahead of her. Oyéré's blade lances through Sumi's chest.

Someone cries out as Sumi sinks to the ground. I stumble to my feet, realizing the cry came from my lips. But her eyes are already closed, her aura wisping away. She's dead.

Suddenly, the cries grow louder. Several red-clad soldiers collapse, mouths gaping like hooked fish, blood streaming from their mouths and nostrils. The soldiers fighting beside them back away, suddenly afraid. Their fallen brethren lie unmoving, dead.

"I told you," I announce, gathering as much energy into my voice as I can. "The blood you spill will be answered. For every Oluso life you take, Ajes will pay the price." I nod at the fallen soldiers—there are at least a hundred of them.

Danou whistles. "Then we've won. They can't kill us."

The soldiers, hearing my words, abandon their weapons and break for the city gates.

"What did you do?" Mari shrieks, staggering back. "What did you do to us?"

Oyéré whips out a small dagger. "I don't care if I die for this," she says.

"Wait!" I yell. "The binding is reciprocal. For every Aje life you take, an Oluso will pay the price."

Danou stiffens. "What?"

"It was the only way. The spirits wanted the bloodshed to end. The only way for us to have peace is if our lives are treated as equally precious. There is no other way."

"There are fewer of us than them," he growls. "They've been killing us all this time and you bound our fates to theirs?"

Jonas tightens a protective arm around me, and I lay my fingers on his arm, grateful. "There is a balance. There is no way to know what the spirits will decide, but now they can no longer just kill us. Killing one of us might mean they lose a thousand. Husbands, wives, children, grandchildren—there will be a sacrifice each time and no way to control it. Unless we all stop killing each other."

Oyéré rams her elbow into Mari's throat, knocking her down. "I just want her to know pain," she says, punctuating each word with a kick to Mari's ribs.

"This is the peace you brokered for us?" Danou asks.

Drawing in a breath, I lift my head high. "This is the only peace we could have. You forget, the K'inu were born of spirits we all maligned. They needed peace too. And the only peace is a world where we no longer fail to see each other. Now your life is as worthy as an Aje's and so is mine. No one can deny that. Now we have to learn to live with each other."

He looks as though he wants to say more, then he sighs, shoulders drooping. "All right."

"Then what must I do?" Oyéré shouts, turning away from a bloody Mari. "Who will pay the price for everything she's done?"

"What happens if she takes her own life?" Elodie calls out. She stands on the platform, tossing a dagger with her working arm like a gambler's coin, flipping between two faces of the hilt.

I stiffen. Even I don't know the answer to that.

"If she takes her own life, surely the spirits might understand she wants to die," she says. She flings her dagger at Mari. The blade impales a swath of hair fanning out from her face.

"Why would she do that?" Jonas asks, eyes narrowed.

Wheezing, Mari eases herself up. "What's my alternative, sitting around in your dungeons?" She grins, a gruesome smile that stains her lips with blood. "Sorry, but I'd rather take some of you out."

Then she yanks the dagger out and rips it across her throat. She falls, eyes wide open, dead.

The Oluso examine one another with bated breath, but no one falls. They let out a collective sigh of relief.

Elodie shrugs. "It was a theory worth testing." She raises her hand. "If it isn't clear though, I'm surrendering. There are some considerations for those who surrender, are there not? Concessions that mean I won't end up in prison?"

Jonas snorts. "You forget, El, the laws are made by those in power. You no longer have any."

Elodie's smile remains in place. "We'll see about that."

Pain erupts in my head then, and I sink against Jonas as the world swims before my eyes.

"Dèmi," Jonas shouts. "Hey, hang on. Stay with me."

But my body feels like iron, longing for nothing more than to sink into the earth's embrace and lie still. I let my eyes droop closed as the world collapses to dust. It's finally over.

EPILOGUE

Six months later . . .

"Your Highness, this is a matter of the gravest importance," the former Lord Ottamen sniffs. His once-rosy cheeks are now as cracked and weather-beaten as a bruised heel. He's arrayed in a wool vest with a cotton undershirt and soft breeches, a far cry from the ostentatious garments he once favored.

As he speaks again, he stamps his foot, nearly causing himself to stumble. "The newly freed meas—" He catches himself when I raise my eyebrow at the intended insult, and clears his throat. "The newly freed Oluso and the former commoners I once gave patronage as tenants have no rights to my ancestral lands."

"Your ancestral lands?" I quip, leaning closer. The iron-and-wood monstrosity Ayaba fashioned for me as a crown slips over my curls, threatening to spill the magical flowers woven into it onto the floor. I groan and shove it back on my head. Lord Ottamen lets out what sounds like a sigh of relief and I shoot him a glare.

Jonas's lips tremble as he tries not to smile. Instead he crosses his legs and settles against the grasping branches of the wooden nests we use as thrones, also courtesy of a grateful Ayaba. "Heinrik Ottamen, you received those lands from my uncle, did you not?"

The disgraced Council member flushes before answering. "Yes, for services rendered to the Crown."

Jonas nods matter-of-factly, then he gestures to the eleven other people in the room, the new members of our Council. We are a council of thirteen, with one ceremonial seat—mine—and twelve governing seats, three from each region, all appointed by the people of those regions.

"Ottamen, can you explain to the Council what those duties were?" Jonas asks. "I'm certain Danou and Zafira would like to hear how you came to possess Berréan lands, and what your system of patronage looked like for the local people of Manapané."

Danou cracks several kola nuts with his fist, splitting the tough, brown exterior to reveal a meaty, earthy fruit. "I'm very excited to hear about this," he declares, throwing two kola nuts into his mouth at once. "I've heard there are plenty of Berréan half-castes in Eingard, but I never knew we had some in nobility." He pulverizes another five nuts with a slam of his fist and shifts the bowl toward Ottamen. "Care for some? They're fresh from the fields. Manapané still has the best kola."

Ottamen shakes his head frantically. "My—My—Liege," he stammers, "per-perhaps we lay the m-matter to r-r-rest."

Zafira bursts into a bout of laughter, showing off toothless gums. "Maybe he's from an area with no kola, Danou," she says, wiping the tears from her eyes. For once, the scarred eldest member of the kunkun is smiling, and it's a delight to see. After finding them new settlements in more fertile areas of Ismar'yana, the other kunkun are finally learning to smile too.

I beam, recalling Malala's joy when she saw her new home, filled with all the necessities she, Samira, Ga Eun, and Adaeze would ever need. One day, she'll discover the letters her father wrote her, full of his wishes for her future, the little spark of hope he never could quench, and finally Ekwensi's soul will be at peace.

Danou glowers. "Soon you'll tell me this fool has never had yerba."

Mikhail claps him on the back, pushing a teacup his way. "Just drink yours, my friend. Don't worry yourself about deceitful lords; you'll get a headache."

Danou flushes and accepts the cup, stealing glances at the Guard commander over the rising steam.

Katharine takes a small sip of her tea, then passes it to Mikhail, a bright smile warming her ruddy cheeks. "We drink cornflower tea in Aedyn. You might find this a little sweeter than the yerba."

Mikhail sniffs at the tea before taking a sip. "I do like this, thank you."

I laugh, hiding my mirth with a hand. One would think by the way Danou is glaring at her that Katharine is a confident Igbagbo Oluso, capable of drawing others in with her silver tongue rather than an Eingardian Aje who has never left her region. Perhaps all people, Ajes included, have magic of their own.

"You understand that those lands have been redistributed for common use, Sir Ottamen," Baba announces, getting to his feet. His easy smile is nowhere to be found. Today his face is all hard angles and a morose stare. Grief. It hasn't been long, after all, since we lost Colin, Nana, and Will.

The sight sobers me. I plunge my fingers into the rough netting of my seat, stroking the splintered brambles. A particularly sharp end nicks my finger, and I hiss, pulling my hand away.

"I know I can't even live in my own home!" Ottamen cries. "Those spirits keep appearing in my bedroom, keeping me up at night."

"Have you tried changing rooms?" Baba asks. His voice holds a little bit of lightness, just enough to make me believe he might be joking, but his expression is still stern.

Ottamen blusters, "They come to every room of the house I'm in, chasing me around. I get no peace unless I leave the territory."

Hanae tuts, checking on the sleeping Haru curled in her lap. "You know the law, Sir Ottamen." She pauses, and I know she is thinking of Ataya who sacrificed herself for her, of all the others who died to protect her family. "Those spirits are those who lost their lives unjustly on that land. They have as much a right to be there as you do."

The older man stamps his foot again. "But why do they bother me? Why not go for anyone else?"

"You must ask the land if it will bear you," I answer. "Those who plague you only come because their lives are bound to the land, just as we are now all bound to each other. If they're after you, perhaps consider what you did for them to hound you so."

Rising, I take a moment to inhale, let the tension in my head ebb to a dull ache before stepping off the dais. Twelve pairs of eyes lock onto me, each asking the same question, but I wave them away. I've held court for long enough today.

Ottamen sniffs, turning towards Jonas. "Can you do nothing to grant me reprieve, my liege? Please, in the days of King Alistair—"

"I am the queen's consort," Jonas snaps. He sweeps past the man, taking my hand, then he calls over his shoulder. "I would suggest two things. Remember whose court you petition to, and move for your peace of mind. Perhaps there are no mistreated spirits in Eingard who seek vengeance against you."

Then he pulls me out of the room, and into the solar opposite. The palace at T'Lapis is a winding maze of narrow corridors and even narrower stairs, but there are enormous rooms with staggered roofs that hold an intricately crafted window above.

We settle under one of those windows, bathing in the light of the sun, warding off the chill and dry Berréan air.

"I thought this new Council meant I didn't have to attend these things."

Jonas strokes my cheek. "It's going to take a while, oko mi. We've got eleven new Council members from all the regions, and four of them have never worked with let alone been close to an Oluso before."

"Mikhail figured things out easily," I mutter, crossing my arms.

"Mikhail has known us for two years. He's not just any Aje on the street." He brushes a kiss against my forehead. "Give it a season; everything will come together."

He snaps his fingers, and the wind knocks open the window above our heads.

"You've been practicing," I say, lips curling into a smile.

He grins. "My wife is the most fearsome Oluso that ever lived. Grown men tell stories of her prowess. Children tell tales of how she descended from the sky to pass judgment on the people. The Oluso sing of how you undertook great trials, wagered your life, and won."

My smile melts in an instant and I find my fingers going to my ear, finding the earring curved around it. Every time I touch its silvered body, pass my fingers over the wings and the curved blade that dangles from its end, I think of Colin.

Jonas places his head on my shoulder, pressing the twin earring on his ear to mine. We'd agreed to wear them as a pair, in Colin's honor.

"We should go see him," he whispers now, breath tickling my ear.

I steal a glance over his shoulder, looking out to the dusty corridor we emerged from. No one. Then I twine my arms around his waist. "Let's go."

We touch the ends of our paired earrings together again and magic sparks between our bodies, setting us ablaze.

The journey to the Spirit Realm is quick—just a blink and we are in Iya's garden, staring out at a glade.

My mother emerges from underneath one of the dancing willows in the glade, eyes brightening with delight when she catches sight of me. She runs, and I mirror her, laughing as we collide and fall into a heap.

"Welcome back," she whispers, pressing a kiss on my hair. Her lips pass through my hair, but I have a sense of her aura nonetheless. It is not quite the same, interacting with what is left of my mother's spirit, knowing my ancestral line was nearly vanquished and my mother will never quite be able to hold me in her arms again, but that is all right. I still have her.

"I wish I could see you all the time," I say. She beams, rich color flooding her near translucent skin.

"I'm happy you can't. I'm happy you're living well, my dear. That is all I ever wished for you."

My father appears beside her, grabbing her by the waist. "There you are, trying to escape to the Physical Realm without me."

She giggles and swats him away. "I wouldn't dream of it. You'd follow me wherever I went anyway."

Jonas saunters over, a handful of flowers in his fist. He lays the flowers at the edge of the pond in the midst of the glade and closes his eyes, wishing his mother well. Unlike my brother, Délé, who disappeared along with the K'inu, we never found Arianne's spirit walking through the Spirit Realm. But we know that she is somewhere, whether born into a new life or preparing until she can let go of the pain of the last one. He has hope he'll see her again, just as I hope that my brother, wherever he is, can now be happy.

Jonas nods to my parents, and they wave back. Then I go to him, grabbing his hand and squeezing it tight.

We venture further into the glade, to the low rushes where the wind spirits make their nests and the smallest omioja reach up from between reeds to snare unsuspecting spirits and steal a piece of their hair to use for flower crowns.

Colin is there, just around the bend, knee-deep in water. He is wading through, hair unbound, chasing young omioja who wave pieces of his tresses around like a trophy. He doesn't take notice of us right away, so we watch him for a bit, see him fight and play as freely as a child with an unfettered fate. The man who only knew pain and sacrifice, who was forced to kill to protect himself and those he loved, is healing.

He spreads his arms, imitating wings, just as one of his friends catapults into the sky, the wings at her waist whipping her around like a kite.

He laughs with abandon as the other two omioja splash water at him, drenching him completely. When he finally notices us, he runs up to me first, sweeping me up in his arms.

I laugh and hold fast to him in a tight hug. The scent of dew and salt tickles my nostrils, and I breathe it fully in, relishing the moment. Then his skin flickers and I start to fall. Jonas catches me just in time.

"Sorry," Colin mumbles as his sunned skin flashes between solid and transparent. "It's a new thing."

His skin rematerializes as he speaks. Jonas opens his arms wide. "Can I get one of those?" he quips.

Colin smirks. "I actually do want to see if I can lift you high. Care to try?"

They throw their arms around one another, like lost brothers who have finally found their way back to each other. Then Colin's skin flickers again, and they pull apart.

"Colin," I say softly, brows furrowed.

He turns his attention to Jonas, eyeing him. "She's starving you, isn't she?"

"The stress is eating us up," Jonas explains. "It doesn't matter that we appointed the Council as governing body. Everyone sees us as the rulers instead."

Since the battle in the capital, the Kingdom of Ifé is enjoying an uneasy peace. The Oluso are freed from their shackles, and living new lives, empowered by the knowledge that their lives are protected by the binding I made. The Ajes, too, are learning to accept their new reality, one where they can no longer value themselves by devaluing Oluso lives, one where they have to face their fears and find out who they are without the gifts they've pillaged from the Oluso all this time. Our world is changing, but it will take time, generations even, to heal the hurt that still lingers and redistribute resources that were unfairly concentrated in the hands of the powerful. But I know we're up to the task.

"That's to be expected," Colin says. "Dèmi just gives off a queenly aura, you know?"

The two share a grin.

I tut at them. "I have no idea why I love you both."

"We love you too," they cry, voices in unison.

I roll my eyes at them, but it's hard to keep the joy from my face.

Colin's skin dissolves a third time, but this time, I round on him. "Colin, explain, please. Why are you disappearing?"

He sighs, the sound like a pot letting out steam. "Take a look at this," he says, voice growing smaller and higher in pitch. One moment his muscled body is looming over me, then his form shifts and I'm peering at a mischievous grinning urchin. His eyes are still level with mine, and I'm reminded now that Colin at ten name days is my height at twenty.

But before I can remark on our heights or anything at all, he blurts, "I'm being reborn. Very soon actually."

"What do you mean?" I ask, grabbing his shoulders. They're frailer than I remember.

"Dèmi," Jonas says softly, "give him a chance to explain."

"My spirit will disappear as soon as you go," Colin announces. "Iya is sending me to a new life."

Shocked, I drop my hands and edge back. "You're going away," I accuse. "You're leaving us."

Jonas and Colin share a look. Then Colin sighs and darts forward, enveloping me in another hug. I'm too stunned to react, so I just accept it.

He squeezes me tight as his body grows to its former shape. Then he pulls away, drawing my fingers to his lips. "I love you. I always will. But I think it's time I find my own way."

I open my mouth, but I can't think of what to say. He folds my fingers, places them in Jonas's. "I want to live in a world where I can be free, where I live as the sun from the start rather than a shadow."

He pauses, staring off at the glade and the undulating waters. "I want to love so deeply and be loved so deeply that the person I love would slay death itself for me."

Tears gather in my eyes, and all I want to do is sob. He's leaving us. I'm losing him.

"Colin," I start.

He shakes his head, his expression resolute. "Go back, Dèmi. Go back to the world of the living."

"Colin," I plead, "how will we see you? We can't follow you into this new life. We—"

I break off, trying desperately not to sob. Despite all the mourning I did this past year, I never once truly thought that I'd lose Colin. But now that day is here.

"You'll be all right," he says, grinning. "You have someone who will choose you now. Someone you chose."

He and Jonas share another look, and I'm tempted for a moment to kick both of them.

"You knew about this," I accuse, stabbing a finger at Jonas as realization dawns. "You knew he was leaving."

Jonas nods. "I wanted you to hear it from him, so you could have a chance to say goodbye."

Yanking my hand from his, I storm off. I want to scream, stoop low and pound the earth with my fists until all the sorrow wrenching my heart is gone.

"I know you're angry," Colin says, appearing in front of me. "But I need you to understand this—I want to be free. I deserve that. To start a life where I'm sure someone will choose me and only me."

He falls to his knees, grabbing my hands. "So please let me go, Dèmi. Please. It's hard enough leaving you as it is, knowing I won't be here waiting when you come."

I cry in earnest now, throwing my arms around him, burying my face in his neck. He's right. This isn't about me, or my grief. This isn't about me losing the person I trusted and loved most after Jonas. This isn't about holding on to the joy of the man who saw me as I truly was before anyone else knew how to. I need to let him go.

"Does it have to happen now?" I whisper.

"I told Iya I wanted to have a real family this time. So she recommended this day."

I straighten. "So by the time we return, you'll be in another realm altogether."

He nods. "It'll be another Physical Realm, just not yours. Another life."

Jonas comes over to us. "I'm sorry for not telling you sooner. It wasn't my secret to tell."

"I know that," I say, resigned. "So what do we do now?"

Colin gets to his feet. "Now I want you two to give me your best wishes. Those will help in the next life." He holds out his hands. "Just think of all the things you want me to experience."

Sighing, I take his hand while Jonas takes the other. Then, I think of what I want Colin to experience most.

Love—the kind that is sure and unwavering. The kind that is willing to keep fighting for him, even when it seems impossible.

Jonas's voice steals into my mind: *Truth, that he will have a sense for what is true, though he may not have the courage to face it.*

Hope, an enduring flame that will sustain him on the wintriest of nights.

Loyalty, from all those blessed to truly know him.

We go on and on like this, the voices of our heart and our minds tangling together like needles pulling threads together, weaving the bountiful fate we hope for our friend.

As we name each thought, Colin's aura brightens, shimmering like a diamond reflecting the sunrise until finally he is little more than a pale whisper, as thin and transparent as smoke.

"You'd better hope I don't catch you in the next life," he says, flashing me one last grin. "I won't let you go then."

Jonas lets out a bark of laughter. "What makes you think I'll let go?"

"Just testing you."

Then Colin disappears and we are alone.

We blink and find ourselves back in the solar, moonlight now streaming through the window above. The castle is brimming with noise, people bustling about and voices carrying through the floors.

"Son of a horse lover," Jonas curses. "We're never going to hear the end of this. The queen and her consort disappearing for a whole day?"

"We can just tell them we were making love, working on an heir."

Jonas tugs me to him. "I'd be happy to do that all night if you're up for it."

But my heart is still tight, still thinking of Colin being gone. "Jonas, what if, what if Colin's not happy where he's going? What if—"

He presses a finger to my lips. "I'll stop you here. Colin will be happy. We gave him our blessings and our hopes for his life. He knows what he's doing. Trust that he'll find what he's looking for in his next life."

I lick my lips. "Are you sure?"

He trails a finger to my ear, then leans in close until his lips are just a breath from mine. "As sure as I am that I love you." He kisses me lightly, sucking lightly, tasting me, then he pulls the front knot of my blouse and watches it fall away from my body. "It's as I said before," he whispers, eyes drinking me in. "Give it a season, everything will come together."

Then he pulls me in, snaking a hand through my curls, kissing me as though I am air to his lungs and he is dying to breathe. I sink into him, wrapping my arms around his neck, pressing my body tight against his. He lifts me in his arms and carries me over to the bed in the center of the room. We rock together, heat passing between our bodies, hands snaking over every inch of each other until I am not sure where he ends and I begin. We make love until we are drunk on each other's scent and the tight coil of need in my belly has settled into a dripping warmth.

As I lie with him under the moonlight, its rich glow bathing our bodies, I turn to him and ask, "Did you think when we met ten years ago that we'd be here someday? Married? In love? Ruling a kingdom together?"

He pulls me in for a deep kiss before answering, "No. But I knew the moment I could understand what love meant, the moment I saw you again two years ago, that I'd do everything to be yours and make you mine."

"You were that confident?"

"I was that enamored."

He kisses the ring on my finger—the ring I can wear proudly now for all to see. Then we kiss again, twining our bodies together, marveling at the miracle of what we have.

Years from now, our story may recede into legend. It may become a tale of good and evil, light and darkness, far from the tangled tale of bloodshed and anguish and violence and hope. But we will do our best to show our people the path forward. We will walk side by side, hand in hand, and fight for a world in which every life is as precious as another— a world where hope is more than a foolish dream and hate has no room to blossom.

But for now, we are two hearts beating as one, singing under the light of the moon, weaving a new world together.

DRAMATIS PERSONAE

(In alphabetical order)

ADAEZE: An Igbagbo Oluso and member of the kunkun, once a pregnant prisoner at Nordgren.

AFÈNI: Grandmother to Yetundé and great-grandmother to Dèmi who harnessed Shango's fire in an attempt to defeat the kokulu during the Great War. Her act of kindness in sparing Osèzèlé's life preserved her future bloodline. Age sixty in the prologue.

ALISTAIR SORENSON: The Eingardian king who hated magic and the Oluso. Conquered most of the kingdom during a war known as Alistair's Betrayal. Was in love with Yetundé when they were teens but didn't have his affections reciprocated. Has always held a grudge toward Iron Blood Osèzèlé, Yetundé's mate. He attempted to kill Jonas when he was a child, and was also Mari's onetime lover.

AMARA: A former okri who is a merchant and Dèmi's friend.

AMINA: An okri girl whom Dèmi rescued from a merchant. She can freeze water. Rollo's sister.

ANNIKA: Former handmaiden of Ta'atia's who defected to join Oyéré. Addicted to koko.

ARIANNE: Jonas's mother, injured when Jonas was a young child. In a frozen state, but passes on when Jonas travels to the Spirit Realm.

ATAYA: An elderly attendant of Lady Hanae's who often takes the form of a bird.

BABA SYLVANUS: An old Oluso master in Benin who helped Will and Nana raise and train Dèmi and Colin. A telekinetic Igbagbo Oluso with minor Cloren abilities.

BRIGITTE: Afèni's former vanguard, an Eingardian woman whom she trusted more than anyone else.

CADENA: Mikhail's childhood friend who grew up with him in an orphanage. She is now vice chancellor of Mattiasjord.

CARIADHE: The head attendant in Château Nordgren assigned to monitor and watch Dèmi. She is having a secret affair with Elodie.

COLIN (NICOLÁS AL'ÉYANI): Dèmi's best friend and confidant, as well as a Madsen Oluso with strong but unstable magic. He's a second lieutenant for the kunkun and the son of Lord Kairen of Berréa and the Scourge of T'Lapis, Eyani Al'hia. Age twenty.

CROIDEN AURELIUS SCHULSON: Jonas's ancestor, his great-great-grandfather who was a Fèni-Ogun and former Eingardian ruler. He lost his power after slaughtering an Aje village in a bid to control the Ajes, and his children were poisoned against the idea of magic ever since.

CREE NATAKI: Elu's younger sister. An Angma Oluso who hid in Lokoja for most of her life before sacrificing herself to allow Dèmi and some Lokoja Oluso to escape.

DAMINI: Afèni's third youngest child who died after being sacrificed to the spirits.

DANOU: Vice general of the kunkun who harnesses his transformation power to aid them in any way possible. Fancies Mikhail.

DARA: An onyoshi assassin who was broken by Sorenson's torture. She later allies with the Council to kill Dèmi once Sorenson is dead.

DÉLÉ (AYODÉLÉ): Dèmi's elder twin brother who resents her for surviving when he died at birth. He was raised in the Spirit Realm by the K'inu, who nurtured him since his parents were not there to care for him.

DÈMI (ABIDÈMI ADENEKAN): A Fèni-Ogun and Ariabhe Oluso who is Jonas's mate, the daughter of Iron Blood Osèzèlé and Princess Yetundé Adenekan as well as descendant of Queen Afèni, who once vanquished the kokulu. Dèmi grew up in hiding with her mother before being taken in by Nana and Will. Once she defeated Alistair Sorenson in battle, she became Jonas's betrothed and potential queen. Age nineteen.

DRAGZBY: A member of Oyéré's gang of guards. In a triad relationship with Moloi and Katsa. Presumed dead. Dèmi assumes their identity using Ekwensi's magic.

EDITH: An Eingardian woman who was Jonas's nanny when he was a boy. She holds strong prejudices against other regions until Alistair cuts out her tongue as punishment. Once she realized the Oyo-born and Gomae were the only ones who could help her, she allied herself to Ekwensi.

EDWINA: An old Oyo-born woman who was once Yetundé's nanny. She alone knew Yetundé was pregnant when she escaped the palace. She also nursed Osèzèlé when he was smuggled off Sayaji Island and hidden as the last iron-blood.

ELODIE: Jonas's former fiancée, a beautiful painter who is Lady Ayn's daughter. She is graceful and well versed in politics. She is very curious about other regions, and possesses many hidden talents. Mari is her aunt. Age twenty-one.

ELU OYERA: Prisoner woman in Lokoja. She is a rare Angma and Cloren Oluso who died protecting the Lokoja Oluso. Wife to Haroun and mother to young Haroun.

EMPRESS REN (LADY YAKI): A powerful Oluso and a former ruler of Goma who once took in young, orphaned noblewomen. She had a tragic love affair with Elegua and birthed Sanaa. She later became the ferryman of the Egun River of Souls known as Lady Yaki.

EMPRESS YOMI: Afèni's mother and Dèmi's great-great grandmother who refused to act when the Fèni-Ogun were murdered by the other Oluso.

ENIKO: Oluso sister of a kunkun member who died in Wellstown. Also sister to Kilem.

ETERA: Friend of Ekwensi in Lokoja. An executioner Aje who is in love with a Cloren and Basaari Oluso named Sanaa. He is the father of Tuléa.

ÉYANI AL'HIA: Colin's mother, aka the Scourge of T'Lapis. A feared warlord who boasted a harem of seventy concubines, including Lord Kairen. She valued only strength and taught Colin how to fight. She died with her regrets.

FOLAKÉ: Former queen of Ifé. Yetundé's mother and Dèmi's grandmother who deeply disapproved of Yetundé's relationship with Osèzèlé and hated her mother, Afèni, for sacrificing her siblings for power.

FOX BEAD (MARANYA): Dèmi's name for an Ashkenayi assassin who wields bead magic and is a master of poison and combat. Silver is his brother.

GA EUN: A general of the kunkun who was once an abused Gomae-born prisoner in Nordgren. Ekwensi treats her as his niece. A Cloren-Igbagbo Oluso who has resonance with both objects and earth. She's willing to do whatever it takes for freedom. Age twenty-four.

GENERAL MINA: A Lani tribe warrior from northern Oyo who serves as a general in Jonas's guard.

GENERAL TENJUN: An Oluso general who once held the Eingardian forces off from invading Goma without killing a single person. He is also Nana's father and Lady Hanae's husband. A cautious yet exacting man. Age fifty-seven.

GIDEON: A teenage shipper whom Amara fancies.

LADY HANAE: Nana's mother, and General Tenjun's wife, was raised by Empress Ren. She has mourned many of her children and does not wish to lose more. Age fifty-three.

HANIFF: An Ariabhe Oluso and Danou's friend who died in Wellstown.

HAROUN (THE YOUNGER): Elu's son, and a powerful Basaari Oluso who can manipulate peoples' bodies using shadow.

HARU: Will and Nana's baby daughter. Magical gifts are unknown.

HEINRIK OTTAMEN: A former Council member and Eingardian lord who loses everything once Dèmi comes into power.

JAE HYUK: A member of Afèni's vanguard and a strong Basaari Oluso.

JONAS (JONAS AURELIUS SORENSON): Son of Arianne and Markham Sorenson. An Eingardian man from the Maven Keep who is king-elect. He is in love with Dèmi and after helping her overthrow his tyrannical uncle, he works to create a network of allies who will aid the Oluso in their quest for freedom. Age twenty-two.

KATHARINE: An Eingardian woman from a smaller city who is elected as a member of the ruling Council. Fancies Mikhail.

KATSA: A guard in Oyéré's camp and one-third of a triad love relationship with Moloi and Dragzby. Engages in an affair with someone else while Moloi and Drgazby are on the surface.

KILEM: Oluso sister of a kunkun member who died in Wellstown. Also sister to Eniko.

LADY CAMILLA AYN: An Eingardian courtier on the Royal Council, Elodie's mother. She values profit and respectability above everything else. She is prejudiced against the Oluso and regions other than Eingard.

LI'UOA: Omioja sister to Ta'atia who is masquerading as human by living in Miri's body. Cares deeply about her younger sister, Ta'atia, but also feels drawn to care for Nana. Also a daughter of Olokun.

LOLA: Youngest child of Afèni who died at age one after being sacrificed to the spirits.

LORD FERDINAND KAIREN: A Berréan politician and retired commandant of Alistair's guard. He is also Colin's and Matéo's father and was once a concubine of Eyani Al'hia, the Scourge of T'Lapis. He has complicated feelings about Colin and has considered both murdering him and using him to cement his legacy. He is from the secretive desert tribe of Ismar'yana, who were tasked with caring for Mount Y'cayonogo.

MALALA: Ekwensi and Samira's daughter, who was born in a prison at Nordgren. Age four. She is actually a very strong Basaari Oluso who loves her father.

MALULY: Vanguard of Afèni's who had a strong talent for battle but preferred cooking.

MAMA ALADÉ: Dèmi's mother's best friend and Biola's mother, she is a Cloren Oluso. Also mother to Tolu and Wunmi.

MAMA SEITA: An Aje woman who ran a needle shop next to Nana's stall in Benin.

MARI (MARI STRUMBLUD): Yetundé's best friend and former lover who betrayed her to become Alistair's second in command and romantic partner. She is obsessed with power, having come from a low-status family. She would rather kill her loved ones than let them become her weakness. She escapes after Alistair's defeat, becomes Oyéré's lover, and uses her to secure resources and power in Gaeyak-Orin. She is also Elodie's aunt.

MARKHAM (MARKHAM DENARIUS SORENSON): Jonas's father and Arianne's husband. He is also a member of the Royal Council and the king regent. He fears losing control over his tenuous hold on power.

MARTINE: A maid and lower attendant in Château Nordgren.

MATÉO: Colin's seven-year-old half-brother.

MATTIAS JONAS SORENSON: Alistair's late father who envied and feared the Oluso. He also had prejudices and anger towards other regions. He rose to power despite being the youngest of a family of twelve. He struggled with impotence.

MIKHAIL: Jonas's commander of the Royal Guard who hails from Wyldewood. He grew up as a poor Aje, and Ekwensi was the first person to give him an opportunity to succeed. Holds no prejudice toward other regions or the Oluso.

MIRI: Nana's sister, a powerful Cloren Oluso who once connected with the K'inu. Overwhelmed by the pain of their suffering, she killed herself, and Nana delivered her body to the sea rather than let their parents discover the truth.

MOLOI: A member of Oyéré's gang, and one of the triad lovers that includes Dragzby and Katsa. Presumed dead. Elodie assumes their identity using Ekwensi's magic.

NADINE: A guard and member of Oyéré's gang who is seduced by Elodie.

NAMIZ'EN: A young Oluso from Manapané who is possessed by the K'inu. Age thirteen.

NANA: A Cloren Oluso and the daughter of General Tenjun and Lady Hanae who runs away to become Will's mate and raises Dèmi as her own. She is also Haru's mother and once masqueraded as an unassuming artisan. She has strong visions and is proficient with weaponry. After Alistair's death, she ferries information to the capital for Dèmi.

NELLIE: A young Aje woman who is part of Ekwensi's network in Nyzchow. Sports a blue butterfly tattoo.

OSÈZÈLÉ: Known as Iron Blood Osèzèlé. Dèmi and Délé's biological father and Yetundé's mate who is believed to be the key to Alistair's victory during the war. He is believed to have murdered 50,000 Oluso, including Yetundé's family. It is later revealed his actions protected the Oluso from total defeat, and he is an iron-blood who possessed the rare power of resurrection.

OYÉRÉ: The Aje lover of Ta'atia, she leaves her to consolidate power with Mari out of a sense of betrayal.

QUEEN FOLAKÈ: The ruler prior to Sorenson. Yetundé's mother and Afèni's daughter, she despised Afèni for sacrificing her siblings and disapproved of her daughter's choice of mate.

RALEK: A member of the kunkun who is willing to do whatever it takes for freedom.

ROLLO: An okri boy and Amina's younger brother. He has the rarer Igbagbo ability and can shapeshift.

SAMIRA: A deaf Oluso member of the kunkun. She is Malala's mother and Ekwensi's mate. She gave birth to Malala in prison.

SANAA: Hidden daughter of Elegua, the trickster spirit of the pathways, and Empress Ren, the last ruler of Goma. She was once Etera's Oluso fiancée and is now the mother to Tuléa. She has strong Cloren abilities, as well as other hidden shadow magic.

SHATU: A middle-aged member of the kunkun who becomes possessed by the K'inu during a ritual.

SILVER BEAD: The brother of Fox Bead (Maryana) who attempts to assassinate Dèmi and Jonas. Dies when Dèmi loses control and kills him.

SUMI: A member of the kunkun who fights to avenge her Oluso mother who was enslaved by her Aje father and killed by his proper wife.

TA'ATIA: An okun-omo, a hybrid between an omioja and an Oluso, daughter of Olokun, one of the premier spirits of the waters, and an unnamed Oluso. Was sold as a slave in her youth and rescued by Yetundé. She rules Gaeyak-Orin as a warlord, watching over one-half of the city. She takes in orphaned children and raises them as handmaidens who use poisonous whips woven of her hair as weapons. Honorable and kind.

THERU AL'JAI: A chancellor from Berréa who sends Dèmi and Jonas obsidian as part of a pledge to help connect their network.

TOBIAS EKWENSI: The founder and revolutionary leader of the kunkun who was once a regional lord over the Ikwara and Ogun areas and Alistair Sorenson's trusted retainer. He is prepared to do anything to secure Oluso freedom. Samira is his lover, and Malala his hidden child.

TS'ALISI: Afèni's Berréan vanguard who died to buy Afèni time to escape.

TULÉA: Child of Etèra and Sanaa, powers unknown.

UNAGBONA: Vanguard of Afèni's, an Oyo born Cloren who died during the Great War.

WARLORD UZAI: A lower Oyo-Berréan half-caste warlord who aids refugees escaping the effects of Ekwensi's rebellion and Sorenson's reign of tyranny.

WILLARD (ALSO KNOWN AS WILL): An Eingardian-Oyo Oluso and Nana's mate. He has strong Masden abilities and masquerades as an instrument maker. He is also Haru's father, Dèmi's guardian, and Colin's mentor. He is tall and grew up in Eingard, passing as full Eingardian from time to time. Since Alistair's death, he's used his passing skills to spy for Dèmi and Jonas. He has heterochromia.

YETUNDÉ: Dèmi and Délé's mother, an Ariabhe Oluso and the former princess of Ifé. She grew up with Alistair and Mari. Though she and Mari were intimately involved, she gave her up once court politics made Mari a target. She later fell in love with Iron Blood Osèzèlé and ran away while she was pregnant to protect her children.

YGRITTE: A guard in Nyzchow who is wary of non-Eingardians.

ZAFIRA: The scarred eldest member of the kunkun.

ZETIAN: A taciturn attendant of General Tenjun's, an Oluso who often transforms into a bird.

SPIRITS AND CREATURES

AGIDI: The spirit remnant of the diduo Yetundé raised in her youth. Sought to care for Délé when he was born in the Spirit Realm alone.

AUNTIE ANOZIÉ: An elder gwylfin. Ogié and Osemalu's mother.

AYABA: The Aziza queen. Gave up her unborn child to harness enough power to save Dèmi's life.

ELEGUA (ESHU): The premier spirit of the pathways and a trickster who is known as the father of Madsen Oluso. He granted them the gift of teleportation and water manipulation. He takes on the form of Eshu, who appears to be a child, but is a denizen of chaos. His colors are red, black, and white. Fell in love with Ren, but feared having his child, Sanaa, in the Spirit Realm, so he sent her to a good family.

JAGUN JAGUN: Keepers of Time who are also guards to the Court of Spirits. They appear as twelve women of varying appearance and prowess who serve Ososhi.

IKÉ: A koriko who lives in the Spirit Realm, a lion-boy.

ÌYÁ-ILÉ: The Mother Tree who watches over all life.

OBATALA: An egbon, an elder premier spirit, who disappeared from Dèmi's realm to rule as a sun serpent spirit in a different realm. Granted all the Basaari Oluso their shadow magic.

OGECHI (CHI CHI): A young tree spirit seeker who has a strong affinity with creatures and can change her speech to communicate with them.

OGIÉ: A gwylfin. Chi Chi's best friend.

OGUN: The premier spirit of metals and iron. Father of the Fèni-Ogun, who demanded Afèni pay a dire price as recompense for the Oluso slaughtering the iron-bloods. Husband to Oya.

OLOKUN: A premier spirit of the water, who birthed the deep waters of Ifé. Father to Ta'atia and Li'uoa. Takes on various gender forms as they will.

OLORUN: Father of Spirits and Skies. Also known as Y'l- shad, the All-Seeking Mother. The premier spirit who rules the Spirit Realm and holds balance for the world.

ORUNMILA: The premier spirit of divination who manages relationships and is the parent of all Clorens.

OSHUN: The premier spirit of the shallow waters (rivers), sister to Yemaya. In a relationship with the spirit of fire and war, Shango.

OSHOSI (GREAT HUNTER): The premier spirit of the fields who watches over animals and creates the rules for honorable battle and hunting. Rules the Jagun Jagun and grants power to all Igbagbo Oluso.

OSEMALU: A gwylfin. Ogié's twin brother.

OYA: Premier spirit of the winds, and the ruler of Egun, the River of Souls. Also known as the mother of healing, who grants power to all Ariabhe Oluso. Wife of Ogun.

SHANGO: Premier spirit of fire and lightning who is known for his fiery temper. Lover to Oshun. Granted all the Angma Oluso their explosive magic.

XIAOQING: An omioja elder who once became mami wata but now presides over the rituals for all omioja. She once helped Afèni when she sought to smuggle Osèzèlé away.

YEMAYA: A premier spirit of the waters, as well as Oshun's sister and Olokun's twin, she left Dèmi's realm to enter another realm in the form of two moons.

APPENDIX

OLUSO MAGIC FAMILIES AND ATTRIBUTES:

Fèni-Ogun (Iron-Blood)

Fèni-Ogun (pronounced Feh-knee-oh-goon) are born with the power to manipulate metals. They can transform iron into gold or silver and can shape iron as they please. Iron magic takes tremendous will to wield and can often take a toll on lifespan. Those who possess iron magic are incredibly powerful, but also highly susceptible to losing control, making them the most likely to lose their spirit bonds. They also often suffer from side effects such as severe muscle pain, migraines, and mental strain. A few iron-bloods possess the power of resurrection, meaning they can restore spirit bonds with a spirit/soul sacrifice, or bring people back from the brink of death with a physical sacrifice. In rare cases, the iron-blood can lose their soul in the Spirit Realm and become permanently trapped.

Ariabhe (Healers, Wind-Magic Users)

The Ariabhe (pronounced Ah-ree-ah-vey) Oluso can use healing magic, but they have to be careful about who they heal. Iron-bloods and shadow-bloods leach energy and life from an Ariabhe who heals them. Ariabhe Oluso are born with either healing magic or wind magic. In rare cases, they can be born with both, especially if their souls have high resonance with the Spirit Realm.

FUN FACT: They are most likely to be multiple-birth children.

Cloren (Seers, Realm-Breakers)

Cloren (pronounced Claw-wren) Oluso are born with the ability to see possible futures and revisit the past. Their future visions could be correct or incorrect, but their ability to wander the past is powerful. They can go back hundreds of years, but the further they go from their current time, the greater the chance that they will become un-anchored and lose themselves in the past while their bodies die. Clorens can enter the Spirit Realm the easiest of all Oluso.

Madsen (Water- and Ice-Shapers, Teleportation)

Madsen (pronounced Mad-sen) Oluso can use ice and water magic. Their form of water magic is usually defensive, as opposed to the omioja who embody water itself and can be both offensive and defensive. Most Madsens tend to prefer either water or ice, but some develop their skills in both. Madsens tend to be stamina-bound since their bodies have to be in good condition to control the elements. Madsen's also possess the power of teleportation, a gift from Elegua, the spirit of the pathways. They can teleport from place to place, but risk leaving a portion of their bodies behind every time.

Fun fact: Many Madsens become crafters, using their powers to create tools that can be imbued with magic.

Angma (Lightbringers)

Angma (pronounced Ahng-mah) Oluso are born with devastating explosive power that is often sealed at birth. They shine brightly enough to blind their mothers when they are born, and a sealing ritual marks their bodies with a unique tattoo that is difficult to remove. Once an Angma decides to unseal itself, it cannot be resealed. When their magic senses a threat, they detonate, destroying everything around them. Some Angma survive this detonation, but their stamina and state of health plays a huge role in whether or not they survive. If they live, they glow faintly all the time. They have to prevent themselves from getting angry or struggling mentally or they risk detonation.

Basaari (Shadow- and Skin-walkers)

Basaari (pronounced Bash-aar-ree) possess the power of skin-walking and short-range shadow manipulation. Once they form a soul contract with someone, they can take over their bodies for a short period of time in exchange for a portion of their lives. They can also render multiple people immobile by possessing their opponents' shadows, but this magic only lasts as long as there is sun, and the Basaari using the magic doesn't move too far away. Every time they skin-walk, they pick up an aspect of the person whose body they inhabited.

Fun fact: Some Basaari possess the power of appearance manipulation, and can retain the appearance of someone they've previously possessed for a short period of time.

Igbagbo (Truth-seekers and Transformers)

Igbagbo (pronounced Ee-'Ba-baw) can call the truth out of people and manipulate them into acting on their deepest desires. They can also call lightning, but it is hard to contain so their magic often causes destruction of a greater area than they may have intended. Some Igbagbo who have high affinity with animal spirits possess the power of transformation, allowing them to take on the shape of the creatures they encounter. A few others possess telekinesis, exerting their will on objects.

Fun fact: Igbagbo who spend more time in their animal forms tend to lose all sense of their humanity with time.

DAY/NIGHT/HOUR SYSTEMS

Day and Night:

There are seven days, each with historical and regionally sourced names:

Midé's Day (The Day of the Hopeful) is the first day of the week

Yèmè's Day (The Day of Weepers) is the second day of the week

Ruko's Day (The Day of the Relentless) is the third day of the week

Tifè's Day (The Day of the Stubborn) is the fourth day of the week

Nabi's Day (The Day of the Free) is the fifth day of the week

Gura's Day (The Day of the Beautiful) is the sixth day of the week

Elù's Day (The Day of the Bright) is the seventh day of the week

Time system:

Famous rhyme that children sing in the Kingdom of Ifé:

"Elephant rises to meet the day

Snake comes to chase it away

Tiger hunts in dead of night

But rabbit runs ahead in spite

Crow snatches sleep from weary eyes

Bear lures it back though you be wise

Pig dances in when spirits rise

And wolf will howl when your soul dies"

Each time block is a two-hour period marked with an animal name.

Tiger Hour: 3–5 a.m.

Rabbit Hour: 5–7 a.m.

Crow Hour: 7–9 a.m.

Elephant Hour: 9–11 a.m.

Antelope Hour: 11 a.m.–1 p.m.

Bear Hour: 1–3 p.m.

Lizard Hour: 3–5 p.m.

Gull Hour: 5–7 p.m.

Pig Hour: 7–9 p.m.

Fox Hour: 9–11 p.m.

Snake Hour: 11 p.m.–1 a.m.

Wolf Hour: 1 a.m.–3 a.m.

ACKNOWLEDGEMENTS

———

If you've reached this point in the book, you've finished *Exiled by Iron*, or you got curious and wondered if you'd find your name here, so you skipped to the end of the book. No matter. Either way, thank you! I decided to switch up the order of my acknowledgments, so you may have to dig a bit long to find your name, or you might find it on the first page. Who knows? ;)

As with anything I strive to publish, I am always aware and eternally grateful for all the loving hands, voices, and hearts it took to bring this book into the world, and once it arrived, to put it into the hands of the curious, the devoted, and the longing.

So, first, and foremost, I want to say thank you to my mighty publishing and editorial teams, my booksellers, librarians, readers, and champions. Thank you, for picking this one up, for giving it a chance to breathe, and for letting it live in and affect your world, whether just for a moment, some days, or even years. Thank you.

Thank you to Kiki, my first agent, who graciously ran with it when it turned out we were going to sell a fantasy first. You did your best to show up for me then, and I will always be grateful for that.

Thank you also to my once agent sibs, Emily, Anna, Becca, and Ruby! You are all so lovely (and very very funny!), and we're still dancing through this industry together, one step at a time.

Thank you to my phenomenal editor, David Pomerico, who is as hilarious as he is kind, and as meticulous as he is imaginative! You are really so intentional, so careful when we work on projects, and you always find ways to challenge me to make the work stronger, smarter, and more daring. You are the reason I'm never afraid to "go there," push until we get to the bottom of these characters, and do my best to honor who they are. Thank you, for all the encouragement, the care, and the funny notes. I swear, I'm always cackling during edit time.

Thank you to Natasha B., and Elizabeth V., who are out living their best lives and being the best mums ever. You two are shepherds of some fantastic literary work, and I am so grateful for your vision and care!

Thank you to my other amazing editor, Aje, who is always cheering and in my corner. My goodness, it's so wonderful to work with you, and to gush about books we love and things we're excited about! I feel absolutely fortunate to have you on my team. I can't wait to spend more time together, and to continually learn from you and David pushing me to be my best self.

Thank you to my fearsome publicist, Lara, who I firmly believe knows all the best lunch spots, and has the best taste in books that make your toes curl in delight! You are such a joy to work with, and so full of life! I feel like we could spend a whole day getting into scrapes and figuring our way out of it, and we would regret nothing!

Thank you to the rest of the team:

Mireya, who had the biggest smile, and always made me feel like I was on the verge of something earthshaking! Miss you, and I am wishing the best for you on your next journey. You are a joy!

Chloe who is really lovely, and who I totally will run around with next time I'm back to the UK. Take this as a promise, Chloe!

Sian who I have yet to meet in person. One of these days, it'll happen!

The Harper Art team, who is strong, mighty, and full of amazing vision. You are all amazing, and I owe you homemade cookies. Seriously, you all deserve it.

To Liate, who cares for all of Harper and Morrow with vision, compassion, and poise, thank you, thank you, thank you. As you said, there's no way to know which book or books will go high, but we keep pushing so we can make it happen!

To every hand that worked on this book from copyedits to typesetting, thank you. I cannot overstate your influence and care. I am ever grateful!

Thank you to gari, my phenomenal artist, who is always up for a challenge and blows my mind every single time. Thank you for reading the pages of notes, accepting my little sketches here and there, making adjustments as you see fit, but always keeping the goal in mind. You are a talent above talents, and we are so fortunate to have you. Seriously. I've been your fan for years, and I remain your fan.

To Sean, Kathy, Betsey, and so many other librarians who have rallied and championed this book, thank you, for more than I can ever say.

To my booksellers and bookstores:

Cathy and Valerie at Blue Willow who took a teen immigrant me to her first ever US book event and made her fall in love, thank you so much. I love y'all. I am still crying.

Eric and Katrina at Black Pearl, you are doing the work, leading the way, and we're going to keep doing it!!!!

Luca and the team at BookPeople, you manage to make intimate events into amazing productions and massive events into a cozy setting. Thank you!

Chanecka and Nia at Kindred, you are phenomenal every single time! Thank you for the support!

Jane, Shakeria, Meghan, and the team at large at Lark and Owl, you are all amazing, and those baked treats keep us coming back!

Shout-out to Kel, bookseller extraordinaire who keeps championing our books!

Amanda Johnston who runs Torch Lit with heart and a continual fierce advocacy that makes me want to cry—thank you!!!

To my readers, reviewers, and bloggers—thank you so very much. This book wouldn't have been loved and screamed about without you all. Special shout-out to Fantasy Café and Bookish Brews—y'all are the realest. Also to Danzi, Briana, Ash, and Jenn, y'all are the best and so much fun!

Also, Jenn and Evan forever (yes, I went there and y'all better write that meet cute women's fiction about your romance or I will).

To Jess, my mighty and formidable agent, who is always up for a challenge and wants me to grow and tell all the stories of my heart, thank you. I can't wait to see all the things we do together. The world isn't ready, but storms never give warning, so let's go!!!!

To my lovely friends who are always down to indulge in madness with me—Becky, Shirlene, Kanksh, Mari, Gabi, Gabs, Nia, Saara, Alice, Marve, Thea, Hannah K, Sarah, Em, George, Mia, Suyi, Ali, Yume, Marshall, and Angel—you are brighter than the stars, and I am so fortunate to call you all friends. Seriously, I am forever laughing with you, and thankful that I get to spend this time with you all.

To Alexia, Cynthia, Daisy, and Lillie, we may be fewer now, but we are still loving, still warm, still here for each other all the time. Thankful for you all, each and every day! Also, shout-out to Mikey Mike, Will (Guillaime, hehehe), Reagan (Kansas, what's up!) and my boy Jin because we all know it's either you or Park Bo Gum who will win our French madam's heart! Talha, we will speak (insert curious eyes emoji).

To Becky and Benny, Kanksh and JJ, and our Shirly Girl, thank you for being my people. We love y'all so much and are grateful to experience life with you. Yup, I mentioned y'all twice—deal with it!

To Nicky, Des, and Sim, I miss our Friday four-hour chats, but I am ever grateful and blessed to know you three. In the best of moments and the worst of times, you are all always there, encouraging me to remember I am a person worth loving and seeing, and I appreciate you all so much for it.

To Connor, Kyle, and Angie Pants—ayyyyy! Thank you for keeping us all together even though we live so far apart. One day soon we'll be in closer proximity, and it will be glorious!

To Haena, who is living it up in Greenland, I miss you so much my belly aches. You'd best come back before I name someone after you. But come back whole and hale, and full of smiles. Know that unnie loves you always.

To Auntie Naae and Uncle Stan, I hope you still save me all the kimbap ends because this is your advance notice that I'm coming over to sit in the house and eat while working on my next book. I'll bring the Bean!

To Cynthia Leitich Smith, Sam Clark, Jason June, Kelis Rowe, Gayleen—we may not be able to still hang every Saturday, but your influence and love will never fade. Thank you all for being my mentors, friends, colleagues, and champions!

To Ellen Oh, the OG, the one and only, thank you for everything you are, and for how much you continue to encourage, share, and love. You are amazing.

To Sarah Rees Brennan, thank you for your candor and courage, and for lifting up a young teen who wanted to believe she could be something more. We're here now!

To Daniela, Eric, and Lucy—thank you always for being there for us. You truly are family, and we are so grateful to know you. Also, Lucy, you should write. I'll keep saying it.

To Jun Woo and the fam, we're going to keep making it day by day. Thankful for you always, and I can never overstate it.

To Mon and Tiff (and Ethan and Greg), thank you for always being ready to enjoy tacos and Summer Moon at a moment's notice, and for being the wisecracking, life-loving people you are.

To Rachel and Misa, you know we're still here!!! Life is a lot these days, but true love is enduring and constant. I'm sending you both some.

To all the cousins, so many we may be, I am thankful for you all. Thank you for cheering for this baby cousin! Thank you for always being ready to answer my questions, and for switching language with me at the drop of a hat!

To Lael and the boys, thank you for cheering for me even from afar. I am so blessed to have such an amazing family and I'm glad you're part of it.

To Mom and Dad, thank you for being my family. Thank you for every prayer, tear, hug, and board game. Thank you for protecting my voice, and loving me in all the ways I need. I am so grateful every day for you.

To Mummy and Daddy, there are not enough words to thank you. For all the love and care you put into raising me, for every sacrifice, sleepless night, hospital visit, language change, life shift you went through to take care of all of us, thank you. I am forever grateful. This book is just as much your victory as it is mine. Also, Daddy, I keep telling people that, if they think my language skills are impressive, they need to hear yours. It would actually be funny if we did one of those telly things where you race the world. We would win on languages alone.

To my padees—yes I did it, my A, O, E, (and AOE of healing, haha, see what I did there?), I love you all. You know it. You know it won't change even though we're spreading out more now. Thanks for taking care of me and my Ks. Thanks for being the OG audience, and for telling me that I needed to put some of these ideas into a book. Here we are on Book 2!

To my Big K, who is my heart, I love you. In every lifetime, in every world, in every form, it's you and me. You know I would've kept trying to be your friend if we'd met sooner. But when we met was just as perfect. Thank you for being my person. Blessed to have you.

To my Professor, my little K, my strong and wonderful one—you are the greatest treasure I have ever been blessed with. Never forget that. I will try my best every day to show you that you matter, and to remind you, that you are made for greatness and true, encompassing love.

Finally, to You who birthed my voice, who made me all I am, who continues to make me every single day and make me new, thank you. I will live my life well in eternal thanks.